KU-125-519

THE NOVELS AND SELECTED WORKS OF
MARY SHELLEY

VOLUME
5

EDITED BY
DOUCET DEVIN FISCHER

THE FORTUNES OF PERKIN WARBECK
A ROMANCE

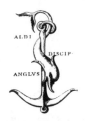

LONDON
WILLIAM PICKERING
1996

Published by Pickering & Chatto (Publishers) Limited

21 Bloomsbury Way, London, WC1A 2TH

Old Post Road, Brookfield, Vermont 05036, USA

All rights reserved. No part of this publication may be
reproduced, stored in a retrieval system, or transmitted in
any form or by any means, electronic, mechanical,
photocopying, recording, or otherwise without prior permission
of the publisher.

© Pickering & Chatto (Publishers) Limited 1996
© Introduction and notes Doucet Devin Fischer 1996

BRITISH LIBRARY CATALOGUING IN PUBLICATION DATA
A catalogue record for this book is available from the British Library

LIBRARY OF CONGRESS CATALOGING-IN-PUBLICATION DATA
Shelley, Mary Wollstonecraft, 1797–1851.
    The fortunes of Perkin Warbeck : a romance / edited by Doucet
Devin Fischer.
       p. cm. –– (The novels and selected works of Mary Shelley ; v.
5) (The Pickering masters)
    Includes bibliographical references (p.).
    ISBN 1–85916–076–7 (set) –– ISBN 1–85196–081–3 (v. 5)
    1. Warbeck, Perkin, 1474–1499––Fiction.   2. Imposters and
imposture––Great Britain––Fiction.   I. Fischer, Doucet Devin.
II. Title.   III. Series: Shelley, Mary Wollstonecraft, 1797–1851.
Selections. 1996 ; v. 5.
PR5397.A1   1996 vol. 5
823'.7 s––dc20
[823'.7]   96–1539
                                                     CIP

This publication is printed on acid-free paper that conforms to the American
National Standard for the Permanence of Paper for Printed Library Materials

Typeset by Waveney Typesetters
Norwich

Printed and bound in Great Britain by
Biddles Limited
Guildford

KING ALFRED'S COLLEGE
WINCHESTER

823.7SHE | 01984977

CONTENTS

ABBREVIATIONS

Abinger/Palacio	The copy of *The Fortunes of Perkin Warbeck*, annotated by Mary Shelley, now in the possession of Lord Abinger; emendations have been cited from Palacio (see below).
Ab. MSS, Pf. Film	Abinger Manuscripts, microfilm in the Carl H. Pforzheimer Collection of Shelley and His Circle, Rare Books and Manuscripts Division, New York Public Library, Astor, Lenox, and Tilden Foundations.
Bacon	Francis Bacon, *The Historie of the Raigne of King Henry the Seventh* (London: Matthew Lownes and William Barret, 1622); often reprinted before 1830.
Barante	Amable G. P. Brugière, baron de Barante, *Histoire des ducs de Bourgogne de la maison de Valois, 1364–1477* (Paris: Ladvocat, 1824–6).
Bayley	John Bayley, *The History and Antiquities of the Tower of London, with Biographical Anecdotes of Royal and Distinguished Persons* [etc.] (London: T. Cadell, 1821–1825; 2nd ed. 1830).
Buchanan	George Buchanan, *Rerum Scoticarum Historia* [etc.] (Edinburgh: A. Arbuthnet, 1582); *The History of Scotland, Written in Latin* [etc.], tr. J. Fraser (London: Awnsham Churchill, 1690); often translated and reprinted before 1830.
Campion	Edmund Campion, *A Historie of Ireland, Written in the Yeare 1571* (see Ware, below).
CC Journals	*The Journals of Claire Clairmont*, ed. Marion Kingston Stocking, with the assistance of David Mackenzie Stocking (Cambridge, Mass.: Harvard University Press, 1968).
Chastellain	Georges Chastellain, *Chronique des ducs de Bourgogne* [...] *publiée pour la première fois par J.-A. Buchon* (Paris: Verdière, 1827).
Chastellain and Molinet	*Récollection de merveilleuses avenues en nostre temps, commencée par très élégant orateur messire George Chastelain* [...] *et continuée jusques à présent par maistre Jehan Molinet* ([?Paris]: Guillaume Vorsterman, n. d.).
Chaudon	Esprit Joseph Chaudon, *Les Imposteurs de masques, et les*

vii

usurpateurs punis, ou Histoire de plusieurs aventuriers [etc.] (Paris: Nyon, 1776).

Comines   Philippe de Comines, *Cronicque et histoire faicte et composée par feu messire Philippe de Commines* [...] *contenant les choses advenues durant le règne du roy Loys unziesme et chronicques du roy Charles huictiesme* [...] (Paris: A. Langellier, 1539; the histories of Louis XI and Charles VIII were first published separately, but later combined, corrected, supplemented, translated, and frequently reprinted before 1830; see, e.g., *The Historical Memoirs of Philip de Comines; containing the Transactions of Lewis XI. and of Charles VIII. of France; and of Edward IV. and Henry VII. of England* [etc.] (London: J. Davis, 1817).

Croker   Thomas Crofton Croker, *Researches in the South of Ireland, Illustrative of the Scenery, Architectural Remains, and the Manners and Superstitions of the Peasantry* [etc.] (London: John Murray, 1824).

Croyland   *Ingulphi Abbatis Croylandensis Historiaram* (see Savile, below).

DNB   *Dictionary of National Biography.*

Dugdale   William Dugdale, *The Baronage of England* [etc.] (London: Abel Roper, John Martin, and Henry Herringman, 1675–6); Arthur Collins, *The Peerage of England* [...], *Being the Substance of Sir William Dugdale's Baronage; Improv'd and Continu'd* [etc.] (London: A. Collins, 1714).

Faerie Queene   Edmund Spenser, *The Faerie Queene* (1590–6).

Ford   John Ford, *The Chronicle Historie of Perkin Warbeck: A Strange Truth* (London: H. Beeston, 1634); *The Dramatic Works of John Ford* [etc.], ed. William Gifford (London: John Murray, 1827).

Gainsford   Thomas Gainsford, *The True and Wonderfull History of Perkin Warbeck, Proclaiming Himselfe Richard the Fourth* [etc.] (London: N. Butter, 1618).

Gairdner   James Gairdner, *History of the Life and Reign of Richard the Third, to which is Added the Story of Perkin Warbeck from Original Documents*, rev. edn (Cambridge: Cambridge University Press, 1898).

Grafton   Richard Grafton, *A Chronicle at large* [...] *of the Affayres of Englande from the Creation of the Worlde, unto the First Yere of the Reigne of* [...] *Elizabeth* (London: R. Tottle and H. Toye, 1568–9); often reprinted and abridged before 1830; see, e.g., *Grafton's Chronicle; or History of England* [...] (London: J. Johnson [etc.], 1809).

Hall	Edward Hall, *The Union of the Two Noble and Illustrate Famelies of Lancastre and Yorke* [etc.] (London: R. Grafton, 1548); often reprinted before 1830; see, e.g., *Hall's Chronicle; containing the History of England* [etc.] (London: J. Johnson [etc.], 1809).
Hanmer	Meredith Hanmer, *The Chronicle of Ireland, Collected by Meredith Hanmer* [...] *in the yeare 1571* (see Ware, below).
Henry	Robert Henry, *The History of Great Britain from the First Invasion of it by the Romans under Julius Caesar* (London, 1771); 3rd edn, rev., on a new plan, by Malcolm Laing, 12 vols (London: A. Strahan, 1799–1800).
Herrera	Antonio de Herrera y Tordesillas, *The General History of the Vast Continent and Islands of America* [...], tr. Capt. John Stevens (London: J. Batley, 1725–6).
———	Antonio de Herrera y Tordesillas, *General Observations and an Account of the First Discovery of America, by Christopher Columbus* [...], in A. and J. Churchill, *A Collection of Voyages and Travels* (London, 1746).
Holinshed	Raphaell Holinshed, *The First Volume of the Chronicles of England, Scotlande, and Irelande* [etc.] (London: G. Bishop, 1577); *The Whole Volume of Chronicles* [...] *Newlie Enlarged and Amended* (London: John Harrison [etc.], 1587); often reprinted and abridged before 1830; see, e.g., *Holinshed's Chronicles of England, Scotland, and Ireland* [etc.], ed. Henry Ellis, et al., 6 vols (London: J. Johnson [etc.], 1807–8).
Hume	David Hume, *The History of England* [etc.], 6 vols (London: A. Millar, 1754–62); new edn, With the Author's Last Corrections [etc.] (London: T. Cadell and T. N. Longman, 1789); often reprinted and abridged before 1830.
Irving	Washington Irving, *A Chronicle of the Conquest of Granada, from the MSS. of Fray Antonio Agapida*, 2 vols (Paris: A. and W. Galignani, 1829).
Laing	Malcolm Laing, *The History of Scotland from the Union of the Crowns to the Accession of James VI*, 2 vols (London, 1800; 2nd corrected edn, London: J. Mawman, 1804); often reprinted before 1830; see also, Henry, above.
Leland	Thomas Leland, *The History of Ireland from the Invasion of Henry II, with a Preliminary Discourse on the Antient State of that Kingdom*, 3 vols (Dublin: J. Moncrieffe, 1743); a Dublin edition (Brett Smith, 1814) has been used here, but the title was often reprinted before 1830.
Lindsay	Robert Lindsay, *The History of Scotland; from 21 February,*

	1436. to March, 1565 [etc.] (Edinburgh: Freebairn; London: Andrew Millar, 1728).
Lyles	W. H. Lyles, *Mary Shelley: An Annotated Bibliography* (New York and London: Garland Publishing, 1975).
Marleburrough	Henry Marleburrough, *Chronicle of Ireland* (see Ware, below).
Molinet	(see Chastellain, above).
More	Sir Thomas More, *The History of the Reigns of Edward V. and Richard III. Written in Part by Sir T. Moor, and Finished from the Chronicles of Hall and Hollinshead* [sic], *with Notes and Additions by the Editor of the Historical Magazine* (London: C. Stalker, 1789).
MWSJ	*The Journals of Mary Shelley, 1814–1844*, eds Paula Feldman and Diana Scott-Kilvert, 2 vols (Oxford: Oxford University Press, 1987).
MWSL	*The Letters of Mary Wollstonecraft Shelley*, ed. Betty T. Bennett, 3 vols (Baltimore and London: Johns Hopkins University Press, 1980–8).
OED	*Oxford English Dictionary.*
Oxford History	J. D. Mackie, *The Earlier Tudors, 1485–1558*, vol. VIII of *The Oxford History of England* (Oxford: Clarendon Press, 1952).
Palacio	Jean de Palacio, *Mary Shelley dans son œuvre: Contribution aux études shelleyennes* (Paris: Editions Klincksieck, 1969).
PBS 1824	*Posthumous Poems of Percy Bysshe Shelley*, ed. Mary Wollstonecraft Shelley (London: John and Henry L. Hunt, 1824).
Perez de Hita	Gines Perez de Hita, *The Civil Wars of Granada: And the History of the Factions* [...] *to the Final Conquest by Ferdinand and Isabella*, tr. Thomas Rodd (London: Thomas Ostell, 1803).
Pforzheimer Collection	The Carl H. Pforzheimer Collection of Shelley and His Circle, Rare Books and Manuscripts Division, The New York Public Library, Astor, Lenox, and Tilden Foundations.
Pinkerton	John Pinkerton, *The History of Scotland from the Accession of the House of Stuart to that of Mary, with Appendixes of Original Papers*, 2 vols (London: C. Dilly, 1797).
Polidori	John Polidori, *The Diary of Dr. John William Polidori, 1816* [etc.], ed. William Michael Rossetti (London: Elkin Mathews, 1911).
Polwhele	Richard Polwhele, *The History of Cornwall* [etc.], 7 vols in 2 (London: Cadell and Davies, 1803–16).

Prescott	William H. Prescott, *History of the Reign of Ferdinand and Isabella the Catholic*, ed. Wilfred Harold Munro, and comprising the notes of E. F. Kirk, 4 vols (Philadelphia: J. B. Lippincott, 1904).
Savile	Sir Henry Savile, *Rerum Anglicarum Scriptores post Bedam praecipui* [etc.] (London: G. Bishop, R. Nuberie & R. Barker, 1596); contains works by Henry Huntindon, Roger Hoveden, and Etherwerd, as well as *Ingulphi Abbatis Croylandensis Historiaram*.
Shelley and Mary	*Shelley and Mary*, 3 vols (London: Privately Printed, 1882).
Spenser	Edmund Spenser, *A View of the State of Ireland, Written Dialoguewise between Eudoxus and Irenaeus* [...] *1596* (see Ware, below).
Stafford	Thomas Stafford, *Pacata Hibernia, Ireland Appeased and Reduced* [etc.] (London: R. Milbourne, 1633); reprinted, Dublin: Hibernia Press, 1810, 1820.
Stow	John Stow, *A Summarie of Englyshe Chronicles. Collected by J. Stow* (London: T. Marsh, 1565); abridged, updated, expanded, and frequently reprinted before 1830; often referred to as *The Annales of England, from Brute unto* [different dates].
Sunstein	Emily W. Sunstein, *Mary Shelley: Romance and Reality* (Boston and London: Little, Brown, 1989; 2nd edn Baltimore and London: Johns Hopkins, 1991).
Vergil	Polydore Vergil, *Anglica Historia libri vigintisex* (1559); *An Abridgement of the Notable Worke of Polydore Vergile* [...], compendiously gathered by T. Langley (London: R. Grafton, 1546).
Walpole	Horace Walpole, *Historic Doubts on the Life and Reign of King Richard the Third* (London: J. Dodsley, 1768).
Ware	Sir James Ware, *De Hibernia et antiquitatibus* [etc.] (London: Joseph Crook and Thomas Heath, 1654); *The Antiquities and History of Ireland* [...] (Dublin: E. Dobson and M. Gunne, 1705).
Ware	Sir James Ware, *The Historie of Ireland, Collected by three Learned Authors viz. Meredith Hanmer* [...] *Edmund Campion* [...] *and Edmund Spenser* [but also containing Marleburrough's history] (Dublin: Societie of Stationers, 1633); reprinted as *Ancient Irish Histories: The Works of Spenser, Campion, Hanmer, and Marleburrough* [etc.] (Dublin: Hibernia Press, 1809).

xi

INTRODUCTORY NOTE

The Fortunes of Perkin Warbeck, A Romance (3 vols, London: Printed by J. B. Nichols and Son, 25, Parliament Street; for Henry Colburn and Richard Bentley, 1830), was the fourth of Mary Wollstonecraft Shelley's six novels and her second work of historical fiction. By January 1827, less than a year after publishing *The Last Man*, she had found her new subject: the pretender to the English throne who claimed to be the younger of the two princes allegedly murdered by Richard III.[1] Exactly when she began working on the novel remains uncertain,[2] but by mid-September 1827 she was 'steal[ing] an hour for writing in the morning', and before the end of the month Godwin had sent her an account of the children of Edward IV and details concerning the aftermath of the battle of Bosworth Field, the novel's opening incident.[3] Her father continued to assist her by fulfilling small research commissions at the British Museum, supplying books from his library, and untangling factual knots.[4] He remained her devoted partisan, offering encouragement as she worked on *Perkin Warbeck* after recovering from smallpox, which she had contracted in the spring of 1828. 'I am transported with your manuscript', he wrote in August of that year, '& long for more'.[5]

By then Mary Shelley had probably studied the major sources named in her Preface (Bacon, Hall, Holinshed, Hume, and Pinkerton) and had examined the revisionist arguments of a few 'modern writers' (Bayley and Walpole), whom she used to subvert the prevailing historical orthodoxy.[6] To these may be added some literary precursors, whose works inevitably form a context for her own. Many of the characters in her novel appear in the *Henry VI* trilogy and *Richard III* of Shakespeare as well as in John Ford's *The Chronicle History of Perkin Warbeck*, a copy of which she had acquired in February 1828.[7]

In the summer and early autumn of 1828 Mary Shelley made a series of requests related to her hero's progress from Flanders, to Spain (rather than to Portugal, where the historical Warbeck travelled), Ireland, and France. First, she sought John Bowring's advice about a suitable 'History of Spain' covering the period 1482–92, questioning him about the 'wars of Grenada [sic]' and 'Herrera' as well as soliciting his suggestions about other titles she might borrow or consult.[8] Next, on 20 August, she asked Byron's old publisher John Murray for Thomas Leland's history of Ireland, Philippe de Comines's account of the French kings Louis XI and Charles VIII, and a 'description of Cork' that 'treated [...] of the antiquities'. Three weeks later she appealed for 'some travels in Andalusia' that portrayed 'the *Scenery* – & [...] the Antique Moorish remains'.[9] Before the end of September she had also sought information about French sources from her admirer and suitor, the writer Prosper Mérimée, whom she had met in Paris.[10]

When Mary Shelley wrote to P. B. Shelley's old publisher Charles Ollier on 14 October 1828, she asked him to procure for her historical accounts by Barante (recommended by Mérimée), 'Ware' ('one of Leland's [...] Authorities'), and the Abbot of Croyland.[11] At the end of October she also made a direct appeal to Thomas Crofton Croker, the Anglo-Irish antiquarian whose depiction of Cork in *Researches in the South of Ireland*[12] she had found 'quite to my purpose'. Confiding her fear of making 'a thousand mistakes' about Ireland, which she had never visited, she won Croker's sympathy.[13] In November 1828 he lent her some books and suggested others. The following May she requested that he furnish her with works he had mentioned – histories of Ireland by Campion, Hanmer, and Stafford – and asked as well to borrow a volume of Leland, an account of the earls of Desmond, and a map of London from the time of Elizabeth I. Her correspondence with Croker also makes clear that he volunteered to check the Irish chapters of *Perkin Warbeck* before publication, a promise he apparently kept.[14]

Mary Shelley next approached Sir Walter Scott. Having discovered in old forgotten writers 'a glimmering of the truth' about her hero, she asked in a letter of 25 May 1829 for his advice about sources other than Buchanan, Lindsay, and Pinkerton, whose histories of Scotland she had already examined. By this time she was by her own account 'far advanced', perhaps up to or beyond the point in Chapter xi of Volume II where Perkin appears at the court of James IV of Scotland.[15]

Perkin Warbeck was completed in the autumn of 1829. By 4 November, having 'written altogether enough for five vols', she was cutting her manuscript to the standard three that publishers expected. She claimed to have already revised and copied one volume, and anticipated finishing the remainder 'in two or 3 weeks'.[16] She may have continued to make changes in the first volume, however, even after she submitted a copy of it to prospective publishers, because on 7 December she asked Murray to lend her Washington Irving's 'exquisitely written and interesting' *Conquest of Granada*, the work that enabled her to abridge the Spanish episodes in *Perkin Warbeck*.[17]

Mary Shelley's hopes that Murray would take on her novel – he had previously lent her £100 which she considered an advance – were extinguished by 12 November.[18] Undaunted, she applied the next day to Henry Colburn, publisher of *The Last Man*. Colburn, who had recently formed a partnership with the printer Richard Bentley, was slow to respond, as Mary Shelley's increasingly anxious letters indicate.[19] Repeated inquiries to Ollier, by then in Colburn and Bentley's employ, yielded nothing until after the new year, when she agreed to the sale of the copyright to 'Poor Perkin Warbeck for £150', payable in three installments. The contract dated 21 January 1830 specified that the novel be ready for publication by 1 March.[20]

Colburn and Bentley continued to be dilatory. Mary Shelley complained of their neglect, and it was only on 5 March that she could tell Murray that at last 'Colburn is in a great hurry [...] so I shall be very busy for two or three weeks'. Three weeks turned into six, however, and *Perkin Warbeck* still was not printed, at least in part because the only copy of the first forty-four pages of Volume III – 'given to the Printer's boy some time back' – had been mislaid and not yet located by 19 April.[21]

When *Perkin Warbeck* had been printed, but not yet published, news of a rival three-decker arrived: Alexander Campbell's *Perkin Warbeck; or, the Court of James the Fourth of Scotland*, issued by A. K. Newman. Campbell, whose narrative focused on a single episode in Warbeck's career, presented him as an impostor but drifted far from the historical roots of the story.[22] Mary Shelley did her best to reassure her publishers, arguing that 'no one would dream of putting [a novel] from Mʳ Newman's press in competition with one issueing from Mess. Colburn & Bentley'; moreover, the words 'By the Author of Frankenstein' on her title page would excite interest. Although she suggested an alternative title, *The White Rose of England; or Perkin Warbeck* – the name of her protagonist had already been printed as the running title on every page – the novel was published on 13 May under the name she had originally chosen.[23]

When Mary Shelley had offered *Perkin Warbeck* to her publishers, she mentioned that Scott, Thomas Moore, and her father each considered her subject 'highly interesting'.[24] And it was on the subject that Colburn and Bentley concentrated when they tried to distinguish their title from Newman's. Their promotional blurbs advertised Perkin Warbeck as the perfect romance hero and praised the author's 'stirring picture [...] of that mysterious claimant of the British throne'.[25]

Colburn and Bentley's methods precipitated some hostile reaction and fewer than a dozen reviews. Reviewers for two journals passed judgement without even reading the Shelley novel: the *Spectator* praised Campbell at her expense and complained about the price of her *Warbeck*, while the *Monthly Magazine* excused its sin of omission because 'so little confidence have we that a tolerable story, merely historical, concerning persons actuated by the common feelings and aspirings of mortals, can come from her hands'.[26] There was also, however, some unequivocal praise: the *Edinburgh Literary Gazette* situated Mary Shelley among the masters of the popular genre of historical fiction; and the *Literary Gazette and Journal* found *Perkin Warbeck* 'full of strange incident and mysterious interest', considering its title character 'admirably' suited for the novelist, who 'flings over her subject all the attraction belonging to the innocent and unfortunate'.[27]

For the most part, however, contemporary reviewers balanced praise and stricture. The *Athenaeum* critic typified those who lauded Mary Shelley's powers of description and character portrayal but expressed reservations about her handling of plot and historical detail. Despite a confessed antipathy to historical novels, the reviewer commended the author for 'a noble energy of thought – a deep concentration of feeling – a fervid glow of expression, and sweet purity of sentiment which display [. . .] the very highest capabilities'. The 'noble conceptions' of Clifford, Frion, and de Faro, were admired. The only defect lay in the reader's 'unavoidable knowledge, that every effort of the hero will fail, and that destruction must overtake him at the last'.[28] The *Edinburgh Literary Journal* similarly blended praise for the 'bold vigour and fine discrimination' of her character sketches and observations with complaints that there was little in the career of Warbeck – impostor or not – to justify 'undivided attention to it through three long volumes'.[29]

Weighing in with a comparable split decision, the reviewer for the *New Monthly Magazine and Literary Journal* preferred the novel's early invented episodes to the 'series of disasters' that constitute the remaining action. Yet there is praise for the author's 'powerful' descriptions and 'beautiful love passages' and for the commingling of 'great energy' of thought and expression with 'feminine delicacy of feeling and perception'.[30] Like his colleagues, the reviewer for the *Sunday Times* (London) admired Mary Shelley's characterisation, but reversed the common judgement regarding plot and description: 'thinking she is sometimes too profuse of her reflections, we are captivated with the situations she has imagined'.[31] The *Intelligence*, on the other hand, recommended *Perkin Warbeck* as a romance, lauded its 'elegant and perspicuous' style, and took exception only to some historical liberties and inaccuracies.[32]

The present text is based on the first edition of 1830, the only one seen through the press by the author.[33] A guide to the principles of textual treatment will be found in volume I of this edition. Explicatory footnotes point out many of Mary Shelley's departures from her known sources and in some conspicuous instances her fidelity to them, but these are not exhaustive. A copy of the first edition, now owned by Lord Abinger, contains her annotations and corrections, most likely made with a second edition in mind, and possibly after studying the *Intelligence* review.[34] The authorial emendations – correction of typesetting errors, adjustments of matters of fact, and marginal indications clarifying the chronology – are listed either in the 'Endnotes' or among the footnotes, as appropriate. All other textual interventions are listed among the 'Silent Corrections'. The comparatively large number of printers' errors and spelling inconsistencies visible in *Perkin Warbeck* may well be the result of Mary Shelley's publishers' 'great hurry', the temporary loss of a portion of her manuscript, or possibly to difficulties stemming from the recent merger of Colburn with Bentley.[35]

NOTES

[1] She described her subject as 'a good one' (*MWSL*, I, p. 538). How good it was emerges from a survey of holdings of major libraries in the USA and the UK. Although Richard III has been a perennial favourite since the fifteenth century (few historical figures have inspired so many writers or have had more *in memoriam* notices inserted in newspapers), Perkin Warbeck, his self-proclaimed nephew, has also had an ample share of glory and ignominy. For a pre-1970 selection of works on Warbeck, some of which may have been known to Mary Shelley, see Palacio, pp. 148–50. Since 1970 Warbeck has appeared – among other places – in a drama by Wallace Johnson (*Don't Leave Me Alone*, 1971), and in novels by Philip Lindsay, Marian Palmer, Rosemary Hawley Jarman, Philippa Wiat (*A Princely Knave*, 1971; *The Wrong Plantagenet*, 1972; *The Courts of Illusion*, 1984; *Prince of the White Rose*, 1984). His name also occurs in the title of a collection of poems by Keith Dersley (*The Perkin Warbeck Blues*, 1974). Twentieth-century historians consider the question of Warbeck's legitimacy to have been conclusively resolved against him by James Gairdner in 1898 (see *Oxford History*, VII, p. 116n); nevertheless, his claims continue to be debated.

[2] Palacio (p. 141), to whose detailed study of *Perkin Warbeck* I am greatly indebted, speculates that Mary Shelley's interest originated in her reading of Hume's *History of England* (in 1818; see *MWSJ*, II, p. 654). Sunstein (p. 274) suggests that she began her research in the summer of 1826.

[3] *MWSL*, II, p. 6; Godwin to Shelley, 26 September 1827 (Ab. MSS, Pf. Film, reel V, file 7; *Shelley and Mary*, III, pp. 1106C-D).

[4] On 13 August 1828, he identified the father of her villain, Sir Robert Clifford; and in letters dated 29 and 30 May 1829, he transmitted genealogical details about the Dukes of Norfolk (incorporated into Volume II, Chapter viii), promising further to 'consult Dugdale' at the British Museum. In the letter of 30 May he complained mildly that she had 'deprive[d] me of some of the books I might consult respecting Yorkists and Lancastrians' (Ab. MSS, Pf. Film, reel V, file 7; *Shelley and Mary*, III, pp. 1122A-B).

[5] Ab. MSS, Pf. Film, reel V, file 7.

[6] To this short list of mainstream historians and Tudor chroniclers can be added the authors of Scotch and Irish histories mentioned in letters written during the time she was writing *Perkin Warbeck*. She probably also read the histories of John Stow, Malcolm Laing, Robert Henry, and William Dugdale (all mentioned to her by Godwin) and may have examined the accounts of Polydore Vergil, Sir Thomas More, Thomas Gainsford, Richard Grafton, and Esprit Joseph Chaudon, among others. Mary Shelley identifies the source of her epigraph as the rhymed chronicle of Chastellain and Molinet, and she may have known Chastellain's *Chronique des ducs de Bourgogne* as well. For bibliographical data concerning these works and other probable sources mentioned in this 'Introductory Note', see the 'Abbreviations' list. Palacio (pp. 153–4) first identified the 'modern writers' (*MWSL*, II, p. 78) as Horace Walpole and John Bayley, the best-known apologists for Warbeck's claims. The matter of Mary Shelley's sources – definite, probable, and possible – and the editions she used still awaits a thorough investigation, but the available evidence indicates that she carefully researched Warbeck's life and times.

[7] In William Gifford's edition of Ford's works; *MWSL*, II, p. 27.

[8] Her undated letter to Bowring, editor of the *Westminster Review*, is postmarked '16 A[ ] | 1828' (manuscript in the Pforzheimer Collection). Given that she left for Paris on 11 April and that the manuscript contains only domestic stamps, the letter must have been written in August ('A[U]') rather than April ('A[P]'). Exactly which history (or histories) initially formed the basis for the Spanish episodes of *Perkin Warbeck* cannot yet be determined, but several titles in English and French would have been available before 1830. Mary Shelley's description of Granada and its environs – and the footnote she herself supplied in her text (see p. 85) – indicate, however, that she found only Irving's *Conquest of Granada* satisfying for 'romantic detail'. Herrera wrote principally about Spanish conquests in the Americas (see 'Abbreviations' for two possible titles); the book about the Granadan wars was probably by Perez de Hita.

[9] *MWSL*, II, pp. 56, 59.

[10] Mérimée affirmed the importance of Comines's work and added a brief bibliography of other chroniclers and historians: Olivier de La Marche, Francesco Guicciardini, Pierre Matthieu, Pierre du Terrail (seigneur de Bayard), and Amable G. P. Brugière, Baron de Barante. See Betty T.

Bennett and William T. Little, 'Seven Letters from Prosper Mérimée to Mary Shelley', *Comparative Literature*, XXXI, No. 2 (Spring 1979), 146, where descriptions, titles, and dates are provided. Although direct evidence indicates that she pursued Barante only, further study may reveal that she examined other authors on Mérimée's list.

[11] *MWSL*, II, p. 63 and n. The Croyland work was included in Savile's compendium of 'Monkish' chronicles; Ware wrote about Irish history and antiquities and published a collection of accounts of Ireland written by Campion, Hanmer, Marleburrough, and Spenser (see n. 14). Mary Shelley was still searching for Barante's book on 1 July 1829 (*MWSL*, II, p. 80). See 'Abbreviations' for the Ware and Savile titles.

[12] Gareth W. Dunleavy ('Two New Mary Shelley Letters and the "Irish" Chapters of *Perkin Warbeck*', *Keats-Shelley Journal*, XIII [Winter 1964], 6–10) discovered the use Mary Shelley made of Croker's description of Cork in Chapter xi of *Researches* in *Perkin Warbeck*, Vol. I, Chapter xiv, and Vol. III, Chapter iii. She may also have read Croker's *Fairy Legends and Traditions of the South of Ireland*, 3 vols (London: John Murray, 1825–8), but would not have found it so much to her purpose.

[13] *MWSL*, II, pp. 59, 65. Croker was a friend of the Irish poet Thomas Moore, then working on *Letters and Journals of Lord Byron: With Notices of His Life* (London: John Murray, 1830). Mary Shelley gave Moore considerable assistance.

[14] If Ollier had procured 'Ware' for her when she asked in October 1828 (see n. 11), it must have been *The Antiquities and History of Ireland*. She otherwise would have already been familiar with the titles by Campion and Hanmer (included in Ware's *The Historie of Ireland, Collected by three Learned Authors viz. Meredith Hanmer* [...] *Edmund Campion* [...] *and Edmund Spenser*) which she requested from Croker in May 1829. (*MWSL*, II, pp. 88, 105 and n; III, pp. 410–11 and n, 413.)

[15] *MWSL*, II, pp. 77–8. A record of Scott's response has not been located, but she invoked his approval of her subject when she was searching for a publisher; see p. xv.

[16] *MWSL*, II, p. 88.

[17] *MWSL*, II, p. 91. Irving's book had not been published when Mary Shelley asked Bowring about Spanish sources in 1828. The adjectives she uses to describe Irving's work when she makes her request to Murray in December 1829, however, demonstrate that *The Conquest of Granada* (published in April of that year) was familiar to her by then. Given her statement in early November that she had completed revisions for Volume I, and her fear (expressed in her letter of 13 November to Henry Colburn) that the first volume might appear 'scanty', it seems evident that the excisions in the Spanish episodes (see p. 85) had already been made. Perhaps she merely wanted to recheck some details as she worked to cut Volumes II and III. It is also possible, of course, that she merely returned to Irving's work for pleasure.

[18] *MWSL*, II, p. 27 and n; II, p. 89 and n.

[19] Mary Shelley wrote to Colburn on 12 December, and to Ollier three times that month, in an effort to discover the firm's intentions (*MWSL*, II, pp. 91–2, 96–7).

[20] *MWSL*, II, p. 98 and n.

[21] *MWSL*, II, pp. 106–7.

[22] For an extended comparison of the two novels, see Palacio, pp. 172–8.

[23] *MWSL*, II, pp. 107–8. Godwin noted the publication date in his Journal, but had already begun *Perkin Warbeck* on 12 May and continued reading sections every day until finishing it on 23 May (Ab. MSS, Pf. Film, reel III).

[24] *MWSL*, II, p. 90.

[25] Quoted in Palacio, p. 665, who notes that caveats about Campbell's novel and 'puffing advertisements' appeared in *Bell's Weekly Messenger*, the *Globe*, the *Morning Journal*, the *Morning Post*, the *Observer*, and the *Standard*, among other places (pp. 665–7).

[26] *Spectator*, No. 97 (8 May 1830), 295; *Monthly Magazine, or British Register of Literature, Sciences, and the Belles Lettres*, No. 10 (October 1830), 470.

[27] *Edinburgh Literary Gazette*, II, No. 57 (12 June 1830), 369–72, cited from the summary in Palacio (p. 665); *Literary Gazette, and Journal of the Belles Lettres*, No. 696 (22 May 1830), 335.

[28] *Athenaeum*, No. 135 (29 May 1830), 323.

[29] *Edinburgh Literary Journal; or Weekly Register of Criticism and Belles Lettres*, No. 84 (19 June 1830), 350–1. In spite of a strong preference for the Shelley novel, the reviewer suggests that Mary Shelley should, like Campbell, have concentrated on a striking aspect of Warbeck's career, for example, his residence and marriage in Scotland.

[30] *New Monthly Magazine and Literary Journal*, XXX, No. CXIX (November 1830), 457.

[31] *Sunday Times*, No. 400 (20 June 1830), 1.

[32] *Intelligence*, No. 11 (30 May 1830), 83; cited from descriptions in Palacio (p. 665) and Lyles (p. 178).

[33] *Perkin Warbeck* was pirated by Carey, Lea & Blanchard of Philadelphia in 1834 (2 vols) and reprinted twice: in 'London, N[ew] Y[ork]' in 1857 by G. Routledge and Company (1 vol.); and in photofacsimile by Norwood Editions in 1976 (3 vols). The piracy corrected some, but by no means all, of the typographical errors, leaving in place the erroneous numeration of the chapters in Volume I (see 'Endnotes').

[34] Because Lord Abinger's copy of *Perkin Warbeck* was unavailable for examination before this edition went to press, I relied in the 'Endnotes' and 'Footnotes' on the census of changes given by Palacio (pp. 637–8).

[35] *MWSL*, II, p. 106.

THE WHITE ROSE ❋ The House of York

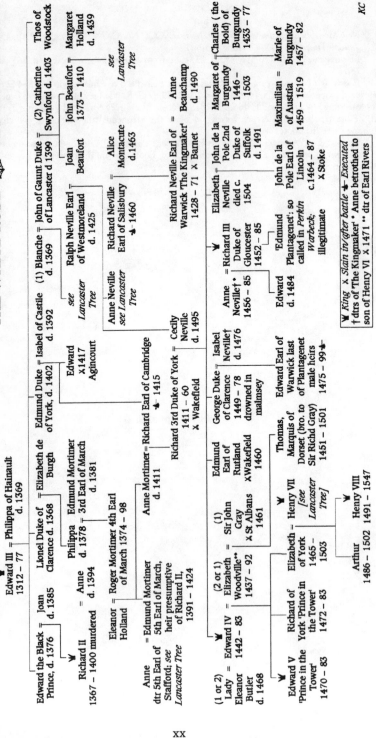

KC

THE RED ROSE ✦ The House of Lancaster

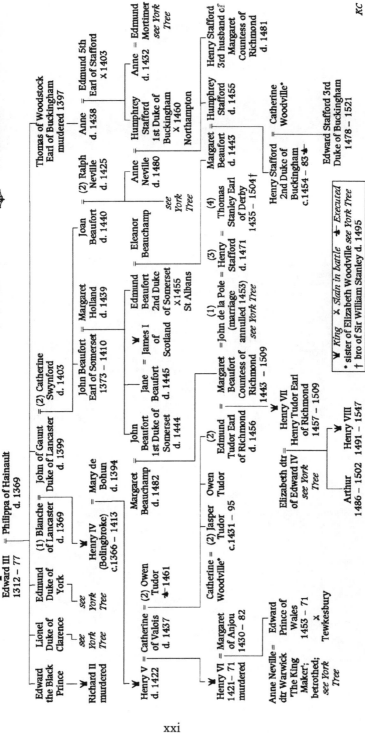

KC

The Fortunes of Perkin Warbeck
A Romance

ᵃ Epigraph: 'I have seen the son of England, named Richard of York (who people in the world said was defeated and destroyed) undergo great suffering; and [yet] by his noble accomplishments live in great hope to become king of the English' [translation supplied by Marcelle Thiébaux]; see Preface (p. 6 and n).

THE

FORTUNES

OF

PERKIN WARBECK,

A ROMANCE.

BY THE

AUTHOR OF " FRANKENSTEIN."

J'ai veu filz d'Angleterre, Richard d'Yorc nommé,
Que l'on disoit en terre, estinct et consommé,
Endurer grant souffrance ; et par nobles exploitz,
Vivre en bonne esperance, d'estre Roy des Angloys.

Old French Chronicle.

IN THREE VOLUMES.

VOL. I.

LONDON:

HENRY COLBURN AND RICHARD BENTLEY,
NEW BURLINGTON STREET.

1830.

PREFACE.

The story of Perkin Warbeck[a] was first suggested to me as a subject for historical detail. On studying it, I became aware of the romance which his story contains, while, at the same time, I felt that it would be impossible for any narration, that should be confined to the incorporation of facts related by our old Chroniclers, to do it justice.

It is not singular that I should entertain a belief that Perkin was, in reality, the lost Duke of York. For, in spite of Hume,[b] and the later historians who have followed in his path, no person who has at all studied the subject but arrives at the same conclusion. Records exist / in the Tower, some well known, others with which those who have access to those interesting papers are alone acquainted, which put the question almost beyond a doubt.[c]

This is not the place for a discussion of the question. The principal thing that I should wish to be impressed on my reader's mind is, that whether my hero was or was not an impostor, he was believed to be the true man by his contemporaries. The partial pages of Bacon, of Hall, and Holinshed and others of that date, are replete with proofs of this fact.[d] There are some curious letters, written by Sir John Ramsay, Laird of Balmayne, calling himself Lord Bothwell,

---

[a] Perkin Warbeck (?1474–99), born in Tournai (now in Belgium, south-west of Brussels). He won support in Ireland (1491) and from other domestic and foreign opponents of England's first Tudor king, Henry VII. The nominal leader of unsuccessful invasions of England in 1495, 1496, and 1497, he was defeated, captured, and executed after two attempted escapes.

[b] David Hume (1711–76), empiricist philosopher, political economist, and historian; alluding to his magisterial, politically conservative *History of England*. Mary Shelley told Sir Walter Scott on 25 May 1829 that she discovered in older historians information 'entirely passed over by Hume' (*MWSL*, II, p. 78).

[c] Almost certainly referring to works by Horace Walpole, 4th Earl of Orford (1717–97), and the antiquarian John Bayley (d. 1869). Bayley castigates the 'violent prejudices' of earlier commentators.

[d] Francis Bacon, 1st Baron Verulam and Viscount St Albans (1561–1626), philosopher, essayist, Lord Chancellor, and author of *Henry the Seventh*; Edward Hall (or Halle, c.1498–1547), whose *Union of* [...] *Lancastre and Yorke* was continued and updated by Richard Grafton (d. 1572); Raphael Holinshed (d. c. 1580), whose *Chronicles* (like Hall's account) were among the sources of Shakespeare's history plays. Throughout, Mary Shelley uses evidence furnished by such supporters of Tudor legitimacy to undermine their own position.

addressed to Henry the Seventh himself, which, though written by a spy and hireling of that monarch, tend to confirm my belief, and even demonstrate that in his eagerness to get rid of a formidable competitor, Henry did not hesitate to urge midnight assassination. These letters are printed in the Appendix to Pinkerton's History of Scotland.[a] / The verses which form the motto to these volumes, are part of a rythmical Chronicle, written by two subjects of Burgundy, who lived in those days; it is entitled "Recollection des Merveilles, advenues en nostre temps, commencée par très élégant orateur, Messire Georges Chastellan, et continuée par Maistre Jean Molinet."[b]

In addition to the unwilling suffrage of his enemies, we may adduce the acts of his friends and allies. Human nature in its leading features is the same in all ages. James the Fourth[c] of Scotland was a man of great talent and discernment: he was proud; attached, as a Scot, to the prejudices of birth; of punctilious honour. No one can believe that he would have bestowed his near kinswoman, nor have induced the Earl of Huntley[d] to give his daughter in marriage, to one who did not bear evident signs of being of royal blood.

The various adventures of this unfortunate Prince in many countries, and his alliance with a / beautiful and high-born woman, who proved a faithful, loving wife to him, take away the sting from the ignominy which might attach itself to his fate; and make him, we venture to believe, in spite of the contumely later historians have chosen, in the most arbitrary way, to heap upon him, a fitting object of interest – a hero to ennoble the pages of a humble tale. /

---

[a] John Pinkerton (1758–1826), Scottish antiquarian and historian, whose history contains letters concerning Warbeck's 1496 invasion of England. For Ramsay (or Ramsey), see p. 221 and n.
[b] Georges Chastellain (1403–75), poet and chronicler in the Burgundian court of Philip the Good; his *Récollection de merveilleuses avenues en nostre temps, commencée par très élégant orateur messire George Chastelain* [...] *et continuée jusques à présent par maistre Jehan Molinet* was completed by his disciple and secretary Jean Molinet (d. 1507).
[c] For James IV, see pp. 209–10.
[d] For the Earl of Huntley, see p. 219n.

PERKIN WARBECK.

CHAPTER I.

He seemed breathless, heartless, faint and wan,
And all his armour sprinkled was with blood,
And soiled with dirty gore, that no man can
Discern the hue thereof. He never stood,
But bent his hasty course towards the idle flood.

SPENSER.[a]

After a long series of civil dissension – after many battles, whose issue involved the fate of thousands – after the destruction of nearly all the English nobility in the contest between the two Roses, the decisive battle of Bosworth Field was fought on the 22d of August, 1485,[1] whose result was to entwine, as it was called, the white and red symbols of rivalship, and to restore peace to this unhappy country.[b] /

The day had been sunny and warm: as the evening closed in, a west wind rose, bringing along troops of fleecy clouds, golden at sunset, and then dun and grey, veiling with pervious network the many stars. Three horsemen at this hour passed through the open country between Hinckley and Welford in Leicestershire.[c] It

---

[a] Edmund Spenser (?1552–99), *Faerie Queene* (Books I–III, 1590; Books IV–VI, 1596), II. vi. 41.

[b] The wars (1455–85) were fought by the Houses of Lancaster and York (rival descendents of Edward III, 1312–77; ruled 1327–77), symbolized respectively by the Red and White Rose. The victorious Lancastrian Henry Tudor, acclaimed Henry VII (1457–1509; ruled 1485–1509) on Bosworth field, married the Yorkist Elizabeth (1465–1503), daughter of Edward IV and niece of Richard III, thus uniting the two Roses (1486).

[c] Small towns about six and twenty miles south-east of Bosworth. The precision with which this journey may be traced suggests an unrecorded visit to the area or the use of road maps to extrapolate a medieval route.

7

was broad day when they descended from the elevation on which the former stands, and the villagers crowded to gaze upon the fugitives, and to guess, from the ensigns they bore, to which party they belonged, while the warders from the near castle hastened out to stop them, thus to curry favour with the conqueror; a design wholly baffled. The good steeds of the knights, for such their golden spurs attested them to be, bore them fast and far along the Roman road, which still exists in those parts to shame our modern builders. It was dusk when, turning from the direct route to avoid entering Welford, they reached a ford of the Avon.[a] Hitherto silence had prevailed with the party – for until now their anxiety to fly had solely occupied their thoughts. Their appearance spoke of / war, nay, of slaughter. Their cloaks were stained and torn; their armour was disjointed, and parts of it were wanting; yet these losses were so arbitrary, that it was plain that the pieces had been hacked from their fastenings. The helm of the foremost was deprived of its crest; another wore the bonnet of a common soldier, which ill accorded with the rest of his accoutrements; while the third, bareheaded, his hair falling on his shoulders, lank and matted from heat and exercise, gave more visible tokens of the haste of flight. As the night grew darker, one of them, and then another, seemed willing to relax somewhat in their endeavours: one alone continued, with unmitigated energy, to keep his horse at the same pace they had all maintained during the broad light of day.

When they reached the ford, the silence was broken by the hindmost horseman; he spoke in a petulant voice, saying: – "Another half mile at this pace, and poor Fleur-de-Luce founders; if you will not slacken your speed, here we part, my friends. God save you till we meet again!" /

"Evil betide the hour that separates us, brother!" said the second fugitive, reining in; "Our cause, our peril, our fate shall be the same. You, my good lord, will consult your own safety."

The third cavalier had already entered the stream: he made a dead halt while his friends spoke, and then replied: – "Let us name some rendezvous where, if we escape, we may again meet. I go on an errand of life and death; my success is doubtful, my danger certain. If I succeed in evading it, where shall I rejoin you?"

"Though the event of this day has been fatal to the king," answered the other, "our fortunes are not decided. I propose taking refuge in some sanctuary,[b] till we perceive how far the Earl of Richmond[c] is inclined to mercy."

---

[a] The ford is presumed to be where Watling Street (the Roman Road) crosses the Avon, exactly at the convergence of three 'Heart of England' counties: Warwickshire, Leicestershire, and Northamptonshire. The knights join Watling Street near the present Mancetter and gallop for about fifteen miles.

[b] Sanctuary, a religious place of refuge designated by royal charter, protected fugitives from punishment.

[c] Henry Tudor's title before his victory at Bosworth.

"I knew the Earl when a mere youth, Sir Humphrey Stafford,"[a] said the foremost rider, "and heard more of him when I visited Brittanny, at the time of King Louis's[b] death, two years ago. When mercy knocks at his heart, suspicion and avarice give her a rough reception. / We must fly beyond sea, unless we can make further stand. More of this when we meet again. Where shall that be?"

"I have many friends near Colchester,"[c] replied the elder Stafford, "and St. Mary boasts an asylum there which a crowned head would not dare violate. Thence, if all else fail, we can pass with ease to the Low Countries."[d]

"In sanctuary at Colchester – I will not fail you. God bless and preserve you the while!"

The noble, as he said these words, put spurs to his horse, and without looking back crossed the stream, and turning on the skirts of a copse was soon out of sight of his companions. He rode all night, cheering his steed with hand and voice; looking angrily at the early dawning east, which soon cast from her cloudless brow the dimness of night. Yet the morning air was grateful to his heated cheeks. It was a perfect summer's morn. The wheat, golden from ripeness, swayed gracefully to the light breeze; the slender oats shook their small bells in the air with ceaseless motion; the birds twittering, alighted from the full-leaved trees, scattering dew-drops / from the branches. With the earliest dawn the Cavalier entered a forest, traversing its depths with the hesitation of one unacquainted with the country, and looked frequently at the sky, to be directed by the position of the glowing east. A path more worn than the one he had hitherto followed now presented itself, leading into the heart of the wood. He hesitated for a few seconds, and then, with a word of cheer to his horse, pursued his way into the embowering thicket. After a short space the path narrowed, the meeting branches of the trees impeded him, and the sudden angle it made from the course he wished to follow served to perplex him still further; but as he vented his impatience by hearty Catholic exclamations, a little tinkling bell spoke of a chapel near, and of the early rising of the priest to perform the matin service at its altar. The horse of the fugitive, a noble warsteed, had long flagged; and hunger gnawed at the rider's own heart, for he had not tasted food since the morning of the previous day. These sounds, therefore, heard in so fearless a seclusion, bore with them pleasant tidings / of refreshment and repose. He crossed himself in thankfulness; then throwing himself from his horse (and such change was soothing to his stiffened limbs), he led

---

[a] These Staffords (Sir Humphrey and his brother Thomas) are not the Staffords of Shakespeare's *Henry VI* plays or *Richard III*.

[b] Louis XI of France (1423–83; ruled 1461–83), known as the 'universal spider' for his intrigues.

[c] Town in Essex; Richard I had granted special privileges to the hospital of St Mary Magdalene in 1189.

[d] The county of Flanders, duchy of Brabant, county of Holland, and bishopric of Liège made up the Low Countries (today, Belgium, Luxembourg, and the Netherlands) in the Tudor period.

him through the opening glade to where a humble chapel and a near adjoining hut stood in the bosom of the thicket, emblems of peace and security.

The Cavalier tied his horse to a tree, and entered the chapel. A venerable priest was reading the matin service; one old woman composed his congregation, and she was diligently employed telling her beads. The bright rays of the newly risen sun streamed through the eastern window, casting the chequered shadow of its lattice work on the opposite wall. The chapel was small and rustic; but it was kept exquisitely clean: the sacred appurtenances of the altar also were richer than was usual, and each shrine was decked with clusters of flowers, chiefly composed of white roses. No high praise, indeed, was due to the rude picture of the Virgin of the Annunciation, or of the announcing Angel, a representation of whom formed the altar-piece: but in barbaric England, / in those days, piety stood in place of taste, and that which represented Our Lady received honour, however unworthy it might be of the inspiress of Raphael or Correggio.[a] The cavalier took his disornamented casque from his head, placed it on the ground, and knelt reverentially on the bare earth. He had lately escaped from battle and slaughter, and he surely thought that he had especial motive for thanksgiving; so that if his lips uttered a mere soldier's "Ave," still it had the merit of fervour and sincerity.

Had he been less occupied by his own feelings, he might have remarked the many glances the priest cast on him, who dishonoured his learning and piety by frequent mistakes of language, as his thoughts wandered from his breviary, to observe with deep attention his unexpected visitor. At length the service ended: the old dame rose from her knees, and satisfied her curiosity which she had excited by many a look askance, by a full and long gaze on the cavalier. His hewn armour, torn cloak, and, unseemly for the sacred spot, the dread stains / on his garments and hands were all minutely scanned. Nor did his personal appearance escape remark. His stature was tall, his person well knit, shewing him to be a man of about thirty years of age. His features were finely moulded, his grey eyes full of fire, his step had the dignity of rank, and his look expressed chivalrous courage and frankness. The good woman had not been long engaged in surveying the stranger, when her pastor beckoned her to retire, and himself advanced, replying to the soldier's salute with a benedicite,[b] and then hastily enquiring if he came from the field.

"Even so, Father," said the Cavalier; "I come from the field of the bloody harvest. Has any intelligence of it travelled hither so speedily? If so, I must have wandered from the right road, and am not so far on my journey as I hoped."

"I have only heard that a battle was expected," said the priest, "and your

---

[a] Raffaello Sanzio (1483–1520) and Correggio (Antonio Allegri, 1494–1534). Both depicted the Annunciation (see Luke 1:26–38) and were admired by Mary Shelley, the former as 'the Prince or rather God of painting' (*MWSL*, I, p. 90; III, pp. 38–9).
[b] A blessing.

appearance tells me that it is over. The fortunes, nay, perhaps the life, of a dear friend are involved in its issue, and I fear that it is adverse – for you / fly from pursuit, and methinks, though stained with dust and blood, that emblem on your breast is the White Rose."

The warrior looked on the old man, whose dignity and language were at variance with his lowly destination; he looked partly in wonder, and partly to assure himself of his questioner's sincerity. "You are weary, Sir Knight," added the Monk, whose experienced eyes had glanced to the golden spurs of his visitant; "come to my hermitage, there to partake of such refreshment as I can bestow. When your repast is ended, I will, by confidence on my part, merit yours."

This invitation was that of worldly courtesy, rather than the rustic welcome of a recluse monk. The Cavalier thanked him cordially, adding, that he must first provide food and water for his horse, and that afterwards he would gratefully accept his host's invitation. The old man entered with the spirit of a soldier into his guest's anxiety for his steed, and assisted in purveying to its wants, ingratiating himself meanwhile with its master, / by discovering and praising scientifically its points of beauty. The poor animal shewed tokens of over fatigue, yet still he did not refuse his food, and the Cavalier marked with joy that his eye grew brighter and his knees firmer after feeding.

They had entered the cottage, and the soldier's eye was attracted from more sacred emblems by a sword which was suspended over a picture of the Virgin: – "You belong to our Chivalry!" he exclaimed, while his countenance lighted up with joyful recognition.

"Now I belong to the holy order whose badge I wear," the Monk replied, pointing to his Benedictine dress.[a] "In former days I followed a brave leader to the field, and, in his service, incurred such guilt, as I now try to expiate by fasting and prayer."

The Monk's features were convulsed by agitation as he spoke, then crossing his arms on his breast, he was absorbed in thought for a few moments, after which he raised his head and resumed the calm and even serene look that characterized him. "Sir Knight," said he, motioning / to the table now spread for the repast, "I have but poor fare to offer, but a soldier will not disdain its meagreness. My wine I may praise, as being the produce of a generous vintage; I have kept it sealed, to open it on occasions like the present, and rejoice that your strength will be recruited by it."

Bread, fruits, cheese, and a flagon of the wine, which merited the giver's eulogium, composed the fugitive's breakfast, whose fatigue required cordial and repose. As he was occupied by his repast, his host eyed him with evident agitation, eager yet fearful to question him on the subject of the battle. At

---

[a] The black habit of the religious order founded by St Benedict, c.529.

length he again asked, "You come from the field on which the forces of the King[a] and of the Earl of Richmond met?"

"I do."

"You fought for the White Rose, and you fly?"

"I fought for the White Rose till it was struck to the ground. The king has fallen with his chief nobility around him. Few Yorkists remain to mourn the success of the Lancastrians."

Deep grief clouded the old man's countenance, / but accustomed to subdue his feelings, as one on whom, being stricken by an overwhelming misery, all subsequent disasters fall blunted, he continued with greater calmness: "Pardon me, noble gentleman, if I appear to ask an indiscreet question. You are of lordly bearing, and probably filled a place near the royal person. Did you hear, on the night before last, aught of the arrival of a stranger youth at the King's tent?"

The knight eyed the old man with a quick glance, asking, in his turn, "Are you, then, the foster-father of King Richard's son?"

"Did you see my boy?" cried the priest, "Did his father acknowledge him? – Where is he now? – did he enter the ranks to fight and fall for his parent?"

"On the night of which you speak," said the stranger, evading the immediate question, "the King placed his son's hand in mine, as I vowed to protect and guard him if ill befell our party, as it has befallen."

"Surely some presentiment of evil haunted the King's mind." /

"I do believe it; for his manner was solemn and affecting. He bade the youth remember that he was a Plantagenet,[b] and spoke proudly of the lineage from which he sprung. The young esquire listened intently, looking at his father with such an ingenuous and thoughtful expression, that he won my heart to love him."

"Now bless thee, Sir Knight, whoever thou art, for this praise of my poor Edmund![c] I pray you, hasten to tell me what more passed."

The Cavalier continued his account; but his manner was serious, as if the conclusion of his tale would afflict his auditor. He related how, on quitting the royal tent, he had led Edmund Plantagenet to his own, there to converse with him awhile, the better to learn whether his bearing and speech shewed promise of future merit. King Richard had enjoined his son to return to his seclusion early on the following morning; but as soon as he entered his conductor's tent, he knelt to him and asked a boon, while tears gathered in his eyes, and his voice

---

[a] i.e., Richard III (1452–85; ruled 1483–5). On becoming Protector of the Realm when his brother Edward IV died, he arrested and executed supporters of Edward's widow, and questioned the legitimacy of her children, the young Edward V and his brother, Richard, Duke of York. Despite Shakespeare's portrayal of him as usurper and evil incarnate, he was not guilty of all the crimes attributed to him.

[b] Family name of the fourteen kings who ruled England between 1154 and 1485.

[c] Richard III's only legitimate son was dead, but a reviewer (for the *Intelligence*) noted that Richard fathered a bastard named after himself.

was broken by the fervour of his desire. The noble was moved by his entreaties, and / promised to grant his request, if it did not militate against his honour and allegiance. "It is for honour that I speak," said Plantagenet; "I am older in years than in seeming, for already I number twenty summers; and spite of my boyish look I am familiar with martial exercises, and the glorious promise of war. Let me draw my sword for my father to-morrow – let me, at your side, prove myself a worthy descendant of the conquerors of France! Who will fight for King Richard with greater courage, fidelity, and devotion, than his acknowledged and duteous son?" The Cavalier yielded to his noble yearnings. Clothed in armour he entered the ranks, and hovered a protecting angel near his parent during the bloody contest. And now, as his venerable guardian watched with trembling eagerness the countenance of his guest while he told his tale, and the stranger, with bitter regret, was about to relate that he had seen Plantagenet felled to the ground by a battle-axe, quick steps, and then a knocking, was heard at the cottage door. The stranger / started on his feet, and put his hand upon his sword; but a bright smile illuminated the Monk's face, as the very youth of whom they spoke, Edmund Plantagenet, rushed into the apartment. His soiled garments and heated brow spoke of travel and fatigue, while his countenance wore an expression of wildness and even of horror. He started when he saw the stranger, but quickly recognized him as his new friend. "Thank God!" he cried, "that you, my dear Lord, have not fallen into the hands of the sacrilegious usurper! It is my father's spirit that has saved you for his son's sake, that I may not be utterly abandoned and an orphan."

With milder accost he bent his knee to his holy guardian, and then turned to answer the Cavalier's questions of how he had escaped death from the blow he had received, and what new events had occurred since he had quitted the field early on the preceding day? – while the Monk chid him for his disobedience to his father's commands, in having mingled with the fray. The eyes of Plantagenet flashed fire at / this reproach. – "Could I know that my father's crown and life," he exclaimed impetuously, "depended on the combat, and not bring to his aid my weak arm? God of Heaven! had there been five hundred true as I, we might all have fallen round him: but never, never, should I have seen the sight which last night I saw – nor heard the sounds I last night heard!"

The youth covered his face with his hands, and the boiling tears trickled between his fingers. "Tell me," cried the noble, "what has happened? – and swiftly tell me, for I loiter here too long."

Almost suffocated by emotion, Plantagenet related, that when he recovered from the trance into which the fearful blow he had received had thrown him, the Earl's camp-followers were busy among the slain; and that he had seen the body of King Richard – of his father – thrown half naked across a mule,[a] thus

---

[a] A horse, according to Mary Shelley's known sources.

to be borne to be exposed to the public gaze and mockery in Leicester, where, but the day before, he had ridden with the royal crown upon his head, the acknowledged sovereign of England. And that / crown, base ill-bartered bauble, having been found in the tent by Lord Stanley,[a] he had brought and placed on Richmond's head, while the soldiers, with one acclaim, hailed him Henry the Seventh, King of England.

The last words more than the others, for the death of his royal master was already known to him, moved the knight: – "Is this the end of our hopes?" he cried; "Am I then too late? Farewell, my friends! Plantagenet, I shall never forget my oath to the King; I shall become, I fear, an outcast and a soldier of fortune, even if I escape worse fate; but claim when you will, and it shall be your's, whatever protection I can afford you."

"Yield then, Lord Lovel,"[b] said the youth, "to my first request. You are in peril, let me share it: permit me to accompany you. If you refuse, my plan is already formed; I repair to the Earl of Lincoln,[c] whom King Richard named his successor, and offer myself as a soldier in his attempt to discrown the usurping Henry, and to raise again the White Rose to its rightful supremacy." /

"To the Earl of Lincoln – the successor of Richard – to him you would repair? It is well – come with me now, and I will present you to that nobleman. If your foster-father consents, bid adieu to this seclusion for a time, and accompany me to London, to new contests – to the combat of right against might – to success and honour, or to defeat and death!"

The sun had risen high when, having taken leave of the venerable Monk, who would not oppose his pupil's gallant spirit of enterprize, Lord Lovel and young Plantagenet threaded the forest paths, which, by a safer and a shorter route than the highway, took them on their road to London. For a time they led their horses with difficulty through the entangled thicket, when at last reaching the open road, they mounted, and Lord Lovel, who was desirous of estimating the abilities and disposition of his companion, entered into conversation with him. They first conversed on the sad changes which were the work of the eventful day of battle; afterwards the Cavalier led Edmund to speak of / himself, his early life, his acquirements, and his hopes.

---

[a] Sir Thomas Stanley, later 1st Earl of Derby (?1435–1504) supported every ruler during the Wars of the Roses, including his stepson, Henry VII. Mary Shelley's account is closer to the chronicles than to Shakespeare, whose Stanley plucks the crown from the temples of the dead Richard (*Richard III*, V. v. 5–6).

[b] Francis, Viscount Lovel (1454–?87), a loyal Yorkist who takes Hastings to his execution and brings back his head to the king in *Richard III*, III. iv, v. After Bosworth he took sanctuary, escaping in 1486 to mount an unsuccessful rebellion. He then fled to the continent, where he continued to conspire against Henry VII. He either died at the battle of Stoke (16 June 1487), drowned fleeing from it, or survived in hiding.

[c] John de la Pole (or Poole), Earl of Lincoln (?1464–87), eldest son of the 2nd Duke of Suffolk and Elizabeth, sister to Edward IV and Richard III, who named him heir presumptive. After Bosworth, he joined the Yorkists in exile and later died at Stoke.

When Plantagenet was but ten years old his mother died, and her last request to the father of her boy, founded on a deep knowledge of the world, was, that her son might be educated far from the court, nor be drawn from the occupations and happier scenes of private life, to become a hanger-on of princes and nobles. There was a man, a gentleman and a knight, who had been a partizan of the White Rose, and who had fought and bled for it in various battles between the Duke of York[a] and Henry VI. In one of these, the misery of the times, and horrible consequences of civil dissension, caused him unwittingly to lift his armed hand against his twin brother, nor did he discover the mistake till, with his dying voice, that brother called on him to assist him against his slayer. A life of seclusion, penance, and prayer, alone blunted his sense of remorse, and quitting the world, he retired to a monastery, where after due noviciate he took vows, and then shrinking / from commerce with his kind, followed by visions that spoke for ever to him of his unnatural crime, he retreated to the forest of Leicestershire, to dwell alone with his grief and his repentance.

His retreat was known to many of his friends, and chance had brought the Duke of Gloucester at one time to visit him; when the ancient warrior rejoiced with enthusiasm at the exaltation of the party to which he was attached. The death of the mother of Edmund had the effect of softening the Duke's heart, of making for a short interval worldly cares and objects distasteful to him, and of filling him with a desire of seclusion and peace. If he was unable to enjoy these himself, he resolved that at least his child should not be drawn by him into the thorny path of rivalship and ambition. His mother's last injunction strengthened this feeling; and the Duke, visiting again the hermit of the wood, induced him to take charge of Edmund, and bringing him up in ignorance of his real parentage, to bestow such education on him as would enable him to fill with reputation / an honourable, if not a distinguished station in society. This order of things was not changed by Richard's exaltation to the crown. On the contrary, the dangers he incurred from his usurpation, made him yet more anxious to secure a peaceful existence for his offspring. When, however, his legitimate son, whom he had created Prince of Wales,[b] died, paternal affection awoke strong in his heart, and he could not resist his desire of seeing Edmund: a memorable visit for the priest-bred nursling of the forest! It gave him a link with society with which before he had felt no connexion: his imagination and curiosity were highly excited. His revered friend, yielding to his eager demands, was easily enticed to recur to the passed scenes of an eventful life. The

---

[a] Richard Plantagenet, 3rd Duke of York (1411–60), had a more solid claim to the throne than the Lancastrian Henry VI (1421–71; ruled 1422–61, 1470–71), a pious, weak man who became the pawn of powerful, rival ministers. York served as protector twice, and won from Parliament the right to succeed Henry VI. He was murdered after the battle of Wakefield (30 December 1460), but two of his sons (Edward IV and Richard III) became kings. He is prominent in all three parts of *Henry VI*. Even in the plays which bear his name, the ineffectual Henry's role is subordinate.

[b] Edward (d. 1484), his only legitimate son.

commencement of the wars of the two Roses, and their dreadful results, furnished inexhaustible topics of discourse. Plantagenet listened with breathless interest, although it was not till the eve of the battle of Bosworth, that he knew how indissolubly his own fortunes were linked with those of the house of York. /

The events of the few last days had given him a new existence. For the first time, feeling was the parent of action; and a foregoing event drove him on to the one subsequent. He was excited to meditate on a thousand schemes, while the unknown future inspired him with an awe that thrilled his young heart with mingled pain and pleasure. He uttered his sentiments with the ingenuousness of one who had never been accustomed to converse with any but a friend; and as he spoke, his dark and thoughtful eyes beamed with a tempered fire, that shewed him capable of deep enthusiasm, though utter want of knowledge of the world must make him rather a follower than a leader.

They rode on meanwhile, the noble Cavalier and gentle Squire indulging in short repose. The intense fatigue Edmund at first endured, seemed to be subdued by the necessity of its continuance, nor did it prevent him from conversing with Lord Lovel. He was anxious thoroughly to understand the immediate grounds of the Earl of Richmond's invasion, and to ascertain the relative position of the remaining / chiefs of the White Rose: "Where," he asked, "are Edward the Fourth's children?"[a]

"The elder of these," Lord Lovel replied, "the Lady Elizabeth, is, by direction of her uncle, at Sheriff Hutton, in Yorkshire."

"And where the princes? Edward, who was proclaimed king, and his younger brother?"

"They were long imprisoned in the Tower.[b] Young Edward died there more than a year ago."

"And the Duke of York?"

"He is supposed to have died also: they were both sickly boys."

Lord Lovel said these words in a grave voice, and suspicion would have been instilled into any but the unsuspecting Edmund, of some covert meaning. After a short pause, he continued: – "The question of the succession stands thus. Your father, the Duke of Gloucester threw the stigma of illegitimacy on King

---

[a] Edward IV (1442–83; ruled 1461–70; 1471–83), eldest surviving son of Richard, 3rd Duke of York, won the throne with the help of Richard Neville, Earl of Warwick ('the Kingmaker', 1428–71). Enraged when Edward married Elizabeth Woodville, Warwick then allied himself with the Lancastrians and secured the help of France to restore Henry VI in 1470. Edward IV fled to the continent, but returned in 1471 to vanquish the Lancastrians. He executed their leaders, and (probably) arranged the murder of Henry VI, usually attributed by Tudor historians to Richard III. Of the five daughters and two sons of Edward and Elizabeth Woodville, the following are mentioned here: Elizabeth, who married Henry VII; Edward V (1470–83); Richard, Duke of York (1472–83). Edward IV figures in parts 2 and 3 of the *Henry VI* plays, and dies in *Richard III.*

[b] The Tower of London served through the centuries as a citadel, palace, prison, armoury, treasury, respository of records, and menagerie.

Edward's children, and thus took from them their right of inheriting the crown.[a] The attainder of the Duke of Clarence[b] was considered reason sufficient why his children should be excluded / from the throne, and their uncle in consequence became, by right of birth, King of England: his son he created Prince of Wales. We submitted; for a child like Edward the Fifth could scarcely be supported against an experienced warrior, a man of talent, a sage and just king, but at the expense of much blood. The wounds inflicted by the opposing houses of York and Lancaster were yet, as the late successful rebellion proves, unhealed; and had the Yorkists contended among themselves, they would yet sooner have lost the supremacy they so hardly acquired: Richard therefore received our oaths of allegiance. When his son died, the question of who was the heir to the crown became agitated; and the king at first declared the Earl of Warwick,[c] the son of the Duke of Clarence, to be his successor. It was a dangerous step – and the imprudent friends of the young Earl made it more so – to name him to succeed, who, if he were permitted at any time to wear the crown, might claim precedence of him who possessed it. Poor Warwick paid the penalty of youth and presumption: / he is now a prisoner at Sheriff Hutton; and John de la Poole, Earl of Lincoln, son of Richard's sister, and by the removal of the children of his elder brothers, his heir by law, was nominated to succeed his uncle. I am now proceeding to him. I am ignorant of the conduct he will pursue; whether he will make head against this Lancastrian King, or ——— Lincoln is a noble cavalier; a man whom bright honour clothes; he is brave, generous, and good. I shall guide myself by his counsels and resolves; and you, it appears, will follow my example."

After a pause, Lord Lovel continued: "After the death or disappearance of his princely nephews, the king, wishing to confirm his title, was ready to take the stigma thrown on their birth from his brother's daughters, and to marry his niece, the Lady Elizabeth. Her mother at first resisted, but the prospect of seeing her children restored to their rights, and herself to her lost dignity, overcame her objections, and the princess yielded a willing consent. Meanwhile the Yorkists, who joined the Earl of / Richmond, extorted from him a vow that he would make King Edward's daughter his queen; and even the Lancastrians, thinking thus to secure a king of their own, are eager for this union: yet the Earl hates us all so cordially that he was hardly brought to consent. Should he, now

---

[a] Richard III used the notorious promiscuity of Edward IV and the rumours concerning his prior marriages to argue that his marriage with Elizabeth Woodville was bigamous.

[b] George Plantagenet, Duke of Clarence (1449–78), memorably murdered in *Richard III* (I. iv) by drowning in a butt of malmsey, was brother of Edward IV and Richard III. For conspiring against Edward IV he was attainted and sentenced to death. Attainder is the extinction of civil and political rights, including the transmission of titles and property to heirs, which follows a sentence of death or outlawry, usually for treason.

[c] Edward Plantagenet, Earl of Warwick (1475–99), son of the Duke of Clarence and grandson of Warwick 'the Kingmaker'. The last of the legitimate male Plantagenets, he spent most of his life in captivity and was eventually executed.

17

that he has declared himself king, evade his promise, the children of Elizabeth Woodville[a] will suffer the stain of illegitimacy; but if the marriage has place, and this unhappy race is restored to their honours and rights, our self-named sovereign may find that his own hands have dug the pit into which he will fall."

A long silence succeeded to these explanations. The last expression used by Lovel inspired Edmund with wonder and curiosity; but the noble pressing his horse to a swifter pace, did not hear his observations, or hearing them, replied only by saying, "Three hours' good riding will bring us to London. Courage, Plantagenet! slacken not your speed, my good boy; soft ease will follow this hard labour."

The young moon in its first quarter was near its setting when they arrived at London. They / approached from Edgware: without entering the town, they skirted its northern extremity, till Lord Lovel, checking his horse, remarked to his companion, that he judged it fitting to delay approaching the residence of the Earl of Lincoln, until the setting of the moon and subsequent darkness secured them from observation. /

CHAPTER II.

_____

Yes, my good Lord,
It doth contain a king; King Richard lies
Within the limits of yon lime and stone.
SHAKESPEARE.[b]

_____

The Earl of Lincoln, declared by Richard the Third, heir to the crown, did not join the royal forces, nor appear at the battle of Bosworth. This distinguished prince was a man of singular abilities and strength of mind, which chivalrous generosity adorned with a lustre superior even to that which he derived from his high rank. Lord Lovel was possessed of knightly courage, untarnished

_____

[a] Elizabeth Woodville (1437–92), daughter of Earl Rivers, married Edward IV (her second husband) in 1464, and succeeded in advancing her numerous family, thus alienating many Yorkists. Shakespeare portrays her as succumbing to Richard's flattery in *Richard III*, IV. iv.

[b] *Richard II*, III. iii. 24–26.

honour, and gentlemanly accomplishment. To these military and graceful qualities Lincoln added the wisdom of a statesman, and the moral energy resulting
from inflexible / principle. He felt himself responsible to mankind and to all
posterity for his actions. He was brave – that was a virtue of the times; but he
was just, in a comprehensive sense of the word, and that exalted him above
them. His manly features did not so much wear the stamp of beauty, though,
like all the offspring of the House of York, he was handsome, as of the best
quality of man, a perception of right, and resolution to achieve that right.

Lord Lincoln disapproved decidedly of the usurpation of his uncle, Richard
the Third, over the children of Edward the Fourth. He allowed that the
evidence was strong in favour of that king's former marriage, and their consequent illegitimacy; but he said, that Elizabeth Woodville had so long been held
Queen of England, and her children heirs to the crown, that it was impossible
to eradicate the belief of the English people, that their allegiance was due to
him who had been proclaimed even by his uncle, Edward the Fifth. Even if
they were put aside, the attainder passed against the Duke of Clarence was an
insufficient reason to deprive his son of his / lawful inheritance. He saw
England wasted, and her nobility extirpated by civil contest; and he perceived
the seeds of future strife in the assumption of the crown by the Duke of
Gloucester. When the son of Richard the Third died, and the Earl of Warwick
was named his successor, the superior right of the nephew before the reigning
uncle became so eminent a subject of discussion, that the king was obliged to
recall his declaration, and to confine the young Prince in a castle in Yorkshire.
The Earl of Lincoln, then seven and twenty years of age, was next named. He
remonstrated with his uncle privately; but fear of dividing the House of York
against itself, and a disdain to make common cause with the dowager Queen's
relations, made him outwardly submit; but his plan was formed, and secretly all
his efforts tended towards the restoring the children of Edward to their
paternal rights.

The boys were sickly. Edward the Fifth, irritated by the extinction of the
hopes which the intrigues of his mother had kept alive in his breast, wasted by
imprisonment in the Tower, / and brooking with untamed pride the change
from a regal to a private station, pined and died. Richard, Duke of York, was
between ten and eleven;[a] a sprightly ingenuous boy, whose lively spirit wore
out his frame, and this, added to confinement and attention to his dying
brother, brought him also near the grave. It was on the death of Edward that
the Earl of Lincoln visited the Tower, and saw young Richard. The accounts
given by the attendants of his more than a child's devotion to his brother, his

---

[a] 'born 1475' (marginal note in *Abinger/Palacio*); modern sources give 1472. Other marginal
notes indicate concern about internal inconsistencies regarding the protagonist's age: overt and
buried references on pp. 63, 64, 66, fit with a 1472 date, but passages on pp. 24–6, 34, and 42 point
toward 1475; other descriptions (p. 76) fit either date.

19

replies full of sportive fancy, his beauty, though his cheek was faded and his person grown thin, moved the generous noble to deep compassion. He ventured, under the strong influence of this feeling, to remonstrate warmly with his royal uncle, reproaching him with needless cruelty, and telling him how in fact, though not in appearance, he was the murderer of his nephews, and would be so held by all mankind.[a] Richard's ambition was satisfied by the success of his measures to obtain the crown; but his fears were awake. The Duke of Buckingham[b] was in arms against him – the Queen / and her surviving relatives were perpetually employed in exciting discontents in the kingdom. Richard feared, that if they obtained the person of his nephew, he would be turned into an engine for his overthrow; while to obtain possession of him, was the constant aim of their endeavours. He earnestly desired to reconcile himself to the Queen, and to draw her from the sanctuary in which she had immured herself – she refused all his offers, unless her son was first placed in her hands.

His head, ripe with state plots, now conceived a scheme. He consented that Lincoln should take the Duke of York under his charge, if he would first engage to keep his removal from the Tower, and even his existence, a secret from his enemies. Lincoln made the required promise; the young Prince was conveyed to a country seat belonging to the Earl, and Richard, in furtherance of his plan, caused a rumour to go abroad that he also was dead. No one knew with whom this report originated. When, to assure themselves, various nobles visited the Tower, the boy was no longer there. The Queen gave / credit to the tale. At this moment, Richard set on foot a negociation of marriage with the eldest daughter of Edward the Fourth, the Lady Elizabeth. The partizans of the Earl of Richmond sought to ensure the success of his enterprize by the same means: and while little Richard grew in health and happiness in his country retreat, his own nearest and most attached relatives were giving away his inheritance – his uncle unwittingly laid the foundation stone of the reputation of cruelty and murder ever after affixed to him; and his mother, endeavouring to exalt her daughter, and to restore herself to her lost station in the kingdom, sealed the fatal decree that first deprived her son of his rights, and afterwards of his life.

On the evening that Lord Lovel and Edmund Plantagenet entered London, the Earl of Lincoln remained waiting intelligence from the field, in a palace he inhabited not far from Tottenham Court,[c] a secluded habitation, surrounded by a garden and a high wall. This was an irksome situation for a warrior; but

---

[a] The plot requires that Richard be acquitted of actual murder.

[b] Henry Stafford, 2nd Duke of Buckingham (c.1454–83), a Lancastrian descendent of Edward III, married the Queen's sister, Catherine Woodville. He was first Richard III's co-plotter, as depicted in Shakespeare, but defected, was captured, and beheaded.

[c] The Manor House of the estate of Tottenham, outside the boundary of the City of London, in which Edward IV installed his mistress, Jane Shore; it formerly stood near the edge of Somers Town, where Mary Shelley lived from her birth until 1807.

though his uncle loved, he distrusted him: his / projected marriage with the Lady Elizabeth, would probably cause him again to be father of an heir to the crown, and knowing that Lincoln possessed, in the young Duke of York, a dangerous rival, he refused to allow him to take up arms against Richmond. Lord Lincoln was alone, pacing his large and vaulted hall in deep and anxious meditation. He, who with conscience for his rule, takes, or endeavours to take, the reins of fate into his own hands, must experience frequent misgivings; and often feel, that he wheels near the edge of a giddy precipice, down which the tameless steeds he strives to govern, may, in an instant, hurl him and all dependent upon his guidance. The simple feeling of compassion, arising from the seeing childhood lose its buoyancy in undue confinement, had first led the princely noble to take charge of his young cousin. Afterwards, when he beheld the boy grow in health and years, developing the while extraordinary quickness of intellect, and a sweet ingenuous disposition, he began to reflect on the station he held, his rights and his injuries; and then the design / was originated on which he was now called to act.

If Richard gained the day, all would stand as before. Should he be defeated – and that second sense, that feeling of coming events, which is one of the commonest, though the least acknowledged of the secret laws of our nature, whispered the yet unrevealed truth to him – who then would assume England's diadem, and how could he secure it for its rightful owner, the only surviving son of Edward the Fourth? All these reflexions coursed themselves through his brain, while, with the zeal of a partizan, and the fervour of one wedded to the justice of his cause, he revolved every probable change of time and fortune.

At this moment a courier was announced: he brought tidings from the field. As is usual on the eve of a great event, they were dubious and contradictory. The armies faced each other, and the battle was impending. The doubts entertained on both sides, as to the part that Lord Stanley would take, gave still a greater uncertainty to the anticipations of each. /

Soon after the arrival of this man, the loud ringing at the outer gate was renewed; and the trampling of horses, as they entered the court, announced a more numerous company. There was something in the movements of his domestics, that intimated to the Earl that his visitor was of superior rank. Could it be the king, who had fled; conquered, and a fugitive? Could such terms be applied to the high-hearted Richard? The doors of the hall were thrown open, and the question answered by the entrance of his visitant: it was a woman; and her name, "Lady Brampton!"[a] in a tone of wonder, burst from the noble's lips.

"Even I, my good Lord," said the lady; "allow me your private ear; I bring

---

[a] A marginal figure in the chronicle sources, wife of Sir Edward Brampton, a converted Portuguese Jew. The historical Warbeck may have learned much from the Bramptons, whom he accompanied to Lisbon in 1487. Brampton was pardoned by Henry VII in 1489, and may later have informed about Warbeck's real origins.

intelligence from Leicestershire. All is lost," she continued, when the closing of the door assured her of privacy; "all is lost, and all is gained – Richard is slain. My emissaries brought swift intelligence of this event to me at Northampton, and I have hastened with it hither, that without loss of time you may act."

There was a quickness and a decision in the / lady's manner, that checked rather than encouraged her auditor. She continued: "Vesper hour has long passed – it matters not – London yet is ours. Command instantly that Richard the Fourth be proclaimed king of England."

Lord Lincoln started at these words. The death of his uncle and benefactor could not be received by him like the loss of a move at chess; a piece lost, that required the bringing up of other pieces to support a weak place. "The king is slain," were words that rung in his ears; drowning every other that the lady uttered with rapidity and agitation. "We will speak of that anon," he replied; and going to the high window of his hall, he threw it open, as if the air oppressed him. The wind sighed in melancholy murmurs among the branches of the elms and limes in the garden: the stars were bright, and the setting moon was leaving the earth to their dim illumination. "Yesternight," thought Lincoln, "he was among us, a part of our conversation, our acts, our lives; now his glazed eyes behold not these stars. The / past is his: with the present and the future he has no participation."

Lady Brampton's impatience did not permit the Earl long to indulge in that commune with nature, which we eagerly seek when grief and death throws us back on the weakness of our human state, and we feel that we ourselves, our best laid projects and loftiest hopes, are but the play things of destiny. "Where-fore," cried the lady, "does De la Poole linger? Does he hesitate to do his cousin justice? Does he desire to follow in the steps of his usurping predeces-sor? Wherefore this delay?"

"To strike the surer," replied Lincoln. "May not I ask, wherefore this impatience?"

Even as he spoke, steps were heard near the apartment; and while the eyes of both were turned with inquietude on the expected intruder, Lord Lovel entered: there was no triumph, no eager anticipation on his brow – he was languid from ill success and fatigue. Lincoln met him with the pleasure of one who sees his friend escaped from certain death. He was overjoyed to be assured of his existence; he / was glad to have his assistance on the present emergency. "We know," he said, "all the evil tidings you bring us; we are now deliberating on the conduct we are to pursue: your presence will facilitate our measures. Tell me what other friends survive to aid us. The Duke of Norfolk, the Staffords, Sir Robert Brakenbury, where are they?" [a]

---

[a] John Howard, 1st Duke of Norfolk (?1430–85), treasurer of the royal household under Edward IV and Earl Marshall of England under Richard III. Sir Robert Brackenbury was in charge of the Tower of London when the Duke of Clarence and the sons of Edward IV were killed, although his degree of complicity is unresolved. Both died at Bosworth.

Lovel had seen the Duke fall, the Staffords had accompanied his flight; uncertainty still hung over the fate of many others. This detail of the death of many of their common friends, subdued the impetuosity of the lady, till an account of how Richard himself had fought and been slain, recalled her to their former topic of discussion; and, again, she said, "It is strange that you do not perceive the dangers of delay. Why is not the king proclaimed?"

"Do you not know," asked Lord Lovel, "that the king is proclaimed?"

Lady Brampton clasped her hands, exclaiming – "Then Richard the Fourth will wear his father's crown!"

"Henry the Seventh," said Lovel, "possesses / and wears the English crown. Lord Stanley placed the diadem on the head of the Earl of Richmond, and his soldiers, with one acclaim, acknowledged him as their sovereign."

"This is mere trifling," said the lady; "the base-born offspring of Lancaster may dare aspire so high, but one act of our's dethrones him. The Yorkists are numerous, and will defend their king: London is yet ours."

"Yes," replied Lincoln, "it is in our power to deluge the streets of London with blood; to bring massacre among its citizens, and worse disaster on its wives and maidens. I would not buy an eternal crown for myself – I will not strive to place that of England on my kinsman's head – at this cost. We have had over-much of war: I have seen too many of the noble, young, and gallant, fall by the sword. Brute force has had its day; now let us try what policy can do."

The council these friends held together was long and anxious. The lady still insisted on sudden and resolute measures. Lord Lovel, a soldier in all his nature, looked forward to the calling / together the Yorkists from every part of the kingdom. The Earl, with a statesman's experience, saw more of obstacle to their purpose in the elevation of Henry the Seventh than either of his companions would allow; the extreme youth of the Duke of York, the oblivion into which he had sunk, and the stain on his birth, which was yet unremoved, would disincline the people to hazard life and fortune in his cause. Henry had taken oath to marry his sister, the Lady Elizabeth, and when thus the progeny of Edward the Fourth were freed from the slur under which they now laboured, the whole country would be alive to the claims of his only son. It was necessary now to place him in safety, and far away from the suspicious eyes of his usurping enemy. That morning Lord Lincoln had brought him up from his rural retreat to the metropolis, and sheltered him for a few hours under safe but strange guardianship. He was left at the house of a Flemish money-lender well known at court. It was agreed that Lord Lovel should take him thence, and make him the companion of his journey to Colchester, where they should / remain watching the turn of events, and secretly preparing the insurrection which would place him on the throne. Lady Brampton was obliged to proceed immediately northwards to join her husband; the north was entirely Yorkist, and her influence would materially assist the cause. The Earl remained in

London; he would sound the inclinations of the nobility, and even coming in contact with the new king, watch over danger and power at its fountain-head. One more question was discussed. Whether the Queen, Elizabeth Woodville, should be made acquainted with the existence of her son. All three, from various reasons decided in the negative. A personal enmity existed between the widow of Edward the Fourth and Lady Brampton: her party was detested by the two nobles. It would be more popular with the nation, they thought, if her kinsmen, whose upstart pretentions were the object of the derision and scorn of the old aristocracy, had no part in bestowing the crown on the heir of the House of York. Time wore away during these deliberations; it was past midnight before the friends separated. / Lord Lovel presented his young friend, Edmund Plantagenet, to the Earl, and recommended him to his protection. Refreshment was also necessary after Lovel's fatiguing journey; but he was so intent on accomplishing his purpose, that he wasted but a few minutes in this manner, and then being provided with a fresh horse from Lincoln's stables, he left the palace, to proceed first to the present abode of Richard of York, and afterwards, accompanied by him, on his road to Essex.

Lord Lovel threaded his way through the dark narrow streets of London towards Lothbury.[a] The habitation of the money-lender was well known to him, but it was not easily entered at past midnight. A promised bribe to the apprentice who hailed him from the lofty garret-window, and his signet-ring sent in to his master, at length procured admission into the bed-chamber of Mynheer Jahn Warbeck.[b] The old man sat up in his bed, his red cotton night-cap on his head, his spectacles, with which he had examined the ring, on his nose; his chamber was narrow and dilapidated, his bed of ill condition. / "Who would suppose," thought Lovel, "that this man holds half England in pawn?"

When Warbeck heard that the errand of Lovel was to take from him his princely charge, he rose hastily, wrapping a robe round him, and opened a small wainscot door leading into a little low room, whence he drew the half-sleeping and wondering boy. There was a rush taper in the room, and daylight began to peep through the crevices of the shutters, giving melancholy distinctness to the dirty and dismantled chamber. One ray fell directly on the red night-cap and spectacles of old Jahn, whose parchment face was filled with wrinkles, yet they were lines of care, not of evil, and there was even benevolence in his close mouth; for the good humour and vivacity of the boy had won

---

[a] An ancient London street where the Bank of England (founded 1694), still stands.

[b] Mary Shelley arranges her story to bring the hero together with the Warbecks. The historical Perkin confessed that his parents were Catherine de Faro and Jehan Osbeck, a converted Jew from Tournai, who apprenticed him to merchants in Antwerp and Middleburgh to learn Flemish and English. He later worked for an English family and a one-eyed Portuguese knight. His career as pretender began in 1491 when he travelled to Ireland in the service of a Breton merchant. (Bacon mentions an old tradition that made London Warbeck's birthplace and named Edward IV as his 'godfather', insinuating that the King's blood may have run in the pretender's veins.)

on him. Besides he had himself a son, for whom he destined all his wealth, of the same age as the little fellow whose plump roseate hand he held in his own brown shrivelled palm. The boy came in, rubbing his large blue eyes, the disordered ringlets of his fair hair shading a face replete with vivacity and intelligence. / Mynheer Jahn was somewhat loth to part with the little prince, but the latter clapped his hands in extacy when he heard that Lord Lovel had come to take him away.

"I pray you tell me, Sir Knight," said old Warbeck, "whether intelligence hath arrived of the victory of our gracious sovereign, and the defeat of the Welch rebels."

Richard became grave at these words; he fixed his eyes enquiringly on the noble: "Dear Lord Lovel," he cried, "for I remember you well, my very good Lord, when you came to the Tower and found me and Robert Clifford[a] playing at bowls – tell me, how you have fought, and whether you have won."

"Mine are evil tidings;" said Lovel, "all is lost. We were vanquished, and your royal uncle slain."

Warbeck's countenance changed at these words; he lamented the king; he lamented the defeat of the party which he had aided by various advances of money, and his regrets at once expressed sorrow for the death of some, and dread from the confiscation of the property of others. / Meanwhile, Richard of York was full of some thought that swelled his little breast; taking Lovel's hand, he asked again, "My uncle, Richard the Third, is dead?"

"Even so," was the reply; "he died nobly on the field of battle."

The child drew himself up, and his eyes flashed as he said proudly, – "Then I am king of England."

"Who taught your Grace that lesson?" asked Lovel.

"My liege – my brother Edward. Often and often in the long winter nights, and when he was sick in bed, he told me how, after he had been proclaimed king, he had been dethroned; but that when our uncle died he should be king again; and that if it pleased God to remove him, I should stand in his place; and I should restore my mother's honour, and this he made me swear."

"Bless the boy!" cried Warbeck, "he speaks most sagely; may the saints incline my lord, the Earl of Lincoln, to do his royal cousin justice!" /

"Your Grace," said Lovel, "shall hear more of this as we proceed on our journey. Mynheer Jahn, the Earl bade me apply to you; you are to repair to him

---

[a] Godwin informed Mary Shelley on 13 August 1828 that 'Warbeck's Sir Robert Clifford was the son of the Lord Clifford who killed Rutland', i.e., John, 9th Baron Clifford (?1425–61), who fell at Towton, 29 March 1461 (Ab. MSS, Pf. Film, reel V, file 7); other sources (*DNB*, e.g.) suggest he was the son of Thomas, 8th Baron Clifford (1414–55), who died at the first battle of St Albans, 22 May 1455. Perhaps Mary Shelley confused the Lancastrian defeat at Towton with that at Tewkesbury (4 May 1471), because internal references are consistent with the 1471 date for Clifford's birth. A birth date in either 1455 or 1461 would not have made him a suitable playfellow for a young Duke of York, born in either 1472 or 1475.

before noon; meanwhile, fill this long empty purse with gold coins. He will be my guarantee."

"Lend me the money," cried the little Duke, "I will repay you. We will repay you, when we have our crown."

This was an inducement not to be resisted. Warbeck counted out the gold; the boy with light steps tripped down the creaking old staircase, and when Lovel had mounted, taking his hand, he sprung in the saddle before him. The fresh morning air was grateful to both, after the close chambers of the Fleming. The noble put his horse to a quick trot, and leaving London by a different road from that by which he had entered, took his way through Romford and Chelmsford to Colchester.[a]

The news of the Earl of Richmond's victory and assumption of the crown reached London that night. The citizens heard it on their awakening. The market-people from the west / related it to those who came in from the east; but it had not hitherto travelled in that direction. Lovel knew that the storm was behind him, but he outrode it; on the evening of the second day he was safe in sanctuary at Colchester. His young charge was lodged at a farmhouse belonging to a tenant of Sir Humphrey Stafford. They all awaited impatiently for the time when the Earl of Lincoln would put a period to their confinement, by informing them that the hour was arrived when they might again take arms against the upstart Lancastrian King. /

CHAPTER III.

———

Small joy have I being England's Queen!
SHAKSPEARE.[b]

———

Henry the Seventh was a man of strong sense and sound understanding. He was prudent, resolute, and valiant; on the other hand, he was totally devoid of generosity, and was actuated all his life by base and bad passions. At first the

---

[a] Towns lying along a major old Roman road leading north-eastward out of London. Colchester was an estuary port for the continent.

[b] *Richard III*, I. iii. 109; 'Shakspeare', a contemporary alternative spelling, is consistently used; the one exception occurs on p. 18.

ruling feeling of his heart was hatred of the House of York – nor did he wholly give himself up to the avarice that blotted his latter years, till the extinction of that unhappy family satisfied his revenge, so that for want of fuel the flame died away.[a] Most of his relatives and friends had perished in the field or on the scaffold by the hands of the Yorkists – his own existence / had been in jeopardy during their exaltation; and the continuance of his reign, and even of his life, depended on their utter overthrow. Henry had a mind commensurate to the execution of his plans: he had a talent for seizing, as if instinctively, on all the bearings of a question before him; and a ready perception of the means by which he might obviate difficulties and multiply facilities, was the most prominent part of his character. He never aimed at too much, and felt instantaneously when he had arrived at the enough. More of cruelty would have roused England against him; less would have given greater hopes to the partizans of his secreted rival. He had that exact portion of callousness of heart which enabled him to extricate himself in the admirable manner he did from all his embarrassments.

It is impossible to say what his exact views were, when he landed in England, and made head against Richard the Third. His right of succession, even through the House of Lancaster, was ill-founded, and probably he would scarcely have dared to decorate his brows with the royal / circlet but for the happy boldness of Stanley, and the enthusiasm felt by his soldiers in the hour of victory, which had bestowed it on him. Once a king, as it was impossible, without risk of life, to sink to a private station, he did not hesitate, but bent every energy of his mind to the contriving the means to seat himself firmly on his newly-acquired throne.

The illegitimacy of Edward the Fourth's children had removed them from the succession. But though no doubt was entertained as to the fact of Edward having married Lady Eleanor Butler,[b] yet Henry had the taint of illegitimacy on his own race; and, moreover, Elizabeth Woodville having so long filled the station of Queen of England, the public voice went in her favour, and the majority of the English people looked upon the tale which deprived her children of their rights, as a contrivance of their usurping uncle. What then was to become of them? Edward the Fifth was dead: of this fact there was no doubt. It had been rumoured that the Duke of York had not long survived his brother. To ascertain the truth of this report, Henry / dispatched one of his most staunch adherents to the Tower. The boy was not there; but a mystery hung over his fate which did not quite assure the new king of his death. Henry feared that he was in the hands of the Yorkists, and this dread gave fresh vigour

---

[a] The hatred and avarice are attested by the chroniclers.

[b] Lady Eleanor Butler (d. 1468) was rumoured to have been secretly married or contracted to marriage with Edward IV when he wed Elizabeth Woodville in 1464, thus making Elizabeth's children by him illegitimate.

to his distrust and abhorrence of the partizans of the White Rose. He formed a scheme to defeat their projects; he caused it to be disseminated that both the princes had been found dead – murdered – in the Tower.

The competitors for the crown, whose claims ranked next, were the daughters of Edward the Fourth. Henry immediately saw the necessity of agreeing to the treaty entered into by the Countess of Richmond,[a] for his marriage with the eldest of these princesses. He hated to owe his title to the crown to any part of the House of York; he resolved, if possible, to delay and break the marriage; but his own friends were urgent with him to comply, and prudence dictated the measure; he therefore promised to adopt it – thus effectually to silence the murmurs of the party of the White Rose. /

But if the young Duke of York re-appeared meanwhile, it would be necessary not to repeal the Act of Parliament that cast a stigma on his birth. If the children of Elizabeth Woodville and Edward the Fourth, were debarred from the crown, the Earl of Warwick was the next heir. He was confined by Richard the Third at Sheriff Hutton, in Yorkshire. He was the especial object of Henry's fear, and now he commanded him to be brought from his northern prison to the Tower of London, to be kept a close prisoner in that melancholy and ill-fated place. There was one other rival, the Earl of Lincoln, named by Richard to succeed him; but his pretensions came so far behind the others, and he enjoyed so high a reputation for sagacity and virtue, that Henry believed it best to let him alone for the present, only surrounding him with spies; and resolved, on the first note of danger, to destroy him.

Fortune smiled on the new sovereign. The disappearance of the two children from the Tower, caused the Yorkists to settle their affections on the young Elizabeth. She was at / Sheriff-Hutton, waiting impatiently for her union with her uncle;[b] now she received commands to proceed to London, as the affianced bride of that uncle's conqueror. Already the common talk ran on the entwining of the two Roses; and all the adherents of her family, who could gain access, recommended their cause to her, and entreated her, in the first days of power, not to forget her father's friends, but to incline the heart of her husband to an impartial love for the long rival houses of Lancaster and York.

Two parties arrived on the same day at Sheriff-Hutton, on the different missions of conducting the Lady Elizabeth and the Earl of Warwick to London. On the morning of their departure, they met in the garden of their abode to take leave of each other. Elizabeth was nineteen years old, Warwick was the exact age of her brother, Edward the Fifth; he was now sixteen.[c]

---

[a] Lady Margaret Beaufort (1443–1509), Countess of Richmond and Derby; mother of Henry VII, she later wed Sir Thomas Stanley and conducted the marriage negotiations for her son.

[b] Elizabeth's anticipation of the proposed union with Richard III, roundly condemned in the chronicles, is Mary Shelley's invention.

[c] Mary Shelley takes her chronology from Godwin, who had (mistakenly) informed her (26 September 1827; Ab. MSS, Pf. Film, reel V, file 7; *Shelley and Mary*, III, p. 1106C) that Elizabeth

"We are about to travel the same road with far different expectations," said Warwick. "I go to be a prisoner; you, fair Cousin, to ascend a throne." /

There was a despondency in the youth's manner that deeply affected this Princess. "Dear Edward," she replied, clasping his hand, "we have been fellow-prisoners long, and sympathy has lightened the burthen of our chains. Can I forget our walks in this beauteous park, and the love and confidence we have felt for each other? My dearest boy, when I am Queen, Esther will claim a boon from Ahasuerus,[a] and Warwick shall be the chief noble in my train."

She looked at him with a brilliant smile; her heart glowed with sisterly affection. She might well entertain high anticipations of future power; she was in the pride of youth and beauty; the light spirit of expected triumph lighted up her lovely face. She was about to become the bride of a conqueror, yet one whose laurels would droop without her propping; she was to be Queen of her native land, the pearly clasp to unite the silken bond with which peace now bound long discordant England. She was unable to communicate this spirit of hope to her desponding friend; he gazed on her beauty with admiration / and deep grief, asking, with tearful eyes, "Shall we ever meet again?"

"Yes! in London, in the Court of Henry, we shall again be companions – friends."

"I go to the Tower, not to the Court," replied Warwick, "and when those gloomy gates close on me, I shall pray that my head may soon repose on the cold stone that pillows my cousin Edward. I shall sleep uneasily till then."

"Fie, Cousin!" said Elizabeth; "such thoughts ill beseem the nearest kinsman of the future Queen of England. You will remain but a short time in the Tower; but if you nurse thoughts like these, you will pine there as you did before I shared your prison here, and the roses with which my care has painted your cheeks, will again fade."

"Wan and colourless will my cheek be ere your bright eyes look on it again. Is it not sufficient grief that I part from you, beloved friend!"

A gush at once of sorrow, of affection, of long suppressed love, overpowered the youth. "I shall think of you," he added, "in my / prison-house; and while I know that you regret my fate, I cannot be wholly a wretch. Do you not love me? And will you not, as a proof, give me one of these golden hairs, to soothe poor Warwick's misery? One only," he said, taking from her braided locks the small gift he demanded, "I will not diminish the rich beauty of your tresses, yet they will not look lovelier, pressed by the jewelled diadem of England, than under the green chaplet I crowned you with a few months past, my Queen of May!"

And thus, the eyes of each glistening with tears, they parted. For a moment

---

was born in 1466 and Warwick in the same year as Edward V (1470). Actually Elizabeth (b. 1465) was ten years older than Warwick (b. 1475).

[a] Esther, the Jewish wife of the Persian king Ahasuerus, charmed her husband into rescinding his orders for the destruction of the Jews.

Warwick looked as if he wished to press his cousin to his heart; and she, who loved him as a sister, would have yielded to his embrace: but before his arms enfolded her, he started back, bent one knee, pressed her hand to his lips, his eyes, his brow, and bending his head for an instant towards the ground, sprang up, and rushed down the avenue towards the gate at which his guard awaited him. Elizabeth stood motionless, watching him till out of sight. The sun sparkled brightly on a tuft of wild flowers at her feet. The glittering light / caught her eye. "It is noon," she thought; "the morning dew is dry; it is Warwick's tears that gem these leaves." She gathered the flowers, and, first kissing them, placed them in her bosom; with slow steps, and a sorrowing heart, she re-entered the Castle.

The progress of the Lady Elizabeth from Sheriff Hutton to London was attended by every circumstance that could sustain her hopes. She was received with acclamation and enthusiasm in every town through which she passed. She indeed looked forward with girlish vanity to the prospect of sharing the throne with Henry. She had long been taught the royal lesson, that with princes, the inclinations are not to bear any part in a disposal of the hand. Her imagination fed on the good she would do for others, when raised to the regal dignity; the hope of liberating Warwick, and of fulfilling her mother's wishes in conferring benefits on various partizans of the White Rose, filled her bosom with the purest joy; youth, beauty, and the expectation of happiness caused the measure of her content to overflow. /

With a fluttering heart she entered London: small preparation had been made to receive her, and she was immediately conducted to her mother's abode at the Tower Royal, in the Parish of Walbrook.[a] The first check her hopes received arose from the clouded brow of the Queen, as she embraced her daughter, and welcomed her arrival. Many fears in truth occupied the thoughts of the illustrious widow. She could not forget her sons; and the mystery that hung over the fate of the younger, pressed heavily upon her. It was now the eighteenth of October, and the preparations for the coronation of Henry were in great forwardness; Parliament had recognized his title without any allusion to the union with the heiress of the House of York. She had endeavoured to fathom his purposes, and to understand his character. She knew that he entertained a settled hatred for the White Rose, and that his chief pride lay in establishing himself on the throne, independent of the claim he might acquire by his marriage with the Lady Elizabeth. The common people murmured, the Yorkists were discontented, – the / neighbour stage before they should break out into open rebellion. Thus dark clouds interposed before the sun of peace, which had been said to have risen on the event of the battle of Bosworth Field.

---

[a] In his letter of 26 September 1827 (see p. 28n) Godwin speculated that Elizabeth's mother was lodged at Tower Royal, in the heart of the City of London.

Henry the Seventh was crowned on the thirtieth of October. The queen looked on this ceremony as the downfall of her hopes. Roused by this fear, she entered into a sea of intrigue, in which, after all, she had no certain aim, except that of re-animating the zeal of the Yorkists, and of exciting such discontent in the public mind, on the postponement of her daughter's marriage, as to force Henry to consent to an immediate union. The gentle Elizabeth had meanwhile submitted patiently to her destiny. She dismissed regality from her thoughts, and devoted herself to her mother; recreating herself in the society of her sisters, and now and then contemplating the faded leaves she had brought from Sheriff Hutton, and lamenting the fate of Warwick. She had learned to fear and almost to hate Henry; and, but for the sake of her suffering party, to rejoice / that he had apparently relinquished his intention of marrying her.

The dissatisfaction manifested by the English people, forced Henry to comply with the universal wish entertained of seeing the daughter of Edward the Fourth on the throne: yet it was not until the beginning of January that the Princess received intimation to prepare for her nuptials. This prospect, which had before elated, now visited her coldly; for, without the hope of influencing her husband, the state of a Queen appeared mere bondage. In her heart she wished to reject her uncourteous bridegroom; and once she had ventured to express this desire to her mother, who, filled with affright, laid aside her intrigues, devoting herself to cultivate a more rational disposition in her daughter. Henry paid the doomed girl one visit, and saw little in her except a bashful child; while his keener observation was directed towards the dowager queen. She, with smooth brow and winning smiles, did the honours of reception to her future son-in-law – to her bitter foe. The cold courtesy of Henry chilled / her; and a strong desire lurked under her glossy mien, to reproach the usurper with his weak title, to set up her daughter's claim in opposition to his, and to defy him to the field. As soon as Henry departed, her suppressed emotions found vent in tears. Elizabeth was astonished: she knelt before her, caressed her, and asked if all were not well now, since the plighted troth had passed between her and the King.

"Has it passed?" murmured the Queen, "and is your hapless fate decided? Why did I not join you at Sheriff Hutton? Why did I not place your hand in that of your noble cousin? Ah, Warwick! could I even now inspire you with my energy, you would be free, in arms; and England to a man would rise in the cause of Edward the Sixth, and my sweet Elizabeth!"

The colour in the Princess's cheeks varied, during the utterance of this speech: first they flushed deep red, but the pale hue of resolution succeeded quickly to the agitation of doubt. "Mother," she said, "I was your child; plastic clay in your hands: had you said these words / two hours ago, Warwick might have been liberated – I perhaps happy. But you have given me away; this ring is the symbol of my servitude; I belong to Henry. Say no word, I beseech you, that can interfere with my duty to him. Permit me to retire."

31

On the eighteenth of January her nuptials were celebrated.[a]

The forbidding manners of Henry threw a chill over the marriage festival. He considered that he had been driven to this step by his enemies; and that the chief among these, influenced by her mother, was Elizabeth herself. The poor girl never raised her eyes from the moment she had encountered at the altar the stern and unkind glance of the king. Her steps were unassured, her voice faltering: the name of wife was to her synonimous with that of slave, while her sense of duty prevented every outward demonstration of the despair that occupied her heart.

Her mother's indignation was deeper, although not less veiled. She could silence, but not quell the rage that arose in her breast from / her disappointment; and there were many present who shared her sentiments. As far as he had been able, Henry had visited the Yorkists with the heaviest penalties. An act of attainder had been passed against the Duke of Norfolk, Lord Lovel, the Staffords, and all indeed of note who had appeared against him. Those with whom he could not proceed to extremities, he wholly discountenanced. The Red Rose flourished bright and free – one single white blossom, doomed to untimely blight, being entwined with the gaudier flowers. /

CHAPTER IV.

———

My noble Queen, let former grudges pass,
And henceforth I am thy true servitor.
                                SHAKSPEARE.[b]

———

Meanwhile the Yorkists were impatient for action. The existence of Prince Richard was a secret to all save Lincoln and Lovel – even the Staffords were kept in ignorance: their purpose, therefore, was merely to put down the

---

[a] '1486' (marginal note in *Abinger/Palacio*); Henry VII delayed his marriage until after he had been crowned and his title recognized by Parliament to avoid appearing to depend upon his queen's hereditary rights. Henry's claims rested on his muddied descent from John of Gaunt, Duke of Lancaster, third son of Edward III. His mother sprang from Gaunt's legitimised Beaufort family; his father, from the union of the Welshman Owen Tudor and the dowager queen Catherine (of France), widow of Henry V.

[b] *3 Henry VI*, III. iii. 195–6.

Lancastrians, and to raise their own party, with Warwick or Lincoln at their head; they cared not which, so that they got a king who would, in his turn, uproot the Red Rose. Lincoln would consent to no decisive step; but from the day of his cousin's marriage, all his emissaries and friends were on foot to cause insurrectionary movements in the kingdom, rousing in the old / Yorkists their ancient party spirit, and inspiring the young with hopes of future aggrandizement and victory.

As the spring advanced, Henry sent the young Queen, with her mother and sisters, and the Countess of Richmond, to hold her court at Winchester, while he resolved on a progress through the northern counties of England, the most affected towards the House of York, to endeavour, by the royal presence, to awaken affection towards the reigning sovereign. He passed the festival of Easter at Lincoln, and there he heard that Lord Lovel, and the two Staffords, had escaped from sanctuary. The sound of insurrection is fearful to a newly anointed king; but as no explanation was given to their movements, and no name of import mingled in the tale, he felt less perturbation at this intelligence. As he proceeded on his journey, the affair took a more serious aspect. The Staffords advanced to besiege Worcester;[a] and Lovel, with an increasing army of three or four thousand men, was in the neighbourhood of York. /

Sir Edward Brampton joined the forces of Lord Lovel, and he and Lady Brampton again met. The history of this lady was singular. Ten years before the time of which we write, being then eighteen, she married, and attended the Court of Edward the Fourth. She had talent and vivacity: her dark laughing eyes, the animation of her countenance, her gay and *naïve* manners, attracted her sovereign; and she was soon distinguished as one whose advancement, if so it might be called, to the highest influence over him, depended on her own choice between honour and such preferment. She did not hesitate: but her rejection won Edward as much as her beauty. A kind of friendship, kept up under the chivalrous phraseology of the day, was established between them, that gave, perhaps, more umbrage to the Queen than a less avowed connexion would have done. All was open; and if the good humour of her young rival never permitted her to assume haughtiness, there was something even more revolting in her girlish assumptions of power and consequence. The Queen hated / and affected to despise Lady Brampton; Lady Brampton felt that she injured the wife of Edward the Fourth. At first she had earnestly sought to gain her favour, but when rebuffed, she resorted to the weapons of youth, beauty, and wit, and set at defiance the darkened brow of Elizabeth. Ten years had passed since then.

Edward the Fourth died, and under Richard the Third Lady Brampton returned to her natural place in society; nay, the vivacity of speech with which

---

[a] Winchester, Lincoln, and Worcester, three wealthy, ancient cathedral cities whose support was essential to Henry.

she defended the rights of his nephews, made him absolutely discountenance her. In her days of pride she had refused every mark of favour from Edward, thus to place their avowed friendship far above the petty intrigues of the courtiers. It might have been thought that the Queen and her rival would now, on the grounds of affection for Edward's children, have leagued together: but, on the contrary, the mother expressed contempt and indignation at the presumption of Lady Brampton in assuming a personal interest in her children, and that lady too well remembered / how often her manner and speech must have offended the Queen to make any vain attempt at reconciliation. The Earl of Lincoln and Lady Brampton had always been friends; her liveliness amused him, her integrity and real goodness of heart won his esteem. Her passionate love for the princes in the Tower, had caused him when he withdrew thence the young Richard, whose ill-health demanded constant feminine attentions, to confide him to her charge: thus she alone became possessed of the secret of his existence, and now with Lord Lovel she debated how best his interests could be furthered.

Lord Lincoln[a] feared by rash measures to endanger the safety of his cousin.[2] He desired to place him on the throne, but he preferred bringing him up in freedom and obscurity to any ill-judged attempt that might throw him into his enemy's hands, and make him prisoner for life. His plans were all laid upon this principle: he commanded Lord Lovel, who submitted wholly to him, not to breathe the name of the son of Edward till he had gained / a decided advantage over the reigning sovereign. If victorious, he might set up the royal standard and proclaim Richard the Fourth, while the Earl, still in London, would call together all the Yorkists, and, in the absence of the king, seize, in his cousin's[3] name, upon the capital of the kingdom. If Lord Lovel's attempt proved unsuccessful, it was decided that the prince should escape immediately to the Continent, there to remain till some new insurrection was organized; for, though cautious, he was resolute, and he had determined never to relinquish his purpose, but to excite rebellion and discontent against Henry till the rightful heir possessed his own.

These plans were in contradiction to Lady Brampton's views, but she was obliged to submit. Her quick woman's wit discovered her another danger. The absolute silence observed concerning the young Prince, then only eleven years of age, might in the end cast a doubt over the justice of his pretensions, and she told Lord Lovel, that, if after a failure Richard quitted England, he must first be seen / and acknowledged by his mother. She resolved, therefore, on immediately going to Winchester to prepare Elizabeth for the reception of her son; and Lord Lovel, who agreed in the wisdom of this proposal, promised at all hazards

---

[a] The marginal note in *Abinger/Palacio* keyed to this sentence refers back to 'p. 26' (p. 17), where Lincoln is identified as the son of a sister of Edward IV and Richard III; see Endnotes 2 and 3.

that ere leaving the kingdom the Duke of York should cross the country to that town, whence by Southampton he might escape to France. While therefore Lord Lovel increased his army and marched in high hopes towards York, Lady Brampton proceeded southward, meditating the safest and best manner of introducing herself to the Queen.

There was a man, Richard Simon or Symond,[a] who afterwards figured in the chronicles, that had long been secretly concerned in the course of events. He was the son of a tenant of Sir John Gray,[b] and had been the playmate of the Lady Elizabeth Gray's elder children. His love of books, his sedentary habits, and quick wit on matters of learning, led those interested in his fate to consider him fitted for the church, and therefore he took priest's orders. But his mind, though not attuned to action in its / noblest sense, was not one that could remain at rest. He loved power; he was sagacious, astute, and intriguing: when the Lady Gray became Queen, he being still too young for high promotion, preferred an unnoticed but influential situation near her person to more lucrative employ, which would remove him from the pleasures and dignity of the Court. When Edward died he devoted himself to the service of his royal patroness, and hardly escaped being imprisoned for life by Richard, when the latter was most exasperated against the Queen Dowager's relations. From that time Richard Simon found full occupation for his plotting head, in endeavouring to bring about the overthrow of the usurping Gloucester, and to raise the hopes of Henry the Seventh, who requited ill his active zeal: and now again he busied himself in exalting the Queen's party. He looked the man he was – a prier into secrets – one who conducted the drama of life by back-stairs and tell-tale valets: his small grey eyes were quick to discern the meaning of each smile or frown; his young brow was already / wrinkled through care and thought; craft lurked in the corners of his lips; and his whispering voice betokened habitual caution. He continued to hover near the Queen; now dispatched to sound some Yorkist, now closeted to discuss some expression of the King's, in which to find a secret meaning. Repose was the thing he hated; and for ever with some plan on foot, some web to weave or unravel, he was seen with brows a little elevated by self-conceit, with a courtly bend of the body and insinuating address, now assuring a Lancastrian of the perfect satisfaction of the Queen, now whispering to a Yorkist a tale of slights and injuries practised by King Henry against his consort and her friends. All the communication that had taken place between Elizabeth Woodville and the Earl of Lincoln had been carried on through this man, though each knew not that he communicated to the other what either said. But Lincoln respected his undeviating fidelity

---

[a] Richard Symonds, a young Oxford priest, created a false Edward VI out of a handsome local youth; see p. 49.

[b] The first husband of the future queen of Edward IV, Elizabeth Woodville ('Lady Elizabeth Gray'), was killed fighting for the Lancastrians in 1461. She bore him two sons.

towards his patroness, and valued his talents. It was to this man that Lady Brampton addressed herself on / her arrival at Winchester, to procure for her a private audience with the Queen. Her dark hints respecting the insurrection of Lovel and the Staffords excited his curiosity, yet he experienced more difficulty than he expected in bringing the royal dowager to consent to receive her rival. When our days of prosperity are fled we cling fondly to all that reminds us of their brightness, and turn with augmented distaste from every thing that marred their splendour. Elizabeth loved to remember herself as the chosen bride of Edward, and any circumstance that spoke of his inconstancy, or detracted from the entireness of her influence over him, then inspired her with indignation, now with abhorrence. It required all Simon's dexterity to allay her anger, and excite her curiosity, sufficiently to induce her to admit her rival to her presence.

It was at the hour of vespers that the priest introduced Lady Brampton into the Queen's cabinet. Elizabeth was assured that she had secrets of importance to communicate, and she designed by affability to win her to a full / disclosure of them. Yet her heart and manner grew cold as she entered the closet where the lady and her guide already were, and bending her head slightly, she said, "The Lady Brampton desired an audience with me – I grant it."

With all her vivacity and consciousness of the importance of her disclosures, the lady felt herself awed and chilled; and the memory of Edward came across her, who had before shielded her from such unkindness, and filled her eyes with tears. A long pause ensued; the Queen looked as in expectation, and Richard Simon, who had retired to an embrasure of a window, was about to come forward, when Lady Brampton, conquering her emotion, said, "Your Grace is the happy mother of the Queen of England, and the hope of an heir, which you now entertain, may make my intelligence distasteful."

"Say on," replied Elizabeth haughtily; "I listen to your words."

The lady felt much inclined not to say another word, but assuming almost equal coldness of manner, she continued, "Would your Grace / prefer that your fair daughter should still bear the sceptre, or that Richard the Fourth should wrest it from the husband's grasp?"

Now indeed the Queen started, and cried impetuously, "I charge you, trifle with me no longer! Explain your words; who would supplant my child?"

"Her brother," Lady Brampton replied; and seeing the Queen lost in a mixture of amazement and terror, she added, "The Duke of York still lives: he is now, I trust, at the head of forces sufficient to enforce his rights. In a few days England will acknowledge him as sovereign."

In reply to these words, spoken with rapidity, as if they were pregnant with supreme delight to their auditress, the Queen with an angry look, said, "I shall league with no plotters to establish an impostor."

"Beware," said Lady Brampton indignantly; "let your Majesty bethink yourself, before you consign your son to misery and an early grave. Will his mother be his chief enemy?"

"Who vouches for him?" /

"Himself! He is the very Edward who once was yours: his young features are but the miniature mirror of his royal father; his princely grace, his wit, his courage, are all derived from him."

"I must see the boy," said the Queen, "to end at once this silly masque. How do you pretend that he escaped from the Tower?"

The independence and sensibility of Lady Brampton's disposition would not permit her to answer a question asked thus ironically. Had she looked at the Queen, she might have seen, by her change of countenance, that it was nearly all put on by the jealous instinct that would not permit her to acknowledge herself under so great an obligation to her rival. Lady Brampton turned to Simon, saying, "I am ready to depart, Sir Priest; I see her Grace sorrows that the same cold bed does not entomb Richard of York and Edward the Fifth. Poor prince! My Lord of Lincoln counselled well, and I was to blame in not acting on his advice."

"Stay," cried Elizabeth, "speak again. Is the Earl of Lincoln a party to this tale?" /

"Your Majesty insults me," said the lady; "I came here to please a mother's ear by assurances of her child's safety, and to conduct the tempest-tost fortunes of this ill-starred boy into the safe harbour of maternal love. I came with a full heart and an ardent desire to serve you; no other motive could have led me hither. You receive me with disdain; you dismiss me with contumely. I fear that so much you hate me, that, for my sake, your heart is steeled against your princely son. But as you already know so much as to make it necessary that you should know all, I will hasten to London, and intreat the noble de la Poole to communicate with you, and to avert a mother's enmity from her child. I take my leave."

She was about to depart; but Simon, who knew that a feud between the prince's partizans must ruin his cause, entreated her to remain; and then addressing the Queen, tried to soothe her, for she was pacing the rushes of her chamber in excessive agitation. "Peace, good friend," said she, "I will speak to Lincoln; I will ask him why I, who was deemed by his / honoured uncle fit partaker of his councils, am kept by him in ignorance of the alleged existence of this poor boy? Even now he might be sitting on the throne, had I been consulted: Instead of this, to what has this distrust brought him? He is a crownless king, a fugitive prince, branded as an impostor; a seal is put on his fate, which nothing probably will ever remove. I, even I, have called my son, if such he be, a counterfeit!"

Maternal tenderness touched to the quick the royal lady's heart, and she wept. Lady Brampton was all impulse and goodness of disposition: she felt that Elizabeth had wronged her, but in a moment she forgave the offence: she advanced, and kneeling at her feet, touched her hand gently, as she said, "Let not your Grace judge too harshly of our proceedings. We poor faulty human

37

beings, hurried hither and thither by passion, are for ever jostling against and hurting each other, where more perfect natures would coalesce, and thus succeed where we fail. Forgive, forget the past: it cannot now be changed. Forgive the Earl, / who, long bound by an oath to his uncle Gloucester, could only save your son's life by feigning his death. Forgive the humblest of your servants, even myself, who acted under his commands, and who now, in disobedience to them, attempts to bring the royal exile to his mother's arms. Would that my humility could appease your displeasure, and that you would acknowledge me your faithful follower. My life should be at the disposal of you and the princely York."

Lady Brampton, full of vivacity, energy, and even of imperiousness, had so much grace in her manner and sweetness in her voice, when she laid these keen weapons aside to assume those of gentleness and love, that she was irresistible. The Queen, at once softened, stretched out her hand, which the lady pressed respectfully to her lips; then, as friends bent on one design, they conversed unreservedly together. Lady Brampton entered into long details concerning the past history of the Duke of York, and the schemes then on foot for his advancement. This was / not their sole interview; they met again and again, and mutual affection confirming the link which the fate of Richard caused to exist between them, the Queen named the Lady Brampton one of her ladies, and henceforth they lived together under the same roof. /

CHAPTER V.

———

Poor orphan! in the wide world scattered,
As budding branch rent from the native tree.
SPENSER.[a]

England, farewell! thou, who hast been my cradle,
Shalt never be my dungeon or my grave!
SHELLEY.[b]

———

The historical account of Lord Lovel's insurrection[c] is contained in a few words. While the two Staffords besieged Worcester, this nobleman advanced against Henry in York. The Duke of Bedford[d] was sent against him, who published a general pardon for all the rebels who should submit. The soldiers of Lord Lovel had no powerful watch-word to ensure their union; the existence of Edward the Fourth's son was a profound secret; they were therefore / easily induced to abandon an almost nameless cause; and in three weeks Lord Lovel found himself with only one hundred adherents, or rather personal friends, who at his earnest entreaty disbanded, while he, chiefly bent on saving the life of his princely charge, felt greater security in being left singly with him.

He had promised to traverse England, and to conduct him to Winchester; but the hot pursuit on foot forced him to delay this journey. Meanwhile a present refuge was to be sought. He had a staunch friend in a zealous Yorkist, Sir Thomas Broughton, who resided in Lancashire, to whose residence he directed his steps. Still, even during this short journey, great precaution was necessary. Lord Lovel and his charge travelled disguised, avoiding high roads

---

[a] *Faerie Queene*, II. ii. 2.

[b] Percy Bysshe Shelley (1792–1822), 'Charles the First', iv. 1–2; Mary Shelley published some surviving fragments of this unfinished drama in *PBS* 1824.

[c] '1486' (marginal note in *Abinger/Palacio*).

[d] Jasper Tudor, Earl of Pembroke and 1st Duke of Bedford (?1431–95), uncle and guardian of the future Henry VII, accompanied his nephew into exile in 1471, and commanded the royal forces upon Henry's accession.

39

and great towns. On the second evening, when the red aspect of the setting sun threatened an inclement night, they took shelter in a lone cot on one of the wild moors of that county.

A long habit of personal attendance had instilled into Lovel's mind a parental affection for the little prince. They had journeyed far that / day, and Richard was overpowered by fatigue; his friend strewed for him a bed of leaves – he stretched himself on it, and quickly fell into a sound sleep, while the noble kept up the fire he had lighted, and paced the hut, revolving in his mind a thousand schemes. It was a chill February evening;[a] and, as night came on, a thick sleet beat against the windows, while the wind, sweeping over the wide heath, howled round the miserable shepherd's cot. Some time passed thus, and fear in Lovel's mind gave place to the sense of security, inspired by the desolation of the spot and the inclemency of the elements. He needed rest, and as soon as he had thrown himself on the ground, drowsiness overpowered him – the wind sang a wild lullaby to both the sleepers.

Though still lost to the outer world, a change passed over Lovel's countenance – again his features relaxed into sleep, and again expressed disquietude. The tramp of horses' feet was around the hut – voices mingled alien sounds with the raging blast; – at last a loud knocking at the door caused the noble at once to start on his feet wide awake. Richard still slept on. / Lord Lovel cautiously withdrew into the shadow behind the door, listening intently to divine the motives of these unwelcome intruders. He felt assured that they were emissaries of Henry, who had traced him hither; he endeavoured to form in his mind some plan of conduct to save the duke, whom he was about to awaken and put on his guard, when a woman's voice struck upon his ear. The knocking at the door was changed into a violent beating, the rude hinges gave way, and it swung back. The fugitive's heart beat quick; it was a moment full of fate; such a one, as when passed, we seem to have concentrated a life into its small space. The man that entered calmed his fears; low in stature, broadly built, a cloak lined with furs added to his bulk, and a Flemish hat completed his peaceable appearance; though he was too much muffled to shew his face. Glancing at Lovel a look which was, doubtless, intended to convey reproach, he muttered some words in a foreign guttural language, and went back to his companions. Two women now entered, both enveloped in furs. One stept lightly on, and drew the bench / which had lately pillowed the head of Lovel, closer to the fire, while the other, bending under the burthen in her arms, approached slower, and sitting down on the seat prepared for her, threw back her cloak, and discovered that she bore in her arms a sleeping child, about six years of age. The first, meanwhile, disencumbered herself of her rich furs, and

[a] An unresolved chronological difficulty; this chill February evening comes after Lovel's failed insurrection, placed at Easter time on p. 33.

then leaning over the child, kissed its little hands, and regarded its sleeping form with mingled anxiety and tenderness, speaking to the other in a foreign dialect, evidently about the risk the poor babe had ran from exposure to the weather. Lovel remained a mute spectator; he resolved not to come forward, till he should see who their male attendants were. After a brief interval the first intruder again entered; he threw off his cloak, and looking round with keen eyes, the fugitive discovered the well-known features of a friend. His heart now relieved, his countenance lighted up, and he stept forward, saying: "Mynheer Jahn Warbeck, God be with you! you travel on a stormy night."

"And you, Lord Lovel," replied the money-lender, / angrily, "are sufficiently discourteous to wanderers at such a season. Why even vipers are harmless during a storm."

"But fair weather returns, and they again find their sting. I might bare my own breast, but – " he pointed to the bed of leaves, on which, in spite of the tumult, young Richard still slept.

Warbeck started: but before he could reply one of his companions turned to speak to him, and a conversation ensued, begun in Dutch, and continued in French, concerning the circumstances which had divided them from their attendants, and their fatiguing wanderings during the storm. A small saddle-bag was produced by Warbeck, containing a few provisions. A bed for the sleeping child was formed, and the travellers sat round the fire, enjoying their simple fare. From time to time the fair blue eyes of the younger lady, who was evidently the mistress, and the other an attendant, turned to look on the chivalric form and manly beauty of Lovel; a few smiling observations escaped her in her native language, which Warbeck answered / drily and succinctly. The bench on which the lady sat was soon sacrificed for firing – the cloaks of the party were dried, and the women, wrapt in them, sought repose on the bare ground, which was the sole flooring of the hut, the younger drawing to her bosom the sleeping child. Lovel and Warbeck kept silence, till the deep breathing of their companions shewed that they slept: then, in reply to the Fleming's questions, Lovel related the history of the last months, and at the conclusion frankly asked his advice and assistance in accomplishing his design of conveying the Duke of York to Winchester. Warbeck looked thoughtful on this demand, and after a pause said "I cannot say wherefore this unfortunate prince excites so strong an interest in me; for in truth my heart yearns towards him as if he were akin to me. Is it because he bore for a time my poor boy's name?"

Warbeck paused; his hard features were strongly marked by grief – "I and my sister," he continued, "crossed the country to visit my / Peterkin, who was ill – who is lost to me now for ever."

A pause again ensued: the young soldier respected too much the father's grief to interrupt it. At length the Fleming said, "Lord Lovel I will – I trust I can – save Duke Richard's life. My sister is kind-hearted; and the silence you have observed concerning the very existence of King Edward's son, makes the task more easy. Madeline is about to return to her own country; she was to have taken my Peterkin with her. Let the Prince again assume that name: it shall be my care to escort him in this character to Winchester; and at Portsmouth[a] they may embark, while you follow your own plans, and take refuge with the friends you mention in these parts."

As Warbeck spoke, Lovel motioned to him to observe his sister,[b] who, unable to sleep, was observing them with attention. "Madeline does not understand our English," said her brother; "but it were well that she joined our counsels, which may continue in French. I / have your leave, my Lord, to disclose your secret to her? Fear her not: she would die rather than injure one hair of that poor child's head."

On Warbeck's invitation, the lady rose; and he, taking her hand, led her to the low couch of the Duke of York. Sleep and gentle dreams spread an irradiation of beauty over him: his glowing cheek, his eyes hardly closed, the masses of rich auburn hair that clustered on a brow of infantine smoothness and candour, the little hand and arm, which, thrown above his head, gave an air of helplessness to his attitude, combined to form a picture of childish grace and sweetness, which no woman, and that woman a mother, could look on without emotions of tenderness. "What an angelic child," said the fair sister of Warbeck, as she stooped to kiss his rosy cheek; "what a noble looking boy. Who is he?"

"One proscribed," said the Cavalier, "one whom he who reigns over England would consign to a dungeon. Were he to fall into the hands of his enemies, they might / not, indeed dare not cut him off violently; but they would consume and crush him, by denying him all that contributes to health and life."

"Can this sweet boy have enemies?" cried the lady: "Ah! if he have, has he not friends also to guard him from them?"

"With our lives!" he replied emphatically; "but that is a small sacrifice and a useless one; for to preserve him we must preserve ourselves. My life, – such acts deserve no record, – I have, and will again and again expose for him; but the will to save him is not enough without the power; and that power you possess, lady, to a far, far greater extent than I."

"The will I have most certainly," said the fair one, regarding the boy with anxious tenderness. "Command me, Sire Chevalier; my power, small as I must believe it to be, and my will, shall unite to preserve this sweet child."

Warbeck disclosed briefly to his sister the secret of young Richard's birth, and detailed his plan for his safe journey to Winchester; / nay, and after that, for his crossing the sea, and continuing to personate, in Flanders, the nephew of Madeline, if so his royal mother deemed fitting, till the moment should

---

[a] Major Channel port on England's Hampshire coast.
[b] Mary Shelley's invention.

arrive, when the schemes of his partizans being crowned with success, he could be restored to his country and his birthright. The fair Fleming joyfully assented to this proposition, and entered cordially into the details. Lovel was profuse of thanks: so suddenly and so easily to be relieved from his worst fears, appeared like the special interposition of some guardian saint. His heart overflowed with gratitude; and his glistening eyes gave token of greater thanks than even his emphatic words. Madeline felt all the excitement of being actively employed in a deed of benevolence: her calm features were animated with an angelic expression. The discussion of details, demanding the coolest prudence and most vigilant observation long occupied them; and the lady brought a woman's tact and keen penetration to arrange the crude designs of her brother. All was rendered smooth; every obstacle foreseen and obviated; every pass of / danger reconnoitred and provided for. When, at last, their plans were perfected, the lady again returned to her hard couch to seek repose: for some time the Cavalier and the Fleming kept watch, till they also, in such comfortless posture as they might, stretched on the bare ground, yielded to drowsiness; and grey morning found all the dwellers in the sheep cot sunk in profound sleep. Fear, charity, hope, and love, might colour their dreams; but quiet slumber possessed them all, driving care and thought from the heart and brain, to steep both in oblivion of all ill.

When Madeline awoke in the morning, the first sight that met her eyes was the lovely boy she had promised to protect, playing with her dark-eyed girl, who displayed all the extacy of childish glee with her new playmate. Madeline was a blonde Fleming, with light blue eyes and flaxen ringlets – she was about five-and-twenty years of age; an expression of angelic goodness animated her features, bestowing on them an appearance of loveliness, which of themselves they did not possess. It could / hardly be guessed, that Richard's playmate was the daughter of the fair-haired Fleming: but the husband of Warbeck's sister was a Spaniard, and the child resembled her father in every thing except the soft mouth and sweet smile, which was all her mother's: her large full dark eyes, gave to her infantine face a look of sensibility, far beyond her years. The little girl ran to her mother when she awoke; and Madeline caressed both her and the Prince with the greatest tenderness. They stood at the door of the cottage; the early sun shone brightly on the hoar frost that covered the moor; the keen air was bracing, though cold; the morning was cheerful, such as inspires hope and animation, a lively wit to understand, and a roused courage to meet difficulties.

Madeline turned from the glittering scene to look on her young charge – his eyes were fixed on her face. "How beautiful and good you look," said the boy.

"I am glad that you think me good," replied the lady smiling; "you will have less fear in trusting yourself with me: your noble friend / has confided your Grace to my care, if, indeed, you will condescend to live with me, and be as a son to me. I have just lost a little nephew whom I fondly loved; will you supply his place, and take his name?"

43

"Fair cousin," said the Prince, caressing his kind friend as he spoke; "I will wait on you, and serve you as no nephew ever served. What name did your lost kinsman bear? Quickly tell me, that I may know my own, and hereafter call myself by it."

"Perkin Warbeck," said Madeline.

"Now you mock me," cried Richard, "that has long been my name; but I knew not that it gave me a claim to so pretty a relation."

"This courtly language," replied the lady, "betrays your Grace's princeliness. What will our Flemish boors say, when I present the nursling of royalty as mine? You will shame our homely breeding, Duke Richard."

"I beseech you, fair Mistress," said Lovel, who now joined them, "to forget, even in private, such high-sounding titles. It is dangerous to play at majesty, unaided by ten thousand / armed assertors of our right. Remember this noble child only as your loving nephew, Perkin Warbeck: he, who well knows the misery of regal claims unallied to regal authority, will shelter himself gladly and gratefully under the shadow of your lowly bower."

And now, as the wintry sun rose higher, the travellers prepared for their departure. Warbeck first left them to find and to dismiss his domestics, who would have been aware of the deception practised in the person of Richard. He returned in a few hours for his sister. The Duke and Lord Lovel then separated. The intervening time had been employed by the noble in schooling the boy as to his future behaviour, in recounting to him his plans and hopes, and in instructing him how to conduct himself with his mother, if indeed he saw her; for Lovel was ignorant how Lady Brampton had succeeded at Winchester, and how far it would be possible to bring about an interview between the Queen and her son. At length Warbeck returned; the travellers mounted; and Lord Lovel, watching from the / cottage door, beheld with melancholy regret the Prince depart: the long habit of intercourse, the uncertain future, his high pretensions and his present state, had filled the Cavalier with moody thoughts, unlike his usual sanguine anticipations and energetic resolves. "This is woman-ly," at last he thought, as the reflection that he was alone, and had perhaps seen his beloved charge for the last time, filled his eyes with unwonted tears. "To horse! To my friends! – There to plan, scheme, devise – and then again to the field!"

Days and weeks past, replete with doubt and anxiety to the Queen and her enthusiastic friend at Winchester. Each day, many, many times, Lady Bramp-ton visited the Cathedral to observe whether the silver heart was suspended near the altar, which she had agreed with Lord Lovel, should be the sign of the Duke's arrival. The part Elizabeth Woodville had to play meanwhile was difficult and painful – she lived in constant intercourse with the Countess of Richmond; the wishes and thoughts of all around were occupied by the hope of an heir to the crown, which the young / Queen would soon bestow on England. The birth of a son, it was prognosticated, would win her husband's affection, and all idea of future disturbance, of further risings and disloyalty, through the existence of this joint offspring of the two Roses would be for ever at an end. While these hopes and expectations formed, it was supposed, the most flattering and agreeable subject of congratulation for the dowager Queen, she remained sleepless and watchful, under the anticipation of seeing her fugitive son, the outcast and discrowned claimant of all that was to become the birthright of the unborn child.

At length the unwearied cares of Lady Brampton were rewarded; a small silver heart, bearing the initials of Richard, Duke of York, was suspended near the shrine; and as she turned to look who placed it there, the soft voice of Madeline uttered the word of recognition agreed upon; joy filled Lady Brampton's heart, as the brief answers to her hurried questions assured her of Richard's safety. The same evening she visited, in disguise, the abode of Warbeck, and embraced, in a transport of / delight, the princely boy in whose fate she interested herself with all the fervour of her warm heart. She now learnt the design Lord Lovel had of placing Richard in safety under Madeline's care in Flanders, until his friends had prepared for him a triumphant return to England. She concerted with her new friends the best mode of introducing Richard into his mother's presence; and it was agreed that early on the following morning, Madeline and the Duke should seek one of the small chapels of the Cathedral of Winchester, and that Elizabeth should there meet her son. With an overflowing heart, Lady Brampton returned to communicate this intelligence to the royal widow, and to pass with her the intervening hours in oft-renewed conjectures, and anticipations concerning the Duke of York.

To modern and protestant England, a cathedral or a church may appear a strange place for private assignations and concealed meetings. It was otherwise in the days of our ancestors, when through similarity of religion, our manners bore a greater resemblance than they now do to those / of foreign countries. The churches stood always open, ready to receive the penitent, who sought the stillness of the holy asylum the more entirely to concentrate his thoughts in prayer. As rank did not exempt its possessors from sin nor sorrow, neither did it from acts of penitence, nor from those visitations of anguish, when the sacred temple was sought, as bringing the votarist into more immediate communication with the Deity. The Queen Dowager excited therefore no suspicion, when, with her rosary formed of the blessed wood of Lebanon encased in gold in her hand, with Lady Brampton for her sole attendant, she sought at five in the morning the dark aisle of the Cathedral of Winchester, there to perform her religious duties. Two figures already knelt near the altar of the chapel designated as the place of meeting; Elizabeth's breath came thick; her knees bent under her; she leaned against a buttress, while a fair-haired boy turned at the sound. He first looked timidly on her, and then encouraged by the smile that visited her quivering lips, he sprung forward, and kneeling at her feet, buried his face in her / dress, sobbing, while bending over him, her own tears fell on

45

his glossy hair. Lady Brampton and Madeline retired up the aisle, leaving the mother and child alone.

"Look up, my Richard," cried the unfortunate widow; "look up, son of King Edward, my noble, my out-cast boy! Thou art much grown, much altered since last I saw thee. Thou art more like thy blessed father than thy infancy promised." She parted his curls on his brow, and looked on him with the very soul of maternal tenderness. "Ah! were I a cottager," she continued, "though bereft of my husband, I should collect my young ones round me, and forget sorrow. I should toil for them, and they would learn to toil for me. How sweet the food my industry procured for them, how hallowed that which their maturer strength would bestow on me! I am the mother of princes. Vain boast! I am childless!"

The Queen, lost in thought, scarcely heard the gentle voice of her son who replied by expressions of endearment, nor felt his caresses; but collecting her ideas, she called to mind / how brief the interview must be, and how she was losing many precious moments in vain exclamations and regrets. Recovering that calm majesty which usually characterized her, she said: "Richard, arise! our minutes are counted, and each must be freighted with the warning and wisdom of years. Thou art young, my son! but Lady Brampton tells me that thy understanding is even premature; thy experience indeed must be small, but I will try to adapt my admonitions to that experience. Should you fail to understand me, do not on that account despise my lessons, but treasure them up till thy increased years reveal their meaning to thee. We may never meet again; for once separated, ten thousand swords, and twice ten thousand dangers divide us perhaps for ever. I feel even now that it is given to me to bless thee for the last time, and I would fain to the last be the cause of good to thee. I have lived, ah! how long; and suffered, methinks, beyond human suffering; let the words I now utter, live in thy soul for ever; my soul is in them! Will not my / son respect the sacred yearnings of his mother's heart?"

Touched, penetrated by this exordium, the tearful boy promised attention and obedience. Elizabeth sat on a low tomb, Richard knelt before her; one kiss she imprinted on his young brow, while endeavouring to still the beating of her heart, and to command the trembling of her voice. She was silent for a few moments. Richard looked up to her with mingled love and awe; wisdom seemed to beam from her eyes, and the agitation that quivered on her lips gave solemnity to the tone with which she addressed her young auditor.

She spoke of his early prospects, his long imprisonment, and late fortunes. She descanted on the character of Henry Tudor, describing him as wise and crafty, and to be feared. She dwelt on the character of the Earl of Lincoln and other chiefs of the house of York, and mentioned how uneasily they bore the downfal of their party. No pains, no artifice, no risk, she said, would be spared by any one of them, to elevate an offspring of the White Rose, and to / annihilate the pretensions and power of Lancaster. "Still a boy, unmeet for such contest, noble blood will be shed for you, my son," she continued; "and while you are secluded by those who love you from danger, many lives will be spent for your sake. We shall hazard all for you; and all may prove too little for success. We may fail, and you be thrown upon your own guidance, your unformed judgment, and childish indiscretion. Alas! what will then be your fate? Your kinsmen and partizans slain – your mother broken-hearted, it may be, dead! – spies will on every side environ you, nets will be spread to ensnare you, daggers sharpened for your destruction. You must oppose prudence to craft, nor, until your young hand can wield a man's weapon, dare attempt aught against Henry's power. Never forget that you are a King's son, yet suffer not unquiet ambition to haunt you. Sleep in peace, my love, while others wake for you. The time may come when victory will be granted to our arms. Then we shall meet again, not as now, like skulking guilt, but in the open sight of day I shall present my / son to his loyal subjects. Now we part, my Richard – again you are lost to me, save in the recollection of this last farewell."

Her own words fell like a mournful augury on her ear. With a look of agonized affection she opened her arms, and then enclosed in their circle the stripling form of her son. She pressed him passionately to her heart, covering him with her kisses, while the poor boy besought her not to weep; yet, infected by her sorrow, tears streamed from his eyes, and his little heart swelled with insupportable emotion. It was at once a sight of pity and of fear to behold his mother's grief.

Lady Brampton and Madeline now drew near, and this effusion of sorrow past away. The Queen collected herself, and rising, taking Richard's hand in hers, with dignity and grace she led him up to the fair Fleming, saying "A widowed mother commits to your protection her beloved child. If heaven favour our right, we may soon claim him, to fill the exalted station to which he is heir. If disaster and death follow our attempts, be kind to my orphan son, protect / him from the treachery of his enemies; preserve, I beseech you, his young life!"

Madeline replied in a tone that shewed how deeply she sympathized in the Queen's sorrows, while she fervently promised never to desert her charge. "Now depart," said Elizabeth, "leave me, Richard, while I have yet courage to say adieu!"

Elizabeth stood watching, while the forms of the prince and his protectress disappeared down the dark aisle. They reached the door; it swung back on its hinges, and the sound, made as it closed again, reverberated through the arched cathedral. The unfortunate mother did not speak; leaning on her friend's arm she quitted the church by another entrance. They returned to the palace in silence; and when again they conversed, it was concerning their hopes of the future, the schemes to be devised; nor did the aching heart of Elizabeth relieve itself in tears and complaints, till the intelligence, received some weeks afterwards of the safe arrival of the travellers in France, took the most bitter sting from her fears, and allowed her again to breathe freely. /

47

CHAPTER VI.

———

"Such when as Archimago him did view,
　He weened well to work some uncouth wile;
Eftsoon untwisting his deceitful clew,
　He 'gan to weave a web of cunning guile."
SPENSER.[a]

———

The birth of Arthur, Prince of Wales,[b] which took place in the month of September of this same year, served to confirm Henry Tudor on the throne, and almost to obliterate the memory of a second and resisting party in the kingdom. That party indeed was overthrown, its chiefs scattered, its hopes few. Most of the principal Yorkists had taken refuge in the court of the Duchess / of Burgundy:[c] the Earl of Lincoln only ventured to remain, preserving the appearance of the greatest privacy, while his secret hours were entirely occupied by planning a rising in the kingdom, whose success would establish his cousin Richard Duke of York, the fugitive Perkin Warbeck, on the throne. The chief obstacle that presented itself was the difficulty of exciting the English to any act of rebellion against the king, without bringing forward the young Prince as the principal actor on the scene. The confirmed friendship between the Queen and Lady Brampton had produced a greater degree of intercourse between the former and the Earl; but their joint counsels had yet failed to originate a plan of action: when chance, or rather the unforeseen results of former events, determined their course of action, and brought to a crisis sooner than they expected the wavering purposes of each.

Richard Simon had quitted Winchester to fulfil his duties as priest in the town of Oxford. No man was better fitted than Simon to act a prominent part in a state-plot. He was / brave; but the priestly garb having wrested the sword

———

[a] *Faerie Queene*, II. i. 8 (adapted).

[b] Henry VII's first-born son (1486–1502); '1486' (marginal note in *Abinger/Palacio*).

[c] Margaret (1446–1503), sister of Edward IV, became in 1468 the third wife of Charles the Bold (or Rash), Duke of Burgundy (1433–77). Burgundy achieved its greatest power under Charles, who strove to make it independent of France.

from his hand, circumstances had converted that active courage, which might have signalized him in the field, to a spirit of restless intrigue; to boldness in encountering difficulties, and address in surmounting them. To form plans, to concoct the various parts of a scheme, wedging one into the other; to raise a whirlwind around him, and to know, or to fancy that he knew, the direction the ravager would take, and what would be destroyed and what saved in its course, had been from youth the atmosphere in which he lived. Now absent from the Queen, he was yet on the alert to further her views, and he looked forward to the exaltation of her son to the throne as the foundation-stone of his own fortunes. In what way could this be brought about? After infinite deliberation with himself, Simon conceived the idea of bringing forward an impostor, who, taking the name of Richard of York, whose survival, though unattested, was a current belief in the kingdom, might rouse England in his cause. / If unsuccessful, the safety of the rightful prince was not endangered; if triumphant, this counterfeit would doff his mask at once, and the real York come forward in his place.[a]

In the true spirit of intrigue, in which Simon was an adept, he resolved to mature his plans and commence his operations before he communicated them to any. He looked round for a likely actor for his new part, and chance brought him in contact with Lambert Simnel, a baker's son at Oxford.[b] There was something in his fair complexion and regular soft features that was akin to York; his figure was slight, his untaught manners replete with innate grace; he was clever; and his beauty having made him a sort of favourite, he had grown indolent and assuming. His father died about this time, and he was left a penniless orphan. Simon came forward to protect him, and cautiously to point out the road to fortune without labour. The youth proved an apt scholar. To hear speak of princes, crowns, and kingdoms as objects in which he was to have an interest and a share, dazzled his young / eyes. He learnt speedily every lesson the priest taught him, and adopted so readily the new language inculcated, that Simon became, more and more enamoured of his scheme, and sanguine as to its results. The next care of Simon was to confirm, in the partizans of the House of York, the suspicion they already entertained of the existence of its noblest scion; he dispatched anonymous letters to the chief nobles, and it became whispered through the country, though none knew the origin of the tale, that the surviving son of Edward the Fourth was about to appear to claim the crown. The peaceful sighed to think that the White and Red Roses would again be watered by the best blood of England. The warlike and ambitious, the

---

[a] Mary Shelley blends two separate Yorkist plots; the Warbeck impersonation began only in 1491.

[b] Lambert Simnel (?1475–?1525), a Yorkist pawn who was a son of an Oxford tradesman; his major impersonation was of the Earl of Warwick (see p. 17n). Crowned Edward VI in Ireland, he re-entered England with a mercenary army furnished by Margaret of Burgundy. His forces were defeated at Stoke (1487), and he was set to work in the royal kitchens.

partizans of York, who had languished in obscurity, walked more erect; they regarded their disused armour with complacency, for war and tumult was then the favourite pastime of high-born men.

It was at this period that, through the intervention of Lady Brampton, Sir Thomas Broughton, a most zealous Yorkist[a] and chief / friend of Lord Lovel, was introduced to the Dowager Queen's presence, then residing in London. He came full of important intelligence. He had been roused from his usual repose by one of Simon's anonymous letters, which hinted at the existence of the Duke of York, and counselled a drawing together of such forces as would be willing to support him: Lord Lovel was with him, and at the name of Richard at once prepared for action. He was busied in raising adherents in the south, sending Sir Thomas to London, that he might there receive the commands of the Prince's mother. Scarcely had he entered the metropolis, when in one of its narrowest alleys he was accosted by Richard Simon, who had earnestly besought him to obtain an audience for Simon himself from the Queen; acknowledging that he was the author of the reports and commotions, and that he had important secrets to disclose.

All this inspired the Queen with the deepest disquietude. She readily arranged with Sir Thomas the desired interview, which, at Simon's / request, was to take place that very night, and agreed that he should enter the palace by a private door, Lady Brampton giving him admittance. Broughton departed, and Elizabeth, disturbed and agitated, counted the hours impatiently which must intervene before the riddle was explained.

Even this interval was full of wonder. A report was circulated, which soon reached the palace, that the Earl of Warwick, in endeavouring to escape from the Tower in a boat, had fallen into the river, and was drowned before assistance could be afforded. Such was the current tale; but many suspected that the King was privy to a more guilty termination of his unhappy prisoner, of whose death none entertained a doubt. This circumstance added to the Queen's impatience – Life was bound up in the event of the next few hours.

The time arrived – all was quiet in the palace (the Queen inhabited Tower Royal); and the royal dowager and her friend prepared for their visitor. At the signal given the door was opened; but Simon came not alone; the Earl of / Lincoln, Lord Lovel, Sir Thomas Broughton, and an unknown youth, it was Edmund Plantagenet, entered. The tale of the imposture of Lambert Simnel was disclosed, and with it a change of plan, the result of the death of Warwick. Simnel's age and appearance accorded better with this prince than with his younger cousin; it were easy to spread abroad that the report of his death was a fiction contrived by the king; that he had escaped in fact, and was in arms. If a more sinister fate had befallen him, guilt would impose silence on his

---

[a] 'p. 84' (marginal note in *Abinger/Palacio*), referring to p. 39, where the same words are used to describe Broughton.

murderer; if the attempt failed, no evil would occur; if successful, he would give instant place to the superior claims of the Duke of York.

Lincoln unfolded these schemes with sagacity and deliberation, and the Queen eagerly adopted his ideas as he disclosed them. It was also the Earl's suggestion that Simnel should first appear in Ireland. The Duke of Clarence had been Lieutenant there, and was much beloved throughout the island: through neglect and forgetfulness all the counsellors and officers appointed by Clarence had / been unremoved by the new government, and might easily be induced to favour his persecuted son. The Duchess of Burgundy was also to be applied to, and counsel was held as to who should be informed of the truth, who deceived in this hazardous attempt; night wore away, while still the conspirators were in deliberation; they separated at last, each full of hope, each teeming with gallant resolution. Henceforth the false smile or ill-concealed frown of their enemy was indifferent to them; their good swords were their sure allies; the very victory gained by Henry at Bosworth raised their expectations; one other battle might give them again all that then they lost. /

CHAPTER VII.

———

Within these ten days take a monastery;
A most strict house; a house where none may whisper,
Where no more light is known but what may make you
Believe there is a day; where no hope dwells,
Nor comfort but in tears.

BEAUMONT AND FLETCHER.[a]

———

With the consciousness of this plot weighing on her mind, Elizabeth Woodville continued her usual routine of life, and made a part of the Court of Henry the Seventh. She had long been accustomed to pass from one evil to the other, and to find that when one cause for unhappiness died away, it gave instant place to

---

[a] *The Tragedy of Thierry King of France, and his Brother Theodoret* (1621), I. i.; now believed to be by John Fletcher (1579–1625), probably with the collaboration of Philip Massinger (1583–1640), and (possibly) Francis Beaumont (1584–1616).

another. She felt, with all the poignancy of a mother's disappointed pride, the situation of her / daughter. Neglect was the lightest term that could be applied to the systematized and cold-hearted tyranny of Henry towards his wife.[a] For not only he treated her like an unfavoured child, whose duty it was to obey without a murmur, and to endeavour to please, though sure of being repulsed. At the same time that he refused to raise her above this state of degradation, he reproached her with the faults of maturity, and stung her womanly feelings with studied barbarity. He taunted her with her attachment to her family and its partizans; spoke with triumph of its overthrow; and detailed with malignant pleasure every severe enactment passed by himself against the vanquished Yorkists. Then, again, he accused her of participating in her parent's intrigues, and though proud of the son she had given him, as the heir of his crown, he divided, as much as possible, the infant from the mother, under the avowed, though ridiculous pretence, of preventing her from inculcating principles of rebellion towards his liege and father.

This last blow sunk deep. She had hitherto / borne his harshness meekly, sustained by the hope of overcoming his flinty nature by softness and yielding. She had anticipated that the fresh enmity conceived against her on the event of Lord Lovel's rebellion, would be entirely allayed by her pretty Arthur, whose birth was solemnized by many rejoicings. But when she found this last hope fail, every expectation of good died away with it. Among other acts of duty, she had for a long time pursued a system of self-denial, deeming it a breach of duty to complain of her husband, even to her mother. But this mother, acquainted with the secrets of the human heart, and desirous of detaching her entirely from her husband, exerted all the influence that one experienced and firm can exercise over the young and vacillating; she brought her to lament her situation, and to complain of each fresh token of the King's disregard. The barrier of self-restraint once broken through, the sympathy and remonstrances of her parent emboldened her to such a change of conduct towards Henry, as at first excited his surprise, then his contempt. The many rumours afloat concerning / the existence of the Duke of York served also to rouse his angry mood: if at first he appeared somewhat complaisant towards his mother-in-law, it was from an endeavour to put her off her guard, and to attract or surprise her confidence on the point which lay nearest his heart; but, when he found that his attacks were vain, his undisguised arrogance and her ill-concealed resentment produced scenes, disgraceful in themselves, and agonizing to the wife and daughter who was their witness.

At this moment, when suspicion was abroad, the Lancastrians fearful, the Yorkists erect with renewed hopes, like the bursting of a thunder-storm came the intelligence of the appearance of the Earl of Warwick in Dublin, his

---

[a] A judgement supported by contemporary chronicles and the more recent histories available to Mary Shelley.

enthusiastic reception there, the rising of the people in his favour, and the menaces held out by him of his intention to wrench the sceptre of England from the hand of him who held it.

Henry alone heard these momentous tidings with contempt. The Earl of Kildare, Lord Lieutenant of the kingdom,[a] had received the pretender with princely honours; yet the very / circumstance of a false son of Clarence being supported by the Yorkists was the occasion of satisfaction to him; his only fear arose from the probable mystery covered by these designs. He was angry at the disloyalty manifested, but it was in a distant province, and so came not home to him. There appeared no falling off, no disturbance among his English subjects. Still caution and policy were the weapons he best loved to wield, and he dispatched several spies to Ireland, to endeavour to fathom the extent and nature of the rebellion. The chief among them was his own secretary, Frion, a Frenchman, a crafty and experienced implement.[b] He succeeded in bringing back irrefragable proof that the Dowager Queen mingled deeply in the plot.

Henry hated Elizabeth Woodville. He considered that it was principally through her restless scheming, that he had been forced to marry the portionless (her detested claim to his crown her only dower) daughter of York, instead of forming an union with a foreign princess; perhaps Mary of Burgundy, or Anne of Britanny, either of whom would have brought gold to his / coffers, or extensive domains to his empire.[c] He hated her, because he deeply suspected that she was privy to the existence of a formidable rival to his state. He *knew* that the young Duke of York had not died in the Tower. In every way she was his enemy; besides that linked to her ruin, was the sweet idea of confiscation, one ever entertained with delight by the money-loving king.

He assembled a council in his palace at Shene, which stood near where Richmond now stands.[d] The chiefs of the English nobility were his counsellors. The Duke of Buckingham,[e] son of him who first favoured, and then rose

---

[a] Gerald Fitzgerald, 8th Earl of Kildare (d. 1513), Lord Deputy of Ireland, who in effect ruled from 1477 until his death. Although Kildare abetted both Simnel and Warwick, Henry VII pardoned him twice, allegedly declaring that if all Ireland could not rule the Earl, the Earl should rule all Ireland.

[b] Stephen Frion, Henry VII's secretary for the French language. He defected to Margaret's court at Burgundy, and procured support for Warbeck from the French king, Charles VIII (1470–98; ruled 1483–98), only son of Louis XI.

[c] Marie (1457–82), daughter and heiress of Charles the Bold of Burgundy and stepdaughter of Margaret, was not a possible bride. Married to Maximilian of Austria in 1477, she died in 1482. Mary Shelley here alters or overlooks the historical record. Anne of Brittany (1477–1514) was in 1486 heiress-presumptive to her father, Francis II. Although Henry hinted that he might marry her, she became the contracted wife by proxy to Marie's widower Maximilian (1490), and later became queen to two French kings: Charles VIII (1491), and Louis XII (1499).

[d] Godwin informed Mary Shelley on 26 September 1827 (see p. 28n) that Henry VII 'immediately built Richmond Palace' when that at Sheen (or Shene) burned in 1498. Richmond, Surrey, is about eight miles from Westminster Bridge.

[e] The 3rd Duke of Buckingham (1478–1521), was a child in 1486. He became Henry VIII's Lord Constable, but, like his father, was undone by ambitions for the throne.

against Richard the Third. The lords Dawbeny and Broke, who had been raised to the peerage for their services in the same cause.[a] Lord and Sir William Stanley,[b] men to whom Henry principally owed his crown. Others there were of high rank and note; but the king paid most attention to two priests: John Morton, Bishop of Ely, and Richard Fox, Bishop of Exeter, were his private advisers and friends, as well as public counsellors.[c] Morton had watched over / his interests while in exile; he first had excited the Duke of Buckingham to revolt, and hatched the plot which placed Richmond on the throne.

The council held was long and solemn, and the results, brought about more by insinuation than open argument, were different from those expected by most of the persons present. First it was resolved that a general pardon should be proclaimed to the insurgents. No exceptions were to be made; those persons then in the very act of setting up his adversary were included; for as, by the second decree, that the real Earl of Warwick should be shown publicly in London, the deception would become manifest; if indeed they were deceived, it was thought more politic to reclaim them by clemency, than by severe measures to drive them to despair.

The third and last enactment was levelled against the Queen Dowager. Many of the council were astonished to hear it proposed, that she should forfeit all her goods and lands, and be confined for life in a convent, for having consented to the marriage of her daughter and Richard the Third, while the ready acquiescence / of the King and his chief advisers made them perceive that this measure was no new resolve. These three decrees past, the council separated, and Henry returned to Westminster,[d] accompanied by Sir William Stanley. To him he spoke openly of the treason of the Queen: he even ventured to say, that he was sure that some mystery lurked beneath; he commissioned Stanley, therefore, to notify the order of council to her Majesty; but at the same time to shew her, that disclosure, and reliance on the King, would obtain her pardon. Sir William Stanley was a courtier in the best sense of the term; a man of gentle

---

[a] Sir Giles Daubeney (d. 1508) and Sir Robert Willoughby (1452–1502) were attainted by Richard III for participating in Buckingham's rebellion. Both fled to Brittany, and returned to fight at Bosworth. Daubeney succeeded William Stanley as Lord Chamberlain in 1495.

[b] Sir William Stanley (d. 1495), like his brother Thomas ('Lord Stanley'), frequently changed sides. At Bosworth he threw his 3,000 men into battle on the side of the future Henry VII at the eleventh hour. Stanley was made Lord Chamberlain, but was later beheaded for plotting with Warbeck's partisans. He figures both in 3 Henry VI and in Richard III, IV. v.

[c] John Morton (?1420–1500), a Lancastrian, accommodated to Edward IV, who made him bishop of Ely. After Buckingham's rebellion, he escaped to the continent, where he helped to save the future Henry VII's life. Named Archbishop of Canterbury (and later, made a cardinal), he became Henry's Lord Chancellor, extracting taxes from the frugal and profligate alike by a strategy that became known as 'Morton's fork'. Richard Fox (1448–1528), Secretary of State and Lord Privy Seal under Henry VII, held four successive bishoprics and helped craft and execute Henry's financial policies; Fox actually devised 'Morton's fork'.

[d] Principal palace of English kings from the reign of Edward the Confessor to that of Henry VIII, its halls accommodated councils, early parliaments, and the courts of Chancery and Exchequer.

manners; desirous of doing right, easily excited to compassion, but ambitious and timid; one in truth than whom none could be more dangerous; for his desire to please those immediately before him, led him to assume every appearance of sincerity, and perpetually to sacrifice the absent to the present.

Elizabeth heard, with utter dismay, the sentence passed against her; courage was restored only when she found that her freedom could be purchased, by the confession of her son's existence, / and place of abode. She repelled Stanley's solicitations with disdain; answered his entreaties with an appeal to his own feelings, of how far, if such a secret existed, it were possible that she, a mother, should entrust it to the false and cruel king. Stanley speedily found his whole battery of persuasion exhausted; he withdrew in some wonder as to what the real state of things might be, and full of the deepest compassion. She had indeed scarcely veiled the truth to him; for, calling to mind the fate of the wretched Margaret of Anjou, she asked him, whether, like her, she should expose the young orphan York to the fate of the Lancastrian Prince Edward.[a] But Stanley shrunk from being privy to such disclosures, and hastily withdrew.

Henry had not exhausted all his hopes: glad as he was to wreak his vengeance on the Queen, and to secure her possessions to himself, he was not so blind as not to see that the knowledge of her secret were a far greater prize. His next implement was her eldest son, the Marquess of Dorset.[b] Lord Dorset had been so active in his / opposition to Richard the Third, and had done such good service to his adversary, that Henry overlooked his near kindred to the Queen Dowager, regarding him rather, as the representative of his father, Sir John Gray, who had fallen in the cause of Lancaster. He became indeed a sort of favourite with the King. Dorset was proud, self-sufficient, and extravagant, but his manners were fascinating, his spirit buoyant, and Henry, who was accustomed to find the storms of party lowering like winter over his domestic circle, found relief only when Dorset was present. The present occasion, however, called forth other feelings in the haughty noble; he might be angry with his mother's plotting, but he was more indignant at the severity exercised against her; and far from furthering Henry's designs, he applauded her resistance, and so irritated the King, that it ended by his sudden arrest, and being committed to the Tower.

And now all hope was at an end for the unhappy lady. The various acts of her tragic history were to close in the obscurity and poverty / of a convent-prison.

---

[a] Margaret of Anjou (1430–82), queen of Henry VI, was captured with him at Tewkesbury, where their only son Edward (1453–71) perished; soon after, Henry was murdered in the Tower. In the *Henry VI* plays Shakespeare displays her ruthlessness and ambition; in *Richard III* she curses the king and his house.

[b] Thomas Grey (or Gray; 1451–1501), 1st Marquess of Dorset, had joined Buckingham's rebel forces, then fled to France, where he remained until after Bosworth. He fell under suspicion during Simnel's insurrection, and was briefly imprisoned in the Tower. He was released when his half-sister was crowned late in 1487.

Fearful that her despair would lead her to some deed that might at least disturb the quiet and order he loved, Henry had resolved that no delay should have place, but that on the very morrow she should be conveyed to Bermondsey.[a] She was to be torn from her family – her five young daughters with whom she resided. The heartless tyrant was callous to every pang that he inflicted, or rejoiced that he had the power to wound so deeply one whom he abhorred. Lady Brampton was with her to the last; not to sustain and comfort her; the Queen's courage and firmness was far greater than that of her angry friend: she pointed out the hope, that the cruelties exercised towards her might animate the partizans of York to greater ardour; and tears forced themselves into her eyes only, when she pictured Richard, her victorious sovereign and son, hastening to unbar her prison doors to restore her to liberty and rank. The night was spent in such discourses between the ladies. With early dawn came the fated hour, the guard, the necessity for instant departure. She disdained to shew regret before Henry's / emissaries; and with one word only to her friend – "I commit *him* to your guidance," she yielded to her fate; submitting to be torn from all she loved, and, without an expressed murmur, entered the litter that bore her singly to her living grave.

The same sun that rose upon the melancholy progress of Elizabeth Woodville towards Bermondsey, shone on a procession, more gaudy in appearance, yet, if that were possible, more sad at heart. This was the visit, ordered by the King, of the Earl of Warwick to St. Paul's Cathedral; thus to contradict to the eyes of all men the pretender in Ireland. Warwick had spent a year in the Tower, in almost solitary imprisonment. Hopeless of freedom, worn in health, dejected from the overthrow of all the wild schemes he had nourished at Sheriff Hutton, linked with the love he bore his cousin, the Lady Elizabeth, now Queen of England, he could hardly be recognised as the same youth who had been her companion during her residence there. He was pale; he had been wholly neglectful of his person; carking sorrow had / traced lines on his young brow. At first he had contemplated resisting the order of being led out as a show to further his enemies' cause: one futile and vague hope, which could only have sprung up in a lover's heart, made him concede this point. Perhaps the Court – the Queen would be there.

He met several noble friends, commanded by Henry to attend him; for it was the King's policy to surround him with Yorkists, so to prove that he was no counterfeit. Alas!

"These cloudy princes, and heart-sorrowing peers,"[b]

assembled like shadows in the dim abyss, mourning the splendour of the day

---

[a] A Cluniac monastery, commemorated by Abbey Street, Bermondsey, about one mile from the Tower on the south side of the Thames.

[b] *Richard III*, II. ii. 112 (loosely quoted).

for ever set. They entered the cathedral, which stood a heavy gothic pile, on a grassy mound, removed from all minor edifices. There was a vast assemblage of ladies and knights; all looked compassionately on this son of poor murdered Clarence, the luckless flower, brought to bloom for an hour, and then to be cast into perpetual darkness. The solemn religious rites, the pealing organ, the grandeur of the church, and chequered painted light thrown from the windows, for a / moment filled with almost childish delight the Earl's young heart; that this scene, adapted to his rank, should be so single and so transient, filled his soul with bitterness. Once or twice he thought to appeal to his noble friends, to call on them to resist the tyrant – Elizabeth's husband. His heart chilled at the idea; his natural timidity re-assumed its sway, and he was led back to the prison-fortress, despairing, but unresisting.

Yet, at this hour, events were in progress which filled many hearts with hope of such change as he would gladly hail. On the news of the Queen's arrest, Lord Lincoln had departed with all speed to Flanders, to his aunt, the Duchess of Burgundy, to solicit her aid to attack and overcome the enemy of their vanquished family. The Lady Margaret, sister of Edward the Fourth of England, and wife of Charles the Rash of Burgundy, was a woman distinguished by her wisdom and her goodness. When Charles fell before Nancy, and his more than princely domains descended into the hands of his only child, a daughter – and the false Louis the Eleventh of France, on one hand, and the turbulent / Flemings on the other, coalesced to rend in pieces, and to prey upon, the orphan's inheritance – her mother-in-law,[a] the Lady Margaret, was her sage and intrepid counsellor; and when this young lady died, leaving two infant children as co-heirs, the Dowager Duchess entirely loved, and tenderly brought them up, attending to their affairs with maternal solicitude, and governing the countries subject to them with wisdom and justice. This lady was warmly attached to her family: to her the Earl of Lincoln and Lord Lovel resorted, revealing the state of things – how her nephew, young Richard, was concealed in poor disguise in French Flanders, and how they had consented to Richard Simon's plots, and hoped that their result would be to restore her brother's son to the throne of their native land.[b]

The Duchess of Burgundy possessed a proud and high spirit. The abasement in which her niece, the Lady Elizabeth, was held by the Earl of Richmond; she, the real giver of his crown, not having herself been crowned; the rigour exercised towards the Yorkist chiefs, many of / whom had been her defenders and friends in time of flight and defeat; the calumnies heaped on the various members of her royal house; made a prospect of displanting Henry, and of revenge, grateful to her. She acceded to the Earl's request, gave him an aid of

---

[a] Stepmother (common nineteenth-century usage).
[b] Tudor chroniclers, by contrast, adopt a hostile attitude towards Margaret's solicitude.

two thousand Germans, led by Martin Swartz,[a] a man of family and note in Germany, providing them with vessels to take them to Ireland, and blessing their expedition with her best and earnest wishes.

On their arrival in Dublin a gay and brilliant scene was acted, which raised the enthusiasm of the Irish, and spread a glory round the impostor they supported. The exhibition of the real Earl of Warwick had produced no effect in Ireland; Thomas Geraldine, Earl of Kildare,[b] asserted that Henry had brought forward a counterfeit, and Lambert Simnel lost no credit among them. He was proclaimed King of England; he was crowned by the bishop of Meath[c] with a diadem taken from an image of the Blessed Virgin; a parliament was convoked in his name, and every measure taken to ensure / his power in Ireland, and to gather together forces wherewith to invade the sister island.

The English lords felt far more anxiety than their allies in the result of this insurrection. Although it had been disregarded by the Irish, the effect produced in England by the visit of Warwick to St. Paul's was such as Henry had anticipated, and the counterfeit in Ireland found few supporters among the Yorkists. Still it was necessary to end as they had begun; to acknowledge the imposture, so to bring forward the young son of Edward, would have been to all appearance too barefaced a cheat. Lovel, as a gallant soldier, was ready to spend his blood in any enterprize that promised to advance the White Rose; but he, as well as the Earl of Lincoln, mingling sad memories of the past with careful forethought, looked forward to the result of Richard Simon's contrivance with well-founded dread. Still they entertained no thought of retreat, but mustered their forces, and counselled with their associates for the furtherance of the cause. On the 4th of June, Lambert Simnel, under the name of Edward the Sixth, with his, / so called, cousin, De la Poole, Lord Lovel, and their constant attendant young Edmund Plantagenet, the Lords Thomas and Maurice Geraldine,[d] with their force of savage scarce-armed Irish, and Martin Swartz with his German auxiliaries, landed at the pile of Foudray[e] in Lancashire, where they were soon after joined by Sir Thomas Broughton, who brought some few English to fight and die for this unhappy conspiracy.

Henry was prepared for their arrival: to gain grace in his subjects' eyes, he

---

[a] '1487', the year of the Swartz (or Swart) expedition (marginal note in *Abinger/Palacio*).

[b] The FitzGeralds (or Geraldines), a complicated kinship group that included the Earls of Kildare and Desmond. Gerald, not Thomas, was Earl of Kildare during this period.

[c] The Hill of Tara, legendary site of the ruined palace of Irish kings, familiar to a contemporary audience from the Thomas Moore (1779–1852) song, 'The Harp that once through Tara's Halls', was situated in Meath. Having Simnel crowned King Edward VI by John Payne, its bishop, would have helped to legitimise his claims in Irish eyes.

[d] Maurice Bacach FitzGerald, 10th Earl of Desmond (d. 1520), succeeded his murdered brother James in 1487.

[e] On what is now Piel Island, off the Isle of Walney in Morecambe Bay, where a fortress (pile) had been built in the thirteenth century by the monks of Furness Abbey. After landing in the north-west, Simnel's forces proceeded south-east toward London.

first made a pilgrimage to Our Lady of Walsingham,[a] and then, proceeding to the midland counties, held council to know whether it were best to encounter his foes out of hand, or to let them drag on; so to weary them by delay. A number of nobles and their followers joined the King, and it was agreed among them to press forward, before the enemy should gather force in England. Henry had a further view in this: he could not tell how far the secret of their plot, which he felt assured was the design to advance the young son of Edward, was / divulged among the Yorkists, and how far believed; as yet the enterprize bore no ill guise for him, having at its head a manifest impostor; so he hastened onward to crush it utterly, before it assumed a more fearful form. The Earl of Lincoln, eager to try the fortune of battle, advanced also on his side, and the rival armies drew nigh each other at Newark-upon-Trent. The King pitched his tents three miles beyond the town; and on the same night the Earl encamped at Stoke,[b] but a few miles distant. And now, after a reign of two years, as he had forced King Richard to fight for his crown against him, an adventurer and an invader in his realm, did Henry Tudor find himself in his adversary's position, about to risk life and kingdom on one cast of the die against troops as ill-assorted but as desperate and brave as his had been. Henry felt in his heart's core the thrilling pang, which a conviction that all is in the hands of fortune must ever impart to a human being who is her slave. He felt that his crown was but an usurpation, that his anointed / and sacred head claimed no reverence from these enemies; he was degraded in his own eyes from being a sceptred king upheld by the laws, to a wild adventurer, his good sword his right; a fierce but disciplined anger filled his heart; his brows were bent, his voice was attuned to harshness, his thoughts were conversant with overthrow and death. The hour was come; he was impatient for its passing, and he led forth his troops, all well-appointed English soldiery, in such hope as the sight of a noble army might well inspire, in such dread as was the natural offspring of the many chances and changes that had occurred to the sovereigns of England during the late struggles.

The Earl of Lincoln cherished still mightier fears: yet there was more of calm and dignity in his meditations than in the impatient misgivings of Henry. His heart sickened at the idea of battle and bloodshed; he felt himself responsible for the lives of all; and, while this nerved his heart to courage, it took rest from his eyes, and planted sorrow deep in his / manly breast. The morrow! oh, the morrow! hours full of fate! whoso looks forward and sees in the morrow the crown or ruin of the hopes of many, may well pray the swift-pacing hours to lag, and night to remain for ever as a spell to stop the birth of time.

---

[a] Walsingham in northern Norfolk, the major shrine of the Virgin Mary in medieval England.

[b] Now East Stoke, site of the battle, about four miles south-west of Newark-on-Trent (Nottinghamshire). Had Simnel's forces taken it, they could have fought their way south along a major road to London.

But the morrow came; a day of slaughter and captivity for the Yorkist party. The battle was hard fought: the German auxiliaries were veteran soldiers, who spared neither blows nor blood; their leader, Martin Swartz, for valour, for strength, and for agility of body, was inferior to none among the warlike captains of those times. The Irish, though half naked and ill-armed, fought with desperate bravery. In vain: the valour of Henry's soldiers was equal, their discipline and numbers superior. First the noble Lincoln fell, and his comrades were slaughtered around him avenging his death. The Lords Geraldine, Swartz, and Sir Thomas Broughton were found among the slain; Lord Lovel was never heard of more; the young Edmund Plantagenet, struck in the side by a dart, lay for dead / upon the ground.[a] Richard Simon and his false-seeming pupil were among the prisoners.

Such was the event of the last attempt of the Yorkists to raise the bruised White Rose to its old supremacy. All of high rank and power that owned this symbol were gone; Lincoln, the best column of its fortunes, was destroyed; nothing remained, save the orphan Prince, the royal exile, a boy of thirteen years of age, brought up as the child of a Flemish money-lender. To hide himself in safe obscurity was his only wisdom, till time should give strength to his arm, sagacity to his plans, and power to his acts; happy if he could find any concealment sufficiently obscure, to baffle the discernment of Henry, and to save him from the arts of those whom he would employ to discover and seize on him.

Henry again felt himself secure on his throne: he deeply lamented the death of Lincoln, as he had hoped to learn from him the secret of the conspiracy. He found in Lambert Simnel the mere tool of others, and in contempt made him a scullion in his kitchen, so to throw derision / on the attempt which had been made to exalt him. He dealt otherwise with Richard Simon. In the secrecy of his prison every art was practised to induce him to make a full confession. Simon played a dastardly and a double part, half revealing, half disguising the truth. Henry became assured that his rival, the Duke of York survived, and he was led in some sort to guess at the place of his abode. He had promised liberty to Simon when the young Prince should be in his hands; meanwhile he was imprisoned in the monastery in which he was fated to close his existence. /

---

[a] The list of casualties follows chronicle sources except for the fictional Edmund. The 'Lords Geraldine' may be assumed to be kin of the Earls of Desmond and Kildare.

CHAPTER VIII.

———

Our king he kept a false stewarde,
     Sir Aldingar they him call;
A falser stewarde than he was one,
     Servde not in bower nor hall.

OLD BALLAD.[a]

———

Whoever writes concerning the actions of the men of the olden time, must sadden the reader by details of war, descriptions of fields of battle, narrations of torture, imprisonment, and death. But here also we find records of high virtues and exalted deeds. It is at first sight strange, that men, whose trade was murder, who habitually wore offensive weapons, whose chief happiness was derived from the glory they acquired by inflicting misery on others, should be among those who live in our memories as / examples of what is most graceful and excellent in human nature. Too great security destroys the spirit of manhood, while the habit of hazardous enterprize strengthens and exalts it: it was not because they destroyed others that the warriors of old were famous for honour, courage, and fidelity; but because, from some motive springing from the unselfish part of our nature, they exposed themselves to danger and to death.

It was at times such as these that friendship formed the chief solace of man's life. The thought of his lady-love supported the knight during his wanderings, and rewarded him on his return, but the society of his brothers-in-arms shortened the weary hours, and made peril pleasure. Death, the severer of hearts and destroyer of hope, is in its actual visitation the great evil of life – the ineffaceable blot, the tarnisher of the imagination's brightest hues – but if he never came, but only hovered, the anticipation of his advent might be looked upon as the refiner of our nature. To go out under the shadow of his dark banner; hand in hand, to / encounter a thousand times his grim likeness; to

---

[a] 'Sir Aldingar', *Percy's Reliques*, 2nd series, I, 9, ll. 1–4; Thomas Percy (1729–1811) published his first ballad collection in 1765; others followed in 1767, 1775, and 1794.

travel on through unknown ways, during starless nights, through forests beset with enemies; over mountains, whose defiles hid him but to assure his aim; to meet him arrayed in his full panoply on the field of battle; to separate in danger; to meet on the verge of annihilation; and still through every change to reap joy, because every peril was mutual, every emotion shared, was a school for heroic friendship that does not now exist. In those times also man was closer linked with nature than now; and the sublimity of her creations exalted his imagination, and elevated his enthusiasm – dark woods, wild mountains, and the ocean's vast expanse, form a stage on which, when we act our parts, we feel that mightier natures than our own witness the scenes we present, and our hearts are subdued by awe to resignation.

Edmund Plantagenet, the forest-bred son of Richard the Third, the late companion of the illustrious Lincoln and gallant Lovel, lay long insensible on the field of battle, surrounded by the dead – he awoke from his swoon to the consciousness / that they lay strewed around him dead, whom he had worshipped as heroes, loved as friends. Life became a thankless boon; willingly would he have closed his eyes, and bid his soul also go on her journey to the unknown land, to which almost all those to whom he had been linked during his past existence had preceded him. He was rescued by a charitable friar from this sad state – his wound was dressed – life, and with it liberty, restored to him. After some reflection, the first use he resolved to make of these gifts was to visit the young Duke of York at Tournay.

Edmund's mind, without being enterprizing, was full of latent energy, and contemplative enthusiasm. The love of virtue reigned paramount in it; nor could he conceive happiness unallied to some pursuit, whose origin was duty, whose aim was the good of others. His father – his ambition and his downfall – were perpetual subjects for reflection; to atone for the first and redeem the last in the person of his nephew, became, in his idea, the only fitting end of his life. Fostering this sentiment, he speedily formed / the determination of attaching himself to the exiled Duke of York: first, to devote himself to the preserving and educating him during childhood – and secondly, to fight and die for him when the time was ripe to assert his rights.

During his hazardous journey to Flanders, Edmund was supported by that glowing sensation which borrows the hues and sometimes the name of happiness: it was an extatic mood that soared above the meaner cares of life, and exalted him by the grandeur of his own ideas. Self-devotion is, while it can keep true to itself, the best source of human enjoyment: there is small alloy when we wholly banish our own wretched clinging individuality, in our entire sacrifice at the worshipped shrine. Edmund became aware of the value of his own life, as he planned how in future he should be the guardian and protector of his un-friended, peril-encircled, orphan cousin. A religious sentiment of filial love also influenced him; for thus he could in some sort repair the wrongs committed by his father. There was much in Edmund's temperament that might have rendered him a mere / dreamer. The baser ends of common men possessed no attractions for him; but a lofty purpose developed the best points of his character.

It was early dawn, when, a month after the battle of Stoke, Plantagenet, in pursuance of his design, arrived at the cottage of Madeline de Faro, where, under the lowly name of Perkin Warbeck, dwelt the noble scion of the House of York. It was a lovely spot – trees embowered the cot, roses bloomed in the garden, and jessamine and woodbine were twined round the porch. The morning breeze and rising sun filled the atmosphere with sweets. Already the cottagers were enjoying its fragrance, and Edmund, as he alighted, beheld the object of his journey – the fair-haired stripling Prince and his protectress Madeline. Edmund was one-and-twenty, but his brow was more bent, his eye more thoughtful, his cheek more pale and sunk than befitted his age; it was only when he smiled that frankness displaced solemnity, and those who conversed with him were ever eager to call forth those smiles, which, like sunbeams that chase the shadows on a green hill-side, made / darkness light. Confidence readily springs up between the open-hearted and good; and Edmund and the inhabitants of the cottage found no impediment to entire reliance on each other. Madeline was overjoyed that her young charge should find manly guardianship in his cousin, and mentioned how often her fears had been awakened on his account, and how suspicions had got abroad concerning him among the citizens of Tournay.

Madeline, the sister of the Fleming, John Warbeck, was married to a Spaniard in the service of Portugal. In those days, just previous to the discovery of America by Columbus,[a] while that illustrious man was offering his unesteemed services at Lisbon, the Portuguese were full of the spirit of enterprize and maritime adventure. Each year new vessels were sent southward along the unexplored shores of Africa, to discover beyond the torrid zone a route to India. Hernan de Faro[b] was a mariner – it was during one of his voyages to Holland that he had seen and married Madeline, and he left her in her native country, while he pursued his fortunes / down the Golden Coast as far as the Cape of Good Hope. He had been absent longer than she had anticipated, and each day might bring the wanderer back, when he purposed taking her with him to his native Spain. What, then, must become of Richard? Plantagenet saw at once the necessity of visiting the court of Burgundy, and of placing her nephew at the disposition of the Duchess Margaret.

---

[a] Mary Shelley proposed in August 1830 to write a work on 'the Conquests of Mexico & Peru', hoping that John Murray might publish it as a sequel to a life of Columbus (*MWSL*, II, p. 113).
  [b] Mary Shelley gives the fictional de Faro the birth name of the historical Warbeck's mother. De Faro is reminiscent of Edward John Trelawny and also of the merchant seadog, De Ruyter, the narrator's mentor in Trelawny's invented autobiography, *Adventures of a Younger Son* (1831). The figure of De Ruyter was almost certainly already known to Mary Shelley, Trelawny having entertained the Shelley circle at Pisa with his exploits (*MWSL*, I, p. 218). The character also had an established literary pedigree in Byron's Turkish Tales.

The young prince was now fourteen[a] – he had shot up in height beyond his years, beautiful in his boyhood, and of greater promise for the future. His clear blue laughing eyes – his clustering auburn hair – his cheeks, whose rosy hue contrasted with the milk-white of his brow – his tall and slender but agile person, would have introduced him to notice among a crowd of strangers. His very youthful voice was attuned to sweetness. If Edmund found the Lady Margaret lukewarm, he need only lead the noble boy into her presence to interest her in his favour. Richard heard with tearful eyes of the imprisonment of his mother, and the slaughter of his kinsmen and friends. His heart for the moment / desired vengeance; he would himself seek his aunt of Burgundy, and aided by her attack the usurper. With difficulty he permitted his cousin to depart alone; but he was obliged to yield, and Plantagenet set out for Brussels, promising a speedy return.

About a week after Edmund's departure, another visitor arrived at the cottage of the exile. A violent storm had overtaken Duke Richard and his constant companion, Madeline's daughter, in one of their wanderings in the fields near Tournay. As they stood for shelter under a half-ruined building, a traveller came to share the asylum. He was a Frenchman – A Provençal by his accent – for he immediately entered into conversation with them. As he is a man spoken of in the Chronicles, he shall receive his name at once: this apparently chance-traveller was Frion, Stephen Frion,[b] King Henry's secretary. He had been employed to search out the young prince by such tokens as Richard Simon had given, and chance had caused him to fall in with Edmund, whom he had before remarked in attendance on the Earl of Lincoln. / Easily guessing that Edmund's journey might have connection with his own, he tracked him to Tournay, and then by some untoward chance lost sight of him. The indefatigable spy had spent the last week in a particular survey of every spot round the town and in the neighbouring cities, to discover his lost clue. Overtaken by a storm on his return from Lisle,[c] he suddenly found himself under a shed with a youth whose appearance at once excited his strongest curiosity.

What Frion loved beyond all other things was power and craft. He had been a subject of the poetical King René of Provence;[d] but, dispatched on some occasion to Louis the Eleventh, he entered into the service of that monarch, whose subtlety and faithlessness were a school of wisdom to this man. On one subject did he love to dwell – the contrast between Charles of Burgundy and Louis of France; the first commencing his reign by combating and vanquishing

---

[a] 'fourteen' (marginal note in *Abinger/Palacio*).

[b] 'p. 121' (marginal note in *Abinger/Palacio*), marking a previous reference to Frion.

[c] Modern Lille, in France, c. fifteen miles west of Tournai.

[d] René I (1409–80) attempted to revive the troubadour poetry of Provence. He figures as a poet in Sir Walter Scott's *Anne of Geierstein* (1829).

the latter, and dying miserably at last by a traitor's hand, his armies cut to pieces, his domains the unresisting prey of his rival; while / Louis, by serpent ways, by words – not deeds – gained every point, won every follower, and established his rule at last over the greater part of the wide territories of the fallen duke. In a minor way Frion aimed at imitating Louis, but he was naturally more fiery and rash. He had visited Italy also, and studied there the wiles and cruelties of the Italian lords; crossing back to Marseilles, he had been seized by corsairs and carried to Africa: – here he put in practice some of his lessons, and contrived to make himself a favourite with his Mahometan master, who afterwards crossed to Spain to serve under the Moorish king of Grenada. Frion was quickly distinguished for his sagacity in the divided counsels of this distracted kingdom, and became the trusty adviser of him called Boabdil El Chico.[a] When this unfortunate sovereign was taken prisoner by the Spaniards, Frion was a chief mediator between them and the Sultana Ayza.[b] At the court of Ferdinand and Isabella[c] he met several Frenchmen, who awakened in his heart a keen desire to revisit his native country. He took / advantage of an embassy thither from the court of Spain, to fulfil his wishes, but arrived at Plessis only in time to witness Louis's death.[d] Two years afterwards he was found in the train of the Earl of Richmond – the future secretary, spy, and favourite of Henry the Seventh – now travelling by his order to find, seize, or destroy, the last blossom of the uprooted White Rose.

Frion was rather handsome in appearance, with bright black eyes and dark hair, a complexion embrowned by the sun, a look of gaiety – unless when controled by the will of a superior, he was always laughing – a quiet kind of sarcastic laugh; he looked not the man Cæsar would have feared, except that his person was rather inclined to leanness, but he was active and well versed in martial exercises, though better in clerkly accomplishments. His early youth had been chiefly employed in copying poetry for King René – he wrote beautifully, and his small white hands were the objects of his own very great admiration. Such was his outward look; he had stores of science and knowledge within, which he seldom displayed, / or, when necessary, let appear with all the modesty of one who deemed such acquirements were of little worth – useful sometimes, but fitter for a servitor than his lord. No words could describe his wiliness, his power of being all things to all men, his flattery, his knowledge of human nature, his unparalleled artifice, which, if it could be described, would

---

[a] Boabdil, el rey chico ('the little king') was the Spanish name of the last sultan of Granada, Abu Abd Allah Muhammad (Muhammad XII; d. 1527). Moorish rule in Spain ended with his surrender to Ferdinand and Isabella after an interrupted reign (1482–92).

[b] Sultana Ayza (or Aixa, 'la Honesta') supported her son Boabdil when he seized power from his father, Abu-al-Hasan 'Ali (d. 1485) in 1482.

[c] The marriage in 1469 of Ferdinand (1452–1516) and Isabella (1451–1504) united the kingdoms of Aragon and Castile, which they ruled jointly from 1479.

[d] Plessis-les-Tours, Louis's chateau near Tours in the Loire valley, where he died in 1483.

not have been the perfect thing it was: it was not silken, it was not glossy, but it wound its way unerringly. Could it fail – the rage and vengeance to follow were as certain as dire, for, next to love of power, vanity ruled this man; all he did was right and good, other pursuits contemptible and useless.

Such was the serpent-spirited man who contrived to partake Richard's shelter; he eyed him keenly, he addressed him, and the Prince replied to his questions about an asylum for the night, by a courteous invitation to his home. "The boy speaks not like a cotter: his eye beams with nobleness. What a freak of nature, to make one in appearance a king's son, the plodding offspring of a rude Fleming!" As these thoughts passed through Frion's mind, the truth / came not across him; and he even hesitated for a moment whether he should not, now the storm had passed, pursue his way: but his garments were wet, the ways miry, night at hand. At a second thought he accepted the invitation, and leading his horse, he accompanied the youthful pair to their cottage home.

Madeline, unsuspicious of one obviously a Frenchman, received him without fear, and after a fire had dried the visitor's dress, they sat down to a frugal supper. Frion, according to his usual manner, strove to please his hosts. His gay discourse, the laughable yet interesting accounts he gave of various adventures that had befallen him, made all three – the fair Madeline, the ardent princely boy, and the dark-eyed daughter of de Faro – sit in chained attention. When he heard that Madeline was united to a Spaniard, he spoke of Spain, of Granada and the Moorish wars; Richard's eyes flashed, and the dark orbs of the girl dilated with wonder and delight.

At length he spoke of England, and his words implied that he had lately come thence. "How / fares the poor island?" asked the youth; "such stories of its tyrant reach us here, that methinks its fields must be barren, its people few."

"Had you been my comrade, young master, through merry Kent," said Frion, "you would speak in another strain. Plenty and comfort, thanks to King Harry and the Red Rose, flourish there. The earth is rich in corn, the green fields peopled with fat kine, such as delight yon islanders. 'Give an Englishman beef and mustard,' says our French proverb, 'and he is happy:' they will find dearth of neither, while the sage Henry lives, and is victorious."

"Yet we are told here," cried the youth, "that this Welch Earl, whom you call King, grinds the poor people he has vanquished to the dust, making them lament him they named Crook-back,[a] who, though an usurper, was a munificent sovereign."

These words from a Fleming or a Frenchman sounded strange to Frion; the doubt, which he wondered had not before presented itself, now / came full-fledged, and changed at its birth to certainty; yet, as the angler plays with the hooked fish, he replied, "I, a stranger in the land, saw its fair broad fields, and

---

[a] Sobriquet of Richard III; his deformity is disputed.

thought their cultivators prosperous; I heard that the king was victorious over his foes, and deemed his subjects happy. Yet, I bethink me, murmurs were abroad, of taxes and impositions. They spoke, with regret, of the White Rose, and scowled when they said that Elizabeth of York was rather a hand-maiden in her husband's palace, than Queen of fertile England."

"Now, were I an English knight, with golden spurs," said the stripling, "I would challenge to mortal combat that recreant Tudor, and force him to raise fair Elizabeth to her fitting elevation: woe the while, all England's good knights are slain, and the noble Lincoln, the last and best of all, has perished!"

"You speak unwisely and unknowingly of things you wot not of," said Madeline, alarmed at the meaning glance of Frion; "good nephew, Perkin, your eyes see not even the / English white cliffs, much less can your mind understand its dangerous policy."

"Nay, dear mother," remarked her little daughter, "you have told me that the noble Earl and the good Lord Lovel had been kind guardians to my cousin Peterkin; you chid him not when he wept their death, and you may suffer him to reproach their foe."

"I know nothing of these lords," said Frion, "whose names are a stumbling block to a Frenchman's tongue. But methinks it is well for us that they aim at each other's hearts, and make booty of their own provender, no longer desolating the gay fields of France with their iron hoofs."

And now, since that he had found him whom he sought, Frion talked again of other matters, and, as before, his smooth and gay discourse gained him pleased auditors. At length the peaceful cottagers retired to rest, and Frion sunk to sleep under their hospitable roof, after he had thought of various plans by which he might possess himself of the prince's person; – the readiest / and safest way was to entice him to accompany him alone some little space, no matter how short; he trusted to his own skill to draw him still further and further on, till he should be put on board the boat that would ferry him to his own revolted England. /

67

CHAPTER IX.

———

In the high chamber of his highest tower
Sate Conrad, fettered in the Pasha's power.
BYRON.[a]

Gilderoy was a bonny boy,
  Had roses tull his shoone;
His stockings were of silken soy,
  With garters hanging doon.
OLD BALLAD.[b]

———

It was a simple scheme, yet with the simple simplicity succeeds best. A new face and talk of distant lands, had excited York beyond his wont. He could not rest during the long night, while the image of his disastrous fortunes haunted him like a ghost. "Were I the son of a falconer or hind,"[c] he thought, "I could don my breast-plate, seize my good cross-bow, and away / to the fight. Mewed up here with women, the very heart of a Plantagenet will fail, and I shall play the girl at the sight of blood. Wherefore tarries Sir Edmund, our gentle coz?[d] If he be a true man he shall lead me to danger and glory, and England, ere she own her king, shall be proud of her outcast child."

To a mind thus tempered – heated like iron in a smith's forge – Frion, on the morrow, played the crafty artizan, fashioning it to his will. He and the Prince rose early, and the Secretary prepared for immediate departure. As he hastily partook of a slight repast, he renewed the conversation of the preceding night, and like the Sultaness Scheherezade,[e] (perhaps he had heard of her device

---

[a] George Gordon Byron, 6th Baron Byron (1788–1824), *The Corsair: A Tale* (1814), II. 366–7.

[b] 'Gilderoy', Percy's *Reliques*, 1st series, III, 12, ll. 1–4.

[c] falconer, a keeper or trainer of hawks; hind, a farm worker.

[d] coz, cousin.

[e] The resourceful sultana in the *Arabian Nights* who saves her life by spinning tales which she interrupts at crucial points, continuing her narrative from night to night. The work became generally familiar to Europeans only with the French translation (1704–17) of Antoine Galland (1646–1715), hence the parenthesis.

among the Moors) he got into the midst of the quarrels of El Zagal[a] and El Chico, the kings of Granada, at the moment it was necessary for him to hasten away – "Good youth," said he, "I play the idle prater, while mine errand waits for me – lead me to the stable, and help me to saddle my nag; if you will serve me as a guide to Lisle, you will do a good deed, / and I will reward it by finishing the strange history of the Moorish kings."

The horse was quickly in order for departure. "I will but say good day to my kinswoman, and go with you," said Richard.

"That were idle," replied the Secretary, "the sun has hardly peeped out from his Eastern window, and dame Madeline and her dark-eyed daughter sleep; we kept them waking yester-night; they will scarce have risen ere you return."

The Duke suffered himself to be persuaded – with his hand on the neck of the horse, he strode beside his tempter, listening to his cunning tales of Moorish ferocity and Christian valour. The walls of Lisle at length appeared – "Here we part," said the Duke, who remembered the caution given him, never to enter these border towns, where the English nobles often resided for a space, and the appearance of the gallant stripling, and his close resemblance to other members of the princely house of York, might beget suspicion and danger. /

"Wherefore this haste, Sir Perkin?" said Frion, "cooped up under a thatched roof from Lent to Shrovetide,[b] methinks you should be glad to stretch your chain. I remain brief space in yonder walls; leave me not till I depart."

"Who told you I was cooped up?" said the Prince, hastily; "if I am chained, the key of my fetters is in my own hand."

"Put it swiftly in the wards then, and cast away the heavy iron; come on with me, to where thou shalt ruffle bravely with satin-coated squires."

Frion judged his prize already won, and almost threw aside his usual caution. Richard liked not the expression his sharp, black eye assumed, nor the wrinkling of his brow; he began to wonder what there had been in this man so to allure him into friendly converse; now that in a familiar tone he invited him to continue his companion, his haughty spirit revolted, "Good sir," said he, "I now have done a host's duty by you. I saved you from a storm, restored you to your road – yonder path, shaded by poplars, leads at once to the town's gate – farewell!" /

"I am but an unmeet comrade for you, gay gentleman," said Frion; "pardon me if I have said aught unfitting the cottager of Tournay to hear. I now go to[4] the noble knight, the Sire de Beverem,[c] and I would fain have shown him what striplings these swamps breed; methought his gilt palace were fitter dwelling than yonder hut for one, who, if his face lie not, aspires to nobler acts than

---

[a] Muhammad ibn Sa'd, el Zagal ('the valiant'), seized power from his brother, the father of 'El Chico' (Boabdil), and then ruled Granada from 1485–7 under the title Muhammad XIII.

[b] Proverbial for 'from one end of the year to the other'.

[c] Probably Corneille of Burgundy, bastard brother of Charles the Bold, or his nephew Philippe.

weeding a garden or opening a drain. Come, my Lord – how tript my tongue? but your eye is so lordly that the word came of itself – gentle youth, trust yourself with one, who loves to see the fiery youngster amid his mates, the gallant boy looked on with love and favour by the noble and valiant."

Prudence whispered to Richard that this was dangerous sport; pride told him that it were unfit, nameless, and ushered thus, to appear before the high-born – but thoughtless youth urged him on, and even as Frion spoke, at a quick pace they approached the town-gate. The Sire de Beverem too, whom the wily Frenchman named, had been favoured by / Edward the Fourth, and was his guest in London – "Let the worst come, and it were well to have made such a friend. I will bear myself gallantly," thought York, "and win the good knight's smile; it may profit me hereafter. Now I shall see how the world goes, and if any new device or fashion have sprung up among our chivalry, that I may seem not quite untaught when I lead the sons of my father's friends to the field. Be it as you please," he said to his seducer, "before now my hand has grasped a foil, and I will not shame your introduction."

Frion went forward conning his part; he felt that his task was not so easy as he had imagined: the boy was wild as a bird, and so gave into the lure; but, like a bird, he might away without warning, and speed back to his nest ere his wings were well limed.[a] It was many miles to the coast: Frion's resolution had been hastily formed. The Lord Fitzwater,[b] a partizan of Henry, was then sojourning at Lisle. He had been to Brussels, and on his return towards Calais a sickness had seized him, which forced him to remain some weeks under the / roof of the Sire de Beverem; he was recovering now, and on the eve of his departure: without confiding the whole secret to him, the papers and tokens Frion bore must vouch that the King would thank any of his lieges who should aid him in bringing by force or decoy a pretended son of the traitor Earl of Lincoln (for thus Frion resolved to name his victim) to the English shores.

Yet the decoyer had a difficult part to play; there was a quickness in the Prince's manner which made him fear that, if his intentions changed, his acts would not lag behind; and though he did not betray suspicion, he was so perfectly alive to every thing said and done, that any circumstance of doubt would not fail immediately to strike him. Although they had hitherto discoursed in French, yet it was certain that his native English had not been forgotten by him; nay, the appearance of the Lord Fitzwater's attendants, their livery, their speech, must awaken the Prince's fears, and confound the wiles of his enemy. Frion pondered on all these obstacles, as he rode gently through the / narrow streets of Lisle; at length, they reached the abode of the French noble, and here Frion halted; while the Duke, beginning to be ill-satisfied with the

---

[a] Smeared with bird-lime, a gluey substance used in trapping birds.
[b] John Radcliffe, 1st Baron Fitzwater (or Fitzwalter, 1452–96), served as joint high steward with Jasper Tudor before defecting to Warbeck. He was later attainted and executed.

part he played and his promised presentation by such a man, almost resolved to break from him here and to return; shame of appearing feeble of purpose alone prevented him. At last, passing through the court-yard up a dark and massy stair-case, he found himself in a hall, where several men at arms were assembled, some furbishing pieces of armour, others engaged in talk, one or two stretched along the benches asleep: pride awoke in the youth's breast, he had gone too far to retrace his steps, and he resolved to bear himself gallantly towards the noble to whom he was about to be presented: yet pausing for a moment, "My memory," he thought, "leads me far a-field, or some of these men bear English badges, and their wearers seem grey-eyed Englishmen." Frion meanwhile, selecting with quick tact one of the followers of the Sire de Beverem who chanced to be among these men, requested an instant introduction to Lord Fitzwater, / using such golden arguments that the man, half afraid of being called on to divide the spoil, motioned him quickly to follow, and, passing through a suite of rooms, as he approached the last, said, "He is there, I will call his page." "It needs not," said Frion; "await me here, Sir Perkin," and pushing forward, to the astonishment of the attendant, entered unannounced to the Baron's presence: Richard thought he heard a "By St. Thomas!" uttered as the door closed hastily; but some Englishman might be with the French noble, and though a momentary wonder crossed him, no doubt of Frion's integrity was awakened.

"By Saint Thomas!" exclaimed the Lord Fitzwater, as Frion almost burst into his apartment, "what rude varlet is this? Are serfs so used to enter a Baron's chamber in France?"

"Most noble Sir," said Frion, "if in three words, or, if you refuse me these, if in one eye-glance, I do not satisfy you, bid your men beat me with staves from the door. I am here in King Henry's service." /

"God save him!" said the noble, "and you, Sir knave, from the fate you name; which will be yours undoubtedly, if you do not give me good reason for your ill-mannered intrusion."

Frion looked round. Except the Baron there was no one in the room, save a stripling of about sixteen years. The lad, though short in stature, was handsome; yet there was a look that indicated the early development of qualities, which even in manhood detract from beauty. He seemed conversant in the world's least holy ways, vain, reckless, and selfish; yet the coarser lines drawn by self-indulgence and youthful sensuality, were redeemed in part by the merry twinkling of his eye, and the ready laugh that played upon his lips. "My words are for your ears alone, my Lord," said Frion, "and be assured they touch your liege nearly."

"Go, Robert," said Fitzwater, "but not further than the ante-chamber."

"There is one there," said Frion anxiously: "he must not quit it – he must not escape, nor learn in whose hands he is." /

"Your riddles, Sir, ill please me," replied the noble.

71

"Look at this paper, my Lord, and let it vouch for the heavy import of my business."

Lord Fitzwater recognized his royal master's signature, and with an altered tone he said, "Leave us, Robert; tarry not in the ante-chamber, but bear my greeting to my noble host, and ask him when I may, at his best leisure, pay my thanks to him and my kind lady. I depart to-morrow at dawn; and mark, speak not to the stranger who waits without."

The youth made obeisance, and departed. A piece of tapestry hung before the door, which, together with the massy boards themselves, prevented any sounds from piercing to the other side; the lad was about to proceed on his errand, when curiosity prompted him to look on the stranger, with whom he was commanded not to parley. Richard stood in the embrasure of one of the windows, but turned quickly as the folding door shut with no gentle sound; his candid brow, his bright blue eyes, his frank-hearted smile, who that had ever seen could forget them, / nor were the traits of the other's countenance less marked, though less attractive. The words burst at the same instant from either – "My Lord of York!" "Gentle Robin Clifford!"

"My prison play-fellow," cried the Prince, "this for me is a dangerous recognition. I pray you be wise, and – as you were ever – kind, and keep my secret close."

"Alas! my Lord," said Robert, "you have opened your hand, and let the winged fool fly unwittingly, if you think it has not been discovered by yonder false loon. Know you where you are?"

"Then I am betrayed! I see it, feel it. Farewell, Robin, my fleet legs will outrun their slow pursuit."

"Nay, an' that were possible," said Clifford – "but it is not; let me better advise your highness; trust me you shall be free: but, hark, they come; I must not be found here. Show no suspicion; yield to your fate as if you knew it not, and confide in me; my hand on it, this night you are at liberty."

Clifford quitted the apartment by the opposite / door, while Frion entered from the other, beckoning the Duke to approach. He took him by the hand, and led him to Lord Fitzwater, who started back when he saw him, and was about to exclaim; but Frion, in French, addressing him as the Sire de Beverem, entreated his kind favour for Perkin Warbeck, the gallant youth before him. The Baron evidently was ill-pleased at the part he had consented to play; he said a few words with an ill grace, and bidding Perkin welcome, promised him favour, and permission for the present to remain in his abode. Richard saw through the flimsy disguise which the Englishman threw over his native speech, though he did not know who his receiver was; but, feeling that it was best to follow his young friend's counsel, he replied, also in French, that, at his guide's invitation, he had eagerly sought an interview with the renowned Sire de Beverem; that the honour done him would be deeply engraven in his heart; that on some future occasion he would gratefully avail himself of his offers; but that, at the present time, he had left his home without intimating any intention of a prolonged absence, and that he owed it to a kind / kinswoman not to disquiet her by delaying his return. He prayed the noble to dismiss him therefore, craving leave only to attend him some other day.

"Be it so," said Fitzwater, "to-morrow at dawn you shall depart hence; but you must not refuse my proferred hospitality. I shall introduce you to my household as one who ere long will be admitted into it, and show my friend, Sir Lalayne,[a] who is now here, what gentle boors our Flanders breeds."

"I can return to-morrow, my good Lord," Richard began; but the noble not heeding him, added, "Stay till my return; I now go to hear mass," and passed hastily from the chamber.

The Prince's first impulse was to reproach Frion's knavery, assert his freedom, and, ere any measures had been taken to secure his person, to quit his new prison. But he did not know how deep-laid the plot might be; he was inclined to think that all was prepared for his reception and safe custody, so that any open attempt to regain his liberty would be resisted by force; while, through the assistance of his / friend Clifford, he might hope to escape, if, giving in to the stratagem, he took occasion by the curb, and forced it to his purpose. "Are you mad," said Frion, "my rustic, that you resist the proffers of a high and powerful man of your native land?"

Richard wondered, when he beheld Frion's sneer and crafty glance, how he had not mistrusted him from the moment he beheld him; the double meaning of his words, and the familiar tone in which they were uttered, grated him like a personal insult. He repressed the angry reply rising to his lips, and said: – "It seems I must submit, yet I should be beholden to you if you contrived an excuse, and lent me your horse, that I might ride back and inform Dame Madeline. To-morrow I might return."

Frion opposed this intention, and led the Prince to a chamber at some distance from any other, at the end of a corridor, saying, "that it had been assigned to him;" and after a short conversation left him. Richard heard the shooting of the bolt as the door closed: "Son of King Edward," he thought, "thy folly disgraces / thy parentage: thus at once to have run into the gin. Yet I am of good cheer, and my heart tells me that I shall relate the merry tale of my escape to Madeline and my sweet coz, and dry this night the tears my disappearance has caused them to shed." It soon appeared, by the long absence of his betrayer, that it was not intended to continue the farce longer; but that, from the moment he had entered that chamber, he was in treatment as well as in fact a prisoner. After several weary hours had elapsed, his blithe spirit began to sink; he reflected that Clifford had probably promised more than he could perform: but courage awoke with the sense of danger; he resolved to be true to

---

[a] Sir Roderic de Lalayne (or Lalaing), a Burgundian envoy who supported Warbeck's claims and brought German troops to Scotland to fight for him in 1496.

himself, and to effect his escape singly, if he could gain no assistance. "Men have ears and hearts," he thought, "and I can work on these; or they may be neglectful while I am on the alert, and I can profit by their carelessness. In all forms my fortune may take, I will not fail to myself; and there is small danger in any change for a true man. With my light spirit and resolved will, I could, I doubt not, persuade an armed band to / make way for me, or open prison bolts with charming words, though my witchcraft be only that of gentle courtesy, moulding with skilful hand the wax of soft humanity." Pacing the apartment, he continued these meditations, imagining every circumstance that might and would arise, and how he was to turn all to the best advantage. He framed persuasive speeches, wily answers to ensnaring questions, cautious movements, by which he might withdraw himself from the hands of his enemies; and while he thus occupied himself, his eyes gleamed, and his cheeks glowed, as if the moment of action had come, and his life and liberty depended on instant deed.

At two hours past noon the door was unclosed, and a servant entered bearing food; impatient to begin his plans of escape, Richard was about to speak to him, when, in the doorway, he beheld the slight figure[5] of Clifford, whose forefinger was pressed on his lips, and who, after exchanging one glance with his friend, cast aside his stealthy expression of countenance, entering with a half-swaggering look, and saying, in / French, "my Lord, young Sir, has sent me on a pleasant embassage, even that of dining with your pageship, saying, two boys like us were better and merrier together, than in the great hall with the arrogant serving-men."[a] Richard felt no great appetite; but taking the tone from his friend, he thanked him, and they fell to on the viands. "Now, kind Thomas," said Clifford, "of your bounty bring us a stoup of wine; the day is rainy, and we cannot abroad; so my gossip and I will tell long stories over our bottle, and lay some plan of merry mischief which you and your fellows may in good time rue."

The domestic obeyed, nor till the wine was brought, the servant fairly dismissed, and the door closed, did Clifford put aside the character he had assumed of a stripling page, in a noble master's abode, entertaining a stranger visitant of his own years. At length, when they were quite alone, the merry boy put his hands to his sides and indulged in so gay a peal of laughter, that the Prince, who at first stared in wonder, at last caught the infection, and laughed too, while tears from superabundant glee, streamed down / their cheeks. Once, twice, and thrice, did Richard check himself, and turn seriously to enquire the cause of this merriment, and Clifford strove to answer, but laughter bubbling up choked his voice, and both again yielded in accord to the overpowering fit. At last gasping, holding their sides, and by degrees commanding their muscles, the Duke said, "I would ask you, friend Robin, what this means? but at the

---

[a] Mary Shelley removed a belittling adjective from this sentence in *Abinger/Palacio*; see Endnote 5.

word, lo, you! your very voice is lost. Now prithee feel half as weary as I do of this folly, and you will be as grave as tumble-down Dick. Do you remember the simpering fellow we made good sport of in the Tower?"

"You have broke the spell, my Lord," said Clifford; "that word suffices to make me as grave as Brakenbury himself, when he looked on your brother's corpse. Ah dear, your Highness, the name of the Tower is worse than a raven's croak! God and St. Thomas preserve you from ever getting the other side of its moat!"

"Amen, Robin, with all my heart," said Richard; "a shudder runs through my limbs down to my finger tips, making the skin on my / head creep, when I think there is any chance of my passing long years in those dreary cells, with their narrow deep windows; the court yards, which the sun seldom visits; the massy dark walls, whose black stones seemed to frown angrily, if our childs' voices were ever heard in sport."

"There your cousin, my Lord of Warwick, pines out his melancholy days," replied Clifford, "and that is your destined abode. My grandfather was slain by Queen Margaret's side,[a] and stained the Red Rose with a blood-red die, falling in its cause. Your father and his brothers did many a Clifford much wrong, and woe and mourning possessed my house till the line of Lancaster was restored. I cannot grieve therefore for the exaltation of the Earl of Richmond; yet I will not passively see my playmate mewed up in a cage, nor put in danger of having his head laid on that ungentle pillow in Tower Yard. The daughter of Warwick, our Edward's affianced bride, your crook-backed uncle's wife,[b] loved my pranks and nurtured my youth; and by her good leave, many a mirthful hour I spent in the dark / place you name. May neither of us ever see it more!"

"You will then assist my escape?" asked Richard.

"As faithfully, gossip Dickon, as God his grace shall await me at the last day! – and now I will tell you a merry tale." /

---

[a] Shakespeare (*3 Henry VI*) shows her on the battlefield.

[b] Lady Anne Neville (1456–85), daughter of Warwick the Kingmaker, first betrothed to the son of Henry VI and later married to Richard III. Shakespeare (without warrant) makes her the widow of young Edward, over whose corpse she is wooed and won by Richard after initially cursing him.

CHAPTER X.

———

– It is thy merit
To make all mortal business ebb and flow
By roguery.

HOMER'S HYMN TO MERCURY.

And then, with you, my friends, and the old man.
We'll load the hollow depth of our black ship,
And row with double strokes from this dread shore.

THE CYCLOPS.[a]

———

Notwithstanding the promise Clifford made of a merry tale, both he and his auditor looked grave as he commenced. Richard expected, with some anxiety, an explanation from his friend, and the other assumed the self-consequence resulting from having achieved a victory. No two beings ever displayed, in their way, a greater contrast than these youths. The prince was many inches taller than his companion, and / his slim make promised increase of height. His brow was smooth as infancy, candid as day; his bright blue eyes were lighted up with intelligence, yet there was a liquid lustre in them that betokened tenderness; nor did his lips, that nest of the heart's best feelings, bely his eyes. They were full, a little curled, can we say in pride, or by what more gentle word can we name a feeling of self-elevation and noble purpose, joined to benevolence and sweetness? His oval cheeks were rounded by the dimpled chin, and his golden hair clustered on a throat of marble whiteness, which, as the white embroidered collar thrown back over the doublet, permitted the out-line to be seen, sustained his head as the Ionic flute rears its graceful capital. Clifford was shorter, but firm set and more manlike in form, his grey eyes were bright or dull as his soul spoke in them; his brow slightly scowled, pending over, and, even thus early, lines were delved in it, hardly seen when he was in repose, but which, as

———

[a] In P. B. Shelley's translations, first printed in PBS 1824 (lxxxviii. 697–9; ll. 466–8); the poems were favourites of young Percy Florence Shelley (MWSL, II, p. 209).

he spoke, showed deep and distorted; his smile was tinctured by a sneer, his voice attracted / no confidence, yet Richard now hung intently on it as he spoke:

"When I returned from doing my Lord's bidding, I found him moving about the room, more like a parched pea than a stately noble; for now he stood still, and then shot off with a quick step, showing every sign of being ill at ease. Now, boy as I am, for I can number but sixteen summers, my Lord more than loves me, he trusts me, and not without cause – for when at hazard – but my story will be too long – enough that ere now I have done him service. Had I not known the cause of his disquiet I should have asked it, but, believing myself fully aware of what this all meant, I went to my post, and busied myself in making some flies for angling, seeming most intent upon my work. My Lord stood over me, and twice or thrice fetched a sigh, and then strode away, and came again, saying, "I am a fool, a dolt – the King can mean no ill to this lad – and yet – " I cannot tell you how long this indecision lasted, while I patiently toiled at a fly of green and gold, bright as those which trouts / love to snap at in clear streams during May. At length he asked me, 'Robin, did you mark the boy that stood in the ante-chamber?' 'Aye, my good Lord!' 'And what thought you of him?' 'Thought, my Lord?' I spoke enquiringly, for it suddenly came across me that he did not know you, and it was not for me to betray your secret. 'Aye,' he replied, 'thought? Does he resemble any one you ever knew? Of what country do you divine him to be?' 'These Flemings are sandy-haired,' I said, 'yet he does not look of Flanders. Methinks he seems English born.'

"'You are right,' said he, 'English he is confessedly. This Frion calls him a natural son of De la Poole – of the late Earl of Lincoln. He says that he has knowledge of a secret treasure concealed by his father before this last rebellion, and the king wishes to get him into his hands, thus to secure the gold. The tale is not unlikely, for the Tudor ever loved the glitter – nay, the very dust of the precious metal, – and the boy resembles strangely the House of York. Yet, I care not for the task put upon / me of kidnapping a child, and of betraying him into his enemy's hands – perhaps of delivering him up a prisoner for life, for the sake of —— Poor fellow! if he know aught of a concealed treasure, in God's name, let him confess it while on this side the fatal channel that now divides him from tyranny or death.' 'Let me deal with him,' I said, 'let me throw out some toy, such as is this gold and green thread to a silly fish, and learn the truth; if he discover the hiding-place of this so coveted coin, we may spare him the trouble of his enforced journey.' 'I know not that,' answered my patron; 'Master Frion is earnest for his safe keeping; and no one is nearer our liege's inner wishes than this Provençal, who served him in exile, and who followed him in his expedition thence; and yet there is a noble daring in the boy, a mountain freshness in his cheek, a springy freedom in his gait, that it were a thousand pities to fetter and limit within narrow prison bounds.' Seeing that my lord was thus favorably inclined, I used all my poor eloquence to urge him further, and at last brought him to / consent that I should converse with you; learn, if possible, your secret; inform you of your danger, and advise you to escape. One only difficulty remained: my Lord had promised this Master Secretary that none should be admitted to talk with you; but when the subtle fiend, the double-dealing Frenchman entered, I told him with a long visage, that our noble host, the Sire de Beverem, had heard that we were carrying off, by force, a Fleming; and that, considering his hospitable mansion stained by the act, he had commanded strict watch to be kept on the morrow, that if any of the English suite were unwilling to go, or appeared in durance,[a] he should be rescued. It was advisable therefore, that you should be kept in good-humour till fairly beyond the gates of Lisle; and this my wisdomship offered to do, if admitted to parlance with you. You look grave, Sir Prince, but had you seen Frion's sage look of hesitation, and heard his many exhortations that I would by no means betray my knowledge of who you really were; and how I, with a bow, careful as if my curls were white from years, promised discretion, you / would laugh as I did, when, the mime over which I played before the servitor, I doffed my page's seeming equality, and in duteous phrase to his Highness of York, offer my best services to liberate him."

"That seems already done," said Richard; "usher me to the Lord Fitzwater. I will declare myself to him; his compassion already excited – "

"Would then be cool as snow at Christmas. Wise young Sir, Baron Fitzwater wears the blushing Rose; and for him there is wormwood in the name of York. Now, as a chance off-shoot of the white thorn, he only sees in you a harmless boy, whom it were sin to injure; but give yourself a name whose very echo would bring St. Albans, Tewkesbury, Bosworth Field,[b] and a thousand scaffolds streaming with his kinsmen's blood before him, and without remorse he would let Frion have his will of you. Even I, Duke Richard, I am sprung from those who fell for Lancaster – "

"Enough," replied the prince haughtily. "I / am content to stand alone, to achieve my freedom singly, or to submit to my fate."

"Not so, my noble playmate," said the other. "I will not offer you my knee, my oath, my sword, for my allegiance belongs to the anointed King of England; but, I beseech you, suffer Robin Clifford to assist high-born Plantagenet to escape from a prison or from death; permit him to pay, if not the duty of a subject, yet that of a loving friend to the former companion of his childish sports."

Richard listened somewhat sullenly to these offers; he ill brooked the

---

[a] Archaic for detention or imprisonment.
[b] Important battle sites. At St Albans, twenty miles north-west of London, Yorkist forces captured Henry VI on 21 May 1455; on 17 February 1461 the army of Margaret, Henry's queen, overcame the Yorkists but she failed to follow up her victory and Edward IV was proclaimed king. The Lancastrians experienced a bitter defeat at Tewkesbury, Gloucestershire, on 4 May 1471, after Henry VI's brief return to the throne in 1470.

thought that any of English parentage should, knowing who he was, refuse to acknowledge him for his liege; but Clifford would not be refused; while it was hardly worth while to contend with his light spirit, which appeared incapable of a serious or profound idea. After a short resistance, therefore, the duke entered willingly into a discussion of the best means of effecting his escape in such a way, that he should have several hours the start of Frion, and be distant from danger, / before his seducer could discover that he was not still safe in his hands.

In the midst of this discussion, Frion suddenly entered. The stake for which he played was too momentous to trust it wholly to the stripling page, and distrust of the wily boy entered also into his calculations; he broke in therefore, not only unannounced, but with such stealthy quiet as shewed that he meant to pounce on his victim unawares. The youths sat, their stools drawn close; Clifford was leaning forward earnestly propounding his schemes, and Richard listened, his whole soul in his countenance. Frion was close upon them before he was perceived by either, his eyes glimmering with their usual suspicious look. The artless Richard started, and would with a conscious mien have drawn back; but Clifford, more used to the wiles and watchfulness of others, and his own double mode of action, continued to speak in the same tone the same words, without moving a muscle. The Prince wondered, and regained his self-possession; not from entering into the deceit of his companion, but from the / haughty sentiment of his own dignity, which even in danger refused to cower.

Clifford had been saying – "I will hence to the Sire: a word to him, of whose secretary this Provençal is, and insinuation that he is now on a secret expedition to the Flemish towns, will awaken his curiosity; he will send for him; fortunately the good knight speaks so slow that a mass can be said while he is introducing the subject of his enquiries; as each word expires, he pauses while a requiem might be sung for its death; our antagonist will writhe and – " and a glance askance informed the speaker that this man was at his side: he continued – "and strive vainly to escape; the heavy weight will be too much for him, he. must submit. Such feints suit well us boys who have not strength nor skill for more declared warfare. Tomorrow's dawn I will practise with you in the court of the castle ere you depart. But indeed, my gossip, you must promise to be at Calais[a] on the sixteenth, when we shall see a combat of good knights fit for royal princesses to look on. And now, fair Sir, farewell; here is your friend. / The Sire de Beverem commanded my presence at this hour. If I see you not again to-night, the saints have you in their keeping!"

When Clifford with his pagelike vivacity ran from the room singing a gay romance, Frion felt himself embarrassed; and more so when Richard said – "My guest, it is hard, after giving you harbourage last night, that I should be

---

[a] Port city where the continental part of Mary Godwin's elopement journey began on 29 July 1814.

forced, whether I will or not, to tarry here, leaving my kinswoman in dread and doubt. Make you my excuse to the Chevalier, and delay me no longer, I beseech you."

Frion, without directly replying, said, "Anon I will speak of that; meanwhile I have news for you:" – and he entered into a long account of an unexpected sedition in Flanders, and how the Sire de Beverem had promised to enlist Perkin Warbeck in his particular troop, when with courage and good fortune he could not fail to rise. While he was talking, one of the men at arms of the noble entered, and notified to Frion that his lord desired an instant interview with him. The Secretary hastened to obey; he thought that good-fortune itself provided this / excuse for him to escape from his victim, and resolved not again to present himself before him. He was scarcely gone when Clifford returned – "Now quick," he cried, "down the back stair-case! My own steed stands saddled for you; ride fast and far – but whither – whither do you intend to go?"

"In the first place to Dame Madeline's cottage."

"That were midsummer madness," cried Clifford; "Frion will never rest till he ensnares his bird again – nay, though I trust he will not discover your escape till to-morrow morning, that part of my scheme may fail; and his papers from the King are such that my lord could not refuse to aid him. I pray you set space and cloudy mystery between you."

"It shall be so. Probably I shall seek refuge at Brussels; but I must see my gentle guardian and my sweet cousin, calm their fears, and bid them farewell."

They had descended a narrow winding stair-case; Clifford unlocked a postern, opening on a dark alley. A small light-limbed horse stood / without, held by a stout, almost gigantic fellow. "Here, Bryan," said Clifford, "this is the smuggled article of which I spoke. Convey it in safety to the gate; once without, the road is known. How now, sweeting! you sit your steed as if you were used to this gear – in truth thou art a false one – yet take care, fold your cloak thus – not one kiss ere we part?" He sportively snatched the Prince's hand, and pressing it to his lips, continued, "No weeping, lovely: my merry heart hates tears like verjuice. The Blessed Virgin protect you; I must in. Remember in every ill Robin Clifford is your fast, your sworn friend. Look at her, Bryan: one would swear by her bearing it were a beardless page, and not a long-haired girl; remember, though gamesome, she is gentle, and respect her on your life."

Laughing at his own deceits, the guileful boy re-entered the mansion; nor could Richard avoid smiling at the merry and ready subterfuges which his friend had at command on every occasion. Bryan demurely held the rein, and hardly hazarded a look or covert joke, as with a pace that put the poney to a trot, he led the / Prince through the narrow streets to the western gate. The youth breathed freely when, after having passed the hollow sounding drawbridge, he saw the dark wall of the town behind him, and before, the green plain. In his haste he scarcely bestowed a benison on his guide; but snatching the rein from his hand, and with the other throwing some money at his feet, and exclaiming "Beware of prating, as thou art willing to save thyself from the whipping-post!" he impatiently struck his unarmed heel against the horse's sides, and bounded swiftly forward. Bryan picked up the angels,[a] and told them slowly, as he said "I meant to have paid myself in other coin; but, by St. Julian,[b] she rides more like a trooper than a gentle dame – and her speech – Master Robert has before now entrusted a damsel to my guidance, but they ever spoke me lovingly, with 'fair Sir,' and 'sweet Bryan!' Forsooth, Flemish girls ruffle[c] more like pranksome pages than soft-cheeked wenches!"

The thought of his conductor had passed as swiftly from the Prince's thoughts, as he made the ground fly from under his horse's hoof. He / was aware that he did neither the safest or best thing in seeking, like a hunted hare, the form from which he had been roused in the morning; but the desire of calming Madeline's anxiety, and imprinting a farewell kiss on the sweet lips of her daughter, prevented him from altering his first purpose. The night was cloudy and very dark, but the road was known to him, and he continued at full speed till a voice, calling aloud, attracted his attention – the words could not be mistaken – his own name, "Perkin Warbeck!" sounded through the night. His first thought was, that he was pursued, but reflection told him that assuredly his pursuers would not halloo to him, while any sent in search of him by Madeline, might naturally so try to stop him as he rode so fast through the dark. He checked his speed, therefore, and in a few moments a Cavalier, a stranger, was at his side, mounted on a tall black horse; his form seemed gigantic, and little else could be discerned: the stranger spoke to him in French, with a foreign accent. He asked him, "Are you not he they call Perkin Warbeck?" This address was / sufficiently startling; and the youth haughtily replied, "My name imports not to you, while to me this interruption is unseasonable."

"Enough; you go towards the cottage of Madeline de Faro; I follow your Highness thither."

Richard grasped the small poinard which hung from his belt; yet how could he, a child, contend with the tall and muscular form beside him? "Whoever thou art," he cried, "and whoever I may be, follow me not; I am no serf to be seized and carried back to his suzerain. Depart in God's name, that the fingers of neither may receive an ill stain!"

"Thou art a gallant boy!" cried the stranger, as placing his hand on the youth's arm, his most gentle touch was felt as an iron vice pressing on his flesh: "Pardon, my Lord, the interference of one unknown to you, though I will not call myself a stranger. I am Hernan de Faro, the husband of Dame Madeline; now stay not your speed, while we hasten to relieve her thousand fears. I am come in search of you."

---

[a] Old English coins stamped with a figure of the archangel Michael slaying a dragon.
[b] i.e., St Julian the Hospitaller, patron of wayfarers, innkeepers, and boatmen.
[c] ruffle, swagger (OED).

The heart of Richard warmed towards his / new friend: he felt, that with him on his side, he might defy Frion, Fitzwater, and all their followers; for there was something in de Faro's mien, which spoke of a thousand combats, and as many victories; his deep voice out-roared the elements; his hand might arrest a wild horse in mid career. When they arrived at the wicket entrance to the cot, he lifted the boy from the saddle, as a child would handle a toy, and shouted aloud in his own language, "Viva el Duque de Inglatierra y el Marinero, Hernan de Faro."[a]

The dangers Richard had run, and the delight she experienced in seeing him, when again under her roof, stopped all Madeline's reproaches. "Is he not worthy all my fears?" she said to her husband, who stood eyeing the boy as he caressed his daughter. De Faro stretched out his hand, saying, "Will you, Señor Don Ricardo,[b] accept my services, and my vow to protect you till the death, so help me the Blessed Virgin and the Holy Trinity."

De Faro was a mariner who had sailed in / the service of the King of Portugal, along the unsounded shores of Africa, and sought beyond the equator a route to the spicy Indian land. His dark skin was burnt to a nearly negro die; his black curled hair, his beard and mustachios of the same dusky hue, half hid his face; his brow somewhat lowered over eyes dark as night; but, when he smiled, his soft mouth and pearly teeth, softened the harshness of his physiognomy, and he looked gentle and kind. Every nerve, every muscle, had been worn and hardened by long toilsome navigation; his strong limbs had withstood the tempest, his hands held unmoved the cordage, which the whirl-wind strove vainly to tear from his grasp. He was a tower of a man; yet withal one, to whom the timid and endangered would recur for refuge, secure of his generosity and dauntless nature. He heard the story of Richard's dangers; his plan was formed swiftly: he said, "If you choose, Sir Prince, to await your foes here, I am ready, having put these girls in safety, to barricade the doors, and with arquebus and sword to defend you to the last: but there is a safer and / better way for us all. I am come to claim my Madeline and our child, and to carry them with me to my native Spain. My vessel now rides off Ostend.[c] I had meant to make greater preparation, and to have laid up some weeks here before we went on our home-bound voyage; but, as it is, let us depart to-night."

The door suddenly opened as he spoke – Madeline shrieked – Richard sprung upon his feet, while de Faro rose more slowly, placing himself like a vast buttress of stone before the intruder. It was Clifford.

"All is safe for the night," he cried; "your Grace has a few hours the start, and but a few; dally not here!"

---

[a] 'Long live the Duke of England and the sailor, Hernan de Faro'.

[b] Mary Shelley asked John Bowring 'what *Richard* is in Spanish' in an unpublished letter of 1828 (MS in the Pforzheimer Collection).

[c] North Sea port, now in Belgium.

Again the discussion of whither he should fly was renewed, and the Duke spoke of Brussels – of his aunt. "Of poison and pit-falls," cried Robert; "think you, boy, as you are, and under pardon, no conjuror, that the King will not contrive your destruction?"

Probably self-interested motives swayed Clifford; but he entered warmly into de Faro's idea of hastening to the sea-coast, and of sailing direct / for Spain. "In a few years you will be a man – in a few years –"

"Forgotten! Yes – I may go; but a few months shall mark my return. I go on one condition; that you, Clifford, watch for the return of my cousin, Sir Edmund, and direct him where to find me."

"I will not fail. Sir Mariner, whither are you bound?"

"To Malaga."[a]

And now, urged and quickened by Clifford, who promised to attend to all that this sudden resolve left incomplete, the few arrangements for their departure were made. Favoured by night, and the Prince's perfect knowledge of the country, they were speedily on their way to Ostend. Clifford returned to Lisle, to mark and enjoy Frion's rage and Fitzwater's confusion, when, on the morrow, the quarry was found to have stolen from its lair. Without a moment's delay, the Secretary followed, he hoped, upon his track: he directed his steps to Brussels. A letter meanwhile from Ostend, carefully worded, informed Clifford of the arrival / and embarkation of his friends: again he was reminded of Plantagenet; nor had he long to wait before he fulfilled this last commission.

Edmund had found the Lady Margaret glad to receive tidings of her nephew; eager to ensure his safety and careful bringing up, but dispirited by the late overthrow, and deeply grieved by the death of the noble and beloved Lincoln; no attack could now be made; it would be doubly dangerous to bring forward the young Richard at this juncture. She commissioned Plantagenet to accompany him to Brussels that she might see him; and then they could confer upon some fitting plan for the privacy and security of his future life, until maturer age fitted him to enter on his destined struggles.

Edmund returned with brightened hopes to Tournay, to find the cottage deserted, his friends gone. It may easily be imagined that this unexpected blank was a source of terror, almost of despair to the adventurer. He feared to ask questions, and when he did propound a few, the answers only increased his perplexity and / fears. It was not until his third hopeless visit to the empty dwelling, that he met a stripling page, who with an expression of slyness in his face, spoke the watchword of the friends of York. Edmund gladly exchanged the countersign, and then the boy asked him, whether he called himself cousin to the fugitive Duke of York, laughing the while at the consternation his auditor exhibited at the utterance of this hidden and sacred word: "You come

---

[a] Port city in the province of the same name, on Spain's Mediterranean coast.

to seek your prince," he continued, "and wonder whither he may be flown, and what corner of earth's wilderness affords him an abode. He is now, by my calculations, tossing about in a weather-beaten caravel, commanded by Hernan de Faro, in the Bay of Biscay;[a] in another month he may anchor in the port of Malaga; and the dark-eyed girls of Andalusia[b] will inform you in what nook of their sunny land the fair-haired son of England dwells. The King is defeated, master Frion balked, and Lord Fitzwater gone on a bootless errand: the White Rose flourishes free as those that bloom in our Kentish hedges." /

Without waiting for a reply, but with his finger on his lip to repel further speech, the youth vaulted on his horse, and was out of sight in a moment. Edmund doubted for some time whether he should act upon this singular communication. He endeavoured to learn who his informant was, and at last became assured that it was Robert Clifford, a young esquire in Lord Fitzwater's train. He was the younger son of the Lord Clifford who fell for Lancaster at the battle of St. Alban's.[c] By birth, by breeding he was of the Red Rose, yet it was evident that his knowledge was perfect as to the existence of the Duke of York; and the return of Lord Fitzwater and King Henry's secretary to Lisle, disappointed and foiled, served to inspire confidence in the information he had bestowed. After much reflection Plantagenet resolved to visit Paris, where he knew that the brother of Madeline, old John Warbeck, then sojourned; and, if he did not gain surer intelligence from him, to proceed by way of Bordeaux[d] to Spain. /

---

[a] Between the north coast of Spain and the contiguous west coast of France; caravel, a small, broad-bowed, lateen-sailed ship common in the fifteenth and sixteenth centuries.

[b] Region of southern Spain including the Sierra Nevada and the valley of the Guadalquivar.

[c] Here Clifford appears as the son of Thomas Clifford, who fell at St Albans, but the allusion on p. 75 to a grandfather 'slain by Queen Margaret's side' suggests that he was Thomas's grandson and the son of John (see p. 25n). By referring to Clifford as a 'younger son' Mary Shelley may be playing off her readers' awareness of the 'younger son's' elder brother, 'The good Lord Clifford' of Wordsworth's 'Song at the Feast of Brougham Castle' (1807), who finds love 'in huts where poor men lie'.

[d] Estuary port on the Garonne, in south-west France.

CHAPTER XI.

———

A day will come when York shall claim his own;
Then York be still awhile, till time do serve.
SHAKSPEARE.[a]

———

The further Edmund journeyed from the late abode of his lost cousin, the more he felt displeased at the step he had taken; but on his arrival in Paris his uncertainty ended. Warbeck had received intimation of the hurried embarkation of his sister, and here also he found Lady Brampton, whose husband had taken refuge in Paris after the battle of Stoke. Like the Queen Dowager, the fate of Margaret of Anjou's son haunted this lady, and she warmly espoused the idea of bringing the / Duke of York up in safe obscurity, until his own judgment might lead him to choose another line of action, or the opposing politics of Europe promised some support to his cause. She agreed to repair herself to Brussels, to take counsel with the Duchess, to use all her influence and arts, and as soon as time was ripe to proceed herself to Spain to announce it to the Prince. Meanwhile Plantagenet, following his former purpose, would take up his abode with Richard in Spain; teach him the science of arms, and the more difficult lessons of courage, self-command, and prudent conduct. In pursuance of this plan, Edmund lost no time in going to Bordeaux, whence he embarked for Malaga, and following his friend's steps, arrived shortly after him at the retreat de Faro had chosen among the foldings of the mountains on the borders of Andalusia.* /

———

*I had originally entered more at large on a description of Andalusia, and the history of the conquest of Granada. The subsequent publication of Mr. Washington Irving's very interesting work has superseded the necessity of this deviation from the straight path of my story. Events which, in their romantic detail, were before only to be found in old Spanish folios, are now accessible to every English reader, adorned by the elegance of style, and arranged with the exquisite taste, which characterize the very delightful "Chronicle of the Conquest of Granada."[b]

———

[a] *2 Henry VI*, I. i. 239, 248.

[b] Irving (1783–1850), prolific author of classic American tales such as 'The Legend of Sleepy Hollow', and 'Rip Van Winkle', travelled widely in Europe in the 1820s, and served as a diplomatic

85

De Faro's was a singular history. In those days that part of Andalusia which comprised the kingdom of Granada, was the seat of perpetual wars, and even when armies did not meet to deluge its fertile plains and valleys with their blood, troops led by noble cavaliers and illustrious commanders overran its districts in search of plunder and glory. During one of these incursions, in the year 1452, some impulse of religion or humanity made a Spanish soldier snatch from a couch in the country-house of a noble wealthy Moor, already half consumed, an infant hardly a year old; the band was already in full retreat, and, fortunately, this incident took place on the very frontiers of Granada, or the benevolence of the soldier would hardly have been proof against the trouble his little charge occasioned him. Toiling up the mountains on their return to the / kingdom of Jaen, they entered the little town of Alcala-la-Real,[a] where on the side of the mountainous road rose the walls of a monastery. "How better," thought the soldier, "save the soul of this boy than by giving him to the monks?" It was not perhaps the present they would most readily have selected, but compassion and piety forbade them to refuse it: the little Moor became a Christian by the name of Hernan, and was brought up within the sacred precincts of the convent. Though the monks were able to make a zealous Catholic of their nursling, they did not succeed so well in taming his fiery spirit, nor could they induce him to devote himself to the inactive and mortifying life of a priest. Yet he was generous and daring, and thus acquired their affection; next to being a recluse vowed to God, the vocation of a soldier for the faith, in the eyes of these holy men, was to be selected. Hernan advancing in life, and shooting up into strong and premature manhood, was recommended by the Abbot to his cousin, the illustrious Don Rodrigo Ponce de Leon, Marquess of Cadiz.[b] He fought several / times under his banners, and in the year 1471 entered with him the kingdom of Granada, and was wounded at the taking of Cardela.[c] In this last action it was, that a sudden horror of taking up arms against his countrymen sprung up in Hernan's breast. He quitted Spain in consequence; and, visiting Lisbon, he was led to embrace a sea-faring life, and entered the marine service of the king of Portugal; at one time visiting Holland, where he sought and won the hand of Madeline: and afterwards, with Bartholomew Diaz,[d] he made one of the crew that discovered the Cape of Good Hope. He sailed with three vessels, one of which lost company of the others,

---

attaché in Spain (1826–9). For his romantic history of Granada he invented a source (Antonio Agapida) to give himself free scope. Mary Shelley met Irving in 1824, but her hopes that a friendship might develop were not fulfilled; see *MWSL*, I, p. 423.

[a] In the province of Jaen, which forms the northern border with the province of Granada.

[b] Roderigo Ponce de Léon (1443–92), described by Irving (I, pp. 30–1) as 'the mirror of chivalry' of his times'.

[c] Not further identified.

[d] Bartholomew Diaz (or Dias, c.1450–1500), the Portuguese explorer, led the first European expedition around the Cape of Good Hope at the southernmost tip of Africa in 1488.

and its crew underwent various and dreadful perils at sea, and from the blacks on land: after nine months they again fell in with their companions, three sailors only remaining. One of these was Hernan de Faro; his skill, valour, and fortitude had saved the vessel; he was exalted to its command, and now, in safer voyage over seas more known, he had freighted it with the fugitives from Tournay. /

During all his wanderings, even in the gay and rich Portugal, Hernan turned with fond regret to his mountain home. To its rugged peaks, its deep and silent dells; its torrents, its verdure, its straggling and precipitous paths; its prospect over the rich and laughing Vega of Granada. He had promised himself, after weary toils, a long repose in this beloved spot; and hither he now led his wife, resolving to set up his tent for ever in the land of his childhood, his happy childhood. It was a strange place to choose, bordering on Granada, which at that time was as lists in which Death and Havock sat umpires. But the situation of Alcala-la-Real preserved it secure, notwithstanding its dangerous neighbourhood. It was perched high upon the mountain, overlooking a plain which had been for many years the scene of ruthless carnage and devastation, being in itself an asylum for fugitives – a place of rest for the victor – an eagle's nest, unassailable by the vultures of the plain.

Here then Plantagenet found his cousin; here in lovely and romantic Spain. Though defaced and torn by war,[a] Andalusia presented an aspect / of rich and various beauty, intoxicating to one whose life had been spent in the plains of England, or the dull flats of Flanders. The purple vineyards; the olive plantations clothing the burning hill-side; the groves of mulberry, cork, pomegranate, and citron, that diversified the fertile vegas or plains; the sweet flowing rivers, with their banks adorned by scarlet geranium and odoriferous myrtle, made this spot Nature's own favoured garden, a paradise unequalled upon earth. On such a scene did the mountain-home of the exiles look down. Alcala too had beauties of her own. Ilex and pine woods clothed the defiles of the rugged Sierra, which stretched far and wide, torn by winter torrents into vast ravines; variegated by a thousand intersecting lines, formed by the foldings of the hills; the clouds found a home on the lofty summits; the wandering mists crept along the abrupt precipices; alternate light and shadow, rich in purple and golden hues, arrayed each rocky peak or verdant slope in radiance all their own.[b]

All this fair land had been under the dominion / of the Moors. Now, town by town, stronghold by stronghold, they had lost it; the riches of the land belonged to the Christians, who still, by military conquest or policy, pressed the realm of the Moorish sovereign into a narrower compass; while, divided in itself, the unhappy kingdom fell piecemeal into their hands. De Faro was a

---

[a] Paralleled by the ravages of the Peninsular War (1808–14), observed by the melancholy hero of Byron's *Childe Harold's Pilgrimage*, I (1812).
[b] Mary Shelley builds on Irving's rhapsodic description of the Vega of Granada (I, pp. 5–6).

devout Catholic; but, with all his intrepidity, more humanity than belonged to that age, warmed his manly heart. He remembered that he was a Moor: whenever he saw a Moslem prisoner in chains, or a cavalgada[a] of hapless women driven from their native towns to slavery, the blood in his veins moved with instinctive horror; and the idea that among them might pine and groan his parents, his own relatives, burned like living coal in his breast. He had half forgotten this, when he came to Alcala, bringing his wife and child, and resolved to set up here his home; but when, in the succeeding spring, the Spanish army assembled on the frontiers of Murcia,[b] and swept on towards the south; when deeds of Moorish valour and Moorish suffering reached Alcala, when the / triumph of the Christians and their ravages were repeated, the gallant mariner could endure no longer. "It is a fruitless struggle," he said, "Granada must fall, and God, who searches hearts, knows that his victory will be dear to me when the cross floats from the towers of the Alhambra.[c] But I cannot behold the dark, blood-stained advances of the invader. I will go – go where man destroys not his brother, where the wild winds and waves are the armies we combat. In a year or two, every sword will be sheathed; the peace of conquest will reign over Andalusia. One other voyage; and I return."

He went without fear, for Alcala appeared a safe retreat, and left his family spectators of the war. What a school for Richard! Edmund rejoiced that he would be accomplished in knightly exercise in the land of chivalry; but he was not prepared for the warlike enthusiasm that sprung up in his cousin's heart, and even in his own. It was the cause of God that armed the gentlemen of Spain, that put daring into the politic Ferdinand's heart, and inspired with martial ardour the magnanimous Isabella. The / veteran Cavaliers had lost many relatives and companions in arms, in various defeats under the rocky castles, or within the pathless defiles of Andalusia; the holy zeal possessed them, to avenge their deaths, or to deliver those who pined in bondage. The younger knights, under the eye of their sovereigns, emulated each other in gallantry and glory. They painted war with pomp, and adorned it by their virtues.

Not many months before, the Earl of Rivers, with a band of Englishmen, aided at the siege of Loxa, and distinguished himself by his undaunted bravery;[d] his blunt but gay humour; his eager emulation with the Spanish commanders. The Duke of York heard, with a leaping heart, his mother's

---

[a] Ancient Spanish word embracing the meanings 'troop' and 'booty'; see Prescott, II, p. 119n.

[b] Neighbouring province north-east of Granada.

[c] Fortress and palace situated on the plateau above the city of Granada, begun in 1238 and enlarged by successive Moorish kings.

[d] Castilian forces ravaged Loxa (or Loja), in western Granada in May 1486. Irving's chs xxxix and xl cover 'the doughty achievements of the English earl', slain in 1488 fighting for the Duke of Brittany. The Englishman was Edward Woodville, brother of the 3rd (and last) Earl Rivers (Richard); see Prescott, II, pp. 133–5 and notes.

brother's name. Had he still been there – but no, he had returned to fall in affray in Britanny, the victim of Tudor's heartless desertion – this circumstance had given distinction and honour to the name of Englishman, nor did Edmund feel inclined to lower the national character by keeping away from the scene of glory. What was to be done? York was a mere boy; yet, when Plantagenet spoke / of serving under one of the illustrious Catholic chieftains, York said, "I follow you: I will be your squire, your page, your stirrup-boy; but I follow!"

In 1489 the siege of Baza[a] was formed. – It was defended with desperate valour by the Moors, while every noble Spaniard, capable of bearing arms, assembled in Ferdinand's camp, which glittered in silks and gay caparisons, yet the very luxury of the warriors was ennobled by their valour. The sallies on the part of the besieged were furious; the repulse they sustained, determined and successful. When closely hemmed in, the Moors relaxed in their desperate efforts; the younger Christian cavaliers used the leisure so afforded them, to unite in making incursions in the surrounding country, to cut off supplies, and to surprise the foraging parties of the enemy. Two youths became conspicuous in these exploits; both proclaimed their English origin. One bore a knight's golden spurs (Edmund had been knighted on the eve of the battle of Stoke by the Earl of Lincoln), and boasted of his royal, though / illegitimate, descent; the other, a beardless, fair-haired, blooming boy, was nameless, save by the Christian appellation of Ricardo, to which was added the further designation of el Muchacho,[b] from his extreme youth. It was a lovely, yet an awful sight, to behold this pair. The elder, whose dark eyes and dun complexion gave him a greater resemblance to his Southern comrades, never lost sight of his young friend; side by side, his shield before Richard's breast, they went to the field. When Edmund would otherwise have pressed forward he hung back to guard his cousin; and when the boy was hurried forward in the ardour of fight, still his kinsman's gaze was on him – his sword protecting him in every aspect of danger. If the stripling were attacked, Edmund's eyes flashed fire, and mortal vengeance fell upon his foe. They became the discourse of the camp; and Plantagenet's modesty, and Richard's docility in all, save avoiding peril, advanced them still further in the favour of the grave courteous Spaniards. "Art thou then motherless?" Isabel asked, "if thou art not, thy gentle parent must pass many wakeful nights / for thee!"[c] At length, in one skirmish, both the youths got surrounded by the foe. Richard's young arm, wearied by the very sword he bore, gave ineffectual blows – forgetting that he left himself unguarded, Edmund rushed between him and his assailant – others came to their

---

[a] '1489' (repeated in marginal note in *Abinger/Palacio*), the year Baza (north-east of the city of Granada) fell; cf. Irving, chs lxix–lxxxi.

[b] Spanish for 'the Boy'.

[c] Cf. Irving's description of Isabella as 'the very soul, the vital principle, of this great enterprise' against the Moors (II, p. 235).

assistance: but Plantagenet was already struck to the ground; and for many weeks York forgot even the glorious emulation of arms, while watching over his best and dearest friend. Meanwhile Baza surrendered, and the cousins returned to Alcala, to Madeline and her fair child; and domestic peace succeeded to the storms of war. Richard loved Madeline as his mother; her daughter was his sister, his angel sister, whose tenderness and heroism of character commanded deep affection.

Monina de Faro[a] was, even in childhood, a being to worship and to love. There was a dreamy sweetness in her countenance, a mystery in the profound sensibility of her nature, that fascinated beyond all compare. Her characteristic was not so much the facility of being impressed, as the excess of the emotion produced / by every new idea or feeling. Was she gay? – her large eyes laughed in their own brightness, her lovely countenance became radiant with smiles, her thrilling voice was attuned to lightest mirth, while the gladness that filled her heart, overflowed from her as light does from the sun, imparting to all around a share of its own essence. Did sorrow oppress her? – dark night fell upon her mind, clouding her face, oppressing her whole person, which staggered and bent beneath the freight. Had she been susceptible of the stormier passions, her subtle and yielding soul would have been their unresisting victim – but though impetuous – wild – the slave of her own sensations, her soft bosom could harbour no emotion unallied to goodness; and the devouring appetite of her soul, was the desire of benefiting all around her. Her countenance was the mirror of her mind. Its outline resembled those we see in Spanish pictures, not being quite oval enough for a northern beauty. It seemed widened at the forehead, to give space for her large long eyes, and the canopy of the darkly fringed and veined lid; her hair was not / black, but of a rich sunny chesnut, finer than carded silk, and more glossy; her skin was delicate, somewhat pale, except when emotion suffused it with a deep pink. In person, she was not tall, but softly rounded; and her tapered, rosy-tipped fingers, and little feet, bespoke the delicate proportion that moulded her form to a beauty, whose every motion awakened admiration and love.

With these companions Richard passed the winter.[b] The following spring brought war still nearer to the English exiles – Baza had fallen: one of the kings of Granada, surnamed El Zagal, the Valiant, had submitted to the Spaniards; and now Ferdinand commanded his former ally, Boabdil el Chico, to deliver up to him proud Granada, the loved city of the Moors. Poor Boabdil, whose misfortunes had been prophesied at his birth, and whose whole career had been such as to affix to him the surname of el Zogoybi, or the Unfortunate,[c]

---

[a] Mary Shelley's invention, like her father Hernan.
[b] '1490' (marginal note in *Abinger/Palacio*).
[c] A 'dark prediction' that Granada would fall during his reign hung over Boabdil from his birth; from this stemmed his father's aversion and his nickname (Irving, I, pp. 77–8).

THE FORTUNES OF PERKIN WARBECK: VOLUME I

was roused from his state of opprobrious vassalage by this demand, and followed up his refusal by an inroad into the Christian country, near Jaen. / Count de Tendilla,[a] a veteran warrior of high reputation and brilliant exploits, command- ed this district. His head quarters were in the impregnable fortress of Alcala-la- Real itself; and when the cry came, that the Moors had passed his border, he resolved to stoop from his eagle's eyrie, and to pounce upon the insolent foe, as they returned from their incursion. He chose one hundred and fifty men, and lay in ambush for them. Plantagenet was of the number, and our young warrior also; though with sage entreaties Edmund, and with tears Madeline, had besought him to stay. The Count succeeded to his wish – the Moors fell into his toils – few escaped slaughter or capture: but while the Christian hero exulted in victory, a messenger, pale with horror, spent with weariness, came to tell that a band of Moors had taken advantage of his absence, to fall upon Alcala. Indignation and fury possessed the noble captain: he left half his troop to protect his spoil, and with the rest, all weary as they were, he hurried back to Alcala, eager to fall upon the marauders before they should have secured their prey in a neighbour- ing / fortress. Edmund and Richard were among the foremost; their rage could only be calmed by the swiftness with which they returned to deliver or avenge their friends. The sun was sinking in the west when they arrived at the foot of the Sierra. At first Tendilla desired that his wearied troop should repose; but several stragglers among the enemy, perceiving them, gave the alarm to their comrades, who, laden with booty, were preparing to depart. Harassed as the Christians were, they had no choice, while their position, on the lower ground, rendered their attack very disadvantageous. But nothing could check their fury: with loud cries and flashing weapons they fell upon the enemy, who burthened by their prey, and wearied by their very outrages, could ill resist men fighting to avenge their desolated hearths. Still, so accustomed to war, so innately brave was every soldier on either side, that the combat was long and sanguinary. Night, the swift-walking darkness of the nights of the south, came suddenly upon the combatants: the casques of the one party, and the / turbans of the other, were scarce perceptible, to guide the scimetar, or to serve as an aim for the arquebus.[b] The discomfited Moors, leaving their booty, dispersed along the defiles, and, forgetful of their prisoners, availed themselves of the obscurity to make good their flight. Alcala was retaken; and through the shadows of the night, husbands and fathers called aloud on their wives and children to tell them if they were safe, while many a sound of woman's wail arose over the corpse of him who had died to save her.

---

[a] Cf. Irving, II, pp. 312–19. Diego (or Inigo) Lopez de Mendoza, Count of Tendilla, from his 'cloud-capt hold among the rocks' at Alcala-la-Real, 'kept an eagle eye upon Granada and had his scouts and spies in all directions'.

[b] casque and harquebus, the headgear and weapon of the Catholic soldier; turban and scimitar, those of the Moor.

The troop, diminished in number, was drawn up the following morning in the square of Alcala. "Where," asked the Count, "are my two English soldiers? I saw the elder leading five others across a steep mountain-path, so as to fall on the enemy's rear: it was a sage measure, and succeeded well. Ricardo I beheld contending with two bearded Moors, who held in their fierce grasp a young and fainting girl. I sent Diego to his rescue: Diego they say was slain: night prevented me from knowing more: have both these strangers fallen? I would pay / them a Spaniard's thanks for their aid – a knight's praise for their gallantry."

Alas! both thanks and praise would have visited their ears coldly. They had forgotten Tendilla, his troop, the very Christian cause, in the overwhelming calamity that had befallen them. Assisted by Diego, who was cut down in the conflict, Richard had delivered Monina; and, forcing his way through the enemy, now already scattered, clambered with her in his arms to their mountain abode: he was guided towards it by the glaring light of the flames that destroyed it. Meanwhile the fight still raged; York placed Monina in safety, and returned to share its perils.

The peace of desolation that came with the morning, united the cousins; and they sought the ruins of their home, and their miserable friend, whose broken and harrowing tale recorded how Madeline had fallen a victim to the savage cruelty of the enemy, as she strove to defend her daughter from impending slavery.

This was the result of Moorish wars – death and misery. Richard's young heart had bounded / to the sound of trump and clarion; and he returned to hear the melancholy bell that tolled for death. Their very home was in ruins; but it was long before, amidst deeper woe, they remembered to lament the destruction of many papers and hoarded objects, the relics and the testimonies of Richard's royal descent.[a] /

---

[a] Mary Shelley elaborates Irving's account (II, pp. 312–19), confined to the ambush itself. The invented attack upon Alcala disposes of Madeline de Faro and tangible evidence of Warbeck's claims. For Mary Shelley's witness to the desolation following war, see *MWSJ*, I, pp. 12–14.

CHAPTER XII.

———

Ah! where are they, who heard in former hours
The voice of song in these neglected bowers?
                 They are gone!
                                    MOORE.[a]

The chain is loos'd, the sails are spread,
    The living breath is fresh behind;
As with dews and sunrise fed,
    Comes the laughing morning wind.
                                    SHELLEY.[b]

———

This was a gloomy lesson for these young and affectionate beings: they consoled one another, and wept as they consoled. At first Monina despaired: her
ceaseless laments and unassuaged grief appeared to undermine her very life;
but, when she marked the sorrow she communicated, when she heard Richard
exclaim, / "Oh! for spring and battle, when I may avenge Monina's grief or die!
Death is a thousand times preferable to the sight of her woe!" and felt that the
fate and happiness of those about her depended on her fortitude: she forced
smiles back to her lips, and again her sweet eyes beamed, undimmed by tears.

Spring came at last, and with it busy preparation for the siege of Granada:
troop after troop defiled through Alcala, bearing the various ensigns of the
noble commanders; the Count Tendilla, leaving his mountain nest, united
himself to the regal camp before the devoted city; Isabella joined her royal
husband, accompanied by her children. Where women looked on the near face
of war, even the timid were inspired to bear arms. The reputation the English
warrior youths had gained, forbade inglorious ease, even had they not aspired
with their whole hearts for renown; yet Plantagenet looked forward with
reluctance to the leading forth his brave, dear cousin to new dangers; divided

---

[a] 'They Are Gone,' from *Evenings in Greece* (1826); see also *MWSJ*, II, p. 501 n.
[b] 'The Boat on the Serchio', ll. 88–91, dated July 1821 in *PBS* 1824.

between pride in his valour, satisfaction at his thus being schooled to arms, and terror from the perils to which he / would be exposed in a war, on the side of the enemy, of despair and fury – his thoughtful eyes rested on the young Prince's glowing cheek, his unsullied youth; if wound or fatal hurt maimed his fair proportion, how should he reply to his widowed mother's agony? If, snapt like a poor flowret, he fell upon the death-strewn Vega, what tale should he report to the ardent Yorkists? None! At least he should be pierced only through him, and Edmund's corse would rampart his heart, even when he had died to save him.

Thus they again appeared in the Spanish army, and were hailed as among its ornaments. Whatever desperate enterprize kindled the young Spaniards to heroic frenzy, found the English pair among their numbers. At the beginning of the siege, the Moors, few in numbers, and often defeated, cheated victory of its triumph by various challenges to single combat, where many a Spaniard fell: their frays resembled, in the splendour of their armour and their equipments, the stately ceremonial of the tournaments, but they were deadly in the event. / Ferdinand, sure of victory, and reluctant to expose the noble youth of his kingdom to needless peril, forbade these duels; and the Moors enraged, multiplied their insults and their bravadoes, to draw their enemies to the field; nor lost any opportunity of committing the defence of their beloved city to the risk of battle, rather than the slow progress of famine. One memorable engagement took place on occasion of the visit of Queen Isabella to the hamlet of Zubia, there to obtain a nearer view of beautiful Granada. The Moors seeing the Spanish troops in array before their walls, came out to attack them; a battle was fought under the very eyes of the Queen,[a] wherein it was the good fortune of Richard to make so gallant a figure, that on the very spot the Count Tendilla conferred on him the honour of knighthood.

Proud was the young Duke of York, and eager to paint his maiden shield with worthy device: he was now nearly eighteen, boyish in aspect, yet well-knit in person, and accustomed to the fatigue of arms. He no longer burst on his foes, like an untrained dog, seeking only to / slay: there was forethought in his eye, and a most careful selection of worthy and valorous opponents. Edmund still was to be found within a javelin's throw of him; but he no longer feared his untaught rashness, as before he had done.

In July occurred the conflagration of the Christian camp. The day following, Ferdinand led forth his troops to make a last ravage among the gardens and orchards, the emerald girdle of Granada. During the fray, it was the young Duke's chance to throw his javelin so as to slay on the spot a veteran Moor, whose turban having fallen off, exposed him thus. His companion in arms, a tall fierce Moslem, rushed forward to fell the insolent youth: others interposed.

---

[a] Irving (II, pp. 351–69) provided details about both single combat and the episode at Zubia, 'built on the skirts of the mountains, to the left of Granada'.

Still the Moor kept his eye upon his boyish foe; a thousand times he threw his dart; twice or thrice he rushed on him with uplifted scimetar: the battle raged among the orchard-paths and flowery hedges of the thickly-planted gardens, and ever some obstruction thwarted the infidel. Plantagenet had marked his rage and his purpose; he watched him keenly, and / the fierce Gomelez boiled with impatient indignation, as some impediment for ever baffled his design. His last effort was to fling an arrow, which stuck in the ground quivering at Richard's feet: a label was affixed – "Dog and infidel," thus was the cartel worded – "if thou hast courage, meet me at dawn at the Fountain of Myrtles."[a]

The following morning, at the hour when Plantagenet was wont to see his cousin, the Prince was absent. Noon approached; the troops reposed after the battle of the day before, or were employed in clearing the dark ruins of the camp: some thoughtless project might occupy the Duke: some excursion to the other side of Granada. The shades of evening gathered round the lofty towers, and dimmed the prospect of its Vega: still Richard came not. Sad, anxious night drew near. Edmund roved through the camp, questioning, seeking; at last, on the morrow he heard the report, that the previous evening a Cavalier had seen Almoradi Gomelez issue from a little wood half a league from the city, and ride towards a postern; that / he was galloping up to him, when he saw the Moor totter in his saddle, and at last fall from his horse: before succour could come, he died. His last words only spoke of the Fountain of Myrtles; in agony of spirit, for Gomelez had surely stricken to death his stripling foe, ere he left the place of combat, Edmund hurried to the spot: the herbage round the fountain was trampled and torn, as by horses' hoofs. It was moistened, but not with water; a bank, thickly overgrown with geraniums, bore the print of a man's form, but none was there.

Monina had been left in Alcala-la-Real, a prey to fear, to gaze from the steep summit on the plain, whereon, beyond her sight, was acted the real drama of her life; to question the wounded, or the messengers that visited Alcala, and to address prayers to the Virgin, were the sad varieties of her day. In the midst of this suspense two unexpected guests visited her abode – her father, and an Irish chieftain; a Yorkist, who came to lead the Duke from his Spanish abode, to where he might combat for his lost crown. De Faro had not heard of the death of Madeline; / and with awe his child beheld the tears that bedewed his rugged cheeks at this sad termination of his ocean-haunting vision. He embraced his daughter – "Thou wilt not desert me; we will leave this fated spot: and thou, Monina, will sail for ever with thy father on the less barbarous sea."

De Faro's companion was named Lord Barry. He was Baron of Buttevant, in

---

[a] Probably Mary Shelley's invention, and emblematically opposing love to glory, the myrtle being sacred to Venus. Irving (II, p. 353) describes the Moorish system for delivering challenges.

the county of Cork, and allied to the Geraldines, chiefs of that soil.[a] He had fought at Stoke, and been attainted by Henry; so that he was forced to wander a banished man. Eager to reinstate himself, every Yorkist plot numbered him among its warmest partizans. He had for some time resided either at Paris or at Brussels, where he often held counsel with Lady Brampton. Weary of delay he at last stole back to Ireland, to see whether his noble kinsmen there would abet and rise in favour of the Duke of York. He came away, proud and delighted with his success: promises of service for the White Rose had been showered on him – his eloquence and enthusiasm conquered even Lady Brampton. / War also seemed impending between France and England: if that were once declared, every objection would be obviated. At any rate, the times seemed so fair, that she agreed with Lord Barry to visit the present home of the young English Prince; and, as if to further their designs, Sir Edward Brampton was at that moment requested by the Archduke Maximilian[b] to undertake a private embassy to Lisbon. Thither they had sailed, and now, leaving this lady in Portugal, Lord Barry had continued his voyage to Andalusia, with the intention of returning again to Lisbon accompanied by the promise and hope of the House of York. He met de Faro in the port of Malaga: the name was familiar to him. They journeyed together to Alcala-la-Real.

Lord Barry was all eagerness that the English Prince should immediately join Lady Brampton at Lisbon. It was agreed that they should proceed thither in de Faro's caravel. The mariner abhorred the name of warfare between Spaniard and Moor; and Madeline's death only added poignancy to this sensation. He would not look / on the siege of Granada. While the Irish noble and Monina proceeded to the camp to prepare the cousins, he returned to Malaga to bring round his vessel to the nearer port of Almeria.[c] Lord Barry and the fair Moor commenced their journey on the morning of a most burning day; they wound down the steep declivities of the Sierra, and entered upon the bright blooming plain. Noon with all its heat approached. They rested under a grove of mulberries, reposing by a brook, while Lord Barry's horse and Monina's mule were tied to the nearest shrubs. Slight accidents are the wires and pullies on which the machinery of our lives hang. Stung by flies, the noble's horse grew restive, broke his rein, and galloped away; through the thick shade his master pursued, till tramp of feet and crackling of branches died on Monina's ear. A quarter of an hour, half an hour passed, when on her solitude came a Moorish voice, an exclamation in the name of Allah, and the approach of several men

---

[a] John, Lord Barry, chief of the Barrymores, an ally of Lambert Simnel. Barry was pardoned in June 1488; there is no evidence that he supported Warbeck. For Buttevant, see p. 112n.

[b] Maximilian I (1459–1519), Archduke of Austria and Holy Roman Emperor (after 1493), secured Habsburg control of sixteenth-century Europe through adroit marital and military moves. He had gained the Burgundian territories and the Netherlands by marrying Marie, daughter of Charles the Bold.

[c] Mediterranean port on the Costa de la Luz.

whom already she painted as enemies. To take to her mule, to ride swiftly through the grove, was the impulse of her fear; and, when again silence gave her token of security, / she found that she had lost her way. It was only after many vain attempts that she extricated herself from the wood, and then perceived that she had wandered from the direct road to Granada, whose high towers were visible at a distance. The burning July noonday sun scorched her. Her mule lagged in his pace. As a last effort she sought a plantation of elms, not far distant. The grateful murmur of flowing waters saluted her ears as she approached. For a few minutes more she was exposed to the glaring sunshine, and then entered the cool umbrage of the trees – the soft twilight of woven leaves and branches; a fountain rose in the midst, and she hastened to refresh herself by sprinkling herself with cool waters. Thus occupied she thought she was alone in this sequestered nook, when a crash among the underwood startled her; the mule snorted aloud, and from the brake issued a mare caparisoned with saddle and bridle. She had lost her rider; yet her distended nostrils, the foam that flaked her sides, the shiver that made her polished skin quiver, spoke of recent contest or flight. She looked on her – could it be? She / called her "Daraxa," and the animal recognized her voice; while in answer to the dreadful surmises that awoke in her heart, a low groan was heard from the near bank. Turning, she beheld the form of a man lying on the herbage; not dead, for he groaned again, and then stirred, as if with returning sense. Quick as lightning she was at his side; she unlaced his helmet, nor did she need to look at his pallid countenance to be assured of what she already knew, that Richard of England lay there, but for her help, expiring. She filled his helm with water, and sprinkled it over him, he opened his eyes, and groaning again, strove to clasp his head with his unnerved hand. With light fairy fingers she released him from his coat of mail, and saw on his right side a mass of congealed blood, which his faintness had made cease to flow from his wound. Fearing that it would bleed again as he revived, she bound it with his scarf and her own veil, and then gave him water to drink; after which he showed still more certain signs of recovery.

It was wonder to him to find himself alive, when already he had believed the bitterness of / death to be passed; still greater wonder was it to behold his own sweet Monina, like a spirit of good, hovering over to recover him. He tried to raise himself, and she bent down to support him, resting his head on her gentle heart; he felt its beating, and blest her with a thousand soft thanks and endearing names. Though the wound in his side was deep, yet now that the blood was staunched, it did not seem dangerous. The immediate cause of his swoon was a stunning blow on his head, which had beat in the iron of his helm, but inflicted no further injury. It was long however before he could move; and the evening shades had made it almost night, before he could sit his horse and slowly quit the wood. Wishing to conduct him to where they might find succour, Monina directed his steps to a village, east of the grove. They had hardly ridden half a mile, when Richard felt dizzy; he faintly called her to his side – she received him as he fell, and, supporting him to a bank, called aloud in agony, in hopes that some wandering soldier or peasant might be near to aid them. It happened to her wish; several countrymen, who / had been carrying fruit to the Christian camp, passed them – she conjured them in the Virgin's name, to assist a soldier of the faith, a crusader in their cause. Such an appeal was sacred in their ears; they contrived, with the poles and baskets in which they had carried their fruit, covering them with a part of their habiliments and the saddle-cloths of the animals, to form a sort of litter on which they placed Richard. Monina followed on foot, clasping his hand; the men led the horses: and thus they proceeded up the mountains to a village about two leagues from Granada, where every house was open to them. The Prince was permitted to repose in the habitation of the Alcalde,[a] and the deep sleep into which he soon fell was a dear assurance to his friend's anxious heart, of the absence of danger, and a promise of speedy recovery.

Yet the night that began so well for the patient, wore a less prosperous appearance towards the conclusion. Monina sat beside his couch, and perceived with alarm symptoms of pain and fever. According to the custom of the / time, she had acquired some little skill in surgery; this, when the wound came to be dressed, made her acquainted with its irritated and dangerous appearance. As the heat of the day came on, the Prince's sufferings increased. In this little village there was neither physician nor medicaments necessary for the emergency; and the place itself, low-built, hedged in by mountains, and inhabited by peasants only, was ill suited for the patient. She resolved that he should that night be removed to a town on the eastern side of the mountains, overlooking the plain bordering the sea. A litter was prepared; and she, fatigued by her journey, and by long and painful solicitude, yet walked beside it, listening to his low breathing, catching the smallest sound he made in complaint or questioning. Before she quitted the village, she employed a peasant to seek Plantagenet, and convey to him intelligence of the actual state of his friends.

After three days of fear and anxious care, the wound began to heal, and Richard became convalescent. Who could tell, during the long hours / that composed those days and nights, the varying emotions that agitated poor Monina? That he should die, was a thought in which, in its extent and reality, she never indulged; but an awful fear of what of suffering the coming hours might produce, never for a moment slept within her. She spent long intervals of time kneeling by his couch – her soft fingers on his pulse, counting the rapid vibration – her cool hand alone tempered the burning of his brow; and often, supported by her, he slept, while she remained in the same position, immovable.

---

[a] In Spain and Portugal a town magistrate, sheriff, or justice (*OED*).

The very pain this produced was a pleasure to her, since it was endured for him who was the idol of her innocent and pure thoughts; she almost lamented when he no longer needed her undivided attention: the hours she gave to repose came like beggars following in a procession of crowned heads; they were no longer exalted by being devoted to him.

After the lapse of three anxious days he grew rapidly better, and at evening-tide enjoyed at the open casement the thrilling sweetness of the mountain air. How transporting and ineffable / are the joys of convalescence! – the calm of mind – the voluptuous languor – the unrebuked abandonment to mere pleasurable sensation – the delight that every natural object imparts, fill those hours with a dream-like, faint ecstacy, more dear to memory than tumultuous joy. Monina sat near him, and it was dangerous for their young hearts thus to be united and alone in a fairy scene of beauty and seclusion. Monina's ardent spirit was entranced by delight at his recovery; no thought of self mingled with the single idea that he was saved – saved for youth, for happiness, and for his long-lost rights. Darkness crept around them, the clumps of chesnut trees grew more massy and indistinct – the fire-fly was alive among the defiles of the hills – the bat wheeled round their humble dwelling – the heavy-winged owl swept with huge flapping wings out of the copse. "Are ye here?" were the first sounds that broke the silence; it was the voice of Edmund. Monina sprung up, and glad to disburthen her full heart, welcomed with an embrace this beloved friend. "Guardian angel of our lives," he cried; "you are destined / at all times to save us!" Dear, soothing expressions, which then formed the joy, long afterwards the master-impulse of her fervent and devoted spirit.

Each told their tale; the one of hazard and mischance, the other of agonizing inquietude. For Richard, Edmund had feared; but when, wearied, terrified, and in despair, Lord Barry had brought intelligence of Monina's disappearance from the streamlet's side where he had left her, and of a distant view he had caught of Moorish horsemen who took refuge in Granada – heaven seemed at once to empty on him its direst curses, and his fate was sealed with misery for ever.

The peasant dispatched by Monina had delayed; not for three days did he deliver her letter to Plantagenet, who still, trembling in recollection of his past terror, and what might have been the ultimate event of the Prince's wound, departed on the moment for ———.

And now farewell to Spain! to romantic Spain, to Moorish and Christian combat, to the gay fields of the Vega, to the sunny mountains / of Andalusia! De Faro's caravel, true to its appointment, arrived at Almeria. They embarked; their immediate destination was Lisbon; but their thoughts were fixed on the promised termination of their wanderings. Soon they would bend their course far away to the islands of the turbid Northern sea, where nature veils herself in clouds, where war assumes a sterner aspect, and the very virtues of the inhabitants grow stubborn and harsh from the struggle they make to be enabled to bear the physical ills of existence.

Farewell to Spain! to boyhood's feats, to the light coursing of shadows as he ran a race with the swift-footed hours. A kingdom calls for Richard! the trials of life attend him, the hope of victory, the fortitude of well-endured defeat. /

CHAPTER XIII.

———

To England if you will!

SHAKSPEARE.[a]

———

A thousand recollections and forgotten thoughts revived in Richard's bosom when he saw his childhood's friend, the Lady Brampton. He was reminded of his sufferings in the Tower, of his noble cousin Lincoln, of her maternal tenderness, when under her care he quitted the gloomy fortress, his brother Edward's tomb. His mother's last embrace again thrilled through his frame, and Lovel's parting blessing: what sad changes had chanced since last he saw her! / Sad in all, but that he, then a boy, had sprung up into the riper age of youthful prowess.

Even with the banished Prince we must recur to the state of affairs in the north of Europe. The French king, Charles the Eighth, had directed all his attempts to the subjugation of Britany, which was now under the dominion of the youthful Anne, its orphan Duchess. The English nation espoused her cause, watched with jealousy and indignation the progress of the French arms, and clamoured loudly for war in her support. Henry, on the contrary, was obstinately bent upon peace, though he took advantage of his subjects' appetite for war, to foist subsidies upon them, which were no sooner collected than his armaments were disbanded, and an ambassador, sent on a mission of peace, was substituted for the herald ready apparelled for defiance. This could not last for ever. French policy triumphed in the marriage of Charles the Eighth with Anne of Britany;[b] and that duchy became finally annexed to the crown of France. England was roused to / indignation: the King, forced to listen to their murmurs, promised to invade the rival kingdom the following spring: a

———

[a] *King John*, III. iv. 68.
[b] '1491' (marginal note in *Abinger/Palacio*), the year the marriage occurred.

benevolence was granted him; all his acts tended to the formation of an expedition, which was the best hope of York.

Lord Barry was urgent against delay, while the English partizans wished that Richard's landing in Ireland, and Henry's in France, should be consentaneous. Nay, they had deeper views. Ireland, since Simnel's defeat, appeared but a forlorn hope, and they fostered the expectation of being able to make England itself the scene of their first attempt, so soon as its king should be fairly engaged in hostilities on the other side of the channel. The Duke himself, eager as he was to begin his career, warmly supported this project; communication with the North was slow meanwhile, and months wore away – not fruitlessly. Richard gained in every way by the delay; his knowledge of English affairs grew clearer; his judgment formed; his strength, weakened by the events / of the summer, was restored during the repose and salubrious coolness of the winter months.

Accident furthered their designs:[a] a visitor arrived from England, who brought with him accounts so encouraging, that hope blossomed into certainty in the hearts of the warm-hearted followers of York. But ere we introduce this new and seemingly important personage, we must return awhile to England, to speak of Henry's suspicions, his fears, his artful policy.

All that Frion had achieved through his abortive attempt, had been but to ascertain the existence of the Duke of York, and to spread still wider the momentous secret; so that Henry, suspicious and irritated, received him on his return with anger, resenting his failure as the result of treachery. Frion had been dismissed: and now years passed over, without the occurrence of any circumstances that spoke of the orphan heir of the English crown. The King brooded over the secret, but spoke of it to no one. The royal youth grew to his imagination, as in reality he did, passing from boyhood to almost man's estate. Yet, when Henry reflected / on the undisturbed state he had enjoyed for years, on the firmness with which he was seated on the throne, and the strong hold he had acquired through the lapse of time on his subjects' minds, he sometimes thought that even Richard's friends would advise him to continue in an obscurity, which was, at least, void of danger. Nevertheless, whenever there had been a question of attacking France, the feeling that his rival was ready to come forward, and that, instead of a war of invasion, he might have to fight for his own crown, increased his unwillingness to enter on the contest.

Now rumours were afloat – none knew whence they came, from France or Ireland – of the existence of King Edward's younger son, and that he would speedily appear to claim his succession. Henry, who was accustomed to tamper with spies and informers, was yet the last to hear of a circumstance so nearly affecting his interests. The name of Lady Brampton at length reached him, as

---

[a] '1492' (marginal note in *Abinger/Palacio*).

being abroad on a secret and momentous expedition. This name had made a considerable figure in Richard / Simon's confessions; it was connected with Lincoln, Lovel, the Dowager Queen, all whom the Tudor feared and hated. Yet he paused before he acted; his smallest movement might rouse a torpid foe: he only increased his vigilance; and, from past experience knowing that to be the weak point, he dispatched emissaries to Ireland, to learn if any commotion was threatened, any tale rife there, that required his interference. As the time approached, when it was expected that the English Prince would declare himself, the policy of his friends greatly changed; and, far from maintaining their former mysterious silence, the circumstance of his abode in Spain, and the expectation of his speedy appearance in Ireland, made, during the winter of 1491–92, a principal topic among such of the native nobility as the Earl of Desmond had interested in his cause. Henry's spies brought him tidings beyond his fears; and he saw that the struggle was at hand, unless he could arrest the progress of events. Meanwhile, he continued to defer his war with France; he felt that that would be the signal for his enemy's attack. /

As he reflected on these things, a scheme developed itself in his mind, on which he resolved to act. The enemy was distant, obscure, almost unknown; were it possible to seize upon his person where he then was, to prevent his proposed journey to Ireland, to prepare for him an unsuspected but secure prison – no cloud would remain to mar his prospect; and, as to the boy himself, he could hope for nothing better than his cousin Warwick's fate, unless he had preferred, to the hazardous endeavour of dethroning his rival, a private and innocuous life in the distant clime where chance had thrown him. This was to be thought of no more: already he was preparing for the bound, but ere he made it he must be crushed for ever.

In those times, when recent civil war had exasperated the minds of men one against the other, it was no difficult thing for a Lancastrian King to find an instrument willing and fitting to work injury against a Yorkist. During Henry's exile in Britany, he had become acquainted with a man, who had resorted to him there for the sole purpose of exciting him against / Richard the Third; he had been a favourite page of Henry the Sixth, he had waited on his son, Edward, Prince of Wales, that noble youth whose early years promised every talent and virtue; he had idolized the heroic and unhappy Queen Margaret. Henry died a foul death in the Tower; the gracious Edward was stabbed at Tewkesbury; the royal Margaret had given place to the widow Woodville; while, through the broad lands of England, the sons of York rioted in the full possession of her wealth. Meiler Trangmar[a] felt every success of theirs as a poisoned arrow in his flesh – he hated them, as the mother may hate the tiger, whose tusks are red with the life-blood of her first-born – he hated them, not

---

[a] Mary Shelley's invention.

with the measured aversion of a warlike foe, but the dark frantic vehemence of a wild beast deprived of its young. He had been the father of three sons; the first had died at Prince Edward's feet, ere he was taken prisoner; another lost his head on the scaffold; the third – the boy had been nurtured in hate, bred amid dire curses and bitter imprecations, all levelled against Edward the Fourth and his brothers – his mind had become distorted by the ill food / that nurtured it – he brooded over the crimes of these men, till he believed that he should do a good deed in immolating them to the ghosts of the murdered Lancastrians. He attempted the life of the King[a] – was seized – tortured to discover his accomplices: he was tortured, and the father heard his cries beneath the dread instrument, to which death came as a sweet release. Real madness for a time possessed the unhappy man, and when reason returned, it was only the dawn of a tempestuous day, which rises on the wrecks of a gallant fleet and its crew, strewn on the dashing waves of a stormy sea. He dedicated himself to revenge; he had sought Henry in Britany; he had fought at Bosworth, and at Stoke. The success of his cause, and the peace that followed, was at first a triumph, at last almost a pain to him. He was haunted by memories which pursued him like the hell-born Eumenides;[b] often he uttered piercing shrieks, as the scenes, so pregnant with horror, recurred too vividly to his mind. The priests, to whom he had recourse as his soul's physicians, counselled him the church's discipline; he assumed / the Franciscan habit,[c] but found sack-cloth and ashes no refuge from the greater torture of his mind. This man, in various ways, had been recalled to Henry's mind, and now he selected him to effect his purpose.

To any other he would have feared to entrust the whole secret; but the knowledge that the destined victim was the son and rightful heir of King Edward, would add to his zealous endeavours to crush him. Besides that Trangmar had a knowledge of the fact, from having been before employed to extract in his priestly character this secret from a Yorkist, Sir George Nevil, who had been entrusted by Sir Thomas Broughton.[d] Every thing yielded in this wretch's mind to his hatred of York; and he scrupled not to hazard his soul, and betray the secrets of the confessional. Nevil fortunately was informed in time of the danger that menaced him, and had fled; while Trangmar, thunder-struck by the magnitude of his discovery, hastened to reveal it to the King. It were long to detail each act of the crafty sovereign, and his scarcely human tool. By his order, the friar introduced / himself to the Dowager Queen, at Ber-mondsey, with a plausible tale, to which she, in spite of her caution, was

---

[a] 'Edward IV' (marginal note in *Abinger/Palacio* referring to 'the King', which is underscored).

[b] 'The kindly ones', euphemistic name given to the Furies of Greek mythology, who rise from the underworld to punish the wicked.

[c] The simple garb worn by the order of friars established in 1209 by St Francis of Assisi.

[d] The chronicles place Nevil (or Neville) among Warbeck's supporters at the French court. Mary Shelley lets the reader infer that Broughton confided in Nevil before dying at Stoke.

induced to give ear, and entrusted a message by him, as he said that he was on his way to Spain, to seek and exhort to action the dilatory Prince. He then departed. Henry had rather to restrain than urge his furious zeal. The scheme projected, was, that Richard should be entrapped on board a vessel, and brought with secrecy and speed to England, where he might be immured for life in some obscure castle in Wales. Trangmar promised that either he would accomplish this, or that the boy should find a still more secret prison, whence he could never emerge to disturb the reign of Henry, or put in jeopardy the inheritance of his son.

Such was the man who, in the month of April, 1492, following Lady Brampton's steps, arrived at Lisbon, and found to his wish the Prince there also, and easy access afforded him to his most secret counsels. He brought letters from the Dowager Queen, and some forged ones from other partizans of York, inviting the Prince / without application to any foreign sovereigns, or aid from distant provinces, at once to repair to England, and to set up his standard in the midst of his native land, where, so these letters asserted, the Earl of Surrey,[a] and many other powerful lords anxiously awaited him. All this accorded too well with the wishes of the little conclave not to ensure assent; nay, more, when Trangmar urged the inexpediency of the Duke's being accompanied by such notorious Yorkists as Plantagenet and Lady Brampton; it was suddenly agreed that Richard should embark on board a merchantman, to sail with the next fair wind for England, while his friends dispersed themselves variously for his benefit. De Faro, in his caravel, was to convey Lord Barry to Cork. Plantagenet resolved to visit the Duchess of Burgundy, at Brussels. Lady Brampton departed for the court of France, to engage the King at once to admit young Richard's claim, and aid him to make it good. "You, sweet, will bear me company;" and Monina, her whole soul – and her eyes expressed that soul's devotion to Richard's success – remembered starting, that the result of / these consultations was to separate her from her childhood's companion, perhaps for ever. As if she had tottered on the brink of a precipice, she shuddered; but all was well again. It was not to be divided from the Prince, to remain with Lady Brampton, to proceed to Paris with her; on his earliest triumph to make a part of it, and to join his court in London. All these words, king, victory, and court, wove a golden tissue before the ardent girl's eyes; she had not yet

"Lifted the painted veil, which men call life;"[b]

as a child who chases the glories of the west, she knew not that night was falling

---

[a] Thomas Howard, 1st Earl of Surrey and 2nd Duke of Norfolk (1443–1524), supported Edward IV and Richard III. Imprisoned after Bosworth, he later became a valued military advisor of the Tudors. Surrey appears briefly in *Richard III*; in *Henry VIII* he is conflated with his son.

[b] Adapted from P. B. Shelley's sonnet, 'Lift not the painted veil', first published in *PBS* 1824.

upon her, while still she fancied that she advanced towards the ever-retreating splendour of the sky.

Lady Brampton and Plantagenet trembled, as they committed their beloved charge to other hands; they importuned Trangmar with their injunctions – their entreaties, their thousand last words of care and love – the Friar heard, and smiled assent to all. Monina had need of all her courage for the hour, which she knew not that she dreaded till it came. He was going; the / truth flashed suddenly upon her – he, from whom since childhood she had scarcely been absent for a day. So blind had she been to her own sensations, that it was not until he leaped into the boat, and put off from shore, that she became aware of the overwhelming tide of grief, disquiet, almost of despair, that inundated her heart. Where was her gaiety, her light etherial spirit, flown? Why lagged the hours thus? Why did ceaseless reverie seem her only refuge from intolerable wretchedness?

She had one other solace; she was still with his friends, whose whole thoughts were spent upon him; his name enriched their discourse; the chances of his voyage occupied their attention. Little knew they the strange and tragic drama that was acting on board the skiff that bore afar the idol of their hopes. /

CHAPTER XIV.

———

This Friar boasteth that he knoweth hell,
And God it wot that is but litel wonder;
Friars and fiends ben but litel asonder.
                                    CHAUCER.[a]

———

Richard meanwhile sailed fearlessly, with treachery for his nearest mate. Trangmar had at once exhibited audacity and prudence in the arrangement of his plan. He had made no great preparation, nor confided to any the real object of his intents. His only care had been, that the Duke should sail on board an English vessel; and chance had brought into the Tagus[b] one whose captain was

---

[a] Geoffrey Chaucer (c.1343–1400), *Summoner's Tale*, Prologue, ll. 1672–4, loosely quoted.
[b] The longest river in the Iberian peninsula; Lisbon is on its estuary.

inclined to the party of Lancaster. He also contrived to have two hirelings of his own engaged on board as part of / the crew, who knew that it was their employer's design to carry to England a prisoner for the King. He was besides provided with a warrant from Henry, empowering him to seize on his rebel subject – the name a blank, for the Monk to fill up – alive or dead. The paper ran thus; so, in case of struggle, to afford warranty for his darker purpose.

Richard was now a prisoner. The vessel belonging to any country is a portion of that country; and the deck of this merchantman was virtually a part of the British soil. The Prince, not heeding his position, was so far from fearing his enemy's power, that he felt glad to find himself among his countrymen. He looked on the weather-beaten countenances of the honest sailors, and believed that he should find friends and partizans in all. He spoke to Trangmar of his purpose of declaring himself, and gaining them over; making this tiny offshoot of wide England his first conquest. Trangmar had not anticipated this. He was ignorant of the versatile and active spirit of the youth with whom he had to deal; nor had he, by putting himself / in imagination in the Prince's place, become aware how the project of acquiring his own was his sleepless incentive to every action, and how he saw in every event a stepping stone in the prosecution of his enterprize. He started at the proposal, and in his own heart said, "I must lose no time; that which I thought to do next week, were better done to-morrow." With Richard he argued against this measure: he showed how the captain was bound to the present English government by his fortunes; how far more likely it was that, instead of gaining him and his crew, he would be made a prisoner by them, and delivered up to his enemy. Richard lent no great credence to this, but he yielded to the authority of the elder and the priest.

It was not in the power of his wily adversary to prevent him from ingratiating himself in the hearts of all around him. Besides his gentleness, his unaffected sympathy, and noble demeanour, his gay and buoyant spirit was congenial to the reckless sailors, who, during the dead calm that succeeded their first day's sail / after quitting the Tagus, were glad of amusement to diversify their monotonous lives. He interceded with their captain when any fault was committed; he learned their private histories, promised his assistance, and scattered money among them. Sometimes he called them around him to teach him their art, discoursing about the stars, the magnet, the signs of the weather; he climbed the shrouds, handled the ropes, became an adept in their nautical language. At other times he listened to tales of dreadful shipwrecks and sailors' hardships, and recounted in turn de Faro's adventures. This made them talk of the new African discoveries, and descant on the wild chimeras, or sage conclusions of Columbus, who, at last, it was said, was to be sent by the sovereigns of Spain in quest of the western passage to India, over the slant and boundless Atlantic.[a] All this time,

---

[a] Columbus (1451–1506) was granted three ships on 17 April 1492 for his first voyage of discovery.

with flapping sails, they lay but at a short distance off the mouth of the Tagus; and Trangmar, impatient of delay, yet found it prudent to postpone his nefarious purpose.

After the calm had continued for nearly a / week, signs of bad weather manifested themselves; squalls assailed the ship, settling at last in a gale, which grew into a tempest. Their little vessel was decked, yet hardly able to resist the lashing waves of the Bay of Biscay. A leak, which had shewn itself even during the calm, increased frightfully; the men were day and night employed at the pumps, exposed to the beating rain, and to the waves, which perpetually washed the deck, drenching their clothes and bedding; each hour the wind became more furious; dark water-spouts dipping into the boiling sea, and churning it to fury, swept past them, and the steep sides of the mountain-high billows were ready at every moment to overwhelm them. Their tiny bark, which in these days would scarcely receive a more dignified name than a skiff, was borne as a leaf on the stream of the wind, its only safety consisting in yielding to its violence. Often at the worst the men despaired. The captain himself, frightened at the danger, and, strange inconsistency, still more fearful of the ruin that must attend him if his vessel were wrecked, lost all presence of / mind. The Prince displayed meanwhile all his native energy; he commanded the men, and they obeyed him, looking on him as a superior being; when, by following his orders, the progress of the leak was checked, and the tost bark laboured less among the surges. "Sailors have short prayers," he said; "but if they are sincere ones, the Saints will not the less intercede for us before God. Join me, my men, in a pious vow. I swear by our Lady's precious name, to walk barefoot to her nearest shrine the first land we touch, and there to make a gift of incense and candles at her altar. This, if we escape; if not, here is Father Meiler, a holy Franciscan, to give us short shrift; so that, like devout Catholics, we may recommend our souls to the mercy of Jesus. And now to the pump, the ropes; bring me a hatchet, our mast must overboard."

Three days and nights they worked unremittingly; the lull that then suc-ceeded was followed by another tempest, and the exhausted mariners grew desperate. They had been borne far into the Atlantic, and now the wind shifting, drove them with the same fury into the Bay of / Biscay. Every moment in expectation of death, the heart of Trangmar softened towards his victim in spite of himself; he was forced to admire his presence of mind, his unvanquish-able courage; his light, yet gentle spirit, which made him bear up under every difficulty, yet pity those who sunk beneath, cheering them with accents at once replete with kindness and fearless submission to the decree of Providence. Feeling the crew bound to him as his natural subjects, he extended towards them a paternal love, and felt called upon to guard and save them. After, for a fortnight, they had thus been the sport of the elements, the gale decreased; the violent breakers subsided into one long swell, which bore them into a sheltered cove, in the wild coast that surrounds the Bay of Biscay. The men disembarked, the vessel was drawn up; all hands were employed in unlading and repairing her. "Ye do ill," said Richard; "do you not remember our vow? Doubtless some village is near which contains a shrine where we may pay it."

This piety was in accord with the spirit of the times, and the men rebuked, revered still more / the youth who had saved them in danger, and who now in safety, paid, with religious zeal, the debt incurred towards their heavenly patroness. A little village lay secluded near the creek, and above it, on a high rock, was a chapel dedicated to Saint Mary of the Ascension,[a] erected by a noble, who had vowed such offering, on escaping, as the Prince of England had, from death on those perilous seas. Bare-headed, bare-footed, bearing lights, following the Franciscan who led the way, the crew of the St. George proceeded towards the shrine. Next to the blessed Virgin, Richard claimed their gratitude; and after due Aves had been said at the altar, still in the sacred place they gathered round him, offering their property and their lives, imploring him to accept from them some pledge of their thankfulness. The heart of the outcast sovereign swelled within him. "I reign here, in their breasts I reign," was the thought that filled his bright eyes with a dew springing from the fullness of his soul; with a smile of triumph, he looked towards Father Meiler, as if to appeal to his judgment, whether now he might not declare / himself, and claim these men's allegiance. He was startled by the dark and even ferocious expression of Trangmar's countenance. His coarse brown Franciscan dress, belted in by a rope; the cowl thrown back, displaying the monkish tonsure; the naked feet; these were symbols of humility and Christian virtue in strong contrast with the deep lines of his face, and the glare of his savage eyes: he met the glance of his victim, and became confused, while the Prince in wonder hastened to ask what strange thoughts occupied him, painting his visage with every sign of fierce passion.

"I was thinking," said Trangmar, hesitating, "I was deliberating, since God has cast us back on the land, whether it were not wiser to continue our journey through France, bidding farewell to the perils of the ocean sea?"

"That will I not," cried the Prince. "Father Meiler, I watched you during the storm; you acted no coward's part then; why do you now?"

"When danger is near, I can meet it as a / man of courage," said Trangmar; "When it is far, I can avoid it like a prudent one."

"A good clerical distinction, fit for a monk," replied the Duke; "but I, who am a Cavalier, Father, love rather to meet danger, than to avoid it like a woman or a priest."

"Insulting boy!" cried Meiler; "dare you taunt me with cowardice? That I was a soldier ere I was a monk, some of your race dearly rued!"

Before these words were fully uttered, Trangmar recollected himself; his

---

[a] The Assumption (the Catholic doctrine of the bodily removal of Mary into heaven) seems intended.

voice died away, so that his last expression was inaudible. The Duke only beheld his burst of passion, and sudden suppression of it, and said gently: – "Pardon me, Father, it is my fault that you forgot the respect due to me. I forgot reverence meet from youth to age, most meet from a sinful boy to a holy monk."

"I thank your Highness," said the Friar, "for recalling to my memory a truth that had half escaped it. Henceforth be assured that I will not forget that you are the undoubted offspring / of the Earl of March[a] – of Edward of England."

Fate thus urged this wicked and miserable man to his fiendlike purpose. Awakened again to deadly vengeance, he resolved to delay no longer; to trust no more to chance: he saw now all the difficulties of his former scheme of taking his enemy a prisoner to England; and this soothed his conscience as he recurred to more fatal designs. During the short delay that intervened before they again put out to sea, he watched an opportunity, but found none. At length they weighed anchor; and, with a favourable wind, bore down the coast of France. The time was come he surely thought: for during this long voyage he could frame an opportunity; during some dark night, when the ship sailed cheerily before a fair breeze, he would engage the Prince in engrossing talk concerning the conduct he should pursue when in England, taking advantage of his victim's incautiousness to allure him near the brink, and then push him overboard. His single strength was more than a match for his slight adversary; but to render / his scheme doubly sure, he would have the two men in his pay near him, to assist in the case of struggle, and vouch for his innocence if he were accused of foul play.

It is the fortune of those hurried into crime by violent passion, that they can seldom find accomplices as wicked as themselves. Thus was it with Trangmar. The men whose assistance he relied upon, partook of the enthusiasm[6] of their fellow-sailors for their noble passenger. After they had again set sail, the wind blowing gently from the south, bore them onwards with a favourable navigation, till, shifting a few points eastward, it began to freshen. It was then, that the Franciscan, not wholly betraying his purpose, but hinting that their presence would be necessary, ordered his men to contrive that the rest of the crew should be below, and they near at hand, while he that night should be alone with Richard upon deck. One of the men replied by stoutly declaring that if any evil was threatened the Prince, he would not be a party in it. "You possess King Henry's warrant," he said, "to make this Fitzroy[b] a prisoner. I will not oppose / his Majesty's command. You have him safely; what would you more?"

The other apparently yielded an assent to his employer's commands, and then found a speedy opportunity to warn Richard of his danger. A veil fell from the Prince's eyes. "Surely I knew this before," he thought; "ever since I was in

---

[a] Edward IV's title before he became king.
[b] King's son; the prefix often implied noble bastardy.

Saint Mary's chapel, I must have known that this dastard monk was my enemy. I am indeed betrayed, alone, friendless, on board an English vessel, surrounded by an English crew. Now let the trial be made, whether simple honesty be not of more avail than cruelty and craft. But first let me fathom the full intention of this man, and learn whether he have a worse design than that of delivering me over defenceless to my adversary. It cannot be that he would really murder me."

The breeze had rather sunk towards sunset, but it arose again with the stars; the vessel's prow struck against the light waves, and danced gaily on through the sea. One man stood at the helm; another, one of the Friar's hirelings, loitered near; the other kept out of the way. / Still, beneath the thousand stars of cloudless night, the little bark hurried on, feeling the freshening of the wind; her larboard beam was deep in the water, and close at the deck's leeward edge, Meiler and his intended victim paced. One thoughtless boy, high among the shrouds, whistled in answer to the winds. There was at once solitude and activity in the scene. "This is the hour," thought Richard; "surely if man's sinful heart was ever touched with remorse, this man's may now. God's throne, visible in all its beauty above us – beneath, around, the awful roaring waters, from which we lately so miraculously escaped." He began to speak of England, of his mother, of the hopes held out to him by his companion; eager in his desire of winning a traitor to the cause of truth, he half forgot himself, and then started to find that, ever as he walked, his companion got him nearer to the brink of the slant, slippery deck. Seized with horror at this manifestation of the worst designs, yet scarcely daring to credit his suspicions, he suddenly stopt, seizing a rope that swung near, and steadying himself by winding / his arm round it, an act that escaped his enemy's observation, for, as he did it, he spoke: "Do you know, Father Meiler, that I suspect and fear you. I am an inexperienced youth, and if I am wrong, forgive me; but you have changed towards me of late, from the kind friend you once were. Strange doubts have been whispered: do you reply to them. Are you my friend, or are you a treacherous spy? – the agent of the noble Yorkists, or Henry Tudor's hireling murderer?"

As he spoke the Friar drew still nearer, and the Prince recoiled further from him: he got on the sheer edge of the deck. "Rash boy!" cried Trangmar, "know that I am no hireling: sacred vengeance pricks me on! Son of the murderer! tell me, where is sainted Henry? where Prince Edward? where all the noble martyrs of his cause? Where my brave and lost sons? There, even where thou shalt be: quick, look back, thy grave yawns for thee!"

With the words he threw himself furiously on the Prince: the stripling sprung back with all the force lent him by the rope he held, and / pushed at the same time Trangmar violently from him, as he cried aloud on the sailors, "What, ho! treason is among us!" A heavy splash of the falling Meiler answered his call: the strong man was cast down in his very pride; the waters divided, and sucked him in. In a moment the crew were on deck; Trangmar's hireling, scared, cried out, "He is King Henry's prisoner! seize him!" thus increasing the confusion. The friar, his garments floating, now appeared struggling among the waves; a rope was thrown to him; the vessel sped on meanwhile, and it fell far short; Richard, horror-struck, would have leapt in to save his enemy; but the time was gone. One loud shriek burst on the ear of night, and all was still; Trangmar, his misery, his vengeance, and his crimes lay buried in the ocean's hoary caves.

What explanation could follow this tremendous incident? The Prince spoke of his life attacked; the men of the warrant their master had for his seizure: what was his crime none knew; "That will I declare freely," said the royal youth; "that unhappy man has sealed / my truth by his death. In my childhood I was nurtured in a palace, and bore the title of the Duke of York. Edward the Fourth was my father, Edward the Fifth my brother."

"Why this is foulest treason," cried the trembling captain.

"Aye, or fairest loyalty; speak, my friends; which of you will lay hands on your liege, on Richard the Fourth of England?"

The reckless and ignorant sailors, riotously and with one acclaim, swore to die for him; but their commander shuddered at the peril that beset him: while his men were hanging round their idolized Prince, he retired with his mate to lament the ugly chance of Trangmar's death, and to express terror at the very name of York. If the captain was a coward-friend of Tudor, the mate was a sturdy Lancastrian; he recommended to his chief[7] to seize the boy, and convey him a welcome gift to his sovereign; the clamours of the delighted crew showed that this was vain advice. He had said to them, with all the ingenuousness of youth, "My life is in your hands, and I know that it is safe." / Yet, when they spoke of seizing their unwilling commander, and of delivering the vessel in his hands, he said, "My good friends, I will not make lawless acts the stepping-stones to my throne; it is grief enough for me that my young hands have unwittingly destroyed the life of one who, not as an armed knight, but in holy garb set himself against me. I myself will persuade your captain to do me all the service I require."

This poor man was willing enough to hear what he called reason; at first he would fain have entreated Richard to suffer himself to be carried a prisoner to England; and, when he found his discourse vain, he yielded timid obedience to York's wishes, in spite of the lowering brow of his mate: thus, at least, his cargo would be saved, and his crew preserved from mutiny. Richard simply requested to be set on shore in Cork harbour, suddenly relinquishing every thought of England, now that he saw the treachery that awaited him there, and recurring to the former plans of Lord Barry. In Ireland, in the county of the Desmonds,[a]

---

[a] The 'county' was the province of Munster in southern Ireland.

111

he should find friends, adherents, / almost prepared for his arrival; and there also, if Barry forgot not his promise, this staunch partizan would speedily join him; the captain gladly assented to any project, that did not force him to land this dangerous pretender on the English shores.

For one week they ran before the wind; and Ireland, far and low, was discernible on the horizon; the dear land of promise to the weary exile, the betrayed, but high-hearted Prince: during this short navigation it had required all his fortitude to banish from his mind the image of the friar struggling in the waves, of a man precipitated in the very act of crime "unhouseled, unanointed, unannealed,"[a] into the life-quenching waters. Besides all other expectations, Richard longed to get on shore, that in a confessional he might lift this burthen of involuntary guilt from his soul.

At length the iron-bound coast was right a-head; the ponderous rocky jaws of the creek were open, and they sailed up Passage, past beautiful and woody islands, under forest-crowned hills, till they cast anchor before the / picturesque and hill-set city of Cork,[b] whose quay was crowded by multitudes, gazing on the newly-arrived vessel.

The Duke of York stood on the prow of his skiff, reflecting on the first step he ought to take. He knew little of Ireland, and that little had been gleaned from Lord Barry: he heard from him of its warlike chiefs, its uncivilized septs,[c] and English settlers, scarce less wild, and quite as warlike as its aboriginal inhabitants. He called to mind the names most familiar to him – the Earl of Kildare, abettor of Simnel, pardoned by Henry, and continued in his office of Lord Deputy; the Earl of Desmond, whom Lord Barry had particularly interested in his favour, who affected the state of an Irish chieftain, or rather king, and who, in his remote abode in Munster, disdained to attend the Dublin parliament, or to make one of the lawful governors of the land.[d] Other names he remembered of less note: Plunket, the Lord Chief Justice,[e] whom, with infinite reluctance, Henry had pardoned; Keating, Prior of Kilmainham, / who had been constable of Dublin Castle,[f] and who, ejected from his office after the battle of Stoke, had saved himself by flight, and was now concealed in an Abbey near Buttevant.[g] Much however of what he had heard, escaped his

---

[a] *Hamlet*, I. v. 77 (adapted).

[b] On Ireland's southern coast. Mary Shelley drew information on Cork from Croker.

[c] septs, 'a division of a nation or tribe; a clan; originally in reference to Ireland' (*OED*).

[d] Warbeck sought support from Desmond and Kildare on arriving. According to Leland (II, p. 94), Kildare did not respond openly, but Desmond 'without restraint, at once declared in favour of the new adventurer'.

[e] Thomas Plunket, a supporter of Simnel mentioned in the chronicles.

[f] Sir James Keating, described in Leland as 'a turbulent ecclesiastic' and 'zealous adherent' of Kildare (II, pp. 64, 71); he seems to have been pardoned in 1489, and would thus not have been in hiding. Dublin Castle was built early in the thirteenth century.

[g] The Abbey (founded c.1229 by Philip de Barry) and Buttevant (a town north of Cork) are described in Croker, pp. 112–18.

memory; and he stood on the threshold of this unknown land, vainly seeking in his recollection for the dim and shadowy forms, which were to guide him in the new and unexplored world before him. Another reflection also presented itself: Lord Barry had quitted[8] Ireland the year before, and communication there had been none since then – was Kildare still Deputy? did incursions of the natives, or turbulence among themselves, occupy the Lords of the Pale?[a] Should he find a band of nobles and their followers ready to assist him, or the motley population of a barbarous wild, whose sole ideas were internal struggles for power, whose watch-words for enterprize were names and things in which he had no portion?

In a hurried manner, York resolved on his plan of action. He had, on their approach to / land, arrayed himself in gay and rich apparel. The Spain from which he came was parent of this act: there embroidery, housings[b] inlaid with gold, and arms encrusted with jewels, formed the pride of the high-born Cavaliers. He stood prepared to land; he thanked the captain for his enforced courtesy; he held out his hand to the crew who gathered round him with their prayers and blessings. "My own!" was his first thought as he set his foot on shore: "Hail, realm of my fathers! Hear the vow of the fugitive who claims your sway! Justice, mercy, and paternal love, are the gifts with which I will repay your obedience to my call; your submission to my rule."

"Heave the anchor, and away!" thus spoke the captain of the craft he had left.

"For England; to warn our king of this springal's[c] insolent presumption;" said the mate.

"To any quarter of the wide world, save England," replied the timid captain: "Would you have me run my neck into the noose for not having clapped under hatches this / mercurial spark? Master mate, learn from an old sailor, that the best you can do with kings and grandees, is to have nought to do with them." /

---

[a] The part of Ireland over which England exercised jurisdiction. At this period it extended about sixty miles north and forty miles west of Dublin.

[b] housing, 'a cloth covering put on a horse or other beast for defense or ornament' (*OED*).

[c] springal, a young man, stripling.

CHAPTER XV.

Then Paridell, in whom a kindly pride
Of gracious speech, and skill his words to frame
Abounded, being glad of so fit tide
Him to commend to them, thus spake, of all well eyed.

SPENSER.[a]

Cork was an asylum for civilization in the centre of a savage distict. The cautious burghers, made wealthy by trade, and ever in fear of incursions from the surrounding septs, kept the strictest guard upon their city, as if they had a continual siege laid to it. They forbade all intercourse or intermarriage between those within and without the walls, till every citizen became linked together by some sort of kindred. It is true, that the / country around was peopled to a great degree by English lords; but they were the degenerate English, as they were styled, who imitated the state and independance of the native chiefs. Such was the Earl of Desmond, of the family of the Geraldines, who ruled as a king over Munster, and with whom the Barrys, the De Courcys, the Barretts, and the Mac Carthys, Mac Swineys, and other native chiefs, were connected by marriage, or struggling with him for "Chieferie" in the mutable chance of war.[b]

There was no appearance of timidity in the frank and assured aspect of the unfriended adventurer, as without entering the city, but merely passing through its suburbs, he proceeded to the cathedral church. It was twelve o'clock on the twenty-fourth of June, the feast of Saint John the Baptist;[c] and

---

[a] *Faerie Queene*, III. ix. 32 (adapted).

[b] English control over Ireland was unstable in the late fifteenth century, when Anglo-Irish and Gaelic Irish alike swore fealty to the crown only while it served their interests. Local alliances were often broken, as rival factions within families contracted strategic marriages to secure power and land. The families listed figure in chronicle accounts of Yorkist plots. 'Chieferie', 'the dues belonging to the chief or tanist of a clan or district' (*OED*).

[c] Warbeck landed in Ireland in November 1491, not in early summer of 1492, although Mary Shelley's sources differ on this point.

high mass was celebrating. The Duke of York entered the church – his soul was filled with pious gratitude for his escape from the dangers of the sea, and the craft of his enemies; and, as he knelt, he made a vow to / his sainted Patroness, the Virgin, to erect a church on the height which first met his eyes as he approached shore, and to endow a foundation of Franciscans – partly, because of all monkish orders they chiefly venerate her name, partly to atone for his involuntary crime in the death of Meiler Trangmar, who wore that habit. The appearance of this young, silken-suited, and handsome Cavalier, drew the eyes of Erin's blue-eyed daughters: – the men whispered together that he must be some Spanish grandee or English noble; but wherefore, unannounced and unattended, he came and knelt in their church before the shrine of Saint Finbar,[a] was matter of vague conjecture. The congregation passed out; then, impelled by curiosity, formed a wide semicircle round the gates of the cathedral, watching the motions of the graceful stranger. Master John Lavallan[b] the Mayor, John O'Water[c] the wealthiest citizen, and former Mayor of the town, and other rich burghers, stood close to the Round Tower within the walls of the Garth,[d] in expectation of being addressed by their distinguished visitor. The Duke of York / cast a quick glance around; and then, as the Mayor advanced, the youth stept forward to meet him. The citizen, as one habituated to exercise hospitality, bade the knight welcome, beseeching him to honour his abode with his presence, and to command his services. The Duke frankly accepted the invitation, and descended with the Mayor into the main street, where the officer resided; and here again Richard was made welcome to the city of Cork.

It was a gala day at the Mayor's; and now, at the dinner hour, twelve o'clock, the long tables groaned under the weight of viands, and round the hospitable board were seated the principal families of the town. No questions were asked the visitor – his golden spurs bespoke his honourable rank; he was placed at the right hand of Lavallan: and, while the clatter of knives and trenchers went on, he was only remarked by the younger guests, who gazed even to the injury of their appetites, on his burnished ringlets, his fair, open brow, his bright, blue eyes, and smile of courteous affability: but time went on; the dishes were carried away, the goblets placed; when the / Mayor, rising, drank welcome to the stranger, and asked, if no reason forbade him to reply, his name and mission. Already Richard had become acquainted with most of the countenances of his entertainers – that is, of those nearest him; for, far through the long hall, almost out of sight, the table extended, crowded by city retainers, and a

---

[a] Founded the city and see of Cork in the seventh century.

[b] John Lavallan (or Lewellyn), mentioned in Warbeck's confession.

[c] John O'Water (or Walters or Water or Atwater or a'Water), a fervent Warbeck supporter, executed with him in 1499.

[d] Croker (pp. 260–2) supplies legends and anecdotes concerning Ireland's distinctive towers, probably originally constructed for refuge and often located close to churches; garth, open court enclosed by a cloister.

few of the mere "Irishry," whose long hair and loose saffron-coloured mantles,[a] contrasted with the doublet, hose, and trimmed locks of the townsmen. Those near him bore the latter character, though their vivacious glances and quick gestures were more akin to the inhabitants of the South, among whom he had been accustomed to live, than to the steady, dull demeanour of English traders.

When Lavallan drank to the stranger, every eye turned to the object of the toast. Richard arose – his plumed cap was doffed; his shining hair, parted on his brow, clustered round his throat; his sunny countenance was full of confidence and courage – "Sir Mayor," he said, "my most kind entertainer, and you, my friends, men of Cork, may the grateful thanks / of the homeless adventurer be as kindly received by you, as they are gladly paid by him. Who am I? you ask. Wherefore do I come? My name is the best in the land; my coming is to claim your aid, to elevate it to its rightful place of pride and honour. Were I craven-hearted, or you less generous, I might dread to declare myself; but fear never entered the heart of a Plantagenet; and, when, unreservedly, I place my life in your hands, will you betray the trust?"

A murmur quickly hushed, the sound of suppressed emotion, as the winds of thought passed over the minds of those around, for an instant interrupted the speaker –

"Neither is my name nor lineage unknown to you," he continued: "you honour both and have obeyed them; will you refuse to submit to me, their descendant and representative? Did you not vow fealty to Richard Duke of York, who, driven from his own England by false Lancaster, found refuge and succour here? Was not Clarence your ruler, and Edward of England monarch of your isle? In the name / of these, in the name of the White Rose and Mortimer[b] and Plantagenet – I, the son of Edward the Fourth, the victim of my uncle Gloster's[c] treachery, and low-born Tudor's usurpation; I, named in my childhood Duke of York and Lord of Ireland, now, if rightly styled, Richard the Fourth of England, demand my lieges of Cork, to acknowledge my rights, to rise in my cause. I, a Prince and an outcast, place myself in their hands, through them to be a fugitive for ever, or a King."

Had Richard planned this scene, with deep insight into the dispositions of those with whom he had to deal, he could not have projected a better arrangement. They had learned of his existence from Lord Barry, and were prepossessed in his favour. Their fiery hearts were lighted at the word – his name, with a thousand blessings attached to it, rang through the hall: by means of the

---

[a] Details probably taken from Leland (I, pp. xxxv-xxxvi).

[b] Yorkist claims ultimately rested on a marriage connection with the Mortimers, descendents of the second son of Edward III. The maternal uncle of Richard, 3rd Duke of York, was Edmund Mortimer, 5th Earl of March (1391–1424), recognized as heir presumptive by Richard II (1367–1400; ruled 1377–99). In 1 *Henry IV* Shakespeare mistakenly assigns his claim to his uncle, another Edmund (?1376–1409), who joined forces with Owen Glendower and Hotspur against the king.

[c] Acceptable alternative spelling.

servants and followers at the lower end of the table, it reached the outer apartments and avenues of the Mansion-house;[a] while, with a kind of exalted rapture, the Mayor and his guests hung over their new-found / Prince. The citizens began to gather without, and to call aloud for the White Rose of England; the day was finished in festal tumult; the Mayor led forth his princely visitor – he was hailed Lord of Ireland with one acclaim. Some elders, who had known his grandfather, or had been followers of the Duke of Clarence, and others who, visiting England, had seen Edward the Fourth, were struck by the likeness he bore to his progenitors, and enthusiastically vouched for his truth. To see and hear the mad exultation of the moment, an uninterested spectator must have thought, that a messenger from heaven had arrived, to bestow liberty on the groaning slaves of some blood-nurtured tyrant. The Duke was installed in the castle with princely state, a town-guard appointed him, and the night was far advanced, before he was permitted to repose, and wondering to collect his thoughts, and feel himself an acknowledged sovereign in the first town of his alienated dominions in which he had set foot.

The morrow brought no diminution to the / zeal of his partizans. The first measure of the day was his attending high mass, surrounded by the mayor and citizens: when the holy ceremony was finished, he took oath on the Gospels, that he was the man he had declared himself. The eager people clamoured for him to assume the name of King; but that he said he would win with his good sword, nor, till he possessed its appanage,[b] assume a barren title: he was the Duke of York, until at Westminster he received his paternal crown.

From the church the mayor and citizens attended his council at the Castle, and here Richard more fully explained to them the projects of Lord Barry, his hopes from the Earl of Desmond, and his wish to attach to his cause the Earl of Kildare, Lord Deputy of Ireland. He learned the changes that had taken place but a month or two ago before: some suspicion having entered Henry's mind, the Earl of Kildare had been dismissed from his high office, and Walter, Archbishop of Dublin,[c] substituted in his room. The Baron of Portlester,[d] who had been treasurer for forty years, was obliged to resign in / favour of a Butler,[e] hereditary and bitter enemies of the Geraldines, while the exaltation of Plunket, from the office of Chief Justice to that of Chancellor, only proved that he was entirely gained over to the Lancastrians. The acts of this new government tended to mortify the late deputy, who bore ill his own degradation and the

---

[a] Mansion-house, here simply 'an official residence' (*OED*).

[b] Here used in the sense of 'rightful endowment' (*OED*).

[c] Walter FitzSimons (d. 1511), Archbishop of Dublin, served at different periods as Lord Chancellor and Lord Deputy of Ireland, in spite of earlier support for Simnel.

[d] Rowland FitzEustace, Baron Portlester, father-in-law of Gerald FitzGerald, 8th Earl of Kildare, lost his post after he supported Simnel; he was later pardoned.

[e] The Butlers controlled the borderlands between Munster and Leinster, ruled respectively by the earls of Desmond and Kildare.

triumph of his enemies. On various occasions brawls had ensued; and when Sir James of Ormond,[a] wished to place a creature of his own in a castle over which Kildare claimed seignory, the latter defended it by arms. This turbulent state of things promised fair for the adventurer; and his first deed was to dispatch letters to the Earls of Kildare and Desmond, soliciting their assistance, setting forth the ready zeal of the city of Cork, and the promises and attachment of Lord Barry, whom he daily expected to see arrive.

In all that the English Prince did, nothing spoke louder for him to his Irish friends, than his fearless confidence, and artless, yet not undignified reliance on their counsels. He had gained a warm friend in the former / Mayor, O'Water, a man reverenced throughout Munster. In his youth he had served in the army, and his spirit was hardly yet tamed to the pacific habits of a burgher. He was sixty years of age; but he bore his years lightly, and remembered, but as the occurrence of yesterday, the time when the Duke of York, grandfather of young Richard, was Lord of Ireland. He had attached himself particularly to his person, and followed him to England, returning to his own country after his patron's death. He saw in the descendant of his chief, his rightful lord, to refuse obedience to whom was a sin against the laws of God and man. He fervently swore never to desert him, and dispatched emissaries on all sides to spread the tidings of his arrival, and excite the partizans of the White Rose to his active assistance.

When the letters were written, council held, and a course of conduct determined on, still the caravel of de Faro did not appear, and Richard grew weary of his state of indolence. A week passed; and during the second, at the conclusion of which, the answers from the noble chieftains / were expected, the Duke of York announced to O'Water his intention of visiting Buttevant, the seat of Lord Barry, where, in the Abbey of Ballybeg, he hoped to find the Abbot of Kilmainham; a man, who in exile and poverty, exercised great influence over the Irish Yorkists. He had been insolent and cruel towards his enemies in power, but he was endowed with popular qualities for his followers; while among his friends, he was valued for his boldness, sagacity, and un- daunted courage. His career had been turbulent: he had supported himself against his sovereign by acts of lawless violence, till, obliged at last to yield, he found himself, in his old age, a poor brother in a distant monastery, obliged, for safety's sake, to veil his lofty pretensions in the obscurest guise. Lord Barry had offered him an asylum in the Abbey of Ballybeg; venerating, with the blind admiration of a soldier, the learning and craft of the priest, conjoined, as it here was, to dauntless courage. O'Water, on the contrary, disliked the subtle prior, and endeavoured to dissuade the Prince from the journey; but he / spurned the city laziness, and in spite of his friends' entreaties, and their fears for his safety

---

[a] Sir James Butler (d. 1497), an illegitimate nephew of Thomas, 7th Earl of Ormond, and ardent supporter of Henry VII.

among the followers of Desmond, Barry, and Macarthy, departed on his intended visit, attended only by Hubert Burgh,[a] the foster-brother of Lord Barry.

The way from Cork to Buttevant was not far, but more desolate than Granada during the Moorish war. Summer and the sun adorned that smiling land, casting a verdurous mantle over her deep wounds, painting the rude visage of war with brilliant hues. The forests, dark hills, and uncultivated wilds of Munster, showed nakedly the deep traces of the sovereign ill. But lately this neighbourhood had been the seat of war between the Earl of Desmond and the Chief of the Macarthy's; the latter had fallen in battle, but his brother and Tanist[b] had succeeded to him, and was already gathering together his sept for a more desperate struggle. Never in Spain had Richard seen such wild strange figures, as crossed his path during this short journey: whether it were the native kern,[c] wrapt in his mantle, disguised by his *glibb*,[d] or / long shaggy hair, or the adherents of Desmond, who affected the state of an Irish chieftain, whose leather-quilted jackets, long saffron-coloured shirts, cloaks and shaggy mustachios, riding without stirrups, bearing spears, formed objects not less uncouth and savage: the very women bore a similar appearance of incivilization. And as a comment on such text, Burgh told, as they rode, the history of the late wars of Desmond with O'Carrol, Prince of Ely, and with Macarthy; and, a still more dread tale, the incursion of Murrogh-en-Ranagh, an O'Brien; who, rising first in Clare, spread through the country, overrunning Munster, and bold from success, advanced into eastern Leinster.[e] All these accounts of battle were interwoven with tales of feuds, handed down from father to son, of the natural hatred of the native chiefs to the lords of English origin; interspersed with such strange wild tales, where the avowedly supernatural was intermingled with deeds of superhuman prowess and barbarity, that the English-born Prince, nursling of romantic Spain, felt as if he were transplanted into a / new planet, and stopped the speaker at each moment, to obtain some clearer explanation, or to have interpreted words he had never before heard, the names of customs and things found only in this land.

Thus entertained, the way to Buttevant, or as the Irish called it, Kilnemullagh,

---

[a] The de Burghs (or Burkes), the ruling family of Connaught, in western Ireland; Warbeck mentioned Hubert in his confession.

[b] Tanistry, system by which 'possessions descended not according to birthright but to the strongest and most skilful' of an Irish chieftain's kinsmen (Leland, I, p. 10).

[c] kern, an Irish foot soldier or someone from the poorer class from which such soldiers came (*OED*).

[d] glibb, 'a thick mass of matted hair on the forehead and over the eyes, formerly worn by the Irish' (*OED*).

[e] The earls of Desmond feuded (usually) with the MacCarthys, the Butler earls of Ormond, and the O'Briens. The Butlers, in turn, often struggled against the O'Carrolls of Ely (in modern county Offaly). The fearsome Murrogh-en-Ranagh flourished when George, Duke of Clarence, was Lord Lieutenant of Ireland (1462–9).

which was about twenty miles, seemed short. One thing was evident in all these details, that it was easy to rouse the English lords in Ireland to any act of turbulence and revolt; but that it would be difficult nevertheless for their ill-armed followers, and undisciplined bands, to compete with the soldiery of England. /

CHAPTER XVI.

————

Sisters, I from Ireland came.
COLERIDGE.[a]

————

The Duke, immediately on his arrival at the Castle of Buttevant, dispatched Hubert Burgh to the Prior of Kilmainham, with a message from himself and a token from Lord Barry, announcing his intention of visiting him at the Abbey the next day. But Keating feared thus to draw the eyes of some enemy upon him, and appointed a meeting in a secluded dell, near the bank of the Mullagh, or Awbeg, the river which Spenser loves to praise.[b] Early in the morning Richard repaired alone to this rural presence-chamber, and found Keating already there. Hearing of / the priest's haughty pride, Richard, with a sensation of disgust, had figured a man something like the wretched Trangmar, strong of limb, and with a ferocious expression of countenance. Keating appeared in his monk's humble guise; his light eyes were still lively, though his hair and beard were snowy white; his brow was deeply delved by a thousand lines; his person short, slender, bent; his step infirm; his voice was silver-toned; he was pale, and his aspect in its lower part sweetly serene. Richard looked with wonder on this white, withered leaf – a comparison suggested by his frail tenuity; and again he almost quailed before the eager scrutiny of the prior's eye. A merchant at a Moorish mart he had seen thus scan a slave he was about to purchase. At length, with a look of great satisfaction, the monk said, "This fits exactly; our

————

[a] Samuel Taylor Coleridge (1772–1834), 'Fire, Famine, and Slaughter: A War Eclogue', l. 46, published in the *Morning Post*, 8 January 1798, and recited by Mary Godwin on 1 June 1816 during her stay on the shores of Lake Geneva (see Polidori, *Diary*, p. 113).
[b] Mentions occur in *Colin Clout*, *Epithalamion*, and *Faerie Queene*.

friends will not hesitate to serve so goodly a gentleman. The daughter of York might in sooth mistake thee for a near kinsman. Thou comest from Portugal, yet that could not have been thy native place?"

Richard started. This was the first time he / had heard an expression of doubt of his veracity. How could he reply? His word alone must support his honour; his sword must remain sheathed, for his injurer was a priest. Keating caught his haughty glance, and perceived his mistake. It was with an effort that he altered his manner, for he exchanged with pain a puppet subject to his will, for a man (prince or pretender) who had objects and a state of his own to maintain. "Pardon the obscure vision of an old man," he said; "my eyes were indeed dim not to see the true marks of a Plantagenet in your appearance. I was but a boy when your princely grandsire fell; nor has it been my fortune to visit England or to see your royal father. But the Duke of Clarence honoured me with his friendship, and your cousin de la Poole acknowledged my zeal in furthering his projects. I am now neither prior nor commander; but, poor monk as I am become, I beseech your highness to command my services."

This swift change of language but ill satisfied the pride of Richard, and in reply he briefly / recounted such facts as established his right to the name he claimed. The noble artlessness of his tone conquered the priest's lurking suspicions: in a more earnest manner he besought the Duke's pardon; and a cordial intercourse was established between them.

The place where they met was secluded and wild; a bower of trees hid it from the view of the river, and an abrupt rock sheltered it behind. It was apparently accessible by the river only, and it was by its bank that the Duke and Prior had arrived. Nothing could equal the picturesque solitude around them. The waving of the leafy boughs, the scream of the water-fowl, or the splashing they made as they sprung from among the sedge and darted across the stream, alone interrupted the voiceless calm; yet at every moment in his speech Keating stopped, as if listening, and cast his keen eyes, which he libelled much in calling dim, up the steep crag, as if among its herbage and shrubs some dreaded spy or expected messenger might appear. Then again he apologized to the Duke / for having selected this wild spot for their interview. A price, he observed,[9] had been set upon his head, and his only safety lay in perpetual watchfulness and never-sleeping caution. "My zeal in your Highness' cause," he added with a courtier smile, "cannot be deemed a strange frenzy, since your success will not only assure my restoration to the dignity of which I have been unjustly deprived, but prevent an old man from perpetually dreaming of the sword of the slayer, or the more frightful executioner's axe."

Again the Prior fixed his eyes on a fissure in the rock, adding, "I had appointed to meet one in this place before your message was communicated to me; and in good time: for methinks the object of your visit may be furthered by the intelligence I hope soon to receive. Your Highness must have heard at Cork of the war carried on by the great Earl of Desmond and a native sept of this region. Macarthy, their chief, fell during the struggle, but his successor and Tanist mustered his broken forces to avenge him. The Earl is impatient of this resistance, for his / presence is necessary in Thomond[a] to drive the O'Carrolls from that district. At his invitation he and Macarthy meet this day to parley but a few miles hence. I was to have made one among them; but a boding raven told me that danger was abroad."

The tidings of the near presence of the Earl of Desmond were unexpected, and most welcome to the Duke. He immediately resolved not to lose the golden hour. He eagerly asked where the meeting was to be, and how speedily he might reach the spot.

As he was thus earnestly expressing his desire, a slight rustling caught the Prior's ear: he looked up; a human form hovered as in mid-air, scarcely, as it were, alighted on the precipitous rock; quickly, but cautiously, it threaded its steep and tortuous path. A large mantle was wrapt round the mountaineer, a large white kerchief enveloped the head in the manner of a turban, yet the Prince caught the outline of a female figure, which soon descended to the little plain on which they stood and advanced towards them; she was evidently very young, but weather-worn / even in youth: her wild picturesque dress concealed the proportions of her form; her large white sleeves hid her arm, but the emaciated appearance of her face and hands and bare feet struck Richard with pity. She seemed astonished at seeing him, and spoke to his companion in the language of the country, which he did not understand: the Prior's face darkened as she spoke: there dwelt on it a mixture of disappointment and ferocity, of which it could hardly have been deemed capable by one who had hitherto seen it only bland and smiling; swiftly, however, he dismissed these indications of passion, and addressed the Prince calmly. "I cannot go," he said; "my time is still to be deferred, though it shall not be for ever lost. How does your courage hold? if you are not afraid of going alone with a guide whose very dialect is a mystery to you, through a country torn by opposing factions; if you do not fear presenting yourself friendless to a haughty noble who deems himself sovereign in this domain, I will contrive that, ere four hours elapse, you shall find yourself in Desmond's presence." /

"Fear!" the Prince repeated. His eye glanced with some contempt on the priest's cowl, which alone could suggest pardon for such a thought; yet he checked himself from any angry disclaiming of the accusation, as he said, "Whatever in my presumption I may hope, sage forethought tells me that I walk a road strewn with a thousand dangers; leading, it may be, to an early death. Not for that will I deviate one furlong from my path. Sir Prior, where is the guide you promise?"

Keating, after a few minutes' reflection, instead of replying, conversed again

---

[a] Modern county Clare, on the Atlantic coast.

with the girl, and then addressed the Duke: "This hapless child is a victim of the wars; she was born far hence, and is the last surviving of my foster-sister's[a] once blooming family. Her mother saved my life. This child, barefoot as she is, guided me hither. Is not a Keating fallen, when he cannot give succour to an offspring of his fosterer's house? And she, poor girl! she has walked far for me to-day; but she will not slacken in her toil when I bid her proceed. She shall be your guide, and your Grace may rely upon her; / the dog you fed from its birth were less faithful. Now, at the hour of noon, Desmond meets Macarthy of Muskerry,[b] on Ballahourah. But for the bogs and streams that cross your path, it is not far; at the worst, you can reach Mallow, where the Earl will lie to-night.[c] It is best not to delay; for, if there is peace in Munster, very speedily Desmond will be on his way to Thomond."

This was a fresh spur to Richard. He accepted the proffered guide, who listened attentively to Keating's instructions given in her native tongue. He followed the girl but a short distance ere he looked back; the Prior was gone; the solitude of the wild crags and shrubs alone met his eye. Meanwhile his companion stepped forward, motioning him to follow. They plunged into the brake; the sun rose high; the birds winged their glad flight among the trees. Now toiling up a steep, now wading a stream, now entangled in a thicket, now stepping lightly over boggy earth; now meditating on Andalusia, and now wondering at his present position, Richard followed his swift and silent guide / through the wild country between Buttevant and Mallow.

Already the meeting between the Earl of Desmond and Macarthy, the Chief of Muskerry, was at an end. They parted with fair words and exasperated thoughts. The native Lord could ill brook the settler's haughty assumptions; nor Geraldine endure the obstinate pride of the conquered native.[d] Still their relative positions enforced a peace.

They had separated, and after a hasty repast spread on the heathy side of Ballahourah, the Earl proceeded towards Mallow. He was surrounded by warriors, who all claimed the Geraldine name, and who variously distinguished themselves as the White Knight, the Knight of Kerry, and the Knight of the Glen. There was Lord Fermoy, his father-in-law, and others of the Roches. Nor did all the native chiefs absent themselves. One sister of the Earl had married Macarthy Reagh; another an O'Brien, whose daughter had intermarried with an O'Carroll – all this in defiance of the English law, which forbade such

---

[a] Fosterage established bonds more sacred than blood: 'The child of every chief was placed out as soon as born, to be nursed by some of his dependents, and the connection of fosterage was thus formed between that child and those of his nurse' (Leland, I, p. 10).

[b] At this period three MacCarthy chiefs – Muskerry, Reagh, and More – often united against the earls of Desmond. Cormac led the Muskerry MacCarthys from 1461–95.

[c] Hills near Buttevant, which lies about twenty-five miles north of Cork and seven miles north of Mallow.

[d] MacCarthy was Gaelic Irish, the 'native lord'; Desmond, the Anglo-Irish 'settler'.

alliances, through which / the father of the present Earl was beheaded in the year 1467.[a] Their antique costume, tight truise,[b] saffron tunics, and flowing robes distinguished them from the Saxons; yet these had not followed the fashions of the times, but dressed in the garb used by the courtiers of Edward the Third.

Maurice, tenth Earl of Desmond, was brave even to a proverb. He loved war, and deemed himself rather King of Desmond, than a chief of English descent. To extend and secure his possessions, rendering them at once independent of his sovereign and of the native chieftains, was the aim of his life. He now meditated the invasion of Thomond; but Macarthy's angry demeanour showed that he must not be left unchecked in his rear. "Where is my cousin Barry – where the Lord of Buttevant – the Chief of the Barrymores? Flying before a slip of parchment indited in far London, as if my sword held not better sway in these regions than a Parliament attainder! Were he here, the O'Carrolls should hear the thunder of my arms ere this moon waned. Muskerry could make no / gathering in the vales, while Barry sat on his perch at Buttevant."

The Earl had time to waste in thought, as he was borne along – at the age of fifteen, pushing rashly forward an assault, he received a wound in his leg, which lamed him for life, so that he was carried about in a litter, and went by the name of Claudus;[c] yet he was not deemed the less an experienced and gallant warrior. With the virtues of a chieftain he possessed the defects: Munster was his world; his universe was peopled by the Geraldines, the Macarthys, the Barrys, Donegans, Barretts, Roches, O'Briens, O'Carrolls, and the rest; he disdained his noble brethren of the pale. He considered it a mark of distinction to be exempted by a law from attendance of Parliament and the government of the land; he saw in the King of England, not his monarch, but the partizan of Ormond, and therefore an enemy. This, and ancient alliance linked him to the cause of the English outcast Prince, who solicited his aid; he had replied favourably to his request; but his interests and the conquest of a kingdom / must be delayed, while he subdued the half-naked septs who insulted his power.

While thus busied, reflecting upon the events of the day, the Earl sat silent and thoughtful. Suddenly, at a turn in the road, he called on his followers to stop; his eye lighted up, he saw two horsemen swiftly approaching – Lord Barry

---

[a] In 1357 marriages and fosterage between Anglo-Irish and either Gaelic Irish or Anglo-Irish in rebellion, previously regulated, were banned outright by royal decree; the prohibition was widely flouted. The Earl's sister Eleanor (the widow of two Butlers) married an O'Brien, who later became king of Thomond; another sister wed Finghin MacCarthy Reagh, Lord of Carbery, clan leader from 1478–1505. Thomas FitzGerald, 8th Earl of Desmond, served as Lord Deputy of Ireland from 1463–7, but then was declared a traitor and executed in 1468, in part because he had violated the marriage laws.

[b] Probably 'trews', a kind of trouser; OED gives the form 'truis' and 'trouse'.

[c] Latin for 'limping, halting, lame'.

was the foremost rider. Forgetting his lameness in his joy, the noble warrior almost threw himself from the litter, as he cried, "Jesu speed you, my loving cousin! spur on! spur on! remember your badge, *Boutez en avant!*[a] No enemy ever turned his back on your sword to avoid, so eagerly as my arms will open to receive you! Were you bound for Mallow?"

"No, my noble coz," replied Lord Barry, "I am for Kilnemullagh; an eaglet I have nursed, has winged its way thither, and I fear, may suffer injury in my absence; for he is young, and his pinions all untried."

"Leave him to his fate, my Lord," said the Earl; "if he be a faithful bird he will find his way back to his fosterer; meanwhile the King of eagles, thy cousin Desmond himself, has need of thee." /

"One word, dear Maurice, will explain the greater duty that I owe my princely fowl. The White Rose of England, missing him, loses all; you, I, each, and every one of us, are his servants and must become his soldiers."

"Cousin," replied Desmond, "one son of York made my father, whose soul God assoilzie![b] Lord Deputy; another chopped off his head[c] – so much for the White Rose! Still I allow this new Lancastrian king is a bitterer enemy: he is a friend of the Butlers, whom the fiend confound. We will first subdue the O'Carrolls, humble the Macarthys, take Coollong from Clan Cartie Reagh, and root out the Desies;[d] and then, when we are kings of Munster, in good hour let us march with your Duke of York, and set our foot on the necks of the Butlers in Dublin."

The Earl spoke with rapidity and energy; all Munster spread before Lord Barry's mind – city, town, strong-hold, held by ancestral enemies; and it was wonderful what a change was wrought in his mind by his cousin's eloquence, and the names of all these sons of Erin, / with each of whom he had a mortal quarrel. He agreed therefore to go with the Earl to Mallow that evening, postponing his visit to Buttevant till the following day.

Such were the wise counsels, that stayed the mighty power Barry had promised York should rise at his name to vanquish England. It was better thus; so the royal boy thought himself, when, welcomed by Desmond at Mallow, he looked round on kern and gallowglass,[e] hearing a language that was not English, viewing their strange attire and savage countenances. "It is not thus, my England, that I will seize on you. Your own nobles shall place the crown on

---

[a] 'Push forward', the motto of the Barrys and source of the name of their family seat at Buttevant (Leland, I, p. 112).

[b] Alternative form of 'assoil', meaning to absolve or pardon.

[c] The first 'son' was Edward IV; the second, John Tiptoft, Earl of Worcester (?1427-70), appointed Chancellor of Ireland (1464) and later Lord Deputy (1467), with a mandate to subdue the Anglo-Irish aristocracy.

[d] Coollong, unidentified; Clan Cartie Reagh, kin of MacCarthy Reagh; Desies, the most easterly part of Desmond territory.

[e] Retainer of an Irish chieftain.

my head; your people wield the sword that will injure only our common enemy. Shall I make a Granada of my native land, and shed Christian blood, better spilt in the cause of God against infidel dogs?"

When the Earl of Desmond found that the Prince, whom he regretted to receive with such cold hopes, was well content, nothing doubting that the good-will of the English would prove a better ally than the / spears of the Irish, he conceived a sudden affection for him. It was no wonder; for the ingenuousness of untarnished youth is ineffably winning; and here it was added to a quick wit, a grace and gallantry, that shone as a vision of light in this wild region.

A few days brought still greater satisfaction to all parties. An embassy had arrived in Cork from the King of France to the Duke of York to invite him to Paris. Desmond would not relinquish his guest: he carried him to his noble seat at Ardfinnin;[a] and thither repaired in due time the messengers from Charles the Eighth.

The chief of these was our old friend Frion, besides a Frenchman called Lucas, and two Englishmen, Stephen Poytron and John Tiler.[b] The Duke was not well pleased with the selection of Frion; but, while this man by his singular arts of insinuation made good his cause, Barry showed how in two points his cause was benefited by him. First, that having been secretary to Henry, he knew many secrets, and was acquainted with many circumstances that might be turned to use; and, secondly, that his very / attempt to entrap the Prince was a proof that he was fully aware of who he was; that he would prove an useful link between Perkin Warbeck, Richard Fitzroy, and the Duke of York; that he need be no more trusted than was deemed expedient; but that meanwhile it were good to entertain him with fair words. Richard yielded; and Frion made good use of this standing-room by which he meant to move the world.[c] Master of the arts of flattery, cunning and wise, he so ingratiated himself with the Duke, and afterwards with his other friends, that by degrees he was admitted to their confidence; and at last succeeded in his chief wish, of becoming follower, secretary, counsellor, he called himself friend, of the English Prince.

Urged by the Earl of Desmond and Lord Barry, and sufficiently inclined in his own mind, the Duke accepted the French king's invitation, and prepared to cross to France. On the very eve of his departure, he was surprised by a visit from John O'Water of Cork. This warm-hearted old man had conceived a paternal love for the royal youth. He came to recommend / his return to Cork – his taking up a kind of regal residence there – the not deserting a nook of his

---

[a] Town in Tipperary, north-east of Cork.

[b] Names mentioned in Warbeck's confession, incorporated into the chronicle accounts and later histories.

[c] Alluding to the famous saying of Archimedes ('Give me somewhere to stand, and I will move the earth'), a motto of late eighteenth-century radicals. It is one of the epigraphs for P. B. Shelley's *Queen Mab* (1813).

kingdom which acknowledged him. He came too late: – already the Prince was on board the vessel in Youghall Harbour,[a] which was to convey him away. "One day you will return to us, my Lord," said O'Water, "a future day will afford us opportunity to prove our zeal. I am old; I had given up public life: but I will take to the oar again. John O'Water will once more be Mayor of Cork, and his right beloved Sovereign shall command him in his service."

The good man departed; with blessings, thanks, and glad prognostics, Desmond and Barry also took leave of him. The wind was fair, the sea smooth: before morning they lost sight of the hospitable shores of Ireland, and turned their thoughts from its quarrels, its chieftains, its warm hearts, and kind reception, to the civilized land of France, and the more influential protection promised by its king to the Royal Adventurer. /

CHAPTER XVII.

———

She had styled him – the fair White Rose of England.
                                                    FORD.[b]

Long die thy happy days before thy death;
And, after many lengthened hours of grief,
Die neither mother, wife, nor England's queen!
                                        SHAKSPEARE.[c]

———

The voyage of the Duke of York was easy and auspicious. He repaired to Paris; and all the exiled Yorkists, to the number of one hundred gentlemen, instantly gathered round him, offering him their services, and forming his court. Charles assigned him magnificent / apartments in the Tuileries, and appointed a guard of honour, under the command of the Lord of Concressault,[d] who, as was the case with every one who approached him, soon became warmly attached to the

---

[a] Situated midway between the cities of Cork and Waterford.

[b] John Ford (1586–after 1639), *Perkin Warbeck* (1634), I. i. 123–4.

[c] *Richard III*, I. iii. 206–8.

[d] Alexander Monypenny, of Scottish origin. Mary Shelley's sources attest to the royal welcome extended to Warbeck by Charles VIII.

princely youth. Having just concluded a peace with Britany by marrying its young duchess, the King of France found himself in so prosperous a state at home, that he began to look abroad for wars, and resolved to invade Naples, to whose crown he had a claim. Meanwhile, the utmost splendour and gaiety reigned in Paris: – balls, tournaments, and hunting parties, succeeded one to the other; now to celebrate a marriage – now to grace the entrance of some noble gentleman into the order of knighthood. Charles was an amiable prince – his Queen a beautiful and spirited lady – the Duke of Orleans[a] an accomplished and adventurous cavalier. They all vied in acts of courtesy and kindness towards their royal visitor. There was an innocence in Richard's vivacity, an ingenuousness in his reliance on their protection, that particularly / captivated the chivalrous Orleans and the fair Queen Anne. How changed the scene from the wilds of Ireland and the semi-barbarous halls of the Desmond! The courtly and soft grace of the French, different from the dignity of the Spaniard, was irresistible to the inexperienced youth. It seemed to him that his standard was set up here for ever. No change could sully the fair favour of these illustrious friends. All young as he was, to be treated as rightful King of England by this potent government, satisfied for the moment his ambition. He and his English friends welcome every where, all honoured – himself beloved – were the ascendant star in Paris. O'Maurice of Desmond! O'Barry, and good honest-hearted O'Water! – though still he acknowledged your kindness, how did your uncivilized hospitalities fade before the golden splendour of King Charles's court!

York might by the sober be blamed for yielding to the current, for setting his swelling canvas with the favouring wind – exulting. It was a boy's blindness; the unsuspiciousness of inexperience; / the fault lay in the falsehood; and that was not his.

On the sixth of October[b] Henry the Seventh landed at Calais; on the nineteenth he sate down before Boulogne,[c] with sixteen hundred men at arms, and twenty-five thousand infantry. Charles could not much fear the tardy operations of his foe; but the name of English invasion, so associated with defeat and disaster, was portentous to the French: besides, Charles was eager to prepare for his Italian wars. Thus disposed, peace was easily brought about. One only obstacle presented itself. Henry insisted that the newly-arrived Duke of York should be delivered up to him; Charles rejected the proposition with disdain: the negociations were suspended, and the French King grew uneasy; it was no pleasant thing to have thirty or forty thousand of those English in the kingdom, who had disputed it inch by inch, at the expense of so much misery

---

[a] Later Louis XII (1462–1515; ruled 1498–1515); he succeeded Charles VIII as King of France and husband of Anne of Brittany.

[b] '1492' (marginal note in *Abinger/Palacio*).

[c] Boulogne, on the strait of Dover, south of Calais.

and slaughter, with his grandfather.[a] Their King was averse to war; but the body of the army, the nobles and leaders, ardently desired it: some intrigue, some accident, might / light up a train to be quenched only by seas of blood; and all this for a Prince, in whom, except that he was gallant and unfortunate, Charles took no concern.[b]

Richard, basking in the noon-day of regal favour, of a sudden felt a cloud spread athwart his sun-shine, and a chill take place of the glowing warmth. The complaints of his followers, principally of Lady Brampton, opened his eyes; for the King and Princes, on the eve of betraying him, were in manner kinder than ever. First, Queen Anne asked this lady, if it were not the Duke's intention to repair to Flanders, to claim the support of the Lady Margaret. It seemed as if nothing was to be spoken of but Brussels, the Low Countries, Maximilian of Austria, and, above all, the virtues and sagacity of the illustrious widow of Charles the Rash. In youth we are slow to understand the covert language of duplicity. Frion was next put in requisition; he arrived in Paris after ten days' absence, with an invitation to her so-named nephew from the Duchess of Burgundy; and when, from the disinclination of the French to / an act of glaring inhospitality, and of the English so to pain the confiding spirit of their Prince, he was still kept darkling, suddenly one night his friend, the Sire de Concressault, visited him. He brought many sugared words from his sovereigns; but the end was, that their ever dear friend, and most honoured guest, the Duke of York, would render them especial pleasure, if, for some short time, he would visit Brussels. The fiery spirit of youth blazed forth at a dismission, still more when Concressault added, that horses were already prepared, and every thing arranged for his immediate departure. To qualify this insult, Concressault could best bring his own warm, affectionate feelings. He loved the English Prince, and by the frankness of his explanations, soothed him, while he made the wound deeper, by shewing whence it was directed, and that Henry Tudor's was the master-hand.

This name calmed York by elevating his thoughts above the actual evil. "It is well, my Lord: I shall obey," he said; "I had forgotten myself; and your monarch's kindness was an / opiate to my unripened purpose. I might have lived his happy guest; reigning over the English hearts around me, forgetful like Dan Ulysse of old in the Lotus land, of my native isle, and rightful kingdom.[c] I thank my enemy he has not permitted this: his insults rouse me; his injuries place the sword in my hand; on him fall the harm."

The French sovereigns did all they could to salve this ill-favoured wound.

---

[a] Charles VII (1403–61; ruled 1422–61), French sovereign at the conclusion of the bloody Hundred Years War.

[b] The foregoing account faithfully compresses historical sources.

[c] A reference to *Odyssey*, IX, in which Ulysses is tempted to abandon his journey home and live with the Lotus-Eaters in forgetful ease.

The Duke of Orleans visited York at the moment of his departure; his English partizans were loaded with presents; he quitted France; and, on the day following,[a] the treaty of peace with England was signed.

Pride, indignation, and heroic resolve sustained the Duke under this insult; but violent, angry emotion was foreign to his disposition, and only kept alive in his bosom at the expense of much suffering. How gladly he took refuge from these painful sensations in the gratitude and affection inspired by his noble aunt. Margaret had never seen him: the Earl of Lincoln, Lady Brampton, Lovel, Plantagenet, and others / were vouchers for his truth; still his first unsupported appearance in Ireland, and his long absence in Spain engendered doubts, not in her mind, but in Maximilian and other nobles and counsellors around her. She replied to their arguments, but they remained unconvinced; at once therefore to justify her acknowledgment of him in their eyes, and to force them to the same credence as herself, she caused his first audience to be a solemn one, nor gave him a kinswoman's reception until he had proved his right to it.

He, who has heard some one falsely traduced and vilely calumniated, and, if not quite believing the detraction, yet impelled by it to some distaste of its object, and when that object appeared, radiant in innocence, attended by the dignity of truth and conscious worth, at once has yielded to the evidence of sense, will have some understanding of what passed in the mind of Margaret of Burgundy. None could resist the frank, blue, unclouded eye of the Prince; that voice and manner, replete with simplicity and native honour. He replied to the Duchess's questions briefly or otherwise, / as appeared most pertinent, but in a way that vanquished the most sceptical person present. The warm-hearted Duchess had hardly contained herself from the moment she beheld this youthful image of her dead brother. As the tones of a remembered melody awaken from sweet and bitter association unbidden tears, so did his voice, his gestures, the very waving of his glossy curls, strike the mute chords of many a forgotten memory. As soon as she saw belief and satisfaction in the countenances of those around her, she no longer restrained herself; with tears she embraced him; with a broken voice she presented her nephew to all around. Now to heap favours on him was her dear delight: she loved not the name of the Duke of York, because, his pretensions admitted, he was something more; but he objected firmly to the empty title of king, and reiterated his determination to assume that only at Westminster. So she invented other names; the Prince of England, and the White Rose of England, were those he went by; she appointed him a guard of thirty halberdiers[b] in addition to / that formed by his English followers. Nor did she rest here; it was her ardent wish to place him on the throne of his father. The glad welcome she gave to the Yorkists, as, from far exile in distant lands, or obscure hiding in England, they repaired to her nephew's court, her

---

[a] 'Nov. 3' (marginal note in *Abinger/Palacio*).
[b] Soldiers armed with weapons consisting of a battle-axe and pike mounted on a long handle.

discourse of succour, armies, plots quickly raised a spirit that spread to the near island; and the rumour of this new White Rose became a watch-word of hope for York, of fear for Lancaster.

The riches and magnificence of the now extinguished house of Burgundy, almost equalled that of Paris; their cavaliers were as noble and as gallant; their tournaments and feasts as gay and pompous. The Prince felt his situation much changed for the better. His aunt's warm affection was more worth than Charles's politic and courteous protection. There he was an honoured visitor, here one of the family – his interests apparently bound up with theirs. His long tried friends exulted in his position; Plantagenet and Lady Brampton congratu-lated each other. The English exiles, Sir George Neville and Sir / John Taylor, the one proud and discontented, the other extravagant and poor, blessed the day which gave them dignity and station, as chief attendants and counsellors of the noble York. One friend he missed: his childhood's companion, his gentle nurse, his beloved Monina.

She had accompanied Lady Brampton to Paris, when intelligence came of Trangmar's treachery, of the falsehood of his pretensions; and, at the same time, letters were covertly conveyed to Lady Brampton from the Dowager Queen, in which mention was made of this man as a trust-worthy agent: the Yorkists desired much to fathom this mystery, and to have some explicit elucidation from the imprisoned Elizabeth. As they canvassed the various modes by which this might be accomplished – the disguises that might be assumed – Monina preferred an earnest prayer, that she might be permitted to undertake the task; a thousand circumstances rendered this desirable – she would be entirely unsuspected, and she was fully acquainted with the cir-cumstances of the case. Three days before Richard landed in France from Ireland, / Monina crossed to England – she assumed a pilgrim's garb, and without danger or much difficulty, arrived at London from the sea coast.

The sudden apparition of Richard, first in Ireland, and afterwards in Paris, was a stunning blow to Henry. No Trangmar arrived to explain the riddle; and, in spite of his caution and his cruelty, he had been unable to avert the event he dreaded – nothing could he do now better than to scoff at his rival, and to oppose his statements with counter declarations; spreading around his spies to stop at its very outset any symptom of rebellion in England. He caused stricter watch than ever to be set on the unfortunate Elizabeth Woodville, who had been for six years the melancholy inmate of her convent prison. All necessity of caution there was soon to be at an end; her health had long declined – latterly she had wasted to a mere shadow, so that the continuance of life in her attenuated frame appeared a miracle: a feeling of suffocation prevented her from lying down; she sat propped by pillows; her fleshless hands incapable of any office, her cheeks fallen in; / her eyes alone – last retreat of the spirit of life – gleamed brightly amid the human ruin. So long had she been thus, that her death, apparently so near, was hardly feared by those around. Henry almost considered her danger as a new artifice, and absolutely refused her last request, to be permitted to see her daughter and grandchildren once again. Her last hour approached; and none were near save the nuns of the convent, who almost revered her as a saint.

There arrived at the monastery a pilgrim, with relics collected in Araby and Spain. She was admitted into the parlour; and one simple sister asked for some wonder-working relic that might give health to the dying. The pilgrim heard of Elizabeth's hopeless state; she begged to be admitted to her presence, that she might try the virtues of a precious balsam given her by the monks of Alcala-la-Real in Spain. Elizabeth was informed of her request: when last she had heard of her son, he was at Alcala – all the strength that had prolonged her life now roused itself; with earnestness she desired that the Spanish maiden might be admitted to her presence. / It was Henry's express command that none should see her; but she was dying; his power, so soon to be at an end, might well slacken in its rigour at the very verge of its annihilation.

The pilgrim knelt beside the Queen's couch – the nuns, commanded to retreat, observed a miracle – the dying appeared again to live; the grim spectre, who had planted his banner in the chamber, retreated for a moment, as Elizabeth listened to Monina's whispered words, "Oh, for one hour more," she cried, "I have so much to say. He comes then, my son comes! Oh, rouse England with the tale – Sir William Stanley, you must visit him – bid him not draw his sword against my Edward's son. Say to the Dean of St. Pauls[a] – I feel faint," she continued, "my voice fails me – I must leave all unsaid, save this – His sister must not doubt his truth; Henry must not shed the blood of his wife's brother."

"Madam," said Monina, "let me bear some token to my lady the Queen."

"A token! – no words can these weak fingers trace. Yet stay; in this missal there is a prayer which each day I addressed to heaven to preserve / my son. Bear the missal to my Elizabeth, bid her listen to you, and believe."

With trembling hands the young girl took the small, but splendid volume. The Queen then dismissed her with a faintly spoken blessing and a prayer. Before night all was over – the cause of her son moved her no more – her sorrowing heart reposed from every strife – she died. The vase replete with so much anguish was broken – the "silver cord," that bound together a whole life of pain, loosened.[b] Her existence had been woe; her death was the dearest blessing she could receive from Heaven. /

---

[a] Sir William Worseley (c.1435–99), dean under Edward IV, Richard III, and Henry VII, was attainted for treason in 1494 but pardoned the following year.

[b] Ecclesiastes 12: 6.

CHAPTER XVIII.

She was most beautiful to see,
Like a lady of a far countree.
COLERIDGE.^a

While in attendance on the King at his palace of Shene, the Lord Chamberlain Sir William Stanley, was informed that a young and foreign lady requested an audience with him. Monina was ushered in – her extraordinary beauty – her large soft eyes – the fascinating sweetness of her manner, at once charmed the worthy gentleman. She spoke in good but accentuated English, and informed Sir William that she came from the death-bed of the Queen of England. /

"I know," said Stanley, "that her grace has long been ill, but –"

"God take her to his mercy," interrupted Monina, "she died last night."

"Is his majesty informed of this event?" Sir William asked.

"It is not yet noon," replied the maiden, "by that hour the messengers from the convent will arrive. I have reasons for greater speed. I bear the royal lady's last words to her daughter, the Queen Elizabeth; you, my Lord, will favour me by procuring an immediate interview with her majesty."

Stanley knew the aversion the King had to any private intercourse between Elizabeth and her mother. He informed his visitor that she must first obtain the King's permission for this audience, which he did not believe would be granted; but Monina, without hesitation, declared that she would apply for it to the King, and requested the Chamberlain to introduce her. Stanley, good-natured but timid, hesitated – she would not be denied – at last he hit on an expedient. Henry had gone out hawking in the / park; if she would place herself at the gate on his return, she might prefer her prayer – he would be near to insure her being heard.

Noontide approached.[10] The sport was over, and the royal party on their return. Henry rode foremost with Morton, while his retinue followed at a

---

^a *Christabel*, ll. 224–5 (not formally published until 1816, but circulated in manuscript and widely known before then).

slower pace, conversing gaily about the birds; now and then hazarding a remark on the war,[a] so oft delayed, at last declared. They were interrupted by the arrival of Sir William Stanley, who communicated to the King the tidings of the Dowager Queen's death. Six long years had passed since the battle of Stoke, and the commencement of Elizabeth Woodville's imprisonment. She was forgotten at Court. Many there had never seen her; few remembered her as the reigning Queen of England. Her history was almost like a romance of the olden time; yet, forgotten during life, her death clouded the hilarity of those who heard it. Among those most affected by these tidings, as was natural, was her son, the Marquess of Dorset; he hastily rode up to receive from Stanley's own lips confirmation of / the news. Feeling that of late he had almost forgotten and wholly neglected his mother, a sudden visitation of remorse was blended with the grief that choked his voice, and blinded his eyes with tears. Henry, who, was attached to him, viewed with pity the bitter regret of his gay unheeding kinsman, and bade him, ere ruder tongues proclaimed it, bear the melancholy tidings to his royal sister. Dorset, gladly escaping from the throng, rode swiftly forward. Meanwhile the order of the ride was disturbed. The nobles conversed earnestly together. After a few questions, Henry remained lost in thought: eager perhaps to know whether her secret had died with her; and viewing in her demise one master testimony the less in favour of his young competitor. Stanley awaited with some inquietude for the moment when they should encounter Monina. They passed the park gate. She was not there. Henry pursued his way, and entered the palace. Still she did not appear.

Lord Dorset had ridden on with the speed of a man who seeks to escape from himself. Death / has more power in its mere sound, than the enchanting touch of a wizard's rod. She was dead – how awful was that word! – the unfailing friend, his mother! All his remissness towards her took a monstrous form: he felt that if he had wearied Henry with prayers, he might have extorted some mitigation of her suffering; and it would have consoled her in her solitude, to have received the balmy medicine of filial tenderness, which he had neglected to pay. At that moment he would have given his marquisate to a beggar, to have purchased the memory of one action done to sooth her woful end. The pomp of a funeral – masses for her soul – these were small compensations, which her arch enemy, even Henry himself, could and probably would concede. The voice of affection – the duteous affection of a child – he only could have afforded; and he had withheld it.

Monina stood at the park-gate, attended by her Spanish domestic, whose singular costume alone must attract regard. "What do you here, maiden?" cried Dorset; "the King and his / court will speedily pass this way: this is no fitting place for you."

---

[a] Against Charles VIII of France.

"I am here," she replied, "to see and speak to your king. I come to prefer a request in the name of one, whom God take to his place; she can disturb him no more."

"You are from Bermondsey, from – " the words choked Dorset; Monina continued, "I come from the death-bed of the Lady Elizabeth of England."

"What demand would you make on his Majesty?" said the Marquess; "do you seek a guerdon for your pains? Speak then to me – I am her son."

He was about to draw forth his purse, but her look, which grew animated, prevented him, as she said, "I come on a holy errand. The dying lady commanded me to convey her last words to her royal daughter; I seek permission from your King to fulfil her wish."

Dorset was thoughtless and eager. He saw no objection that Henry could have that his sister should have the last message from her now dead parent; so without hesitation he told the / maiden that by Henry's permission he was now about to communicate the sad intelligence to the Queen, and that she might accompany him.

It is thus, by small, invisible threads, that Fate weaves the intricate web of our lives. All hung by the slenderest tissue; had Monina seen Henry, most assuredly he would have prevented the interview she sought, and have used his utmost craft to discover whether the fatal secret made a part of the Queen's message. Now his sagacity, his caution, his severity were of no avail. Monina stood in the presence of his wife.

Six years had considerably altered Elizabeth; habitual fear had engendered a moral timidity, which was not natural to her, for she was the daughter of a proud race: her sweetness, her affectionate disposition still remained; but her soul was sad, and she looked pale and inanimate. The news of her mother's death moved her to tears. One expression of bitter regret burst from her lips; it was mingled with blame of her consort; and she checked herself, while she wept still more abundantly. Dorset felt uneasy at the sight of female tears; he longed to escape. / Monina's request for a private interview came to liberate him; he presented her to his sister, and hurried away.

Elizabeth eagerly asked many questions concerning her mother's dying moments. The Spanish maiden, wondering at her own success, fearful of interruption, presented the missal, and then hastened to declare the motive for which it was sent: she opened the jewelled clasps, and showed the Queen the prayer written in her mother's hand on a blank leaf of the brilliantly illuminated pages: rapidly the enthusiastic girl detailed the escape, the exile of the Duke of York, while Elizabeth, not daring to believe her own senses, astounded, terrified, looked with large open eyes on the animated countenance of her lovely visitant. Before Monina paused, or gave time for an answer, they were interrupted by the entrance of Sir William Stanley. He started when he saw Monina, nor did the confused look of his Queen, as she hastily closed the fatal volume, tend to re-assure him. He came to announce a visit from Henry to Elizabeth.

135

Frightened at what / he saw, he hardly permitted a slight interchange of greeting, but hurried Monina away through a door hid by the tapestry, down a narrow staircase into a garden, and then by a small gate that opened on a court. In this court was placed the entrance to the apartments of the pages and esquires of the King. Stanley unlocked the gate cautiously, hesitating before he permitted his fair companion to pass on, in the fear that some mischievous boy, or prying servitor, might be there to wonder at, and question wherefore he led the maiden from the Queen's garden through a door, sacred, and never opened, into the resort of wild and dissolute youth. As he unclosed the wicket, at its very entrance, standing so that in spite of every caution a full view of Monina was at once afforded, stood a young man, whose countenance bespoke him to be ever on the alert for gamesome tricks, or worse mischief. His first aspect was that of recklessness; his second spoke of baser habits; and athwart both broke gleams, now of better feelings, now of desperate passion. He had heard the rusty bolts move, and perceived / the slow opening of the door: knowing how sacred was the respect enforced towards this ingress to the Queen's retirement, he stood close, to discover and shame any intruder. "In good season, my Lord Chamberlain!" he at first exlaimed, vexed to find no cause for taunt, till perceiving his fair companion, the expression of his countenance changed to irony, as he cried – "Whither so fast and fearfully, my good Lord? Does her Grace deal in contraband: and art thou the huckster?"

"As ill luck will have it, wild Robin Clifford!" cried Stanley, angrily.

"Nay, we are brothers in wildness now, fair Sir," retorted the other, "and I claim my part here."

Clifford approached Monina, but Stanley interposed. "Waste your ribaldry on me, good Knight, but spare this child: let us pass in all speed, I pray you."

Monina drew back, but Clifford still followed. "Child! In good hour she is young; and but that burning suns have made her cheek tawny, I might call her fair. She is well worth your / pains, and I praise them. Sweet mistress, I am beholden to my Lord Chamberlain for making us friends.

He was running on thus, but Monina, collecting her spirits, raised her large eyes on him: his name had caught her ear; she remembered partly having seen him on the night of their flight from Tournay; and frequent mention had subsequently been made of him by the cousins. She began – "Sir Robert Clifford, I know you will not harm me."

"Thanks for that knowledge, pretty one," cried the youth; "old grey beards only, with frozen hearts, (pardon me, Sir William!) could injure thee; thou art sure of good from tall fellows (though in troth, tall I am not) like me."

Sir William writhed with impatience; again and again he would have interrupted the intruder. Monina replied – "We have met before – when you served him I now serve. I speak in his name: for the sake of PERKIN WARBECK detain me no longer. Noble Sir, I attend you: Sir Clifford yields respect to the words I have spoken." /

"They are strange indeed, maiden," he replied, "and I must hear more of this. We have met before, I now believe; and we must meet again. Meanwhile, I will keep off bird-catchers till you and his reverence get clear of these limed twigs. Ah! I see a gallant; I will go draw William d'Aubigny[a] aside while you pass forth."

And now again Sir William proceeded on his expedition, and conducted his gentle companion beyond the precincts of the palace. As they parted one from the other, Monina, in a brief energetic manner, delivered the message of the departed Queen to the good Chamberlain: he was more disconcerted than surprised, and the reflection, that Clifford was a party to the secret, added to his consternation. He felt how far he was compromised by the introduction of Monina to the young Queen; fear for a while palsied his better feelings; he replied only by entreating her not to remain longer in London, but to embark in all haste for France: he then quitted her, yet again came back to ask where she sojourned in town, and / turned away a second time, as if to escape from his better self, and from the interest he felt in King Edward's son, which impelled him to ask a thousand questions.

He returned to the court-yard of the Palace, and found Clifford pacing its length in deep thought. Monina's words had awakened a thousand ideas in his unquiet bosom. Since the event to which she referred, when he delivered Richard from Frion's hands, he had run a headlong, ruinous course. No character can be wholly evil; and Clifford's was not destitute of good, though overgrown and choked up by weedy vices, so that his better nature too often served but as a spur and incentive to folly and crime. He was generous; but that led to rapacity; since, unable to deny himself or others, if he despoiled himself one day, on the next he engaged in the most desperate enterprises to refil the void. He was bold – that made him fearless in doing wrong; and to drown the gentle spirit of humanity, which too often for his own peace sprung up in his heart, he hardened himself in selfishness; then, as his sensitive, undisciplined nature received new impressions, / he was cowardly, cruel, and remorseless. He had never forgotten the princely boy he had saved: he turned to that recollection as to one of the few Oases of virtue in the far extended desart of ill, over which, in hours of satiety or despondency, his sickening memory wandered. Indeed, he was yet too young to be decidedly vicious, for at one-and-twenty a thousand mere human impulses, unrepressed by worldly wisdom, occasion sallies of kindly sympathy. The worst was, that Clifford was a ruined man: his fortunes were nought, his reputation shaken on its base: he veiled, by an appearance of hilarity and recklessness, the real despair that gnawed at his heart, when he considered all that he might have been – the worse than nothing that he was. Hitherto he had, to a great degree, blinded the world, and he

---

[a] For D'Aubigny (or Daubeney or Dawbeny), see pp. 159, 160n.

longed for some adventure, some commotion, either public or private, that should refil his emptied money-bags, and paint him fair in men's eyes: all these considerations mingled incongruously to make him wish to know more of the outcast Duke. He awaited the return of Stanley – he learned the name of the Spanish / girl: as they spoke, both became aware that the other possessed a secret each dreaded to avow. Clifford first dashed through the flimsy barrier of useless discretion, and related his adventure at Lisle; meantime Sir William broke forth in lamentation, that young Richard should have been induced to quit the security of private life, to enter on an unequal and bloody contest, which could only end in destruction to himself and his partizans, while England would again be made the tomb of the Irish (the landing of Richard at Cork was all that was then known), whom he might allure from their woods and bogs to ravage the more gifted sister isle. A new light was let in on Clifford at these words. Was the game already playing – the box shaken – the die about to fall? This required his attention, and determined his half-formed purpose of visiting, that same night, the daughter of de Faro.

END OF VOL. I. /

THE

FORTUNES

OF

PERKIN WARBECK,

A ROMANCE.

BY THE

AUTHOR OF "FRANKENSTEIN."

J'ai veu filz d'Angleterre, Richard d'Yorc nomme.
Que l'on disoit en terre, extinct et consommé,
Endurer grant souffrance ; et par nobles exploitz,
Vivre en bonne esperance, d'estre Roy des Angloys.
Old French Chronicle.

IN THREE VOLUMES.

VOL. II.

LONDON:

HENRY COLBURN AND RICHARD BENTLEY,
NEW BURLINGTON STREET.

1830.

PERKIN WARBECK.

CHAPTER I.

His father was a right good lord,
  His mother a lady of high degree;
But they, alas! were dead him frae,
  And he loved keeping companie.

To spend the day with merry cheer,
  To drink and revel every night;
To card and dice from eve to morn,
  It was, I ween, his heart's delight.

THE HEIR OF LYNNE.[a]

It had been Monina's design to return to the protection of Lady Brampton, immediately on the fulfilment of her task in England. The appearance of Clifford suggested other ideas. It was the duty of every friend of York to declare / his existence, and claim the allegiance of his subjects. It might seem a hopeless enterprise for her, a young foreign girl, to do this in the heart of the usurper's power; and yet she fancied that she might attempt it with success. The most distant prospect of serving her beloved friend was hailed by her with romantic ardour; while the knowledge possessed by Stanley and Clifford, promised to render her undertaking less nugatory in its effects. Her purpose was quickly formed. She resolved to postpone her departure, and to busy herself in replanting, in Tudor's own city of London, the uprooted rose-bush, parent of the spotless flower. None but a woman's fond enthusiastic heart can

---

[a] Percy, *Reliques*, series 2, II, 5, ll. 5–12.

tell the glow of joy, the thrilling gladness, that diffused itself through her frame, as this plan spread itself, clear as a map, beauteous as a champagne country viewed from some overtopping mountain peak, to her keen mind's eye. She rode to London occupied by these thoughts, and on her arrival, announced to the merchant friend, at whose house she resided, her intention of remaining in England: / the vessel that was on the morrow to have conveyed her away would bear instead a letter to Lady Brampton, explanatory of her hopes and intentions; that very night in the seclusion of her chamber, she robbed some hours from sleep to write it; her enthusiasm animated her expressions; her cheek glowed as she wrote, for she spoke of services she might render to him who was the idol of her thoughts; though with this idea she consciously mingled no feeling save that of devoted friendship and an intense desire to benefit. The weariness of spirit that oppressed her in his absence, she did not attribute to him.

Thus intently occupied, she was unaware of a parley in the room beneath growing into a loud contention, till steps upon the stairs recalled her wandering thoughts; she looked up from her task; but her gaze of inquiry was changed to an expression of heartfelt pleasure, when Sir Robert Clifford entered the apartment. Here then her enterprise commenced. There was something that did not quite please her in the manners of her visitant, but this was / secondary to the great good she might achieve through him. Her eyes danced in their own joy, as she cried, "Welcome, gallant gentleman! you are here to my wish: you come to learn how best you may prove your allegiance to your rightful sovereign, your zeal in his cause."

These words grated somewhat on the ear of a man who had hitherto worn the Red Rose in his cap, and whose ancestors had died for Lancaster. He did not, therefore, reply in the spirit of her wish when he said, "We will not quarrel, pretty one, about names; sooth is it, that I came to learn tidings of my princely gossip, and I am right glad that fortune makes thee the tale-bearer. Prolong as thou wilt, I shall never cry hold, while my eyes serve to make true harmony to the sound of your sweet voice."

Much more he said in the same strain of gallantry, as he placed himself beside the maiden, with the air of one whose soft speeches ever found ready hearing. Monina drew back, replying, gently, "I am the partizan, the vowed conspirator for a cause, whose adherents walk as over / the thread-broad bridge spanning an unfathomable gulph, which I have heard spoken of by the Moors in my own Granada; I beseech you, as you are a gentleman, reserve your fair speeches for the fortunate ladies of your native land. I will be a beacon-light to guide you, a clue for your use through a maze, a landmark to point your way; meanwhile, forget me as I am; let me be a voice only."

"As soon forget sunshine or moonshine, or the chance of play when the dice-box rattles," thought Clifford, as she clasped her little fingers in the fervour of her wish, and raised on him her soft, full eyes: but though he gazed with unrepressed admiration, he said nothing as she told the story of Duke Richard's Spanish adventures, and last of his attempt in Ireland and the embassy sent to him by King Charles. How eloquently and well she told his tale! speaking of him with unfeigned admiration, nothing disguising her zealous devotion. "Sir Clifford," she continued, "you are his friend. His cause will sanctify your sword; it will call you from the paltry arts of peace to the / nobler deeds of chivalry; it will give you grace in the eyes of her you love, defending and asserting your king."

She paused breathless from her own agitation; she looked up into his thoughtful face and placed her hand on his; the soft touch awoke him from a reverie in which he had lost himself.

"Maiden," he replied, "you plead your cause even too well; you have cast a spell upon me; so that at this moment I would readily swear to perform your bidding, but that, when I do not see your witch's eyes, nor hear your magic voice, another wind may blow me right to the other side. Do not call this courtly gallantry, would by Saint Cupid that it were! for I am not pleased to behold my sage self fined down into a woman's tool: nor is it love; – Thor's hammer could not knock a splinter from my hard heart, nor the Spanish sun thaw its sevenfold coat of ice. I never have loved; I never shall: but there is some strange sorcery about you. When I next see you, I will draw a circle round, knock my head three times on the eastern floor, and call out 'aroint!' This twinkling light / too, and darkling hour – I must away: – sunshine shall, when next we meet, protect me from your incantations. Will you trust yourself? At tomorrow's noon a servitor of mine shall await you at the gate of St. Paul's, dare you commit yourself to one in the Devil's pay?"[a]

All this incoherent talk was spoken at intervals; he rose, sat down, stood over her as she patiently let him run his tether's length: his last words were said in an insinuating, and, as well as he could command, a soft voice, as he pressed her hand in his. She crossed herself, as she replied, "Our Lady and my cause shall protect me, while I adventure life fearlessly for its sake! Adieu till then, Sir Knight: the saints guard you, and give you better thoughts."

The cavalier proceeded homewards, considering deeply the part he was to act. He thought of what he might gain or lose by siding with the Duke; and he was angry to find that the image of Monina presented itself even more vividly, than his ambitious dreams. "God assoil me," thought he. "I will repeat a paternoster backwards, and so unsay her sorceries. She has / persuaded me, even as my own soul did before, that the best mode to mend my broken fortunes, and better still to regild my faded escutcheon, is to join Duke

---

[a] Clifford's manner of speech discloses his affinities with stage villains and gothic anti-heroes. His awareness of Thor, the Norse god of thunder, presumably stems from his roots in the Lake District counties, where vestiges of Thor worship, a legacy of Norse settlements between AD 800–1000, persisted as late as the mid-eighteenth century.

Richard. Yet, after all, this may be mere magic; for once I will act a wise man's part, and seek old gray-beard, my Lord Fitzwater."

Lord Fitzwater endured impatiently the harsh countenance Henry bore to him, ever since he had permitted his young rival to escape. Some question of right and law which implicated a large portion of his possessions, had, as he believed, been unjustly decided against him through the interposition of the king, who, on every occasion, sought to mortify and injure the old man. He lived as the disgraced and impoverished servants of a court are wont to live, neglected and forgotten. He had no family. He loved Robert Clifford better than any other in the world; and he, when suffering from disappointment or loss, when his own pain reminded him of that of others, sought his ancient friend – too seldom to please him with a show of reverence, often enough to keep alive his affection. /

If it were good for him to aid in the replanting of the White Rose, so also were it well that Lord Fitzwater joined the same party. He talked even to himself of asking his experienced friend's advice; he really meant to endeavour to seduce him into a companionship in the projected rebellion against Henry Tudor. In this spirit he paid his visit; nearly three months had elapsed since his preceding one. The noble received him coldly; so at once to break through the ceremony that fettered their discourse, he cried, "I hear from soft Sir William Stanley, that his Majesty has again said that he will find a way to thank you for a service you rendered him some six years ago."

"I have long had knowledge of his Grace's good memory on that point," answered his Lordship, angrily; "and yours, methinks, might remind you of the part you played. By St. Thomas, Robin, I believe you saw further in the game than I. But what makes the King harp on this out-worn tale?"

"Few know – we may guess. Have you not / heard tell of a new king of kerns and gallowglasses? a phantom duke, whose duchy lies without the English pale in Ireland? a ghost whose very name makes the King's knees knock together as he sits on the throne? This ruffler, who calls himself son of Edward the Fourth, the prince Richard of York, escaped from the Tower, bears a strange resemblance to the hero of Lisle, Perkin Warbeck."

"Would, by St. George, he were the same!" exclaimed the noble; "my dagger should sever the entwined roses, our armed heels tread to dust the cankered red blossom."

"You speak treason, my lord," said Clifford; "but you speak to a friend. Let us talk more calmly. I, the playmate of the imprisoned Prince, know that he, Perkin Warbeck, and the Irish hero are the same – this I can prove: so much for the justice of our cause; as to the expediency, – we, my good lord, are styled Lancastrians, but our meed therefore is small. Tudor is a niggard king; Plantagenet, a young and generous adventurer. What shall we say? / Shall Fitzwater and Clifford place the sacred diadem on this boy's head, and become chiefs in the land where they now pine obscurely?"

144

Lord Fitzwater fastened his keen eyes on his companion, while his hand involuntarily grasped his dagger's hilt. "I am not an old man," he cried; "fifty-seven winters have shed no snows upon my head. I remember when, at Tewkesbury, I smote an iron-capped yeoman who raised his battle-axe against our young Edward, and clove the villain to the throat. I can wield the same weapon – do the same deed now; and I am thrown like a rusty sword among old armour – refused permission to lead my followers to Calais. War in France! – it will never be: the word is grown obsolete in England. Ambassadors thrive instead of valiant captains; crafty penmanship in lieu of straitforward blows. Art sure, Robin, that this youth is King Edward's son?"

This was the first step Clifford took; and the eagerness of Fitzwater quickly impelled him to spread wider the narrow circle of conspirators. The intelligence meanwhile, that the King of France had received in Paris with meet honour / a Yorkist pretender to the crown, burst at once over England, spreading wonder and alarm. Some few despised the pretensions of the youth; the greater number gave to them full and zealous credence. Many, dreading Henry's sagacity and harshness, recoiled from every thought rebellious to him; others hailed with joy the appearance of a rival who would shake his throne, and hold forth hope of disturbance and change. As yet this was talk merely; nay, there was more thought, than spoken. Men expected that some other would make the first move, which would put in play the menacing forces mustered on either side. Monina saw with joy the work well begun. She remembered the Queen's injunction to seek the Dean of St. Paul's: in acquiring him, many reverent and powerful partizans were secured. Her presence added to the interest which the mere name of Richard of York excited. Many who disbelieved his tale, were eager to behold his lovely advocate; they listened to her syren eloquence, and ranged themselves on her side. Clifford watched jealously the influence she acquired. When / he first saw her, she had been an untaught girl in comparison with the graceful, self-possessed being who now moved among them. One feeling in her heart separated her indeed from the crowd – but this was veiled, even to herself; and she appeared courteous, benign to all. Clifford often flattered himself that when she spoke to him her expressions were more significant, her voice sweeter. He did not love – no, no – his heart could not entertain the effeminate devotion; but if she loved him, could saints in heaven reap higher glory? Prompted by vanity, and by an unavowed impulse, he watched, hung over her, fed upon her words, and felt that in pleasing her he was for the present repaid for the zeal he manifested for the Duke her friend. Strange he never suspected that she was animated towards the Prince by a deeper feeling. They had lived like near relations from their childhood; that were sufficient to raise the flame that shed so bright a light over her soul: that he was a prince, and she the daughter of a Spanish mariner, forbade their union; and he paid the just tribute to innocent youth, in not judging of / its upright purity by the distorted reflection his depraved heart presented, whenever he dared turn his eyes inward.

Foundation was thus laid in England for a momentous combination. Intelligence from the continent was gathered with keen interest. Early in December[a] the army of Henry recrossed the Channel: they brought word of the favour and esteem Richard enjoyed at the French court, of the zeal of the exiled Yorkists, of their satisfied assurance of his truth. Next was spread abroad the news of his reception by the Dowager Duchess of Burgundy, and the brilliant figure he made at Brussels. What step would be taken next to advance his cause?

This was a fearful question for the actual King of England. He redoubled his artful policy, while he wore a mask of mere indifference. The Yorkists, not yet considerable enough to act openly, or even covertly to combine for any great attempt, felt fresh bonds thrown over, new and vexatious tyrannies in exercise against them. This served to unite / and animate their chiefs; they each and all resolved that, when fit opportunity armed their Prince, their swords should at the same moment leap from the scabbards, darkly to be dyed ere resheathed, or struck useless from their lifeless hands. The days of St. Albans and Tewkesbury passed in all their grim conclusions before their eyes, but the event was worth the risk: defeated, they lost nothing; victorious, they exchanged a narrow-hearted, suspicious, exacting tyrant for a chivalrous and munificent sovereign; Henry Tudor, the abhorred Lancastrian, for the grandson of York, the lineal heir of Edward the Third – the true representative of the kings of the glorious and long line of the Plantagenets. /

---

[a] '1492' (marginal note in *Abinger/Palacio*).

CHAPTER II.

———

Like one lost in a thorny wood,
That rents the thorns, and is rent with the thorns,
Seeking a way, and straying from the way;
Not knowing how to find the open air,
But toiling desperately to find it out.

SHAKSPEARE.[a]

———

In the days of our earlier history, our commerce led us to have more intercourse with Flanders than with France. That which journeyed slowly and doubtfully from Paris came in all the heat of a first impression from the Low Countries. A train had been laid before, which now took light and blazed through the kingdom. The Duchess of Burgundy's reception of the Duke of York, the honours rendered him at her / court, the glad gathering together of the fugitive English, gave pledge of his truth, and promise of glorious results. Sedition began to spring up in England on every side; even as, after a mild rain in the birth of the year, a black, ploughed field is suddenly verdant with the young blades of wheat. All who had, since the battles of Bosworth and of Stoke, lived in seclusion or fear; all who from whatever reason had taken sanctuary; men of ruined fortunes, who desired to escape bondage; came singly or in small companies to the coast, embarked for the continent, and hastened to the court of the Dowager of Burgundy. All discontented men, who felt themselves looked coldly on by Tudor, to whom they had yielded the throne of their native land; many, whom it grieved and vexed to see the world stagnate in changeless peace, desirous of novelty and glad of any pretence that called them into activity, dashed headlong into revolt; nor were there few, chiefly indeed among the nobility, who had lamented the fall of the House of York, and hailed gladly this promise of its resuscitation. The common adventurers / and soldiers of fortune acted on their single separate resolves; the noble adherents of the White Rose drew together, that there might be plan and strength in their

———

[a] *3 Henry VI*, III. ii. 174–8.

147

schemes. They were cautious, for their enemy was crafty and powerful; they were resolute, for they hated him.

Out,[a] far in the low flats bordering the river Lea,[b] there stood, in a marshy hollow, a straggling village, now effaced from the landscape. At its extremity was a solid, but gloomy, square, brick house, surrounded by a moat, which the low watery soil easily filled even to overflow; and the superfluity was received in a deep stagnant pool at the back of the mansion. The damp atmosphere had darkened the structure, and thrown a mantle of green moss and speckled lichen over the bricks. Its fantastically carved and heavy portal yawned like a black cavern's mouth, and added to the singularly desolate appearance of the mansion. The village was but half inhabited, and looked as struck by poverty and discomfort. The house belonged to the Clifford family. It had been built, it was said, in Henry the Fifth's[c] time, when Sir Roger / Clifford, a stern old man, following his sovereign to the wars, shut up here his beautiful young wife, so to insure her fidelity during his absence.[d] Among her peers and gentle companions, the Lady Clifford had doubtless been true to the bond that linked her to her lord; but, alone in this solitary mansion, surrounded by ill nurtured[11] peasants, pining for her father's pleasant halls and her girlish enjoyments, no wonder that she found her state intolerable. Age and jealousy are ill mates for youth and sprightliness, and suspicion easily begets that which it abhors even to imagine. One who had loved her in her virgin days, introduced himself into her suite; the brief months of stolen happiness passed by, and the green stagnant pool was, they said, the cold sepulchre of the betrayed lovers. Since then, during the wars of York and Lancaster, this house had been the resort of Clifford's followers: and, when the White Rose became supreme, that alone of the family possessions had not been forfeited to the crown: it was the last relic of Sir Robert's fortunes. His few tenantry, hard pressed for rent to satisfy his necessities, / had deserted their abodes; the green acres had passed into other hands; a band of poor cotters alone remained, and this old house haunted by the ghosts of those who slept beneath the waveless pool, dilapidated, disfurnished. Yet here the wild knight had held lawless carousals; hither he sometimes fled to hide after some ruinous loss, or when he was pursued by those who sought to avenge insults committed during drunken brawls.

Now it would seem some orgie was meditated: liveried servants, one or two only bearing Clifford's coat, the rest wearing different badges, as belonging to different masters, had arrived during the previous day. Some of the ruined huts were pulled down to supply firewood, and the old chimnies sent out volumes of smoke; various carts, laden, some with eatables, fat bucks, young calves,

---

[a] '1493' (marginal note in *Abinger/Palacio*).
[b] River in Hertfordshire.
[c] Henry V (1387–1422; ruled 1413–22).
[d] Unidentified.

pheasants, hares, and partridges, piles of bread, seven hooped casks of wine, were unladen in the mildew-stained hall. Other carts followed the first, bearing bedding, apparel, furniture, and, it was whispered by the idling villagers, arms. Several apartments were strewed / thick with rushes, and the blazing fires, in spite of the tattered plaster and stained ceilings, imparted cheerfulness to the rooms. There was need of internal warmth; a thick snow-storm fell, sheeting the low fields, which, uninterspersed by trees, now looked doubly wild and drear. The waters of the moat and pool were frozen; a sharp north-wind whistled round the house. For the first time for many years its poor dependents were cheered during the severe season by the crumbs, or rather large portions of superfluous food, from the mansion of their landlord.

The first guest that arrived came in a close litter, attended by a Moorish servant, and Clifford himself on horseback. Monina had forgotten her Flemish home: bright Andalusia, its orange groves, myrtle and geranium hedges, the evergreen forests which embowered Alcala, and the fertile laughing Vega of Granada, formed her image of such portions of fair earth, as, unincumbered by houses, afforded on its green and various surface sustenance to its inhabitants. She shivered before the northern blast, and / gazed appalled on the white plain, where the drifting snow shifted in whole showers, as the wind passed over it. The looks of the people, sallow, ill-clothed, and stupid, made her turn from comtemplating them, as she yet answered the contemptuous and plaintive remarks of her Spanish attendant in a cheerful, deprecating voice.

For two successive days other guests continued to arrive. They were chiefly men of note, yet came attended by few domestics. There was Lord Fitzwater, dissatisfied at the part of rebel he was forced he thought to play; and on that account he was louder than any against King Henry. Sir Simon Mountford was a Yorkist of the days of Edward the Fourth, he personally hated Richmond, and looked on Richard's as a sacred cause. Sir Thomas Thwaites had been a friend of the Earl of Rivers, and gladly seized this occasion to avenge his death, attributable to the dastardly policy of Henry. William Daubeny was attached to the Earl of Warwick, and entered warmly into projects whose success crowned his freedom. Sir Robert Ratcliffe, cousin / of Lord Fitzwater, had lived in poor disguise since the battle of Stoke, and gladly threw off his peasant's attire to act the soldier again in a new war of the Roses. Sir Richard Lessey had been Chaplain to the household of Edward the Fourth. Sir William Worseley, Dean of St. Paul's, was a rare instance of gratitude outliving the period of receiving benefits; he had been a creature, and was a sincere mourner, of the late Queen. Many others, clergy and laity, entered the plot; a thousand different motives impelled them to one line of conduct, and brought them to Clifford's moated-house, to conspire the overthrow of Tudor, and the exaltation of the Duke of York to the throne. One only person invited to this assembly failed, Sir William Stanley; each voice was loud against his tergiversation, and Clifford's whispered sarcasm cut deeper than all.

149

The debates and consultations lasted three days. After infinite confusion and uncertainty, the deliberations brought forth conclusions that were resolved upon unanimously. First, the house they then occupied, and the village, was to / be a repository for arms, a rendezvous for the recruits of the cause. The conspirators levied a tax on themselves, and collected some thousand pounds to be remitted to the Prince. They regulated a system, whose object was to re-awaken party-spirit in England, and to quicken into speedy growth the seeds of discontent and sedition, which Henry's avarice and extortion had sown throughout the land. Those who possessed estates and followers were to organize troops. And last, they deputed two of their number to go over to the Duchess of Burgundy, and to carry their offers of service to her royal nephew. The two selected for this purpose were, first Sir Robert Clifford, who had known the Duke formerly, and who it was supposed would be peculiarly welcome to him; and secondly, Master William Barley, a man advanced in years; he had combated in nearly all the twelve pitched and sanguinary battles that were fought between York and Lancaster. He had been a boy-servitor to the old Duke of York; a yeoman of Edward's guard; an halberdier in Richard the Third's time. He / had been left for dead on the field of Bosworth, but came to life again to appear at the battle of Stoke. He had risen in the world, and was a man of substance and reputation: he was not noble; but he was rich, zealous, and honest.[a]

The meeting lasted three days, and then gradually dispersed. All had gone well. An assembly, whose individuals were noble, wealthy, or influential, united to acknowledge Richard as their liege. Foreign potentates declared for him; and hope was high in every bosom at all these forerunners of success. Monina's enthusiastic heart beat with ecstacy. Young – the innocent child of unsophisti-cated impulse, her gladness showed itself in wild spirits and unconstrained expressions of exultation. She and Clifford returned to London together, for he contrived tacitly and unsuspected by her, to instal himself as her habitual escort. Happy in expectation of her beloved friend's success, she talked with-out reserve; and the genius, which was her soul's essence, gave power and fascination to every thing she said. She spoke of Spain, of Richard's adventures there, of her father / and his voyages. The name of Columbus was mentioned; and the New World – source of wondrous conjecture. They spoke of the desolate waste of waters that hems in the stable earth – of the golden isles beyond: to all these subjects Monina brought vivid imagery, and bright paint-ing, creations of her own quick fancy. Clifford had never before held such discourse. In hours of sickness or distaste, at moments of wild exhilaration, when careering on a high-mettled horse beneath the stars of night, fanned by a strong but balmy wind, he had conceived ideas allied to the lofty aspirations of

---

[a] The conspirators and their chosen representatives are named in the accounts that Mary Shelley read.

our nature; but he cast them off as dreams, unworthy of a wise man's attention. The melodious voice of Monina, attuned by the divine impulses of her spirit, as the harp of the winds by celestial breezes, raised a commotion in his mind, such as a prophetess of Delphi felt, when the oracular vapour rose up to fill her with sacred fury. A word, a single word, was a potent northern blast to dash aside the mist, and re-apparel the world in its, to him, naked, barren truth. So fervently, and so sweetly did she speak of Richard, that / Clifford's burning heart was in a moment alight with jealousy; and the love he despised, and thought he mastered, became his tyrant, when it allied itself to his evil passions. He looked angry, he spoke sharply – Monina was astonished; but his libellous insinuations fell innocuous on her pure mind: she only felt that she feared him, half disliked him, and, trembling and laughing as she spoke, said, "Well, well; I will not care for your angry mood. You are going soon: ere you return, our Prince will, by his own bright example, have taught you better things. Learn from him diligently, Sir Knight, for he is all courtesy and nobleness."

Clifford laughed bitterly, and a base resolve of lowering the high-hearted York to his own degrading level arose in his breast: it was all chaos there as yet; but the element, which so lately yielded to a regular master-wind of ambition, was tossed in wild and hideous waves by – we will not call the passion love – by jealousy, envy, and growing hate. Short interval was allowed for the gathering of the storm; he was soon called upon to fulfil his commission, and to / accompany Master William Barley on their important embassy to Brussels.

The scene here presented, operated a considerable change on these personages; arriving from England, where the name of the White Rose was whispered, and every act in his favour was hid in the darkness of skulking conspiracy, to his court at Brussels, where noble followers clustered round him, and the Duchess, with a woman's tact and a woman's zeal, studied how best to give importance and splendour to his person and pretensions. The spirit of the Yorkist party, in spite of her natural mildness, still glowed in the bosom of this daughter of Henry the Sixth's unhappy rival, – the child of disaster, and bride of frantic turbulence. Opposed to the remorseless Louis the Eleventh, struggling with the contentious insolence of the free towns of Flanders, war appeared to her the natural destiny of man, and she yielded to its necessity, while her gentle heart sorrowed over the misery which it occasioned.

She first received Clifford and Barley; and with the winning grace of a sovereign, solicited / for her nephew their affection and support: then she presented them to him – this was the fair-haired, blue-eyed boy, whom Clifford saved, the gentle, noble-looking being, whose simplicity awed him; whose bright smile said, "I reign over every heart." The Knight shrunk into himself: how had he dyed his soul in a worldliness which painted his countenance in far other colours. – He was not deficient in grace: his dark-grey eyes, veiled by long lashes, were in themselves exceedingly handsome: the variableness of his face, traced with many unseasonable lines, yet gave him the power of assuming a pleasing expression; and his person, though diminutive, was eminently elegant, while his self-possession and easy address, covered a multitude of faults. Now, his first resolve was to insinuate himself into Richard's affections; to become a favourite; and consequently to lead him blindly on the path he desired he should tread.

The Prince's spirits were high; his soul exulted in the attachment of others, in the gratitude that animated him. Until Clifford's / arrival (Edmund was for the time in England), Sir George Neville, among his new friends, held the first place. He was proud and reserved; but his aristocracy was so blended with honour, his reserve with perfect attention and deference to the feelings of others, that it was impossible not to esteem him, and find pleasure in his society. Clifford and Neville made harsh discord together. Richard, inexperienced in the world, sought to harmonize that which never could accord: Neville drew back; and Clifford's good humour, and apparent forbearance, made him appear to advantage.

At this period ambassadors from Henry arrived at Brussels: they had been expected; and as a measure of precaution, Richard left that place before their arrival, and took up his temporary abode at Audenarde,[a] a town which made part of the dowry of the Duchess Margaret. All the English, save Lady Brampton, attended him to his retreat. The ambassadors, in their audience with the Archduke, demanded the expulsion of Richard from the Low Countries, taunting the Duchess with her support of the / notorious impostor, Lambert Simnel, and speaking of the Duke of York as a fresh puppet of her own making. They received the concise reply – that the gentleman she recognized as her nephew, inhabited the territory of her dowry, of which she was sovereign, and over which the Archduke had no jurisdiction: however, that no disturbance might occur in their commercial relations, which would have roused all Flanders to rebellion, Maximilian was obliged to temporize, and to promise to afford no aid to the illustrious exile.[b]

Their audience accomplished, the ambassadors had only to return. They remained but one night at Brussels: on this night, Sir Edward Poynings and Doctor Warham,[12] who fulfilled his mission,[c] were seated over a cup of spiced wine, in discourse concerning these strange events, the Lady Margaret's majestic

---

[a] Now in Belgium, about fifteen miles south of Ghent and thirty-one miles west of Brussels.

[b] Mary Shelley appears to conflate Philip (1478–1506), Archduke of Burgundy (a title inherited from his mother, Marie), and his father, Maximilian. Henry's exploitation of the trade issue brought father and son to heel. Philip became founder of the Habsburg dynasty in Spain by marrying Joan the Mad, daughter of Ferdinand and Isabella.

[c] When Poynings (1459–1521) served as Ireland's Lord Deputy, the laws (which bear his name) subjecting the Irish parliament to the control of the English king and council were enacted. William Warham (?1450–1532), held many political and ecclesiastical posts before serving as Lord Chancellor and Archbishop of Canterbury under Henry VII and Henry VIII. Mary Shelley made a marginal correction to 'Warham' from 'Wattam' in *Abinger/Palacio* and underscored two more misspellings on page 153; see Endnotes 12, 13, 14.

demeanour, and the strangeness of her supporting this young man, if indeed he were an impostor; when a cavalier, whose soiled dress and heated appearance bespoke fatigue and haste, entered the room. It was Sir Robert / Clifford: they received him as liege subjects may receive a traitor, with darkened brows and serious looks. Clifford addressed them in his usual careless style: – "Saint Thomas shield me, my masters; can you not afford one benizon to your gossip! Good Sir Edward, we have ruffled together, when we wore both white and red in our caps; and does the loss of a blood-stained rag degrade me from your friendship?"

The bitter accusations of the Knight, and the Doctor's sarcasms, which were urged in reply, awoke a haughty smile. "Oh, yes!" he cried, "ye are true men, faithful liege subjects! I, an inheritance of the block, already marked for quartering, because I am for the weak right, you for the strong might. Right, I say – start not – the Mother of God be my witness! Duke Richard is Duke Richard – is lord of us all – true son of the true king, Ned of the White Rose, whom you swore to protect, cherish, and exalt; you, yes, even you, Sir Knight. Where is now your oath? cast from heaven, to pave / the hell where you will reap the meed of your lying treachery!"

Clifford, always insolent, was doubly so now that he felt accused of crimes of which he did not deem himself guilty; but which would (so an obscure presentiment told him) hereafter stain his soul. Doctor Warham[13] interposed before Poynings' rising indignation: "Wherefore come you here, Sir Robert?" he asked. "Though we are envoys of the king you have betrayed, we may claim respect: Sir Edward, as a gentleman and a cavalier – I as an humble servitor of the Lord Jesus, in whose name I command you not to provoke to a bloody deed the messengers of peace."

"Cease to taunt me with a traitor's name," replied Sir Robert, "and I will chafe no further the kindling blood of my sometime friend. Let us rather leave all idle recrimination. I came hither to learn how wagged the world in London town, and, as a piece of secret intelligence, to assure you that you wrongfully brand this stripling for an impostor. Be he sovereign of our land or not – be it right or wrong to side with York / against Lancaster – York he is, the son of Edward and Elizabeth; so never fail me my good sword or my ready wits!"

The best of us are inclined to curiosity. A little fearful of each other, the Ambassadors exchanged looks, to know whether either would accuse the other of treachery if they heard further. "Good Sir," said the Doctor, gravely, "methinks we do our liege service in listening to this gentleman. We can the better report to his Majesty on what grounds the diabolic machination is founded."

So, over another goblet, Clifford sat telling them how Richard had long lived as Perkin Warbeck, in the neighbourhood of Tournay, under the guardianship of Madeline de Faro; and he recounted the history of his escape from the hands of Frion. Doctor Warham[14] carefully conned these names; and then, in reply, he set forth how unworthy it was of a Clifford to desert from Lancaster; how unlikely, even if it were true, which after all his tale hardly proved, it was, that the outcast boy could compete with success / with the sage possessor of England's throne. Poynings asked him how it pleased him to find himself at the same board with a Neville and a Taylor, and hinted that, an exile from his country and a traitor to his sovereign, this was hardly the way to replenish his purse, or to gain anew the broad lands he had lost. The service he might do Henry by a return to his duty, gratitude and reward, were then urged by the priest, while Clifford listened in dogged silence. His brow became flushed; his lips worked with internal commotion. He felt, he knew, that he hated the very man whose cause he espoused; but he was pledged to so many, a whole array of noble and respected names came before him. Could he, in the eyes of these, become a false, foul traitor? He refilled, and quaffed again and again his cup; and at last so wound himself up, as to begin, "My friends, you speak sooth, though I may not listen; yet, if you name one so humble and distasteful, say to my liege –"

A page in green and white – the colours of Lady Brampton, entered, announcing her / speedy arrival. Clifford's wits were already disturbed by wine; instinct made him fear in such a state to come in contact with the subtle lady; he drew his cap over his eyes, his cloak around his person, and vanished from the hall, ere his friends were aware of his intention.

The interview between Lady Brampton and the gentlemen was of another sort. Sir Edward had in her younger days worn her colours. She was changed in person since then: but, when, after a short interval, he got over the shock consequent on the first perception of the sad traces of time on the cheek of beauty, he found that her eyes possessed the same fire, her voice the same thrilling tone, her smile the same enchantment. While the Doctor, who had loved her as a daughter, and she regarded him with filial reverence, rebuked her for what he termed her misdeeds; she replied with vivacity, and such true and zealous love for him whose cause she upheld, that they were both moved to listen with respect, if not conviction, to her asseverations. She could not gain her point, nor win them over to her side; but, when she departed, neither / spoke of young Richard's rights, unwilling to confess to one another that they were converts to his truth. She went. The next day they departed from Brussels, and it became subject of discussion, what step Henry would now take, and whether, by any new measure, he could disturb the ripening conspiracy against his throne. /

CHAPTER III.

———

Oh, what excuse can my invention make?

I do arrest ye of high treason here!

SHAKSPEARE.[a]

———

Henry's ambassadors had wrought little change on any except Clifford. His words had been interrupted; they were nothing in themselves; but their spirit, the spirit of treason, was in his heart. He made up his mind to nothing; he looked forward to no certain project; but he felt that hereafter he might betray his present associates to their arch-enemy. As yet his conscience was not seared; the very anticipation of guilt tortured him, and he longed to fly from thought.[b] Another blind impulse drove him on. He hated the Prince, because / he was his opposite; because, while he was a cankered bloom, his heart a waste, his soul crusted over by deceit, his very person sullied by evil deeds and thoughts, Duke Richard stood in all the pride of innocence. Could he degrade him to his own level, there would be a pang the less in his bosom; could he injure him in the eyes of his friends, render him, as he himself had ever been, an object of censure, he would satisfy the ill-cravings of his nature, and do Henry a wondrous benefit by tarnishing the high character his rival bore, causing him whom his adherents set up as an idol, to become a reproach to them.

Clifford thought that it would be an easy task to entice a gay young stripling into vice. Richard loved hawking, hunting, and jousting in the lists, almost more, some of his elder friends thought, than befitted one on the eve of a perilous enterprize. Governed by Edmund, attended by Neville, watched by the noble Duchess and vigilant Lady Brampton, it was no great wonder that he had hitherto escaped error: but Clifford went wilily to work, and hoped in some / brief luckless hour to undo the work of years. Richard was glad to find in him a defender of his inclination for manly sports; an intimacy sprung up

———

[a] 'The Rape of Lucrece', l. 225; 2 Henry VI, III. i. 97.
[b] Perhaps alluding to William Cowper (1731–1800), The Task (1785), IV. 166.

between them, and it would not[15] be the Knight's fault, if it did not bring about the catastrophe he desired.

What then perpetually opposed all his measures? What, when he thought he had caused the tide of temptation to flow, suddenly made it ebb and retreat back to its former banks? Clifford, an adept in every art, moulded himself to every needful form, and at last won the secret from the deep recess of Richard's heart: he loved, – he loved Monina, that living emblem of innocent affection; never, he had vowed, would he disturb the sacred calm that reigned in her young heart, nor gift ignorance with fatal knowledge. She knew not the nature of her own feelings, and he would not withdraw the veil; but he was himself conscious of being swayed by the tenderest love. He could not marry her; his own misfortunes had arisen from the misalliance of his father; she herself would have refused to injure thus his / cause, and have disdained him, if for her sake he had been inclined to abdicate his rights: he would be her friend, her brother. With passion came sorrow: he fled from sad reflection to the chase, to the exercise of arms. But other temptation became blunted by this very senti- ment: his love grew more ardent by restraint; if he yielded in her absence to the contemplation of her image, his soul was filled with a voluptuous languor, from which he rouzed himself by attention to his duties or hardy pastimes; but to every other form of pleasure he was cold. This was a strange, incomprehensible picture to present to the world-worn Clifford; he fancied that it must be a delusion, but he found all the resistance of firm reality. To embitter his defeat came his own fierce passions, and the knowledge that Monina loved his rival; they would see each other, be happy in each other, and laugh him to scorn! He concealed his jealousy, his disappointment: but double, treble rage gnawed at his heart; hatred awoke in her most viperous shape, fanged by a sense of inferiority, envenomed by envy, sharpened by the / torture of defeat. How little did any know – above all, how not at all did his innocent victim suspect – the storm that brooded in his heart! There was something in the very slightness and grace of his figure that was at variance with the idea of violence and crime; and his glossing tongue added to the deceit. Lady Brampton feared him a little; Frion saw something in him, that made him pay greater court to him than to any other – these were the only indications. Sunshine and calm brooded over the earthquake's birth.

Meanwhile, Henry was not sleeping at his post. He saw the full extent of his danger, and exerted all his energy to provide against it. His immediate attention was chiefly directed to two points. In the first place it was desirable to forge some tale, to account for the circumstances that spoke so loudly for the truth of York's story, and thus to degrade him from the high esteem in which he was universally held; secondly, it became necessary to certify to the public the death of Edward the Fifth and his brother in the Tower. We may well wonder at his ill success as to the first point: – there / never was concocted so ill-fangled, so incongruous, and so contradictory a fable, as that put together by Henry, purporting to be the history of the pretender. He was himself ashamed of it, and tried to call it in. History has in its caprice given more credence to this composition, than its contemporaries gave; it was ridiculed and despised at the time even by the partizans of Lancaster.[a]

He was equally unfortunate in his second effort. To explain his attempts we must go back to the time of Richard the Third. On repeated reports being made to him of his unhappy imprisoned nephew's illness, this monarch had commissioned Sir James Tirrel to visit him. The young Prince had languished without any appearance of immediate danger, and then suddenly drooped even to the grave. Tirrel arrived at the Tower late in the evening, and the first intelligence he received was, that the Lord Edward was dying. At the midnight hour he was admitted into his sick room: his two attendants followed him no further than the ante-chamber. He entered. The glazed eye / and death-pale cheek of the victim spoke of instant dissolution: a few slight convulsions, and it was over – Edward was no more! With wild, loud cries poor little York threw himself on his brother's body. Tirrel's servants, affrighted, entered: they found one of the Princes, whose illness had been represented as trivial, dead; the other was carried off, struggling and screaming, by their master and an attendant priest, the only two persons in the chamber. They departed two hours afterwards from the Tower. Tirrel seemed disturbed, and was silent. They would perhaps have thought less about it; but hearing subsequently of the disappearance and supposed death of the young Duke, wonder grew into suspicion, and in thoughtless talk they laid the foundation of a dire tale out of these fragments. Henry had heard it before; now he endeavoured to trace its origin. Tirrel, who for some time had lived obscurely in the country, came to London – he was immediately seized, and thrown into prison. Emissaries were set to work to find the three others, the priest and Sir James's two servants. Only one was to be / found; and, when Tirrel was asked concerning this man, by name John Dighton,[b] he told a tale of ingratitude punished by him, which was soothing sweet to King Henry's ear: he was speedily discovered and imprisoned. Both master and follower underwent many examinations; and it was suggested to each, that reward would follow their giving countenance to a tale of midnight murder. Tirrel was indignant at the proposal; Dighton, on the contrary – a needy, bad man – while he told the story so as to gloss his own conduct, was very ready to inculpate his master; and it grew finely under his fosterage. Henry saw that without Tirrel's connivance he could not authenticate any account; but he gave all the weight he could to these reports. Few persons believed them, yet it served to confuse and complicate events; and, while people argued, some at least would take his side of the question, and

---

[a] A point made by both Walpole and Bayley.

[b] In *Richard III* (IV. iii. 4–5), after the murder of the princes, Sir James Tirrel (or Tyrrell, d. 1502) identifies Dighton as one he suborned 'To do this piece of ruthless butchery'.

these would be interested to spread their belief abroad: – Duke Richard must be the loser in every way.

The spies, the traitor-emissaries of the fear-struck monarch, were all busy; there was a / whole army of them dispersed in England and Flanders – none could know the false man from the true. To obviate every suspicion, he caused his own hirelings to be proclaimed traitors, and cursed at St. Paul's Cross.[a]

The priests, ever his friends, were impiously permitted to violate the sacrament of confession; and thus several unsuspecting men betrayed their lives, while they fancied that they performed a religious duty. A few names still escaped him – he tampered with Clifford and Frion for them: the former was not yet quite a villain; the latter found that he enjoyed more credit, honour, and power, as the Duke's Secretary, than he could do as Henry's spy; besides, his vanity was hurt – he wished to revenge himself on the master who had discarded him.

In nothing did Henry succeed better than in throwing an impenetrable veil over his manœuvres. Most people thought, so tranquil and unconcerned he seemed, that he did not suspect the existence of an actual conspiracy, fostered in England itself, containing many influential persons among its numbers. All were / sure that he was entirely ignorant of their names and actual purposes. The many months which intervened while he waited patiently, corroborated this belief, and the conspirators slept in security. The winter passed, and they continued to scheme, apparently unobserved; spring came – they prepared for York's landing – for a general rising – for a sudden seizing on many walled towns and fortresses – for the occupation of London itself. A few brief weeks, and Henry's prosperity would be shaken to its centre – his power uprooted – he and his children would wander exiles in a foreign land; and another king, the gallant descendant of the true Plantagenets, reign in his stead.

Thus occupied, thus prepared, were the Yorkists in England; at Brussels, things were carried on more openly, and wore a more promising appearance. The Duchess, Lady Brampton, Plantagenet, triumphed. Sir George Neville anticipated with proud joy a restoration of the fallen race of Warwick, and regarded himself already as another king-maker of that house. Every exile looked northward, and grew / joyful with the thought of home. Frion became more busy and important than ever; he had lately gone disguised to England, in pursuance of some project. In another week they expected Lord Barry to join them from Ireland: Clifford was amazed, vacillating, terrified. He knew that Henry was far from idle; he was aware that some of the loudest speakers in Richard's favour in Brussels were his hirelings, whom he would not betray, because he half felt himself one among them, though he could not quite prevail

---

[a] A pulpit cross in St Paul's churchyard, used for preaching sermons and publishing state information, royal and ecclesiastical proclamations.

on himself to join their ranks. He believed that the King was in eager expectation of his decision in his favour; that nothing could be done till he said the word; he proposed conditions; wished to conceal some names; exempt others from punishment. Messengers passed continually between him and Bishop Morton, Henry's chief counsellor and friend, and yet he could not determine to be altogether a traitor.

Thus stood affairs;[a] a consummation, all thought to be nigh at hand. It was the spring of 1494, and the coming summer was to decide / the fate of York. A ball was given by the Duchess, in honour of her nephew; it was splendidly and gaily attended. Clifford had been conversing with the Prince, when suddenly he left the apartment: it was long ere he came back, and slowly joined the principal groupe in the room, consisting of the Duchess, the Prince, Lady Brampton, Neville, Plantagenet, Taylor, and several others. Clifford's countenance was marked by horror and surprise; so much so, that Lady Brampton looked at him a moment without knowing him. Suddenly she started up and seized his arm – "Holy Virgin!" she cried, "what had dressed your face, Sir Robert, in this pale livery? what tale of death have you heard?"

The brow of Clifford became flushed, his lips grew whiter, as quivering they refused to form the words he attempted to utter. Barley had before this quitted the apartment: he rushed in now, crying aloud, "Treason!"

"Treason!" Neville repeated, laying his hand heavily on Clifford's shoulder; "hear / you that word, Sir Knight? Where is the traitor?"

Clifford in a moment recovered himself, answering, composedly, "Aye, would I could point out the man – would that I could drag him forth, the mark, the very target for the shafts of vengeance. We are lost; the cause is lost; our friends; the good Lord Fitzwater. I would have hid his name in the bowels of the earth!"

Already the festal hall was deserted; already the guests were dispersed, to learn how wide the destruction had spread. By the Prince's orders, the messenger from England was introduced before himself and his principal friends: it was Adam Floyer, Sir Simon Mountford's chaplain; escaped himself, he was the bearer of a frightful tale. On one day, almost at the same hour, the Yorkist conspirators were arrested. Lord Fitzwater, Sir Simon Mountford, Sir Thomas Thwaites, Robert Ratcliffe, William Daubeny, Thomas Cressenor, Thomas Astwood, two Dominicans, by name William Richford and Thomas Poyns, Doctor William Sutton, Worseley the / Dean of Saint Paul's, Robert Langborne, and Sir William Lessey, were all seized and cast into prison. Others had escaped: young Gilbert Daubeny, brother of William, and Sir Edward Lisle, had arrived in Flanders.[b] Others made good speed and had fled to Ireland. /

---

[a] '1494' (marginal note in *Abinger/Palacio*).

[b] The conspirators are catalogued in Hall, Holinshed, and Hume, who are, however, silent about the names of escapees.

CHAPTER IV.

Oh, Clifford! but bethink thee once again,
And in thy thought oerrun my former time,
And if thou can'st for blushing, view this face!

SHAKSPEARE.[a]

"Where is the traitor?" Neville's question resounded through Flanders, and was re-echoed in groans from the English shores. Each man feared the other; and saw the mark of Henry's malice on the brow of all. It was a worse scene in England; executions followed imprisonment; the scaffolds flowed with blood, and suspicion was still greedy of prey. Among the papers seized by the King, there was found a letter from Clifford to Lord Fitzwater, containing / these words: "I do protest, my Lord, that the proof of York's truth is most pertinent. You know this; and yet he who cut the crooked rose-bush to the roots, still doubts: forsooth, he is still at his 'ifs' – 'if he were sure that that young man were King Edward's son, he would never bear arms against him.'[b] Pray, deprive my Lord of his 'if;' for arms he must never bear: he is too principal to any cause."

Henry tormented himself to find who this doubter might be: again he sought to bribe Clifford, who was at first dogged that so much was done without him, and then tried to barter his intelligence for Lord Fitzwater's life. Such grace had he left, that he was ready to exert his wits to save his former patron; this was granted. This noble alone of the conspirators, who were laymen, was spared; he was sent prisoner to Calais.[c]

At the first word of discovery Monina's friends had endeavoured to ensure her escape to Flanders; but her name was known to Henry, and there was none

---

[a] *3 Henry VI*, I. iv. 44.

[b] The sentiment that sealed Stanley's fate, according to the chronicles.

[c] Only a few conspirators (Mountford, Thwaites, and William Daubeney) were executed. Mary Shelley alters her sources to darken Henry's character. Fitzwater was beheaded in 1496 after an attempted escape.

whom he was more desirous to get into his power. She remained concealed at /
a little distance from London; she grew mad in inaction; the work of death and
misery around, wound up her tender spirit to torture; and the execution of her
former friends filled her with such horror, as made day hateful, night the parent
of frightful visions. After several weeks' seclusion, she all at once resolved to
visit London, to seek some one of her former friends: to learn whether the
tragedy was over, and what further mischiefs despair might have engendered.
She inhabited a solitary mansion, with one old woman, who opposed her going,
but vainly. Monina was too young to bear uncertainty with any degree of
patience. Some slight joy visited her as she found herself on her road to
London: before she arrived a heavy rain fell, but she was not to be discouraged.
Sir Edward Lisle, she knew, had not been arrested; she was unaware of his
escape, and thought perhaps that he had not been discovered: she might get
intelligence from him. His house was deserted and empty: another hope
remained; Sir William Stanley. She knew his timidity, and resolved to be
cautious as to the manner of her visit. / Sir William had ever been peculiarly
kind to the gentle maiden: fearing to see her openly, she had often come to him
by water: his mansion, near the Palace of Westminster, had a garden upon the
Thames: without exciting any remark, she could land here: it was already night,
and this favoured secrecy. With some difficulty, in the city, where she then was,
she contrived to find her way to an obscure wharf, and embarked in a wherry;
fortunately, it was high water, and she landed without difficulty in the garden,
and dismissed the men. Now she began to be puzzled as to how she should
make her way, dripping with rain, unexpected, to Sir William's presence. She
had been accustomed to be admitted by a little door opening on stairs which
led to her old friend's library; this was shut now. Suddenly she thought she
heard voices, and then perceived a thread of light that streamed through the
key-hole of the summer-house in the garden: there was a noise on the water
too, and a boat was paddled to the landing-place. Bewildered, yet believing that
all this secresy was connected / with the grand conspiracy, she moved towards
the summer-house; the door was opened, and the light falling full upon her, she
saw several figures within, and a female shriek burst upon her ear: quick steps
were heard behind: to retreat or go forward equally terrified her; when one of
the persons in the summer-house, a man in an uncouth foreign garb, cried –
"Thou here, Monina! What miracle is this? Come, come in, there is danger in
all we do."

Monina recognized the voice of Frion, and entered; there she saw one, a lady
richly attired, yet half disguised in a large black cloak. Fear was painted on her
cheek; her blue eyes were cast up to Heaven. A female attendant with her
seemed yet more terrified. About the room were scattered globes and astro-
labes, and all the gear of an astrologer. In the lady, Monina recognized York's
sister, Tudor's Queen, the fair Elizabeth of England. At once compassion and
respect entered her heart; she addressed the royal lady with reverence, and all

that touching grace that was her sweetest charm; she / assured her of inviolable secrecy; she reminded her of their former interview. Elizabeth grew calmer as she recognized her visitor at Shene: she stretched out her hand to the Spaniard, saying – "I do indeed believe and trust thee; thou shalt hear again from me:" then folding her mantle round her, and leaning on her attendant, she quitted the house, and with trembling haste embarked.

For many weeks after this scene Monina continued concealed in Sir William Stanley's mansion. When the arrest of the conspirators had taken place, Frion, balked in an attempt to escape, for safety's sake had assumed the habit and character of an astrologer, and so far worked upon Stanley's fears, and won him by his flattery, that he permitted him to take up his residence in his summer-house. Frion was a clever prophet, and too restless not to become notorious: it was a good mode, he averred, to put hope in the hearts of the Yorkists, by prognosticating all manner of success to them. His fame spread; the Queen questioned Stanley about his new astrologer, and the confusion the / poor Chamberlain evinced, served only to excite her curiosity. She sent one of her attendants to see what manner of man he might be, and the subtle Frion profited by this little artifice, which Sir William in his terror divulged, to entice the Queen herself to his cell; she came, and the result of her visit was to bring Monina again before her.

Such were the agents still at work for York in London. Such the materials Clifford strove to mould into a purpose of his own. There was no reason, so many of the White Rose thought, to forego all their plans, because one had come to a fatal end. Still Richard might land in England, and make head against Tudor. On a smaller scale, with lessened hopes and diminished ardour, a scheme of this kind was canvassed. Clifford appeared its chief abettor, and encouraged it by every means in his power; none were averse; it was not an enterprize of such high expectation as the discovered one; but, undertaken with speed, and prosecuted with energy, it might turn out as well. England was by no means tranquil; the metropolis itself was / the scene of tumults: these were raised to a ferment by the embargo Henry had found it necessary to place on all communication with Holland, a measure fraught with ruin to many of the richest merchants in London.

At this time, towards the end of summer, the King came up from his palace at Shene, and held a court at Westminster. One of the immediate subjects that brought him up, was a tumult in the city, to which the embargo had given rise. A vast number of apprentices and journeymen belonging to the ruined merchants, were out of employ, while the traders from Hans, and other free German towns, who went among us by the name of the Easterlings, got the commerce into their own hands, and grew rich upon it.[a] The sight of their

---

[a] The Hanse (or Hans), a forceful commercial and political league of German towns (*OED*).

prosperity was to the starving Londoners, as the pressed rowel of a spur in a horse's side; with the usual barbarism of the untaught and rude, they visited on these men the fault of their governors – the discontent augmented till it became loud, furious, and armed. Multitudes of those deprived of their usual means, met, and, in a moment of / rage, proceeded from words to acts. They endeavoured to force and rifle the warehouses of the Easterlings, who repulsed them with difficulty; nor did they disperse, till the Mayor arrived with men and weapons, from whom they fled like a flock of sheep. When tidings of this event was brought to Henry, he, who saw in all things the multiplied image of the abhorred White Rose, believed the Yorkists to be its secret cause. The day after his arrival he gave audience to the Mayor, who reported that, from every examination made, none appeared to have a part in it, except servants and apprentices, nearly a hundred of whom were imprisoned in the Tower.

In giving a detail of this circumstance, the Mayor related that the Easterlings declared, that at the first onset their richest store-chambers must have become the prey of the rioters, but for the interposition of one man. He was a sea captain, and had arrived but the day before with his caravel, from Spain – they represented him as a person of gigantic stature and superhuman strength. Entangled by the mob / in his progress through the city, he had no sooner discovered their intent, than he contrived to make his way into the stilyard;[a] and, there combining the forces of the defenders, more by his personal prowess than any other means, he beat back the invaders, and succeeded in closing the gates. At the representation of the Mayor, Henry commanded that this man should be brought before him, partly that he might thank him for his services; and partly, for Henry was curious on such points, to learn from him the news from Spain, and if more had been heard of the wild visionary Columbus and his devoted crew, since they had deserted the stable continent, to invade the hidden chambers of the secret western ocean.

The King received the mariner in his closet. None were in attendance save Urswick.[b] There was something grand in the contrast between these men. The courtier priest – the sovereign, whose colourless face was deep-lined with careful thought, whose eyes were skilled in reading the thoughts of men, and whose soul was perpetually alive to every thing that was passing / around him – and the ocean rock, the man of tempests and hardships, whose complexion was darkened and puckered by exposure to sun and wind, whose every muscle was hardened by labour, but whose unservile mien bespoke no cringing to any power, save Nature's own. He received Henry's thanks with respect, and replied simply: he answered also several questions put to him concerning his

---

[a] Variant of 'steelyard', 'the place on the north bank of the Thames above London Bridge where the Merchants of the Hanse had their establishment' (*OED*).

[b] Sir Christopher Urswick (1448–1522), trusted advisor who negotiated the terms of Henry VII's marriage; he figures briefly in *Richard III*, IV. v.

voyages; it appeared that he had but lately arrived from Spain – that he came to seek a relative who resided in England. During this interview a thought flashed on Henry's mind. In his late transactions with Clifford, the base purpose had been formed of enticing the Duke and his principal adherents to England, and of delivering them up to their enemy; there had been some discussion as to providing, at least, one vessel in Henry's pay, to make part of the little fleet which would bring the Duke of York over. This was difficult, as suspicion might attach itself to any English vessel; but here was one, with a stranger captain, and a foreign crew, a man who knew nothing of White or Red Rose, who would / merely fulfil his commission. Slow on all occasions to decide, the King appointed another interview with the stranger.

It so happened, that the news of the appearance of the Spanish Captain, had penetrated to the Queen's apartments; and little Arthur, her gentle and darling son, was desirous to see the countryman of Columbus, whose promised discoveries were the parent of such wonder and delight throughout the world. The Prince of Wales must not be denied this pleasure, and the Spaniard was ushered into the Queen's presence. An enthusiast in his art, his energetic, though simple expressions enchanted the intelligent Prince, and even compelled the attention of his little sturdy brother Henry.[a] He spoke in words, borrowed from Columbus's own lips, of translucent seas, of an atmosphere more softly serene than ours, of shores of supernal beauty, of the happy natives, of stores of treasure, and the bright hopes entertained concerning the further quest to be made in these regions. Elizabeth forgot herself to listen, and regretted the necessity of so soon dismissing him. She asked a few / questions relative to himself, his vessel; "She was a gallant thing once," replied her commander, "when I took her from the Algerines,[b] and new christened her the Adalid;[c] because like her owner, being of Moorish origin she embraced the true faith. My own name, please your Grace, is Hernan De Faro, otherwise called the Captain of the Wreck, in memory of a sad tedious adventure, many years old."

"De Faro – had he not a daughter?"

Anxiety and joy showed itself at once in the mariner's countenance. Monina! – Where was she? How eagerly and vainly had he sought her – faltering, the Queen had only power to say, that Sir William Stanley, the Lord Chamberlain, could inform him, and, terrified, put an end to the interview.

Two days after – already had de Faro found and fondly embraced his beloved child – Urswick, at the King's command, sent for the hero of the stilyard, and after some questioning, disclosed his commission to him; it was such, that, had De Faro been in ignorance, would have led him to suspect

---

[a] Arthur (1486–1502) and Henry VIII (1491–1547; ruled 1509–47).

[b] Corsairs from the Algerian coast.

[c] 'armed guard' (Irving, I, p. 242).

nothing – he was simply to sail for / Ostend; where he would seek Sir Robert Clifford, and deliver a letter: he was further told that he was to remain at Sir Robert's command, to receive on board his vessel whoever the Knight should cause to embark in her, and to bring them safely to England. To all this De Faro, aware of the dread nature of these orders, assented; and, in Stanley's summer-house, with the Lord Chamberlain, Monina, and Frion, it was discussed how this web of treason could best be destroyed. There was little room for doubt; Monina resolved to sail with her father, to denounce Clifford to the Prince, and so save him and his friends from the frightful snare. Frion still remained in England, to try to fathom the whole extent of the mischief intended; though now, fearful of discovery, he quitted his present abode, and sought a new disguise. Stanley trembled at Clifford's name, but he saw no suspicion in his sovereign's eye, and was reassured.

The Adalid sailed, bearing the King's letters to Clifford, and having Monina on board, who was to unfold to the deceived Prince and his followers the dangers that menaced them. /

Already, as the appointed time drew near, most of Richard's partizans were assembled at Ostend; a fleet of three vessels was anchored in the port to convey them to England to fated death; the Prince himself, with Clifford, sojourned in a castle at no great distance. Sir Robert insinuated himself each day more and more into his royal friend's confidence; each day his hatred grew, and he fed himself with it to keep true to his base purpose; among the partizans of York sometimes he felt remorse; beside the bright contrast of his own dark self, never.

Monina landed; and, the Prince being absent, first she sought Lady Brampton – she was at Brussels; then Plantagenet, – he was expected, but not arrived from Paris; then she asked for Sir George Neville, as the chief of the English exiles; to him she communicated her strange, her horrid tidings, to him she showed Henry's still sealed letter to Clifford. What visible Providence was here, laying its finger on the headlong machinery that was bearing them to destruction! Neville was all aghast: he, who did not like, had ceased to suspect Clifford, / seeing that he adhered to them at their worst. He lost no time in bringing Monina to the castle, but ten miles distant, where York then was; he introduced her privately, and, wishing that she should tell her tale herself, went about to contrive that, without Clifford's knowledge or suspicion, the Prince should have an interview with her.

Monina did not wonder that her bosom throbbed wildly, as she remained in expectation of seeing her childhood's playfellow, from whom she had been so long absent. Nor did she check her emotion of intense pleasure when she saw him, and heard him in her native Spanish utter expressions of glad delight at so unexpectedly beholding her. Time had changed him very little; his aspect was still boyish; and, if more thought was seated in his eye, his smile was not the less frank and sweet; she was more altered; her little but feminine form had acquired grace; the girl was verging into the woman – blooming as the one, tender and impassioned as the other; her full dark eyes, which none could behold and not feel the very inner / depths of their nature stirred, were the home of sensibility and love. A few moments were given to an interchange of affectionate greeting, and then York, recurring to the mysterious mode in which Neville had expressed himself, asked if any thing, save a kind wish to visit the brother of her childhood, had brought her hither; she replied, by relating to him the circumstances of her father's commission from Henry, and delivering to him the letter for Sir Robert. The whole wide world of misery contains no pang so great, as the discovery of treachery where we pictured truth; death is less in the comparison, for both destroy the future, and one, with Gorgon countenance, transforms the past.[a] The world appeared to slide from beneath the Prince, as he became aware that Clifford's smiles were false; his seeming honesty, his discourse of honour, the sympathy apparent between them, a lie, a painted lie, alluring him by fair colours to embrace foulest deformity. The exceeding openness and confidence of his own nature, rendered the blow doubly unnatural and frightful; and Monina, / who had half disliked, and latterly had almost forgotten Clifford, was full of surprise and pain to mark the affliction her friend's countenance expressed.

There was no time for regret. Neville interrupted them, and it became necessary to act. Richard held in his hand the sealed proof of his associate's falsehood: Sir George urged him to open it, so to discover the whole extent of the treason. The Prince's eyes were at once lighted up by the suggestion: no, no, because Clifford had been base, he would violate no law of honour – there was no need for the sake of others; his treachery discovered, was fangless; nor would he even undertake the dark office of openly convicting and punishing: his conscience and remorse should be judge and executioner.

Monina and Neville returned to Ostend. The Prince sent a message to Clifford with some trifling commission to execute in the same town; and Sir Robert, who had heard of the arrival of a stranger caravel from England, was glad of an opportunity, to ride over to learn its character. His feet were in the stirrups, when / a page brought him a letter from the Duke, which he was bid not to open till he had departed. A sense of a mysterious meaning came over him. Was he discovered? At the first dawn of this suspicion he clapped spurs to his horse, and was already far away; then, impatient of uncertainty, as soon as half the brief space to Ostend was measured, he took out the packet, eyed it curiously, and, after many qualms and revolutions of feeling, suddenly tore it open. King Henry's dispatch, written in Urswick's well-known hand, first met his eye. Worse in action than in thought, a cold dew mantled on his brow; and,

---

[a] One of three serpent-haired sisters of Greek mythology (the most famous being Medusa), whose appearance turns a viewer to stone. Mary Shelley's own past had been painfully transformed by her discovery in 1827 of Jane Williams's betrayal; see *MWSJ*, II, pp. 502–3; *MWSL*, II, pp. 25–6.

while his heart stood still in his labouring breast, he cast his eyes over a few lines, written in Richard's fair clear Spanish hand:–

"This paper, joined to the mode in which it fell into my hands, accuses you of treason. If wrongfully, accord permission that the seal may be broken, and your innocence proved.

"Even if the mystery which this letter contains cannot be divulged nor exculpated, all is not / lost. Perhaps you are rather weak than guilty; erring but not wicked. If so, return immediately on your steps; by a frank confession merit my confidence. I were unworthy of the mediation of the Blessed Saints, whom each night I solicit to intercede for me before our Heavenly Father, were I not ready to pardon one who has sinned, but who repents.

"If your crime be of a deeper dye, and you are allied in soul to my enemy, depart. It is enough for me that I never see you more. If I remain a fugitive for ever, you will lose nothing by deserting my ruined fortunes; if I win the day, my first exercise of the dearest prerogative of kings, will be to pardon you.

"RICHARD." /

CHAPTER V.

———

> Shall I be the slave
> Of – what? a word? which those of this false world
> Employ against each other, not themselves,
> As men wear daggers not for self offence.
> But if I am mistaken, where shall I
> Find the disguise to hide me from myself,
> As now I skulk from every other eye.
>
> SHELLEY.[a]

———

One of the surest results of guilt is to deprive the criminal of belief in the goodness of others. Clifford was discovered. Even, if Richard continued true to his promise of pardon, his adherents and counsellors might force him to

---

[a] *The Cenci* (1819), V. i. 98–104.

another line of conduct. A dungeon and death floated terribly before his confused vision. Flight, instant flight to England, where by a / full confession of many things he had reserved, and the disclosure of an important unsuspected name, he might still receive welcome and reward from Henry, was the only course left him to pursue.

His thoughts were chaos. Shame and indignation raged in his heart. He was a convicted traitor, a dishonoured man. "Oh, my envied father!" in his wretchedness he exclaimed, "you died gloriously for Lancaster. I live, steeped in obloquy, for the same cause. Abhorred Plantagenet! what misery has been mine since first your name came to drug me with racking poison! What have I not endured while I cringed to the fair-haired boy! Thank the powers of hell, that time is past! Devil as I have stamped myself, his arch crime, lying, is no more my attribute. To the winds and men's thirsty ears I may cry aloud – I hate Plantagenet!"

It was some relief to this miserable man to array his thoughts in their darkest garb, soothing his evil passions with words, which acted on them as a nurse's fondling talk to a querulous / child. His line of conduct was fixed; he remembered Neville's sudden appearance and departure the night before; he had brought the letter; he was waiting for him at Ostend to seize on him, to turn to mockery the Prince's promised pardon. Those were days of violence and sudden bloodshed: the enemy a man could not visit with legal punishment, he thought himself justified in destroying with his own hand; the passions of the Yorkists, who found they had been driven into shambles instead of a fold, must be fierce and dangerous. Without delay, he resolved to embark in one of the vessels then in the roads; he hurried to the beach; the wind seemed fair; there was a poor kind of hostelry, the common resort of sailors near, from whence a signal could be given for a boat to be sent off for him. While waiting for it, he quitted the noisy vulgarity of the inn, and walked towards a kind of ruined tower, that once perhaps had served as a light-house. In all the panic of guilt, a roof, however desolate, appeared a shelter, and he sought it: it was dilapidated and dark; there were some rude, narrow stairs / leading to the upper story; these he ascended, and entered what had been a kind of guard-room, and started at the vision he beheld: leaning against the aperture that had served for a casement, looking on the wide green sea, was Monina. Her lustrous eyes turned on him – eyes before whose full softness his violence, his insolence quailed; till shame, despair, and rage, and the deep-seated arrogance of his nature conquered his better feelings. She knew his crime, witnessed his disgrace; there was no more to lose in the world. What more could he win? His presence occasioned her much emotion. She had just quitted Neville, who somewhat angrily remarked upon the Prince's ill-timed lenity, and spoke bitterly of all the ill Clifford, thus let loose, might do in England. And here he was, about to embark for that very island, where one at least, Sir William Stanley was at his mercy. Gladly Monina seized on this opportunity to dive into his projects, and to inspire by her energetic words the traitor's bosom with some sense of right. She, alas! inspired passion / only, and jealousy, that now at last his rival would see her love-lighted eyes turned affectionately on him; while all the reproach of which they were capable was his meed. What such men as Clifford feel is not love: he had no real friendship for the innocent girl; each feeling that expresses the sympathy of our intellectual nature, was never associated to him with the name of woman. As she spoke therefore of his duties to God and man, violated, but not irretrievably, and with soft persuasion entreated him to spare those whose lives hung upon his word, he recovered his obduracy, and replied in a tone whose hollow vaunting was at discord with the music that fell from her lips – "My pretty maiden, I thank thee for thy good intentions, and if thou wilt wholly undertake my instruction, will prove an apt scholar. Honesty and I are too poor to be messmates; but if thou wilt join us – by God, Monina, I mean what I say – the priest shall say grace for us, and we will partake life's feast or fast together. I will sail with thee to thy Spain, to the Indies of the West. England shall be a forgotten / name; the White or Red Rose, neither worse nor better in our eyes, than any blooms that smell as sweet: if thou refusest this, here ends the last chance for honesty; and be the victim who it may, I care not so my fortunes thrive."

"Unworthy man!" cried Monina; "farewell! I go to England also: I to save, you to destroy. Bounteous Heaven will look on our several intentions, and shape our course accordingly. Henry will visit with poor thanks your blighted purpose, barren now of its ill fruit. Mine will be the harvest; yours the unlamented loss."

She would have passed him, but he seized her slender wrist. "We will run no race," he cried; "if we go to England, it will be together: listen to the splash of oars, it is my boat among the breakers. We enter it together; it is vain for you to resist; you are my prisoner."

Monina trembled in every joint: she felt that in very truth she was in Clifford's power. There rode her father's caravel; but he could not guess her pressing danger: he would behold her / depart, ignorant of the violence she was suffering, ignorant that she was there. No help! – no form of words was there, that might persuade the ill-minded Knight to free her: her proud spirit disdained to bend; her cheek was flushed; she strove to withdraw her hand. "Pardon me," said Clifford; "if my fingers press too roughly; the slight pain you endure will hardly counterbalance the fierce torture your words inflicted. Be patient, my fellows are already here. Let us not act a silly mime before them; do not oblige me to demonstrate too unkindly, that you are wholly in my power."

Hardly had he spoken the words when with a scream she sprung from him. He turned; but before even he could see the gigantic form of De Faro, a blow was struck which made him reel against the wall. It would have been instantly followed by another, but that Monina had flung herself on her father's breast, and he, supporting her, forgot his enemy, who recovered himself, and drew his sword. He met the fierce glare of the injured parent's eye, and shook. "We meet again, recreant!" were / the only words spoken by De Faro; and, as an elephant might snatch a youngling antelope from the pursuit of a tiger, he took his daughter in his arms, descended the steps with her, and, as Clifford stood gazing on the sea, in such bitter mood as is the fruit of baffled malice, he saw the mariner lift his daughter into the boat. It pushed from the shore; and, with long, measured strokes, it swept the waves towards the caravel, whose sails were again unfurled, while every thing bespoke the readiness and anxiety of the crew to depart.

Ere the Adalid had reached the open sea, Clifford in his vessel was but little astern. It was a race they ran. The caravel at first had the best. Night concealed them from each other's view; and, in the morning, already on the tranquil bosom of the Thames Sir Robert's vessel was sailing alone towards London. By one of those strange turns of fortune by which our purposes swim or are wrecked, De Faro, without a pilot, unacquainted with the coast, missed the channel; he gounded on a sand-bank at the river's mouth; and the tide which carried Clifford / so swiftly towards London, had several hours to run, before it reached a height sufficient to float the other's vessel; the situation was not without peril, and no boat even could be lowered to carry the anxious Monina to shore.

The very day (it was now the month of January),[a] that Henry heard of Clifford's arrival in London, he removed his court from Westminster to the Tower. Already he divined that his Lord Chamberlain was to be criminated by Sir Robert; and, as Stanley possessed considerable influence in the state, he wished to make his arrest as unexpected as possible. Another motive worked upon the avaricious sovereign; seized thus, without preparation or forethought, his jewels, his rich plate, his valuable moveables, which might otherwise be secreted, now fell the indiscriminate prey of confiscation; the Tower, at once a palace and a prison,[b] favoured this purpose. Here he received Clifford; Urswick had already conversed with the traitor Knight, and represented to him the necessity of ample confession. There was something in the priest's manner that, like iron, entered Clifford's soul; / he felt himself, too truly, to be the abject slave, the despised tool of power; there was but little need to use cajoleries or bribes with him now; he was there, to be executed as a felon or pardoned as a spy, according as his disclosures satisfied or not the callous-hearted King.

For his greater punishment, there clung to this unfortunate man a sense of what he ought to and might have been, and a burning consciousness of what he was. Hitherto he had fancied that he loved honour, and had been withheld, as by a hair, from overstepping the demarcation between the merely reprehensible

---

[a] '1495' (marginal note in *Abinger/Palacio*).
[b] Perhaps echoing Byron, *Childe Harold's Pilgrimage*, IV (1818), i. 2.

and the disgraceful. The good had blamed him; the reckless wondered at his proficiency in their own bad lessons; but hitherto he had lifted his head haughtily among them, and challenged any man to accuse him of worse, than greater daring, in a career all travelled at a slower and more timid pace.

But that time was gone by. He was now tainted by leprous treachery; his hands were stained by the blood of his deceived confederates; honour disowned him for her son; / men looked askance on him as belonging to a Pariah race. He felt this; and even Monina, who had last conversed with him in the summer house of the inn at Ostend, would hardly have recognized him. He was then a bold-faced villain; his step was haughty; his manner insolent. Now his gait was shuffling, his appearance mean, his speech hesitating and confused. Urswick had known him a gay ruffler; he started back: was this Sir Robert Clifford? He was obliged to use with him the usual style of speech adopted towards men in his situation; to speak of his duty towards his liege; the propriety of delivering up the guilty to condign punishment: hackneyed phrases, which sounded cold to the unhappy man.

There was no resource. At Henry's feet, kneeling before a King who used him as a tool, but who hated him as the abettor of his rival, and despised him as the betrayer of his friend, Clifford spoke the fatal word which doomed the confiding Stanley to instant death, himself to the horrors of conscious guilt, or, what as yet was more bitter to the worldling, relentless outlawry / from the society and speech of all, however depraved, who yet termed themselves men of honour.

Henry heard him with feigned amazement; and with grating words of insulting unbelief, demanded evidence of his chamberlain's treason: these were easily furnished, yet, such as they were, they comprised such irrefragable proof of the identity of the outcast Duke, that Henry found, that, while they confirmed him more than ever in his resolve that Stanley should suffer the severest penalty of his crime, it made it difficult to bring forward the testimonials of his guilt. This was for after consideration: Clifford was dismissed with cold thanks, with promise of pardon and reward, and an haughty command neither to obtrude himself again into the royal presence, nor to depart from London without especial leave.

Henry's first act was to command Stanley not to quit his chamber in the Tower. The next day before the hour of noon, the Bishop of Durham,[a] Lord Oxford,[b] Lord Surrey, Urswick, and Lord Dawbeny, met in the fallen chamberlain's / apartment, for the purpose of examining him. A thousand opposing feelings operated upon Stanley: accustomed to pay deference to the King, even now he said nothing to displease him; and his expressions rather spoke of

---

[a] Richard Fox; see p. 54 and n.

[b] John de Vere, 13th Earl of Oxford (1443–1513), returned from a long exile to fight at Bosworth; he became Chamberlain and Admiral of England under Henry VII.

compassion for him who very possibly was Duke of York, than any falling off from his allegiance to the then King of England.

This monarch was tormented by no doubts, – to be actuated by no pity. Stanley's acknowledgment of the truth of the Burgundian pretender roused his bitterest feelings. In addition, he was rich booty – which weighed heavily against him; so that, when Bishop Fox remarked on the villany and extent of his treason, Henry, off his guard, exclaimed – "I am glad of it; the worse the better; none can speak of mercy now, and confiscation is assured;" – nor did he in the interval before his trial, nor after it, express one regret that the man was about to forfeit his head, who had encircled his own with the regal diadem.

Tried, condemned; but a few days remained before on the fatal block the rich, noble, prudent, / royally-connected Sir William Stanley would expiate his guilt to Henry. All wondered; many pitied; few thought of soliciting for or aiding the fallen man; yet one or two there were, whom this last blow against York filled with bitter regret. In a secluded part of London Lord Barry, who had just arrived, Frion, and Monina met. Barry came with intelligence that there had appeared in Ireland a gentleman from Scotland, commissioned by its young monarch to enquire into the truth of Richard's story; and, if indubitably he were the man he pretended, to counsel him to visit Scotland, where he would find friendship and aid. The Earl of Desmond also had just arrived in London, and Lord Barry was in his company. This downfall of Stanley called their minds from every other consideration. Monina was peculiarly agitated and thoughtful. One evening she joined them late: she was full of some project. "I can, I do believe, save our friend," she said: "the assistance I need is small – you, Master Stephen, will hasten on board the Adalid, and bid my father have all in / readiness for sailing, and to drop down the river as far as Greenwich: you, my dear Lord, must also take a part in my scheme – keep watch on the river, right opposite the Tower, during the coming night and the following: if you see a light upon the shore beneath its dark walls, come towards it with a boat; the Blessed Virgin aiding my design, it shall be freighted with disappointment to the Tudor, joy to us."

Lord Barry and Frion promised obedience, though they would have dissuaded her from the risk; but she was devoted, enthusiastic, firm: she left them, nor did they delay to execute her commission, and both went down the river to De Faro's caravel. Here a new surprise awaited them. The Duke of York and his friends had not been idle in the interim. Each design, as it failed, gave place to another. They were diminished in numbers, but now no traitors were among them. Their hopes were few; but, unless the present time were seized, there would be none. The false expectations Clifford had held out to them of coalition and succour in England were lost, but attachment to York was / alive in many an English bosom: the preparations of arms they had made still existed; it was resolved therefore in early spring to descend on the English shores.

The Duke of York, deeply grieved by the ruin that visited his friends, stung to the heart by Clifford's treachery, resolved meanwhile to seek relief in action. Could not his presence do much? Unknown in England, he might visit the Yorkists, rouse their affection, and form such an union, as, assisted afterwards by his friends and their little fleet, would contribute to ensure success. His friends did not approve of the hazard to which he exposed himself: but every thing they alleged on this score, only confirmed his purpose. "All endanger themselves – all die for me," he cried; "shall I alone be ingloriously safe?" The first sight therefore that presented itself to Lord Barry and Frion on the deck of the Adalid, was Prince Richard and Edmund Plantagenet.

The Duke's presence did not change the purpose of Frion's visit. De Faro got his vessel in readiness for the voyage; and Lord Barry, as / evening closed in, prepared to take his stand – not singly: Richard insisted on sharing his watch; docile as he usually was, remonstrance had now no effect; hitherto he had given himself up to guarded safety, now he seemed in love with peril, resolved to court her at every opportunity. The risk to which Monina exposed herself, made him obstinate. He would have thought himself untrue to the laws of chivalry, a recreant knight, had he not hastened to protect her; and, more than this, for the inborn impulses of the heart are more peremptory than men's most sacred laws – he loved; and a mother draws not more instinctively her first-born to her bosom, than does the true and passionate lover feel impelled to hazard even life for the sake of her he loves, to shield her from every danger, or to share them gladly with her. /

CHAPTER VI.

———

I do not like the Tower, of any place.
SHAKSPEARE.[a]

———

At nine o'clock in the evening, York and Lord Barry took their station on the Thames, at the appointed place. The boat was tethered to the shore; and the rising tide brought them nearer to the banks. All was dark, during the cold

---

[a] *Richard III*, III. i. 68.

night of early February; to the right and left, nothing was apparent save the glimmering water, and the only sound was the rushing and rippling of the Thames, as it sped downward in its course.

"My mother greets me with a cold kiss," said the Prince; "In truth, she has wedded mine enemy, and cast me out from my inheritance."[a] /

A brief pause ensued – a few minutes, which were freighted with the cares and sorrows of years. Back, back young Richard threw his eye over the skeleton shapes of the dead years; and again he sought to penetrate the future. Dark as the starless sky, not one gleam of comfort presented itself to the outcast's hope. But such state of mind was unnatural to the ardent boy, and he sprung from it;

> "Like to a lark at break of day, uprising
> From sullen earth, to sing at heaven's gate,"[b]

he soared from groveling despondency into recollections of the labour and love that had been expended on him. His harvest might never be the crown at which he aimed; but, better still, the ambrosial food of affection and devoted attachment, that filled him even to sweet satiety.

"A light! our beacon!" cried Lord Barry.

A small gleam appeared on the opposite bank. It moved; then returned to its former place, and was stationary. They watched it, till they became satisfied that it was the guide for which they were waiting. The early matin service / rung from several convents, and came pealing faintly across the water. It was the dead of night; and the gentlemen gladly exchanged their inert watch for the labour of contending with the tide and floating ice, which impeded their way, as they rowed across the Thames to where the light was now fixed.

The drear bank of the Tower-moat rose abruptly from the water-side, and the waves lay murky dark beneath the arch of the Traitor's Gate.[c] The tide, which was setting in, carried them above the point where the light was, to this spot. Their beacon indeed had disappeared; and, as they waited its return, they floated idly on the river, merely giving now and then a few strokes, to keep the wherry stationary. They did not perceive that, while they thus curbed the tide, they had drifted into an eddy which carried them fast down, till, jamming them between the wall of the Tower and a near pile, their boat lurched, partly filled with water, and resisted every attempt they made to extricate it. The clouds were getting thinner before the pale waning moon; but their fancied beacon light had vanished. /

Their situation was sufficiently dreary. The cold was piercing. They had difficulty in keeping themselves out of the water that lay at the bottom of the

---

[a] Warbeck's adventures in chs vi–ix are Mary Shelley's invention.

[b] Shakespeare, Sonnet XXIX, ll. 11–12 (loosely quoted).

[c] So called because under it lay 'a private passage by water from the Thames, through which state-prisoners were usually brought' (Bayley, p. 262).

boat. Lord Barry was a soldier, accustomed to hair-breadth escapes and dangerous attempts; Richard a bold youth, who thought that his best safety depended on his own exertions. They were neither of them inclined to linger tamely in their present situation.

"Before our limbs get numbed with this biting breeze, we must use them to our own benefit; your Highness can swim?"

"So say the streams of the Vega," replied Richard: "but the very remembrance of those sweet brooks makes me shudder at the chilly bath this ice-nourished river affords. I will reconnoitre the land, before I attempt the freezing wave." With lithe, sinuous limbs he coiled about the pile, and continued to raise himself to where a beam rested on the upright post, and again was fixed in the turret, which spans and guards the entrance to the Tower by water. He had hardly gained this place, and he felt little cold as with nervous fingers he kept fast in the position / he had attained, when a ray of light fell upon the water, streaming from out a window of the turret. It was but for a moment, and it disappeared; but Richard's eyes had glanced keenly on the illuminated spot. The transverse beam he had attained was but little below the window; it had been grated, but two of the stancheons were broken. This to our adventurer, suspended between the unattainable sky and the icy wave, seemed a place of refuge. Carefully and slowly, he with clinging knees and hands contrived to get along the beam, to raise himself on his feet on it, and then to clutch the broken iron bar, and hoist himself into a chamber of the Tower of London.

The immediate physical dangers that beset our adventurers were so great (the least horrific of which was spending the night exposed to freezing blasts, which Barry already felt chilling his very heart's blood), that they both forgot the dangerous nature of the asylum they were seeking. The Irish noble had, as well as darkness permitted, followed the movements of his / young companion; the same ray which guided Richard to temporary safety, had showed to Barry the mode of following him. He made the attempt; but, though stronger, he was not so agile as his friend; besides, the minutes which had elapsed during Richard's exertions, had enfeebled by numbing the other's powers; he got nearly to the top of the pile – he felt his fingers slip, and that he could hold on no longer. One desperate struggle he made to cling closer; his grasp seemed rather to relax, than tighten, in the attempt; and Richard, after a second, heard with horror his heavy fall into the water. But Barry was more at his ease in the yielding wave; and the very intensity of the cold, burning his skin, set his blood in motion: the tide also had arrived at its height during this interval, and had turned: without great difficulty the noble cleared, after a few strokes, the abrupt banks that fence the Tower, and landed on a quay below.

Richard heard the waters splash from under his strokes. The silence was so entire, that he thought he could distinguish the change of sound when the swimmer emerged, and plainly / heard Lord Barry's shout, in his own native

Irish, of thanksgiving and good cheer. For a moment, like lightning, it flashed into his mind, the thought of the ominous refuge he had found; and he was tempted to leap into the water and to rejoin his friend. But by this time the alarm of some one having plunged into the river, had been spread by the sentinels. The court became thronged; some hastened to the wall, others loosened the boats tethered beneath the gate, and issued in them from under the dark arch, over which Duke Richard had found refuge. By the glare of many torches, they discovered the wherry wedged in, as has been described. The splash attested that some one had fallen into the water: that some one should escape from the fortress, was more readily present to their imaginations, than that any should enter. They called to each other, communicating their surmises and intentions; then one boat remained in guard close at the gate, while the other rowed down the stream. Their exertions must end in nothing, for Lord Barry had had full time to ensure his escape. /

Richard attended to all their motions: several of the men in pursuit, had issued from the lower chambers of the turret in which he was: it was not thus cooped up, that he chose to be found; all seemed still; the only sounds came from the men in the boat; he descended the stairs: he came out upon the court of the Tower; the dark fortress frowned above, casting, in spite of the dull moon, a shadow dark enough to hide him. Steps were heard approaching; he turned under a dim archway; he ascended a narrow, steep staircase; the steps still followed; hurriedly he opened a door, and entered a chamber; the men, whoever they might be, were unaware of his presence; they passed the door, turned down another gallery; the very echo of their steps died away.

Did he recognize the spot where he then stood? Well! – far too well! – with a sickening feeling, an irresistible impulse to penetrate into the very heart of the horror that made his pulses faint, he gazed on the walls around. Was he then alone changed? had he sprung up into manhood, thought, experienced, suffered; / and had the material universe stood still the while? He saw before him a small chamber, enlightened by one deep-set window, half blocked up by projecting buttresses outside: there was the pallet-bed, the prie Dieu, the little crucifix: his infant limbs had reposed there; on that couch his brother had died.

This was the Tower! Ten years before he had escaped from its gloomy walls; and had he done this only to return again, when maturer years gave him a bitterer feeling of the ills he must endure? He had visited England, guided by the traitor-spirit of Clifford it seemed; for he had returned but to render himself a prisoner: yet at first these thoughts were hardly so painful as the memory of his childhood. The superstitous fears of the Tower, which haunted poor Edward, had made it an abode of terror for both: how often had they lain in that bed, curdling each other's young blood with frightful tales! His brother had pined, and died. Now, true to the pious usage of the times, he knelt to say a paternoster for his soul; he said another for his own perilous state; and then, having, / with entire faith committed himself to the protection of his Father in Heaven, he rose with a cheered heart and sustained courage.

What was he to do? He was in the Tower; a fortress so well guarded, that of the unhappy beings confined there for life, none had ever made their escape: high walls, numerous courts, and grated windows, opposed his egress. The clock chimed one. It were as well to remain where he was, as to go on. But it were better still to turn back: quiet would soon be restored; he might attain the same room, the same window, and leap thence into the waters below. He remembered wherefore he had come; the hazardous enterprise of Monina, and the imprisonment of Stanley. Now that he had attained this chamber, the whole Tower presented itself, as in a map, to his memory: he knew where the rooms allotted to state prisoners were situated: confident in his knowledge, his feelings underwent an entire change; instead of considering himself a prisoner in the Tower, he felt lord of its labyrinths. Darkness was his wand of office; the ignorance of all that he was there, was his guard; and his knowledge of the place, better / than the jailor's key, might aid him to liberate the victims of his enemy.

In this temper of mind he rejoiced that he had been unable to follow his first impulse in leaping from the window; and he resolved on making his way immediately to the part of the fortress inhabited by the state prisoners. Blindfold, setting out from the point where he was, he could have found his way; yet several images of barred and locked doors presented themselves to his recollection, as intervening between the spot where he then was, and that which he desired to visit. He descended again into the court – he skirted the edifice, keeping close to the shadowy wall – he saw the door but a few paces distant, which led to the prison-chambers. At dead of night it must be locked and barred, guarded by a sentinel, quite inaccessible to him. He paused – he saw no soldier near – he walked on a few steps quickly; the door was wide open – this looked like success – he sprung up the steps; a man below cried, "Who goes there?" adding, "Is it you, sir? My light is puffed out; I will bring one anon." Above he heard / another voice – there was no retreat – he went on, relying on some chance, that might afford him a refuge under cover of mirky night from the twofold danger that beset him. A man stood at the door-way of the nearest chamber; it was not possible to pass him – as he hesitated he heard the words, "Good rest visit your Lordship – I grieve to have disturbed you." Richard retired a few steps – the man closed, locked the door – "A light, ho!" he exclaimed, and the Prince feared to see the servitor ascend the stairs. The moon just beginning to show its clouded rays threw a brief ray upon the landing, where Richard stood, and he moved out of the partial radiance; the slight movement he made attracted notice, which was announced by a challenge of "Who goes there? is it you, Fitzwilliam? How is this? the word, sir!"

The Duke knew that, among the numerous and various inhabitants of the Tower, many were personally unknown to each other; and that any stranger visitor was not entrusted with the word – so he replied immediately, as his best safeguard. "I was roused by the / calling of the guard. I knew not that such reveilles were usual; good night, sir."

Those pay little attention to the impression of their senses, who are not aware, that family resemblance developes itself in nothing so much as the voice; and that it is difficult in the dark to distinguish relatives. In confirmation of this I heard a sagacious observer remark, and have proved the observation true, that the formation of the jaw, and setting of the teeth is peculiar, and the same in families. But this is foreign – enough, that, caught by the voice, hardly able to distinguish the obscure outline of the speaker in the almost blackness of night – the man replied, "I crave pardon, my good Lord, you forget yourself, this way is your chamber. What, ho! a light!"

"It needs not," said the Prince; "the glare would offend mine eyes – I shall find the door."

"Permit me," said the other, going forward, "I will wait on your Lordship so far. I wonder not you were roused; there was an alarm at the river postern, and the whole guard roused. Sir John thought it might concern poor Sir William;[a] / and I was fain to see all right with him. It irked me truly to break in on his repose; the last he may ever have."

They approached a door; the man's hand was on the lock – Richard's heart beat so loud and fast, that it seemed to him that that alone must be perceived and excite suspicion – if the door were fastened on the inside he were lost; but the man was in no hurry to try – he talked on: –

"The Lieutenant was the more suspicious, because he gave credit and easy entrance to his pretended stripling son, who craved for it even with tears: yet when they met, we all thought that the Lord Chamberlain did not greet him as a parent would a child at such a time; the truth, indeed, we saw with half an eye, be she his daughter, or his light-of-love; yet not the last, methinks, for she seemed right glad to be accommodated for the night in a separate chamber – she is a mere girl besides, and in spite of her unmeet garb, modest withal."

"When goes she? With the dawn?" Richard hazarded these questions, for his silence might / be more suspected than his speech; and the information he sought, imported to him.

"Nay, she will stay to the end for me," said the man: "Sir William was a kind gentleman, as I can testify, in his prosperity; and it is little to let him have the comfort of this poor child's company for a day longer: he dies on the morrow."

"Could I see this fair one?"

"By my troth, fair she is not, though lovely to look on, but somewhat burnt, as if her mother had been a dweller in the south. If you visit and take leave of

---

[a] Sir John Digby, Lieutenant of the Tower of London, and 'Sir William' Stanley.

Sir Stanley to-morrow, you may chance to behold her: but I detain you, my Lord; a good night, rather, a good morning to your lordship."

He unclosed the door; all was dark within, save that the chamber opened into another at the further end, in which evidently a lamp was burning. Kind thanks and a benison passed; Richard stepped within the apartment, and the door shut on him.

What could this mean? Glad, confused, yet still fearful, the Prince was almost deprived of / the power of motion. Recovering himself with a strong effort, he passed on to the inner chamber: it was a bed-room, tapestried, strewed thick with rushes, a silver lamp suspended by a silver chain to the grim claws of a gilt eagle, which was fixed in the ceiling, gave token of rank, as well as the rich damask of the bed-furniture and the curious carving of the couch and seats; the articles of dress also strewed about belonged to the noble born: strange, as yet Richard had not conjectured for whom he had been mistaken! He drew near the bed, and gazed fixedly on its occupier. The short, clustering, auburn curls were tinged with grey, yet the sleeper was young, though made untimely old by suffering; his cheeks were wasted and fallen in; the blue veins on his brow were conspicuous, lifting the clear skin which clung almost to the bones; he was as pale as marble, and the heavy eye-lids were partly raised even in sleep by the large blue ball that showed itself beneath; one hand lay on the coverlid, thin to emaciation. What manner of victim was this to Henry's tyranny? nay, the enigma was / easily solved: it must be the Earl of Warwick. "And such, but for my cousin Lincoln, would have been my fate," thought Richard. He remembered his childhood's imprisonment; he thought of the long days and nights of confinement, the utter hopelessness, the freezing despair, blighting the budding hopes of youth, the throes of intolerable, struggling agony, which had reduced poor Warwick to this shadow of humanity; he felt a choking sensation in his throat as he bent over him: large drops gathered in his eyes; they fell, ere he was aware, on the sleeper's wan cheek.

Warwick turned uneasily, opened his eyes, and half started up, "Whom have we here?" he cried; "why am I disturbed?"

"Your pardon, fair gentleman," Richard began –

"My pardon!" repeated Warwick bitterly; "were that needed, you were not here. What means this intrusion – tell me, and be gone?"

"I am not what you take me for, cousin Edward," said the Prince. /

Now indeed did Warwick start: shading his eyes from the lamp he gazed earnestly on the speaker, murmuring, "That voice, that name – it cannot be – In the name of sweet charity speak again; tell me what this means, and if you are – why this visit, why that garb?"

"My dear Lord of Warwick," said the Prince, "dismiss this inquietude, and if you will listen with patience to the story of an unhappy kinsman, you shall know all. I am Richard of York; those whose blood is akin to yours as well as mine, have y'cleped me the White Rose of England."

The Earl of Warwick had heard of the Pretender set up by his aunt, the Duchess of Burgundy; he had often pondered over the likelihood of his really being his cousin, and the alteration it would occasion in his fortunes, if he were to succeed. Shut out from the world, as he had been so long, the victim of mere despair, he could not even imagine that good could betide to any one, save to the oppressor of his race; to see Perkin, for so he had been taught to call him, within the walls of the ill-fated / Tower, appeared to disclose at once his defeat. Even when the Duke rapidly and briefly narrated the accidents that had brought him thither, and his strange position, Prince Edward believed only that he had been decoyed into the trap, which had closed on him for ever.

Still Richard talked on: his ardour, his confidence in his own measures, his vivacious anxiety already to put them into practice, his utter fearlessness, were not lost upon one who had been dead to outward impressions, not from want of sensibility, but from the annihilation of hope. Some of his cousin's spirit overflowed into Warwick's heart; and, in conclusion, he assented to all he said, promising to do whatever was required of him, though after ten years of lone imprisonment he almost shrunk from emerging from his listless state. /

CHAPTER VII.

———

Let all the dukes and all the devils roar,
He is at liberty! I've ventured for him;
And out I've brought him to a little wood
A mile hence.

TWO NOBLE KINSMEN.[a]

———

Morning, cold and wintry, dawned upon the gloomy chambers of the Tower. York became eager to put in execution some plan of escape in which Warwick should share; but Warwick was full of timidity and fear. His prison was a frightful den; yet all without was a wide, pathless, tiger-infested jungle. He besought his cousin to regard his own safety only. Richard refused; yet the more he meditated, the more did obstacles crowd upon him. After the lapse of

———

[a] Probably a collaboration between Shakespeare and Fletcher, II. vi. 1–4.

an / hour, Warwick was called upon to attend early mass, as usual, in the chapel of the fortress. Here he saw Stanley and the disguised shrinking Monina; and, the service ended, attended them to the prison-chamber of the Chamberlain, relating as he went, in quick low whispers, the history of the preceding night. Both his hearers grew pale: one feared for her friend, the other for himself; though on that score all cause of dread was well nigh at an end. All three entered Stanley's cell, and found there Prince Richard himself, whose active mind had led him to watch his opportunity to pass hither unseen from Warwick's apartment.

The young Earl of March,[a] arming for the battle of Northhampton, looked not so young, so blooming, and so frankly erect, as his uncrowned son. Stanley saw at once who was before him, and, never forgetting the courtier, addressed his Prince with a subject's respect. York was struck by the placid, though somewhat worldly physiognomy of the man, devoted to die, at the age when human beings are most apt to cling to life; when, having weathered the storms and / passions of youth, they desire to repose awhile on the sun-enlightened earth, before they enter the gloomy gates of the tomb.

The Prince spoke eagerly of escape – of safety – of life: Warwick, even timid Warwick, urged an attempt at flight; while Monina kissed her aged friend's hand, and turned her sweet eyes on him, saying: "You will listen to him, though you were deaf to me."

Stanley alone was unmoved[b] – "A thousand heartfelt, useless thanks, my dear and honoured Lord, your poor servant renders; and even when prayer for himself is most needed, earnestly he prays that harm to you arise not from your unexampled generosity. I cannot fly; I do believe that I would not, if I could: and I will spare myself the disgrace of further endangering you, and of being seized myself in the coward's act. Ask me not, with your beseeching eyes, my gentle, venturous child, for it must not be. I die to-morrow; and this fate you would have me avoid. Whither would you drag me from the block? To poverty? to an unhonoured old age? a traitor's reputation, and miserable dependance? I am a sinful man; but / I trust in God's mercy, and he holds out better hopes after the brief spasm of death, than you after the torture of difficult escape."

More he would have said, but they were interrupted; they had not been aware of any one's approach; and suddenly Sir John Digby, Lieutenant of the Tower, entered. He was aghast to see one more than he expected, one whose demeanour spoke nobility. Silence followed his entrance, nor did words readily present themselves to the blunt soldier; at length, addressing the cause of this wonder, he in an ironical tone of voice asked – "May I, Lieutenant of this

---

[a] Edward IV held the title Earl of March when Henry VI was defeated at Northampton on 10 July 1460.

[b] 'Feb. 15' (marginal note in *Abinger/Palacio*), 1495, the day before Stanley's execution.

Fortress, delegated by his Majesty to its keeping, be permitted to ask, fair sir, the name, station, and designs, of my unbidden guest?"

"My answer to your two first questions," replied York, "would little satisfy you; my design was to facilitate the escape of this virtuous and unhappy gentleman."

"The King is infinitely your debtor, and I shall prove unmannered in marring your intent."

"You do not mar it, Sir John," said the / Prince; "my Lord Chamberlain is a true man, and would rather lay his head on the block at his liege's bidding, than carry it in security at the prayer of any other. Sir William has refused to fly; and, my mission ended, I was about to take my leave."

"Do so, young man; take leave – an eternal one – of Sir William, and follow me. My Lord of Warwick, this is an unmeet scene for you to be present at. This holy man comes to bestow the last words of pious comfort my noble prisoner can receive in this world: please your Lordship to leave them together uninterrupted. I am sorry," continued the Lieutenant, addressing Monina, "to retract the permission I gave you yesterday; but this strange incident must be my excuse: say a last farewell to him you have named your father."

Monina dreaded too much the fate that might befall her friend, to entreat for any change in this decree. Soon poor Sir William found himself separated from the busy scene of life, shut up with the chaplain. He was bid to remember and repent, and to prepare to die. / A dark veil fell before the vista of coming years, which was apparent to the eyes of his late companions. He saw in the present hour – one only, almost superfluous, added to the closing account. They beheld in it the arbiter of their undivined destinies.

It is an awful emotion, when we feel that the "very shoal of time"[a] on which we stand, is freighted with the good and ill of futurity – that the instant birth of the hour inherits our entire fortunes. Yet Richard was proof against this rough testimony of our powerless mortality. The ill had not yet arrived, with which he did not believe he could cope; and more – now he was bent upon endeavouring to save Stanley; for his own fate, though about to expose it to the most unquestioned shape of peril, he had no fears.

Sir John Digby, followed by his new prisoners, paced back to his own chamber, and then addressed his uninvited guest. "Fair gentleman," he said, "again I crave to be informed of your name and degree, that his Majesty may be duly made aquainted on whom to bestow his thanks. Your speech and appearance are English?" /

"Whoever I may be," replied York, "I will reveal nothing except to your King. If he is willing to listen to disclosures nearly touching his throne and safety, I will rouse him by a tale to shake sleep from one who has steeped his eyes in poppy juice. To no other will I vouchsafe a word."

---

[a] 'bank and shoal of time', in *Macbeth*, I. vii. 6.

Monina listened in terror. She would have given her life to beseech her friend to retract that foolish word, but it was too late; while his questioner, startled by his unforeseen reply, said "You make a bold demand; think you that his Grace is of such common use, that it is an easy matter to attain his presence?"

"I have said it, Sir John," answered York; "your liege may hereafter visit with poor thanks the denial you give me."

The Lieutenant fixed his eyes on him; his youth and dignity impressed him favourably; but he hesitated, confused by doubts of who and what he might be. At last he said, "His Majesty is at present at his palace of Shene, ten miles hence."

"The less reason, Sir Lieutenant," replied / Richard, "that you should dally in the execution of your duty. The life of your prisoner, the fortunes of your King, depend upon this interview."

This was a riddle difficult for Sir John to solve; and he was about to order his enigmatical visitant to the guard-room, while he should consult upon the fitting conduct to pursue; when a beating at the gates, the letting down of the draw-bridge, and the clatter of hoofs announced fresh arrivals at the fortress.

The attention of every one was suspended, till, the usher announcing the excellent Prince, the Earl of Desmond, that noble, attended by followers, almost with regal pomp, entered. He cast his penetrating glance around, and then unbonneting to the Duke, he said respectfully, "Your Highness will believe that as soon as I heard of the position into which, pardon me, your generous rashness has betrayed you, I hastened hither to vouch for you, and deliver you from it."

To such a speech, so unexpected, so portentous, what answer? Richard felt inclined to / laugh, as he heard himself spoken to, in terms which seemed to say that the discovery of who he really was, would occasion his release; but he quickly discerned a hidden meaning beneath this incomprehensible language, and he contented himself with graciously thanking the Earl for his interference, while this noble turned to address the wondering Sir John.

"Sir Lieutenant," said he, "I have a strange story to tell, fitter for his Majesty's ears than those of a subject; but his Grace is absent, and it were not well that this noble gentleman should be kept in durance while messengers go to and fro. Rather dismiss your followers, and I will confide a weighty secret to you, and bring such arguments as will induce you to entrust the high-born youth to my care and escort."

Digby was not much of a statesman; he had a simple heart, and considerable veneration for rank. He knew that the Earl of Desmond had been well received at court, and complied with his desire. The noble then began a long explana-tion / of parties and tumults in Scotland; of the frightful death of James the Third; the accession of James the Fourth; the discontent of several chief nobles, who wished to set up the younger brother of the new king in opposition to him.

"Your Highness," continued Desmond, addressing Richard, "will pardon me for thus introducing your name – this, Sir Lieutenant, is the Duke of Rosse, who has come, and not vainly, to seek the assistance of our liege."[a]

Sir John bowed low and looked puzzled, while Desmond continued to speak of disguise and secresy, of friendship for Stanley, and of the rash design of Lord Barry of Buttevant and the young Duke to liberate him, chiefly under the idea that thus they should best serve King Henry, who must in his heart be loth to have his zealous friend put to death through the falsehood of faction. "And now, gentle Sir," he continued, "be guided by me; the King loves peace; he loves state privacy; the very presence of the Duke in this country is a mystery; you will do agreeable service by hushing up this youthful frolic. Permit his / Highness to accompany me; I will make fitting report to his Majesty, who will be grateful withal."

There was a kind of confused tallying in the story; for Richard's mysterious words were at no discord with Desmond's explanations; and his excessively youthful and perfectly noble appearance were further corroboration. Digby liked not the responsibility of keeping him: he spoke of sending for the Bishop of Durham. Desmond exclaimed, "A soldier have recourse to a priest – this England is a strange country! Do as you will; only until the thumber of missals arrive, this is no place of entertainment for the Prince. We will receive you and your clericus[b] at Walbrook;[c] and I will entertain the royal gentleman till you come."

Digby still looked blank and uncertain. Richard, who had remained silent, now spoke: "Farewell, good Sir; in truth, I need your excuse for my impertinent visit; but here it ends. When I travel to Scotland, I will report the favour I met at your hands."

This sufficed. Sir John sullenly yielded: with / a mixture of fear and deference, he attended his visitors to the court; they crossed the draw-bridge; and ere the Tower-gates closed behind them, they heard the lieutenant order out a guard and his own horse, that without loss of time he might communicate with the Bishop.

The Duke and his preserver rode gently enough down Tower Hill: scarce had they reached the foot, before the Earl gave a sudden command to his followers, who turned one way, as he, York, and Monina, who had left the Tower at the same time, and was mounted on one of Desmond's attendants' horses, went another. "*Au galoppe*, dear, my lord!" cried the Earl, "we have but a short hour's grace – this way – still the river to our left."

---

[a] For James III and James IV, see pp. 209–10 and n. The Duke of Ross (1476–1504), also named James, later became Archbishop of St Andrew's.

[b] clericus, Latin for clergyman or priest.

[c] Named for the stream – and later street – that ran through the centre of the City of London into the Thames.

They galloped along with loosened reins. Arriving at the vale of Holborn, they followed the upward course of the Fleet, so to reach the open country; and many a wild field they crossed, and briary lane they threaded – the country was flat, marshy, wild; skirted in various directions by brown wintry woods, rarely interspersed by hamlets. The river was their / only guide; they followed its course for several miles, till they reached the shelter of Caen Wood.[a] Thank St. Patrick[b] for this cover!" cried the Irish chieftain; "may my cousin Barry find no let nor hindrance – yon troubled stream will guide him well. We have done a daring deed: for me, I have not ridden so far since my father, God sain[c] him! died – I am well nigh *hors de combat*."

The Prince assisted both his companions to dismount. Lord Desmond's tale was soon told, of how Lord Barry had sought him and suggested this mode of effecting York's escape. "With the help of your Moorish friend," said the Earl, "no ill wind betide me – I shall be in Munster before the riddle be half told; that is, if ever we reach the vessel. By my faith! I would rather be knee-deep in a bog in Thomond, than dry shod where I am!"

As day advanced, the situation of the fugitives became still more disquieting. All was tranquil in the leafless wood; but, in spite of the sun, it was very cold. Besides, they were in an unknown spot, without guide; their sole hope / being, that each passing minute would bring Lord Barry to their assistance. Earl Maurice was thoroughly disabled; he grumbled at first, and at last wearied out, lay on the cold ground, and fell into a slumber. Monina, serious, timid, and yet in spite of herself happy in her friend's safety, and in her own being near him, was silent; while Richard, to escape from his own thoughts, talked to her. When, for a moment, his conversation languished, his eyes were fondly fixed upon her downcast face, and a strife of sentiment, of ardent long-restrained love, and a torturous, but severe resolve to protect her even from himself, battled in his heart; so that, in all-engrossing love, every sense of danger was lost.

Desmond at last roused himself: "The shadows grow long; herbage there is little for our horses, pasture for ourselves there is none – if we stay we starve; if we stir, we –"

He was interrupted; strange voices came upon the wind; then the crackling of boughs, and the sound of steps. Through the vista of bare trees the intruders at length appeared, in / strange array. There was a band of ill-attired, ruffian-looking men, followed by women and children; their swart visages, their picturesque, but scant and ragged garb, their black hair and dark flashing eyes

---

[a] The trio, riding westward out of London along the north bank of the Thames, passes through what was later to be the Skinner Street neighbourhood of the Godwin household, and then northward to the present Ken Wood in Highgate. Coleridge lived in Highgate (1816–34).
[b] Ireland's patron saint.
[c] Archaic for bless.

were not English. Some were on foot, some on asses, some in a cart, drawn by two rough ill-assorted colts – their very language was foreign. Richard and Monina recognised a horde of Gitani,[a] Bohemians, or Gypsies; while Desmond looked in wonder on something almost wilder than the Irish kern.

The savage wanderers were surprised to perceive the previous guests the barren woods had received – they paused and looked around in some fear; for the noble appearance of the gentlemen made them imagine that they must be accompanied by numerous attendants. York's quick wit suggested to him in a moment of what good use such humble friends might be. He addressed them; told them that they were travellers who had lost their way, "And so we have encroached on your rightful domain; but, like courteous hosts, I beseech you, gentlemen, welcome us to your / green-wood palace, and make happy, as you will grateful, guests of us."

Thus invited, the whole horde gathered round – the women, fancying all three of an opposite sex, were forward with their prophetic art.

"My fortune," cried Desmond, "shall not be told before supper; it is an ill one, by the rood! at this hour. I have fasted since yesternight."

Preparations were speedily made for a repast, while Richard, alive to his situation, looked around for the most fitting object to address; whose charity and aid he could hope to solicit with the greatest success. One laughing-eyed girl glanced at him with peculiar favour; but near her stood and scowled a tall handsome countryman of her own. York turned to another, fairer, who sat retired apart; she looked more gentle and even refined than the rest. He addressed her in courtly phrase, and her reply, though ready, was modest. The acquaintance was a little in progress, when one of the oldest among the sibyls, with white hair, and a face of wrinkled parchment, hobbled up, / muttering, "Aye, aye, the fairest flower is aye the dearest to pluck; any of those gaudy weeds might serve his turn; but no, my young master must needs handle the daintiest bloom of the garden." Notwithstanding this interruption, Richard still stood his ground, bandying pretty speeches with one, not the less pleased, because, strictly guarded by her duenna, she was unaccustomed to the language of flattery.

"Hast never a word for me, fair sir," said the crone, at last; "no comparison of star and gems for one, who in her day has flaunted with silk-clad dames – whose lips have been pressed even by a king?"

His father's reputation for gallantry, thus alluded to, brought the blood into York's cheeks; forgetful of what import his words bore, he replied hastily, "Sleep King Edward's faults with him, mother; it is neither wise nor well to speak irreverently of those gone to their doom – may God assoilzie him!"

"What voice is that?" cried the old woman; "if I boast, Heaven forgive me, of his Grace's slight favour, your mother may take shame –" /

---

[a] Mary Shelley's use of this word antedates OED's first record, 1834.

"Your words are naught," cried York, interrupting her, "my mother's is a sacred name – yet, tell me in very truth, and give me some sign that indeed you knew my father."

The word passed his lips before he was aware, but being spoken, he felt that it were best not to recede. Seizing the old woman's shrivelled hand, he said, "Look – use thy art – read my palm: read rather my features, and learn indeed who I am: I am in danger; you may betray, or you may save me, choose which you will – I am the Duke of York."

An exclamation checked, a look of boundless surprise, changed into a cautious glance around, attested the Gypsy's wish to serve the venturous youth. "Rash boy," she answered, in a low voice, "what idle, or what mortal words are these! How art thou here? With what hope? What aid?"

"Frankly, none but what I derive from your bounty. I have escaped worse peril, so do not fear but that God will protect me; and even turn to profit my parent's sin, if his kiss purchase his son's life." /

"Young sir," said the Gypsy, with great seriousness, "the flower of love is gay – its fruit too often bitter. So does she know on whose account I wickedly and shamelessly did the Foul Fiend's bidding, and ruined a sinless soul to gratify the pleasure-loving king. But thou hast paid the penalty: thou and thine, who have been called by the ill-word; thrust from thy place by thy crook-back uncle; and now art nearer a dungeon than a throne, through thy father's fault. I will serve and save thee; tell me quickly, who are thy companions – whither thou wouldst go? that I may judge the best to be done."

It is to be observed, that at the very beginning of this colloquy, the young girl, whom York had first addressed, had stolen away. Now he replied by mentioning the lameness of his elder friend, and his resolve not to be divided from the other. He spoke of the Adalid, and of his further wish to be awhile concealed in England. The old woman continued silent, wrapt in thought. At length she raised her head – "It can be done, and it shall," she said, half to herself, / "Come now, they are serving our homely fare. You, who are young, and ill apt for penance, must eat before you go."

The savoury steams of the well-filled and rustic *marmite*,[a] gave force to her words, and to Richard's appetite. The repast was plentiful and gay, and even too long. Evening was far advanced, the fire grew light in the dusk, and threw its fitful rays upon the strange and incongruous feasters. Monina had cowered close to Richard; the cup went round; scarcely did she put it to her lips; a rude companion of the crew made some rough jest on her sobriety. Richard's face lighted up with anger: his watchful old friend stept forward, in her own jargon she made some communication to her associates, which caused a universal pause, and then a stir: it was evident some movement was intended. She

---

[a] A pot or kettle hung over the fire.

meanwhile drew the three fugitives aside. "In a few minutes," she said, "we shall all be on our way hence; listen how I would provide for your safeties." She then proposed that Desmond should assume the disguise of one of the horde, and so be conveyed in safety to the / banks of the Thames, and on board the Adalid. She promised herself to conduct the Prince and his young friend to a secure refuge. The Earl, accustomed to find fidelity and rags near mates, readily acceded to this proposal. In the solitary unknown spot to which chance had directed them, environed by every danger, no step was more perilous than the remaining where they were. York and Monina were familiar with the reports of the gypsy character – its savage honour and untractable constancy. The season was such, though the day had been unusually sunny and warm, as to make a night in the open air no agreeable anticipation; and Richard had a thousand fears on his lovely friend's account. They all readily acceded to the old woman's plan. Desmond was quickly disguised, his visage stained deep brown, his whole person transformed; he was placed in the caravan, and the horde was speedily in movement; the sound of their departing steps died away. They had left a rude cart, to which York's horse, a strong hack, was harnessed. The sibyl undertook to guide it. Richard and Monina ascended the jumbling / fabric. Soon they were on their journey, none but their conductress knew in what direction; but they submitted to her, and through copse and over field they wound their darkling way. /

CHAPTER VIII.

———

So love did vanish with my state,
Which now my soul repents too late;
Then, maids and wives, in time amend,
For love and beauty will have end.

BALLAD OF JANE SHORE.[a]

Oh, it grieves my soul
That I must draw this metal from my side
To be a widow-maker!

SHAKSPEARE.[b]

———

Seated in the rude gypsy-cart, guided, protected, by the uncouth being into whose hands he had so strangely fallen, Richard for the first time felt the degradation and low fortune to which his aspirations, at variance with his means, made him liable. With a strong / effort he dismissed these painful ideas, and fixed his contemplation on mightier objects, which gilded his mean estate, or were rather the "gold o'erdusted"[c] by such extraneous poverty. To rise from this lowliness to a throne were an emprise worthy his ambition. Was he not a few hours ago a prisoner in the terror-striking Tower? And now he was free – free in his England; which, when the battle-day was come and past, would claim him for her own. A few words from Monina interrupted the silence: she sat at his feet, and they conversed in whispers in Spanish. Night had gathered round them; Monina, in all the innocence of her pure heart, was supremely happy: to be near her friend in his disasters, united to him in his peril, was a more rapturous destiny to her than the world's best pomp, and he absent. No busy conscience, no untoward thought, disturbed in her soul the calm of perfect bliss. She grew weary at last; her head sunk on Richard's knee, and, overworn with watching, she fell into a deep sleep. Richard heard her regular

———

[a] Percy, *Reliques*, 2nd Series, II, 26, ll. 101–2, 149–50.
[b] *King John*, V. ii. 15–17.
[c] *Troilus and Cressida*, III. iii. 179 (loosely quoted).

189

breathing; once or twice his fingers played among her / dishevelled ringlets, while his heart whispered to him what a wondrous creation woman was – weak, frail, complaining when she suffers for herself; heroic fortitude and untired self-devotion are hers, when she sacrifices herself for him she loves.

The cart moved on, Richard saw not whither; they almost stuck in some flat low fields, and at last arrived at a solitary, miserable hut. Monina awoke, when they stopt, and the gypsy told them that this wretched dwelling was to be their asylum: the apartment they entered was poor beyond meanness – a bed of straw piled in one corner, a rude bench, formed the furniture; the walls were ragged and weather-stained, and the outer crumbling rafters were visible through the broken ceiling: there appeared to be neither food nor fire. The inhabitant of the hovel alone was there, a white-looking, emaciated female; yet with a look of such sweetness and patience, that she seemed the very enshrinement of Christian resignation, the type of sorrow and suffering, married to meek obedience to the supreme will. She had roused herself from slumber at the voice of the / gypsy, and gathered her scant garments around her – scant and poor they were; her coarse woollen dress was tied by a girdle of rope round her slender waist; her head was wrapt in a kerchief; her feet were bare.

"Jane," said the old woman, "you will not refuse the shelter of your roof to these poor wanderers?"

Such an address seemed strange, for the rich attire of her guests ill-accorded with her poverty-stricken home; but she turned with a smile – she spoke – and then a throb of agony seemed to convulse her frame – her head swam; Richard rushed forward to prevent her falling, but she shrunk from him, and leaned on the old woman, who said with a look of triumph, "I knew how it would be; it is vain to hide a bright light behind a veil of gauze! Yes, Jane, this is his son; and you may save him from danger and death."

Jane Shore, the once lovely mistress of King Edward, now the miserable outcast of the world's scorn, heard these words, as if they had been spoken to her in a dream. After the death of / her royal lover, she had obeyed the impulse that made her cling to the soft luxuries of life, and yielded to solicitations which tended to guard her from the sharp visitation of the world. She had become the mistress of the Marquess of Dorset; but sorrow and penury were destined to pursue her in their worst shape – and wherefore? She had been good and humane; and in spite of her error, even the sternest moralist might have pitied her. But she was all woman, fearful of repulse, dreading insult; more willing to lie down and die, than, fallen and miserable, to solicit uncertain relief: squalid poverty, famine, and lonely suffering, were hers; yet in all she preserved an unalterable sweetness of disposition, which painted her wan face with its own soft colouring.[a]

---

[a] Jane Shore (d. 1527) encouraged Dorset and William, Baron Hastings (?1430–83), to thwart the ambitions of Richard III, who forced her to do public penance after he seized the throne. She died in poverty.

The old woman went forth to seek for food, and the two friends were left for several hours alone with Jane. She gazed affectionately on the youthful Duke; she looked more timidly on Monina, whose sex could not be said to be disguised by her page's dress: the fallen woman fears women, their self-sufficient virtues and / cold reprobation; yet the sensibility of Monina's countenance, and the soft expression of her eyes, so all-powerful in their sweetness, could not be mistaken; and her first shrinking from censure was exchanged for even a more painful feeling. They were a lovely pair, those lone guests of poverty; innocence sat on the brow of each, yet love beamed in their aspect: – love! the two-edged sword, the flower-strewn poison, the dread cause of every misery! More than famine and sickness Jane feared love; for with it in her mind were linked shame and guilt, and the world's unkindness, hard to bear to one, whose heart was "open as day to melting charity;"[a] and she feared that she saw in this sweet girl a bright reflex of her early days. Oh, might the blotted mirror ne'er pourtray a change like hers! "I am a living lesson of the woes of love," thought poor Jane; "may this chance-visit to my hut, which saves young Richard's life, ensure her innocence!" Thus impelled, she spoke: she spoke of the danger of their solitary companionship; she adjured York to fly the delusive charm – for love's own sake he ought to fly; for / if he made her his victim, affection would be married to hate – joy to woe – her he prized to a skeleton, more grim than death. Richard strove to interrupt her, but she misunderstood his meaning; while Monina, somewhat bewildered, fancied that she only alluded to the dangers she incurred in his cause, and with her own beaming look cried, "Oh, Mother, is it not better to suffer for one so noble, than to live in the cold security of prosperity?"

"No, no," said Jane, "Oh, does my miserable fate cry aloud, no! Edward, his father, was bright as he. Libertine he was called – I know not if truly; but sincere was the affection he bore to me. He never changed nor faltered in the faith he promised, when he led me from the dull abode of connubial strife, to the bright home of love. Riches and the world's pleasures were the least of his gifts, for he gave me himself and happiness. Behold me now: twelve long years have passed, and I waste and decay; the wedded wife of shame; famine, sorrow, and remorse, my sole companions."

This language was too plain. The blood / rushed into Monina's face. "Oh, love him not," continued the hapless penitent; "fly his love, because he is beautiful, good, noble, worthy – fly from him, and thus preserve him yours for ever."

Monina quickly recovered herself; she interrupted her imprudent monitress, and calmly assured her that her admonition, though unnecessary, should not prove vain; and then both she and York exerted themselves to engage Jane's

---

[a] *2 Henry IV*, IV. iv. 32 reads '[…] for meting charity' in modern editions which follow the Quarto.

191

attention on topics relative to his cause, his hopes, his partizans, thus exciting her curiosity and interest.

Richard passed the whole of the following day[a] in this abode of penury and desolation. That day, indeed, was big with dire event. The morning rose upon Stanley's death. In Jane's hut the hollow bell was heard that tolled the fatal hour. The ear is sometimes the parent of a livelier sense than any other of the soul's apprehensive portals. In Italy, for three days in Passion Week, the sound of every bell and of every clock is suspended. On the noon of the day when the mystery of the Resurrection is solemnized, they / all burst forth in one glad peal. Every Catholic kneels in prayer, and even the unimaginative Protestant feels the influence of a religion, which speaks so audibly.[b] And, in this more sombre land, the sad bell that tolls for death, strikes more melancholy to the heart, than the plumed hearse, or any other pageantry of woe. In silence and fear the fugitives heard the funereal knell sweep across the desolate fields, telling them that at that moment Stanley died.

Women nurse grief – dwell with it. Like poor Constance,[c] they dress their past joys in mourning raiment, and so abide with them. But the masculine spirit struggles with suffering. How gladly, that very evening, did the Duke hail Frion's arrival, who, in the garb of a saintly pardoner, came to lead him from Jane's dim abode. In spite of his remonstrances, Monina refused to accompany him: she should endanger him, she said; besides that, his occupation would be to rouse a martial spirit among the Yorkists – hers to seek the Adalid and her dear father's protection.

Frion procured a safe asylum for the Prince; / and here, no longer pressed by the sense of immediate danger, his head was rife with projects, his spirit burning to show himself first to the Yorkists, in a manner worthy of his pretensions. The choice was hazardous and difficult: but it so happened, that it was notified that in a few weeks Lord Surrey's eldest sister was to marry the Lord de Walden,[d] and the ceremony was to be graced with much feasting and a solemn tournament.

There was magic in all the associations with this family for Richard. In his early infancy, Thomas Mowbray, the last of the Dukes of Norfolk of that name, died. It almost was beyond his recollection, that he had been married to the little Lady Anne, the Duke's only child and heiress.[e] She died soon after; and the representative of the female branch of the Mowbrays, John Howard, was created Duke of Norfolk by Richard the Third. He fell at Bosworth; and his son, the Earl of Surrey, though attaching himself to Henry the Seventh, and

---

[a] 'Feb. 16' (marginal note in *Abinger/Palacio*), 1495, the date of Stanley's execution.

[b] Religious observances no doubt witnessed during Mary Shelley's residence in Italy (1818–23).

[c] The eloquent, grief-stricken mother of Arthur in *King John*.

[d] Unidentified; Surrey had numerous sisters.

[e] Anne (d. 1483), daughter of John (not Thomas) Mowbray, 4th Duke of Norfolk (d. 1475), the betrothed of young York.

pardoned and taken into favour, was not permitted to assume his father's attainted title.[a] /

At this marriage feast the mother of his Anne, the dowager Duchess of Norfolk, daughter of Talbot, Earl of Shrewsbury,[b] so famous in the French wars, would be present; and others of the Howard and Berkeley[c] families, all Yorkist once. The Prince could not resist the temptation of appearing on the lists that day, where, if success crowned him, as surely it would, he could with prouder hopes call on Surrey to maintain his claims. Frion got gallant armour for him, and contrived to have him, under another name, inserted in the list of combatants.

York's bosom swelled with pride and exultation, when he saw himself among his countrymen – his subjects – with lance in rest and bright shield upon his arm, about to tilt with England's noblest cavaliers. It seemed to him, as if he had never asked more of fortune – and the herald's voice, the clarion's sound, the neigh of steeds, the gallant bearing of the knights, and charmed circle of joyous beauty around, were like a voice from beyond life, speaking of a Paradise he had left, – his own native home. But one emotion of disquiet crossed him: as about to pass the / barrier, Frion put his hand on his rein, and whispered, "Beware of Clifford!" The Duke threw his eyes round the vizored throng. With what gladness would he have singled him out, and met him in fierce, mortal combat! A second thought told him that the dishonoured man could not find place in this gallant company.

We will not dwell on the tilt, the thrust, and the parry, the overthrowing of horses, and defeat of knights. Richard gloried in the recollection of his Spanish combats, and the love he bore for martial exercises, which made him, so boyish in figure, emulate the strong acts of men. Fortune had varied; but, when at noon the pastime of that day ended, the Prince remained victor in the field. From the hand of the Queen of the Feast he was receiving his reward, when Surrey, who had led him to her throne, was suddenly called away. The assembly broke up; and Richard was half occupied by polite attention to the Countess, and half by recollecting his peculiar situation, when the Marshall of the Lists whispered him to follow – he led him to a gallery, where Surrey alone was pacing / backwards and forwards in great agitation. He stopped when the Prince entered – motioned the Marshall to leave them, and then in a voice of suppressed passion, said, "I will not ask thee why with a false appellation thou

---

[a] John Howard (?1430–85) was rewarded for supporting Richard against his nephew, Edward V. Henry VIII restored the Earl of Surrey (see p. 104n) to the dukedom of Norfolk after Surrey's victory at Flodden Field (1513). Godwin untangled the passage of the Norfolk title in his letter of 29 May 1829 (Ab. MSS, Pf. Film, reel V, file 7; *Shelley and Mary*, III, pp. 1122A-B).

[b] John Talbot, 1st Earl of Shrewsbury (?1388–1453), distinguished military commander during the Hundred Years War; he appears in *1 Henry VI*.

[c] William Berkeley, for instance, had supported Edward IV and Richard III, but had earned a marquisate in 1488 after allying himself with Henry VII.

193

hast insulted the feast of nobles? – but well may I ask, what fiend possessed thee to do a deed that affixes the taint of disloyalty to King Henry's liege subject?"

"My good sword, my Lord," said Richard, colouring, "were eloquent to answer your questioning, but that you are much deceived; I am not indeed that which I called myself; but honour, not disgrace, attaches itself to my presence. I came to tell you this, to rouse the old fidelity of the Howards; to bid Lord Surrey arm for the last of the true Plantagenets."

"Saint Thomas speed me! Clifford then spoke true – thou art Perkin Warbeck?"

"I would fain," said the Duke haughtily, "ask a revered lady, who claims kindred with thee, what name she would give to her sainted daughter's affianced husband?"

The language of truth is too clear, too complete, / for the blots and flaws of incredulity; the very anger Lord Surrey had manifested, now turned to his confusion; the insult he had offered demanded reparation; he could not refuse his visitant's earnest demand to be led to the widow of Mowbray, Duke of Norfolk.

Elizabeth, daughter of the gallant Talbot, was proud of her ancestry, and disappointed in the diminution of her house. When her Anne was affianced to the little Duke of York, and the nobility of Norfolk was merged in the royal style of England, she had gloried; since then, attainder and defeat had eclipsed the ducal honours of her race; nor could she forgive the allegiance of its heirs to Lancaster. Often had she pondered on the reports concerning Margaret of Burgundy's White Rose; it was with agitation therefore that she heard that he was to be brought for her to decide on his truth.

The Duke had doffed his helm: his golden hair clustered on the almost infantine candour of his brow, and shaded to softer meaning the frank aspect of his clear blue eyes. The aged / Duchess fixed her dimmed but steady gaze upon him, and at once became aware that this was no ignoble pretender who stood before her. His dignity inspired Surrey with respect: he hesitated as he introduced the subject of his identity with Edward the Fourth's youngest son. The Duke, with a half smile, began to speak of his boyish recollections, and his little pretty play-fellow, and of one Mistress Margery, her gouvernante;[a] he spoke of a quarrel with his infant bride on the very wedding-day, and how nothing would bribe him to the ceremony, save the gift of a pretty foal, White Surrey, which afterwards bore his uncle Gloucester in the battle of Bosworth. As he spoke he saw a smile mantle over the aged lady's countenance; and then he alluded to his poor wife's death, and reminded the Duchess, that when clad in black, an infant widower, he had visited her in condolence; and how the sad

---

[a] governess or chaperon (OED).

lady had taken a jewel-encircled portrait of her lost child, garnished with the blended arms of Plantagenet and Mowbray, from his neck, promising to / restore it on an after day, which day had never come. Tears now rushed into the Duchess's eyes; she drew the miniature from her bosom, and neither she nor Lord Surrey could longer doubt, that the affianced husband of the noble Anne stood before them.

Much confusion painted the Earl's countenance. The Duke of York's first involuntary act had been to stretch out his hand; but the noble hesitated ere he could bestow on it the kiss of allegiance. Richard marked his reluctance, and spoke with gallant frankness: "I am an outcast," he said, "the victim of lukewarm faith and ill-nurtured treason: I am weak, my adversary strong. My lord, I will ask nothing of you: I will not fancy that you would revive the ancient bond of union between York and Norfolk; and yet, were it not a worthy act to pull down a base-minded usurper, and seat upon his father's throne an injured Prince?"

The Duchess answered for him. "Oh, surely, my noble cousin will be no recreant in this / cause, the cause of our own so exalted lineage."

But Lord Surrey had different thoughts: it cost him much to express them; for he had loved the House of York, and honoured and pitied its apparent offspring. At length he overcame his feelings, and said, "And, if I do not this, if I do not assist to replant a standard whose staff was broken on the graves of our slaughtered fathers, will your Highness yet bear with me, while I say a few words in my defence?"

"It needs not, gallant Surrey," interrupted York.

"Under favour, it does need," replied the Earl; "and withal touches mine honour nearly, that it stand clear in this question. My lord, the Roses contended in a long and sanguinary war, and many thousand of our countrymen fell in the sad conflict. The executioner's axe accomplished what the murderous sword spared, and poor England became a wide, wide grave. The green-wood glade, the cultivated fields, noble castles, and smiling villages were changed / to churchyard and tomb: want, famine and hate ravaged the fated land. My lord, I love not Tudor, but I love my country: and now that I see plenty and peace reign over this fair isle, even though Lancaster be their unworthy vicegerent, shall I cast forth these friends of man, to bring back the deadly horrors of unholy civil war? By the God that made me, I cannot! I have a dear wife and lovely children, sisters, friends, and all the sacred ties of humanity, that cling round my heart, and feed it with delight; these I might sacrifice at the call of honour, but the misery I must then endure I will not inflict on others; I will not people my country with widows and orphans; nor spread the plague of death from the eastern to the western sea."

Surrey spoke eloquently well; for his heart was upon his lips. Prince Richard heard with burning emotion. "By my fay!" he cried, "thou wouldst teach me to turn spinster, my lord: but oh, cousin Howard! did you know what it is to be

195

an exiled man, dependant / on the bounty of others; though your patrimony were but a shepherd's hut on a wild nameless common, you would think it well done to waste life to dispossess the usurper of your right." /

CHAPTER IX.

——

Farewell, kind lord, fight valiantly to-day.
And yet I do thee wrong to mind thee of it,
For thou art framed of the firm truth of valour.
SHAKSPEARE.[a]

——

The Duke of York was not of a temperament to sink supinely before the first obstacles. Lord Surrey's deep-felt abjuration of war influenced him to sadness, but the usual habit of his mind returned. He had been educated to believe that his honour called on him to maintain his claims. Honour, always a magic word with the good and brave, was then a part of the religion of every pious heart. He had been nurst in war – the javelin and the sword were as familiar to his / hand as the distaff and spindle to the old Tuscan crone. In addition, the present occasion called for activity. The fleet, armed for invasion, prepared by his noble aunt – manned by his exiled zealous friends – would soon appear on the English coast, giving form and force to, while it necessitated, his purposed attempt.

He possessed in his secretary Frion, a counsellor, friend, and servant, admirably calculated to prevent all wavering. This man's vanity, lion-strong, was alive to ensure his new master's success, and to overthrow him by whom he had been discarded. He was an adept in intrigue; an oily flatterer; a man of unwearied activity, both of mind and body. It was his care to prevent York from suffering any of the humiliations incident to his position. He obtained supplies of money for him – he suffered none to approach who were not already full of zeal – when he met with any failure, he proved logically that it was a success, and magnified an escape into a victory – he worked day and night to ensure that

---

[a] *Henry V*, IV. iii. 12–14.

nothing came near the Prince, except through his medium, which was one sugared / and drugged to please. When he saw Richard's clear spirit clouded by Lord Surrey, he demonstrated that England could not suffer through him; for that in the battle it was a struggle between partizans ready to lay down their lives in their respective causes, so that for their own sakes and pleasure, he ought to call on them to make the sacrifice. As to the ruin and misery of the land – he bade him mark the exactions of Henry; the penury of the peasant, drained to his last stiver – this was real wretchedness; devastating the country, and leaving it barren, as if sown with salt. Fertility and plenty would speedily efface the light wound he must inflict – nay, England would be restored to youth, and laugh through all her shores and plains, when grasping Tudor was exchanged for the munificent Plantagenet.

In one circumstance Frion had been peculiarly fortunate. The part he had played of astrologer during the foregoing summer, had brought him acquainted with a young nobleman zealous in the cause of York, and well able to afford it assistance. Lord Audley was of the west / country, but his maternal relations were Kentish, and he possessed a mansion and a small estate not far from Hythe in Kent. Lord Audley[a] was of a class of men common all over the world. He had inherited his title and fortune early in life, and was still a very young man. He loved action, and desired distinction, and was disposed to enter readily into all the turmoil and risk of conspiracy and revolt. His aim was to become a leader: he was vain, but generous; zealous, but deficient in judgment. He was a Yorkist by birth and a soldier by profession – all combined to render him, heart and soul, the friend of the wandering Plantagenet.

Frion led York to the mansion of this noble, and it became the focus of the spirit of sedition and discontent to the country round. The immediate presence of the Duke was concealed; but the activity of his friends was not the less great to collect a band of partizans, to which, when prepared and disciplined, they might present their royal leader. Their chief purpose was to collect such a body of men as might give / one impetus to the county, when the invading fleet should arrive on these coasts from Burgundy. Time was wanting for the complete organization of their plan; for each day they expected the vessels, and their operations in consequence were a little abrupt. Still they were in hopes that they should be enabled to assemble an armed force sufficient to facilitate the landing and to ensure the success of the expected troops. Day and night these men were occupied in gathering together followers. It was not long, however, before the wily secretary discovered that some one was at work to counteract their schemes. Those he had left transported with zeal for the cause yesterday, to-day he found lukewarm or icy cold. Their enemy, whoever it

---

[a] Perhaps James Touchet, 7th Baron Audley (?1465–97), executed for his role in the Cornwall uprising of June 1497, although Mary Shelley's known sources are silent on his involvement in Warbeck's cause.

might be, observed great mystery in his proceedings; yet he appeared to have intuitive knowledge of theirs. Frion exerted himself to discover the secret cause of all the mischief – he was liberal of promises and bribes. One day he had appointed a rendezvous for a party of recruits, about a hundred men, who had been exercised for the / last fortnight, and promised well – none arrived at the appointed spot. Frion rode sorrowfully through the dusk of the evening towards Lord Audley's dwelling. He was overtaken by a horseman, with a slouched hat, and otherwise muffled up: he rode at his side for a little way, quite mute to all Frion's courteous salutations; and then he suddenly put spurs to his horse, and was out of sight in a moment. Night grew darker; and at the mirk-embowered entrance of a shady lane, Frion was startled by the tramp of a horse – it was the same man: – "Maitre Frion!" he cried.

"Sir Robert Clifford!"

"The same – I knew not that my voice was so treacherous," Clifford began: he went on abruptly to declare that he was the counterminer; he, the secret marplot of the sagacious Frenchman's schemes. He displayed in all that he said a perfect knowledge of every transaction, and of the Prince's present residence. By'r lady's grace, he might have brought King Henry's archers to Lord Audley's very door! Wherefore he had not done this seemed strange; his / own account perplexed. In truth, this wretched man, at war with guilt and with himself, loathed the dishonour he had acquired. Like all evil-disposed persons, he had no idea of purging himself from the foul stain by frank confession and reformation: his project was to begin a new career in a new country: to go where his own tarnished reputation was unknown, where the cankerous name of York would poison no more his native language by its perpetual recurrence. His violent passions led him also to other conclusions; he hated Richard, and loved Monina; his desire to satisfy both these sentiments suggested a project on which he now acted, and which dictated his discourse with Frion. He showed how from that very spot he might ride to London, and make disclosures to the King; his knowledge of every detail of the Yorkist plans was startling – ruinous; – his offer was simply this: – That the Duchess of Burgundy should pay him a thousand golden crowns; that the Spanish maiden, Monina, should consent to wed him; and that they should seek together the / golden isles of the western ocean, leaving the Old World for York to ruffle in.

Frion desired time: it was necessary to consult Richard, and also Monina; where should they meet again? Clifford would appoint neither time nor place: – "I shall find you," he said: "I may draw your curtain at dead of night; come on you with an armed band of men, whom you think all your own. I will choose my own hour, my own audience-chamber. You have but to get the damsel's consent, and to tell her, an' you list, that she were better as Robin Clifford's wife, than as the light-of-love of the son of Jane Shore's gallant." With these words the Knight rode off; and being much better mounted than the Secretary, put all pursuit to defiance.

Frion was full of thought. He said nothing to the Duke or Lord Audley; but the following day hastened to visit Monina at Canterbury, where she had resided latterly, in the character of a pilgrim to St. Thomas-a-Becket's shrine.[a] Frion had flattered himself that he could easily persuade the young inexperienced girl, whose ardour for York he had often admired. Yet he / felt uncomfortable when he saw her. Monina looked a little pale, and her dark religious garb gave no adornment to her beauty; but there was in the innocence and tenderness of her full dark eye, in the soft moulding of the cheek which harmonized with the beautiful lids, and in her

> "sweet lips like roses,
> With their own fragrance pale, which Spring but half uncloses;"[b]

– there was in all this a purity and soft appeal which even the politician felt, who looked on mankind as mere agents in the drama he caused to be acted. With some hesitation he brought out his story, but of course grew bolder as he proceeded. Monina looked pained, but said – "Double the number of crowns, and Sir Robert will content him. My father will make my ransom good."

Clifford's speech and manner had convinced Frion that this would not be the case; he tried to persuade Monina, and even repeated the Knight's insolent message. Her large eyes grew larger, dilating with surprize and indignation. He little knows woman, who thinks to govern / the timid thing by threats. "Answer that bad man," she said, "thus: Monina will wed death, rather than crime and treason. Good master Frion, you have done wrong by so insulting mine ears: it were enough to drive a poor girl to eternal vows and a convent, to dream that such words are spoken of her; and if I do not take that refuge, it is because I will not desert my dear, fond, bereaved father – as soon I shall prove; meanwhile we must not delay to secure our Prince from his enemy's machinations. You know Astley, the poor scrivener in this town?[c] I defy Clifford to win him. Bring his Highness there, I will prepare him. We must show a boldness to Clifford matching his own: let us be fearless for ourselves; and for the White Rose we need not fear. Stay; Clifford watches you; I will provide for the Duke's safety."

That very night by secret, unknown means (it might be through her gypsy friend), Monina had communicated with York, and induced him to take refuge with the man she named. Astley's father had been a soldier in the cause of York, / and had died on Bosworth Field, leaving an unprovided widow and five children, one only among them being a son. From his youth upward, the boy

---

[a] The goal of Chaucer's pilgrims, a popular devotional site from 1170 when Becket was murdered in the cathedral by men attached to Henry II (1133–89; ruled 1154–89) until it was destroyed in 1538 during the reign of Henry VIII.

[b] P. B. Shelley, *The Revolt of Islam* (1818), VI. xxxiii. 8–9, but with 'eager' lips softened to 'sweet'.

[c] So described in the chronicles and histories.

had struggled, not with privation on his own account, to that he submitted without a murmur, but for the sake of his mother and sisters, whom he loved with an ardour peculiar to his sensitive and affectionate disposition. Weak in health and strength, he had betaken himself to the occupation of a scrivener, so meagrely to support them. It is probable that, in the frame of all, there was a delicacy of organization that unfitted them for penury. One by one they died. That spring had left Astley comparatively rich, because he could well support himself, but miserable beyond words, for he idolized all and every one of his lost relatives. Frion, had with unwearied care, made an accurate enumeration of all in Canterbury who had ever favoured the White Rose. Astley was on this list; he saw him, and passed him over as useless. Chance brought him and Monina together, who instantly detected his latent, unpractised talents, his integrity and enthusiasm; now his habitation / occurred as an unsuspected and faithful asylum for her persecuted friend.

Frion was still at work; Clifford came on him suddenly, and heard with unrepressed rage his rejection by Monina; his threats were unmeasured; but the moment for putting them into execution to their full extent had gone by. On the very day that York arrived in safety at Canterbury, his fleet was seen off Hythe. In the morning the vessels hove in sight; towards evening they bore down upon land, and anchored in the offing. The land-breeze rising at evening tide secured them from the dangers of a lee shore.

Hythe is situated at the water's edge. The cliffs, which at Dover beetle so fearfully over the tremendous deep, have by degrees receded from their apparent task of paling in the ocean, and as they retire inland, lose their barren, precipitous aspect, and become green, wooded hills, overlooking a grassy plain, which extends from their feet to the sands, a distance of about half a mile. In the neighbourhood of Hythe a ravine, the bed of a stream, divides / these acclivities, which on one side are abrupt, on the other softly rounded as they gradually disappear. Arcadia seems to breathe from the fertile landscape; the sunny uplands, the fringed banks of the rivulet, the darker shadows of the wooded hills, are contrasted with the verdant meadows, on which cattle and sheep graze. But the sea, the dark, dangerous sea, with barking waves and vast encircling barrenness, suddenly checks the beauty of the earth, adding magnificence to the pastoral prospect.[a]

A few days before, some gypsies had pitched their tents near the stream: some of the wanderers had strolled down to Hythe; but they were looked on for the most part with suspicion and fear. Now, while at the close of day most of the inhabitants of the little town were collected on the beach, gazing on the anchored vessels, two stout-looking gypsy-men, with one old woman of their

---

[a] Mary Shelley spent time on the coast of Kent as a child, and again in 1828 when she was recovering from smallpox. Dover was her departure point for the continent in 1814, 1818, and 1828.

tribe, were lying on the sands, occupied in their lazy way, by the same object, the vessels in sight. The people of Hythe, fishers, or such poor traders as supplied the fishermen with a few coarse necessaries, were rouzed from the / usual monotony of their lives by the aspect of this fleet. Added to these, there were three or four mendicant friars; an old soldier or two, disabled in the wars of the two Roses, and a few dependents on neighbouring nobles or Franklins; while women and children of various ages filled up the group. They all spoke of the fleet: it consisted of five armed vessels; two of these were weather-beaten caravels, two were low-decked Flemish smacks, but the fifth was one of prouder build, and it bore a flag of pretension on its mizen. The French king and the Spaniard were spoken of first: some thought it was a fleet which had sought the unknown, golden lands, driven back upon the old world by the continuous west winds of the last month; some said, they belonged to the Duchy of Burgundy; there was a spell in that word; no one knew who first whispered the name; none could guess whence or wherefore the conjecture arose, but the crowd broke into smaller groups; their talk declined into whispers as "York," "Duke Perkin," "The White Rose," "The Duchess of Burgundy," / were mentioned; and the fleet grew as they spoke into a mighty armada, freighted with invasion, ready to disembark an army, to ravage and conquer the island.

As soon as the appearance and nature of these vessels became confirmed, the gypsies arose from their indolent posture and retreated to their encampment. A few minutes afterwards, a wild-looking youth on a shaggy horse, without a saddle, trotted off at a quick pace through the ravine to the inland country. Lord Audley and Frion heard from him of the arrival of their friends who they had expected would have been delayed[16] for another month. Frion instantly set off for Canterbury to apprize the Prince; and the noble lost no time in collecting his retainers and hastening to Hythe. Clifford's spies brought him word also of the arrival of the fleet. Ill luck attended his guiles. King Henry was in the north: there was no time to apprize him, and Clifford's underhand proceedings might turn out bitterly to his disadvantage. He had nothing for it but to endeavour to be the first to convey the already-blown news to Sir John Peachy, / sheriff for Kent:[a] his pains were rewarded by his being detained prisoner as a suspected person, while Sir John mustered his yeomanry, and, together with the neighbouring gentry and their retainers, marched towards Hythe. The wavering people, awed by this show of legal and military power, grew cool towards the White Rose, whose name, linked to change and a diminution of taxation, had for a moment excited their enthusiasm. Some had assumed the snowy badge, and collected in groups; but they tore it off when the magistrate appeared: he thanked them for arming for their King, and they in much fear and some wonder joined his standard.

---

[a] Peachy's historical role was as Mary Shelley describes it.

Sir John advanced with his increasing troop towards the village in question. He was informed that a band of the Prince's friends was there before him, consisting of a few Yorkist gentlemen and their retainers. His first idea was to disperse them; his second, "No; this will serve as a decoy: every coast may not be prepared; driven too speedily hence, the armament may make good their landing elsewhere: if we appear unguarded, they will disembark, and fall / into our hands." This policy had good effect; the two smaller Dutch vessels and one of the caravels ran as close in shore as their soundings permitted, and hastily landed a part of the troops. The commanders of the expedition on board the fleet had been in considerable anxiety; they had hoped to find the country raised to receive them; they saw but a handful of men: still signs were made to them to disembark; and, eager to ensure the safety of their Prince, they in part obeyed, landing about two hundred and fifty men, with Mountford, Corbet,[a] and some other distinguished exiles, at their head. York and Frion had not yet had time to arrive from Canterbury; Lord Audley and his friends received the troops, and held consultation with their chiefs. It was resolved to go forward, and penetrate into the country, to raise it if possible; and, as they had not yet heard of Sir John Peachy's advance, to forestal resistance by their speed.

They marched forward in good order for nearly ten miles, when they halted; their scouts here brought intelligence of a regular force of / at least two thousand men who were near at hand, advancing against them. Audley advised a deviation from their line of march, so to enter the county in a different direction; Mountford proposed to fortify themselves in Hythe; Corbet to re-imbark with all speed on board their vessels. While they deliberated, it was reported that another troop of the King's men were posted in their rear, while an herald from the Sheriff called on them to lay down their arms and to submit. Already a panic ran through this knot of men; already their coward hands dropped their weapons, ready to be held out for servile cords, signs of terror, increased by the near tramp of Peachy's soldiers, and the sound of martial music.

At this moment of irresolution, four persons were seen at the top of a neighbouring eminence; one was a knight in complete armour, the others were more peacefully attired; they paused a moment gazing on the scene below; then the three pursued their way over the hills towards the sea; the cavalier came riding down / at a furious pace; Lord Audley advanced towards him, "All is lost!" he cried.

"Or won!" exclaimed the Prince, "surely Neville and my good cousin will send us reinforcements. How strong are ye on board, Mountford?"

"About six hundred; two of which are German well-trained auxiliaries; but we hoped to find an ally army."

---

[a] Two rebels singled out in the chronicles; both were captured and later executed.

"Treason, Sir John, is stronger to break, than truth to bind. Ye are mad: better not have landed at all than thus."

A few scattered shot from Peachy's advanced guard broke in upon these regrets; Richard in a moment recollected that this was a time for action, not for words. He issued a few commands as to the position of his troops, and riding to their front, addressed them: "My merry men, and very good friends," he cried, "let us recollect that we are soldiers; our lives depend upon our swords; draw them for the right, and be strong in it. Our enemies are chiefly raw recruits; cold friends of a tyrant-usurper; but they are many, and death is before / us; behind our vessels, the wide ocean, safety and freedom: we must retreat, not as cowardly fugitives, but as men who, while they see, fear not their danger."

The order of the march was speedily established. While the rear retrograded, Richard, with a hundred chosen men, made a stand, receiving so well the first onset of their assailants, that they were staggered and driven back.

"In good hour, spare neither whip nor spur," cried York; and turning his horse's head, he galloped towards his retreating friends. Peachy, who believed that he had them in his toils, followed slowly and in good order. For the first five miles all went well; but when the hills approached and grew more abrupt, forming by degrees a narrow ravine, they found this post guarded by the enemy. "Betrayed!" cried Audley; "we ought to have traversed the hills; now we are between two fires."

"Silence!" said Richard, sternly; "we must give courage to these poor fellows, not deprive them of it – fear you for your life, / Baron? By my fay, I had rather mine were spilt, than that of the meanest of our men!"

Combat like this York had shared in the ravines of Andalusia: he remembered that warfare, and founded his present operations upon it. His onset was impetuous: the enemy recoiled, but formed again. The horsemen dismounted, and presented a frightful bulwark of iron-headed lances to the horses of the little troop; while, from the intervals in the ranks, the archers and men armed with matchlocks, kept up a rain of arrows and bullets, that spread consternation among his troop. It was necessary to break through this formidable defence: thrice the Prince charged in vain; the third time his standard-bearer fell; he wore a white scarf; he fixed it to his lance, and drawing his sword, he waved this emblem of his cause as again he dashed forwards, and with greater success; yet, as he drove the enemy before him, the whiz of bullets and arrows from behind showed that their previous resistance had given Sir John Peachy time to come up. York grasped Audley's hand: "Farewell," he cried, "forgive my hasty / speech, my valiant friend: may we meet in paradise, where surely, through God's grace, we shall sup this night."

With the words he charged again, and overcame the last faint resistance. Followed by all his troop, pursuing the flying, Richard dashed through the defile: soon the open plain was before them, and he saw the wide, calm, free ocean, with his vessels riding at anchor. The decks were crowded with men, and the water covered with boats, hovering near shore, as they waited to receive tidings of their friends.

Before in the van, Richard now hung back to secure the retreat of those behind. Audley urged him to embark; but he moved slowly towards the beach, now calling his men to form and gather round him, now marking the motions of those behind, ready to ride back to their aid. At length Peachy's troops poured through the defile; the plain was covered by flying Yorkists: it only remained for him to assemble as many as he could, to protect and ensure the embarkation of all. /

"One word," cried Audley; "whither do you propose to sail?"

"It is doubtful: if Barry still be true, and my voice be heard, not to Burgundy and dependence, but rather to Ireland, to Cork and Desmond."

"Meanwhile, dear your Highness," said the noble, "I will not believe that all is lost in England. I shall make good speed to the West, and gather my friends together; we shall not be distant neighbours; and if I succeed to my wish, Audley will call you from your Irish fastnesses to your own native England. Our Lady preserve you meanwhile – farewell!"

Audley, swift in all his proceedings, put spurs to his horse, and was away. A few minutes brought Richard to the sands: he guarded the embarkation of his diminished numbers; nor, till Peachy's troop was within bowshot, and the last straggler that arrived was in the last boat, did he throw himself from his horse and leap in: he was rowed to the chief vessel. He cast an anxious glance at the Adalid just under weigh: a green and white flag was hoisted: Monina / was on board. Further to re-assure him of his friends' safety, Frion received him as he mounted his own deck. Evening was at hand – the late balmy, summer evening; a land breeze sprung up; the vessels had already weighed their anchors, and swiftly, with swelling sails, they gained the offing. How tranquil and sweet seemed the wide-spread waters; how welcome these arks of refuge, sailing placidly over them, after the strife, the blood, the shouts, the groans of battle. "Farewell England," said the royal exile; "I have no country, save these decks trodden by my friends – where they are, there is my kingdom and my home!"[a] /

---

[a] Mary Shelley heroicizes Warbeck, whom the historical record places offshore during the unsuccessful Kent invasion.

CHAPTER X.

Why, it cannot choose but be a noble plot:
And then the power of Scotland and of York
To join ——
In faith it is exceedingly well aimed!

SHAKSPEARE.[a]

The Duke of York found Lord Barry, Sir George Neville, Plantagenet, and several other distinguished friends, on board his vessel. In consultation with them, it was agreed to sail immediately for Cork. The loss of many brave friends, killed or prisoners, on the Kentish coast, saddened them: while the diminution of their numbers forbade the idea of a second descent upon England. Towards Ireland they sailed, with such alternation of calm and contrary winds, as made them linger for several weeks / upon their way. Here, for the first time, Richard heard from Frion of Clifford's machinations, and of his message, and insolent threat to Monina. Every drop of blood in his veins was alive with indignation: before, he had despised Sir Robert as a traitor; and, while he looked on him as the cause of all his disasters, and of the death of so many of his noble and gallant adherents, his abhorrence was mingled with contemptuous pity. The unchivalrous wrong offered to a woman, that woman his sweet sister-friend, animated him with other feelings: to avenge her, and chastise the arrogant braggart, was his knightly duty, his fervent, impatient wish. He saw her not meanwhile; she was in one of those dark hulls, among which love alone taught him to discern the lighter build and more sea-worn frame of the Adalid.

Ireland was at this time[b] very differently situated, from when the Prince first landed on her shores. After Lambert Simnel's success there, still the King of England had neglected its internal policy. A more terrible name awakened his caution; and he sent Sir Edward / Poynings, as the deputy of his infant son

----

[a] *1 Henry IV*, I. iii. 279–82.
[b] '1496' (marginal note in *Abinger/Palacio*).

Henry, whom he had nominally appointed to the government. Poynings was resolute and successful. He defeated the natives, quelled the Earl of Kildare, and forced the Earl of Desmond to renew his oaths of allegiance. A free pardon was afterwards granted to all, with the exception of Lord Barry.

York was received at Cork most cordially by his old friend O'Water, and immediately, at the Earl of Desmond's invitation, repaired to Ardfinnin. The Earl had found no great difficulty in escaping from England, and returning to his native island. The timely assistance he had afforded Henry's enemy in the Tower, was an impenetrable mystery, though the consciousness of it had made him more yielding, than he would otherwise have been in his concessions to Poynings. He received York with the hospitality of an Irish Chieftain, and the kindness of a friend. But he held out no inducement for him to remain: on the contrary, he was the first to counsel him to turn his eyes, where a new and brighter prospect presented itself. Sir Patrick / Hamilton[a] had left Munster a few months before, with a firm belief in Richard's truth; he had assured the Earl of the favourable reception his adventurous friend would obtain from his royal master, and had declared his intention of proceeding to Brussels to see the Prince, and personally to enforce his invitation. York was absent; but the Duchess gave a cordial reception to the renowned Scottish cavalier. He had been present at the sailing of the fleet; and his last words were wishes for their success, and an offer of secure and honourable refuge in Edinburgh, in case of failure. It had been agreed, that on his own return thither, he should be accompanied by messengers from the Duchess, to thank the King of Scotland for the interest he manifested towards her beloved nephew. Sir Edward Brampton was chosen as the chief of these, accompanied of course by his Lady, York's long-tried and zealous friend.

All these circumstances were decisive of the course it became the exile to pursue. He was at that moment in a condition to appear under advantageous circumstances at the Scottish / Court. He had lost several valued friends during the late attempt; but many remained of noble birth and good renown. Above a hundred knights graced his train. The treasure his aunt had bestowed for his English struggle remained, besides a considerable sum of money, services of valuable plate and valuable jewels, the munificent gift of the Dowager Duchess of Norfolk. In fine, not a dissentient voice was raised; and the attention of every one was turned towards preparations for the voyage. York continued to be the Earl of Desmond's guest: in his princely halls he received all the honour due to his rank and pretensions. The Countess, a lady of the noble family of Roche, distinguished him by her kindness, and conceived a peculiar friendship for the Spanish maiden, Monina.

The moment arrived for York's embarkation. He had visited his vessels, and

---

[a] For Sir Patrick Hamilton, see p. 220 and n.

seen that all was in readiness; but his surprise was excited by perceiving that no preparations were made for sailing on board the Adalid. This was explained on his return, by the Countess telling him that a friend of his desired to take leave of him before / he sailed, and that she had been besought by her to explain in some measure the reasons of their separation. De Faro's whole soul was set upon becoming one of those immortal pioneers who opened new paths across the unexplored West. He could be of no use to Richard in Scotland; but he could not prevail on himself to leave his lovely, unprotected girl behind. She had at last consented to accompany him in his far and dangerous voyage.

Many had been this poor child's struggles, sad her reflections, ere she wrought herself to this purpose. "Alas!" such were her reveries, "that innocence should be no safeguard in this ill world! If indeed I loved him sinfully, or he sought me wrongfully, I should simply obey the laws of God in flying him; but he is noble, and I know my own heart. Spotless Mother of God, thou knowest it! – there is no single feeling in my woman's soul that I dare not avouch to thy all-blessed gentleness! I ask only to live in the same land, to breathe the same air, to serve him at his need, to associate with his friends; so that when I see him not, I may feed upon discourse / of him. This is all I ask – all! – and this must not be! I cannot bear a tainted name; I cannot endure that, linked with any slightest stain of calumny, my image should haunt his dreams; nor that he or any human being should suffer through me, which may so easily happen: for if words like those Frion reported should reach my father's ears, he would clothe his tempest-shaken limbs in arms, and expose his breast to the sharp sword's point, to vindicate my honour. No! – no tragedy shall be associated with poor Monina's name; nor agony nor woe shall visit those I love, through me: they shall not even commiserate my sufferings; these shall be garnered up in my own heart, watched with a miser's care. I will not enrich the tell-tale air by one sigh; nor through my broken heart, shall the gloom of my despair appear. I will paint my face with joy's own hue; put sunshine in my eyes: my hapless love shall be no tale of pity for any, save my own desolate thoughts. Nor let me forget every lesson of resignation, nor the dear belief I cherish in the protection and goodness of my sainted guardianess. Let me rejoice / at much that exalts my destiny in my own eyes. The Prince's friendship, affection, gratitude and esteem are mine: I have been able to serve him I love – am I not sufficiently fortunate? He needs me no more; but I am no alien upon earth. I shall give delight to my dear father by accompanying him over the untrod watery deserts: through me – for, if I went not, he would remain behind – the name of De Faro will be added to the list of those who bestow a new creation of supernal beauty on our out-worn world. He will call me the partner of his glory: and, though that be a vain word, his dark eyes will flash with joy. My dear, dear father! Should the Prince succeed and ascend his rightful throne, more impassable than that wide sea would be the gulph which ceremony would place between us; and if he fall – ah! mine is no summer day's voyage; the tornados of that wild region may wreck me; the cold sea receive me in her bosom; and I shall never hear of Richard's overthrow, nor endure the intolerable pang of knowing that he dies."

Fortified in some degree by such thoughts, / anxious to conceal her sorrows from one who might compassionate, yet not wholly share them, Monina met Richard with an air of gaiety: glad, in spite of his involuntary mortification, that she should be spared any pain, he copied her manner; and a spectator would have thought, that either they parted for a few hours, or were indifferent to each other. He could not help betraying some anxiety however, when Lady Desmond, who was present, solicited him to make his friend change her purpose, and drew a frightful picture of the hazardous voyage, the storms, the likelihood that they might be driven far, far away, where no land was, where they would perish of famine on the barren, desolate ocean. Monina laughed – she endeavoured thus to put aside her friend's serious entreaties; and, when she found that she failed, she spoke of the Providence that could protect her even on the wastes of innavigable ocean; and proudly reminded him, that she would trust her father, whose reputation as a mariner stood foremost among those in the King of Portugal's employ. / Richard looked perplexed – sorrow and pain spoke in his countenance; while she, true to herself to the last, said, "I have now told you my purpose – but this is no farewell; to-morrow we meet again; and another to-morrow will come also, when I bring treasure from my Indian isle to dazzle the monarch of fair, happy England."

On that morrow Richard sought in vain among the Countess of Desmond's companions for his sweet Spaniard; he imaged her as he last saw her, light, laughing, her soft-beaming eyes hardly daring to glance towards him, while he fancied that a shower of precious drops was shaken from their fringed lids. He had meant to say, "Ah! weep, Monina, weep for Andalusia – for our happy childhood – for the hopes that leave us: thy tears will seem to me more glad than thy untrue smile." But she was not there. Could he have seen her from the deck of his vessel, marking its progress from the watch-tower of Youghall, he had been satisfied. The anguish of bitter tears, the heart's agonizing / gaspings, were hers, to be succeeded by the dull starless night of despair, when his sail vanished on the glittering plains of the sunny sea.

Farewell to her who mourned; to her who saw neither day nor joy, whose heart lived with him, while she prepared for her melancholy separation from the very world which he inhabited.

The scene shifts to Scotland;[a] and hither, to a new country, a new people, almost to a new language, our royal adventurer is transported. Dark, tumultuous, stained with blood, and rendered foul by treason, are the pages of early

---

[a] During her girlhood Mary Shelley lived for extended periods (June–November 1812, June 1813–March 1814) in the household of her father's associate, William Baxter, near Dundee. For the historical sources of the Scottish episodes, see Introductory Note, p. xiv.

Scottish history. A wild and warlike people inhabited its mountainous districts, whose occupation was strife, whose religion was power and revenge. The Lowlanders, a wealthier race, were hardly more cultivated or less savage. One course of rebellion against the sovereign, and discord among themselves, flows, a sanguinary stream from the hidden sources of things, threading a long track of years, or overflowing it with its pernicious waves. Discord, hate and murder were the animating spirits of the scene. /

James the Third was a weak, unhappy man. A prophecy had induced him to distrust all the Princes of his house – he extended this distrust to his son, who was brought up consequently in a kind of honourable and obscure imprisonment. He fostered unworthy favourites; and many bold and sanguinary revolts had been the consequence. On one occasion, while encamped, during a foray into England, his nobles had seized on all his personal friends and adherents, and hanged them over Loudon Bridge. The last rebellion cost him his life. The insurgents seized on, and placed at their head, his eldest son, then only sixteen years of age – they met their sovereign in the field – he fled before them; and his death was as miserable and dastardly as his life.

James the Fourth succeeded to the throne. The mean jealousy of his father had caused him to be untutored; but he was one of those beings, who by nature inherit magnanimity, refinement and generosity. His faults were those that belong to such a character. His imagination was active, his impulses warm but capricious. / He was benignant to every other, severe only in his judgment of himself. His father's death, to which he had been an unwilling accessary, weighed like parricide on his conscience. To expiate it, in the spirit of those times, he wore perpetually an iron girdle, augmenting the weight each year, as habit or encreasing strength lightened the former one. He devoted much of his life to penance and prayer. Here ended however all of the ascetic in his disposition. He was a gallant knight and an accomplished gentleman. He encouraged tourneys and passages of arms, raising the reputation of the Scottish cavaliers all over Europe, so that many noble foreigners repaired to Edinburgh, to gain new trophies in contests with the heroes of the north. He passed edicts to enforce the schooling of the children of the nobles and lairds. His general love of justice, a little impaired it is true by feudal prejudices, often led him to wander in disguise over his kingdom; seeking hospitality from the poor, and listening with a candid and generous mind to every remark upon himself and his government.[a] /

He was singularly handsome, graceful, prepossessing, and yet dignified in his manners. He loved pleasure, and was the slave of the sex, which gives to

---

[a] James III (1451–88; ruled 1460–88); six years after the incident at Loudon (or Lauder, in Berwick, south-east of Edinburgh), he was murdered following the battle of Sauchieburn, 11 June 1488, and succeeded by his son, James IV (1473–1513; ruled 1488–1513). Mary Shelley extracts details for the brief portraits from her acknowledged sources.

pleasure all its elegance and refinement; he partook his family's love for the arts, and was himself a poet and a musician; nay more, to emulate the divine patron of these accomplishments, he was well-skilled in surgery and the science of healing. He was ambitious, active, energetic. He ruminated many a project of future glory; meanwhile his chief aim was to reconcile the minds of the alienated nobles – his murdered father's friends – to himself; and, succeeding in this, to abolish the feuds that raged among the peers of Scotland, and civilize their barbarous propensities. He succeeded to a miracle. His personal advantages attracted the affection of his subjects; they were proud of him, and felt exalted by his virtues. His excellent government and amiable disposition, both united to make his reign peaceful in its internal policy, and beneficial to the kingdom. The court of Holyrood[a] vied with those of Paris, London and Brussels: to which capitals many of his high-born / subjects, no longer engaged in the struggles of party, travelled; bringing back with them the refinements of gallantry, the poetry, learning and science of the south of Europe. The feuds, last flickerings of the dying torch of discord, which lately spread a fatal glare through the land, ceased; if every noble did not love, they all obeyed their sovereign – thus a new golden age might be said to have dawned upon this eyrie of Boreas, this tempestuous Thule of the world.[b]

We must remember that this was the age of chivalry; the spirit of Edward the Third and the princely Dukes of Burgundy yet survived. Louis the Eleventh in France had done much to quench it; it burnt bright again under the auspices of his son. Henry the Seventh was its bitter enemy; but we are still at the beginning of his reign, while war and arms were unextinguished by his cold, avaricious policy. James of Scotland laboured, and successfully, to pacify his subjects, children of one common parent; but he, as well as they, disdained the ignoble arts of peace. England formed the lists where they desired to display their courage; war with / England was a word to animate every heart to dreadful joy: in the end it caused the destruction of him and all his chivalry in Flodden Field;[c] now it made him zealous to upraise a disinherited Prince; so that under the idea of restoring the rightful sovereign to the English throne, he might have fair pretext for invading the neighbour kingdom. At the hope, the soldiers of Scotland – in other words, its whole population – awakened, as an unhooded hawk, ready to soar at its accustomed quarry.

Sir Patrick Hamilton, the most accomplished and renowned of the Scottish cavaliers, and kinsman of the royal house, had returned laden with every testimony of the White Rose's truth, and a thousand proofs of his nobleness and virtue. Sir Edward Brampton delivered the Duchess's message of thanks;

---

[a] Palace of the Scottish kings at Edinburgh.

[b] Boreas, Greek god of the northwind; Thule, the northernmost part of the habitable ancient world.

[c] Near Branxton, Northumberland, where he perished in 1513.

and his lady had already awakened the zeal of many a gentleman, and the curiosity and interest of many a lady, for the pride of York, the noble, valiant Plantagenet. Woman's sway was great at Holyrood; as the bachelor king, notwithstanding his iron girdle, and his strict attention to his religious duties, / was a devout votary at the shrine of feminine beauty.

There was a hawking party assembled in the neighbourhood of Stirling,[a] which he graced by his presence. All was apparently light-heartedness and joy, till a dispute arose between two damsels upon the merits of their respective falcons. One of these was fair Mary Boyd, daughter of the Laird of Bonshaw. Mary Boyd was the first-love of the young sovereign, and the report went that he was no unsuccessful suitor; it spoke of offspring carefully concealed in a village of Fife,[b] whom James often visited. When afterwards this young lady's example was imitated by others nobly born, this became no secret, and of her children one became Archbishop of St. Andrews, the other, a daughter, married the Earl of Morton.[c]

But these were days of youthful bashfulness and reserve; the mind of Mary Boyd balanced between pride in her lover, and shame for her fault; a state of feeling, that ill-brooked the loss of what gilded her too apparent frailty – the exclusive attention of the King. Mary was older / than the King; the dignity which had captivated the boy's imagination, lost its charm, when the tyranny of assumed right took place of that of tenderness. He grew cold, then absent, and at last ventured to fix a regard of admiration on another, sliding easily from the restraint to which he at first submitted, into all of devotion and soft, gallant courtesy, by which kings win lady's love, and in which none grew to be a greater adept than James. The new object that attracted him, was the young, gay and lovely Lady Jane Kennedy, daughter of the Earl of Cassils.[d] Her sparkling eyes, her "bonny brent brow,"[e] her dark, clustering hair, contrasted with the transparency of her complexion – her perfect good humour, her vivacity and her wit – made her a chief beauty in the Scottish court, and in all this she was the reverse of the fair, light-haired, sleepy-eyed Mary. Lady Jane saw and gloried in her triumph over the King. Innocent then, she only desired the reputation of such a conquest, fully resolved not to tread in the steps of her rival. It is something of fool's play to strive to enchain fire by links of straw, / to throw silken fetters on a bounding torrent, to sport with the strong lion, Love,

---

[a] James III had erected a great hall and elaborate chapel in the palace at Stirling, north-west of Edinburgh.

[b] County on Scotland's east coast, north of Edinburgh.

[c] Alexander and Catherine Stuart, the children of Mary (or Marion) Boyd, daughter of Archibald Boyd of Bonshaw.

[d] Lady Jane (or Janet) Kennedy, daughter of John, Lord Kennedy (according to *DNB*), not an ingenue, but the former mistress of the Earl of Angus (see p. 216n), whom she may have married after James IV discarded her. James fathered her son James Stuart (1499–1544), created Earl of Moray in 1501. It was probably Jane's brother David who was created Earl of Cassillis in 1509.

[e] Echoing Robert Burns, 'John Anderson My Jo', st. 1, l. 4: 'Your bonie brow was brent'.

as he were a playful whelp: some, secure in innocence and principle, may at last discover their mistake and remain uninjured; but not the vain, heedless, self-willed Lady Jane. The courtiers were divided in their attentions; some for shame would not forsake Mary Boyd; some thought that still she would regain her power; one or two imagined that Lady Jane's resistance would restore the king to her rival; but the greater number caught the light spirit of the hour, and gathered round the laughing, happy girl.

The contention between these ladies made many smile. The King betted a diamond against a Scotch pebble on Lady Jane's bird. Mary had thwarted him, and forced him to her side during the first part of the day – now he took this revenge. A heron rose from the river banks. The birds were unhooded; and up soared Lady Jane's in one equal flight through the blue air, cleaving the atmosphere with noiseless wing. Mary's followed slower; but, when Lady Jane's pounced on the quarry, and / brought it screaming and flapping to the ground, the rival bird darted on the conqueror, and a sharp struggle ensued. It was unequal; for the Lady Jane's hawk would not quit its prey. "Let them fight it out," said Mary, "and the survivor is surely the victor."

But the spectators cried shame – while Lady Jane with a scream hastened to save her favourite. The other, fiery as a borderer, attacked even her; and, in spite of her gloves, drops of blood from her fair hand stained her silken robe. James came to her rescue, and with one blow put an end to the offender's life. Jane caressed her "tassel gentle;"[a] while Mary looked on her "false carrion's"[b] extinction with unrepressed indignation. They returned to Stirling: immediately on their arrival they received tidings that the Duke of York's fleet had been descried, and was expected to enter the Frith on the following day. None heard the words without emotion; the general sentiment was joy; for Richard's landing was to be the signal of invasion. King Henry had one or two friends / among the Scottish nobles, and these alone smiled contemptuously.

"We must have feasts and tourneys, fair mistress," said the King, "to honour our royal visitor. Will your servant intrude unseemingly if while his arms extol your beauty, he wears your colours?"

Lady Jane smiled a reply, as she followed her father towards his mansion. She smiled, while feminine triumph beamed in her eye, and girlish bashfulness blushed in her cheek. "Has she not a bonny ee?"[c] cried James to him, who rode near him. It was Sir Patrick Hamilton, his dear cousin and friend, to whom James often deferred, and respected, while he loved. His serious look recalled the King. "This is not the time, good sooth!" he continued, "for such sweet gauds[d] – but for lance and broad-sword: – the coming of this Prince of Roses

---

[a] Peregrine falcon.
[b] A worthless bird.
[c] 'ee', Scottish form for 'eye'.
[d] *Two Noble Kinsmen*, IV. ii. 53 (loosely quoted).

will bring our arms into play, all rusty as they are. I wonder what presence our guest may have!"

The friends then conversed concerning the projected war, which both agreed would be well-timed. It would at once give vent to the fiery / impulses of the Scotch Lords, otherwise apt to prey upon each other. But lately a band of the Drummonds had burnt the kirk of Moulward, in which were six-score Murrays, with their wives and children; all of whom were victims. But foray in England – war with the land of their hate – the defiance would be echoed in glad shouts from Tweed to Tay; from the Lothians to the Carse of Gowrie; while it should be repeated in groans from the Northumberland wilds.[a] /

CHAPTER XI.

———

Cousin of York, thus once more we embrace thee;
Welcome to James of Scotland! For thy safety,
Know, such as love thee not shall never wrong thee.
Come, we will taste awhile our court delights,
Dream hence afflictions past, and then proceed
To high attempts of honour.

FORD.[b]

———

The Duke of York arrived off Leith.[c] While the messengers were going to and fro, and preparation was made to disembark, he and his principal friends were assembled on the deck of their vessel, regarding this strange northern coast with curiosity, wonder, and some contempt.

"I see horses," cried Lord Barry; "By'r / Lord's grace, grass grows hitherward – that is much!"

---

[a] Mary Shelley refers to places along Scotland's eastern coast: the river Tweed, which runs along its southern border separating Berwick from English Northumberland; the Firth of Tay, near Dundee, far north of Edinburgh; the Lothians, embracing the modern counties of East, West, and Midlothian; the Carse of Gowrie, between Perth and Dundee.

[b] *Perkin Warbeck*, II. i. 108–13.

[c] Port on the Firth of Forth, near Edinburgh.

"I see kye," exclaimed Frion, "so we may hope for buttered sowans at least, if not beef, at the palace of feasts."[a]

"Aye," cried Sir Edward Brampton, who had come on board, "you may hope for choice cheer. I promise ye shall live well, ye that are noble – these unclad rocks and desart moors are the home of many an earl and belted knight, whose gorgeousness may vie with the cavaliers of France or Burgundy. In this it differs from England, ye will not find stout franklins or fat burgesses; there are no men of Ghent, nor London Alderman: the half-naked kern tills the stony soil. Next to the palace is the hearthless hovel. Wealth and penury, if not mates, are joint masters of the land."

"I have heard," said York, "that there is much paternal love and filial duty between the rich and poor in this country."

"Among the northern mountains thus it is," said Brampton; "a strange and savage race, / which, my good Lord Barry, some name Irish, dwell on the barren heights, along the impassable defiles, beside their vast stormy lakes; but the Lowlander looks askance on the Highland clanship. List ye, gentlemen; all bears a different aspect here from the gentle southern kingdoms; but they are men, proud, valiant, warlike men, as such they claim our respect. His Majesty and a few others are moreover right gallant cavaliers."

"Mark these words," said York, earnestly, "and remember, dear friends, that we, the world's wanderers, seek refuge here of our own will, which if we find, we must not disdain our hosts. Remember too the easy rage of the fiery Scot; and that we boast gentler customs: suffer no brawling to mar our concord; let not Richard of York, who of all his wide realm possesses your hearts only, find his dominions narrowed, or violently disturbed by your petulance and pride."

The Duke's associates listened with respect. Hitherto the spirited boy had been led by a Barry, a Clifford, a Neville, or a Plantagenet. / They had counselled, spoken for him; his sword only had been as active as theirs. A new light seemed to have broken in upon his soul; it assumed a seriousness and power that exalted him in their eyes, while it took nothing from the candour and single-hearted reliance on their loves, which was his dearest charm.

On landing, the Duke of York was escorted to Edinburgh by the Earl of Errol,[b] Sir Patrick Hamilton, and others. The attire, arms, and horses, with their caparisons, of these gentlemen, were little inferior to those displayed at Paris. King James awaited him at the Castle of Edinburgh. The monarch received his guest in state on his throne. The Prince was struck at once by his elegance, his majesty, and sweet animated aspect: his black bonnet, looped up by a large ruby, sat lightly on his brow, his glossy black curly hair escaping in ringlets from underneath; his embroidered shirt collar thrown back, displayed his throat, and the noble expression of his head; his dark grey eyes, his manly

---

[a] kye, dialect for cow; sowans (or sowens), a porridge extracted from oats.
[b] One of the Hays of Errol, hereditary constables of Scotland.

sun-burnt complexion, the look of thought, combined with goodness, mingled with dignity, gave an air of / distinction to his whole person. Various were the physiognomies, various the guises, of those around him. The swart, gaunt Highlander, in his singular costume; the blue-eyed, red-haired sons of the Lowlands were there; and in each and all were remarkable a martial, sometimes a ferocious expression.

The Prince of England entered, surrounded by his (to the Scotch) foreign-looking knights.

James descended from his throne to embrace his visitant, and then re-assumed it, while all eyes were turned upon the royal Adventurer, whose voice and mien won every heart, before his eloquence had time to move them. "High and mighty King," said Richard, "your grace, and these your nobles present, be pleased to hear the tragedy of one, who, born a prince, comes even as a beggar to your court. My Lords, sorrow and I were not twins: I am the elder, and for nine years I beheld not the ill-visage of that latest birth of my poor but royal mother's fortunes. It were a long tale to tell, what rumour has made familiar to every ear: my uncle Gloucester's usurpation; my brother's / death; and the sorrows of our race. I lost my kingdom ere I possessed it; and while yet my young hands were too feeble to grasp the sceptre of my ancestors, and with it, the sword needful to defend the same, capricious fate bestowed it on Henry of Richmond; a base-born descendant of ill-nurtured Bolingbroke;[a] a scion of that Red Rose that so long and so rightfully had been uprooted in the land, which they had bought with its children's dearest blood.

"Good, my lords, I might move you to pity did I relate how, in my tender years, that usurer King sought my life, buying the blood of the orphan at the hands of traitors. How, when these cruelties failed him, he used subtler arts; giving me nick-names; meeting my gallant array of partizans, not with an army of their peers, but with a base rout of deceits, treasons, spies, and blood-stained decoyers. It would suit me better to excite your admirations by speaking of the nobleness and fidelity of my friends; the generosity of the sovereigns who have shed invaluable dews upon the fading White Rose, so to refresh and restore it. /

"But not to waste my tediousness on you, let this be the sum. I am here, the friend of France, the kinsman of Burgundy; the acknowledged Lord of Ireland; pursued by my powerful foe, I am here, King of Scotland, to claim your friendship and your aid. Here lies the accomplishment of my destiny! The universal justice to be rendered me, which I dreamed of in my childhood, the eagle hopes of my youth, my better fortunes, and future greatness, have fled me. But here they have found a home: here they are garnered up; render them

---

[a] base-born, implying that Henry VII is of bastard race; see p. 32n. Henry IV (Bolingbroke; ?1366–1413; ruled 1399–1413), eldest surviving son of John of Gaunt by his wife Blanche, gained the throne by usurpation after Richard II abdicated in his favour, legitimizing his claim through his descent from Henry III (1207–72).

back to me, my lord; unlock with the iron key of fatal battle, the entrance to those treasures, all mine own, whose absence renders me so poor. Arm me, Scotland; arm for the right! Never for a juster cause could you buckle breast-plate, or poize your lance. Be my captain, and these your peers, my fellow-soldiers. Fear not, but that we vanquish: that I gain a kingdom; you eternal glory from your regal gift. Alas! I am as an helmless vessel drifting towards the murderous rock; but you, as the strong north-wind, / may fill the flapping sails, and carry me on my way with victory and gladness."

A murmur filled the presence-chamber; dark Douglas[a] grasped his sword; Hamilton's eyes glanced lightnings; not one there but felt his heart beat with desire to enforce the illustrious exile's right. The tide of rising enthusiasm paused as James arose; and deep attention held them all. He descended from his throne. "My royal brother," he said, "were I a mere errant knight, so good and high I esteem your cause, without more ado I would don my armour, and betake me to the field. The same power which enables me to afford you far better succour than the strength of one arm, obliges me to pause and take counsel,[17] ere I speak what it is in my heart to promise. But your Highness has made good your interests among my counsellors; and I read in their gestures the desire of war and adventure for your sake. Deem yourself an exile no more. Fancy that you have come from merry England to feast with your brother in the north, and we will escort you back to your capital in triumphant procession, showing the gaping / world how slighter than silky cobwebs are the obstacles that oppose the united strength of Plantagenet and Stuart. Welcome – thrice, welcome to the Scottish land – kinsmen, nobles, valiant gentlemen, bid dear welcome to my brother England!" /

---

[a] Archibald Douglas, 5th Earl of Angus (?1449–1514), powerful border chieftain who served James IV as Lord High Chancellor from 1493–8.

CHAPTER XII.

———

A lady, the wonder of her kind,
Whose form was upborne by a lovely mind;
Which dilating had moulded her mien and motion,
Like a sea-flower unfolded beneath the ocean.

SHELLEY.[a]

———

A few days made it apparent that York acquired a stronger power over the generous and amiable King of Scotland, than could be given by motives of state policy. He became his friend; no empty name with James, whose ardent soul poured itself headlong into this new channel, and revelled in a kind of extacy in the virtues and accomplishments of his favoured guest. Both these Princes were magnanimous / and honourable, full of grandeur of purpose, and gentleness of manner: united by these main qualities, the diversities of their dispositions served rather to draw them closer. Though Richard's adventures and disasters had been so many, his countenance, his very mind was less careworn than that of James. The White Rose, even in adversity, was the nursling of love: the Scottish Prince, in his palace-fostered childhood, had been the object of his father's hatred and suspicion: cabal, violence, and duplicity had waited on him. James governed those around him by demonstrating to them, that it was their interest to obey a watchful, loving, generous monarch: Richard's power was addressed to the most exalted emotions of the human heart, to the fidelity, self-devotion, and chivalric attachment of his adherents. James drew towards himself the confidence of men; Richard bestowed his own upon them. James was winning from his courtesy, Richard from his ingenuousness. Remorse had printed a fadeless stamp of thought and pain on the King's countenance; an internal self-communion and self-rebuke / were seated in the deep shadows of his thoughtful eyes. Richard's sorrow for the disasters he might be said to have occasioned his friends, his disdain of his

---

[a] 'The Sensitive Plant' (1820), II. 5–8.

217

own vagabond position, his sadness, when his winged thoughts flew after the Adalid, to hover over his sweet Monina; all these emotions were tinged by respect for the virtues of those around him, conscious rectitude, pious resignation to Providence, gratitude to his friends, and a tender admiration of the virgin virtues of her he loved: so that there arose thence only a softer expression for his features, a sweetness in the candour of his smile, a gentle fascination in his frank address, that gave at once the stamp of elevated feeling and goodness to his mien. He looked innocent, while James's aspect gave token, that in his heart good and ill had waged war: the better side had conquered, yet had not come off scatheless from the fight.

In the first enthusiasm of his new attachment, James was eager to lavish on his friend every mark of his favour and interest: he was obliged to check his impatience, and to submit / to the necessity of consulting with and deferring to others. His promises, though large, continued therefore to be vague; and York knew that he had several enemies at the council-board. The intimacy between him and the King prevented him from entertaining any doubts as to the result; but he had a difficult task in communicating this spirit of patient forbearance to his friends. Sometimes they took sudden fright, lest they should all at once meet a denial to their desires; sometimes they were indignant at the delays that were interposed. None was more open in his expressions of discontent than Master Secretary Frion. He, who had been the soul of every enterprize until now, who had fancied that his talents for negociation would be of infinite avail in the Scottish court, found that the friendship between the Princes, and Richard's disdain of artfully enticing to his side his host's noble subjects, destroyed at once his diplomatic weaving. He craftily increased the discontent of the proud Neville, the disquietude of the zealous Lady Brampton, and the turbulent intolerance of repose / of Lord Barry; while Richard, on the other hand, exerted himself to tranquillize and reduce them to reason: he was sanguine in his expectations, and above all, confident in his friend's sincere intention to do more than merely assist him by force of arms. He saw a thousand projects at work in James's generous heart, every one tending to exalt him in the eyes of the world, and to rescue him for ever from the nameless, fugitive position he occupied. Nor was his constant intercourse with the King of small influence over his happiness: the genius, the versatile talents, the grace and accomplishments of this sovereign, the equality and sympathy that reigned between them, was an exhaustless source of more than amusement, of interest and delight. The friends of James became his friends: Sir Patrick Hamilton was chief among these, and warmly attached to the English Prince: another, whom at first ceremony had placed at a greater distance from him, grew into an object of intense interest and continual excitation.

"This evening," said the King to him, soon / after his arrival, "you will see the flower of our Scottish damsels, the flower of the world well may I call her;

for assuredly, when you see the Lady Katherine Gordon,[a] you will allow that she is matchless among women."

Richard was surprised: did James's devotion to Lady Jane Kennedy, nay, his conscious look whenever he mentioned her, mean nothing? Besides, on this appeal to his own judgment, he pictured his soft-eyed Spaniard, with all her vivacity and all her tenderness, and he revolted from the idea of being the slave of any other beauty. "Speak to our guest, Sir Patrick," continued the King, "and describe the fair earthly angel who makes a heaven of our bleak wilds; or rather, for his Highness might suspect you, let me, not her lover, but her cousin, her admirer, her friend, tell half the charms, half the virtues of the daughter of Huntley.[b] Is it not strange that I, who have seen her each day since childhood, and who still gaze with wonder on her beauty, should yet find that words fail me when I would paint it? I am apt to see, and ready to praise, the delicate / arch of this lady's brow, the fire of another's eyes, another's pouting lip and fair complexion, the gay animation of one, the chiseled symmetry of a second. Often, when our dear Lady Kate has sat, as is often her wont, retired from sight, conversing with some travelled greybeard, or paying the homage of attention to some ancient dame (of late I have remarked her often in discourse with Lady Brampton), I have studied her face and person to discover where the overpowering charm exists, which, like a strain of impassioned music, electrifies the senses, and touches the hearts of all near her. Is it in her eyes? A poet might dream of dark blue orbs like hers, and that he had kissed eyelids soft as those, when he came unawares on the repose of young Aurora,[c] and go mad for ever after, because it was only a dream: yet I have seen brighter; nor are they languishing. Her lips, yes, the soul of beauty is there, and so is it in her dimpled chin. In the delicate rounding of her cheeks, in the swanlike loveliness of her throat, in the soft ringlets of her glossy hair, down to the very tips of her roseate-tinged fingers, there is proportion, / expression and grace. You will hardly see all this: at first you will be struck; extreme beauty must strike; but your second thought will be, to wonder what struck you, and then you will look around, and see twenty prettier and more attractive; and then, why, at the first words she speaks, you will fancy it an easy thing to die upon the mere thought of her: her voice alone will take you out of yourself, and carry you into another state of being. She is simple as a child, straight-forward, direct: falsehood – pah! Katherine *is* Truth. This simplicity, which knows neither colouring nor deviation, might almost make you fear, while you adore her, but that her

---

[a] Daughter of Princess Annabella Stuart, and granddaughter of James I; Katherine's merit and beauty were universally praised by early chroniclers and later historians.

[b] George Gordon, 2nd Earl of Huntley (or Huntly; d. ?1502), supported James III but later switched allegiance to his son, the future James IV. After Sauchieburn Huntley served as the young king's Privy Counsellor, Lieutenant of the North, and Lord High Chancellor. Byron's mother was descended from the Earl's third son, William, ancestor of the Gordons of Gight.

[c] Roman Goddess of dawn.

goodness brings you back to love. She is good, almost beyond the consciousness of being so: she is good, because she gives herself entirely up to sympathy;
and, beyond every other, she dives into the sources of your pleasures and pains,
and takes a part in them. The better part of yourself will, when she speaks,
appear to leap out, as if, for the first time, it found its other half; while / the
worse is mute, like a stricken dog, before her. She is gay, more eager to create
pleasure than to please; for to please, we must think of ourselves, and be
ourselves the hero of the story, and Katherine is ever forgetful of self: she is
guileless and gall-less; all love her; her proud father, and fiery, contentious
Highland brothers, defer to her; yet, to look at her, it is as if the youngest and
most innocent of the Graces[a] read a page of Wisdom's book, scarce understanding what it meant, but feeling that it was right."

It was dangerous to provoke the spirit of criticism by excessive praise; Richard
felt half inclined to assert that there was something in the style of the King's
painting that showed he should not like this lauded lady; but she was his cousin,
he was proud of her, and so he was silent. There was a ball at court that night; and
he would see many he had never seen before; James made it a point that he should
discover which was his cousin. He could not mistake. "She is loveliness itself!"
burst from his lips; and from that moment he felt what James had / said, that there
was a "music breathing from her face,"[b] an unearthly, spirit-stirring beauty, that
inspired awe, had not her perfect want of pretension, her quiet, unassuming
simplicity, at once led him back to every thought associated with the charms and
virtues of woman. Lady Brampton was already a link between them; and, in a few
minutes, he found himself conversing with more unreserve and pleasure than he
had ever done. There are two pleasures in our intercourse in society, one is to
listen, another to speak. We may frequently meet agreeable, entertaining people,
and even sometimes individuals, whose conversation, either by its wit, its profun-
dity or its variety, commands our whole rapt attention: but very seldom during
the course of our lives do we meet those who thaw every lingering particle of ice,
who set the warm life-springs flowing, and entice us, with our hearts upon our
lips, to give utterance to its most secret mysteries; to disentangle every knot and
fold of thought, and, like sea-weed in the wave, to spread the disregarded herbage,
as a tracery matchlessly fair before another's eyes. Such / pleasure Richard felt
with Katherine; and, ever and anon, her melodious voice interposed with some
remark, some explanation of his own feelings, at once brilliant and true.

Richard knew that Sir Patrick Hamilton loved the Lady Katherine Gordon;
he also was related to the royal family.[c] Hamilton in the eyes of all, fair ladies

---

[a] Euphrosyne, Aglaia, and Thalia, offspring of Zeus and Eurynome.

[b] Byron, *The Bride of Abydos. A Turkish Tale* (1813), I. 179; Byron defended the expression in
an explanatory note.

[c] Illegitimate son of Sir James Hamilton of Cadzow (d. 1479), once married to Mary, a sister of
James III. Like Ford, Mary Shelley supplies her heroine with an unsuccessful suitor.

and sage counsellors, was acknowledged to be the most perfect Knight of Scotland; what obstacle could there be to their union? Probably it was already projected, and acceded to. Richard did not derogate from the faith that he told himself he owed to Monina, by cultivating a friendship for the promised bride of another, and moreover one whom, after the interval of a few short months, he would never see again. Satisfied with this reasoning, York lost no opportunity of devoting himself to the Lady Katherine.

His interests were the continual subject of discussion in the royal council-chamber. There were a few who did not speak in his favour. The principal of these was the Earl of Moray,[a] the King's uncle: the least in consideration, for he / was not of the council, though he influenced it: but the bitterest in feeling, was Sir John Ramsay, Laird of Balmayne, who styled himself Lord Bothwell. He had been a favourite of James the Third. His dark, fierce temper was exasperated by his master's death, and he brooded perpetually for revenge. He had once, with several other nobles, entered into a conspiracy to deliver up the present King to Henry the Seventh; and the traitorous intent was defeated, not from want of will, but want of power in his abettors. Since then, Lord Bothwell, though nominally banished and attainted, was suffered to live in Edinburgh, nay, to have access to the royal person. James, whose conscience suffered so dearly by the death of his father, had no desire to display severity towards his ancient faithful servant; besides, one who was really so insignificant as Sir John Ramsay. This man was turbulent, dissatisfied: he was sold to Henry of England, and had long acted as a spy; the appearance of York at Edinburgh gave activity and importance to his function: / his secret influence and covert intrigues retarded somewhat the projects and desires of the King.[b]

When the first opposition made to acknowledging this pretender to the English crown was set aside, other difficulties ensued. Some of the counsellors were for making hard conditions with the young Duke, saying, that half a kingdom were gift enough to a Prince Lackland:[c] a golden opportunity was this, they averred, to slice away a bonny county or two from wide England; he whom they gifted with the rest could hardly say them nay. But James was indignant at the base proposal, and felt mortified and vexed when obliged to concede in part, and to make conditions which he thought hard with his guest. After a noisy debate, these propositions were drawn out, and York was invited to attend the council, where they were submitted for his assent.

These conditions principally consisted in the surrender of Berwick,[d] and the promised payment of a hundred thousand marks. They were hard; for it would

---

[a] Andrew Stuart, Bishop (not Earl) of Moray, great-uncle of James IV; see pp. 244, 271n.

[b] Ramsay (d. 1513), the lone favourite to escape hanging at Loudon Bridge, was a pliant tool of Henry VII; see pp. 5–6.

[c] Name traditionally applied to a ruler without a kingdom.

[d] Border county then under English control. James's display of shame is Mary Shelley's invention.

touch the new monarch's / honour not to dismember his kingdom; and it were his policy not to burthen himself with a debt which his already oppressed subjects must be drawn on to pay. The Duke asked for a day for consideration, which was readily granted.

With great zeal for his cause on one side, and perfect confidence in his friend's integrity on the other, these difficulties became merely nominal, and the treaty was speedily arranged. But the month of September was near its close; a winter campaign would be of small avail: money, arms, and trained men, were wanting. The winter was to be devoted to preparation; with the spring the Scottish army was to pass the English border.[a] In every discussion, in every act, James acted as his guest's brother, the sharer of his risks and fortunes: one will, one desire, was theirs. Sir Patrick Hamilton went into the west to raise levies: no third person interposed between them. It was the King's disposition to yield himself wholly up to the passion of the hour. He saw in Richard, not only a prince deprived of his own, and driven into exile, but a youth of royal lineage, exposed / to the opprobrium of nick-names and the accusation of imposture. The King of France acknowledged, but he had deserted him; the Archduke had done the same: how could James prove that he would not follow in these steps? He levied the armies of his kingdom in his favour; he was to fight and conquer for him next spring. The intervening months were intolerable to the fervent spirit of the Stuart – something speedy, something now, he longed, he resolved to do; which, with a trumpet-note, should to all corners of the world declare, that he upheld Richard of York's right – that he was his defender, his champion. Once he penned a universal challenge, then another specially addressed to Henry Tudor; but his invasion were a better mode than this. Should he give him rank in Scotland? – that would ill beseem one who aspired to the English crown. Should he proclaim him Richard the Fourth in Edinburgh? – York strongly objected to this. Money? – it were a base gilding; besides, James was very poor, and had melted down his plate,[b] and put his jewels to pawn, to furnish forth the intended / expedition. Yet there was one way, – the idea was as lightning – James felt satisfied and proud; and then devoted all his sagacity, all his influence, all his ardent soul, to the accomplishment of a plan, which, while it ensured young Richard's happiness, stampt him indelibly as being no vagabond impostor, but the honoured prince, the kinsman and ally of Scotland's royal house.

King James and the Duke of York had ridden out to inspect a Lowland regiment, which the Earl of Angus proudly displayed as the force of the Douglas. As they returned, James was melancholy and meditative. "It is strange

---

[a] 'The invasion was in October 1496' (marginal note in *Abinger/Palacio*). In fact, there were two invasions: the first in September 1496, according to modern sources; the second, coincident with the Cornwall uprising in 1497; see p. 238n.

[b] Details reported to Henry VII by Ramsay.

and hard to endure," he said at last, fixing on his companion his eyes at once so full of fire and thought, "when two spirits contend within the little microcosm of man. I felt joy at sight of those bold followers of the Douglas, to think that your enemy could not resist them; but I do myself foolish service, when I place you on the English throne. You will leave us, my Lord: you will learn in your bonny realm to despise our barren wilds: it will / be irksome to you in prosperity, to think of your friends of the dark hour."

There was sincerity in these expressions, but exaggeration in the feelings that dictated them. Richard felt half-embarrassed, in spite of gratitude and friendship. The King, following the bent of his own thoughts, not those of others, suddenly continued: "Our cousin Kate at last finds grace in your eyes; is she not good and beautiful, all cold and passionless as she is?"

"Cold!" the Lady Katherine, whose heart felt sympathy, was a sunny clime in which he basked – whose sensibility perpetually varied the bright expression of her features – York repeated the word in astonishment.

"Thou findest her wax?" enquired James, smiling; "by my troth, she has proved but marble before."

"I cannot guess even at your meaning," replied York, with all the warmth of a champion; "the lady is in the estimation of all, in your own account, the best daughter, the most devoted friend, the kindest mistress in the world. How can we call that spirit cold, which animates / her to these acts? It is not easy to perform, as she does, our simplest duties. How much of self-will, of engrossing humour, even of our innocent desires and cherished tastes, must we not sacrifice, when we devote ourselves to the pleasure and service of others? How much attention does it not require, how sleepless a feeling of interest, merely to perceive and understand the moods and wishes of those around us! An inert, sluggish nature, half ice, half rock, cannot do this. To achieve it, as methinks your fair kinswoman does, requires all her understanding, all her sweetness, all that exquisite tact and penetrative feeling I never saw but in her."

"I am glad you say this," said James. "Yes, Kate has a warm heart: none has a better right to say so than I. There are – there were times, for the gloom of the dark hour is somewhat mitigated – when no priest, no penance, had such power over me as my cousin Katherine's sweet voice. Like a witch she dived into the recesses of my heart, plucking thence my unholy distrust in God's mercy. By St. Andrew![a] when / I look at her, all simple and gentle as she is, I wonder in what part of her resides the wisdom and the eloquence I have heard fall from her lips; nor have I had the heart to reprove her, when I have been angered to see our cousin Sir Patrick driven mad by her sugared courtesies."

"Does she not affect Sir Patrick?" asked Richard, while he wondered at the thrilling sensation of fear that accompanied his words.

---

[a] Scotland's patron saint.

"'Yea, heartily,' she will reply," replied the King; "'Would you have me disdain our kinsman?'[18] She asks when I rail; but you, who are of gender masculine, though, by the mass! a smooth specimen of our rough kind, know full well that pride and impertinence are better than equable, smiling, impenetrable sweetness. Did the lady of my love treat me thus, 'sdeath, I think I should order myself the rack for pastime. But we forget ourselves; push on, dear Prince. It is the hour, when the hawks and their fair mistresses are to meet us on the hill's side. I serve no such glassy damsel; nor would I that little Kennedy's eye darted fires on / me in scorn of my delay. Are not my pretty Lady Jane's eyes bright, Sir Duke?"

"As a fire-fly among dark-leaved myrtles."

"Or a dew-drop on the heather, when the morning sun glances on it, as we take our mountain morning-way to the chace. You look grave, my friend; surely her eyes are nought save as nature's miracle to you?"

"Assuredly not," replied[19] York; "are they other to your Majesty – you do not love the lady?"

"Oh, no," reiterated James with a meaning glance, "I do not love the Lady Jane; only I would bathe in fire, bask in ice, do each and every impossibility woman's caprice could frame for trials to gain – but I talk wildly to a youthful sage. Say, most revered anchorite, wherefore doubt you my love to my pretty mistress?"

"Love!" exclaimed Richard; his eyes grew lustrous in their own soft dew as he spoke. "Oh, what profanation is this! And this you think is love? to select a young, innocent and beauteous girl – who, did she wed her equal, would become an honoured wife and happy / mother – to select her, the more entirely to deprive her of these blessings – to bar her out for ever from a woman's paradise, a happy home; you, who even now are in treaty for a princess-bride, would entice this young thing to give up her heart, her all, into your hands, who will crush it, as boys a gaudy butterfly when the chace is over. Dear my Lord, spare her the pain, yourself, remorse; you are too good, too wise, too generous, to commit this deed and not to suffer bitterly."

A cloud came over James's features. The very word 'remorse' was a sound of terror to him. He smote his right hand against his side, where dwelt his heart in sore neighbourhood to the iron of his penance.

At this moment, sweeping down the near hill-side, came a gallant array of ladies and courtiers. The King even lagged behind; when near, he accosted Katherine, he spoke to the Earl of Angus, to Mary Boyd, to all save the Lady Jane, who first looked disdainful, then hurt, and at last, unable to struggle with her pain, rode sorrowfully apart. James tried to see, to / feel nothing. Her pride he resisted; her anger he strove to contemn, her dejection he could not endure: and, when riding up to her unaware, he saw the traces of tears on her cheek, usually so sunny bright with smiles, he forgot every thing save his wish to console, to mollify, to cheer her. As they returned, his hand was on her saddle-bow, his head bent down, his eyes looking into hers, and she was smiling, though less gay than usual. From that hour James less coveted the Prince's society. He began a little to fear him: not the less did he love and esteem him; and more, far more did he deem him worthy of the honour, the happiness he intended to bestow upon him. /

CHAPTER XIII.

———

She is mine own;
And I as rich in having such a jewel,
As twenty seas, if all their sand were pearl,
Their water nectar, and the rocks pure gold!
SHAKSPEARE.[a]

———

The threads were spun, warp and woof laid on, and Fate busily took up the shuttle, which was to entwine the histories of two beings, at whose birth pomp and royalty stood sponsors, whose career was marked by every circumstance that least accorded with such a nativity. A thousand obstacles stood in the way; the King, with all his fervour, hesitated before he proposed to the Earl of Huntley to bestow his daughter, of whom he was justly proud, on a fugitive / sovereign, without a kingdom, almost without a name. Fortune, superstition, ten thousand of those imperceptible threads which fate uses when she weaves her most indissoluble webs, all served to bring about the apparently impossible.

The Earl of Huntley was a man of plain, straightforward, resolved ambition. His head was warm, his heart cold, his purpose one – to advance his house, and himself as the head of it, to as high a situation as the position of subject would permit. In the rebellion which occasioned the death of James the Third, he had vacillated, unable quite to ascertain which party would prove triumphant; and when the rebels, rebels then no more, but lieges to James the Fourth, won the day, they looked coldly on their lukewarm partizan. Huntley grew discontented: though still permitted to hold the baton of Earl Marshal, he saw a cloud of royal disfavour darkening his fortunes; in high indignation he joined in the

---

[a] *Two Gentlemen of Verona*, II. iv. 168–71.

nefarious plot of Buchan, Bothwell, and Sir Thomas Todd, to deliver his sovereign into the hands of Henry of England, a project afterwards abandoned.[a] /

Time had softened the bitter animosities which attended James at the beginning of his reign. He extended his favour to all parties, and reconciled them to each other. A wonder it was, to see the Douglas's, Hamiltons, Gordons, Homes, the Murrays, and Lennoxes, and a thousand others, at peace with each other, and obedient to their sovereign. The Earl of Huntley, a man advanced in life, prudent, resolute and politic, grew into favour. He was among the principal of the Scottish peers; he had sons to whom the honours of his race would descend; and this one daughter, whom he loved as well as he could love any thing, and respected from the extent of her influence and the perfect prudence of her conduct, she was his friend and counsellor, the mediator between him and her brothers; the kind mistress to his vassals; a gentle, but all powerful link between him and his king, whose value he duly appreciated.

Her marriage was often the subject of his meditation. Superstition was ever rife in Scotland. James the Third had driven all / his brothers from him, because he had been told to beware of one near of kin; and his death, of which his son was the ostensible agent, fulfilled the prophecy. Second-sight in the Highlands was of more avail than the predictions of a lowland sibyl. The seer of the house of Gordon had, on the day of her birth, seen the Lady Katherine receive homage as a Queen, and standing at the altar with one on whose young brow he perceived all dim and shadowy, "the likeness of a kingly crown."[b] True, this elevation was succeeded by disasters: he had beheld her a fugitive; he saw her stand on the brow of a cliff that overlooked the sea, while the wild clouds careered over the pale moon, alone, deserted; he saw her a prisoner; he saw her stand desolate beside the corpse of him she had wedded – the diadem was still there, dimly seen amid the disarray of his golden curls. These images haunted the Earl's imagination, and made him turn a slighting ear to Sir Patrick Hamilton and other noble suitors of his lovely child.[c] Sometimes he thought of the King, her cousin, or one of his brothers: flight, desolation and / death were no strange attendants on the state of the King of Scotland, and these miseries he regarded as necessary and predestined; he could not avert, and so he hardly regarded them, while his proud bosom swelled at the anticipation of the thorny diadem which was to press the brow of a daughter of the Gordon.

Lord Huntley had looked coldly on the English Prince. Lord Bothwell, as he called himself, otherwise Sir John Ramsay of Balmaine, his former accomplice, tampered with him on the part of Henry the Seventh, to induce him to oppose

---

[a] Huntley seems to have had no role in the plot designed in 1491 by James Stuart, 1st Earl of Buchan, Ramsay, and Todd to kidnap the king and his brother.

[b] John Milton (1608–74), *Paradise Lost* (1667, 1674), II. 673.

[c] Cf. Ford's depiction of Huntley as an ambitious father.

warmly the reception of this "feigned boy,"[a] and to negative every proposition to advance his claims. King Henry's urgent letters, and Ramsay's zeal, awakened the Earl's suspicions; a manifest impostor could hardly engender such fears, such hate; and, when midnight assassination, or the poisoned bowl were plainly hinted at by the monarch of wide England, Huntley felt assured that the enemy he so bitterly pursued was no pretender, but the rightful heir of the sceptre Henry held. He did not quite refuse to join with Bothwell, especially / when he heard that he was listened to by the Bishop of Moray and the Earl of Buchan; but involuntarily he assumed a different language with regard to York, became more respectful to him, and by his demeanour crushed at once the little party who had hitherto spoken of him with contempt. The King perceived this change; it was the foundation-stone of his project. "Tell me, you who are wise, my lord," said the Monarch to his Earl Marshal, "how I may raise our English Prince in the eyes of Scotland. We fight for him in the spring, for him, we say: but few of ours echo the word; they disdain to fight for any not akin to them."

"They would fight for the Foul Fiend," said Huntley, "whom they would be ill-pleased to call cousin, if he led them over the English border."

"Aye, if he took them there to foray; but the Duke of York will look on England as his own, and when the nobles of the land gather round him, it will be chauncy work to keep them and our Scots from shedding each other's blood; / they would spill Duke Richard's like water, if no drop of it can be deemed Scotch."

"It were giving him a new father and mother," replied the Earl, "to call him thus."

"When two even of hostile houses intermarry, our heralds pale their arms; the offspring pale their blood."

"But what Scottish lady would your Grace bestow on him whose rank were a match for royalty? There is no Princess of the Stuarts."

"And were there," asked James quickly, "would it beseem us to bestow our sister on a King Lackland?"

"Or would your Majesty wait till he were King of England, when France, Burgundy and Spain would compete with you? I do believe that this noble gentleman has fair right to his father's crown; he is gallant and generous, so is not King Henry; he is made to be the idol of a warlike people, such as the English, so is not his rival. Do you strike one stroke, the whole realm rises for him, and he becomes its sovereign: then it were a pride and a glory for us, for him a tie to bind him for ever, did he / place his diadem on the head of a Scottish damsel."

"You are sanguine and speak warmly," replied the King: "see you beyond your own words? to me they suggest a thought which I entertain, or not, as is

---

[a] So called in the chronicles and Pinkerton (II, p. 27).

your pleasure: there is but one lady in our kingdom fitting mate for him, and she is more Gordon than Stuart. Did your Lordship glance at the Lady Katherine in your speech?"

Lord Huntley changed colour: a sudden rush of thought palsied the beatings of his heart. Was he called upon to give his child, his throne-destined daughter, to this king-errant? Nay, nay, thus did fortune blindly work; her hand would insure to him the crown, and so fulfil to her the dark meaning of the seer: hesitating, lost to his wonted presence of mind, Huntley could only find words to ask for a day for reflection. James wondered at this show of emotion; he could not read its full meaning: "At your pleasure, my Lord," he said, "but, if you decide against my honoured, royal friend, / remember that this question dies without record – you will preserve our secret."

Every reflection that could most disquiet an ambitious man possessed the Earl Marshal. That his daughter should be Queen of England was beyond his hopes; that she should be the errant wife of a pretender, who passed his life in seeking ineffectual aid at foreign courts, was far beneath them. He canvassed every likelihood of York's success; now they dwindled like summer-snow on the southern mountain's side – now they strode high and triumphant over every obstacle; the clinging feeling was – destiny had decreed it – she being his wife, both would succeed and reign. "There is fate in it," was his last reflection," and I will not gainsay the fulfilment. Andrew of the Shawe was the Prince of Seers, as I have good proof. Still to a monarch alone shall she give her hand, and I must make one condition."

This one condition Lord Huntley communicated to his royal master. It was that York should, as of right he might, assume the style and title of King. James smiled at his Earl / Marshal's childish love of gauds, and did not doubt that the Duke would pay so easy price for a jewel invaluable as Katherine. But granting this, the King, knowing the noble's despotic character, required one condition also on his part, that he should first announce the intended union to the lady, and that it should not have place without her free and entire consent. Huntley was surprised; "Surely my liege," he began, "if your Majesty and I command –"

"Our sweet Kate will obey," interrupted James; "but this is no mere marriage of policy; hazards, fearful hazards may attend it. Did I not believe that all would end well, by the Holy Rood he should not have her; but she may see things with different eyes – she may shrink from becoming the wife of an exile, a wanderer without an home: yet that need never be."

York little guessed the projects of his royal friend. Love, in its most subtle guise, had insinuated itself into his soul, becoming a very portion of himself. That part of our nature, which to our reflections appears the most human, and / yet which forms the best part of humanity, is our desire of sympathy; the intense essence of sympathy, is love. Love has been called selfish, engrossing, tyrannic – as the root, so the green leaf that shoots from it – love is a part of us – it is our manifestation of life; and poisonous or sweet will be the foliage, according to the stock. When we love, it is our aim and conclusion to make the object a part of ourselves – if we are self-willed and evilly inclined, little good can arise; but deep is the fount of generous, devoted, godlike feeling, which this silver key unlocks in gentle hearts.[a] Richard had found in the Lady Katherine a magic mirror, which gave him back himself, arrayed with a thousand alien virtues; his soul was in her hands, plastic to her fairy touch, and tenderness and worship and wonder took his heart, ere passion woke, and threw a chain over these bosom guests, so that they could never depart. A mild, yet golden light dawned upon his soul, and beamed from it, lighting up creation with splendour – filling his mind with mute, yet entrancing melody. He walked in a dream; but far from being / rendered by his abstraction morose or inattentive to others, never had he been so gay, never so considerate and amiable. He felt that, beneath the surface of his life, there was the calm and even the bliss of paradise; and his lightest word or act must be, by its grace and benevolence, in concord with the tranquil spirit that brooded over his deeper-hidden self. All loved him the better for the change, save Frion; there was something in him that the wily Frenchman did not understand; he went about and about, but how could this man of "low-thoughted care"[b] understand the holy mysteries of love.

Katherine accompanied her father to Gordon Castle, in Aberdeenshire. Where was the light now, that had made a summer noon in Richard's soul? There was memory: it brought before him her cherub-face, her voice, the hours when at her side he had poured out his overbrimming soul in talk – not of love, but of ideas, feelings, imaginations he had never spoken before. Two days past, and by that time he had collected a whole volume of things he wished to say – and she was far: then hope claimed entrance to his / heart, and with her came a train he dreamt not of – of fears, anticipations, terror, despair; and then a tenfold ardour for his enterprize. Should he not win Katherine and a kingdom?

On the third day after her departure, King James informed the Prince, that Lord Huntley had invited them to visit him at his castle. "Will your Grace venture," he asked, "so far into the frozen circles of the icy North? You will traverse many a savage defile and wild mountain-top; torrents and dark pine forests bar the way, and barrenness spreads her hag's arms to scare the intruder. I speak your language, the effeminate language of an Andalusian, who loves the craggy heights, only when summer basks upon them; and the deep sunless dell, when myrtles and geranium impregnate the air with sweets. I love the mist and snow, the tameless winds and howling torrent, the bleak un-adorned precipice, the giant pines where the North makes music. The grassy upland and the cornfield, these belong to man, and to her they call Nature, the

---

[a] Cf. P. B. Shelley, 'On Love', first published by Mary Shelley in *The Keepsake for MDCCCXXIX* (published 1828).

[b] John Milton, *A Maske presented at Ludlow Castle, 1634* ('Comus'), published 1637, l. 6.

fair, gaudy dame; but God takes to himself, and lives among, these sublime rocks, / where power, majesty and eternity are shaped forth, and the grandeur of heaven-piercing cliffs allies us to a simple but elevating image of the Creator."

King James was a poet, and could feel thus – York might smile at his enthusiasm for the bleak and horrific. But had the path to Gordon Castle been ten times more frightful, the thoughts of love were roses, the hopes of love vernal breezes, to adorn it with beauty. "Say, my Lord," continued James, "shall we go, throwing aside the cumbrous burthen of pomp? We are here in Perth. Yonder, over those peaks, lies our direct path. Shall we, two woodland rovers, with bows in our hand and quivers at our back, take our solitary way[a] through the wild region? It is my pastime ofttimes so to do; and well I know the path that leads me to the abode of my cousin Kate. We will send our attendants by the easier path to the eastern sea-shore, at once to announce our approach, and bear such gear as we may need, not to play too humble a part in Huntley's eyes." /

A thousand motives of policy and pride had induced the Earl to desire that this marriage should be celebrated in the Highlands. Here he would appear almost a sovereign to his royal son-in-law; here also he should avoid the sarcasms of the Tudor party, and the anger of those who had pretended to fair Katherine's hand. James consented to his wish, and now led his friend and guest, through the very heart of his craggy kingdom over the Grampians, towards Aberdeen.[b] It was the end of October; a few sweet autumnal days still lingered among these northern hills, as if to light on their way the last feathered migrators, hastening towards the south; but dark mists invested their morning progress. The rivers were swollen; and the mountain peaks often saluted the rising sun, garmented in radiant snow. It was a little drear, yet grand, sublime, wondrous. York suppressed his chilling distaste, till it grew into admiration; the King played the guide featly; and the honoured name of the Bruce,[c] which peopled this region with proud memories, was the burthen of many a tale; nor was his account / of the fierce people of these wilds unwelcome to a warrior. York remarked that the King was generally known to them, not, indeed, as a monarch, but as a hunter, a traveller, sometimes as a skilful mediciner, or as a bard, and always hospitably received.

After three days they drew near their journey's end: curiosity as to the cause of their visit, anxiety concerning his reception, all faded in Richard's heart; dimmed by the glad expectation of seeing her again, who had dawned, the glowing orient of his darkened heart. They had departed from their rude

---

[a] Echoing the final line of *Paradise Lost*, XII. 649.

[b] About seventy miles from Perth by James's 'direct path'.

[c] Robert the Bruce (1274–1329), Scotland's liberator, who crushed England's Edward II at Bannockburn in 1314.

shelter before the sun rose: the mountain peaks were awake with day, while night still slumbered in the plain below: some natural sights speak to the heart more than others, wherefore we know not: the most eloquent is that of the birth of day on the untrodden hill-tops, while we who behold it, are encompassed by shadows. York paused: the scene appeared to close in on him, and to fill him, even to overflowing, with its imagery. They were toiling up the mountain's side: below, above, the dark pines, in many a tortuous / shape, clung to the rifted rocks; the fern clustered round some solitary old oak; while, beetling over, were dark frowning crags, or the foldings of the mountains, softened into upland, painted by the many coloured heather. With the steady pace of a mountaineer, King James breasted the hill-side; nor did York bely his rugged Spanish home. As a bravado, the King in the very sheer ascent trolled a ballad, a wild Scottish song, and Richard answered by a few notes of a Moorish air. A voice seemed to answer him, not an echo, for it was not his own, but taking the thrilling sweetness of Monina's tones. Ah! ungentle waves, and untaught winds, whither bear ye now the soft nursling of Andalusia? Such a thought darkened York's brow; when the King, pausing in his toil, leaned against a jutting crag – both young, both gallant, both so noble and so beautiful; of what could they think – of what speak? Not of the well governed realm of the one, nor the yet unconquered kingdom of the other; of such they might have spoken among statesmen and warriors, in palaces or on the battle plain; but here, in this wild / solitude, the vast theatre whose shifting scenes and splendid decorations were the clouds, the mountain, the forest and the wave, where man stood, not as one of the links of society, forced by his relative position to consider his station and his rank, but as a human being, animated only by such emotions as were the growth of his own nature – of what should they speak – the young, the beautiful – but love!

"Tell me, gentle Cavalier," cried James suddenly; "hast thou ever been in love? Now would I give my jewel-hilted dagger to tear thy secret from thee," continued the King laughing; for York's eyes had flashed with sudden light, and then fell downcast. Where were his thoughts? at his journey's goal, or on the ocean sea? If he smiled, it was for Kate; but the tear that glittered on his long eyelashes, spoke of his Spanish maid. Yet it was not the passion of love that he now felt for his childhood companion; it was tenderness, a brother's care, a friend's watchfulness, all that man can feel for woman, unblended with the desire of making her his; but gratitude and distance had / so blended and mingled his emotions, that thus addressed, he almost felt as if he had been detected in a crime.

"Now, by the Holy Rood, thou blushest," said James, much amused; "not more deeply was fair Katherine's cheek bedyed, when I put the self-same question to her. Does your Grace guess, wherefore we journey northwards?"

Richard turned an inquiring and unquiet look upon his royal companion. A kind of doubt was communicated to James's mind; he knew little of his friend's

231

former life: was it not possible that engagements were already formed, incompatible with his plans? With some haughtiness, for his impetuous spirit ill brooked the slightest check, he disclosed the object of their visit to Castle Gordon, and the proposal he had made to the Earl to unite him in marriage to the Scottish Princess.

"When I shall possess my kingdom – when I may name my wife, that which she is, or nothing – Queen!" Richard exclaimed.

"Nay, I speak of no millenium, but of the present hour," said James. /

The enthusiastic King, bent upon his purpose, went on to speak of all the advantages that would result from this union. York's silence nettled him: the Prince's thoughts were indeed opposed to the exultation and delight which his friend had expected to see painted on his face. The first glad thought of a lover, is to protect and exalt her he loves. Katherine was a princess in her native land; – and what was he? – an outcast and a beggar – a vagabond upon the earth – a man allied to all that was magnificent in hope – to all that imagination could paint of gallant and true in himself, and devoted and noble in his friends. But these were idealities to the vulgar eye; and he had only a title as unreal as these, and a mere shadowy right, to bestow. It had been sinful even to ally Monina to his broken fortunes; but this high offspring of a palace – the very offer, generous as it was, humbled him. A few minutes' silence intervened; and, in a colder tone James was about to address him, when York gave words to all the conflicting emotions in his breast – speaking such gratitude, love, hope, and despair, / as reassured his friend, and made him the more resolve to conquer the difficulties unexpectedly given birth to by the disinterestedness of his guest.

A contest ensued; Richard deprecating the rich gift offered to him – the King warmly asserting that he must accept it. The words vagabond and outcast were treason to his friendship: if, which was impossible, they did not succeed in enforcing the rights to his ancestral kingdom, was not Scotland his home – for ever his home – if he married Katherine? And the Monarch went on to describe the happiness of their future lives – a trio bound by the ties of kindred – by affection – by the virtues, nay, even by the faults of each. He spoke also of the disturbances that so often had wrecked the fortunes of the proudest Scottish nobles, and said, that a princess of that land, united, it might be, to one of its chiefs, trimmed her bark for no summer sea. "Like these wild Highlands are our storm-nursed lives," continued James. "By our ruder thanes the beautiful and weak are not respected; and tempest and ruin visit ever the / topmost places. Kate is familiar to such fears, or rather, to the resignation and courage such prospects may inspire. Look around on these crags! listen! the storm is rising on the hills – howling among the pines. Such has been my cousin's nursery – such the school which has made her no slave of luxury; no frail flowret, to be scared when the rough wind visits her cheek."

In such discussions the travellers beguiled the time. The day was stormy; but, eager to arrive, they did not heed its pelting. York had a sun in his own heart, that beamed on him in spite of the clouds overhead. Notwithstanding his first keen emotion of pain at the idea of linking one so lovely to his dark fate, the entrancing thought of possessing Katherine – that she had already consented to be his – animated him with delight, vague indeed; for yet he struggled against the flattering illusion.

After battling the whole day against a succession of steep acclivities, as evening drew near, the friends gained the last hill-top, and stood on its brow, overlooking a fertile plain or strath – / an island of verdure amidst the black, precipitous mountains that girdled it. The sun was hidden by the western mountains, which cast their shadow into the valley; but the clouds were dispersed, and the round full silvery moon was pacing up the eastern heaven. The plain at their feet was studded by villages, adorned by groves, and threaded by two rivers, whose high, romantic banks varied the scene. An extensive, strongly-built castle stood on the hill that overhung one of the streams, looking proudly down on this strath, which contained nearly thirty-six square miles of fertile ground. "Behold," said James, "the kingdom of Lord Huntley, where he is far more absolute than I in my bonny Edinburgh. The Gordon fought for the Bruce; and the monarch bestowed on him this fair, wide plain as his reward. Bruce flying before his enemies, on foot, almost alone, among these savage Grampians, then looked upon it as now we do."

King James's thoughts were full of that wild exhilaration of spirit, which none, save the inhabitant of a mountainous country, knows, when desolation is around – a desolation which is to / him the pledge of freedom and of power. But York had other ideas: he had been told that the Lady Katherine had yielded a willing consent to the proposal made; and she whom he had before conversed with only as a gentle friend – she, the lovely and the good – his young heart beat thick, – it had no imagery, far less words, expressive of the rapture of love, tortured by the belief that such a prize he ought to – he must – resign.

The petty tyranny of trivial circumstance often has more power over our best-judged designs, than our pride permits us to confess. From the moment York entered Castle Gordon, he found an almost invisible, but all-conquering net thrown over him. The Gordon, for thus the Earl of Huntley preferred being called, when surrounded by his clan in his northern fastness, received the Princes with barbaric, but extreme magnificence: his dress was resplendent; his followers numerous, and richly clad according to Highland ideas of pomp. But no Lady Katherine was there, and it soon became apparent that Richard was first to see her at the altar. Sounds of nuptial / festivity rang through the Castle; instead of grace or generosity attending his meditated declining of the honour, it would have borne the guise of an arrogant refusal. There was also something in the savage look of the clansmen, in the rude uncivilization of her native halls, where defence and attack formed the creed and practice of all, that reconciled him to the idea of leading her from the wild north to softer milder scenes;

233

where every disaster wears a gentler shape; soothed, not exasperated by the ministrations of nature.

At midnight, but a very few hours after his arrival, he stood beside her in the chapel to interchange their vows. The Earl had decorated the holy place with every emblem that spoke of his own greatness, and that of his son-in-law. The style of royalty was applied to him, and the ambitious noble, "overleaping"[a] himself, grasped with childish or savage impetuosity at the shadowy sceptre, and obscure cloud-wrapt crown of the royal exile. York, when he saw the Princess, summoned all his discernment to read content or dissatisfaction in her eyes; if any of / the latter should appear, even there he would renounce his hopes. All was calm, celestially serene. Nay, something almost of exultation struggled through the placid expression of her features, as she cast her eyes up to Heaven, till modest gentleness veiled them again, and they were bent to earth.

The generosity and pride of woman had kindled these sentiments. The Lady Katherine, a princess by birth, would scarcely have dreamed of resisting her father's behests, even if they had been in opposition to her desires; but here she was to sacrifice no inclination, nothing but prosperity; that must depart for ever she felt, she knew, when she became the bride of England's outcast Prince. Yet should aught of good and great cling to him, it was her gift; and to bestow was the passion of her guileless heart. It was not reason; it was feeling, perhaps superstition, that inspired these ideas. The seer who foretold her fortunes, had been her tutor and her poet; she believed in him, and believed that all would be accomplished; even to the / death of the beautiful and beloved being who stood in the pride and strength of youth at her side. All must be endured; for it was the will of Heaven. Meanwhile, that he should be happy during his mortal career was to be her study, her gift, the aim of her life. In consenting to be his, she also had made a condition, that, if defeat awaited his arms, and that again a wanderer he was obliged to fly before his enemies, she was not to be divided from him; if no longer here, she was to be permitted to join him; if he departed, she should accompany him.

As the priest bestowed his benediction on the illustrious and beauteous pair, a silent vow was formed in the heart of either. Doomed by his ill-fate to hardship and dependence, he would find in her a medicine for all his woes, a wife, even the better, purer part of himself, who would never suffer him to despair: but who would take the bitterer portion of his sorrow on herself, giving in return the heroism, the piety, the serene content which was the essence of her being. His / vow, it depended not on himself, poor fellow! "Never through me shall she suffer," was the fervent resolve. Alas! as if weak mortal hands could hold back giant Calamity, when he seizes the heart, and rends it at his pleasure. /

---

[a] Alluding to *Macbeth*, I. vii. 25–8.

CHAPTER XIV.

But these are chimes for funerals: my business
Attends on fortune of a sprightlier triumph;
For love and majesty are reconciled,
And vow to crown thee Empress of the West.

FORD.[a]

The royal party returned to Edinburgh, where the nuptials of Richard of England and the Lady Katherine were celebrated with splendour. Festivities of all kinds, tournaments, hunting parties, balls, succeeded to each other; but far beyond every outward demonstration was the real happiness ensured by this marriage. Graced by Katherine, the little English court became a paradise. The Princess assumed her new character among the exiles with facility; yet the phrase is bad, for Katherine could / assume nothing, not even a virtue, if she had it not. In every position she was not princess, queen, patroness, or mistress; but woman merely – a true-hearted, gentle, refined woman. She was too young for the maternal character to be appropriate to her, yet the watchfulness and care she had for all resembled it. Her new subjects felt as if before they had been a disconnected, vagabond troop, and that dignity and station were assigned to them through her: through her the charities and elegances of life hallowed and adorned them. The quality most peculiarly her own was the divine simplicity which animated her look, her manners, her acts. Taintless simplicity, that best of fascinations, whose power is not imperious and sudden, but gradual and changeless, where every word spoken is but the genuine interpreter of the feelings of the heart, to which not only falsehood, but even the slightest disguise or affectation, is wholly foreign; and which is the more delicate, winning, and kind, from being spontaneous – so that, as in describing her, her royal cousin had said, "you almost questioned her authority / from its want of pretension, yet yielded to it in all its extent."

----

[a] *Perkin Warbeck*, III. ii. 159–62.

Richard's political position stood higher than ever. The ever-watchful Duchess of Burgundy had sent a renowned Burgundian captain, Sir Roderick-de-Lalayne, with two hundred German mercenaries. The King of France, at the request of Henry the Seventh, had dispatched an embassy to King James, to advise a peace between England and Scotland. The ambassador was the Sire de Concressault, York's ancient friend, who continued to espouse his cause warmly, and gave it all the grace and honour of his high influence. King James was eager to collect his army, and to prepare for an invasion. If Richard had lost any part of his open-hearted confidence and personal friendship, he had gained in his esteem and consideration. The change that had been operated was imperceptible to York, who naturally found in his marriage a barrier to the hourly intercourse they had formerly had, when both were free. Yet change there was, greater even than the King himself suspected: the causes were easily traced. /

The Tudor party in Scotland, instigated by bribes and large promises, were very active in their enmity to the White Rose. They had been obliged to let the torrent of royal favour force its headlong way, but they watched the slightest pause in its flow, to throw impediments in the way of the abundant stream. Soon after his return from the North, it became apparent that the King continued no unsuccessful suitor to the Lady Jane Kennedy. This a good deal estranged him from his English friend, who no longer reproved, but whose tacit condemnation he feared, as well as that of his fair cousin. Nay more, Lady Jane had drawn from him the cause of their transient quarrel, and, now that she had yielded, felt angry and disdainful at the attempt made to estrange her lover. One of those lower eddies or currents of intelligence, so in use at courts, had reported an angry expression of hers to the Earl of Buchan, one of York's most active enemies. This grasping-place in their difficult way was eagerly laid hold of by the conspirators. A coalition was formed between Lady Jane and this party, which / ensured the aggravation of any ill-feeling that might arise between the late brothers in heart. Soon after another agent or tool was added to their number.

The most subtle, the most politic, the most wily, are sometimes the slaves of impulse; nay, very often those who fancy that they measure their actions the most narrowly by the rules, either of self-interest or ambition, are more easily influenced to unwise passion by any obstacle thrown in their path. The Secretary Frion had hitherto considered himself of primal import to the English Prince: no project was conceived, that was not first concocted in his brain, and insinuated by him; every new partizan had been enticed by his silvery speeches; whatever of difficult, crooked and hidden was to be done, Frion was consulted, and employed, and deeply trusted in its accomplishment. On his first arrival in Scotland, the intimacy between the King and York destroyed half his influence. James's discernment and experience was not duped by the insinuating flatteries of Frion: as a proud man he disdained, as a / conscientious and pious one, he disliked him. It was worse when Katherine's influence became paramount; she put him exactly in his right place, yet was so kind that there was no room for complaint: all his former patrons were her worshippers; her praises were re-echoed from all; and assuredly no intrigue could exist where she was. Yet it was neither comprehensible, nor to be endured, that this banished Prince and his friends should walk straight forward in their allotted route, unaided by plot or manœuvre. The subtlety of the man quickly revealed to him the existence of the opposing party; he was ready to foment it, were it only to gain reputation afterwards by its destruction. He made one step, and became the confidant of Balmayne, and apparently the tool of the higher confederates: at first he rather perplexed than served them, spinning spiders' webs in their way, and elevating himself in their eyes by brushing them off at his pleasure. He was exactly the man to shine in a dark conspiracy: soon nothing could be done but by his advice, nothing known but as he informed them, nothing / said but as he dictated. Balmayne, who, fierce and moody, entered more zealously into these discontents than any other, yet took his counsel – little knew they Maitre Etienne Frion: he only watched the while, sage fisher of men as he was, for the best opportunity of betraying them for his own advantage. In the midst of festivity, of gallant, warlike preparation, Frion had, like a witch gathering poisonous herbs by the silvery light of the quiet moon, sought to extract all that was baleful in what, but for the uses to which he strove to put it, had died innocuous.

The winter grew into spring: these were the happiest months of young Richard's life. He had traversed many a pass of danger and tract of sorrow – falsehood had blotted – loss of friends who had died for him, had darkened the past years: often during their course he had believed that he gave himself up to despair; he had fancied that he had doubted every one and every thing; he imagined that he was tired of existence – vain ideas! Sanguine, confiding, full to the very brim of that spirit of life which is / the happiness of the young, he sprung up a fresh Antæus, each time that fortune with Herculean power had thrown him to the earth.[a] And now he congratulated himself even on every misery, every reverse, every sentiment of despondency that he experienced: they were so many links of the chain that made him what he was – the friend of James, the husband of Katherine. It was this best attribute of sunny-hearted youth, this greenness of the soul, that made Richard so frank, so noble, so generous: Care and Time had laboured in vain – no wrinkle, no deforming line marked his mind, or, that mind's interpreter, his open, candid brow.

With the spring the Scottish troops drew together, and encamped near Edinburgh. The occasion seemed seasonable; for news arrived of disturbances which had taken place in England, and which had caused Henry the Seventh to recall the Earl of Surrey, (who was conducting an army northward to oppose

---

[a] Antaeus, the giant of Greek mythology whose strength was restored every time he touched his mother, Earth; when Hercules learned the secret, he held him aloft and crushed him to death.

237

the expected attack from Scotland) to check and defeat enemies which had arisen in the west of his kingdom. The inhabitants of Cornwall, vexed / by increasing taxes, had long been in a state of turbulence; and now, instigated by two ringleaders from among themselves, combined together, and rose in open and regulated rebellion – sedition, it might have been called; and had perhaps been easily crushed, but for the interference of one, who acted from designs and views which at first had made no part of the projects of the insurgents.[a]

Lord Audley had not forgotten the White Rose. On his return westward, however, he found all so quiet, that no effort of his could rouze the rich and satisfied men of Devon, from their inglorious repose. His imprudence attracted attention; he had notice of the danger of an arrest, and suddenly resolved to quit the post he had chosen, and to join the Duke of York in Ireland. He came too late; the English squadron had sailed; and he, changeful as the winds and as impetuous, despising a danger now remote, resolved to return to England, and to Devonshire. His voyage from Cork to Bristol[b] was sufficiently disastrous; contrary and violent winds drove him from his / course into the Atlantic; here he beat about for several days, till the wind, shifting a point or two in the west, he began to make what sail he could in the opposite direction. Still the weather was tempestuous, and his skiff laboured frightfully amidst the stormy waves: not far from them, during the greatest fury of the gale, was a larger vessel, if such might be called the helmless, dismasted hull, tossed by the billows, the sport of the winds, as it rose and fell in the trough of the sea. At length the wind lulled; and the captain of the caravel, which indeed might be called a wreck, lowered a boat, and came alongside Lord Audley's vessel, asking whither he was bound? To England, was the answer; and the vast reef of clouds lifted on the southern horizon, and showing beyond a streak of azure, gave promise of success in their voyage. The questioner, who spoke English imperfectly, went on to say, that in spite of the miserable state of the caravel, he was resolved not to desert her, but to carry her, God willing, into the nearest French port he could make. But there was on board one sick, a woman, / whom he wished to spare the dangers and privations of the voyage. Would the Commander take her to England, and bestow her in some convent, where she might be tended and kept in honourable safety? Lord Audley gave a willing consent, and the boat went off speedily, returning again with their stranger passenger. She was in the extremity of illness, even of danger, and lay, like a child, in the arms of the dark, tall, weather-beaten mariner, who, though squalid in his appearance from fatigue and want, stood as a rock that has braved a thousand storms; his muscles seemed iron – his countenance not

---

[a] '1497' (marginal note in *Abinger/Palacio*), year of the Cornwall uprising. This notation, coupled with that on p. 222n, shows that Mary Shelley recognized that she had collapsed two Scottish invasions into one.

[b] Severn estuary port, on the west coast of England.

stern, but calm and resolved – yet tenderness and softness were in the expression of his lips, as he gazed on his fragile charge, and placed her with feminine gentleness on such rude couch as could be afforded; then addressing Lord Audley, "You are an Englishman," he said, "perhaps a father?"

"I am an English noble," replied the other; "confide in my care, my honour; but, to be doubly sure, if you feel distrust, remain with us; yonder wreck will not weather another night." /

"She has seen the suns of two worlds," said the sailor proudly, "and the Blessed Virgin has saved her at a worse hazard; if she perish now, it were little worth that her old captain survived; better both go down, as, if not now, some day we shall, together. I will confide my poor child to you, my Lord. If she recover, she has friends in England; she would gain them, even if she had them not. Not one among your boasted island-women is more lovely or more virtuous, than my poor, my much-suffering Monina."

Lord Audley renewed his protestations. De Faro listened with the ingenuous confidence of a sailor; he placed several caskets and a well-filled bag of gold in the noble's hand, saying, "The Adalid fills a-pace. You but rob the ocean. If my child survives, you can give her the treasure you disdain. If she does" – and he bent over her; she almost seemed to sleep, so oppressed was she by feebleness and fever. A tear fell from the father's eye upon her brow: "And she will; Saint Mary guide us, we shall again." /

Such was the strange drama acted on the wide boundless sea. Such the chances that restored the high-minded Andalusian to England, to the White Rose, to all the scenes, to every hope and fear which she had resolved to abandon for ever. For good or ill, we are in the hands of a superior power:

> "There's a divinity that shapes our ends,
> Rough-hew them how we will."[a]

We can only resolve, or rather endeavour, to act our parts well, such as they are allotted to us. Little choice have we to seek or to eschew our several destinations.

With Monina at his side, and his own restless ambition as a spur, it may be easily imagined what Lord Audley's projects were in joining the Cornish insurgents. He led them from the Western extremity of the island towards Kent, where he hoped to find the seeds of rebellion to Lancaster, which he had sown the year before, ripened into harvest. News of the unimpeded march of the insurgents from Cornwall to the neighbourhood of London was brought to Edinburgh / freshening the zeal and animating the preparations for war.

Already the Scottish army was encamped south of Edinburgh. The English troops set up their tents among them. The day was fixed for the departure of

---

[a] *Hamlet*, V. ii. 10.

239

the King, the Prince, and the noble leaders. They quitted Edinburgh in all the pompous array of men assured of victory. James loved the hopes and stirring delights of war: Richard saw his every good in life dependent on this expedition, and fostered sanguine expectation of triumph. The burning desire of asserting himself, of rewarding his faithful friends, of decorating Katherine with the rank and honours due to her – the belief that he should achieve all this – gave dignity, and even gladness, to his last adieu to his lovely wife. Her heart mirrored his hopes; not that she entertained them for her own, but for his sake: yet the quicker sensibilities of a woman imparted fears unknown to him. She concealed them, till when, as her last office and duty, she had fastened an embroidered scarf around him. Softly, whisperingly, as fearful of paining him, / she said, "You will return – you have a kingdom here: though England prove false, you must not disdain to be sole monarch of Katherine."

These words had been spoken – earl, baron, and gallant knight thronged the courts of Holyrood. There was the sound of warlike trump and the streaming of painted banners, among which that of the White Rose waved conspicuous. The King vaulted on his saddle; the Prince of England rode at his side. He was surrounded by the rude northern warlike chiefs, ancient enemies of his native land, whose fierce eyes were lighted up by the expectation of meeting their old adversaries in the field; could he fancy that, through such aid, he might win back the crown usurped from him?

King James and Richard rode side by side. At this moment, when the one was spending the riches of his kingdom and the lives of his subjects for the other's sake, while the hearts of both were softened by regret for their abandoned home, and both anticipated the joys of victory or perils of defeat to be shared between them, the / sentiment of friendship was rekindled. Never had they been more cordial, more confidential, more happy in each other's society. After several hours' ride, the short spring day declined to evening, which was accompanied by a drizzling rain: the bad roads, and the darkness impeded their progress; and it was night before the twinkling camp-lights appeared in the distance, and the hum of men was heard. To the right of the camp, surrounded by the tents of his nobles, the royal pavilion was pitched. On their arrival the Earl of Buchan was in readiness to hold the King's stirrup. "Nay," said James, "first we will see our royal guest lodged; where is the tent of his Grace of England? we commanded it to be pitched in close neighbourhood to our own."

"Please you, my liege," said Buchan,[a] "Lord Moray gave direction it should be placed out of our line; it is set up a mile eastward of us."

"My uncle forgot himself; and you also, Sir Earl, were bound rather to obey our order," said the King. /

"There were reasons," returned Buchan: "your Majesty, I dare aver, will

---

[a] 'See p. 27' (marginal note in *Abinger/Palacio*), probably a miswritten reference to the first mention of Buchan on p. at II, 227 (p. 226).

approve the change, and his Highness of England also. There was a brawl between the Scottish borderers and the English; blood has been shed. We feared that the peace of the encampment, not to say the life of his Highness, would be endangered if he were in the midst of our savage Southrons."[a]

"I like not this," said James moodily, "but it is too late to change to-night. The rain-drops begin to freeze upon my hair; your Highness would rather be in your tent, far though it be from mine, than quarrel about its position at this inclement hour. Lord Buchan, you will attend him thither. Prince, good night; to-morrow we will be more brotherly in our fashion; now the fiat of my Lord of Moray must be obeyed."

The King dismounted and entered his pavilion: as the cloth was raised, a blazing fire, the apparel of silver flagons and golden cups, the trim appearance of silken-suited pages were visible, making strong contrast with the cheerless / blank without. One slight glimpse revealed the cause, and partly excused the inhospitality of James, in not inviting his guest to partake his warm cheer. One in a kirtle sat somewhat retired from view; the quick motion of her head, the glance of her dark eye, showed that the monarch had been impatiently expected, and was gladly welcomed by the lovely daughter of the Earl of Cassils.[b]

Lord Buchan accompanied Richard, Lord Barry, and Plantagenet, to their quarters; talking, as he went, of the contention, which had terminated fatally to several. They rode down the elevated ground on which the King's tent was placed, over a plashy low plain, through a little of wood of stunted larch, across a narrow dell, in whose bottom a brook struggled and murmured, to the acclivity on the other side, on which the tents of the English troops were pitched: considerably apart from the rest was Richard's own pavilion: all looked tranquil and even desolate, compared to the stirring liveliness of the Scotch camp. Richard was received by Sir George Neville, who looked more than usually / cold and haughty as he bent to Lord Buchan's salutation: the Scotchman uttered a hasty good night, galloped down the upland, and across the dell, and was lost to sight in the wood.

"What means this, Sir George?" was the Prince's first remark: "what discipline is yours? – brawling and bloodshed with our allies!"

"Did your Highness name them our enemies," said Neville, "it were more appropriate. Suspend your displeasure, I beseech you, until I can lay before you the reality of what you name a brawl; my honour, and I fear all our safeties are concerned in the discovery. Now, your Grace is wet and fatigued, you will repose."

Richard desired solitude, not rest: he wished to be alone; for a thousand intricate ideas possessed him, clamouring to be attended to. He dismissed his

---

[a] Scottish appellation for 'southerners', or Englishmen (OED).

[b] Jane Kennedy (see p. 211 and n), who had by this time been supplanted by Margaret Drummond (?1472–1501), fated to be poisoned with her sisters.

friends. Frion only remained – Frion, who lately had almost become surly, but who was now smooth, supple as ever; his eye twinkling as of yore, and his ready laugh – that most characteristic part of him – again showing / the old secretary returned. To the Prince's warm heart the appearance of discontent and moodiness was peculiarly grating; the smile or frown even of Frion had power over him; and he felt grateful to the man for his glossy and satisfactory speeches, now that, spite of himself, a feeling – it was not fear, but an anticipation of evil – disturbed his mind.

At length, he dismissed him;[a] yet still he felt utterly disinclined for sleep. For some time he paced his tent; images of war and battle floated before him – and then the vision of an angel with golden hair came, not to calm, but to trouble him with unquiet regret. In vain he strove to awaken the flock of gentle thoughts that usually occupied him; his ideas seemed wolf-visaged: unreal howlings and cries rung in his ears. This unusual state of mind was intolerable: he folded his cloak round him, and stept into his outer tent. Frion, two pages, and his esquire, were to occupy it; but he found it solitary. This seemed a little strange; but it was early yet. He lifted the outer cloth; a sentinel was duly at his post; the prince saluted him, and passed / on. The fitful winds of spring had dispersed the storm: the scarcely waning moon, encircled by the dark clear ether, was in the east; her yellow light filled the atmosphere, and lay glowing on the trees and little hill-side. The Prince stept onwards, down the declivity, across the dell, into the wood. He thought he heard voices; or was it only the swinging branches of the pines? The breeze raised his hair and freshened his brow. Still he walked on, till now he came in view of the Scottish camp, which lay tranquil as sheep in a fold, the moon's bright eye gazing on it. The sight brought proud Granada and all its towers, with the Christian camp sleeping at her feet, before his mind; and he still lingered. Now the tramp of horses became audible: a troop wound down the hill: the leader stopt, exclaiming, in some wonder, "My Lord of York! does your Highness need any service? do you bend your steps to the royal tent?"

"I blush to answer, Sir Patrick," replied the Prince; "for you will scoff at me as the moon's minion: I came out but to visit her. Yet a / knight need not feel shame at loitering beneath her ray, dreaming of his lady-love. You are more actively employed?"

"I was on my way to your Highness's encampment," replied the Knight. "His Majesty is not quite satisfied with Lord Buchan's report, and sent but now his esquire to me, to bid me visit it. With your good leave, I will escort you thither." /

---

[a] 'Frion' (marginal note in *Abinger/Palacio* referring to 'him', which is underscored).

CHAPTER XV.

Traitor, what hast thou done? how ever may
Thy cursed hand so cruelly have swayed
Against that knight? Harrow and weal-away!
After so wicked deed why liv'st thou longer day!
                                        SPENSER.[a]

When he had been dismissed by his royal master, Frion called aside the esquire, and sent him on an errand, it would seem of some import and distance; for the youth uttered a few forcible interjections, and with a lowering brow drew on the riding-boots he had just doffed, muttering, "I must treat my horse better than my Lord treats me; so, master, seek a fresh steed. By my fay! this is to become a Squire of / Dames – a love-token to the Duchess, in good hour!"

Having got rid of this young gentleman, Frion's next care was to give distant employment to the pages, saying he would wait their return. But scarcely had they entered the most crowded part of the camp, before with quick cautious steps the secretary took the same path which the Prince trod half an hour later – he crossed the dell, and arriving at the little wood of larches; instead of traversing, he skirted it, till the gentle eminence on which the English camp was pitched, grew higher and more abrupt, the murmuring brook took the guise of a brawling torrent, grey rocks peeped out from the soil, and the scene became wilder and more mountainous: he walked on, till he arrived where a rustic bridge spanned the stream – under its shadow were three horsemen, two of whom dismounted, and a tall servitor held the bridles. One of these men Frion knew at once to be him who called himself Lord Bothwell, King Henry's spy, and Richard's fierce, motiveless, but ruthless enemy; the other – his bonnet was drawn / over his brow – a cloak obscured his person. Frion's quick eyes scrutinized it vainly, for the moon, cloudy at intervals, gave uncertain light; besides, the man had stationed himself within the deepest shadow of the bridge.

---

[a] *Faerie Queene*, II. viii. 46.

"Good befall your watch," said Frion; "your worship is before your time."

"Is not all ready?" asked Balmayne.

"That question is mine," replied the other. "You know our treaty – not a hair of my Lord's head must be injured."

"Tush! tush! fear not, good conscience-stickler," replied Bothwell with a contemptuous laugh; "no ill will befall the boy; we but ferry him over the Tweed a few hours earlier than he dreamed of, and land him all gently on the shore he seeks. As for thy reward, I have said, name it thyself."

"Fair words are these, Sir John Ramsay," said Frion; "but I said before, I must have surer pledge, both for my reward and my Lord's safety. King Henry will haggle about payment when the work is done, and the steel you wear is a toper in its way." /

"How now, Sir Knave," cried Balmayne; "thinkest thou that I will turn midnight stabber!"

The man in the cloak started at these words. He uttered some sound, but again drew back; while the person who continued on horseback, said, and his voice was that of the Bishop of Moray, King James's uncle, "A truce to this contention, Master Good-fellow – whatever thy name be: I will answer for thy pay, and here is earnest of my truth." He threw a purse at Frion's feet – "The peace of two kingdoms – the honour of a royal, too long dishonoured house are at stake. No time is this to squabble for marks, or the paltry life of a base impostor. I, a prince of Scotland, avouch the deed. It were more friendly, methinks, to unlock his life with the steel key of our friend Wiatt, than to devote him to the gallows. Let Scotland be rid of him, I reck not how."

Again Frion fixed his eyes on the other – the clouds had fallen low in the sky; the moon was clear; the western breeze murmured among the bushes and the trees, and the beams of the / silvery planet played upon the unquiet waters. "We have no time for delay, Sir John," said Frion, "prithee introduce me to our fellow labourer – this is the King's emissary? You call yourself Wiatt, master Black Cloak?"

The other made a gesture of impatience as he stepped aside. Balmayne and Moray discoursed aside, till the former bade the Secretary lead on – as they went, the Scotchman and Frion conversed in whispers concerning their plans, while their companion followed as if doggedly. Once he cast an impatient glance at the moon – Frion caught that look. "Have I found you, good friend," he thought; "then by our Lady of Embrun,[a] you shall acquit you of the debt I claim this night."

With quicker steps the Provençal proceeded, till they reached the opening of the valley, and came opposite the slope on which the English camp was pitched. Furthest off and far apart was the royal pavilion, the banner of

---

[a] The Black Virgin, whose shrine was in the city's cathedral. Embrun, in south-east France, midway between Grenoble and Nice.

England flapping in the breeze, and this the only sign of life – but for this, the white silent tents looked like vast druidical stones piled upon a wild / moor. They paused – "I must go first," said Frion; "we have wasted more time than I counted for – you will await me here."

"Listen, Master Frion," said Balmayne. "I would hardly trust you, but that I think you are a wise man; silver angels and golden marks,[a] as a wise man, you will love: one thing you will hardly seek, a shroud of moonbeams, a grave in the vulture's maw. Look ye, one soars above even now; he scents dainty fare: twenty true men are vowed that he shall sup on thee, if thou art foresworn: thou wilt give some signal, when all is ready."

"That were difficult," said Frion; "I will return anon if there be any let to your enterprize; else, when the shadow of that tall larch blackens the white stone at your feet, come up without fear: have ye bonds ready for your prisoner?"

"An adamantine chain – away!" Frion cast one more glance at him called Wiatt. "It is even he, I know him, by that trick of his neck; his face was ever looking sideways:" thus assured, the Frenchman ascended the hill. Balmayne watched him, now visible, and now half / hid by the deceptive light, till he entered the folds of the pavilion; and then he glanced his eyes upon the shadow of the tree, yet far from the white stone; and then paced the sward, as if disdaining to hold commune with Wiatt. Whatever thoughts possessed this hireling's breast he made no sign, but stood motionless as a statue; his arms folded, his head declined upon his breast. He was short, even slight in make, his motionless, half-shrinking attitude contrasted with the striding pace and the huge, erect form of the borderer. Who that had looked down upon these two figures, sole animations visible on the green earth beneath the moon's bright eye, would have read villany and murder in their appearance; the soft sweet night seemed an antidote to savageness, yet neither moon nor the sleeping face of beauteous earth imparted any gentleness to the Scot; he saw neither, except when impatiently he glanced at the slow-crawling shadow, and the moonlight sleeping on the signal stone. Many minutes past – Bothwell gave one impatient look more – how slowly the dusky line proceeded! He / walked to the edge of the brook; there was no movement about the pavilion; tranquil as an infant's sleep was the whole encampment. Suddenly a cry made him start, it was from Wiatt; the man, heretofore so statue-like, had thrown his arms upward with a passionate gesture, and then, recalled by Bothwell's imprecation, shrunk back into his former quiet, pointing only with a trembling finger to the stone, now deep imbedded in the black shadow of the larch. The Scot gave a short shrill laugh, and crying "Follow!" began the ascent, taking advantage of such broken ground and shrubs, as blotted the brightness of the rays that lit up the acclivity.

---

[a] Old English coins.

Bothwell strode on with the activity of a moss-trooper;[a] Wiatt was scarce able to walk; he stumbled several times. At length they reached the pavilion; the Frenchman stood just within, lifting the heavy cloth; they entered. Frion whispered, "I have cleared the coast; my Lord sleeps; we need but cast a cloak around him, to blind him, and so bear him off without more ado on his forced journey." /

"There is wisdom in your speech," said Balmayne with something of a grin, "My friend Wiatt has a cloak large and dark enough for the nonce."

Frion drew back the silken lining of the inner tent, saying, "Tread soft, my Lord ever sleeps lightly; he must not be waked too soon."

"*Never* were the better word," muttered Bothwell: the dimmest twilight reigned in the tent. The Prince's couch was in shadow; the men drew near; the sleeper was wrapt in his silken coverlid, with his face buried in his pillow: his light-brown hair, lying in large clusters on his cheek, veiled him completely. Ramsay bent over him; his breathing was heavy and regular; he put out his large bony hand, and as gently as he might, removed the quilt, uncovering the sleeper's right side; then turning to Wiatt, who had not yet advanced, he pointed to the heaving heart of his victim with such a glance of murderous callousness, that the very assassin shrunk beneath it; yet he approached; his hand held an unsheathed dagger, but it shook even to impotence; he raised it over his prey, / but had no power to strike. Frion had crept round behind; a sound just then, and tramp of feet was heard in the outer tent; as by magic, in one brief second of time the mute dread scene changed its every characteristic. The assassin cried aloud, "It is not he!" Frion had seized his arm – the dagger fell – the pretended sleeper (one of York's pages) leaped from the couch; and the muffling cloak, dropping from the murderer's shoulders, disclosed the wretched, degraded Clifford. Ramsay drew his sword, and rushed towards the outer tent, when at the same moment Richard of York and Sir Patrick Hamilton showed themselves from beneath the hangings, which their attendants had raised. This sight startled Frion, and Clifford, restored to life and energy, tore himself from his grasp, and in a moment had rushed from beneath the pavilion: he was forgotten; all eyes were turned on Bothwell; the dagger at his feet, his drawn sword, his appearance in the retirement of the Prince of England, all accused him. He saw at once his danger, drew himself proudly up, / and returned Hamilton's look with a fierce, haughty glare.

"Thy act is worse than thy enemies' speech," said Sir Patrick, sternly; "thou wilt answer this, recreant, to thy royal master."

"To him, to any, to you," said Balmayne; "There is my glove. Now, on the hill's side, or in the lists anon, I will avouch my deed."

Hamilton answered with a look of sovereign contempt; he bade his men seize the traitor. "Before I sleep," he cried, "the King hears this treason."

---

[a] 'One of a class of marauders who infested the "mosses" of the Scottish border' (*OED*).

Richard had looked on in silence and wonder; he placed his hand on Hamilton's arm, stopping him, "Pardon me, valiant knight," he said; "but, I do beseech you, disturb not the King to-night, nor ever, with this ill tale. Too roughly already has the English Prince broken Scotland's rest. No blood is shed; and, strange as appearances are, I take Sir John Ramsay's word, and believe that, as a cavalier, he may maintain his cause, nor stain by it his knightly cognizance. I take up your glove, fair Sir, but only to restore it; without one slightest accusation / attaching itself to you therewith. Nay, myself will take up the quarrel, if any blame you. Sir Patrick will not call me to the trial, I am sure. Frion, conduct the gallant gentleman beyond our lines."

Shame for the first time flushed Ramsay's brow as he left the tent. The Prince drew up to let him pass, with a mien so dignified and yet so tranquil, with a smile so bland, that thus it seemed an angelic essence, incapable of wound, might have gazed on a mere mortal, armed to injure him.

"Is this recklessness or nobility of soul?" Sir Patrick thought. He did not doubt, when Richard, changing his look to one of anxious appeal, besought him to omit utterly to report this strange scene. "I much fear," he said, "my wily Secretary to be most in fault; and I caught a glance of one, whose appearance here proves that Ramsay is not alone guilty. Let me enquire, let me learn – punish, if need be. English gold and English steel were the weapons here, and I alone have power over England. You will pledge me your word, Sir Patrick, not / to disquiet our royal cousin by our domestic brawls. We must not put in opposing scales our paltry anger against ruffians like these, and the disquiet of the generous-hearted James. Ramsay was his father's favourite; for his sake he bears with him; and more easily may I. I indeed, who am most in fault, for spending the precious minutes wandering, like a shepherd of Arcadia, in listless foolishness, instead of acting the general, and guarding my tents from such visitors. The brawl last night might have forewarned me."

"Does it not shame Scotland," cried Hamilton warmly, "that you should need any guard but our true hearts, while you tread our soil?"

"Were this true," answered York, yet more earnestly, "remember, what shames Scotland, shames her King. Be assured, dear cousin, I speak advisedly. Were this examined, worse might appear; and I and your liege must be the sufferers: I to excite this treason in his subjects' hearts; he to prove that some near him are not true as they seem."

Hamilton yielded to these many pleas; but / his heart warmed with admiration and love for the noble being who urged the cause of pardon for his enemies. "Be it as your Highness pleases," he exclaimed. "This I the more readily yield, since any new attempt kills Hamilton ere it reach you. I will be your guard, your sentinel, your wide, invulnerable shield; you will not refuse me this post of honour."

"Or let us both fulfil it," cried York, "one to the other; let us be brothers in arms, noble Hamilton. And yet, how can I, a fugitive, almost a tainted man, seek the alliance of one who stands as you do, fair and free in all men's eyes?"

As he spoke, the Prince held out his hand; the Scottish knight raised it respectfully to his lips. But now Frion returned; and the clash of arms and trumpets' sound spoke of the advance of night, and change of guard: the noble friends took leave of each other, and Sir Patrick departed. As soon as they were private, the Prince questioned his Secretary closely and sternly as to the events of the night. Frion had a plausible and ready tale, of artifice and guile, / of how he had a pledge even from the King's uncle that York's life was not to be attempted; and that he had but wished to balk and vex them, by causing the page to be carried off; the discovery of their mistake would shame them from any second enterprize against the Prince of England.

York was but half satisfied; he had caught a transient glimpse of the fugitive. Was it indeed Clifford, who came a hired murderer to his bed-side? A man who had partaken his heart's counsels, long his companion, once his friend? It was frightful, it was humiliating but to imagine how deep the man may fall, who once gives himself over to evil thoughts, and unlawful deeds. Frion here protested his ignorance and surprise. It was almost day before his master dismissed him: and even then, how could Richard repose? That couch, Clifford had marked as his bier – it were a bed of thorns; he threw himself on the bare, hard ground, and innocence had more power than his angelic pity for the vice of others; it shed poppy influence on his lids; and the beams of the morning sun stole softly over, but did not disturb his slumbers.[a] /

---

[a] The unsuccessful snare set by Warbeck's enemies in ch. xiv and sprung in ch. xv has a historical basis.

CHAPTER XVI.

———

Methinks I see Death and the Furies waiting
What we will do, and all the Heaven at leisure
For the great spectacle. Draw then your swords!
BEN JONSON.[a]

———

Faster than the airy slave quicksilver is influenced by the changes of the
atmosphere, does the subtle essence of the mind of one, who from love or
gratitude hangs upon the smile or frown of another, feel the sunshine or frost
of that other's countenance; and an independent disposition speedily revolts
from servile obedience to such alteration. On the following day, and afterwards
on the succeeding ones, Richard felt that the heart of James was no longer the
same. / He was courteous, kind – his friend's interests formed the sole topic of
their conversations – but York could neither say the thing he wished, nor do
that which he desired; the same objects were before him, apparently the same
colouring was upon them; yet a pale sickly hue was cast over the before glowing
picture; a chill had penetrated the summer warmth in which he basked; the
wave was yet calm; but it was clouded, and no longer showed in its limpid
depths that sympathy and affection, which made the White Rose's fortunes
seem truly and intrinsically Scotland's own.

Friendship was now professed, service tendered; before words had seemed
superfluous – the thing was there. James assured his guest that he would not
turn back, nor give ear to Henry's propositions; and York felt, with a start, that
ear had been given to them, or this conclusion had not been noted. The
disunion and continued separation of the camps was another circumstance that
spoke loudly of division of thought and counsel.

Frion believed that he should now resume / his ancient position with his
royal master: he bore his reproofs humbly, and strove to regain his favour by
the importance of his services. The arcana of the Tudor party were, to a great

———

[a] Ben Jonson (1572–1637), *Catiline His Conspiracy* (1611), V. v. 46–8.

249

degree, revealed to York; and it was easy to mark the ascendancy it was gaining. The presence of Lady Jane Kennedy might explain the ceremony and regulations observed in the intercourse between the King and his friend; but it was Frion's part to disclose the enmity this lady entertained for the White Rose, and the influence she exerted to its detriment. Moray and Lord Buchan were her friends, and they were frequent visitors in the royal pavilion.

A short time somewhat changed this state of things. The army drew near the frontier; and the King separated himself from the fair mistress of his heart. On the third day they arrived on the banks of the Tweed. It was but crossing a little river, but stepping from one stone to another – and Richard would stand on English ground.

The troops had passed the day before; some had proceeded southward; others were even / now to be seen defiling in long lines on the distant plain. The sun was up cheerily; the fresh pleasant green of spring had stolen, more like a tinted atmosphere, than in the guise of foliage, over tree and bush; field flowers and crocusses peeped from under the mossy turf. The scene was a wide moor, varied by broken ground; clumps of trees, where many a bird nestled; and here and there thick underwood, where the wild deer made his lair; this had been the scene of a thousand conflicts and of mortal carnage between Scot and Englishman, but the sky-lark above sang of nature's bounty and nature's loveliness, an immemorial and perennial hymn, while nothing spoke of the butchery and wretchedness which once had made the landscape a tragic corpse-strewn stage.

Reining in his pawing courser, King James, in all the gay array of a high-born knight, paused on the Scottish bank – his lips, proud as the Apollo's – spoke of struggle and victory,

> ————"In his eye
> And nostril, beautiful disdain and might
> And majesty flashed their full lightnings by."[a] /

Here was he who, in a later day, led the flower of Scotland to die on the English plains; who himself was doomed to lie with mangled limbs, and in blank, cold extinction, a trophy of victory to his enemy, on Flodden Field: he was alive now, and in his strength; he drank in with buoyant spirit every glorious anticipation, and laughed with fond delight; spurring on his horse, he crossed the ford, and entered England.

In a moment, as by impulse, York, who had lingered, dashed after him; allies they were; friends in seeming, nay, in truth; for the glance of proud enmity Richard cast on the Scot was perhaps the more factitious feeling: it sprung from

---

[a] Byron, *Childe Harold's Pilgrimage*, IV (1818), clxi. 6–8, describing the Apollo Belvedere, a Roman copy (c.AD 130–40) after a Greek bronze original (c.330 BC), attributed to Leochares.

patriotism, but its energy was borrowed from the deadly feuds of their ancestors, that natural hate which is said to exist now between the French and
English, and which was far more envenomed between the near-rival people.
Notwithstanding James's change towards him, York felt in the core of his
affectionate heart, all that was due to him who had raised him when he was
fallen; given him state, power / – Katherine; he saw in him his kinsman – his
benefactor. But the pride of a son of England rose in his breast, when he beheld
the haughty Scot caracol[a] in arrogant triumph on her soil. What was he? What
had he done? He was born king and father of this realm: because he was
despoiled of his high rights, was he to abjure his natural duty to her, as her
child? Yet here he was an invader; not arming one division of her sons against
the other, but girt with foreigners, aided by the ancient ravagers of her smiling
villages and plenteous harvests. He looked on each individual Scot, and on
their gallant king, and felt his bosom swell with rage and hate. These were
unwise, nay, ungrateful sentiments; but he could not repel them. His first
commands were to his cousin, to hasten to Randal of Dacre,[b] to learn what
Yorkists had gathered together to receive him. "If there be any large company," he said, "without more ado we will thank our kind cousin, invite him to
recross the Tweed, and leave us to fight our battles by ourselves."

The satisfaction and triumph James felt made / him, so far from participating
in York's feelings, turn with renewed cordiality towards him. It was his first
care to have the standard of the White Rose set up with martial pomp, to
disperse his proclamations, and to invite, by his own manner, the Scottish
nobles to encrease in observance towards the Prince. Lord Huntley, believing
that the prophecy of his daughter's elevation was on the eve of its accomplishment, was prodigal of his shows of honour and service to his son-in-law. For
some days the pavilions of the brother kings were pitched side by side, and
James each hour thought to hear of the arrival of the Yorkist nobility of
England: he had expected so many that he had given orders that care should be
taken to recall his own troops, when the English visitants outnumbered his own
guard. Day after day passed, and not one came – not one: even Randal of
Dacre, Lord Dacre's brother, who had visited Richard in Scotland, seized with
panic, had gone southward. Nothing came, save intelligence that the Cornish
insurgents had been defeated on / Blackheath, their ringleaders taken and
executed: among them Lord Audley perished.[c]

Another life! – how many more to complete the sad hecatomb, a useless
offering to obdurate fate in Richard's favour! Sir George Neville, gathered up

---

[a] Execute a halfturn to the right or left on horseback.

[b] Mentioned by Ramsay to Henry VII; probably related to Sir Thomas Dacre, who served as
Henry VII's Lieutenant in the North (Pinkerton, II, pp. 30, 442).

[c] On 17 June 1497; the victorious Earl of Surrey then marched north to punish Scotland with a
retaliatory invasion.

in all the cold pride of disappointed ambition, disdained to regret. Plantagenet saw the hopes and purpose of his life crushed, but dared not give words to his despair; Sir Roderick sneered; Lord Barry was loud in his laments; while the Scots grew taller and prouder, and ceased to frequent the tents of the English exiles. Councils were held by James, in which York had no part: it was only afterwards, that he learnt it had been commanded to the Scotch army to lay waste the country. Now indeed all the Englishman was alive in his heart – he gave sudden orders to raise his camp, and to march forward: he had sat still too long; he would enter the kingdom he claimed; discover for himself his chance of success – and, if there were none, his rights should not be made the pretence of a Scotch invasion.

None cried, "Long live King Richard!" as / he passed along. How did his noble, youthful spirit droop at finding that not only he did not meet with, but was judged not to deserve success. It ranks among the most painful of our young feelings, to find that we are justly accused of acting wrong. Our motives – we believed them disinterested or justifiable; we have advanced a wondrous step in life before we can concede even to ourselves that alloy may be mingled with what we deemed pure gold: ignorant of the soil and culture of our own hearts, we feel sure that no base mixture can form a part of what we fancy to be a mine of virgin ore. Richard would have stood erect and challenged the world to accuse him – God and his right, was his defence. His right! Oh, narrow and selfish was that sentiment that could see, in any right appertaining to one man the excuse for the misery of thousands.

War, held in leash during the army's march from Edinburgh, was now let loose; swift and barbarous he tore forward on his way; a thousand destructions waited on him; his track was marked by ruin: the words of Lord Surrey / were fulfilled. What a sight for one, whose best hope in acquiring his kingdom, was to bestow the happiness of which the usurper deprived it. The English troops, about five hundred men, crossed the wide-spread plains in the immediate vicinity of Scotland; they entered a beaten track, where the traces of cultivation spoke of man; a village peeped from among the hedge-row trees – York's heart beat high. Would the simple inhabitants refuse to acknowledge him? A few steps disclosed the truth – the village had been sacked by the Scotch: it was half burnt, and quite deserted; one woman alone remained – she sat on a pile of ashes wailing aloud. The exiles dared not read in each other's eyes the expression of their horror; they walked on like men rebuked. This was England, their country, their native home; and they had brought the fierce Scot upon her. Passing forward, they met trains of waggons laden with spoil, droves of cattle and sheep. They overtook a troop roasting an ox by the burning rafters of a farm-house, whose green palings, trim orchard, and shaved grass-plat, spoke of domestic comfort; / the house-dog barked fearfully – a Lowland archer transfixed him with his arrow.

The English marched on; they dared not eye the ravagers; shame and hate

252

contended – these were their allies; while the sarcasm and scornful laugh which followed them, drugged with wormwood the bitter draught. In vain, west or east or south, did they turn their eyes, a sad variety of the same misery presented itself on every side. A stout yeoman, gashed by an Highlander's claymore, was sometimes the ghastly stepping-stone passed over to enter his own abode; women and children had not been spared, or were only left to perish for want. Often during apparent silence, a fearful shriek, or the voice of lamentation, burst upon the air: now it was a woman's cry, now the shrill plaint of infancy. With the exception of these sufferers, the landscape was a blank. Where were the troops of friends Richard had hoped would hail him? Where the ancient Yorkists? Gone to augment the army which Surrey was bringing against the Scot; attached to these ill-omened allies how could the Prince hope to be met by his partizans? / He had lost them all; the first North Briton[a] who crossed the Tweed trampled on and destroyed for ever the fallen White Rose.

Resolutely bent on going forward till he should have advanced beyond the Scotch, on the following day York continued his march. They entered the ruins of another village; the desolation here was even more complete, although more recent; the flame was hardly spent upon the blackened rafters; the piles which the day before had been smiling dwellings, still smoked; a few domestic animals were skulking about. There was a church at the end of what had been a street; this was not spared. The English entered the desecrated aisle; an aged bleeding monk was lying at the altar's foot, who scowled even in death upon the soldiery; suddenly he recognised his countrymen; pleasure gleamed in his sunken eyes, "Ye will avenge us! Deliver the land! – The hand of God will lead ye on!"

Plantagenet rushed forward, "Father!" he cried, "do I find you here?"

The old man spoke, looked faintly; Edmund / bent over him: "My father, it is I, Edmund, your boy, your murde——"

"My son," said the Monk, "I behold you again, and die content! You are in arms, but by the blessing of the saints your sword's point is turned against the cruel invader. Not one, oh! not one Englishman will fall by his brother's hand, for not one will fight for that base deceit, the ill-nurtured Perkin, to whom God in his wrath has given such show of right as brings the Scot upon us. Once I thought – but no son of York would ally himself to these cruel border-robbers. God of my country, oh curse, curse him and his cause!"

The dying man spoke with difficulty; a few moments more, a spasm crossed his features, and they settled into stony insensibility. Edmund threw himself on the body; a deathlike silence reigned in the building; every heart beat with breathless horror; the curse uttered by the murdered man was even then breathed before God, and accepted. York spoke first with a calm, firm voice,

---

[a] An appellation for 'Scot'.

253

"Arise, my cousin," he said; / "do not thou fix yet more deeply the barbed arrow, which has entered my heart."

There are periods when remorse and horror conquer by their intensity every lesser impulse, and reign kings of the waste; this was no time for words or tears. Oh! welcome the grief or crime, which the bitterest of these could express or extenuate; it would insult this sad effigy of death to imagine that the impiety could be expiated. In silence they bore the reverend corpse to the vaults of the church, and then continued their way; some of the under-officers and men whispered together, but when again the chiefs conversed, they did not allude to this frightful scene, or to the awful imprecation which they felt suspended over their heads, shadowing their souls with unknown horror.

This was but the opening scene to worse wretchedness: hitherto they had seen the waste of war now they came upon its active atrocities. A dense smoke, the flickering of pale flames marked the progress of devastation; fierceness gleamed in the open blue eyes of Richard; he bit his lips, and at a quicker pace went forward; screams and / horrid shrieks, mixed with shouts – oh! may not a veil be drawn over such horrors – flying children, mothers who stayed to die, fathers who unarmed rushed upon the weapons of the foe, fire and sword, animated by man's fellest spirit, were there to destroy. Kindled to fury, York and his chief friends had outspeeded their troops: they came to save; they called on the fierce Scot to spare; and, when their words were unheeded, they drew their swords to beat back their allies. A fresh troop of Borderers, headed by Sir John Ramsay, at this moment poured into the village. The grey eye of the Scot was lighted up to the fiercest rage; but when he saw who and how few were they who had assailed his men, a demoniac expression, half exultation and joy, half deadly hate, animated him. Richard was driving before him a whole troop of camp-followers, cowardly and cruel fellows. Balmayne's hand was on his arm. "Your Highness forgets yourself," he said; "or is the fable ended, and you turned friend of Tudor?"

York's blood was up; his cheek, his brow / were flushed; the word "assassin" burst from his lips, as he wheeled round and assailed his midnight foe. Thus a natural war began; English and Scotchmen, bent on mutual destruction, spurred on by every feeling of revenge, abhorrence, and national rivalship, dealt cruel blows one on the other. Richard's troops began to arrive in greater numbers; they far out-told their adversaries. Lord Bothwell with his marauders were obliged to retreat, and York was left in possession of his strange conquest. The peasantry gathered round him; they did not recognise the White Rose, they but blest him as their deliverer: yet the sufferers were many, and the flames still raged. One woman with a wild shriek for her children, threw herself into the very heart of her burning cot; while, statue-like, amidst a little helpless brood, his wife at his feet a corse, his dwelling in ashes, a stout yeoman stood; tears unheeded flowing down his weather-beaten cheeks. During the whole day Richard had striven against his own emotions, trying to dispel by pride, and indignation, and enforced fortitude, the softness that / invaded his heart and rose to his eyes, blinding them; but the sight of these miserable beings, victims of his right, grew into a tragedy too sad to endure. One young mother laid her infant offspring at his feet, crying, "Bless thee; thou hast saved her!" and then sunk in insensibility before him; her stained dress and pallid cheeks speaking too plainly of wounds and death. Richard burst into tears, "Oh, my stony and hard-frozen heart!" he cried, "which breakest not to see the loss and slaughter of so many of thy natural-born subjects and vassals!"

He spoke – he looked: Plantagenet was there, grief and horror seated in his dark, expressive eyes; Neville, who had lost his lofty pride; it was shame and self-abhorrence that painted their cheeks with blushes or unusual pallor. "We must hasten, my Lord," said Barry, "after those evil-doers: they but quit one carcase, to pounce upon another."

"Do we fight the King of England's battles?" cried the Burgundian Lalayne, in unfeigned / astonishment: "this will be strange intelligence for James of Scotland."

"So strange, Sir Roderick," said Richard, "that we will be the bearers of it ourselves. Give orders for the retreat, gentlemen. His Majesty is engaged in the siege of Norham Castle.[a] We will present us before him, and demand mercy for our unhappy subjects." /

CHAPTER XVII.

———

Why didst thou promise such a beauteous day,
    And make me travel forth without my cloak,
To let base clouds o'ertake me on the way,
    Hiding thy bravery in their rotten smoke?
                                        SHAKSPEARE.[b]

———

It was York's characteristic to be sanguine beyond all men. Pain impressed him more deeply and sorely, than could be imagined by the cold of spirit; but show him the remedy, teach him the path to redress, and he threw off the clogging

———

[a] On the Berwick-Northumberland border; Richard Fox successfully defended it until Surrey's advance forced the Scots to retreat.
[b] Sonnet XXXIV, ll. 1–4 (loosely quoted).

weight of care, and rose free and bright as in earliest youth. His impatience to behold his royal friend, to speak the little word, which he felt assured would recall the Scots from their ravages, and take from him the guilt / of his subject's blood, grew like a torrent in the spring: – he outspeeded his main troop; he left all but his chiefest friends behind; one by one even these grew fewer; he mounted a fresh horse, it was the third that day – "May-Flower is worse than blown," said Neville; "will not your Highness repose till to-morrow?"

"Repose!" – this echo was his only answer, and already he was far and alone upon his way.

The Scottish lines were passed, and the embattled walls of Norham, grey and impenetrable as rock, were before him; the royal pavilion occupied the centre of the camp. The wearied steed that bore York dropt on one knee as he reined him up before it, flushed, with every mark of travel and haste – he threw himself from his saddle, and entered the tent: it was thronged; he saw not one face, save that of the Monarch himself, who was conversing with a churchman, whose dark, foreign countenance Richard had seen before; now it was like a vision before him. James, in an accent of surprise, cried, "My Lord, this is an unexpected visit." /

"Excuse ceremony, my dear cousin," said York; "I come not to speak to the Majesty of Scotland: man to man – a friend to his dearest friend – I have a suit to urge."

James, who was aware that his actual occupation of listening and even acceding to the suggestions of his foreign visitant, in favour of peace with Henry, was treason to York's cause, thought that news of Don Pedro D'Ayala's[a] arrival was the secret of these words: he blushed as he replied, "As friend to friend, we will hear anon – to-morrow."

"There is no anon to my dear plea," said York; "even now the hellish work is about which you must check. Oh, what am I, King of Scotland, that I am to be made the curse and scourge of my own people? The name of Richard is the bye-word of hate and terror, there, where I seek for blessings and filial love. You know not the mischief your fierce Borderers achieve – it is not yet too late; recall your men; bid them spare my people; let not the blood of my subjects plead against my right; rather would I pine in exile for ever, than occasion / the slaughter and misery of my countrymen, my children."

Richard spoke impetuously; his eyes filled with tears, his accents were fraught with passionate entreaty, and yet with a firm persuasion that he spoke not in vain: but his address had the very worst effect. James believed that, hearing that he was in treaty with his foe, he had come to re-urge his suit, to enforce the many promises given, to demand a continuation of the war. James,

---

[a] Shrewd diplomat sent to enlist Scottish support for Spain against France; he urged James IV to abandon Warbeck and to marry an English princess.

a Scotchman, bred in civil strife among fierce Highlanders and ruthless Border-ers, saw something contemptible in this pity and supplication for cottagers and villains: the shame he had felt, or feared to feel, at the idea of being accused of treachery by his guest, was lightened; his lips were curled even to scorn, as in a cold tone he replied, "Sir, methinketh you take much pains, and very much strive to preserve the realm of another prince, which, I do believe, never will be yours."

A momentary surprise set open wide York's eyes; he glanced round him; the Earl of Huntley's brow was clouded; a smile curled / Lord Buchan's lips; the emotion that had convulsed the Prince's features, gave place to the calmest dignity. "If not mine," he said, "let me yield the sway to the lady Peace: the name and presence of a Plantagenet shall no longer sanction the devastation of his country. I would rather be a cotter on your wild Highlands, than buy the sovereignty of my fair England by the blood of her inhabitants."[a]

The warm, though capricious heart of James was quickly recalled by the look and voice of his once dearest friend, to a sense of the ungraciousness of his proceeding: he frankly stretched out his hand; "I was wrong, cousin, forgive me, we will confer anon. Even now, orders have been issued to recal the troops; a few words will explain every thing."

York bent his head in acquiescence. The King dismissed his nobles, and committed to the care of one among them the reverend D'Ayala. With a strong sentiment of self-defence, which was self-accusation – a half return of his ancient affection, which acted like remorse – James set himself to explain his proceedings. / Fearful, unaided by any of the natives, of proceeding with an inadequate force further into the heart of the country, he had set down before the Castle of Norham, which was defended undauntedly by the Bishop of Durham. He had wasted much time here; and now the Cornish insurgents being quelled, the Earl of Surrey was marching northwards, at the head of forty thousand men. Surrey, Howard, might he not be a masked friend? "who," continued James, "has surely some personal enmity to your Highness; for the reverend Father D'Ayala, an embassador from Spain, visited him on his journey northward, and it seems the noble indulged in despiteful language; saying, that he who could bring the fell Scot (I thank him) into England, wore manifest signs of – I will not say – I remember not his words; they are of no import. The sum is, my dear Lord, I cannot meet the English army in the open field; walled town – even those paltry towers – I cannot win: with what shame and haste I may, I must retreat over the border."

Many more words James in the heat of repentant affection said to soothe his English / friend. York's blood boiled in his veins; his mind was a chaos of scorn, mortification, and worse anger against himself. The insult inflicted by

---

[a] Warbeck's revulsion is amply documented in the historical record.

James before his assembled lords, the bitter speech of Surrey; he almost feared that he deserved the one, while he disdained to resent the other; and both held him silent. As speedily as he might, he took leave of the King: he saw signs in the encampment of the return of the foragers; they were laden with booty: his heart was sick; to ease his pent up burning spirit, when night brought solitude, though not repose, he wrote thus to the Lady Katherine: –

"Wilt thou, dear lady of my heart, descend from thy lofty state, and accept an errant knight, instead of a sceptered king, for thy mate? Alas! sweet Kate, if thou wilt not, I may never see thee more: for not thus, oh not thus, my God, will Richard win a kingdom! Poor England bleeds: our over-zealous cousin has pierced her with dismal wounds; and thou wouldst in thy gentleness shed a thousand tears, hadst thou beheld the misery that even now, grim and / ghastly, floats before my sight. What am I, that I should be the parent of evil merely? Oh, my mother, my too kind friends, why did ye not conceal me from myself? Teaching me lessons of humbleness, rearing me as a peasant, consigning me to a cloister, my injuries would have died with me; and the good, the brave, the innocent, who have perished for me, or through me, had been spared!

"I fondly thought that mine was no vulgar ambition. I desired the good of others; the raising up and prosperity of my country. I saw my father's realm sold to an huckster – his subjects the victims of low-souled avarice. What more apparent duty, than to redeem his crown from Jew-hearted Tudor, and to set the bright jewels, pure and sparkling as when they graced his brow, on the head of his only son? Even now I think the day will come when I shall repair the losses of this sad hour – is it the restless ambitious spirit of youth that whispers future good, or true forebodings of the final triumph of the right?

"Now, O sweetest Kate, I forget disgrace, / I forget remorse; I bury every sorrow in thought of thee. Thy idea is as a windless haven to some way-worn vessel – its nest in a vast oak tree to a tempest-baffled bird – hope of Paradise to the Martyr who expires in pain. Wilt thou receive me with thine own dear smile? My divine love, I am not worthy of thee; yet thou art mine – Lackland Richard's single treasure. The stars play strange gambols with us – I am richer than Tudor, and but that *thy* husband must leave no questioned name, I would sign a bond with Fate – let him take England, give me Katherine. But a Prince may not palter with the holy seal God affixes to him – nor one espoused to thee be less than King; fear not, therefore, that I waver though I pause – Adieu!" /

CHAPTER XVIII.

———

Yet, noble friends, his mixture with our blood,
Even with our own, shall no way interrupt
A general peace.

FORD.[a]

———

Pedro D'Ayala was embassador from Ferdinand and Isabella to the King of England. There was something congenial in the craft and gravity of this man with the cautious policy of Henry. When the latter complained of the vexation occasioned him by the counterfeit Plantagenet and the favour he met with in Scotland, D'Ayala offered to use his influence and counsel to terminate these feuds. He found James out of humour with York's ill success among the English, weary of a siege, where / impregnable stone walls were his only enemies, uneasy at the advance of Surrey; pliable, therefore, to all his arguments. A week after d'Ayala's arrival, the Scots had recrossed the Tweed, the King and his nobles had returned to Edinburgh, and York to Katherine.

Richard's northern sun was set, and but for this fair star he had been left darkling. When the English general in his turn crossed the Tweed, and ravaged Scotland, *he* was looked on by its inhabitants as the cause of their disasters; and, but that some loving friends were still true to him, he had been deserted in the land which so lately was a temple of refuge to him. The Earl of Huntley exerted himself to prevent his falling into too deep disgrace in the eyes of Scotland, and was present at the consultations of the exiles to urge some new attempt in some other part of King Henry's dominions. York was anxious to wash out the memory of his overthrow; so that this check, which seemed so final to his hopes, but operated as an incentive to further exertions. Yet whither should he go? the whole earth was closed upon him. The territory / of Burgundy, which had so long been his home, was forbidden. France – Concressault, who was his attached friend, dissuaded him from encountering a mortifying repulse there. Even his own Spain would refuse to receive him, now that

———

[a] *Perkin Warbeck*, IV. iii. 44–6.

d'Ayala had shown himself his enemy; but, no, he was not so far reduced to beg a refuge at the limits of civilization; still he had his sword, his cause, his friends.

A stranger came, an unexpected visitant from over the sea to decide his vacillating councils. The man was aged and silver-haired, smooth in his manners, soft-voiced, yet with quick grey eyes and compressed lips, indications of talent and resolution and subtlety. Frion saw him first, and deceived by his almost fawning manners into an idea of his insignificance, asked his purpose and name. The stranger with the utmost gentleness refused to disclose his object to any but the Prince; and Frion, with great show of insolence, refused to introduce him to his presence. "Then without thy leave, Sir Knave," said the old man calmly, "I must force my way." /

Astley, the poor scrivener of Canterbury, was present. This honest, simple-hearted fellow had shown so much worth, so much zeal, so much humbleness with such fidelity, that he had become a favourite in York's court, and principally with the Lady Katherine. Frion hated him, for he was his opposite, but pretended to despise him, and to use him as an underling. Astley meekly submitted, and at last gained a kind of favour in the Frenchman's eyes by the deference and respect of his manner. The stranger, with the readiness of one accustomed to select agents for his will, addressed him, bidding him announce to his Highness a gentleman from Ireland. "And be assured," he said, "the Duke will ill-requite any tardiness on thy part."

An angry burst from Frion interrupted him. This man, rarely off his guard, but roused now by recent mortifications, forgot himself in the violence he displayed, which strangely contrasted with the soft tranquillity of the stranger, and Astley's modest, but very determined annunciation of his resolve to convey the message to the / Prince. Frion, from loud words, was about to proceed to acts, when Lord Barry entered – Barry, who felt Scotland as a limbo of despair, who was for ever urging Richard to visit Ireland, to whom the court life of the English was something like a trim-fenced park to a new-caught lion. Barry saw the stranger – his eyes lighted up, nay, danced with sudden joy: with no gentle hand he thrust Frion away, and then bent his knee, asking a blessing of the Prior of Kilmainham; and in the same breath eagerly demanded what had brought the venerable man from Buttevant across the dangerous seas.

Keating's presence gave new life to York's councils: he brought an invitation from Maurice of Desmond to the Duke. The Earl had since Richard's departure been occupied in training troops, and so fortifying himself as to enable him to rise against Poynings, whose regular government, and above all whose predilection for the Butlers, caused him to be detested by the Geraldines. Hurried on by hatred and revenge, Desmond resolved to do that which would be most dreaded and abhorred of Henry / – to assume the badge of the White Rose, and to set up the pretensions of young Richard. The tidings were that York was a loved and honoured guest in Edinburgh; and the impetuous Desmond feared that he would hardly be induced to abandon King James's powerful alliance, for the friendship of a wild Irish chieftain. The very invitation must be committed to no mean or witless hands: the difficulties appeared so great, that the measure was on the point of being abandoned, when the Prior of Kilmainham, who in the extreme of age awoke to fresh life at a prospect of regaining his lost consequence, offered himself to undertake the arduous task. His views went far beyond the Earl's: he hoped to make the King of Scotland an active party in his plots, and to contrive a simultaneous invasion of England from the north and from the west. Already his turbulent and grasping spirit saw Irish and Scotch meeting midway in England, and with conjoined forces dethroning Tudor, and dictating terms to his successor. He came too late: he came to find a peace nearly concluded between James and / Henry; the White Rose fallen into disregard; and his arrival looked upon as the best hope, the last refuge of his fallen party.

Richard on the instant accepted his invitation. To a generous heart the feeling of enforced kindness succeeding to spontaneous affection, is intolerable. The very generosity of his own disposition made him recoil from exacting a reluctant boon from his sometime friend. To live a pensioner among the turbulent, arrogant Scots, was not to be thought of. The Earl of Huntley, in fond expectation of his daughter's greatness, would have despised him had he remained inactive. Even Katherine was solicitous to leave Scotland – she knew her countrymen; and, ready as she was to give up every exalted aim, and to make her husband's happiness in the retired quiet of private life, she knew that insult and feud would attend his further tarrying among the Scotch.

York had been for nearly a year the guest of King James;[a] twelve months, in all their long-drawn train of weeks and days, had paced over / the wide earth, marking it with change: each one had left its trace in the soul of Richard. There is something frightful, to a spirit partly tired of the world, to find that their life is to be acquainted with no durable prosperity; that happiness is but a modification of a train of events, which, like the fleeting birth of flowers, varies the year with different hues. But York was still too young to be aweary even of disappointment; he met the winter of his fortunes with cheerful fortitude, so that a kind of shame visited James, inspired by the respect his injured friend so well merited.

The capricious, but really noble heart of the Scottish King was at this time put to a hard trial. One of the preliminaries of peace, most insisted upon by Henry, was, that his rival should be given up to him: – this was, at the word, refused. But even to dismiss him from his kingdom, seemed so dastardly an act towards one allied to him by his own choice, that the swelling heart of the cavalier could not yet tame itself to the statesman's necessity.[b] Some of his subjects, meanwhile, were ready enough to cut / the Gordian knot by which he

---

[a] His stay was in reality longer: from November 1495 to July 1497.
[b] Mary Shelley's sources testify to James's effort to reconcile honour and expedience.

was entangled. Tudor had many emissaries in Edinburgh; and Lord Moray, Lord Buchan, and the dark Bothwell, whose enmity had become fierce personal hate, were still egged on by various letters and messages from England to some deed of sanguinary violence.

Sir John Ramsay was sought out by Frion. That goodly diplomatist must have entertained a high opinion of his mollifying eloquence, when he dared encounter the hot temper of him he had dishonoured in the eyes of the English Prince, and of his own countryman Hamilton. But Frion knew that in offering revenge he bought pardon: he was of little mark in Ramsay's eyes, while the man he had injured, and whom he consequently detested beyond every other, survived to tell the grating tale of the defeated villany of the assassin, and the godlike magnanimity of him who pardoned.

Frion's own feelings, which had vacillated, were now fixed to betray the Prince. He had wavered, because he had a kind of personal affection for the noble adventurer. Somehow / he managed to fancy him a creature of his own: he had worked so long, and at one time so well for him, that he had fostered the vain belief that his dearest hopes, and best pretensions, would vanish like morning mist, if he blew unkindly on them. It was not so: James had been his friend; Huntley had given him his daughter without his interference; and the Irish project, with Keating at its head, who treated Frion with galling contempt, filled up the measure of his discontents. If anything else had been needed, the Lady Katherine's favour to Astley, and some offices of trust in which York himself had used him, sufficed to add the last sting to malice. "If they will not let me make, they shall rue the day when I shall mar; learn shall they, that Frion can clip an eagle's wings even in its pride of flight."

It is common to say that there is honour among thieves and villains. It is not honour; but an acknowledged loss of shame and conscience, and a mutual trust in the instinctive hatred the bad must bear the good, which strongly unites them. In spite of the Frenchman's / former treachery, Balmayne felt that he could now confide, that his guilt would stretch far enough to encircle in its embrace the very act he desired; and he again trusted, and used him as the chief agent of his plots.

The Earl of Surrey was ravaging Scotland; and King James, with the chivalrous spirit of the times, challenged him to single combat. The Earl, in answer, refused to place his master's interests at the hazard of his single prowess, though ready for any other cause to accept the honour tendered him. The herald that brought this reply, Frion reported to Richard to be charged with a letter to him. Its purpose was to declare, that though, while aided and comforted by the enemies of England, the Earl warred against him, yet the Howard remembered the ancient attachments of his house; and that, if the White Rose, wholly renouncing the Scotch, would trust to the honour of the representative of a race of nobles, the army now in the field to his detriment should be turned to an engine of advantage. "Time pressed," the letter concluded by saying –

"and if the Duke of / York were willing to give his sails to the favouring wind, let him repair with a small company to Greenock,[a] where he would find zealous and powerful friends."

At first this intimation filled the Prince with exultation and delight. The time was at last come when he should lead the native nobility of England to the field, and meet his enemy in worthy guise. There was but one check; he could not join Surrey, while Surrey was in arms against his once generous friend; so that, by a strange shifting of events, he now became anxious for peace between Scotland and England; eager that the seal should be set that destroyed the alliance and amity which had so lately been the sole hope of his life. Neville and Plantagenet entered into his views; and, while seemingly at the bottom of Fortune's scale, a new spirit of gladness animated this little knot of Englishmen.

For one thing young Richard was not prepared: the preliminaries of peace he knew were arranged, and he was aware that its conclusion would take the sword out of James's / hand. They had rarely met lately; and this, while it lessened the familiarity, rather added to the apparent kindness of their interviews. There was in both these young Princes a genuine warmth of heart, and brightness of spirit, that drew them close whenever they did meet. James honoured the integrity and the unconquered soul of the outcast monarch, while his own genius, his vivacity, and polished courtesy, in spite of his caprice and late falling off, spread a charm around that forced admiration and affection even from him he injured. It was at this period, that, notwithstanding their real disunion, Richard felt it as strange to find his royal host confused in manner, and backward of speech. They had been at a hunting party, where Lord Moray's haughty glance of triumph, and the sneer that curled the Earl of Buchan's lip, would have disclosed some victory gained by them, had York deigned to regard their aspects. At length, after much hesitation, while riding apart from his peers, James asked – "If there were any news from the Lady Margaret of Burgundy?" /

"Sir Roderick Lalayne returned to her a month ago," replied York, "and with him went my dear and zealous Lady Brampton, to urge fresh succour for one, to whom fortune has so long shown a wintry face, that methinks spring must at last be nigh at hand, herald of bright, blossoming summer."

"What promises then my lady Duchess?" said the King, eagerly.

"Alas! her promises are as blank as her power," replied Richard. "Even when the old Dukes of Burgundy were as Emperors in Christendom, they were but as provosts and city-magistrates in the free towns of Flanders; and these towns resolve on peace with England."

"It is the cry of the world," said James with a sigh; "this Tudor is a mighty man. Why, even I, a Scot, a warrior, and a king, am forced to join the universal

---

[a] Port city on the river Clyde in Renfrewshire.

voice, and exclaim, 'Peace with England,' even though my honour is the sacrifice."

"Your Majesty imparts no strange truth to me," said York. "I have long known that this must be; but surely you speak in soreness of / spirit, when you speak of the sacrifice of honour. I thought the terms agreed on were favourable to Scotland."

"King Henry demanded, in the first place, the delivery of your Highness into his hands." James blushed deeply as he said these words.

"Or he will come seize me," rejoined the Duke, with a laugh. "In good hour I will deliver myself, if he will walk through the bristling lances, and set at naught the wide-mouthed cannon that will bellow in his path."

"Have you then new hopes?" cried the King; "Oh! say but so; and half my shame, and all my sorrow vanishes. Say that you have hope of speedy good in some other country; for I have sworn, ere April wear into May, Scotland shall be made poor by your Highness's absence."

A long pause followed these words. James felt as if he had given words to his own concealed dishonour, and struck his iron-girdled side with the bitter thought. "O! spirit of my father, this may not atone; but I must pay also in shame and torturous self-contempt for my heavy guilt." A sudden blow, a precipitous fall when / unaware his feet had reached the crumbling brink of a beetling precipice, would not have made such commotion in Richard's heart, as the forced and frightful conviction that the friend he had trusted heaped this insult on him. For the first time in his life perhaps, pride conquered every other feeling; for reproach had been more *friendly*, than the spirit that impelled him, with a placid voice, and a glance of haughty condescension, to reply: – "Now that your Majesty dismisses me, I find it fittest season to thank you heartily for your many favours. That you deny me to the suit of your new ally, and send me forth scaithless[a] from your kingdom, is the very least of these. Shall I forget that, when, a wanderer and a stranger, I came hither, you were a brother to me? That when an outcast from the world, Scotland became a home of smiles, and its King my dearest friend? These are lesser favours; for your love was of more value to me than your power, though you used it for my benefit; and, when you gave me the Lady Katherine, I incurred such a debt of gratitude, that it were uncancelled, though you cast me, bound hand / and foot, at Tudor's footstool. That I am bankrupt even in thanks, is my worst misery; yet, if the eye of favour, which I believe Fortune is now opening on me, brighten into noon-day splendour, let James of Scotland ask, and, when England shall be added to his now barren name, Richard will give, though it were himself."

"Gentle cousin," replied the King, "you gloss with horrid words a bitter pill

---

[a] Variant of 'scatheless', unharmed.

to both; for though the skaithe seem yours, mine is the punishment. I lose what I can ill spare, a kinsman, and a friend."

"Never!" cried York; "Scotland bids a realmless monarch, a beggar prince, depart: the King of Scotland, moved by strong state-necessity is no longer the ally of the disinherited orphan of Edward the Fourth: but James is Richard's friend; he will rejoice, when he sees him, borne with the flowing tide, rise from lowness to the highest top at which he aims. And now, dear my Lord, grant me one other boon. I am about to depart, even of my own will; dismiss then every rankling feeling; / lay no more to your generous, wounded heart a need, which is even more mine than yours; but let smiles and love attend your kinsman to the end, unalloyed by a deeper regret, than that fate wills it, and we must separate."

END OF VOL. II. /

THE

FORTUNES

OF

PERKIN WARBECK,

A ROMANCE.

BY THE

AUTHOR OF "FRANKENSTEIN."

J'ai veu filz d'Angleterre, Richard d'Yorc nommé,
Que l'on disoit en terre, estinct et consommé,
Endurer grant souffrance; et par nobles exploitz,
Vivre en bonne esperance, d'estre Roy des Angloys.

Old French Chronicle.

IN THREE VOLUMES.

VOL. III.

LONDON:

HENRY COLBURN AND RICHARD BENTLEY,
NEW BURLINGTON STREET.

1830.

PERKIN WARBECK.

CHAPTER I.

I am your wife,
No human power can or shall divorce,
My faith from duty.
FORD.[a]

———— With
My fortune and my seeming destiny,
He made the bond, and broke it not with me.
No human tie is snapped betwixt us two.
SCHILLER'S WALLENSTEIN.[b]

Frion believed that he held the strings,[c] which commanded the movements of all the puppets about him. The intrigues of party, the habitual use of ill-means to what those around him deemed a good end, had so accustomed him to lying and forgery, that his conscience was quite / seared to the iniquity of these acts; truth to him was an accident, to be welcomed or not according as it was or was not advantageous to his plots.

King James prepared a fleet for the conveyance of the Prince; and the Earl of Huntley, as a matter of course, promised to entertain his daughter royally, until, in a palace in Westminster, she should find her destined title and fit abode. The Lady Katherine thanked him, but declared that she was nothing moved from her bridal vow, and that she never would desert Richard's side. All that her father urged was of no avail. State and dignity, or their contraries,

---

[a] *Perkin Warbeck*, IV. iii. 101–3.
[b] Johann Christoph Friedrich von Schiller (1759–1805), *The Death of Wallenstein* (1799), I, vii (S. T. Coleridge's translation, 1800).
[c] '1497' (marginal note in *Abinger/Palacio*).

humiliation and disgrace, could only touch her through her husband; he was her exalter or debaser, even as he rose or fell; it was too late now to repine at degradation, which it ill-beseemed the daughter of a Gordon to encounter; it was incurred when she plighted her faith at the altar; wherever she was, it must be hers. As a princess she was lost or redeemed by her husband's fortunes. As a woman, her glory and all her honour must consist / in never deviating from the strait line of duty, which forbade her absence from his side.

The Earl disdained to reason with a fond doating girl, as he called the constant-minded lady, but applied to the King, representing how it would redound to his discredit, should a princess of his blood wander a vagrant beggar over sea and land. James had passed his royal word to Katherine, that she should have her will on this point; and when, at her father's suit he tried to dissuade her, he was at once silenced by her simple earnest words; "Ask me not," she said, "to place myself on the list of unworthy women: for your own honour's sake, royal cousin, permit your kinswoman to perform a wife's part unopposed. You and my father bestowed me, a dutiful subject, an obedient daughter, according to your will; you transferred my duty and obedience, and truly as I paid it to you, so will I keep it for my lord."

"What can we reply, my good Earl Marshall," said James, turning to Huntley, "I rebelled against the religion through which I reign, did I deny our sweet Kate free allowance / to follow the dictates of her generous heart. Nor let us grudge the White Rose this one fair bloom. Love, such as Katherine feels, love, and the dearest, best gift of God – alas! too oft denied to poor humanity, and most to me – self-complacency, arising from a good conscience, will repay her every sacrifice."

Huntley retired in high indignation; his will was opposed; his word, which he deemed a law, had but a feather's weight. The blood of the Gordon was stirred to rage; and he broke forth in fierce and cruel expressions of anger, calling his daughter, ingrate – her lord base, and a traitor. Such muttered curses were reported to Lord Buchan: in the scheme on foot they had somewhat dreaded to incur Huntley's displeasure and revenge; knowing how dearly he prized the hope of royalty for his daughter; but now they fancied that they might draw him in, ere he was aware, to approve their deed. The crafty Frion was set on to sound him; the iron was hot, most easily, to their eyes, it took the desired form.[a]

Huntley was a Scot, cunning even when angry / – cautious when most passionate. The first intimations of the conspiracy were greedily received by him. He learnt the falsehood of the letter pretending to come from the Earl of Surrey; and the use that was to be made of this decoy to seize on the Duke of York's person. He did not scruple to promise his assistance; he reiterated his

---

[a] The plot elaborated in this chapter is Mary Shelley's invention.

angry imprecations against his unworthy son-in-law; he thanked Frion with cordial warmth for affording him this opportunity for revenge; he declared his gratitude towards the confederate nobles; and the Frenchman left him, with the full belief that he was ready to lend his best aid to deliver over the English Prince to ignominy and death.

Such was the end of King Henry's last scheme to obtain possession of his too noble, too excelling rival, by means of Scottish fraud, and the treason of York's dependents. The Earl of Huntley conducted the whole affair with the utmost secresy. Apparently he acted the part designed for him by the conspirators. He reconciled himself to the prince; he urged an instant compliance with Surrey's invitation. / The English had asked for some guarantee of Surrey's truth. Huntley obviated this difficulty. Through his intervention a new and sufficing impulse was given. Richard appointed the day when he should repair to Greenock, there to meet the envoy who was to lead him to Lord Surrey's presence. In the harbour of Greenock rode the bark which was to convey him to his English prison. King Henry's hirelings were already there; Frion conducted the victims blindfold into the net: they had meant to have gathered together a troop of ruffian borderers to prevent all resistance; but Huntley promised to be there himself with a band of Highlanders. The whole thing only seemed too easy, too secure.

The wily secretary had overshot his mark in taking so readily for granted Huntley's assent to the ruin of the Duke of York. He had come upon him in his angry hour: his honied words were a dew of poison; his adjurations for peace, oil to fire. Then, as the noble strode through the hall, imprecating vengeance, he slid in words that made him stop in full career. Men are apt to see their wishes mirrored in the object before them; and, when the Earl bent his grey / eyes upon the Provençal, and knit his time-furrowed brow in attention and interest, Frion saw the satisfaction of a man on the brink of dear revenge. He was far a-field. The very rage in which the Earl had indulged, by a natural reaction, softened him towards his children: and, when the traitor spoke of schemes ripe to deliver York into his adversary's hands, he recoiled at once from the path of vengeance opened before him, and listened with horror to the detail of a conspiracy which would tear the very shadow of a diadem from his daughter's brow; yet he listened, and his words still enticed the over wily Frion. "Balmayne," said the Earl, "all must succeed, even to the death. Where he intermeddles, he is ruthless;" thus ran his comments: "My good Lord Buchan, what the Foul Fiend makes him so busy? English gold! Yes: Buchan loves the gilding better than the strong iron that it hides. The honour of the royal house, my most reverend uncle! Is his animosity so stirring? Oh! priests are your only haters.[a] So

---

[a] 'Bishop of Moray/ See vol. II, p. 2[ ]' (marginal note in *Abinger/Palacio*), probably referring to II, 279 (p. 244), where the priestly hater is previously mentioned. He is wrongly titled 'Earl of Moray' on p. 221.

Richard's tale is told. The chroniclers will speak of Duke Perkin, of the canker that ate out the heart / of Gordon's fair rose, the gibbet, instead of a throne, to which she was wed; a fair eminence! My Kate will hardly ascend it with him: she must halt at the gallows' foot." These words, said with bitterness, seemed to Frion the boiling sarcasm of an exasperated parent. The man's vanity was the trap in which he was caught: he could not believe that a savage Scot, an untaught Highlander, could enter the lists with one nurtured in the subtle atmosphere of Provence, with the pupil of Louis the Eleventh; a man schooled in eastern lore, who had passed a whole life of contrivance and deceit.

The Scottish nobles, Moray, Buchan, and Bothwell, were satisfied in having given their countenance to the English hirelings; and, now that the more powerful Huntley promised to watch over the execution of their designs, they were glad enough to withdraw from the rude and inhospitable act. Huntley had every thing in his own hands. He, with a party of Highlanders, escorted the Duke and Duchess of York, with their friends and attendants, to Greenock. Frion had never shown himself so / humble or so courteous; he seemed afraid that any one of his victims should escape: he was particularly[20] anxious to entice his old enemy, the Prior of Kilmainham, into the snare. His readiness and vivacity were remarked by all: it was attributed to the high hopes he entertained of his royal master's success through the alliance of the Earl of Surrey; and, while York expressed his affectionate approbation, he smiled blandly, and painted every feature in the very colouring he wished it to wear.

The vessel rode at anchor; the English sailors, on the arrival of York, went on board, got her under weigh, and dropt down the coast. With the dawn Lord Howard of Effingham,[a] with a chosen troop, was, according to the false hopes of Richard, to arrive at the rendezvous, a wood about two miles south of the town, bordering the sands of the sea. Here the English emissaries were congregated, and here a score of Highlanders were in ambush, to assist in the capture of the White Rose. Hither, even before dawn, the wakeful Frion came, to announce the speedy arrival of his lord. He / found his English friends in some anxiety. Clifford, who, under the name of Wiatt, had been chief among them, was seized with panic or remorse, and had gone on board the vessel, which had cast anchor but a few furlongs from the shore. The others were mean underlings: Frion's presence gave them courage; he was elated; his laugh was free; he had neither doubt nor scruple; no, not even when he turned from the vulgar, brutalized countenances of these ruffians, to behold the princely victim in all the splendour of innocence, with one beside him so lovely, that the spirit of good itself had selected her form for its best earthly bower; or to see Edmund,

---

[a] Two of Surrey's sons, Thomas (1473–1554; 3rd Duke of Norfolk) and Edward (?1477–1513; later Lord High Admiral) fought under their father's command against James IV in 1497 (see p. 251n). William Howard, 1st Baron Howard of Effingham (?1510–73), Surrey's eldest son by his second wife, was not yet born.

whose dark eyes beamed with unknown joy, and Neville, whose haughty glance was exchanged for a glad smile. The man's sole thought was exultation at his own cleverness and success, in having inveigled so many of the noble and the brave to this dark fate.

"What tidings of Effingham?" asked York.

"Are ye ready?" cried Huntley.

"All!" replied Frion; "all save him ye name Wiatt. Sir Robert, forsooth, is but half / a man, and never does more than half deed, though that half makes a whole crime. All is ready. I hear the sound of oars; the boat nears the shore."

Through the tall, bare trunks of the trees, a glimpse of the beach might be gained; the roaring of the surges was distinct, now mingled with the cry of sailors.

"Then lose we no time," said Huntley. "My Lord of York, these words sound strange. You expected a noble countryman, to lead you to victory; you find nameless fellows, and the prince of knaves, most ready and willing to lead you to everlasting prison. Lo, the scene shifts again! Never be cast down, Master Frion; you are as subtle as any of your race – only to be outwitted by a niggard Scotchman, who can ill read, and worse write; except when villainy is blazoned in a man's face, and his sword indites a traitor's fate. Your clerkship will find none among us learned enough to afford you benefit of clergy."

Huntley drew his sword; and at the signal his Highlanders arose from their ambush. Frion was seized and bound. None, who even a moment / before had seen the smooth-faced villain, could have recognized him; he was pale as the snow on Ben Nevis.[a] A Highlander, an adept in such acts, dexterously threw a knotted rope over his head, and cast his eye up to the trees for a convenient branch. Such had been the orders; such the summary justice of the Earl.

Richard meanwhile looked on the blanched visage and quailing form of his betrayer in mere compassion. "Is it even so, Etienne?" he said; "and after long companionship we part thus."

The trembling craven fell on his knees, though he tightened the halter by the movement, so that when Richard turned away, saying, "I had thought better of thee: Jesu pardon thee as readily as I – farewell!" he had scarce voice to cry for mercy.

"Aye," cried the Gordon; "such mercy as we grant the wolf and thievish fox. Short shrift be thine, Master Secretary!"

"By our Lady's grace, stay!" said Katherine; "do not kill the false-hearted knave. He is a coward, and dares survive his honour; let him live." /

Richard looked sternly on the kneeling slave. To the good there is something awful in the sight of a guilty man. It is a mystery to them how the human heart can be so perverted. Is it a spirit from hell, that incorporates itself with the

---

[a] Highest mountain in the British Isles, in the district of Lochaber, Scotland; its peak is snow-covered year round.

273

pulsations of our mortal bosom; a darkness that overshadows; a fiendly essence that mingles with the breath God gave to his own image? York felt a shrinking horror. "Thou hast pursued me since my youth," he said, "forcing thyself into my councils; sometimes as a wily enemy; at others, befriending me in seeming, raising my soul, that flagged beneath the world's unkind ministry; dropping balm by thy words into a wounded heart; to end thy office thus! Was this thy purpose ever; or what demon whispered thee to betray? Die! oh, no! too many, the good, the great, the true, have died for me; live thou a monument – a mark to tell the world that York can pardon, York can despise – not so base a thing as thee – that were little, but even thy employer. Go, tell my sister's husband that I bear a charmed life; that love and / valour are my guards. Bid him bribe those, nor waste his ill-got crowns on such as thee. Unbind him, sirs; make signal to the boat; let him on board; the winds stand fair for England."

The fall of many a hope, roused by the forgery on Surrey's name, was forgotten by Richard, as he sickened at this other mark of man's wickedness and folly. He was surely the dear sport of fortune, a tale to chronicle how faithless friends may be. If such thoughts, like summer clouds, darkened his mind, they vanished, driven by the winds of life that bore him onward. This was no time for mere gloomy meditation. Though he was obliged to return to his forgotten Irish scheme, and to dismiss the glorious anticipation in which he had indulged, of leading the chivalry of England to the field; though no real defeat had ever visited him so keenly as this mockery of one; yet he was forced to forget himself, and to apply himself to console and rouse his downcast friends; but his skill was well repaid, and soon he again awoke to / those feelings of buoyant hope, unwearied energy, and unshaken confidence which were the essence of his character.

In this last trial he felt how much good he might derive from the sweetness and constant spirit of the Lady Katherine. She hoped for none of the world's blessings, except they came in the shape of loves from him to whom she was united; happiness – all her's as centered in her blameless affections; and her confidence was placed in the belief and knowledge, that by devoting herself to her lord, to the wandering outcast who so dearly needed her sacrifice, she fulfilled her destiny upon earth, and pleased the "great Task Master,"[a] who for happiness or misery, but certainly for good, had given her life. All her gentle eloquence was spent in dissuading Richard from those unkind thoughts towards his species, which the treason of these base men, the caprice of James, the harsh sentence (for this was again brought home to him by disappointment) of Surrey, awakened in his bosom. It proved no hard task; soon the princely Adventurer, with eagle flight, soared / from the sad prostration of spirit, the birth of his disasters, to fresh hopes and lofty resolves.

---

[a] John Milton, Sonnet VII, 'How Soon Hath Time' (1632), l. 14.

It was necessary immediately to prepare for his departure. The Earl of Huntley, struck by his magnanimity, no longer opposed his daughter's wish. The English exiles were eager for a new, and, they believed (for untired is Hope in man); for a prosperous career. Scotland grew rude, confined, and remote in their eyes. In Ireland were placed for them the portals of the world, to be opened by their swords; the dancing sea-waves invited them: the winds of heaven lent themselves to their service. "My friends," said Richard, "dear and faithful partners of my wayward fortunes, I would fondly believe that we are favoured of heaven. We are few; but the evil and the treacherous are no longer among us. And does old Time in all his outworn tales tell any truer, than that the many, being disunited, and so false, have ever been vanquished by the loving, bold, and heroic few? That a child may scan with its fingers our bare arithmetic, will therefore be to us the source of success, as assuredly it will be of / glory. The English were few when they mowed down thickly planted French at Cressy and Poictiers.[a] Which among us, armed as we are in the mail of valour, but would encounter ten of Tudor's scant-paid mercenaries? For me! I do believe that God is on my side, as surely as I know that justice and faith are; and I fear no defeat."

It is thus that man, with fervent imagination, can endue the rough stone with loveliness, forge the mis-shapen metal into a likeness of all that wins our hearts by exceeding beauty, and breathe into a dissonant trump soul-melting harmonies. The mind of man – that mystery, which may lend arms against itself, teaching vain lessons of material philosophy, but which, in the very act, shows its power to play with all created things, adding the sweetness of its own essence to the sweetest, taking its ugliness from the deformed. The creative faculty of man's soul – which, animating Richard, made him see victory in defeat, success and glory in the dark, the tortuous, the thorny path, which it / was his destiny to walk from the cradle to the tomb.

Oh, had I, weak and faint of speech, words to teach my fellow-creatures the beauty and capabilities of man's mind; could I, or could one more fortunate, breathe the magic word which would reveal to all the power, which we all possess, to turn evil to good, foul to fair; then vice and pain would desert the new-born world!

It is not thus: the wise have taught, the good suffered for us; we are still the same; and still our own bitter experience and heart-breaking regrets teach us to sympathize too feelingly with a tale like this; which records the various fortunes of one who at his birth received every gift which most we covet; whose strange story is replete with every change of happiness and misery; with every contrast of glorious and disgraceful; who was the noble object of godlike fidelity, and the sad victim of demoniac treason; the mark of man's hate and woman's love;

---

[a] Crécy (1346) and Poitiers (1356), decisive English victories in the Hundred Years War (1337–1453).

spending thus a short eventful life. It is not spent; he yet breathes: he is on the world of waters. / What new scene unfolds itself? Where are they who were false, where those who were true? They congregate around him, and the car of life bears him on, attended by many frightful, many lovely shapes, to his destined end.[a] He has yet much to suffer; and, human as he is, much to enjoy. /

CHAPTER II.

———

One moment these were heard and seen; another
Past, and the two who stood beneath that night,
Each only heard, or saw, or felt the other.

SHELLEY.[b]

———

The hour had now arrived when Richard took leave of Scotland. The King was humbled by the necessity he felt himself under, of sending forth his friend and kinsman into the inhospitable world; and he felt deep grief at parting with his lovely cousin. She grew pale, when for the last time she saw the friend of her youth. But Katherine looked upon life in a mode very different from the usual one: the luxuries and dignities of the world never in her mind for a moment came in competition with her affections and her duty; she saw the plain path before her; whatever her father's or her royal cousin's idea / had been in giving her to the Duke of York, she knew that, being his, her destiny upon earth was to share his fortunes, and soothe his sorrows. This constant looking on, giving herself up to, and delighting in one aim, one object, one occupation, elevated her far above the common cares of existence. She left

——— "All meaner things,
The low ambition and the pride of Kings;"[c]

– to shroud herself in love; to take on herself the hallowed state of one devoting

---

[a] Allusion to ll. 178–81 of P. B. Shelley's unfinished 'The Triumph of Life', edited by Mary Shelley for *PBS* 1824.

[b] *The Revolt of Islam* (1818), VI. xxiv. 1–3.

[c] Alexander Pope (1688–1744), *An Essay on Man* (1733–4), I. 1–2 (adapted).

herself to another's happiness. Cleopatra, basking in sunny pomp, borne, the wonder of the world, in her gilded bark, amidst all the aroma of the east, upon the gently rippling Cydnus,[a] felt neither the pride nor joy of Katherine, as, on the poor deck of their dark weather-beaten skiff, she felt pillowed by the downy spirit of love, fanned by its gentle breath.

The Duke of York was more depressed; he thought of how, since his miserable childhood, he had been the sport of fortune and her scorn. He thought of the false, the cold, the perished: a dark wall seemed to rise around him; a murky vault to close over him: success, glory, honour, the world's treasures, which he had been brought / up to aspire to as his dearest aim, his right, were unattainable; he was the defeated, the outcast; there was a clog in his way for ever; a foul taint upon his name. Thus seated on the deck, his arm coiled round a rope, his head leaning on his arm, while the stars showered a dim silvery radiance, and the sparkling sea mocked their lustre with brighter fires; while the breeze, that swelled his sail, and drove him merrily along, spent its cold breath on him; he, painting all natural objects with the obscure colouring suggested by his then gloomy spirit, distorting the very scenery of heaven and vast ocean into symbols of his evil fate, gave himself up to the very luxury of woe, – meanwhile the shadow of a lovely form fell on him, soft fingers pressed the curls of his hair, and Katherine asked, "Are the nights of Andalusia more glorious than this?"

At the voice of the charmer the dæmon fled: sky and sea cast off the dim veil his grief had woven, and creation was restored its native beauty. Hitherto the halls of palaces, the gaiety of a court, the council-chamber, had been the scenes in which the princely pair had lived together; / linked to an engrossing state of things, surrounded by their partizans, they had been friends, nay lovers, according to the love of the many. But solitary Nature is the true temple of Love, where he is not an adjunct, but an essence; and now she alone was around them, to fill them with sublime awe, and the softest tenderness. In Richard's eyes, the kingdom of his inheritance dwindled into a mere speck; the land of her nativity became but a name to Katherine. It sufficed for their two full hearts that they were together on the dark wide sea; the bright sky above, and calm upon the bosom of the deep. They could ill discern each other in the shadowy twilight; a dream-like veil was cast over their features, as sleep curtains out the soul, so that we look on the beloved slumberer, and say "He is there, though the mystery of repose wraps me from him;" so now darkness blinded and divided them: but hand clasped hand; he felt that one existed who was his own, his faithful; and she rejoiced in the accomplishment of the master-sentiment of her soul, the desire of self-devotion, self-annihilation, for one who loved her. / The passion that warmed their hearts had no fears, no tumult, no

---

[a] Alluding to Shakespeare's *Antony and Cleopatra*, II. ii. 190–201.

doubt. One to the other they sufficed; and, but that the trance is fleeting, Happiness, the lost child of the world, would have found here her home; for when love, which is the necessity of affectionate hearts, and the sense of duty, which is the mystery and the law of our souls, blend into one feeling, Paradise has little to promise save immortality.

For many days this state of forgetful extacy lasted. Plantagenet and Neville spoke of wars in England; Lord Barry and Keating of their Irish schemes – the Prince listened and replied; but his soul was far away – Oh, that for ever they might sail thus on the pathless, shoreless sea! – Nothing mean or trivial or ignoble could visit them; no hate, no care, no fear – this might not be, but to have felt, to have lived thus for a few short days, suffices to separate mortal man from the groveling part of his nature – no disgrace, no despair can so bring him back to the low-minded world, as to destroy the sense of having once so existed. And Richard, marked for misery and defeat, acknowledged that power which / sentiment possesses to exalt us – to convince us that our minds, endowed with a soaring, restless aspiration, can find no repose on earth except in love. /

CHAPTER III.

"Now for our Irish wars!"
SHAKSPEARE.[a]

Again the Duke of York approached the rocky entrance of the Cove of Cork, again he passed through the narrow passage, which opening, displayed a lovely sheet of tranquil water, decked with islands. The arrival of his fleet in the harbour was hailed with joy. Old John O'Water had returned to his civic labours, and had contrived to get himself chosen mayor for this year, that he might be of greater assistance to the White Rose in his enterprize.

As soon as the arrival of his ships off the coast was known, O'Water dispatched messengers / to the Earl of Desmond, and busied himself to give

---

[a] *Richard II*, II. i. 155.

splendour to Richard's entrance into Cork. Tapestry and gay-coloured silks were hung from the windows; the street was strewn with flowers – citizens and soldiers intermixed crowded to the landing-place. York's heart palpitated with joy. It was not that thence he much hoped for success to his adventure, which required more than the enthusiasm of the remote inhabitants of the south of Ireland to achieve it, but Cork was a sort of home to him; here he had found safety when he landed, barely escaped from Trangmar's machinations – here he first assumed his rightful name and title – here, a mere boy, ardent, credulous, and bold – he had seen strangers adopt his badge and avouch his cause. Five years had elapsed since then – the acclaim of a few kind voices, the display of zeal, could no longer influence his hopes as then they had done, but they gladdened his heart, and took from it that painful feeling which we all too often experience – that we are cast away on the inhospitable earth, useless and neglected. /

He was glad also in the very first spot of his claimed dominions whereon he set foot, to see the Lady Katherine received with the honours due to her rank. Her beauty and affability won the hearts of all around, and O'Water, with the tenderness that an old man is so apt to feel towards a young and lovely woman, extended to her a paternal affection, the simplicity and warmth of which touched her, thrown as she was among strangers, with gratitude.

Lord Desmond arrived – he was struck by the improvement in York's manner, still ingenuous and open-hearted: he was more dignified, more confident in himself than before – the husband of Katherine also acquired consideration; as an adventurous boy, he might be used according to the commodity of the hour – now he had place – station in the world, and Desmond paid him greater deference, almost unawares.

But the Earl was sorely disappointed; "Reverend Father," said he to Keating, "what aid does Scotland promise? Will they draw Tudor with his archers and harquebussiers,[a] and well-horsed Knights, to the north, giving our Irish / Kern some chance of safe landing in the west?"

"Peace is concluded between Scotland and England," replied Keating.

Desmond looked moody. "How thrives the White Rose over the water? How sped the Duke, when he entered England? Some aid somewhere we must have, besides yonder knot of wanderers, and our own hungry, naked kerns."

"By my fay!" replied Keating, "every budding blossom on the Rose-bush was nipped, as by a north-east wind. When Duke Richard sowed his hopes there, like the dragon's teeth of Dan Cadmus, they turned into so many armed men to attack him."[b]

"Sooth, good Prior," said the Earl, with a sharp laugh, "we shall speed well thereby: would you a re-acting of the gleeful mime at Stoke?"[21]

---

[a] harquebusier, soldier carrying a portable firearm.
[b] Alluding to the story of the legendary founder of Thebes.

"Wherefore," said Keating, "fix your thoughts on England? The dark sea rolls between us, and even the giants of old broke their causeway, which in the north 'tis said they built, ere it laid its long arm on the English / shore.[a] The name of Ireland reads as fair as England; its sons are as brave and politic, able to defend, to rule themselves: blot England from the world, and Ireland stands free and glorious, sufficing to herself. This springal, valorous though he be, can never upset Tudor's throne in London; but he can do more for us by his very impotence. He is the true Lord of Ireland: we are liegemen in maintaining his right. Plant his banner, rally round it all men who wish well to their country; drive out the good man Poynings; crush the Butlers – aye, down with them; and when Richard is crowned King of Erin, and the Geraldines rule under him, our native land will stand singly, nor want England for a crutch – or, by'r Lady! for a spear to enter her heart, while she leaneth on it; so the wars of York and Lancaster may free us from the proud, imperious English; and the Irish, like the Scotch, have a king and a state of their own."

Desmond's eyes flashed for a moment, as Keating thus presented before them the picture he most desired to behold; but they grew cold / again. "The means, reverend Prior, the arms, the money, the soldiers?"

"A bold stroke brings all: strike one blow, and Ireland is at our feet. We must not tarry; now the Butlers and their party are asleep in their security; gather men together; march forward boldly; strike at the highest, Dublin herself."

"Father," replied the Earl, "long before I were half way there, my litter would be abandoned even by its bearers, and we left alone among the bogs and the mountains, to feed as we may, or die. If there be any sooth in your scheme, it can only prove good, inasmuch as we secure Connaught to ourselves, and turn this corner of the island into a kingdom; but neither one word, nor one blow, will gain Dublin. You are right so far, something must be done and speedily; and, if it be well done, we may do more, till by the aid of the blessed St. Patrick and white tooth'd Bridget![b] we tread upon the necks of the Butlers."

This one thing to be undertaken, after much consultation among the chieftains, was the seige / of Waterford: it had been summoned to acknowledge Duke Richard as its lord, and had refused: Keating was very averse to spending time before a fortified town. "On, on, *boutez en avant!*" He reminded Lord Barry of his device, and strove to awaken ambition in him. The Prior of Kilmainham had spent all his life in Dublin, a chief member of the government, a seditious, factious but influential man: the capital to him was all that was worth having, while, to these lords of Munster, the smallest victory over their

---

[a] The 'Giant's Causeway', a series of great columns off the north coast of county Antrim, formed by cooling lava flows.

[b] St Bridget (d. 525), patroness of all good women, founded an abbey at Kildare.

particular rivals, or the gaining a chief city in a district, which was their world, appeared more glorious than entering London itself victoriously, if meanwhile Waterford, or any one of the many towns of Ireland, held out against them.

On the fifteenth of July, 1497, the Duke of York, the Earl of Desmond, and the other many chief of many names, some Geraldines, all allied to, or subject to them, as the O'Briens, the Roches, the Macarthys, the Barrys, and others, assembled at Youghall, a town subject to the Earl of Desmond, and situated about / mid-way between Cork and Waterford, at the mouth of the river Blackwater.[a]

On the twenty-second of July the army was in movement, and entered the county of Waterford; the chiefs, at the head of their respective followers, proceeded to the shrine of St. Declan at Ardmore, to make their vows for the success of their expedition. The church at Ardmore, the round tower, the shrine, and healing-rock, were all objects of peculiar sanctity.[b] The Countess of Desmond, and her young son, and the fair Duchess of York, accompanied this procession from Youghall. After the celebration of mass, the illustrious throng congregated on the rocky eminence, on which the mysterious tower is built overlooking the little bay, where the calm waters broke gently on the pebbly beach. It was a beauteous summer day; the noon-day heat was tempered by the sea breeze, and relieved by the regular plash of the billows, as they spent themselves on the shore. A kind of silence – such silence as there can be among a multitude, such a silence as is preserved when the winds sing among the pines – possessed the crowd: / they stood in security, in peace, surrounded by such objects as excited piety and awe; and yet the hopes of the warrior, and, if such a word may be used, a warrior's fears, possessed them; it was such a pause as the mountain-goat makes ere he commits himself to the precipice. A moment afterwards all was in motion; to the sound of warlike instruments the troops wound up the Ardmore mountains, looking down on the little fleet, that stemmed its slow way towards the harbour of Waterford. The ladies were left alone with few attendants. The young Duchess gazed on that band of departing warriors, whose sole standard was the spotless rose; they were soon lost in the foldings of the hills; again they emerged; her straining eye caught them. That little speck upon the mountain-side contained the sole hope and joy of her life, exposed to danger for the sake of little good; for Katharine, accustomed to the sight of armies, and to the companionship of chiefs and rulers, detected at once the small chance there was, that these men could bring to terms a strongly fortified city; but resignation supplied the place of hope; / she believed that

---

[a] Mary Shelley alters the historical record. It was in July 1495 that Irish lords had rallied to Warbeck's side when he appeared off the Waterford coast with a fleet supplied by Maximilian. Poynings had crushed the insurgents, who ignored Warbeck when he tried to return to Ireland in July 1497.

[b] Croker (pp. 161–5) supplies a detailed description of the shrine at Ardmore (on the Waterford coast) where St Declan served as bishop in the sixth century.

Richard would be spared; and, but for his own sake, she cared little whether a remote home in Ireland, or a palace in England received them. She looked again on the mountain path; no smallest moving object gave sign of life; the sun-light slept upon the heathy uplands; the grey rocks stood in shadowy grandeur; Katherine sighed and turned again to the chapel, to offer still more fervent prayers, that on this beauteous earth, beneath this bright genial heaven, she might not be left desolate: whatever else her fortune, that Richard might be hers.

The army which the Earl of Desmond led against Waterford, did not consist of more than two thousand men. With these he invested the western division of the city. Richard, with his peculiar troop, took his position at the extremity of this line, nearest Passage, close to Lumbard's Marsh,[a] there to protect the disembarkment of troops from the fleet.

Neither party failed in zeal or activity. The first days were actively employed in erecting works and bringing the canon to play upon / the town. On the third, in the very midst of their labours, while the Earl in his litter was carried close under the walls among the pioneers, and Lord Barry in his eagerness seized a spade and began to work, signals of attack were made from the town, and the troops poured out from the nearest gate. The advanced guard were too few to contend with them; they were driven back on the entrenchments. The citizens were full of fury and indignation; they rushed forward with loud cries, and created a confusion, which Desmond and Lord Barry were not slow to encounter; they brought a few regular troops to stand the assault; a well pointed cannon from the town swept the thin lines; they fell back; a yell of victory was raised by the men of Waterford; it reached the out-post of Duke Richard: he, with a score of men, five among them, with himself, being cavaliers armed at all points, were viewing a portion of the walls that seemed most open to assault; the roar of cannon and the clash of arms called him to more perilous occupation; he galloped towards the scene of action; and, while still the faltering / men of Desmond were ashamed to fly, yet dared not stand, he, with his little troop, attacked the enemy on their flank. The white steed, the nodding plume, the flashing sword of York were foremost in the fray; Neville and Plantagenet were close behind; these knights in their iron armour seemed to the half-disciplined Irish like invulnerable statues, machines to offend, impregnable to offence; twenty such might have turned the fortunes of a more desperate day: their antagonists fell back. The knight of Kerry[b] led on at this moment a reinforcement of Geraldines, and a cannon, which hitherto had been rebel to the cannoneer's art, opened its fiery mouth with such loud injurious speech, that for many moments the dread line it traced remained a blank. Richard saw the post of advantage, and endeavoured to throw himself between the enemy and

---

[a] About five miles from the city of Cork.
[b] Earl of Desmond.

the city: he did not succeed; but, on the contrary, was nearly cut off himself by a reinforcement of townsmen, sent to secure the retreat of their fellows. Those who saw him fight that day spoke of him as a wonder: the heart that had animated him / in Andulasia was awake; as there he smote to death the turbaned Moor; so now he dealt mortal blows on all around, fearless of the pressing throng and still encreasing numbers. While thus hurried away by martial enthusiasm, the sound of a distant trumpet caught his ear, and the echo of fire arms followed; it came from the east – his own post was attacked: now, when he wished to retreat, he first discerned how alone and how surrounded he was; yet, looking on his foes he saw, but for their numbers, how despicable they were; to a knight, what was this throng of half-armed burghers and naked kerns, who pell mell aimed at him, every blow ineffectual? But again the loud bellow of distant cannon called him, and he turned to retreat – a cloud of missiles rattled against him; his shield was struck through; the bullets re-bounded from his case of iron, while his sword felled an enemy at every stroke; and now, breaking through the opposing rank on the other side, his friends joined him – the citizens recoiled. "Old Reginald's tower,"[a] they averred, "would have bled sooner than these Sir Tristans[b] – they were charmed / men, and lead and good arrow-heads were softer than paper-pellets on their sides." The first movement of panic was enough; before their leaders could rally them again to the attack, the English knights were far, riding at full speed towards the eastern gate.

Here Richard's presence was enough to restore victory to his standard – flushed, panting, yet firm in his seat, his hand true and dangerous in its blows, there was something superhuman in his strength and courage, yet more fearful than his sharp sword. The excess of chivalrous ardour, the burning desire to mingle in the thickest fight, made danger happiness, and all the terrible shows of war entrancing joys to York. When reproached for rashness by his cousin, his bright eye was brighter for a tear, as he cried, "Cousin, I must have some part of my inheritance: my kingdom I shall never gain – glory – a deathless name – oh, must not these belong to him who possesses Katherine? The proud Scots, who looked askance at my nuptials, shall avow at least that she wedded no craven-hearted loon." /

With the morrow came a new task. Their little fleet had made its way up Waterford Harbour into the river Suir; and the troops destined to join his were partly disembarked. To protect the landing, he and Neville rode across the marsh to the strand. On their return a fresh sight presented itself – the ponds

---

[a] A large circular tower, once part of the city's walls, occupying the site of a tower built by Reginald the Dane in 1003.

[b] Tristan, valorous hero of medieval romance, healed of poisonous wounds by Isoud, daughter of an Irish king; they later drank a love potion intended for her and her betrothed, King Mark of Cornwall.

of Kilbarry[a] were filled, the besieged having raised a mound of earth to stop the course of the river which flows from Kilbarry into the Suir; and the road back to their camp was completely cut off. There was no mode of getting round save by the road to Tramore;[b] yet to the active mind of Richard, it seemed that even this disaster might be turned into a benefit. He reimbarked the troops; he himself went on board the principal vessel; he called to secret council the captains: – the conclusion was not immediately divulged, but some adventure of peril was assuredly planned among them.

The long summer day went slowly down; the hum of men from Waterford reached the ships; the quay was thronged with soldiers; several vessels were anchored in the advance, / and manned with troops; but the English fleet, their anchors cast, their sails furled, seemed peacefully inclined. As night came on, the quay became a desert; the ships were worked back to their former stations. It grew darker; the city, with its old rough tower and spires, was mirrored indistinctly in the twilight tide; the walls grew dim and gigantic; the sound of fire-arms ceased; the last roll of the drum died away; the city slept, fearless of its invaders. At this moment, the ebbing tide began to flow. Assisted by the rising waters, Richard and Neville ran a small boat under the cover of the opposite bank of the river, to observe what defences the quay might possess. The low tide at that hour was its best defence: a watch-tower or two with their centinels, completed the guard of a part of the town, whose defence on that side was neglected: by midnight also the tide would have risen, but it was necessary to wait for the following night; for first he must communicate with Desmond, that a night attack in the opposite direction might effectually leave the water-side deserted. The vessels meanwhile dropt / down below Little Island,[c] at once to get out of shot of Reginald's tower, which commands the harbour, and to remove from the citizens any apprehensions they might entertain of attack. The winding of the river concealed them entirely from the town.

The next day, a burning August day, declined into a dewy night; imperceptibly during the dark the vessels were nearer the city; and, while the warders of the city fancied that the troops on board the fleet were finding a circuitous path over land to Desmond's camp, the stars of night twinkled through the shrouds upon decks crowded with men, arming themselves in busy silence. Suddenly it was reported to Richard that a stranger caravel was among them; she was the only vessel with set sails, and these were enlarged by night, till as she neared, she seemed a giant, a living thing stalking between heaven and the element beneath. A sudden shiver convulsed the Prince; to his eye it was the likeness of that vessel which long ere this had traversed, he hoped in safety, the western sea, stemming its mountainous waves towards / the beauteous Indian Isles.

---

[a] A parish two miles south of Waterford.
[b] On the coast about seven miles south of Waterford.
[c] In the river Suir, two and a half miles below Waterford city.

Had it been wrecked, and this the spectre? It was the illusion of a moment; but it was necessary to ascertain the nature and intentions of the stranger, who was now close among them. York's vessel, at his command, got alongside of her; he leapt upon the deck, and saw at once him whom the dim night had concealed before, Hernan de Faro upon the deck.

A thousand emotions, wonder, fear, delight, rushed into the youth's heart; while the Mariner, yet more weather-beaten, thin to emaciation, but still erect, still breathing the same spirit of fortitude and kindliness, grasped his hand, and blessed the Virgin for the meeting. The questions, the anxiety of Richard, could not be uttered in this hour of action; he only said, "You will join us, and we will be doubly strong; or must you remain to guard your daughter?"

"I come from her – she is not with me – more of this anon."

Rapidly he asked and obtained information of the meditated attack; in part he disapproved, / and, with all the sagacity of a veteran in such enterprizes, suggested alterations. Now every boat was lowered with silent expedition, each received its freight of troops, and was rowed with the tide up the Suir. One skiff contained York and the Moor. The Prince, in the anticipation of the hazardous contest, looked serious; while every feature of De Faro's face was bright, his animated, glad smile, his flashing eyes – all spoke the exhilaration of one engaged in his elected pleasure. Richard had never seen him thus before: usually he appeared kind, almost deferential; yet, except when he talked of the sea, heavy and silent, and speaking of that in a subdued tone. He now stood the picture of a veteran hero, self-possessed and calm, but for the joyousness that the very feeling of his sword's weight, as his right hand grasped the hilt, imparted to his warlike spirit.

Had an angel, on poized wings of heavenly grain, hovered over the city of Waterford, gazing on its star-pointing spires, the reflecting waters of the Suir, the tranquil hills and woods / that gathered round the river, he would have believed such quiet inviolate, and blessed the sleep that hushed the miserable passions of humanity to repose. Anon there came the splash of waters, the shout of men, the sentinels' startled cry, the sudden rush of the guard, the clash of swords, the scream, the low groan, the protracted howl, and the fierce bark of the watch-dog joining in. The celestial angel has soared to heaven, scared; and yet honour, magnanimity, devotion filled the hearts of those who thus turned to hell a seeming paradise. Led by Richard and De Faro, while a party was left behind to ensure retreat, another rushed forward right through the town, to throw open the western gate, and admit Desmond, before the terrified citizens had exchanged their night-caps for helmets; in vain: already the market-place was filled with soldiers ready for the encounter; guided by a native, they endeavoured to find a way through the bye-streets; they lost themselves; they got entangled in narrow allies; the awakened citizens cast upon their heads tiles, blocks of wood, all they could / lay hands upon; to get back to the square was their only salvation; although the storm and yell that rose behind, assured them that Desmond had commenced the attack. With diminished numbers York regained the market-place; here he was furiously attacked; the crowd still increased, until the knot of assailants might have been crushed, it seemed, by mere numbers; day, bright day, with its golden clouds and swift pacing sun, dawned upon the scene. In one of those pauses which sometimes occur in the most chaotic roar, a trumpet was heard, sounding as it seemed Desmond's retreat from the walls. Richard felt that he was deserted, that all hope was over; and to secure the retreat of his men was a work of sufficient difficulty. Foot to foot the young hero and the veteran mariner fought; one by the quickness of his blows, the other by his tower-like strength, keeping back the enemy; while retreating slowly, their faces to the foe, they called on their men to make good their escape. They reached the quay – they saw the wide river, their refuge; their vessels near at hand, the boats hovering close, their safety was in sight, and yet hope of / safety died in their hearts, so many and so fierce were those who pressed on them. Richard was wounded, weary, faint; De Faro alone – Reginald's old tower, which, dark and scaithless, frowned on them, seemed his type. They were at the water's edge, and the high tide kissed with its waves the very footway of the quay: "Courage, my Lord, a few more blows and we are safe:" the mariner spoke thus, for he saw Richard totter; and his arm, raised feebly, fell again without a stroke. At that moment, a flame, and then a bellowing roar, announced that the tardy cannoneer had at last opened his battery on the fleet, from the tower. One glance De Faro cast on his caravel; the bolt had struck and damaged one of the vessels, but the Adalid escaped. "Courage, my Lord!" again he shouted; and at that moment a blow was struck at Richard which felled him; he lay stretched at De Faro's feet. Ere it could be repeated, the head of the assailant was cleft by a Moorish scymitar. With furious strength, De Faro then hurled his weapon among the soldiers; the unexpected act made them recoil; he lifted up the / insensible form of Richard with the power of an elephant; he cast him into the near waves, and leapt in after: raising him with one hand, he cut the waters with the other, and swam thus towards his vessel, pursued by a rain of missiles; one arrow glanced on Richard's unstrung helmet, another fixed itself in the joint at the neck; but De Faro was unhurt. He passed, swimming thus, the nearest vessels; the sailors crowded to the sides, imploring him to enter: as if it had been schoolboy's sport he refused, till he reached the Adalid, till his own men raised Richard, revived now, but feeble, to her worn deck: and he, on board her well-known planks, felt superior to every sovereign in the world. /

CHAPTER IV.

———

Farewell, Erin! farewell all
Who live to weep our fall!

MOORE.[a]

———

On the height of the tower of Ardmore, the White Rose of young Richard kept her vigils, and looked across the calm sea, and along the passes of the mountains of Drum,[b] in anxious expectation of the event of the expedition. Sad forebodings oppressed her; the sentiment that mastered every other, was that her lord should require her presence, her assistance, while she was far. He had promised to send a post each day; when these failed, her heart sank within her. The only change that occurred, was when she saw the Adalid proceed slowly in the calm towards Waterford. /

One sunny morn she from her watch-tower perceived several straggling groupes descending the mountains. She strained her eyes: no banners waved; no martial music spoke of victory. That was secondary in her eyes; it was for Richard's safety that she was solicitous; yet she would not, did not fear; for there is an instinctive sense in human nature which, in time of doubt, sallies forth from the ark of refuge, and brings back tidings of peace or sorrow to the expectant on the perilous flood; a prophetic spirit which, when it despairs – woe the while! – the omen proves not false. The Lady Katherine watched anxiously but not in despair. At length heavy footsteps ascended the tower-stairs; and, to answer the beatings of her heart, Edmund Plantagenet and the Mayor of Cork presented themselves; they eagerly asked, "Is he not here?"

"Nay, he has not fled?" she replied, while for the first time she grew pale.

"Weigh our words as mere air," said O'Water; "for we know nothing, gentle dame, but that I must to Cork, to bar out the men of Waterford. His Highness left us for the fleet; and the filling / up of those cursed ponds of Kilbarry – ill luck to them! – cut off his return. Last night – Saint Patrick knows the deeds of

———

[a] Thomas Moore, 'Where is the Slave', ll. 11–12, *Irish Melodies*, no. 6.
[b] She gazes toward Waterford, about thirty-three miles east-north-east.

287

the last night! – weary from our labour the day before, we were all too carelessly asleep, when our camp was assaulted. Earl Maurice had ridden to Lismore[a] to hasten his cousin, the Knight of the Valley. There was some report of an attack upon the town from the ships. Havock was the cry that roused the welkin from east to west. The sum I know not, save that we are runaways – the siege of Waterford is raised."

"What skiff is that?" interrupted the Duchess. Round the point of Mine-head[b] first peeped the bowsprit, then the prow; and last the complete form of a vessel in full sail, yet scarcely touched by the wind, weathered the promontory. "Haste we, my friends," she continued; "the Duke may be on board; at least we shall have intelligence."

"I know that craft full well," said O'Water; "her captain is a converted Moorish pagan."

"The White Rose waves from her mast-top," cried Katherine; "oh, he is there!" /

"Holy angels!" exclaimed Edmund; "it is the Adalid! I will on board on the instant."

Already the Duchess was descending the steep narrow stairs; the villagers of Ardmore, with many of the soldiers who had fled from Waterford, were on the shingles, watching the caravel, now full in sight, yet fearful to venture too near the shelving shore. "They are bound for Cork," cried a man.

"Oh, not till I first speak to them," said Katherine; "the day is fair; the sea calm; put off a boat. Ah, my cousin Edmund, take me with thee."

Plantagenet had already got a boat from its moorings. O'Water was beside the Princess to beseech vainly that she would be patient; and poor Astley, who had been left in special attendance on her, waited near with blanched cheeks. Accompanied by these dear or humble friends, the White Rose was borne with the speed of ten oars towards the Adalid. On the deck, half reclining on a rude bed, very pale, yet with lively, wakeful eyes, lay the Prince of England. In a moment Katherine was assisted on board. / There was no death for Richard; she was there, life of his life; so young, so beautiful, and true; the celestial goodness that beamed in her eyes, and dimpled her cherub countenance, was not like that of an inhabitant of this sad planet; except that spirits of beauty and love ever and anon *do* animate the frames of the earth-born; so that we behold in the aspects of our fellow-beings glances and smiles bright as those of angels. De Faro himself looked with admiration on the bending form of this lovely one, till accosted by Edmund, whose first question was, "Don Hernan here – where then is ——"

"My beloved Monina you would ask for," said De Faro; "she, who to please her vagrant father, would have crossed the wild Atlantic to visit the savage

---

[a] About fifteen miles north-north-west of Ardmore, away from the coast.
[b] About seven miles north-north-east of Ardmore, on the Waterford coast.

Western Isles. Poor child, even at the threshold of this adventure we were nearly wrecked. She is now in England; she sent me here – to tell of rebellion against King Henry; to invite Duke Richard to his kingdom."

Thus they were occupied on the sunny deck; the sea was calm, the keel almost stationary in / the water; they were bound for Cork; Plantagenet and the Mayor gathered eagerly from De Faro the history of the combat. They learned that it had been expected that Desmond would have assaulted from land, while York invaded the city from the river; but the fellow sent with Richard's missive had been taken, the city put on her guard. Nothing but the desire of the citizens to do too much, and his own desperate valour, had saved Richard; they resolved at once to receive and destroy him, and to sally unawares on the Earl's camp: they hoped to make prisoners of all the chiefs. They failed in this, but succeeded in raising the seige of their city.

Towards evening a land-breeze sprung up, and two others of York's vessels hove in sight, and passed them quickly; for the Adalid was much disabled, and made slow way. Soon in pursuit appeared a ship and two corvettes, which O'Water recognized as belonging to Waterford. The corvettes proceeded on their way; but the larger vessel spied out the Adalid, and, being now in advance of her, hove to, with the / manifest resolve of attacking her on her watery way towards Cork. De Faro, with his keen eyes fixed on the enemy's movements, stood on the forecastle in silence; while Plantagenet and O'Water eagerly demanded arms, and exhorted the sailors to a most vain resistance. From the vessel of the foe the Moorish mariner cast his eyes upwards; the wind was shifting to the west. With a loud voice he shouted to his crew to man the yards; then, seizing the rudder, gave the swift orders that made the caravel go about. Sailing near the wind, her canvas had flapped lazily, now it filled; the keel felt the impulse, and dashed merrily along, bounding forward like a courser in the race; the ship, which had furled its sails in expectation of the combat, was in an instant left far behind; the other vessels from Waterford were still further to the west, towards Cork.

All these manœuvres were mysteries to the landsmen: they gladly hailed the distance placed between them and a superior enemy; but as with a freshening gale the Adalid still held her swift course towards the east, and the land / began to sink on the horizon, O'Water asked with some eagerness whither they were bound.

"To safety," De Faro replied, laconically.

"An idle answer," said Edmund; "we must judge where our safety lies?"

"I have ever found best safety on the wide ocean sea," cried the mariner, looking round proudly on his beloved element. "Your safeties and your Lord's, are, methinks, English born; if this wind hold, on the third morning we shall see the coast of Cornwall."

The mayor was aghast, exclaiming – "Cornwall! England! we are betrayed?"

De Faro looked on him with contempt: – "I do not command here," he continued; "I obey the Prince of England; let him decide. Shall we engage superior force; be boarded; taken by the enemy: or land, be wrecked, perchance, upon this savage coast; alive with vengeful kerns – defeated men among a victorious angry people? Or go where we are called by your leader's cause, where thousands of men are up in arms to receive you like brothers, to fight for / you, with you; where England, the long desired kingdom, makes you welcome to her green, sunny shores? Ask ye your Prince this question; let his word be law."

This statement, upheld by York, brought conviction to the minds of Plantagenet and O'Water. The latter was aware of the risk he ran from the awakened vengeance of Henry, to pursue his having fostered rebellion in the city of which he was magistrate; and a moment's reflection showed him that there was no security for him, except in flight from Ireland. Meanwhile the wind, increasing in its strength, and right astern, carried them over the foaming waters. The early dawn showed them far at sea: they had outrun or baffled their pursuers; and, though, now and then, with anxious thought, they reflected on the comrades left behind, on the poor equipage and diminished numbers with which they were about to land in England, still there was something so miraculous in their escape, so unforeseen in the destiny that cut them off, and carried them, a remnant merely of the war, away from its dangers, that they felt / as if they were under the immediate direction of a ruling Providence, and so resigned themselves; greedily drinking in the while the highly coloured picture De Faro painted of the Yorkist army which awaited them in Cornwall.

Again upon the sea – again impelled by winds and waves to new scenes – new hopes, tost here and there by Fortune, it was Richard's fate to see one frustrated expectation give place to another, which, in its turn, faded and died. This constant succession of projects kept alive within him that sanguine spirit which never could be vanquished. Eagerly he passed from one idea to another, and almost welcomed the last disaster, which appeared but to pioneer the way to future success. During this voyage, weak as his wounds had made him, he talked of England as his own – the dearer, because he must spend his blood to win it. Circumstances had an exactly contrary effect upon Katherine. The continual change of schemes convinced her of the futility of all. She felt that, if the first appearance of the Duke of York, acknowledged and upheld by various sovereigns and dear high-born / relatives, had not animated the party of the White Rose in his favour, it was not now, after many defeats and humiliations on his side, and after triumphs and arrogant assumptions on that of his enemy, that brilliant success could be expected. This conviction must soon become general among the Yorkists, Richard would learn the sad lesson, but she was there to deprive it of its sting; to prove to him, that tranquillity and Katherine were of more worth than struggles, even if they proved successful, for vain power.

It was strange that a girl of royal birth, bred in a palace, accustomed to a queen-like sovereignty over her father's numerous vassals in the Highlands, should aim at restricting the ambitious York to mere privacy; while Monina, the humble daughter of a Moorish mariner, would have felt honour, reputation, all that is dear to man, at stake, if her friend had dreamed of renouncing his claims to the English crown. His cause was her life; his royalty the main spring of all her actions and thoughts. She had sacrificed love to it – she taught her / woman's soul to rejoice in his marriage with another, because his union with a princess was pledge to the world of his truth. Perhaps, had the time ever come when he renounced his struggles, she had felt with a pang that his lowly fortunes might not incongruously be shared by her, and self had mingled in the religion of her heart, which was virtuous devotion to him; but as it was, the idea never presented itself. He must win, or die. Did he win, her happiness would result from the contemplation of his glory; were he to die, the young hero's grave would not be watered by her tears: she believed that in that hour her life would cease.

The Lady Katherine saw a vain mask in all the common-place pomp of palaces; she perceived that power failed most, when its end was good; she saw that in accomplishing its purpose in the cottage, or in halls of state, felicity resulted from the affections only. It was but being an actor in different scenes, to be a potentate or a peasant; the outward garb is not the livery of the mind: the refinement of taste, which enables us to gather pleasure from / simple objects; the warmth of heart which necessitates the exercise of our affections, but which is content when they are satisfied; these, to her mind, were the only, but they were the complete ingredients of happiness; and it was rarer to find, and more difficult to retain them, among false-hearted, ambitious courtiers, and the luxury of palaces, than among simple-minded peasantry, and a plain natural style of living. There was some romance in this idea; Katherine felt that there was, and subdued herself not to lay too much store by any change or guise of outward circumstance. She taught herself to feel and know, that in the tumult of camps and war, in the anxieties of her present vagrant life, on the throne which she might possess, or in the prison she might share; by devoting herself to the happiness of him to whom she was united, whose heroism, goodness and love merited all her affection, she was performing the part assigned to her on earth, and securing a portion of happiness, far beyond the common lot of those whose colder harder natures require something beyond sympathy to constitute their misnamed felicity. /

CHAPTER V.

————

From Ireland thus comes York to claim his right.
If I am not ashamed of my soldiers, I am a soused gurnet.
                                                    SHAKSPEARE.[a]

————

On the deck of the sea-worn Adalid, watching the renovated strength, and attending on the still remaining weakness of her lord, the soft heart of the Princess possessed to fulness all its desires; while Monina, among the wild rude Cornish rebels, exerted herself, to inspire zeal for his cause, and to increase the number of his partisans, winning them by her thrilling eloquence, ruling them by her beauty and enthusiasm. She had found the whole population ready to second him; but fitting leaders, noble and influential men, were absolutely wanting. She / sent her father to urge Richard to this new attempt, and when he should appear, attended, as she fondly hoped, by a train of high-born Irish lords, of gallant Scotch cavaliers, and devoted English warriors; he would be able to give a martial form to the rout of Cornish insurgents, to discipline their wild, untamed valour, to attract others by name and rank, and Tudor at last must grow pale upon his throne. With eagerness she awaited the fleet that was to bring the chosen band of heroes; when, after a long and calm voyage, on the third of September, the Adalid ran into White Sand Bay, on the western coast of Cornwall, and Plantagenet, at Richard's command, disembarked and proceeded forthwith to Bodmin.[b]

It was strange that the chief partizan of the White Rose should, on his invasion of the island, find a Spanish girl the main source of information – the chief mover of the rebellion by which he was to profit. Yet Plantaganet almost forgot his mortal struggle for a kingdom, in the anticipation of seeing Monina.

————

[a] *2 Henry VI*, V. i. 1 (first line); *1 Henry IV*, IV. ii. 11–12 (second line).

[b] '1497' (marginal note in *Abinger/Palacio*). On September 7 (according to modern accounts), Warbeck sailed into Whitsand Bay on the eastern (not western) side of Cornwall's south coast. He then proceeded to Bodmin about twenty-three miles west-north-west, where he picked up the main road stretching from London to Lands End, at England's south-western tip. His forces grew as he marched north-east to Exeter, Devonshire, fifty-five miles closer to the capital.

Plantagenet, prouder, more ambitious for his cousin, than Richard for himself – Plantagenet, who / had but one object to be the guardian, supporter, defender of York, now wandered in thought far back through many years to their Spanish home; to his tenderness for the sweet child of Madeline; to the developement of the beauty and virtues of the lovely Moor. Thrown apart by their several destinies, he had scarcely seen her since then; and now, in place of the dark, laughing-eyed girl, he beheld a woman, bright with intelligence and sensibility; whose brow wore somewhat the sad trace of suffering, whose cheek was a little sunk, but in whose eyes there was a soul, in whose smile an enchantment not to be resisted. She was all life, vivacity, and yet softness: all passion, yet yielding and docile. Her purpose was steady, stubborn; but the mode of its attainment, her conduct, she easily permitted to be guided. Edmund scarcely recognized her, but she instantly knew him; her elder brother, her kind but serious guardian, whom she had loved with awe, as the wisest and best of men. Now he bore a dearer name, as the unfailing friend of him she loved. To both their hearts this meeting was an unexpected joy. / Monina had thought too much of Richard, to remember his cousin. He had half forgotten his own sensations; or, at least, was quite unprepared for the power and effect of her surpassing beauty.

After the first overflowing of affection, Monina eagerly detailed the forces raised, and dwelt on the spirit and courage of the insurgents. "They are poor fellows," she said, "but true; burning with zeal to right themselves, and to avenge their losses at Blackheath. They are gathered together by thousands. They want merely leaders, discipline, arms, money, ammunition, and a few regular troops to show them the way: these, of course, you bring."

"Alas! no," said Edmund, "we bring merely ourselves."

"Could Ireland, then, furnish no warlike stores?" continued the zealous girl. "But this can be remedied, doubtless. Yourself, your leader, Lord Desmond, Lord Barry, the gallant Neville; tell me who else – who from Burgundy – what Irish, what Scottish knights?"

The last word was said with difficulty: it / made a pause in her rapid utterance; while Edmund, aghast, replied, "Indeed! none of all these, or very few: in a word, we have fled from Waterford in the Adalid. His Highness and myself are the sole English knights. The good old Mayor of Cork must represent all Ireland, gentle and simple, to your eyes – our fair Duchess, Scotland: her attendants will follow in due time, but these are but needy servitors." Monina laughed. "We came to seek, not bring aid," continued Plantagenet gravely.

"Do not be angry," replied Monina. "There is more bitterness and sorrow in my laugh, than in, methinks, a widow's tears. My dear friend, God send we are not utterly lost. Yet his Highness and yourself may work wonders. Only report truly our state, that the Duke be not too dissatisfied with our appearance. Tell him Lord Audley headed a worse organized troop: tell him that Master Heron, the mercer, has no silken soul – that Master Skelton, the taylor, disdains a smaller needle than a cloth-yard shaft."ᵃ /

"And is it to head men like these we have been drawn from our Irish friends?" cried Edmund; "better return. Alas! our path is besieged; the very sea is subject to our enemy; in the wide world the King of England has no refuge."

"That he is King of England," said Monina, "let not him, let none of us forget. The very name is powerful: let him, on his native shores, assume it. Surely, if their liege King stand singly in the land of his forefathers, at his sacred name thousands will congregate. He has dared too little, when he had power: at the worst, even now, let him dare all, and triumph."

Her bold, impetuous language had its effect on Edmund: it echoed his own master passion, which ever cried aloud, "He is a King! and, once give himself that sacred name, submission and allegiance from his subjects must follow." Buoyed up by these thoughts, his report on board the Adalid was free from those humiliating details, which, even if he had wished, he would have found no voice to communicate to his royal cousin. /

Monina's task of imparting to her friends the destitute condition in which their sovereign arrived, was even easier, "He is come among tall men," said the pompous Heron, "who can uphold him for the better king, even to the satin of his doublet."

"And fight for him, even to the rending of our own," cried Skelton.

"And die for him, as he must too, when all's done," said Trereife. "A soldier's death is better than a dastard's life."

"We will have out our men in goodly array," said Heron. "Master Skelton, are the doublets cut from that piece of sad-coloured velvet, last of my wares, slashed with white, as I directed?"

"Slash me no doublets but with a Spanish rapier," squeaked Skelton, "Have I not cast away the shears? Yet, look you now, good lack! I lie. Here in my pouch be a sharp pair, to clip Master Walter of Hornbeck'sᵇ ears – if by the help of the saints we can lay him as flat on the field as his own grey suit was on my board when / a shaping; by the same token that he never paid for it."

"In good hour, Sir Taylor," said Monina: "but the talk now is, how duly to receive his Grace, how induce him to accept your aid."

"Aye, by Saint Dunstan!"ᶜ cried Trereife, "he has ruffled in France and Burgundy, my masters, and will look on you as clowns and base-born burghers; but no man has more to give than his life, and if he waste that heartily, time was

---

ᵃ The chronicles mention John Heron, Richard Skelton, and John Astley (see p. 199 and n); Trereife, Mary Shelley's invention, completes the quartet. Like Ford, she deploys these inept groundlings for comic effect.

ᵇ Probably Hornbach, in Germany.

ᶜ St Dunstan (d. 988), celebrated abbot, royal adviser, and Archbishop of Canterbury, had been educated by Irish monks.

and time may be when villains trod on the necks of knights, as the ghost of Charles of Burgundy could tell us. Courage is the beginning and end of a soldier's catechism."

Such were the chiefs Monina found desirous, and in their own conceit capable, of placing England's diadem on Duke Richard's head. Heron, the bankrupt mercer, who fancied himself the base-born offspring of the late Earl of Devonshire, and whose first deed of arms would find him Heron no more, but Sir John Courtney;[a] Skelton, a luckless wight, whose shears ever / went astray, (the true cause why Walter of Hornbeck paid not for his misshapen suit,) and who, therefore, believed himself born for greater things; and Tre-reife, the younger prodigal son of a rural franklin, who, cast off and disinher-ited, had served in the wars in Flanders, gaining in that country no small reverence for the good Duchess Margaret, and ready therefore to right her nephew; besides, like a true hero, he abhorred this silken time of peace, and hoped to gather spoil, if not laurels, in the meditated insurrection.

The noble passengers disembarked from the Adalid. "Welcome to England, sweet Kate! welcome to the country of which thou art Queen," said York; "and even if her reception be cold or rough, love her for my sake, for she is my mother."

"A step-mother I will not call her, dear my Lord," replied the Princess, "but the maternal embrace is strangely wanting on these deserted sands: the narrow deck of yonder caravel were, methinks, a kindlier home: may we go on and prosper; but, if we fail, my Lord will pardon / me, if I welcome the day when I embark again on board the Adalid; to find, when the wide earth proves false, safety and happiness on the free waves of ocean." /

---

[a] Heron was on the wrong side. Edward Courteney (d. 1509) was created Earl of Devonshire after Bosworth and fought against Warbeck in 1497, as did his son William (d. 1512).

CHAPTER VI.

————

SKELTON. 'Tis but going to sea and leaping ashore, cut ten or twelve thousand unnecessary throats, fire seven or eight towns, take half a dozen cities, get into the market-place, crown him Richard the Fourth, and the business is finished.

FORD.[a]

Am I not king?
Awake, thou coward Majesty! thou sleepest.
Is not the King's name forty thousand names?

SHAKSPEARE.[b]

————

These doughty leaders drew out their followers in a plain just without Bodmin. There were about two hundred men decently clad from the remnants of the mercer's wares, tolerably well armed and disciplined by Trereife; this troop obtained the distinction of being / selected as King Richard's body guard. Skelton was their captain, a rare commander, whose real merit was that he felt happiest when stuck close as a burr to Trereife; for at heart he was an errant coward, though a loud braggart, and talked of slaying his thousands, while the very wounding of his doublet had made him wince.

Heron was brave in his way; a true Cornishman, he could wrestle and cast his antagonist with the strength of a lion; he loved better, it is true, to trust to his arm than to his sword, which, in spite of his strength, Trereife always made fly from his hand in their fencing lessons: not the less did he consider himself a gallant knight, and had cut up many a yard of crimson cramoisy[c] to make a rich suit for himself. He wore Monina's glove in his cap and large yellow roses at his knees; he called himself generalissimo, and marshalled under him full three thousand men, who in truth had

————

[a] *Perkin Warbeck*, IV. ii. 61–6.
[b] *Richard II*, III. ii. 83–5.
[c] crimson cramoisy, the substantive alone means crimson cloth.

> never set a squadron in the field
> Nor the division of a battle knew
> More than a spinster;[a] /

but they were sturdy discontented spirits, who valued life at its worth, which was even nothing to them, who had laboured with all their hearts, till labour was of no avail, and who then left the mine and the furrow to carry their loud complaints to the foot of Henry's throne – they were better pleased with the prospect of overthrowing it.

"Now, my masters, make yourselves heard," cried Heron, as he shuffled down a little eminence on a short-legged Welch pony, the only steed he found he could back in safety. "His Grace is within ear-shot, so you be loud. Long life to King Richard! – down with the taxes – Saint Michael and Cornwall for ever!"[b]

The din was prolonged, ended, began, went on, as the Prince arrived at the summit of the hill with his little train – Fair Katherine was at his side. Plantagenet, O'Water, De Faro, with some dozen soldiers who fled from Waterford; sure never invader came so ill equipped. On the hill-top the illustrious wanderers paused. Richard hastily scanned the rough-suited multitude – then, turning to Plantagenet, "Cousin," / he said, "You told me that the insurgent army would be drawn out for my view; is it not strange that yonder rabble should hide it from us? As far as my eye can reach, I see no martial discipline, no banners, no lordly crest; fie on those drums! they have no touch of military concord. What makes our army so slack of duty, Cousin?"

Though no fault of his, Edmund blushed deeply in very shame – the approach of Heron, Skelton, Trereife, and three or four other principal rebels, cut off his reply. It had been agreed that Skelton, who had a gift of eloquence, should speak, and many words he used to welcome his liege – "We will have every man with a Red Rose in his cap, in a drag chain, please your Grace, and give a sound lesson to the saucy burghers of Exeter withall. Not a knight shall live in the land, but of your Majesty's dubbing. We have but to put to rout King Henry's army, to hang the false loon for a traitor, and to set fire to London and the Parliament. Such nobles as please to doff their silken cloaks, and don miners' jackets, may work, the rest shall / hang. Their mere wardrobes, bless the day! will find us and your Grace in cloth of gold, embroidery, and other rich garniture to the end of our lives."

"We thank your zeal, my worthy master," said Richard, courteously, "if our good troops do half your saying, King Henry must look to it."

"Are those men to be worse than their word?" cried Skelton. "There is not one among us but has the arms of ten. We are of a race of giants, please your

---

[a] Shakespeare, *Othello*, I. i. 22–4 (loosely quoted).
[b] The Archangel Michael, Cornwall's patron saint.

297

Majesty, and could knock the walls of Exeter down with our fists. Please you to enter Bodmin, whose very stones will cry for King Richard louder than King Hal's cannon; – to-morrow, God willing, we are for the wars."

The royal party passed on – the dark ferocity or sturdy obstinacy painted on the faces of the ill-armed rout, struck Richard as he passed – he became meditative, while Edmund, shamed and angry, his cheeks burning, his eyes on the ground, listened in indignant silence to Master Skelton, who fastened on him with such talk, / that whether a soldier spoke of killing doublets, or a tailor prattled of fashioning a field of slaughter, was a riddle ill to be devised. At length they passed the gates of Bodmin; and here was a louder cry of welcome from the shrill voices of women, who held up their thin hands and half-starved children, crying for vengeance on Tudor, blessing the sweet faces of Richard and his lovely wife. York's eyes flashed again with their wonted fires; his creative spirit had found materials here to work some project, all poor and rude as they might seem.

They entered the town-hall; when, by some sudden revulsion in the tide of the crowd, every Cornishman fell back, closed the doors, and left the wanderers alone. Something was forgotten surely; for Heron had paced pompously up to Richard, when suddenly he turned on his heel, crying, "A word, my masters!" and all were gone. The Lady Katherine had marked their backing and hurrying with becoming gravity; but, when the door was fairly shut, she could restrain no longer a heart-felt laugh. Richard joined in her mirth, while Plantagenet / strode through the hall angrily; muttering, "an army – a rout of shirtless beggars; is this England's reception for her King?"

"It were fine mumming," said Richard, "under a hedge with the green sward for a stage."

"By our Lady, this passes patience!" reiterated Edmund, "where are the gentlemen of England? Where the sons of those who fell for York? Are we to oppose these half-naked knaves to the chivalry of Henry?"

"It would seem that such is expected," replied the Prince; "and, verily, Cousin, we might do worse. I pray you, treat the honest rogues well; better may come of it; keep we our secret, and have we not an army?"

"My Lord!" cried Plantagenet, in wonder.

"Patience, dear friend," said York; "I have not been apprentice to adversity so many long years, without becoming an adept in my calling. I say, I have an army; bold, though poor – ragged truly, but exceeding faithful. Methinks it were more glorious to put Tudor down with such small means, than to meet him in / equal terms, like a vulgar conqueror. I do beseech you, Edmund, put a good face on it; speak to our Cornish giants, as if they had souls of mettle, and bodies decked like Ponce de Leon and his peers, when they welcomed Queen Isabel to the Spanish camp. You remember the golden array of the knights, Cousin?"

Edmund was impatient of the Prince's gay humour; while Katherine, seeing in his bright eyes heroism and lofty resolve, felt a dewy moisture gather in her own: there is something at once awful and affecting, when a man, the sport of fortune, meets her rudest blow unshrinking, and turns her very spite into arms against herself. The whole secret of Richard's present thoughts she could not divine, but she saw that their scope was worthy of his birth, his aim; her respect – her love augmented; and her gentle heart at that moment renewed its vow to devote herself to him entirely and for ever.

In the same spirit, York answered the deputation that waited on him. He commanded a proclamation to be made, in which he assumed / the title of Richard the Fourth. He announced his intention of immediately penetrating England, and seizing on some walled town or city, before Henry could be aware of his having landed. Nor did he confine his energy to words: he examined the state of his men; their arms and furniture; he provided for their better discipline, and animated his cousin to take an active part in marshalling them to order. He went among them, learned the causes of their dissatisfaction, promised them better days, and so raised a glad spirit in them, that their hearts overleaping both time and circumstance, paid him the honour and the love he might have claimed, had he already led them through fertile England, and planted his victorious standard on the Tower of London. Trereife swore by his beard, he was a proper youth; the old soldier awoke to the remembrance of harvests of spoil he had gathered in the Netherlands, the stern encounters and the joys of success; he gazed on the rough Cornish men, and wondered how they should withstand the nobility of England: but, when Richard glanced hope and / triumph from his bright eyes, when he spoke of the omnipotence of resolved valour, when he drew a picture of their ghastly poverty, and showed them how, by standing firm merely, they might redeem themselves; – while the poor fellows answered with a prolonged shout, or better still, grasped their arms more fiercely, and trod the earth with free and decided steps; – a thousand facilities seemed to be discovered; a thousand resources for the war displayed, undreamt of before. Were these mere words? or at his voice did soldiers rise from the clods, and victory obey the sound?

Plantagenet, seeing his royal Cousin's resolve, strove to second it. With a party of men he assaulted a near fortress, carried it, and seized on a store of arms. This success looked like a mighty victory; Richard exalted it as such; and the very fellows who handled awkwardly their booty, fancied themselves heroes at the mere sight of it.

On the third day they were to proceed to Exeter, it being determined that they should besiege this city. De Faro offered to sail to Cork to / invite the warlike chieftains of Munster to come over with their power; and at least himself to bring back in the Adalid, Neville, and the rest of the English exiles. While Edmund, who looked glad at the thought, counselled that they should entrench themselves in this corner of England, which was so entirely devoted to them, till these forces were added to their number, and till by discipline, they should have made regular troops of the rabble, by courtesy y'cleped an army.

"Wherefore, Cousin," asked Richard, "do you desire others to share in our disasters?"

"My Lord!" cried Edmund, astounded.

"I have but one wish," continued the Prince, "that you and my good O'Water were even now in Ireland; so that I might stand the brunt of this war alone. You look amazed. Yet it were more amazing if I expected to do battle against the Veres, the Howards, the Berkeleys, the Courtneys, and ten thousand other names of high renown, backed by their train of martial adherents, with ragged regiments like those we are about to lead to the field; – even though the kerns of Ireland made their number double, / and the Geraldines, Barry and Neville added by their nobleness dignity to our victor's conquest. Remember Stoke, my cousin Edmund; you may well remember it. Remember my honoured kinsman the Earl of Lincoln and my lamented Lovel. Ah, that I did not now peril your life, then spared!"

"Yet, if your Grace fight at all," said O'Water, bluntly; "methinks we were not the worse for being better appointed for the fray. For victims, even those poor honest varlets are too many."

"That one other life should be wasted for me," replied Richard fervently, "is my saddest thought. I fear it must be so; some few lives, each as dear to him that spends it, as is the life-blood to our own hearts. I can say no more. I have a secret purpose, I confess, in all I do. To accomplish it – and I do believe it to be a just one – I must strike one blow; nor fail. Tudor is yet unprepared; Exeter vacant of garrison; with stout hearts for the work, I trust to be able to seize that city. There the wars of York shall end. So far I confide in your discretions, / that you may not deem me mad. More is the single property of my own soul. Will you help me so far, dear friends – so far hazard life – not to conquer a kingdom for Richard, but to redeem his honour?"

The warm-hearted, grey-headed Irish O'Water, with gushing eyes, swore to adhere to him to the last.

Edmund replied, "I am but a bit of thee; deal with me as with thyself; and I know thou wilt be no niggard in giving me away to danger."

De Faro cried, "I am a sailor, and know better how to face death on the waves than victory on shore; but Santiago![a] may our blessed Lady herself look shy on me at the great day, if the Mariner of the Wreck prove false to your Grace."

"Now then to our work," cried York, "to speak fair to my faithful fellows and their braggart leaders. They at least shall be winners in our game; for my hand is on my prize; a spirit has whispered success to me; my hope and its consummation are married even at their birth." /

---

[a] Santiago, 'St James'.

CHAPTER VII.

Dost thou hear, lady?
If from the field I shall return once more
To kiss these lips, I will appear in blood;
I and my sword will earn our chronicle;
There is hope in it yet.

SHAKSPEARE.[a]

Richard was obliged to plead his cause yet once again. Katherine had watched all his movements; she had eyed curiously the army he mustered to the field; she talked to its leaders, and while they vaunted her affability, she was diving with earnest mind, into the truth of things. No fear that it could be hid from her; love for Richard was the bright light that dispelled every deceptive shadow from the scene. She saw the bare reality; some three thousand / poor peasants and mechanics, whose swords were more apt to cut themselves than strike the enemy, were arrayed against the whole power and majesty of England. On the morrow they were to set forward. That night, while at the casement of his rude chamber, Richard gazed upon the congregated stars, trying to decipher in their intricate bright tracery the sure omen of the good he was told they charactered for him, Katherine, after a moment's hesitation, with a quivering voice, and hand that shook as it pressed his, knelt on a cushion at his feet, saying, "My sweet Richard, hear me; hear your faithful friend – your true wife; call not my councils weak and feminine, but weigh them sagely ere you resolve. May I speak?"

"Lady of my heart, arise," said Richard; "speak my soft-voiced Katherine – my White Rose of beauty – fair flower, crowning York's withered tree. Has not God done all in giving you to me; yet we must part, love, for awhile. Your soldier is for the wars, Kate, while you sit in your bower, weaving victorious garlands for his return." /

"My ever dear Lord," said Katherine, "I speak with fear, because I feel that

----

[a] *Antony and Cleopatra*, III. xiii. 172–6.

I shall not address myself to your concealed thought. I do not wish to penetrate your secrets, and yet I tremble at their event. You have not so far deceived yourself as to imagine, that with these unfortunate men, you can ride over the pride and the power of this island; did I see on what else you founded the lofty hope, that has, since we came here, beamed in your eyes, I would resign myself to your better wisdom. But, wherever I turn my view, there is a blank. You do not dream of conquest, though you feel secure of victory. What can this mean, save that you see glory in death?"

"You are too quick-sighted, sweet Kate," said Richard, "and see beyond the mark. I do not set my cast upon falling in this fray; though it may well happen that I should: but I have another aim."

"Without guessing at what that may be," replied the lady, "since you seem desirous to withhold the knowledge, permit me to present another object to your choice; decide between / them, and I submit: but do not carelessly turn from mine. There is all to lose, nought to win, in what you now do. Death may blot the future page, so that we read neither disgrace or prison in its sad lines; but wherefore risk to die. While yet, dear love, we are young, life has a thousand charms, and one may be the miserable survivor, whose heart now bleeds at the mere surmise."

She faltered; he kissed her soft cheek, and pressed her to his heart. "Why may we not – why should we not live?" continued Katherine; "what is there in the name or state of king, that should so take captive our thoughts, that we can imagine no life but on a throne? Believe me, careful nights and thorny days are the portion of a monarch: he is lifted to that awful height only to view more clearly destruction beneath; around, fear, hate, disloyalty, all yelling at him. The cold, heartless Tudor may well desire the prize, for he has nothing save the gilt crown to ennoble him; nothing but the supple knees of courtiers to present to him the show of love. But – ah! could I put fire into / my weak words – my heart's zeal into my supplicatory voice – persuasion would attend upon me, and you would feel that to the young, to two united as we are, our best kingdom is each other's hearts; our dearest power that which each, without let or envy, exercises over the other. Though our palace roof be the rafters of a lowly cot, our state, the dear affection we bear each other, our attendants the duty and observance of one to the other – I, so served by King Edward's son – you, by the rightful queen of this fair island – were better waited on than Henry and Elizabeth, by their less noble servitors. I almost think that, with words like these, I might draw you from the uneasy throne to the downy paradise of love; and can I not from this hard struggle, while death yet guards the palace gate, and you will be pierced through and through long ere you can enter?"[22]

"Thus, my gentle love," said Richard, "you would have me renounce my birth and name; you desire that we become the scorn of the world, and would be content that so dishonoured, the braggart impostor, and his dame / Katherine, should spend their shameful days in an ignominious sloth, misnamed tranquillity. I am a king, lady, though no holy oil nor jewelled crown has touched this head; and such I must prove myself."

"Oh, doubt it not," she replied, "it is proved by your own speech and your own nobleness; my heart approves you such; the whole earth, till its latest day, will avouch that the lord of Katherine is no deceiver; but my words avail not with you."

"They do avail, my best, my angel girl, to show me that the world's treasure is mere dross compared with thee: one only thing I prize, not as thy equal, but as that without which, I were a casket not even worthy to encase this jewel of the earth – my honour! A word taught me by my victim brother, by my noble cousin Lincoln, by the generous Plantagenet; I learnt its meaning among a race of heroes – the Christian cavaliers – the Moorish chivalry of Spain; dear is it to me, since without it I would not partake your home of love – an home, more glorious and more blessed than the throne of the universe. / It is for that I now fight, Katherine; not for a kingdom; which, as thy royal Cousin truly said, never will be mine. If I fall, that Cousin, the great, the munificent James, will be your refuge."

"Never," interrupted the lady, "Scotland I shall never see again; never show myself, a queen and no queen, the mock of their rude speech; never put myself into my dear, but ambitious father's hands, to be bartered away to another than my Richard; rather with your aunt of Burgundy, rather in Tudor's own court, with your fair sister. Holy angels! of what do I speak? how frightfully distinct has the bereft world spread itself out as my widowed abode!"

A gush of tears closed her speech. "Think of brighter days, my love," said Richard, "they will be ours. You spoke erewhile of the difficulty of giving true imagery to the living thought; thus, I know not how to shape an appropriate garb (to use a trope of my friend Skelton) for my inmost thoughts. I feel sure of success. I feel, that in giving up every prospect / of acquiring my birth-right, I make the due oblation to fortune, and that she will bestow the rest – that rest is to rescue my name from the foul slur Henry has cast on it; to establish myself as myself in the eyes of England; and then to solicit your patience in our calamity – your truth and love as the only sceptre and glove this hand will ever grasp. In my own Spain, among the orange and myrtle groves, the flowery plains and sun-lit hills of Andalusia, we will live unambitious, yet more fortunate than crowned emperors."

With such words and promises he soothed her fears; to the word honour she had no reply. Yet it was a mere word here; in this case, a barren word, on which her life and happiness were to be wrecked.

The Prince and Monina had met with undisguised delight. No Clifford would now dare traduce her; she need not banish herself from countries where his name enriched the speech of all men; nor even from that which, invited by her, he had come to conquer. He was glad to be able to extend his zealous fraternal protection / over her, to feel that he might guard her through life, despite of the fortune that divided them. He obtained for her the Lady Katherine's regard, which she sought opportunities to demonstrate, while they were avoided by Monina, who honoured and loved her as Richard's wife and dearest friend, yet made occasion to absent herself from both. Nothing beautiful could be so unlike as these two fair ones. Katherine was the incarnate image of loveliness, such as it might have been conceived by an angelic nature; noble, soft, equable from her tender care not to displease others; in spite of the ills of fate, gay, because self-satisfied and resigned; the bright side of things was that which she contemplated: the bright and the tranquil – although the hazards run by him she loved, at this period informed her thoughts with terror. Monina, – no, there was no evil in Monina; if too much self-devotion, too passionate an attachment to one dear idea, too enthusiastic an adoration of one exalted being, could be called aught but virtue. The full orbs of her dark eyes, once flashing bright, were now more serious, / more melancholy; her very smile would make you weep; her vivacity, all concentred in one object, forgot to spend itself on trifles; yet, while the Princess wept that Richard should encounter fruitless danger for a mistaken aim, gladness sat on Monina's brow: "He goes to conquer; God will give victory to the right: as a warrior he treads his native land; as a monarch he will rule over her. The very name of King he bears, will shame the lukewarm English; they will gather round the apparent sun, now that he shows himself unclouded, leaving the false light, Tudor, to flicker into its native nothingness."

"Monina," said the Prince, "you in the wide world can bestow richest largess on the beggar, King Richard." She looked on him in wonder. "I go to conquer or to die: this, lovely one, is no new language for you; a warrior's friend must hear such words unflinching. I die without a fear if you take one charge upon you." Her beaming, expressive eyes replied to him. He continued: "The Adalid and safety are images most firmly united in my mind; if I cannot find security on / board of her myself, let those dear to me inherit my possession there. The hardest thought that I bear with me, is that my fair Queen should become captive to my base-minded foe. May I not trust that if I fall, the Adalid will be her home and refuge to convey her to her native country, or any whither she may direct? I intrust this charge to you, my sister, my far more than sister, my own kind Monina. You will forget yourself in that fateful hour, to fulfil my latest wish?"

"My Prince," she replied, "your words were cruel, did I not know that you speak in over care, and not from the impulse of your heart. In the same spirit, I promise that your desire shall be accomplished: if you fall, my father will protect – die for my lady the Queen. But why speak these ill-omened words? You will succeed; you will hasten the lagging hand of Fate, and dethrone one never born to reign, to bestow on England its rightful king. The stars promise this in their resplendent, unfailing scrowl[a] – the time-worn student in his lore

---

[a] Variant of 'scroll', meaning the expanse of heaven or the sky (*OED*).

has proclaimed it – the sacred name of monarch / which you bear, is the pledge and assurance of predestined victory."

"And you meanwhile will stay, and assure Katherine's destiny?"

"My dear Lord, I have a task to accomplish. If I leave her Grace, it is because all spirits of good and power watch over her, and my weak support is needed elsewhere. I am bound for London."

They parted thus. The temerity of their designs sometimes inspired them with awe; but more usually animated them to loftier hopes. When the thickening shadows of "coming events"[a] clouded their spirits, they took refuge in the sun-bright imaginations which painted to each the accomplishment of their several hopes. Monina felt assured that the hour of victory was at hand. Richard looked forward to a mortal struggle, to be crowned with success: a few short weeks or briefer days would close the long account: his word redeemed, his honour avenged, he looked forward to his dear reward: not a sceptre – that was a plaything / fit for Henry's hand; but to a life of peace and love; a very eternity of sober, waking bliss, to be passed with her he idolized, in the sunny clime of his regretted Spain. /

---

[a] Thomas Campbell (1777–1844), 'Lochiel's Warning', (first published 1802, but later revised and lengthened), l. 56.

CHAPTER VIII.

———

> Oh, that stern unbending man!
> In this unhappy marriage what have I
> Not suffered – not endured!
> SCHILLER'S WALLENSTEIN.[a]

> Once more unto the breach, dear friends, once more,
> Or close the wall up with our English dead!
> SHAKSPEARE.[b]

———

The lapse of years had confirmed Henry on his throne. He was extortionate and severe, it is true; and thus revolts had been frequent during the earlier portion of his reign; but they took their rise in a class which even in modern days, it is difficult to keep within the boundaries of law. The peasantry, scattered and dependant on the nobles, / were tranquil: but artificers, such as the miners of Cornwall, who met in numbers, and could ask each other, "Why, while there is plenty in the land, should we and our children starve? Why pay our hard earnings into the regal coffers?" and, still increasing in boldness, demand at last, "Why should these men govern us?

"We are many – they are few!"[c]

Thus sedition sprung from despair, and assumed arms; to which Henry had many engines to oppose, bulwarks of his power. A commercial spirit had sprung up during his reign, partly arising from the progress of civilization, and partly from so large a portion of the ancient nobility having perished in the civil wars. The spirit of chivalry, which isolates man, had given place to that of trade, which unites them in bodies.

———

[a] *The Death of Wallenstein*, I, iii (Coleridge translation).

[b] *Henry V*, III. i. 1–2.

[c] P. B. Shelley, *The Masque of Anarchy*, ll. 155, 372, substituting 'We' for 'Ye'; the poem, inspired by the Peterloo Massacre of 16 August 1819, was suppressed for political reasons by Leigh Hunt, who first published it in 1832, the year of the Reform Bill.

Among these, the White Rose of England had not a single partizan – the nobles who once had upheld the house of York were few; they had for the last eight years been intent upon restoring their fortunes, and were wholly disinclined / to the endangering them afresh for a stranger youth. When Fitzwater, Stanley, and their numerous fellow-conspirators, and fellow-victims sided with the Duke of York, nearly all England entertained a timid belief in his identity with King Edward's lost son – but those times were changed. Many were glad to soothe their consciences by declaring him an impostor; many so desired to curry favour with Henry; a still greater number either feared to say their thought, or were averse to disturb the tranquillity of their country, by a contest, which could benefit one man alone, and which must entail on them another war like that so lately ended – Abroad, in France, Burgundy, and Scotland, the Prince might be discountenanced from political motives; but he was treated with respect, and spoken of as being the man he named himself: in England it was otherwise – contempt followed hard upon fear, giving birth to derision, the best weapon against the unhappy, which Henry well knew how to wield. He had two motives in this – one was, that by affixing disgrace and scorn to his adversary, he took / away the glitter of his cause, and deterred the young and ambitious from any desire to share in his obloquy. The other was a feeling deeper-rooted in his mind – an intense hatred of the House of York – an exultation in its overthrow and disgrace – a gloating over every circumstance that blotted it with ignominy. If Richard had really been an impostor, Henry had not used half the pains to stigmatise him as low-born – to blast his pride with nicknames, nor have looked forward with the joy he now did, to having him in his power – to the degradation – the mortal stain of infamy he intended to taint him with for ever.

Secure in power – fearless of the result, Henry heard with unfeigned joy that his young rival had landed in England, and was advancing into the interior of the island, at the head of the Cornish insurgents. He himself announced the rising to his nobles. Laughing, he said, "I have tidings for you, gentlemen: a flight of wild geese clad in eagles' feathers, are ready to pounce upon us. Even now they hover over / our good city of Exeter, frighting the honest burghers with their dissonance."

"Blackheath will witness another victory," said Lord Oxford.

"And my kitchen receive a new scullion," replied the King; "since Lambert Simnel became falconer, our roast meat thinks itself dishonoured at not being spitted by a pretender to my crown; for no Audley heads these fellows, but the King of Rakehells himself, the most noble Perkin, who, to grace the more the unwashed rogues, calls himself Richard the Fourth for the nonce. I have fair hope to see his Majesty this bout, if he whiz not away in a fog, or sink underground like Lord Lovel, to the disappointment of all merrry fellows, who love new masks and gaudy mumming."

"Please your Majesty," said the young Lord William Courtney, "it is for the

307

honour of our house that not a stone of Exeter be harmed. With your good leave, my father and myself will gather in haste what force we may: if fortune aid us, we may present your Grace with your new servitor." /

"Be it so, my Lord," replied the King, "and use good dispatch. We ourselves will not tarry: so that, with less harm to all, we may tread out these hasty lighted embers. Above all, let not Duke Perkin escape; it is my dearest wish that he partake our hospitality."

"Yes," so ran Henry's private thoughts; "he must be mine, mine alive, mine to deal with as I list." With even more care than he put in the mustering his army, he ordered that the whole of the southern sea-coast of England should be guarded; every paltry fishing village had its garrison, which permitted no boat to put off to sea, nor any to land, without the strictest investigation; not content with this, he committed it to the care of his baser favourites to forge some plot which might betray his enemy without a blow into his hands.

"Give me your benison, good Bess," said the Monarch, with unwonted gaiety of manner; "with daylight I depart on the ungentle errand of encountering your brother Perkin."

Elizabeth, not less timid than she had ever been, was alarmed by his show of mirth, and by / this appellation bestowed on one she knew to be so near of kin. That very morning she had seen Monina – the enthusiastic Monina, who, confiding in her royal friend's success, visited London to watch over the fate of Elizabeth and her children. The Queen smiled at her offers of service; she felt that no such army could endanger Henry's reign; but she feared for Richard, for her ill-fated brother, who had now entered the net, for whom she felt assured there was no escape. Trembling at her own boldness, she answered the King, "Whoever he may be, you will not destroy him in cold blood?"

"You would have me spare the impostor?" asked Henry. "Spare him who claims your son's throne? By Our Lady of Walsingham, the maternal virtues of the daughter of York deserve high praise."

Elizabeth, dreading more to offend, horror-struck at the idea that her husband should shed her brother's blood, burst into tears. "Silly girl," said Henry, "I am not angry; nay, more, I grant your prayer. Perkin, if not slain by a chance blow, shall live. My word is / passed; trust to it: I neither inquire nor care whether he be the godson or the base brat of the libertine Edward. In either case, my revenge stoops not so low as his paltry life: does this content you?"

"May the saints bless your Grace," said Elizabeth, "you have eased my every fear."

"Remember then that you prove no ingrate," continued the King, "no dupe of report, no traducer of your children's birth. Betray no interest in the knave's downfall, save as he is my enemy. If you display any emotion that awakens a doubt, that this canker rose be aught in your eyes except a base pretender – if you mark any feeling but stern contempt for one so vile – tremble. My vengeance will fall on him; and his blood be on your head."

"Magnanimous Prince!" thought Elizabeth, in bitter scorn, when he had left her: "this is your mercy. You fear! My poor Richard – your sister, a monarch's daughter, is finely taught by this Earl's son. But you will live; then let him do his worst: the Queen of England is not quite a slave; if Henry can bind, / Elizabeth may loose; and the Duke of York laugh in another land at the malice of his enemy."

We return to this Prince, whose lofty spirit was sustained by an aim, an object dearer than a kingdom in his eyes. He arrived before Exeter at the head of seven thousand men. All the discontented in Cornwall and Devonshire joined him. Some of these were younger brothers; some men-at-arms who repined at peace; chiefly they were needy, oppressed men, rouzed by a sense of wrong, as destitute, but not so hardy as the kerns of Ireland. Still they were many, they were valiant; Exeter was ungarrisoned, unprepared for defence, and there was a possibility that by sudden assault, he might possess himself of the town. With this intent he did not allow his troops time to repose, but at once set on for the attack, endeavouring to scale the lofty walls; unaided by any fitting machinery, scarcely possessed of a single scaling ladder, he was driven back with loss. Foiled but not vanquished, for his heart was set upon this prize, for three days, though unpossessed / of artillery or any warlike engine, he exerted his utmost force to win the city; he contrived rude machinery to cast stones, he planted the ladders himself, he multiplied himself to appear every-where, flattering, encouraging, leading his troops again and again to the assault. When they found the walls impregnable, he made an attempt on the gates: with fascines and hewed trees he set one of them on fire; his men shouted as they heard the stout oak crackle, and saw it split and crumble, offering a large opening; but the citizens, made desperate, fearful of the ravages this untamed multitude might commit, were true to themselves; they resisted fire by fire, keeping up a fierce blaze within, till with piles of brick and rubbish they had blocked the passage. Richard saw his last hope fail, "This is not the work of the burghers," he cried, "a soldier's skill is here."[a]

"True as my old yard measure!" cried Heron. "It was but last night that my cousin, the Earl of Devon, clambered into the city; he came to the northern wall, where Skelton keeps watch; when my valiant tailor heard the noise, / ran to look for Master Trereife, who, poor fellow, lies cold within the moat. The citizens heard and answered my Cousin the Earl's call; but they were too frightened to let light through the keyhole of a postern; and his lordship, God save him! was obliged to climb the battlements."

"Climb the battlements, noble Captain?" said Richard; "that is, a ladder was let down?"

"It was a stone ladder he scaled, my liege, said Heron; "your Grace may walk

---

[a] Stratagem employed at the siege of Exeter (17–18 September 1497) and vividly described in the chronicles.

309

up the same. It will scarce budge, seeing that it is the old part of the wall itself."

"Who knows more of this?" asked the Prince.

"I saw the whole," said Skelton; "That is the end. Master Trereife was dead for the nonce, so I came back to lead my men to the fray. There was the Earl, perched like a crow, on the boughs of an old thorn-bush, that grows at the top of the wall. Surely he must have torn his cloak, for the place is thick with all manner of weeds, and rough stones, and brambles. But more than his broad-cloth got a hole; for Clim / of Tregothius handled his bow, and let fly a cloth-yard shaft, which was sticking in his shoulder as he got down the other side."[a]

While the Tailor talked, Richard was proceeding hastily to the spot. It looked tranquil. The old crumbling wall was green with rank grass and tangled weeds. He drew nearer, and then a whole shower of arrows was discharged against him. The Earl had expected that his success would excite their curios-ity, and prepared for them, with not the less zeal on account of his own wound. Richard escaped unhurt; but Edmund, who was scantily armed, received an arrow in his side: he fell. That same hour tidings came of the advance of King Henry at the head of a formidable army.

Plantagenet's wound was dressed; it showed signs of danger, and quite disabled him. "My faithful fellows swear to preserve you in safety, Cousin," said Richard; "I must leave you."

"Do you retreat?" asked Edmund.

"No, by my soul! Truly, my hopes have somewhat quailed; yet it is but a lucky blow, and I gain all. I leave you, my friend; but I / will not leave you in doubt and ignorance. Read this paper: it is to enforce its contents – to oblige my haughty foe to lay aside his worst weapon, detraction, that I, against all probability and wisdom, will urge my cause to the last. My kingdom, it is his: my honour he must restore, and I cry him quits. Now you have my secret. Pardon for my poor fellows; pardon, and some alleviation of their cruel lot. For myself, as you will find, I ask little, but I must show no fear, no retreating, to obtain even that. I march forwards, then, towards Taunton:[b] it is a less place than Exeter. The smallest secure port gained, and Henry may grant my boon."

Plantagenet unfolded the paper, and read these words:

"Richard, legitimate and true son of Edward the Fourth, King of England and France, and Lord of Ireland, to Henry, the reigning Sovereign of these realms. In my infancy I was made a prisoner by an usurping uncle, escaping from his thrawl by aid of the most noble Earl of Lincoln. This uncle, this usurper, you conquered, / and seized upon his crown. You claim the same by right of Bolingbroke, and strengthen your title through your union with my

---

[a] The incident is drawn from the chronicles, where the archer remains anonymous.
[b] Lying about twenty-seven miles north-east of Exeter, along a main road.

sister, the Lady Elizabeth. I am poor, and an outcast: you a King. God has destroyed my house, and I submit. But I will not submit to the vile slander that takes from me my name, and brands me a dishonoured man.

"Henry of Richmond, I neither admit nor combat your claim to the crown. Lancaster has many partizans, and the victory is yours. But as Duke of York, I challenge and defy you. I call on you, either by person or by champion, to meet me in the lists, that I may defend my honour, and maintain the right. Let us spare the people's blood. In single combat let my pretensions be set at issue; and my good sword shall cut to pieces the wicked lies and base traditions you have calumniously and falsely forged to my disgrace.

"Body to body, I will meet you or your champion. Name the day, the hour, and the place. With my lance and my sword, to the death I will maintain my birth. If I fall, I ask / that my wife, the Lady Katherine Gordon, be permitted to return to her royal cousin, James of Scotland; that such of my followers as desire it, may be allowed to go beyond seas; that those of your subjects who, goaded into rebellion by your exactions, have taken up arms, receive free pardon and remission of their imposts. If I conquer, I add but one other demand – that you confess to the wide world how foully you have slandered me; revoke the lies you have published, and acknowledge me to all men, the rightful Duke of York.

"If you deny my just demands, be the blood spilt in defence of my honour on your head; England ravaged, your towns destroyed, your realm subject to all the calamities of war; these evils rest with you. I will not sheathe my sword, nor tread one backward step in my undertaking; but as in the lists, so on the dread battle-field, meet your abettors, and conquer or die in defence of my name. Expecting a fitting answer to this just defiance, I bid you heartily farewell.

"RICHARD. /

"Written under the walls of Exeter, this twelfth day of September, in the year of our Blessed Lord 1497."

Plantagenet was deeply affected by his Cousin's gallantry. He sighed, saying, "Tudor has not, will not reply to your challenge?"

"He has not, but he may," replied Richard. "I have, I know not why, a firm belief that good will come from it. If not, in a few days all will be over. In a very few days you can be conveyed to St. Michael's Mount, where the Queen now is.[a] The Adalid hovers near. Save her, save yourself: save one other, less helpful than my Katherine – be a brother to Monina."

Richard, erring in his mark, was animated by the most sanguine hopes, to which he was seduced by a constant belief that his life was not near its close, and therefore that his claims would be admitted; as otherwise he had resolved

---

[a] See p. 334.

to fall in the assertion of them. Leaving the sick couch of his Cousin, he prepared to advance to Taunton. A conversation meanwhile which he dreamt not of, and would have scorned, had / place in an obscure and gloomy spot in London, fraught with fate to him.

After the base desertion of his royal master, Frion had sailed to England with the other hirelings of Henry; among these was Clifford. Clifford, whose need and whose malice armed him against York's life, but who tried to hide his shame under an assumed appellation. There had always been a false fellowship and a real enmity between Frion and the knight. On his first arrival in Brussels, the secretary looked on him as an interloper; and Clifford, while he used the other, tried to force him into his place as an underling, and to blind him to his own designs. When he betrayed his party, spreading death among the partizans of York, and annihilating the cause, Frion, whose fortunes depended on its success, was unmeasured in his expressions of indignation and contempt. They had worked in direct opposition the year before in Kent; and, when Frion saw the hand of this reprobated man uplifted in midnight assassination, he triumphed in the lowness of his fall. Both were traitors now, both baffled: / Frion looked on Clifford as the worse villain; and Clifford writhed under the familiar impertinence of a menial. They arrived in London; Sir Robert was dismissed with barren thanks, Frion thrown into prison; how far the knight's account gave intimation of the Frenchman's double dealing, and so brought this severity upon him was not known, but for three months this mercurial spirit had languished in confinement.

Addicted to scheming, he had now full leisure to spend his whole thoughts that way; a single, simple plot was too plain for his industrious soul; he wove a whole web of them so intricate, that he sometimes lost the clue himself; not the less did he do his endeavour to put them in action. He intended either to lose Richard or make him; either to be the cause of his overthrowing Henry, or of being overthrown by him; in either case, to reap favour and advantage from the triumphant party.

Sad as is ever a prison-house, it was worse in those days of incivilization: this pen could ill describe the squalid figures and dire visages / that crowded its tumultuous court. Even here Frion reigned umpire; but he broke from a knot of noisy squabblers, who held tattered cards, and appealed to him on a question of fair play, as he saw one enter. Even he a wretch, yet many degrees better than the best of his miserable companions; a scarlet suit, trimmed with gold lace, somewhat tarnished, a cloak of ample folds, but threadbare, a dark plumed bonnet, drawn over his brow, above all, a rapier at his side, distinguished him from the prisoners.

"This is kind, Sir Robert," said Frion in his softest manner, "I half feared you were too proud or politic to visit a disgraced man; for these last three days I have despaired of your worship; by my fay! you are right welcome."

Clifford cast a shuddering look around the walls; his eyes were hollow; his cheek sunk; he was the mere shadow of bold Robert. "Few words are best thanks, Master Stephen," he replied; "I am kind to you because the dice are cruel to me; you promise largely, and my wants are no dwarfs. What are your designs?"

"This is no place for parley," said Frion; / "follow me." He led the way through several narrow passages to a miserable cell; straw was heaped in one corner for a bed; the walls were dank and tattered; the floor broken and filthy. "Welcome to my domicile, Sir Knight," said Frion: whether it were compunction that he had brought him to this, or distrust that the injury would be revenged, Clifford shrunk back and his lips grew livid. "One would not live here from choice," said Frion, "I allow; yet do not grudge me a few moments, it may stead us both."

"To the point then," said the Knight; "it is not the place, Master Frion; but at the hour of noon – "

"No excuses, you like the place as ill as I," said the Frenchman with a bland smile; "but you are more generous, for I would not dwell an instant's space here of my own will to gain any man's salvation. Now, what news from the west? Is it true that the Duke of York is slain? or Exeter taken? both reports are rife. Adam Wicherly and Mat Oldcraft[a] made their escape two days ago, to join the gallant. Mat was / seized again, and says that there were bonfires in Southwark[b] for Richard the Fourth."

Clifford, by a brief detail, answered, and then after some hesitation said, "He is not so low but that the King desires him to be lower: he who could bring him, bound hand and foot, to London, would be a made man. Empson saw Garthe yesterday;[c] and he, who calls me Wiatt, came post to consult with me; but it were hazardous to attempt him; he is ten thousand strong."

"You know me, Sir Robert," said Frion; "there are few things I cannot bring about, so that I have room to ruffle in. I have a plot, King Richard is ours in three days, so one word be said; that word is liberty to me. Take you the reward; I ask no further share in your gains than free leave to set the channel between me and this dingy island."

Each despising, each mistrusting the other, these men conspired for the Prince's fall: like "mousing owls"[d] they hawked at an eagle with too true an aim. York's thoughts were of honour; but through them they were to be / drugged with ignominy and despair. It is melancholy that circumstance and fortune should have power to reach the very shrine of our dearest thoughts; degrading them from their original brightness to a likeness of the foul aspect of

---

[a] Apparently invented adherents.

[b] Borough of London, south of the river Thames.

[c] Sir Richard Empson, much-loathed implementor of Henry VII's tax policies, was attainted and executed in 1510. Thomas Garth had led an army into Ireland in 1491 to suppress a rebellion.

[d] *Macbeth*, II. iv. 13 (adapted).

the outer world. Richard's free and noble spirit was to become plastic to the touch of such men as the fallen Clifford and crafty Frion. Men, whom he had cast from him as unworthy his regard, could besiege the citadel of his hopes, and garrison it with disgrace; forcing him to occupy himself with ideas as base as those which possessed their own minds. It is the high heart's curse to be obliged to expend its deep and sacred emotions in hatred of, or struggle with things so mean, so very alien to its own aspiring nature. /

CHAPTER IX.

———

Ah! Richard, with the eyes of heavy mind,
I see thy glory, like a shooting star,
Fall to the base earth from the firmament.
                                    SHAKSPEARE.[a]

———

Richard proceeded towards Taunton. Although this was in appearance an advance, his ill-success before Exeter, and report of the large force already brought against them by Sir John Cheney, King Henry's Chamberlain,[b] had so far discouraged his followers as to occasion the desertion of many – so that of the seven thousand he had with him in Devonshire, he retained but three on his arrival near Taunton. These consisted of the original body of insurgents, / Cornishmen, who had proceeded too far to go back, and who, partly in affection for their leader, partly from natural stubbornness, swore to die in the cause. Poor fellows! rusty rapiers, and misshapen lances were their chief arms; a few had bows; others slings; a still greater number their ponderous tools, implements of labour and of peace, to be used now in slaughter. Their very dress displayed at once their unmartial and poverty-stricken state. In all these might be gathered a troop of three hundred foot, not wholly destitute of arms and discipline. The horse were not less at fault; yet among them there were about one hundred tolerably mounted, the riders indeed, but too frequently, disgracing their steeds.

———

[a] *Richard II*, II. iv. 18–20.
[b] Sir John Cheney (or Cheyney) had lived in exile with Henry before he became king.

It required all Richard's energy of purpose to hold him back from despair. The bitter sense of degradation visited him in spite of every effort. Had he ever made one of the chivalry of France and Burgundy? Had he run a tilt with James of Scotland, or grasped in knightly brotherhood the mailed hand of Sir Patrick Hamilton? And were these his comrades? unwashed artificers; / ragged and rude peasants; vulgar-tongued traders? He felt, "in disgrace with fortune and men's eyes;"[a] and now to obtain pardon for them, to send them back skaithless to their own homes, was his chief desire, even to the buying of their safety with his own downfall.

After two days march he arrived near Taunton. On reconnoitring the town, its position and weakness gave him hope that he might carry it, even with his sorry soldiery. To check these thoughts, tidings came, that Sir John Cheney was in close neighbourhood, and Henry himself advancing with a chosen body of men. On the evening of their arrival before the town, a detachment of the enemy entered it, cutting off the last hope of Richard.

The next morning it became evident that the crisis of his fortunes was at hand. The whole country teemed with soldiery. As the troops poured towards a common centre, the array and order of a battle-field became apparent in their operations. A battle, between a very myriad of golden-spurred knights, armed at all points, and / the naked inhabitants of Richard's camp! call it rather a harvest; there were the reapers, here the bending corn. When in the north Richard wept over the devastation of the land, he felt that a word of his could counteract the harm – but now, his challenge had proved an airy dagger – substanceless – his resolve to encounter his foe, bringing the unarmed against these iron-suited warriors, grew in his eyes into premeditated murder: his heart heaved in his overcharged breast. To add bitterness to his thoughts there were his companions – O'Water brave in despair; Astley pale with fear for his lord; Heron foolish in his unmeaning boasting; Skelton trembling in every joint, and talking incessantly, apparently to deafen himself to "the small still voice"[b] that whispered terror to his heart.

Richard spent the day among his men. They were prepared to fight; if needs must, to fall: protestations of sturdy devotion, the overflowing of the rude, manly heart, always affecting, met him at every turn. He was beloved, for he was generous and kind. Often he had exposed his life, when before Exeter, to save some one among / them: when dismayed, he had cheered, when defeated, he had comforted them; nor did he leave the body of the meanest camp-follower uninterred; for one of Richard's characteristics was a quick sympathy with his species, and a reverence for all that bore the shape of man. But, while these qualities rendered him dear to all, they inspired him with a severe sense

---

[a] Shakespeare, Sonnet XXIX, l. 1.
[b] 1 Kings 19: 12.

of his duties towards others, and a quick insight into their feelings; thus increasing to anguish the disquietude that agitated him.

Towards evening he was alone in his tent. At first he was confused by the various aspects, all terrible, that his fortunes assumed. By the caprice of destiny, he who was descended from a line of kings, who had so long been the inhabitant of courts, a Cavalier, honourable in his degree, renowned for his prowess, had not one noble-born partizan near him: not one of his ancient counsellors, to whom he had been used to defer, remained; he was absolutely alone; the sense of right and justice in his own heart was all he possessed, to be a beacon-light in this / awful hour, when thousands depended upon his word – yet had he power to save?

An idea, dim at first as a star on the horizon's verge, struggling through vapours, but growing each second brighter and clearer, dawned upon his mind. All then was over! his prophetic soul had proved false in its presumed fore-knowledge; defeat, dishonour, disgrace tracked his steps. To lead his troops forth, and then to redeem them at Henry's hand, by the conditionless surrender of himself, was the thought, child of despair and self-devotion, that still struggling with the affections and weaknesses of his nature, presented itself, not yet full fledged, but about to become so.

He had been several times interrupted during his meditations by the arrival of scouts, with various reports of the situation and proceedings of the enemy: Richard, better than these untaught recruits, knew the meaning of the various operations. As if on a map, he saw the stationing of a large and powerful army in expectation of battle; and was aware how incapable he was to cope with their numbers and force. At last / Astley announced the arrival of two men: one was a Fleming, known to Richard as one of Lalayne's men, but the fellow was stupidly drunk; the other was an English peasant. "Please your worship," he said, "I am this man's guide, and must act as his interpreter besides; nothing would serve the spungy fellow but he must swallow ale at every tavern on the way."

"Speak, then," said Richard; "what is the purport of his journey?"

"Please you, Sir, last night three hundred of them came right pop upon us afore we were aware; sore afraid they made us with their tall iron-shafted poles, steel caps, and short swords, calling each one for bread and beer."

"Do you mean," cried the Prince, his eye brightening as he spoke, "that three hundred men, soldiers, armed like yonder fellow, are landed in England?"

So the countryman averred; and that even now they were but at the distance of twenty miles from Richard's encampment. They were still advancing, when the report was spread that / the Prince's forces were dispersed, himself taken prisoner. The rustic drew from the Fleming's pocket a letter, in French, signed by Swartz,[a] a son of him who fell at Stoke, a man in high favour with the Lady

---

[a] Mary Shelley's invention; for his 'father', see p. 58.

Margaret of Burgundy. It said how he had been dispatched by her Grace to his succour; how intelligence of the large army of Henry, and his defeat, had so terrified his men, that they refused to proceed, nay, by the next morning would take their way back to Poole,[a] where they had landed, unless Richard himself came to re-assure them, and to lead them on. Every word of the letter lighted up to forgotten joy young Richard's elastic spirit. With these men to aid him, giving weight and respectability to his powers, he might hope to enforce the conditions of his challenge. All must be decided on the morrow: that very hour he would set forth, to return before morning with these welcome succours.[b]

It was near midnight; his camp was still; the men, in expectation of the morrow's struggle, had retired to repose; their leaders had orders to visit their commander in his tent / at the hour which now the empty hour-glass told was come. Hastily, eagerly, Richard announced the arrival of these German merce-naries; he directed them to accompany him, that with some show of attendance he might present himself to Schwartz. The camp was not to be disturbed; two or three men alone among them were awakened, and ordered to keep guard – in five hours assuredly he must return. In a brief space of time, the troop who were to accompany him, Heron, Skelton, O'Water, and Astley, with some forty more, led their horses to his tent in silence: – there were few lights through all the camp; their honest hearts which beat within slept, while he was awake to succour and save them. This was Richard's last thought, as, mounted on his good steed, he led the way across the dim heath towards Yeovil.[c]

It was such a night as is frequent at the end of September; a warm but furious west-wind tore along the sky, shaking the dark tresses of the trees, and chasing the broad shadows of the clouds across the plains. The moon, at the / beginning of her third quarter, sped through the sky with rapid, silvery wings; now cutting the dark, sea-like ether; now plunging deep amidst the clouds; now buried in utter darkness; anon spreading a broad halo among the thinner woof of vapours. The guide was at the Prince's side; Heron, upon his short sturdy pony, was just behind; Skelton tried to get his tall mare to an even pace with Richard's horse, but she fell back continually: the rushing, howling wind, and rustling trees drowned the clatter of the hoofs. They reached the extreme edge of the common; Richard turned his head – the lights of his little camp burnt dim in the moonshine, its poor apparel of tents was lost in the distance: they entered a dark lane, and lost sight of every trace of it; still they rode fleetly on. Night, and the obscure shapes of night around – holy, blinding, all-seeing

---

[a] Poole, on the Dorset coast, south-east of Taunton.

[b] According to the historical record, Warbeck and a small band of followers left Taunton at night to avoid engaging Henry's forces, and headed toward Southampton, about seventy-five miles east on the Hampshire coast, hoping to escape by sea. With Lord Daubeney and 500 men in pursuit, he instead sought sanctuary at Beaulieu, a few miles from his destination. Mary Shelley invents an alternative narrative route to Beaulieu (reached in ch. xii).

[c] Yeovil, Somerset, midway between Taunton and Poole.

317

night! when we feel the power of the Omnipotent as if immediately in contact with us; when religion fills the soul, and our very fears are unearthly; when familiar images assume an unknown power to thrill our hearts; and the winds and trees / and shapeless clouds, have a voice not their own, to speak of all that we dream or imagine beyond our actual life.[a] Through embowered lanes, whose darkness seemed thick and palpable – over open, moonshiny fields, where the airy chase of clouds careered in dimmer shapes upon the earth – Richard rode forward, fostering newly-awakened hope; glad in the belief that while he saved all who depended on him, he would not prove a mere victim led in tame submission, an unrighteous sacrifice to the Evil Spirit of the World. /

CHAPTER X.

———

Art thou he, traitor! that with treason vile
  Hast slain my men in this unmanly manner,
And now triumphest in the piteous spoil
  Of these poor folk; whose souls with black dishonour
  And foul defame do deck thy bloody banner?
The meed whereof shall shortly be thy shame,
  And wretched end which still attendeth on her.
With that himself to battle he did frame;
So did his forty yeomen which there with him came.
                    SPENSER.[b]

———

Some miles to the east of Yeovil there was a deep stream, whose precipitous banks were covered by a thick underwood that almost concealed the turbid waters, which undermined and bared the twisted and gnarled roots of the various overhanging trees or shrubs. The left / side of the stream was bounded by an abrupt hill, at the foot of which was a narrow pathway; on the green acclivity flourished a beech grove, whose roots were spread in many directions to catch the soil, while their trunks, some almost horizontal, were all fantastically grown, and the fairy tracery of the foliage shed such soft, mellowed,

---

[a] Cf. P. B. Shelley, 'On Love'.
[b] *Faerie Queene*, VI. vi. 25.

chequered light as must incline the heart of the wanderer beneath the leafy bower, to delicious musings.

Now the moon silvered the trees, and sometimes glimmered on the waters, whose murmurs contended with the wind that sung among the boughs: and was this all? A straggling moon-beam fell on something bright amid the bushes, and a deep voice cried, "Jack of the Wynd, if thou can'st not get to thicker cover, pluck darnels to cover that cursed steel cap of thine."

"Hush!" repeated another lower voice, "Your bawling is worse than his headpiece; you outroar the wind. How high the moon is, and our friends not come; – he will be here before them." /

"Hark! a bell!"

"Matins, by the Fiend! may *he* seize that double-tongued knave! I much suspect Master Frion; I know him of old."

"He cannot mar us now, though it be he who made this ambushment."

"Oh, by your leave! he has the trick of it, and could spring a mine in the broadest way; he can turn, and twist, and show more faces than a die. He laughed this morn – I know the laugh – there is mischief in 't."

"But, your Worship, now, what can he do?"

"Do! darken the moon; set these trees alive and dancing; do! so play the Will o' the Wisp that the King shall be on Pendennis and the Duke at Greenwich, and each fancy he is within bow-shot of the other;[a] do! ask the Devil what is in his compact, for he is but the Merry Andrew of Doctor Frion. Hush!"

"It is he," said the other speaker.

A breathless pause ensued; the wind swept through the trees – another sound – its monotonous recurrence showed that it was a dashing waterfall – and yet again it grew louder. /

"It is he."

"No, Gad's mercy, it comes westward – close, my merry fellows, close, and mind the word! close, for we have but half our number, and yet he may escape."

Again the scene sank into silence and darkness: such silence as is nature's own, whose voice is ever musical; such darkness as the embowering trees and vast island-clouds made, dimming and drinking up the radiance of the moon.

The stillness was broken by the tramp of horses drawing near, men's voices mingled with the clatter, and now several cavaliers entered the defile; they rode in some disorder, and so straggling, that it was probable that many of their party lagged far behind: the principal horseman had reached midway the ravine, when suddenly a tree, with all its growth of green and tangled boughs, fell right across the path; the clatter of the fall deafened the screech which

---

[a] Greenwich, now a borough of London, was the site of an ancient royal palace enlarged by Edward IV; Henry VIII later built a castle on Pendennis, a promontory overlooking Falmouth harbour, in Cornwall.

accompanied it, for one rider was overthrown; it was succeeded by a flight of arrows from concealed archers. "Ride for your lives," / cried Richard: but his path was crossed by six horsemen, while, starting from the coppice, a band of near forty men engaged with the van of his troop, who tried to wheel about: some escaped, most fell. With his sword drawn, the Prince rushed at his foremost enemy; it was a mortal struggle, for life and liberty, for hatred and revenge. Richard was the better swordsman, but his horse was blown, and half sunk upon his haunches, when pressed closely by the adversary. Richard saw his danger, and yet his advantage, for his foe, over-eager to press him down, forgot the ward; he rose on his stirrups, and grasped his sword with both hands, when a blow from behind, a coward's blow, from a battle-axe, struck him; it was repeated, and he fell lifeless on the earth.

Sickness, and faintness, and throbbing pain were the first tokens of life that visited his still failing sense; sight and the power of motion seemed to have deserted him, but memory reviving told him that he was a prisoner. Moments were stretched to ages while he strove to collect his sensations; still it was night; the / view of fields and uplands and of the varied moon-lit sky, grew upon his languid senses; he was still on horseback, bound to the animal, and supported on either side by men. As his movements communicated his returning strength, one of these fellows rode to impart the tidings to their leader, while the other stayed to guide his horse; the word "gallop!" was called aloud, and he was urged along at full speed, while the sudden motion almost threw him back into his swoon.

Dawn, which at first seemed to add to the dimness and indistinctness of the landscape, struggling through the clouds, and paling the moon, slowly stole upon them. The Prince became sufficiently alive to make observations; he and his fellow-prisoners were five in number only, their guards were ten; foremost among them was one, whom in whatever guise he could not mistake. Each feeling in Richard's heart stimulated him to abhor that man, yet he pitied him more. Gallant, bold Robin, the frolicksome page, the merry-witted sharer of a thousand pleasures. Time, thou art a thief; how / base a thief – when thou stealest not only our friends, our youth, our hopes, but, besides, our innocence; giving us in the place of light-hearted confidence – guile, distrust, the consciousness of evil deeds. In these thoughts, Richard drew the colouring[23] of the picture, from the fresh and vivid tints that painted his own soul. Clifford's breast had perhaps never been free from the cares of guilt: he had desired honour; he had loved renown; but the early developement of passion and of talent had rendered him even in boyhood, less single-hearted than Richard now.

Clifford was triumphant; he possessed Monina's beloved – the cause of his disgrace – bound, a prisoner and wounded. Why then did pain distort his features, and passion flush his brow? No triumph laughed in his eye, or sat upon his lip. He hated the prince; but he hated and despised himself. He played a dastardly and a villain's part; and shame awaited even success. The notoriety and infamy that attended on him (exaggerated as those things usually are, in his own eyes), made him fear to meet / in the neighbouring villages or towns, any noble cavalier who might recognize him; even if he saw a party of horsemen on the road, he turned out of it, and thus got entangled among bye-paths in an unfrequented part of the country. They continued the same fast career for several hours, till they entered a wild dark forest, where the interminable branches of the old oaks met high-arched over head, and the paths were beset with fern and underwood. The road they took was at first a clear and open glade, but it quickly narrowed, and branched off in various directions; they followed one of its windings, till it abruptly closed: the leader then reined in, and Clifford's voice was heard. Years had elapsed since it had met Richard's ear; the mere, as it were, abstract idea of Clifford was mingled with crime and hate; his voice, his manner, his look were associated with protestations of fidelity; or, dearer still, the intercourse of friendship and youthful gaiety; no wonder that it seemed a voice from the grave to betrayed York. "Halloo!" cried Clifford, "Clim of the Lyn,[a] / my merry man, thou art to track us through the New Forest[b] to Southampton."

"Please your knightship," said a shaggy-headed fellow, "our way is clear, I am at home now: but, by Saint George,[c] we must halt; a thirty miles ride since matins, his fast unbroken, would have made Robin Hood[d] a laggard."

"What would you eat here?" cried Clifford; "a stoup of canary and beef were blessings for the nonce; but we must get out of this accursed wilderness into more Christian neighbourhood, before we find our hostelry."

Clim of the Lyn grinned. "To a poor forester," said he, "the green-wood is a royal inn; vert and venison,[e] your worship, sound more savoury than four smoky walls, and a platter of beef brought in mine host's left hand, while his right already says – 'Pay!'"

"They would feed me with mine own venison in way of courtesy, even as the Lion Heart,[f] my namesake and ancestor, was feasted of old; mine – each acre, each rood,[g] and every noble stag that pastures thereon; but I am not so / free as they; and, mine though this wild wood be, I must thank an outlaw ere I dine upon my own."

---

[a] lyn (or linn), a waterfall; a pool into which a cascade falls; a deep ravine; or a precipice; also, a variant for linden or lime (*OED*). Mary Shelley probably drew the name Clim (or Clym, p. 324) from 'Adam Bell, Clym of the Clough, and William of Cloudesley' (see p. 325 and n), the ballad from which her father drew the name of the title character of his novel, *Cloudesley*, published the same year as *Perkin Warbeck*.

[b] A few miles south and west of Southampton.

[c] England's patron saint, slayer of the dragon.

[d] The legendary outlaw was already a well-established hero by the late fifteenth century.

[e] woodland and deer; old legal term.

[f] Richard the Lion-Hearted (1157–99; ruled 1189–99), celebrated in ballads and historical romances for his exploits during the crusades.

[g] Measure of land equal to one-quarter of an acre.

Thus thought Richard; and at that moment, with his limbs aching through their bondage, and with throbbing temples, liberty in the free forest seemed worth more than a kingdom. The bright sun was high – the sky serene – the merry birds were caroling in the brake – the forest basked in noon-day, while the party wound along the shady path beneath. The languid frame of York revived; at first to pain alone, for memory was serpent-fanged. What bird-lime was this to ensnare the royal eagle! but soon Despair, which had flapped her harpy wings across his face, blinding him, fled away; Hope awoke, and in her train, schemes of escape, freedom, and a renewal of the struggle.

Meanwhile they threaded many a green pathway, and, after another hour's ride, arrived at the opening of a wide grassy dell; a deer, "a stag of ten,"[a] leapt from his ferny bed and bounded away; a herd of timid fawns, just visible in the distance, hurried into the thicket; / while many a bird flew from the near sprays. Here the party halted; first they unbitted their steeds, and then dismounted the prisoners, binding them for security's sake to a tree. Richard was spared this degradation, for still he was a prince in Clifford's eyes; and his extreme physical weakness, caused by his blow, made even the close watching him superfluous. He was lifted from his horse, and placed upon the turf, and there left. While some of his guards went to seek and slay their repast, others led their animals to a brook, which murmured near: all were variously and busily employed. Clifford alone remained; he called for water; evidently he was more weary than he chose to own; he took off his casque: his features were ghastly; there was a red streak upon his brow, which was knit as if to endurance, and his lips were white and quivering. Never had crime visited with such torment ill-fated man; he looked a Cain after the murder; the Abel he had killed was his own fair fame – the ancestral honour of his race. How changed from when Richard last saw him, but two years before; his hair was / nearly grey, his eyes hollow, his cheeks fallen in; yet, though thin to emaciation, he had lost that delicacy and elegance of feature that had characterized him. Almost without reflection, forgetting his own position in painful compassion, the Prince exclaimed, "Thou art an unhappy man, Sir Robert!" the knight replied with a ghastly smile, which he meant to be disdainful. "But now," continued Richard, "while thy visor screened thy face, I was on the point of taunting thee as a coward, of defying thee to mortal combat; but thou art miserable, and broken-hearted, and no match for me."

Clifford's eyes glared, his hand was upon his sword's hilt: he recollected himself, replying, "You cannot provoke me, Sir, you are my prisoner."

"Thy victim, Robin; though once saved by thee; but that is past, and there is no return. The blood of Stanley, and of a hundred other martyrs, rolls between us: I conquer my own nature, when even for a moment I look upon their murderer." /

---

[a] A stag with ten points on its antlers.

The weakness of the prince gave a melancholy softness to his voice and manner; the deep pity he felt for his fallen friend, imparted a seraphic expression to his clear open countenance. Clifford writhed with pain. Clifford, who, though not quick to feel for others, was all sense and sensitiveness for himself: and how often in the world do we see sensibility attributed to individuals, whose show of feeling arises from excessive susceptibility to their own sorrows and injuries! Clifford wished to answer – to go away – he was spell-bound; his cowering look first animated Richard to an effort, which a moment before he would have ridiculed. "Wherefore," said he, "have you earned all men's hate, and your own to boot? Are you more honoured and loved than in Brussels? Scorn tracks you in your new career, and worst of all, you despise yourself."

"By St. Sathanas[a] and his brood!" fiercely burst from the Knight. Then he bit his lip, and was silent.

"Yet, Clifford, son of a noble father, spare yourself this crowning sin. I have heard from / travelled men, that in Heathenesse[b] the unbaptized miscreant is true to him whose hospitality he has shared. There was a time when my eyes brightened when I saw you; when the name of Robin was a benediction to me. You have changed it for the direst curse. Yours are no common crimes. Foremost in the chronicles, your name will stand as a type and symbol of ingratitude and treason, written with the blood of Fitzwater and Stanley. But this is not all. The young and defenceless you destroy: you have stood with uplifted dagger over the couch of a sleeping man."

Clifford had fostered the belief that this vilest act of his life, to which he had been driven rather by fierce revenge than hope of reward, was a secret. A moment before he had advanced with hasty and furious glances towards his enemy. Scarcely had the words passed York's lips, than a kind of paralysis came over him. His knees knocked together: his arms fell nerveless to his side.

"O, man!" continued York, "arouse thy sleeping faculties. Bid the fiend who tortures / thee, Avaunt! Even now, at the word, he feels his power over thy miserable soul waver. By Him who died on the Cross, I conjure him to leave thee. Say thou 'amen' to my adjuration, and he departs. Cast off the huge burthen of guilt: deliver thy soul into the care of holy men. As thy first act, depart this spot: leave me. It is I who command – Richard of York, thy sovereign. Begone; or kneeling at my feet, seek the grace thou hast so dearly forfeited."

For a moment it almost seemed as if the wretched man were about to obey; but at the moment his groom came from the spring, where he had been watering his horse. The sight of another human being, to witness his degradation, awoke him to phrenzy. He called aloud, "How now, Sirrah! Why[24] unbit Dragon? Bring him here. I must begone."

---

[a] Variant for 'Satanas', an obsolete form of Satan (OED).

[b] Heathenesse, 'the lands outside Christendom, including in Middle English, Mohammedan lands' (OED).

"He can't carry your honour a mile," said the fellow.

"A miracle," cried Richard; "you repent, Sir Robert."

"As Lucifer in hell! Look to the prisoner." / Clifford vaulted on his horse: his head was bare, his eyes wild and bloodshot. Clapping spurs to the jaded animal's side, he put him to his speed, and was gone.

"His fit is on him!" cried his attendant, "and what are we to do? He rides a race with the fiend, leaving us to do both their works." More whisperingly he muttered, "Hold Duke Richard in bonds against his will may I not. He gave me gold in Flanders; he is a King's son and a belted Knight, and I a poor servitor."

Richard had conceived a faint hope of working on Clifford's manifest remorse, and enlisting him again under the banner of the White Rose. His wonder was great when he saw him flying through the forest with uncovered head and dishevelled hair; the bridle of his horse in the groom's hand, while the wearied animal, spurred to speed, threw up his head, snorting with fear. Not a moment was to be lost, the Prince flew to his comrades in captivity. Already Heron and O'Water had their bonds cut by the sword of which he possessed himself. Heron, in whose / two arms lay his chief strength, and O'Water, at home in a fray, fired with the desire of liberty and life, got speedy hold of battle-axes, and stood at bay. Skelton, the next made free, began to run; but finding his flight was solitary, he secured a bow and arrows, and betook himself to a short, sure aim from behind a tree, while he offered up another sigh to the memory of Trereife. Astley threw himself foremost before his master, unarmed. The weapons of their guard were chiefly in a heap, and these, defended by the enfranchised prisoners, were useless to them. Headed by Clifford's groom, who stood in salutary awe of shedding royal blood, a parley commenced. He entreated Richard to submit; he told him that the whole country was in arms against him, his way back to his army beset, the sea-coasts strictly guarded. What then could he do?

"Die, in arms and at liberty. Stand back, sirs; what would you do with me? Your guilty captain has deserted you; is there one of your number who will raise his accursed weapon against a King and a Knight?" /

Clym of the Lyn, and another outlawed forester, (Clifford in mustering a troop had gathered together all manner of wild companions) now appeared dragging in a fat buck. Clym grinned when he saw the altered state of things: "Come, my men," he said, "it is not for us to fight King Henry's battles; the more Majesties there be in England, the merrier for us, I trow; and the wider and freer the range of the King of the New Forest. Put up your rapiers, and let us feast like brethren; ye may fall to with your weapons afterwards. Or, if it please your Grace to trust to me, I will lead you where none of the King's men will follow."

"Wilt thou guide me back to Taunton?" asked the Prince.

"Not for my cap full of rose nobles," replied the outlaw; "the way is beset: and trust me your worship's men are scattered far and wide ere this. You are a tall fellow, and I should ill like to see you in their gripe. Be one of us; you shall be King of the Greenwood-shade; and a merrier, freer monarch than he who lives at Westminster." /

"Hark!" the word, spoken in a voice of alarm, made the party all ear. There was a distant tramp – every now and then a breaking of bushes – and a whole herd of deer came bounding up the glade in flight. A forester who had rambled further than the rest, rushed back, saying, "Sixty yeomen of the royal guard! They are coming hitherward. Sir Harry de Vere[a] leads them – I know his bright bay horse."

"Away!" /

CHAPTER XI.

————

He might have dwelt in green forest,
   Under the shadows green;
And have kept both him and us at rest,
   Out of all trouble and teen.

OLD BALLAD.[b]

————

It had been the policy of Richard's captors, to have remained to deliver up their prisoners to a stronger force. But most of them were outlaws by profession, who held the King's men in instinctive horror: these were the first to fly; the panic spread; those who had no cause to fear, fled because they saw others do so. In a moment the sward was cleared of all save the prisoners, who hastily bridled their horses, and followed York down a narrow path into a glen, in an opposite direction from the approaching troop. With what speed they might they made / their way through the forest, penetrating its depths, till they got completely entangled in its intricacies. They proceeded for several hours, but their jaded horses one by one foundered: they were in the most savage part of the wood; there was no beginning nor end to the prospect of knotted trunks,

---

  [a] Probably an error for John de Vere, 13th Earl of Oxford.
  [b] 'Adam Bell, Clym of the Clough, and William of Cloudesley', Percy's *Reliques*, 1st series, II, ll. 189–92.

which lifted their vast leafy burthen into the air; here was safety and needful repose. Richard, animated to a sudden effort, could now hardly keep his seat: the state of their animals was imperative for a halt; so here, in a wild brake, they alighted near a running brook; and here O'Water slew a buck, while Astley and Skelton unbridled their horses, and all set about preparing a most needful repast. Evening stole upon them before it was concluded: the slant sun-beams lay in golden glory on the twisted ivy-grown trunks, and bathed the higher foliage in radiance. By the time their appetites were satisfied, Heron and Skelton were discovered to be in a sound sleep; it were as well to follow their example; neither men nor horses[25] could proceed without repose; darkness also afforded best safety for travelling. / It was agreed that they should pursue their way at midnight; and so, stretched on the grassy soil, peace and the beauty of nature around them, each gave himself up to a slumber, which, at that extremity of fatigue, needed no courting.

All slept, save the Prince; he lay in a state of feverish disquietude, looking at the sky through the leafy tracery overhead, till night massed and confused every object. Darkest thoughts thronged his mind; loss of honour, desertion of friends, the fate of his poor men: he was to have devoted himself to them, but a stream, driven by a thundering avalanche from its course, had as much power as he to oppose the circumstances that had brought him from his camp near Taunton, to this secluded spot. For an interval he gave himself up to a tumult of miserable ideas, till from the grim troop some assumed a milder aspect, some a brighter hue; and, after long and painful consideration, he arranged such a plan as promised at least to vindicate his own name, and to save the lives of his adherents. Calmed by these thoughts, / soothed to repose by the gentle influence of a south wind, and the sweet monotony of rustling leaves and running water, he sank at last into a dreamless sleep.

A whispering of voices was the first thing that struck his wakening sense: it was quite dark. "Is Master O'Water come back?" asked Heron.

"I am here," replied the Irishman.

"Hast discovered aught?"

"That the night is dark, and the forest wide," replied O'Water; "had we a planet to guide us we might hope to reach its skirts. We are worse off, than the Spanish Admiral on the western sea, for the compass was a star without a cloud to him."

"Saint Mary save us!" said, or rather whined poor Skelton, "our fortunes are slit from top to toe, and no patch-work will make them whole."

"There is hope at the mouth of a culverin,"[a] said O'Water, "or at the foot of the gallows, so that a man be true to himself. I have / weathered a worse day, when the Macarthys swore to revenge themselves on the Roches."

---

[a] An early firearm; also a cannon.

"And by our Lady's grace," interrupted Richard, "shall again, worthy Mayor. My good fellows, fear nothing, I will save you, the ocean cannot be many miles off, for the sun set at our right hand, and blinded our eyes through the day; the wind by its mildness is southerly; we will face it. When once we reach the sea-side, the shore of the free, wide ocean, Tudor's power stops short, and ye are safe; of myself there will then be time to think. Say, shall we proceed now, or give another hour to repose?"

All were eager to start, slowly leading their horses through the tangled paths they could find, the quarter whence the wind blew their only guide: morning found them toiling on, but morning diminished half their labours; and, as the birds twittered, and the east gleamed, their spirits rose to meet and conquer danger. O'Water was in his native element, that of hairbreadth escape and peril. As to Heron and Skelton, they might have flagged, but for Richard; he flattered their pride, raised their / hopes, making weariness and danger a plaything and a jest. As the sun mounted in the sky, their horses showed many a sign of weariness; and, in spite of a store of venison, which the careful Skelton had brought away with him, they needed refreshment: each mile lengthened to ten; each glade grew interminable in their eyes; and the wide forest seemed to possess all England in its extent. Could the Prince's body have conquered his mind, the White Rose had indeed drooped: he was parched with fever, and this, preying on his brain, made him the victim of conflicting thoughts: his heart, his imagination, were in his deserted camp; even fair Katherine, awaiting tidings of him in her far retreat, had not such power to awaken anguish in his heart, as the idea of Henry's vengeance exercised on his faithful, humble friends, whose father and protector he had called himself. There was disease in the fire and rapidity with which these ideas coursed through his mind; with a strong will he overcame them, bent on accomplishing his present purpose, and rescuing these chief rebels, whose / lives were most endangered, before he occupied himself with the safety of the rest.

At length, at noon, his quick ear caught a heavy, distant roar. The trees had begun to be more scattered: they reached the verge of the forest; they were too weary to congratulate each other; before them was a rising ground which bounded their view; some straggling cottages crowned the height; slowly they reached the hill-top, and there beheld stormy ocean, clipping in the circular coast with watery girdle; at a crow's flight it might be a mile distant; a few huts, and a single black boat spotted in one place the else desert beach; a south wind swept the sea, and vast surges broke upon the sands; all looked bleak and deserted.

They stopped at a cottage-door inquiring the road; they heard there was one, which went three miles about, but that the plain at their feet was intersected by wide ditches, which their fagged animals could not leap. Moreover, what hope of putting out to sea, in opposition to the big noisy waves which the wind was hurrying / towards shore! It were safest and best to take a short repose in this obscure village. Heron and Skelton entered the poor inn, while Richard waited on his horse, striving to win him by caresses to taste the food he at first refused. Heron, who was warm-hearted with all his bluster, brought the Prince out a flagon of excellent wine, such, as by some chance, it might be a wreck, the tide had wafted from the opposite coast: Richard was too ill to drink; but, as he stood, his arm on his poor steed's neck, the creature looked wistfully up in his face, averting his mouth from the proffered grain; half playfully his master held out to him the wide mouthed flagon, and he drank with such eagerness, that Richard vowed he should have another bottle, and, buying the host's consent with gold, filled a large can from the wine-cask; the beast drank, and, had he been a Christian man, could not have appeared more refreshed. The Prince, forgetful of his pains, was amusing himself thus, when Skelton, pale and gasping, came from the house, and voiceless through fear, laid one hand on his leader's arm, and with the other / pointed: too soon the hapless fugitive saw to what he called his attention. Along the shore of the sea a moving body was perceptible, approaching towards them from west to east, which soon showed itself to be a troop of horse soldiers. Richard gave speedy order that his friends should assemble and mount, while he continued to watch the proceedings of the enemy.

They were about two hundred strong – they arrived at the huts on the beach, and the Prince perceived that they were making dispositions to leave a part of their number behind. Fifty men were selected, and posted as patrole – the rest then moved forward, still towards the east. By this time the remaining fugitives had mounted, and gathered in one spot – the villagers also were collecting – Skelton's teeth chattered – he asked an old woman if there were any sanctuary near.

"Aye, by our Lady, is there," replied the dame, "sixteen miles along the coast is the monastery of Beaulieu. A sanctuary for Princes; by the same token that the Lady Margaret, / Saint Henry's Queen, lived safely there in spite of the wicked Yorkists, who would have taken her precious life."

Richard turned quickly round as the woman spoke and heard her words, but again his eyes were attracted to the coast. As the troop were proceeding along the sands, the little knot of horsemen perched upon the hill, caught the attention of a soldier. He rode along the lines, and spoke to the commanding officer; a halt ensued, "We are lost," cried Skelton, "we are taken, Lord! Lord! will they grant us our lives?"

"These trees are tempting, and apt for hanging," said O'Water, with the air of a connoisseur.

"Oh, for Bewley – for Bewley,[a] let us ride!" exclaimed Skelton, longing to go, yet afraid of separating himself from his companions.

---

[a] Phonetic rendering of Beaulieu.

Still the Prince watched the movements of the adverse party. Ten men were detached, and began to advance inland – "Oh, dear my Lord," cried Astley, "betake yourself to the forest – there are a thousand ways of baffling / these men. I will meet them, and put them to fault. Ride, for my lady's sake, ride!"

"Master Astley is a cunning gentleman," said Skelton; "our horses are a-weary, and a little craft would help us mightily."

Still Richard's eyes were fixed on the troopers – the men advanced as far as a broad, deep stream, which intersected the plain; here they hesitated; one of the best mounted leapt across, the others drew back, seeking along the steep, shelving banks for a ford, or a narrowing of the stream. The eyes of the troop on the shore were now turned upon their comrades. "Our time is come," cried Richard; "back to the forest." One step took them down the other side of the hill, hiding sea and beach and enemy from their eyes, and skreening them also from observation. They soon reached the forest, and entered its shade; and then proceeded along just within its skirts. "Whither?" respectfully O'Water asked, after Skelton had for some time been muttering many a hint concerning sanctuary.

"To Beaulieu," said the Prince. "We are / barred out from the ocean – we are beset at land – the little island, ycleped sanctuary, is all that is left to ye. God speed us safely hither."

Richard's horse was lively and refreshed after his generous draught, but those of the others flagged. The Prince exerted himself to keep up the spirits of all; he rallied Skelton, spoke comfort to Astley, and good hope to Heron. The sturdy apprentice of danger, flight and trouble, O'Water, treated it all as a matter of course – even hanging, if it so chanced, was but a likely accident – the others needed more encouragement. Astley feared for his Lord, even to an appearance of timidity, which, though disinterested, had a bad effect on the others. Heron complained bitterly that his dinner had been left unfinished; while the poor tailor, now fancying that he would run away from all, now fearful of solitary misadventure, kept up a garrulous harangue, of which terror was the burthen and the sum. Richard's voice was cheerful, his manner gay; but, placing his hand on Astley, it felt scorching; every moment it required more energy to throw off the clinging lethargy that / fell upon him. It was again evening – a circumstance that had caused them to enter deeper into the forest; and it was to be feared they had lost their way. All were weary – all, save Richard, hungry. The breeze had died away; the air was oppressive, and more and more it felt like a load intolerable to the Prince's burning brow. Night began to close in so very dark, that the horses refused to go forward. Suddenly a roaring sound arose, which was not the sea; and, but that the atmosphere was so still, the wanderers would have said that it was a fierce wind among the trees. Such must it be, for now it came nearer; like living things, the vast giants of the forest tossed their branches furiously; and entire darkness and sudden, pouring rain revealed the tempest, which their leafy prison had before hidden – all was so instantaneous, that it would seem that nature was undergoing some great revulsion in her laws. The Prince's horse snorted and reared, while O'Water's dashed furiously on, striking against a tree, and throwing his rider, from whose lips there escaped a shriek. What would have been the last overflowing drop in the bitter cup to a / weak mind, restored Richard – lassitude and despondency vanished. In an instant he was off his horse at O'Water's side, speaking in his own cheerful, kind voice. "Waste no moment on me," cried the generous Mayor. "My leg is broken – I can go no further – speed you, your Highness, to the sanctuary."

This was the end of hope – the raging storm, the disabled man, dark night, and Richard's resolve not to desert his follower, all were causes of terror and of despair.

A voice in the wood was heard calling aloud; no answer could be returned; it was repeated, and Astley went forward to reconnoitre – even an enemy were help in such disaster, yet Heron and Skelton implored him to remain. Another halloo Richard answered; for he recognized Astley's voice, who in the dark could not find his way back. He came at last, accompanied by a monk – this was heaven's favour revealed; for the holy man was a hermit, and his poor cell was near: poor indeed was it, built with logs, the interstices filled with mud; a bed of dried leaves was nearly all the furniture. The hermit / had gone on first, and lit a torch; as they might, they bore along poor O'Water, and placed him in his agony on the low couch. The hermit looked inquisitively on all the party, neglecting to answer Skelton, who asked for the hundredth time the distance to Beaulieu.

Richard still occupied himself with the Mayor, endeavouring to discover if the limb were broken. "By your leave, your Grace," said the hermit, "I am somewhat of a chirurgeon; I boast of my cures of horses, and have saved a Christian man ere now."

Scarcely did the Prince remember to wonder at the title by which the unknown addressed him. By our Lady's love he besought him to attend to his friend. "Trust me," said the hermit, "I will not fail; but you, my Lord, must not tarry here; the forest is beset with troops: but for night and storm, you would hardly attain Beaulieu in safety. It is but two miles distant: I will guide your Highness thither; and then return to your follower. Have faith in me, my Lord; I have served your royal uncle, and was enlisted under your banner last / year in Kent. I made a shift to escape, and took sanctuary; but the stone walls of a monastery are little better than those of a prison; so I betook me to the woods. Oh, I beseech you, waste no time: I will return to your follower: he is safe till then."

"Direct us, and I will thank you," replied Richard; "but you shall not desert your patient even for a moment."

There was no alternative but to comply: the man gave as clear instructions as he might, and Richard again set forward with his diminished party. They were long entangled by trees; and it was now quite night: the excitement over, the Prince had drooped again. Even this interval was full of peril – a tramp of steeds was heard: they drew up among the trees; a party of horsemen passed; one – could it be the voice of the subtle Frion? – said, "At the end of this glade we shall see the abbey spires. Well I know the same; for when Queen Margaret –"

This speaker was succeeded by a woman's voice: yet greater wonder, she spoke in Spanish, in unforgotten accents – Richard's heart stood / still, as he heard them; but soon both voice and tramp of steeds grew faint; and his brain, becoming more and more bewildered, allowed no thought to enter, save the one fixed there even in delirium. The fugitives continued to linger in this spot until it was probable that the travellers should have arrived. True to the information they had overheard, the forest opened at the end of the glade into a leafy amphitheatre; an avenue was opposite, which led to the abbey gates, whose Gothic spires, buttresses and carved arches, rose above the tufted trees in dark masses. One end of the building was illuminated – that was the church, and the pealing organ stole mournfully on the night, sounding a Miserere; the chaunting of the monks mingled with the harmonious swell, adding that pathos, that touch of solemn, unutterable sentiment, which perhaps no music, save that of the human voice, possesses. Richard's companions were rough-suited, vulgar-minded; but they were Catholic and religious men, and were awe-struck by this voice from heaven reaching them thus in their desolation; / a voice promising safety and repose to their harassed, wearied bodies.

A few steps carried them to the very spot; the bell was rung, the gate was opened, sanctuary was claimed and afforded. Skelton sprang forward; the other two hung back; but, on a sign from Richard, they also passed the sacred threshold. "Farewell, my friends," he said, "a short farewell. Astley, I charge you wait for me. Sir priest, close the gate."

The word was said, the order obeyed, Richard was left alone in darkness. "Now for my task – for my poor trusty fellows. The work of murder cannot yet have begun: my life pays for all. Yet awhile bear me up, thou fainting spirit; desert not Richard's breast till his honour be redeemed!"

Vain prayer! – "I must repose," he thought; "it is of no avail to urge nature beyond herself; a few minutes, and I am strong." He dismounted, and, with a sensation of delicious relief, threw himself at his length on the wet grass, pressing the dank herbage to his fevered brow. At first he felt recovered; but in a few / minutes strong spasms shot through his frame; and these yielded to a feebleness, that forced him to sink to the ground, when he endeavoured to rise: he forgot his situation, the near abbey, his friends; he forgot wherefore, but he remembered that his presence was required somewhere, and with a resolved effort he rose and staggered towards his horse – he fell. "A little sleep, and I shall be well." This was his last thought, and he lay in a state between slumber and stupor upon the earth. /

CHAPTER XII.

———

If the dull substance of my flesh were thought,
Injurious distance should not stop my way;
For then, despite of space, I would be brought
To limits far remote, where thou dost stay.

SHAKSPEARE.[a]

———

There is a terror whose cause is unrevealed even to its victim, which makes the heart beat wildly; and we ask the voiceless thing – wherefore, when the beauty of the visible universe sickens the aching sense; when we beseech the winds to comfort us, and we implore the Invisible for relief, which is to speed to us from afar? We endeavour, in our impotent struggle with the sense of coming evil, to soar beyond the / imprisoning atmosphere of our own identity; we call upon the stars to speak to us, and would fain believe that mother earth, with inorganic voice, prophecies. Driven on by the mad imaginings of a heart hovering between life and death, we fancy that the visible frame of things is replete with oracles – or is it true? And does air and earth, divined by the sorrow-tutored spirit, possess true auguries? At such dread hour we are forced to listen and believe: nor can we ever afterwards, in common life, forget our miserable initiation into the mysteries of the unexplained laws of our nature. To one thus aware of the misfortune that awaits her, the voice of consolation is a mockery. Yet, even while she knows that the die is cast, she will not acknowledge her intimate persuasion of ill; but sits smiling on any hope brought to her, as a mother on the physician who talks of recovery while her child dies.[b]

The Lady Katherine had yielded to Richard's wishes, because she saw that he really desired her absence. Alone in a monastery, in a distant part / of Cornwall, she awaited the fatal tidings, which she knew must come at last. She was too

———

[a] Sonnet XLIV, 1–4 (loosely quoted).

[b] Mary Shelley had watched two of her children die: Clara (September 1818), and William (June 1819). In March 1815 she had also discovered the death of her first-born, an unnamed girl then only two weeks old.

clear-sighted not to be aware, that the armed power of a mighty kingdom, such as England, must crush at once his ill-organized revolt. She was prepared for, and ready to meet, all the disasters and humiliations of defeat; but not to be absent from her husband at this crisis. She ordered horses to be kept perpetually in readiness, that she might proceed towards him on the first intimation of change and downfall. She watched from the highest tower of her abode, the arrival of messengers: before she dared open her letters, she read in their faces, what news of Richard? It was a bitter pang to hear that Plantagenet was dangerously wounded; that the Prince had advanced further forward, at the head of his rabble soldiers.

She had no friends, save humble ones, and very few of these: they borrowed their looks from her, yet hoped more than she did. Quickly she was aware of a change in them: they spoke in a low, subdued voice, as if awe-struck by some visitation of destiny. That very day letters / arrived from the Prince: they were of ancient date, nor could she lay his terms of endearment and cheering to her heart and be consoled. In the afternoon a torn soiled billet was brought her from Edmund. In spite of his wound, he had dragged himself as far as Launceston,[a] on his way to her. Forced to stop, he sent her tidings of all he knew – Richard's mysterious flight, Henry's bloodless victory, the eagerness the King expressed to learn where she was, and the dispatching of troops in search of her. He besought her to fly. It might be hoped that the Prince had escaped beyond sea, whither she must hasten; or falling into his enemy's hands, she would never see him more.

Perplexed and agitated, knowing that dishonour would result from Richard's strange disappearance, yet persauded that he had some ulterior view which it behoved her not to thwart, she hesitated what step to take.

An incident occurred to end her uncertainty. Suddenly, in the evening, Monina stood before her. Monina came with the safety-laden Adalid, to bear her to the shores of Burgundy. She / brought the history of the fraud practised upon York, of the ambush laid for his life, of his escape, and the arrival immediately succeeding to hers, of his followers at the Abbey of Beaulieu; how the pawing and trampling of a horse at the gates had brought out the monks, who discovered the hapless Prince senseless on the dark sod. He was carried in, and through her care his name was entered in the sanctuary. She had attended on his sick couch two days and nights, when his first return to reason was to implore her to seek Katherine, to carry her beyond Tudor's power, out of the island prison. Her father's caravel was hovering on the coast. A favouring south-east wind bore her to these shores: she came at his desire: the Adalid was there, and she might sail, not to Burgundy, but even to the spot which harboured Richard. She also could take sanctuary in Beaulieu.

---

[a] In Cornwall, near the Devonshire border.

333

The monastery in which the Duchess of York had taken refuge, was situated on Saint Michael's Mount, not far from the Land's End. The land projects romantically into the sea, forming a little harbour called Mount's Bay. Towards / the land the acclivity is at first gradual, becoming precipitous towards the summit: now, at high water, the tide flows between the rock and the land, but it was in those days connected by a kind of natural, rocky causeway. Towards the sea it is nearly perpendicular. A strong fortress was connected with the church; and a stone lantern was attached to one of the towers of the church. Not far from the castle, in a craggy and almost inaccessible part of the cliff, is situated Saint Michael's Chair, which, on account of its dangerous approach, and the traditions attached to it, became the resort of the pious. Many a legend belonged to this spot. Its thick woods, the hoar appearance of the crags, the wide spread sea, for ever warring against the land, which had thrust itself out into the watery space, usurping a part of its empire, made it singularly grand; while the placid beauty of the little bay formed by the rock, and the picturesque grouping of the trees, the straggling paths, and numerous birds, added every softer beauty to the scene.[a]

Often did Katherine watch the changeful ocean, or turn her eyes to the more grateful / spectacle of umbrageous woods, and rifted rock, and seek for peace in the sight of earth's loveliness. All weighed with tenfold heaviness on her foreboding soul. For the first time, they wore to her the aspect of beauty, when now she hoped to leave them. Hopes so soon to fail. A south wind had borne the caravel swiftly into the bay, but the breeze increased to a gale, and even while the ladies were making a few hasty preparations, De Faro had been obliged to slip his moorings, and run out to sea, to escape the danger of being wrecked on a lee shore. With a pang of intense misery, Katherine saw its little hull hurry over the blackening waters, and its single sail lose itself amidst the sea foam. The mariner had even, on anchoring, anticipated a storm; he had informed his daughter of the probability there was, that he should be driven to seek for safety in the open sea; but he promised with the first favourable change of wind to return. When would this come? Fate was in the hour, nor could even Katherine school herself to patience.

Evening shades gathered round them; the / Princess growing each minute, more unquiet and miserable, sought in some kind of activity for relief to her sufferings. "I will go to Saint Michael's Chair," she said; "good spirits for ever hover near the sainted spot; they will hear and carry a fond wife's prayer to the throne of the Eternal."

In silence Monina followed the lady. They were both mountain-bred, and trod lightly along paths, which seemed scarcely to afford footing to a goat. They reached the seat of the rock; they looked over the sea, whose dark surface was

---

[a] Cf. Polwhele's vivid description and the accompanying engraving (I, pp. 66–8), of St Michael's Mount and Chair, upon which Mary Shelley may have relied.

made visible by the sheets of foam that covered it; the roar of waves was at their feet. The sun went down blood-red, and, in its dying glories, the crescent moon shewed first pale, then glowing; the thousand stars rushed from among the vast clouds that blotted the sky; and the wind tore fiercely round the crag, and howled among the trees. O, earth, and sea, and sky! Strange mysteries! that look and are so beautiful even in tumult and in storm; did ye feel pain then, when the elements of which ye are composed, battled together? Were ye tortured by the strife of wind and wave, even as the soul / of man when it is the prey of passion? Or were ye unmoved, pain only being the portion of the hearts of the two human beings, who, looking on the commotion, found your wildest rage, calm in comparison with the tempest of fear and grief which had mastery over them.

Sickened by disappointment, impatient of despair, each remained, brooding mutely over their several thoughts.

Poor Katherine; her dearest wish was set upon sharing in all its drear minutiæ the fortune of her lord, her gallant knight, her most sweet Richard. He was her husband; he had taken her, timid yet confiding, from the shelter of her father's roof; they had entered the young world of hope and hazard together. Custom, the gentle weaver of soft woman's tenderness, had thrown its silken net over her; his disasters became hers; his wishes, and their defeat, were also hers. She only existed as a part of him; while enthusiastic love made her fondly cling even to the worst that betided, as better in its direst shape than any misnamed good fortune that unlinked them. "My love, my altar-plighted / love! must I then wake and say no good day to thee; and sleep, my rest unbenisoned[a] by thy good night! The simple word, the *we*, that symbolized our common fate, cut in two, each half a nothing, so disjoined."

While Katherine thus struggled with necessity, Monina was given up to patience. The present hour had fulfilled its fear; her busy thoughts fashioned a thousand plans for his escape, or tremblingly painted a dark futurity. He was a part of her being, though no portion of herself was claimed by him. She was not his, as a lover or a wife, but as a sister might be; if in this ill world such heart's concord could exist: a sharing of fate and of affection, combined with angelic purity. As easily might she fancy animal life to survive in her body after the soul had fled, as soon imagine that the beating of her heart could continue when the living impulse which quickened its palpitations was still, as that he, her childhood's playfellow, the golden dream of her youth, the shrine at which she had sacrificed that youth, should die, and she live on in the widowed world without him. /

The stars glittered over their gentle heads, and the moon went down in the west; fitful, thread-like rays were shed upon the raging sea, whose heady

---

[a] unbenisoned, unblessed.

billows foamed and roared at their feet: both these fair gentle creatures remained, careless of the wild wind that swept their limbs, or the spray, which
high as they stood, besprent their hair: both young, both lovely, both devoted
to one, yet confiding in the reality of virtue and purity, trusting fully each other,
the one accepting the heart's sacrifice which the other unreservedly made, they
watched for the Adalid, which, a plaything of the waves, was carried afar. Day
dawned before they could resolve to quit this spot; then they took refuge in the
near monastery; and from its towers, looked out over the sea.

A few anxious hours brought the dreaded consummation of their fears. The
ascent of a troop of horse up the steep, told Katherine that she was discovered.
Their sudden appearance before her proved that she was a prisoner. For the
first time she saw the White and Red Rose entwined; the Earl of Oxford was
announced / to her as their leader, and he soon appeared, to claim his prize.

Katherine received him with dignified sweetness; she conquered her ill fate
by smiling at its blows, and looked a Queen, as she yielded herself a slave. The
watching of the night had all disordered her dress, and deranged her golden
tresses; but her wondrous fairness, the soft moulding of her face, her regal
throat, and arched open brow, bending over her intelligent, yet soft, blue eyes;
her person majestic, even in its slim beauty, were tokens of a spirit, that in
destitution must reign over all who approached it.

Her first words, to ease the awe-struck Earl, were an entreaty to be conducted to the King. She showed more earnest desire than he to present herself
to her royal victor. In a very few hours, they had descended the Mount; and
hastened out of hearing of the roar of the ocean, which had so cruelly deceived
her hopes. In her eyes could only be read the mastery she had obtained over her
thoughts; no lurking weakness betrayed fear, or even disappointment. – Surely
yet she cherished some dear expectation; / yet how, lost to liberty, could she
hope to attain it?

But thus we are, while untamed by years. Youth, elastic and bright, disdains
to be compelled. When conquered, from its very chains it forges implements
for freedom; it alights from one baffled flight, only again to soar on untired
wing towards some other aim. Previous defeat is made the bridge to pass the
tide to another shore; and, if that break down, its fragments become stepping
stones. It will feed upon despair, and call it a medicine which is to renovate its
dying hopes. /

CHAPTER XIII.

———

For, when Cymocles saw the foul reproach
Which him appeached, pricked with noble shame
And inward grief, he fiercely 'gan approach;
Resolved to put away that loathly blame,
Or die with honour and desert of fame.

SPENSER.[a]

———

After the Prince, by the voyage of Monina, had, as he hoped, provided for the escape and safety of the Lady Katherine, he could not, all weak as he was, remain in repose.

From his early childhood he had been nurtured in the idea that it was his first, chief duty to regain his kingdom; his friends lived for that single object; all other occupation was regarded as impertinent or trifling. On the table of his / ductile boyish mind, that sole intent was deeply engraved by every hand or circumstance. The base-minded disposition of his rival king adorned his cause with a show of use and the name of virtue.

Those were days when every noble-born youth carved honour for himself with his sword; when passes at arms were resorted to whenever real wars did not put weapons in their hands, and men exposed their breasts to sharp-biting steel in wanton sport. Often during his green and budding youth Richard had gloried in the very obstacles set before him; to be cast out and forced to redeem his state, was a brighter destiny than to be lapped in the bosom of guarded royalty. The treason of Clifford and the sacrifice of devoted friends but whetted his ambition; vengeance, the religion of that age, being a sacred duty in his eyes. He had been shaken by Lord Surrey's appeal, but cast the awakened pity off as a debasing weakness.

The painted veil of life was torn.[b] His name had not armed the nobles of his

———

[a] *Faerie Queene*, II. viii. 44 (adapted).
[b] Allusion to P. B. Shelley's *Prometheus Unbound* (1820), III. iv. 190–2; cf. his sonnet, 'Lift not the painted veil'.

337

native land, his cause had not been trumpeted with praise / nor crowned by victory; deserted by foreign allies, unsuccessful in Ireland, he had appeared at the head of a rabble army strong only in wrongs and in revenge. Even these he had abandoned, and with nameless hinds taken sanctuary; his story was a fable, his name a jeer; he no longer, so it seemed, existed; for the appellation of Duke of York was to be lost and merged in the disgraceful misnomer affixed to him by the Usurper.

Richard was no whining monk to lament the inevitable, and tamely to await the result. To see an evil was to spur him to seek a remedy: he had given up every expectation of reigning, except such as sprung from his right, and faith in the justice of God. But honour was a more valued treasure; and to his warm heart dearer still was the safety of the poor fellows abandoned by him. On the third day after his arrival at Beaulieu, he arose from his sick couch, donned his armour, and, yet pale and feeble, sent to speak with the cavalier who commanded the party that guarded all egress from the Abbey. With him he held long parley, in conclusion of / which Sir Hugh Luttrel[a] directed three of his followers to be in readiness, and two of his chosen horses to be led to the Abbey gates. Richard took leave of the Abbot; he recommended his poor followers to him, and lightly answered the remonstrance of the holy man, who thought that delirium alone could urge the fugitive to quit the tranquil, sacred spot, where he himself passed his days in quiet, and which held out so secure a protection to the vanquished. His remonstrance was vain; one word weighed more with Richard than a paradise of peace. Infamy, dishonour! No; even if his people were safe – by throwing himself in the self-same peril to which he had apparently exposed them, that stain were effaced. The very gentleman to whom he had surrendered himself, had trespassed on his allegiance to Henry to dissuade him from the fool-hardihood of his adventure. It was a sight of pity to see one so very young walk voluntarily to the sacrifice; and the princely mien and youthful appearance of the self-constituted prisoner, wrought all to compassion and respect. For still this fair White / Rose was in the very opening flower of manhood; he looked, after such variety of fortune, as if evil not only never had, but never could tarnish the brightness of his spirit or of his aspect; illness had a little enfeebled him, without detracting from his youthful beauty, giving rather that softness which made it loveliness, yet painted fairer by his self-immolating resolve,

> "A sweet regard and amiable grace,
> Mixed with manly sternness did appear,"[b]

and eagerness withal: for eager he was, even to almost foolish haste, to redeem the lost hours, and establish himself again no runaway.[c]

---

[a] Listed in the chronicles among those prepared to fight for Henry VII at Taunton.

[b] *Faerie Queene*, II. xii. 79.

[c] Mary Shelley revises the historical record. After Warbeck sought sanctuary, Henry VII dispatched troops to prevent his escape and insure his surrender, which was swiftly achieved.

With fresh joy he addressed himself to retrace his steps to Taunton. Sanctuary and refuge from death – oh! how he trampled on the slavish thought. Death was to him a word, a shadow, a phantom to deride and scorn, not an enemy to grapple with; disgrace was his abhorred foe, and him he thus overthrew. His resolves, inspired by disdain of permitting one taint to blemish his career, were not the expedients of prudence, but the headlong exploit of / daring youth. The iron must indeed have entered our souls, and we be tamed from dear, youthful freedom to age's humble concessions to necessity, before we can bow our head to calumny, smile at the shafts as they rankle in our flesh, and calmly feel that, among the many visitations of evil we undergo, this is one we are compelled to endure.

Thus he, his gentle guide and followers, travelled towards Taunton. In all prudence, from the moment they left sanctuary, Sir Hugh Luttrel ought to have guarded him closely. But even the staid Sir Hugh forgot this duty; rather was Richard the enforcer of this journey, than his guard. Richard it was who at night halted unwillingly, Richard who first cried to horse at morning's dawn; who, in spite of ill-weather, resisted every delay. As they drew near their bourne, the appellation of Perkin first met the Prince's ear; he was unaware that it had ever been applied to him except by Henry's written proclamations. It acted as a galling spur; for he believed, with youth's incapacity of understanding systematized falsehood, that his presence / would put to flight the many coloured web of invention, which his rival had cast over him to mar his truth and obscure his nobility.

After three days they drew near Taunton. The stubble fields, the flowery hedges, the plenteous orchards were passed. From a rising ground they looked upon the walls of the town, and the vacant moor where his camp had stood. Richard halted, saying – "Sir Knight, I will await you here – do you seek your King: say, I come a voluntary sacrifice, to purchase with drops of my royal blood the baser tide of my poor followers. I demand no more – bid him rear the scaffold; let the headsman sharpen the axe, to lop off the topmost bough of Plantagenet. The price I ask, is the despised lives of men, who, but that they loved me, were incapable of merit or of crime in his eyes. For their humble sakes, like my grandfather York, I am prepared to die. If pledge of this be denied me, I still am free. I wear a sword, and will sell my life dearly, though alone."

Sir Hugh Luttrel was perplexed. He knew the stern nature of his royal master, and how / heavily he would visit on him any disappointment in his dearest wish of obtaining possession of his rival's person. The Prince had, during their three days' companionship, gained great power over him: he felt that he was in truth the son of Edward the Fourth, a man he had never loved (for Sir Hugh was a Lancastrian), but one whom he had feared and obeyed as his sovereign. How could he put slavish force upon his gallant offspring? He hesitated, till the Prince demanded – "Wherefore delay – is there aught else that you desire?"

339

"You pledge your knightly word," said Sir Hugh, "not to desert this spot?"

"Else wherefore am I here? – this is idle. Yet, so to content you, I swear by my vow made under the walls of Granada, by our Lady, and by the blessed Saints, I will abide here."

The knight rode into the town with his followers, leaving young Richard impatient for the hour that was to deliver him to servitude.

Sir Hugh first sought Lord Dawbeny, requesting him to obtain for him instant audience of the King. "His Grace," said the / noble, "is at vespers, or about to attend them."

"I dare not wait till they are said," replied Luttrel, who every minute felt the burthen of responsibility weighing heavier on him.

"Nor I interrupt his Majesty – even now he enters the church."

In haste Sir Hugh crossed the street; and, as the King took the holy water from the chalice, he knelt before him. The few words he spoke painted Henry's face with exulting gladness. "We thank thee, good Sir Hugh," he said, "and will make our thanks apparent. By the mass, thou hast deserved well of us this day! Where hast thou bestowed our counterfeit?"

"Please your Majesty, he awaits your Highness' acceptance of his conditions without the eastern gate."

"You have placed strong guard over him?"

"He pledged his oath to await my return. He is alone."

A dark, angry frown chased all glee from Tudor's brow; bending a stern glance on his erewhile welcome messenger, he commanded / Lord Wells,[a] his cousin, to take a strong force and to seize this Duke of Runaways. Sir Hugh, timid as he was, interfered: driven by respect for his prisoner, and fear of what might ensue, he tried to enforce York's stipulation. Henry looked on him with scorn, then said, "Truly, Cousin, I have vaunted of a bloodless conquest; so let not the blood of the misborn traitor stain our laurels, nor Sir Luttrel's Duke Perkin shed one precious ruby drop. Say aye to all he asks; for as it seems his demands are as foolish as himself, and need no chaffering.[b] Tell him that his life is safe, but bring him here; set him within our ward and limitation: do this, while we with a Te Deum thank our Heavenly Father for his watchful mercies. Sir Hugh, accompany our cousin, and then wend your way whither it please you. We have no pleasure in your presence."

Thus duped, even by his own generous proud spirit, the Duke of York became a prisoner – delivering up his sword, and yielding himself an easy prey to his glad victor. Once, twice, thrice, as he waited the return of Luttrel, it had crossed / his mind, not to fly, his vow being pledged, but to remember that he was now free and unconstrained, and would soon be in other's thrall – when farewell to the aspiring thought, the deed of arms, and to the star of his life, to

---

[a] John Wells, 6th Baron Welles, 1st Viscount Welles (d. 1499), uncle of Henry VII.
[b] Archaic for trading, bargaining, haggling.

whose idea, now his purpose was accomplished, he fondly turned! – "Poor Katherine," he whispered, "this is the crown, the fated, fallen youth, the seer foretold." In after-times that scene dwelt on his memory; he called to mind the evening-tide, for the sun was down, and the clouds, lately gold besprent, waxing dun, as the town walls grew high and dark, and the few trees about him waved fitfully in a soft breeze: that wind was free, and could career over the plain; what spell bound the noble knight and stalwart steed, that they coursed not also free as it?

In a few minutes he was a prisoner – and led within those darksome walls. At first, treated with some observance, he was unaware, as is the case in any new position, with whose circumstances and adjuncts we are unacquainted, how utterly he had fallen. He was led to no barred prison; and, for a time, the nobles and knights / who flocked to see him, were no bad exchange for the motley crew he had quitted. But, as if in a dream, he felt gather round him impalpable but adamantine walls – chains hung upon his limbs, not the less heavy, because the iron pierced his soul rather than his flesh. He had been a free man; his name was attended with love and respect, and his aspect commanded the obedience of men. Now, the very appellation given to him was a mortal insult; a stranger seemed to be spoken to when he was addressed, and yet he must answer. He was never alone; and night was the sole suspension from the insulting curiosity of the crowd. He must forego himself; grow an impostor in his own eyes; take on him the shameful name of Perkin: all which native honour, and memory of his Princess bride, made trebly stinging.

To barb the dart came intelligence that the Lady Katherine was a prisoner. King Henry had quitted Taunton, and gone towards Exeter, when, on his arrival there, the Earl of Oxford presented the Scottish Princess to him. Praises of her wondrous beauty became rife, / brought by some of the King's train, returned to Taunton; praises so excessive and warm as could not have been inspired by celestial beauty in adversity, if not egged on by some adventitious stimulant. It was the fashion to speak of her as the Queen of Loveliness; as (for beauty's sake the name belonged to her) the fairest White Rose that ever grew on thorny bush. By this name she was mentioned to York; and it visited his heart as the first gleam of sunshine on his enshadowed misery: dear was the name of the White Rose to the fallen one. It had been his own in fresh and happy days, when first he showed his prowess among the knights of France and Burgundy. Still louder grew the echo of some mighty voice, that gave forth encomium of the prisoner's bride; and the smiles with which some spoke, smiles half of wonder half of mockery, told of some secret charm, which at last was openly commented upon. "Again the King saw the fair one yestermorn; and dallied ere he granted the earnest suit she made, as if he loved so to be entreated." /

"The grave King Henry caught in the net of the wanton boy! Oh, this were subject for a ballad for the nonce."

341

"Blythe news for gentle Perkin; his wife thrives at court. She takes occasion by too slender a hold, if she raise not her husband from the kitchen to a higher place at court."

"Now we shall see our Lady, the Queen, jealous of her liege."

"Our Queen? what midsummer's dream is this? The White Rose will never flower in our court garden."

To falsify this assertion came the next day a messenger, with command to convey the noble prisoner with all speed to London; and for the attendance of the Lady Cheney and the Lady Howard, two noble matrons, to wait on the Lady Katherine, who was about to proceed to Westminster. Smiles and whispers were interchanged; and, when to this was added, that as much courtesy should be shewn the counterfeit youth as might not endanger his safe keeping, the light laugh followed; though, as if to meet and overthrow the raillery, it was added, / this was ordered for his royal wife's sake, who was cousin to England's dear ally, the King of Scotland. These idle tales did not reach York's ear: wherever he showed himself, he enforced such personal respect, that there was no likelihood that any conjecture, linked with his lady's name, would be hazarded before him. He was told that the King entertained her royally; and when he heard that she was to be presented to his sister, the Queen Elizabeth, a thrill of joy passed into his heart. His sister! as a boy, he remembered the fair, kind girl, whom he had called his loved and most sweet sister: he knew that she was conscious of his truth, and, though wedded to his rival, loved not her lord. It was a pleasing dream, to fancy these gentle ladies together; to know that, while the one spoke her affection and praise, the other must feel the kindred blood warm in her heart, and proudly, though sadly, acknowledge him her worthy brother.[a] /

---

[a] Katherine was styled 'the White Rose' at the English court. Mary Shelley exploits the narrative possibilities opened up by Henry VII's willingness to harbour the pretender's wife.

CHAPTER XIV.

———

They are noble sufferers. I marvel
How they'd have looked, had they been victors, that
With such a constant nobility enforce
A freedom out of bondage.

TWO NOBLE KINSMEN.[a]

———

The vulgar rabble, fond of any sort of show, were greedy of this new one. In all parts the name of the Duke of York, of the counterfeit Perkin, drew a concourse of gazers. The appetite was keenest in London; and many a tawdry masque and mime was put in motion, to deck the streets through which the defeated youth was to pass. Vainly; he entered London at night, and was conducted privately to Westminster. / What strange thing was this? What mark of reality did his very forehead wear, that Henry, so prodigal of contumely on his foes, dared not bring him forward for the public gaze?[b] One man was put in the stocks for a similar remark; and on the following day it was suddenly proclaimed, that Perkin would go in procession from Westminster to Saint Pauls, and back again. A troop of horse at the appointed hour left the Palace: in the midst of them rode a fair young gentleman, whose noble mien and gallant bearing gave lustre to his escort: his sweet aspect, his frank soft smile, and lively but calm manner, had no trace of constraint or debasement. "He is unarmed – is that Perkin? No, the Earl of Warwick – he is a prince sure – yet that is he!" Such murmurs sped around; at some little distance followed another burlesque procession; a poor fellow, a Cornishman, was tied to an ass, his face to the tail, and the beast now proceeding lazily, now driven by sticks, now kicking, now galloping, made an ill-fashioned mirth for the multitude. Whether, as York was not to be / disgraced in his own person, the contumely was to reach him through this poor rogue, or whether the eyes of men were to be drawn from

———

[a] Shakespeare and Fletcher, II. i. 31–4.
[b] Both Walpole and Bayley (pp. 352–3) ask why Henry VII concealed Warbeck from those who might have distinguished the true York from the facsimile.

him to the rude mummery which followed, could only be guessed: the last was the effect produced. Richard heard mass at St. Paul's, and returned to Westminster unmolested by insult. It seemed but as if some young noble made short pilgrimage from one city to the other, to accomplish a vow. The visit of ill-fated Warwick to the cathedral, before the battle of Stoke, had more in it of humiliating ostentation.[a]

He returned to the palace of Westminster. A few weeks he spent in mingled curiosity and anxiety concerning his future destiny. It was already accomplished. Modern times could not present any thing more regular and monotonous, than the way of life imposed upon him. It was like the keeping of a lunatic, who, though now sane, might be momentarily expected to break out in some dangerous explosion, rather than the confining of a state-prisoner. Four armed attendants, changed every eight hours, constantly / guarded him, never moving, according to the emphatic language of the old chroniclers, the breadth of a nail from his side.[b] He attended early mass each morning: he was permitted to take one hour's ride on every evening that was not a festival. Two large gloomy chambers, with barred windows, were allotted him. Among his guards, he quickly perceived that the same faces seldom appeared; and the most rigorous silence, or monosyllabic discourse was imposed upon them. Harsher measures were perhaps spared, from respect to his real birth, or his alliance with the King of Scotland: yet greater severity had been less tantalizing. As it was, the corpse in the grass-grown grave was not more bereft of intercourse with the sunny world, than the caged Duke of York. From his windows, he looked upon a deserted court-yard; in his rides, purposely directed to unfrequented spots, he now and then saw a few human beings – such name could be hardly bestowed on his stony-faced, stony-hearted guards.

Richard was the very soul of sympathy; he could muse for hours in solitude, but it must be / upon dear argument, that had for its subject the pleasures, interests or affections of others. He could not entertain a heartless intercourse. Wherever he saw the human countenance, he beheld a fellow-creature; and, duped a thousand times, and a thousand times deceived, "still he must love."[c] To spend the hour in sportive talk; fondly to interchange the gentle offices of domestic life; to meet peril and endure misery with others; to give away himself, and then return to his inner being, laden like a bee with gathered sweets; to pile up in his store-house memory, the treasured honey of friendship and love, and then away to nestle in the bosom of his own dear flower, and drink up more, or gaily to career the golden fields; such was his nature: and now – this was worse than loneliness; this commune with the mutes of office; to be checked by low-born men; to feel that he must obey the beck of an hireling.

---

[a] Warbeck's visit to the cathedral is invented.
[b] Both Hall and Holinshed use this language.
[c] Alluding perhaps to Byron, 'On This Day I Complete my Thirty-sixth Year' (1824), l. 4.

A month, interspersed with hopes of change, he had endured the degradation; now he began to meditate escape. Yet he paused. Where was Katherine? where his many zealous friends? /

The Lady Katherine was in an apartment of the Palace, whose arched and fretted roof, and thick buttresses, were well adapted to impart a feeling of comfortable seclusion from the rough elements without. The dulness of dark November was gladdened by a huge wood fire. The little Prince of Wales was narrating some strange story of fairyland; and bluff Harry was setting two dogs to quarrel, and then beating his favourite for not conquering, which seeing, his sister Margaret drew the animal from him to console and caress it. The gentle Queen bent over her embroidery. Listening she was to her favourite Arthur, interrupting him with playful questions and exclamations, while Katherine now kindly attended to the boy, now turned anxiously at every sound. She rose at last: "Surely vespers are ringing from the Abbey. My lord the King promised to see me before vespers."

"My lord the King is very gracious to you, sweet one," said Elizabeth.[26]

"Methinks by nature he is gracious," replied the Princess; "at least, I have ever found him so. / Surely the shackles of state are very heavy, or ere this he would have granted my prayer, which he has listened to so oft indulgently."

The Queen smiled faintly, and again pursued her work with seeming earnestness. Was it jealousy that dimmed the silk of her growing rose-bud by a tear – or what name shall we give to the feeling? – envy we may not call it, she was too sweetly good – which now whispered, "Even he, the cold, the stern, is kind to her: my brother loves her passionately; and many a lance has been broken for her. Happy girl; happy in adversity; while I, England's miserable Queen, am forgotten even by my fellow-prisoner of Sheriff Hutton, poor Warwick! he might have been my refuge: for the rest, how hard and rocky seem all human hearts to me." Her tears now flowed fast. Katherine saw them: she approached her, saying, "Dear and royal lady, none should weep, methinks, but only I, whose mate is caged and kept away; none sigh but poor Kate, whose more than life hangs on state policy; or is it for *him* these tears are shed?"

Still Elizabeth wept. Accustomed to the excess / of self-restraint, timid, schooled to patience, but with the proud fiery spirit of a Plantagenet, tamed, not dead within her, she could be silent, but not speak by halves. The very natural vivacity of her nature made her disdain not to have her will, when once it was awaked. She struggled against her rising feeling; she strove to suppress her emotion; but at last she spoke; and once again, after the ten years that had elapsed since her mother's imprisonment, truth was imaged by her words. To none could she have addressed herself better. The life of the Scottish Princess had been spent in administering balm to wounded minds: the same soft eloquence, the same persuasive counsels, that took the sting of remorse from her royal cousin's conscience, was spent upon the long-hidden sorrows of the neglected wife, the humbled woman. From her own sensitive mind she culled the knowledge which taught her where and how peace and resignation were to be found. The piety that mingled with her talk was the religion of love; her philosophy was mere love; and it was the spirit of love, now kindling the / balmy atmosphere of charity to many, now concentred in one point, but ever ready to soothe human suffering with its soft influence, that dwelt upon her lips, and modulated her silver voice. Elizabeth felt as if she had wandered long in a wolf-haunted wild, now suddenly changed to a fairy demesne, fresh and beautiful as poet's dream. Timidly she feared to set her untaught feet within the angel-guarded precincts. The first effect of her new friend's eloquence was to make her speak. After years of silence, to utter her very inner thoughts, her woman's fears, her repinings, her aversions, her lost hopes and affections crushed: she spent her bitterest words; but thus it was as if she emptied a silver chalice of its gall, to be refilled by Katherine with heavenly dew.

The weeks of baffled expectation grew into months.[a] It is a dreary portion of our existence, when we set out hearts upon an object which recedes as we approach, and yet entices us on. The king's courtesy and smiles, and evident pleasure in her society, gave birth to warm hopes in the bosom of the princess. She had / asked to share her husband's prison; she had besought to be permitted to see him; it seemed, from Henry's vague but consolatory answers, that to-morrow she would receive even more than her desires. The disappointment of the morrow, which she lamented bitterly at first, then grew into the root, whence fresh hopes sprung, again[27] to be felled by the cruel axe, again to shoot forth: the sickening sensation of despair crept over her sometimes; her very struggles to master it enfeebled her; and yet she did conquer all but the hard purposes of the tyrant. Now a messenger was to be despatched to Scotland; now he expected one thence; now an embassy from Burgundy: he implored her patience, and talked back the smiles into her saddened countenance. He was almost sincere at first, not in his excuses, but in his desire to please her at any sacrifice; but this disinterested wish grew soon into a mere grasping at self-gratification. In a little while he hoped she would be persuaded how vain it was to expect that he should set free so dangerous a rival; and yet he did not choose to extinguish all her / anticipations; for perhaps then she would desire to return to her native country; and Henry would have sacrificed much to keep her where he could command her society. Thus he encouraged her friendship with the Queen, though he wondered how one so wise, so full of reflection and reason as Katherine, could love his feeble-minded wife.

The King underrated the talents of Elizabeth. This hapless woman had perceived that contention was useless; she therefore conceded every thing without a struggle. Her energies, spent upon endurance, made her real strength of mind seem tameness; but Katherine read with clearer eyes. We are all and

---

[a] '1498' (marginal note in *Abinger/Palacio*).

each of us riddles, when unknown one to the other. The plain map of human powers and purposes, helps us not at all to thread the labyrinth each individual presents in his involution of feelings, desires and capacities; and we must resemble, in quickness of feeling, instinctive sympathy, and warm benevolence, the lovely daughter of Huntley, before we can hope to judge rightly of the good and virtuous among our fellow-creatures. /

The strangest sight of all was to see Henry act a lover's part. At first he was wholly subdued,

> "So easy is, t' appease the stormy wind
> Of malice, in the calm of pleasant womankind."[a]

Even generosity and magnanimity, disguises he sometimes wore the better to conceal his inborn littleness of soul, almost possessed him; for a moment he forgot his base exultation in crushing a foe, and for a moment dwelt with genuine pleasure on the reflection, that it was in his power to gratify her every wish, and to heap benefits on one so lovely and so true. When first she was presented to him, in all the calm majesty of her self-conquering mood; her stainless loveliness had such effect, that surely he could deny her nothing; and when she asked that no foul dishonour should be put upon her Lord, he granted almost before she asked: his expressions of service and care were heartfelt; and she lost every fear as she listened. When custom, which, with man, is the devourer of holy enthusiasm, changed his purer feelings into something he dared not name, he continued to / manifest the same feelings, which had bested him so well at first; and to angle with his prey. Though he scarcely knew what he wished, for a thousand worldly motives sufficed to check any dishonourable approach, it was enough that she was there; that, when she saw him, her countenance lighted up with pleasure; that with the sweetest grace she addressed her entreaties to his ear; not in abrupt demands, but in such earnest prayer, such yielding, again[28] to return with another and another argument; that often he thought, even if he had wished to concede, he would hold out a little longer, that still her sweet voice might address him, still her stately neck be bent imploring as she fixed her blue eyes on him.

It was very long before the artless girl suspected that he had any other intent, but to consent at last to her supplications. As it was as easy to him to lure her on with a greater as a lesser hope, she even fancied that, under certain restrictions, York's freedom might be restored; and that with him, in some remote country, she might bless Tudor as a generous adversary. / Elizabeth was afraid to discover the truth to her, for she also dreaded to lose her, and was afraid that, on the failure of her hopes, she would seek to return to Scotland; or at least seclude herself from her husband's jailor. Monina first awoke her to the

---

[a] *Faerie Queene*, II. vi. 8.

347

truth. Monina, who had been to Brussels, to consult with the Duchess Margaret and Lady Brampton, and who came back full of projects for her friend's escape, heard with amazement and scorn the false lures held out by Henry; she impatiently put aside every inducement for delay, and with rash, but determined zeal, framed many a scheme for communicating with him, and contriving means for his flight.

He himself – the chained eagle – was sick at heart. No word – no breath – no hope! Had all forgotten him? Was he, yet living, erased from the lists of memory? Cut off from the beloved beings in whom he had confided, through their own act – no longer a part of their thoughts, their lives, themselves? Stood he alone in this miserable world, allied to it by hate only – the hate borne to him by his foe? / Such gloomy misgivings were so alien to his nature, that they visited him as cruel iron torture visits soft human flesh. That she – the life of his life, should be false and cold! Each friend forgetful – Monina – Plantagenet – all – all! Oh, to stretch his quivering frame upon burning coals, had been to slumber on a bed of roses, in comparison with the agony these thoughts administered. His calmer moods, when he believed that, though tardy, they were true, were scarcely less painful. Then the real state of things grew more galling: the bluntness or silence of his keepers; their imperturbable or rude resistance to his questions; the certainty that, if one answered graciously – that one he should see no more. Often he felt as if he could not endure his present position one hour longer. Fits of hope, meditations on escape, chequered his days; so that all was not so dark – but the transition from one emotion to another, each to end in blank despair, tasked his mercurial soul. Patience died within him – he might perish in the attempt, but he would be free.

Urged by Monina, by her own awakening fears, / and, above all, by the keen burning desire of her heart, the Lady Katherine became very importunate with the crafty monarch to be permitted an interview with her lord. Henry was in no mood to grant her request: the thousand designs he had meditated to disgrace his victim, he had given up for her sake, because he would not refuse himself the pleasure of seeing her, and feared to behold aversion and horror mark an aspect hitherto all smiles towards him. The same fear, nurtured by the expressions of her tender affection, made him hesitate, ere he should endeavour to convince her that she had misallied herself to an impostor. Indeed, when at last he ventured to frame a speech bearing such a meaning, her answer told him, that, if he could have changed the royal York into base-born Perkin, the young and innocent wife would still cling to him to whom she had pledged her vows; to whom she had given herself;[29] whose own, in heaven's and her own eyes, she unalienably was. But now Henry, grown more callous as time elapsed, coined a new scheme, vile as his own soul: he resolved, by acting on / her woman's fears, tenderness and weakness, to make her the instrument of persuading her lord to some damning confession, that must stamp him as a deceiver for ever. This bright project animated him to fresh endeavours to please, and her with fresh hopes; yet he paused a little before he sought to execute it.

Winter crept on into spring, and spring ripened into summer, and still the various actors in this tragic drama were spending their lives, their every thought and heart's pulsation, on one object. Richard had latterly received intimation that he would be permitted an interview with his beloved White Rose; and a week or two more were patiently endured with this expectation. Katherine each day believed, that on the morrow she should see him, whom now she conversed with only in her nightly dreams, and woke each morning to find him fled with them. Some change approached: Henry's promises became more clear in their expression; his assertions more peremptory; he would at last name his conditions, which she was to communicate to her lord; even Elizabeth / almost dared to hope. Monina alone, deeply impressed with a belief in the malice of Tudor, was incredulous, and reluctantly yielded to Katherine's request to suspend yet a little while her plots.

Whitsuntide[a] arrived, and Henry at last would decide. This festival was to be spent at Shene: thither the royal family went, accompanied by the Princess, who vanquished her disappointment at further delay, not to appear an ingrate to the fair-promising King. Indeed, in the secure hope she cherished of again seeing him who was her earthly paradise, she smiled through the very heart-gushing tears expectation caused to flow. On Whit Sunday she awoke, resolving to discard the heavy load of anticipated evil that involuntarily weighed at her heart. She knelt at mass, and fervently strove to resign her dearest wishes to the direction of her God; and yet that she should see him again soon – oh! how very soon – filled her with such dizzy rapture, that her orisons were forgot midway – remembered, and turned to thanksgivings – till she recollected that still her hope was unfulfilled; / and fear awoke, and with tears and prayer she again strove to ease her agitated heart.

That very night a thunder-storm roused her from slumber: with those unexplained emotions, which, in fateful periods, make so large a portion of our lives, she felt as if every clap spoke audibly some annunciation which she could not interpret: as if every lurid flash were sent to disclose a sight which yet she could not see. At length the rain ceased, the thunder grew distant, the lightning faint; a load was lifted from her soul; she slept, with the firm belief that on the morrow tidings, not all evil, would be brought from London.

Some tidings surely came. What they were she was not permitted to know. For the first time Henry made her a real prisoner; she was carefully guarded, and none were allowed to speak to her. Overwrought by her expectations, this seemed a frightful cruelty; and yet, where caution was used, there must be fear: her – his enemy feared – then good had occurred. She dared not permit her

---

[a] The week beginning with Pentecost, which occurs fifty days after Easter.

imagination to picture / forth the thing which yet was for ever present to it; and, while all else were amazed to hear that York had escaped and fled, his lovely, anxious wife, cut off from communication with all, knew only that she alone was ignorant of what she would have given her life to learn. /

CHAPTER XV.

———

Thou, God of winds, that reignest in the seas,
 That reignest also in the continent,
At last blow up some gentle gale of ease,
 The which may bring my ship, ere it be rent,
 Unto the gladsome port of her intent.
SPENSER.[a]

———

During the winter[b] and the untoward late spring, Richard had endured his captivity. The warm happy summer season, calling all nature to a jubilee, at first saddened, then animated him to contrive new projects of escape. The promised interview with his White Rose tempted him to delay; while an inner spirit rebelled even against this dear enticement, and bade him fly.

On the evening of the ninth of June, he was / permitted to attend vespers in a secluded chapel of Westminster Abbey. During the short passage from the Palace to the Cathedral, it seemed to him as if a new life were awake every where; an unknown power, on the eve of liberating him. Never before had he prayed so fervently for freedom: the pealing organ, the dim arched venerable vault above, acted as stimulants to his roused and eager soul; he stood tiptoe, as on the eve of the accomplishment of his desire.

A deep and awful sound suddenly shook the building; a glaring, lurid flash, filled with strange brilliancy the long, dark aisle. A clap of thunder, loud, and swiftly repeated, reverberated along the heavens; the shrill scream of women answered the mighty voice. The priest who read the service, saw his sacred book glared on by so keen a flash, as blinded him to the dimmer light that

---

[a] *Faerie Queene*, III. iv. 10.
[b] '1498' (marginal note in *Abinger/Palacio*).

succeeded. Every being in the church sank on their knees, crossing themselves, and striving to repeat their paternosters and aves; while Richard stood fearless, enjoying the elemental roar, exulting in the peal, the flash, the tempestuous havock, as powers yet rebellious / to his conqueror. Freedom was victorious in the skiey plains; there was freedom in the careering clouds, freedom in the sheeted lightning, freedom in the cataract of sound that tore its way along. On his poor heart, sick of captivity, and enforced obedience, the sweet word liberty hung as a spell: every bird and tiny fly he had envied as being free; how much more things more powerful, the chainless destructions of nature. The voice of God speaking in his own consecrated abode was terrible to all; soothing to himself alone. He walked to the southern entrance of the edifice to mark the splashing shower, as it ploughed the stones: two of his keepers remained on their knees, paralyzed by terror; the two others followed trembling. At that moment a louder, a far, far louder clap burst right above them, succeeding so instantaneously the blinding flash, that, while every object was wrapt in flame, the pavement and fretted roof of the Abbey shook with the sound. A bolt had fallen; the priest at the altar was struck: with mingled horror and curiosity one of York's remaining / guards rushed towards the spot; the only remaining one was kneeling in an agony of terror. York stood on the threshold of the porch; he advanced a few steps beyond; a new fear possessed the fellow. "He will escape! – halloo! – James! – Martin!" The very words imparted the thought to the Prince, who filled erewhile with wonder and religious awe, had forgotten his own sad plight. He turned to the man, who was doubtful whether to rush into the chapel for his comrades, or singly to seize his prisoner – his dagger was drawn. "Put up that foolish steel," said York, "it cannot harm one whom God calls to freedom – listen, he speaks; – farewell!" The lightning again flashed: with blue and forked flame it ran along the blade of the weapon raised against him; with a shriek the man dashed it to the earth. Richard was already out of sight.

The rain poured in torrents: it came down in continuous cataracts from the eaves of the houses. On this sunny festival few had remained at home; and those, terror-stricken now, were on their knees: no creature was / in the streets as the fugitive sped on, ignorant whither he should go.[a] London was a vast, unknown labyrinth to him: as well as he could divine, he directed his flight eastward, and that with such velocity, that he might compete with a horse in full career. If any saw him, as thus with winged heels he flew along, they did not wonder that a person should hasten to shelter out of the storm. It was of slight

---

[a] Warbeck's escape and recapture are historically based, but the details are Mary Shelley's alone. The chronicles report that when Warbeck broke free on 9 June 1498, he planned to flee to the continent, but found the coast well guarded. He proceeded inland, and sought sanctuary in the Priory at Sheen, known as the House of Bethlehem. Henry VII spared his life at the prior's request. After forced recitations of the confession he had made following his capture the previous year, Warbeck was imprisoned in the Tower.

regard to him, that rain and hail ploughed the earth, and continual thunder echoed through the sky; that alone and friendless he fled through the streets of his victor's chief city. His exulting heart, his light, glad spirit told him that he was free; if for a few minutes only, he would joyfully purchase with his life those few minutes' emancipation from his frightful thraldom. No words could speak, no thought image the supreme gladness of that moment.

Meanwhile, dark night, aided by the thick clouds which still poured down torrents of rain, had crept over the dim twilight, and began to imbarrier with doubt the path of the rejoicing fugitive. He found at last, that the lines of houses / receded, and that he was in an open space, in the midst of which rose a gigantic shadow, stretching itself in stillness and vastness on the summit of the rising ground before him; – it was the Cathedral of St. Paul's. Now, cloaked by the dark and inclement night, he began to reflect on his actual situation: London might swarm with his partizans, but he knew not where to find one. Probably all those who were occupied by his fate resided in Westminster, whence he had precipitately fled; whither assuredly he would not return. These reflections perplexed him, but in no way allayed his transport at finding himself free; he felt that if he wandered to the wide fields, and died of hunger there, it were bliss enough to see the sky "unclouded by his dungeon roof;"[a] to behold the woods, the flowers, and the dancing waves; nor be mocked with man's shape, when those who wore it had sold man's dearest privilege – that of allowing his actions to wait upon the free impulses of his heart.

Still therefore he hurried along, and finally became completely bewildered in some swampy, / low fields, intersected by wide ditches. The night was pitchy dark; nor was there any clue afforded him, by which he could even guess whether he might not be returning on his path. Suddenly a small ray of light threaded the gloom; it went and came, and at last remained stationary. With wavering will and irregular steps the Prince proceeded towards it; for he would rather have died where he stood, than discover himself, so to fall again into captivity. Once or twice he lost sight of this tiny earth-star, which evidently shone through some low casement; and, as at last he caught sight of the solitary miserable hut where it was sphered, the recollection of his former asylum, of ill-fated Jane Shore's penurious dwelling, flashed across him; with speedy, re-assured pace he hurried on, leaping a ditch that obstructed his path, careless of every physical obstacle, when the malice of man was no longer to be apprehended. "Poor Jane!" he ejaculated: and again he reflected with some wonder that, in every adversity, women had been his resource and support; their energies, their undying devotion and enthusiasm, were / the armour and weapons with which he had defended himself from and attacked fortune. Even one so fallen and so low as poor Jane Shore, was, through the might of fidelity

---

[a] Byron, *The Lament of Tasso* (1817), l. 188 (adapted).

and affection, of more avail than all his doughty partizans, who, in the hour of need, were scattered and forgetful.

The low-roofed cot was before him unmistaken. The crevice whence the light emanated was too small to admit his enquiring glance; amid the driving, pattering rain he fancied that he distinguished voices within; but, with a boldness which bade him fear nothing, he lifted the latch, and beheld in truth a sight of wonder; – Monina, with a shriek started from her seat; she folded him with wild joy in her fair arms, and then, blushing and trembling, threw herself on the neck of Lady Brampton; and Jane herself rose from her couch of straw, more wan, more emaciated than ever; – yet even over her sad pale face a smile wandered, shewing in yet more ghastly hues the ruin it illumined.

Questions, ejaculations, wonder and delight, burst from every lip: "He is here to our wish; / the means of escape are secured, and he is here! Oh, dearest Lady Brampton, do not the blessed angels guard him?" Monina spoke, and her soft luminous eyes were fixed on him, as if not daring to believe the vision; it was not the chastened delight of age, but the burning, ardent joy of a young heart, who had but one thought, one desire, and that about to be accomplished; her flushed cheeks betokened her rapture: "I have repined, despaired, almost blasphemed; yet he is here: how good is Almighty God! Listen, dear my Lord, how wondrously opportune your arrival is: Lady Brampton will tell you all. Oh, this new miracle is the blessed Virgin's own achievement – you are free!"

Scarcely less animated, the zealous lady detailed the circumstances that united so favourably for him. She had been for some time at Brussels with the Duchess Margaret, who was more grieved than could be imagined at the capture of her beloved nephew. She lived in a state of terror on his account. That his life was awhile spared, availed little to pacify her; the midnight murders and prison-assassinations, so rife / during the wars of York and Lancaster were present to her imagination. She exhausted every device, every bribe, to gain partizans for him to achieve his freedom. Among others, most liberal of promises, was the false Clifford. After Richard had escaped from him in the New Forest, he fell in with Frion, whose double plot being defeated, he strove to capture and accuse the accomplice whom, in fact, he had deceived. The Knight fled; he escaped to the Low Countries; and by a glozing[a] tale easily gained the ear of the Duchess. Lost in England, perhaps he wished to rebuild his fallen fortunes; aided by her munificence, perhaps he prepared some new treachery: however it might be, he was trusted, and was the soul of the present enterprise. De Faro's vessel, refitted and well manned, was now anchored in the mouth of the Thames. Clifford undertook the task of foisting some creature of his own, or even himself, disguised, of undertaking the part of one of Richard's keepers, when he doubted not to be able to secure his flight.

---

[a] Archaic for 'flattering'.

With her usual vivacity Lady Brampton gave / this account; but no explanations on her part could dissipate the horror York felt at the name of Clifford, or inspire him with any thing but distrust of his intentions. Monina, before silenced by her sanguine associates, now gave expression to the terror and abhorrence his interference occasioned; she had come, exposing herself to a thousand perils and pains, merely that she might watch over his acts, and awaken her too credulous friends to a knowledge of his duplicity. But the danger was past; before Clifford could know that he had escaped, York might reach the Adalid.

Almost as an answering echo to these words there was a sound of hurrying steps. "It is he: the traitor comes. Oh, bar the door!" There was no bar, no mode of securing this dwelling of penury; three women alone were his guard: Monina, pale and trembling; Lady Brampton, endeavouring to reassure her; while Richard stood forward, his gaze fixed on the opening door, whose latch was already touched, resolved to meet, with perfect show of frank reliance and intrepidity, the intruders. /

Sir Robert Clifford entered. Confusion, attempted boldness, and, last, sullen malice painted his aspect when he beheld the Prince. He was much changed, and looked almost an old man; his dark and profuse hair was grizzled; his grey eyes hollow; and his dress, though that of a cavalier, exhibited signs of habitual neglect. His person, always slight, had been redeemed from insignificance by its exquisite grace and elegance; every trace of this was flown; and his haggard countenance and diminutive size made even York scarcely credit that this was indeed the gay, reckless Robin. His resolve had been already made; he addressed him kindly, saying, "Sir Robert, I hear that you are willing to renew to me your broken vows: may you hereafter keep them more faithfully."

Clifford muttered a few words; he looked towards the door, as if desirous of escape; he struggled with shame, guilt, and some other emotion. As soon as a consultation began as to the means to be adopted for the Prince to reach the sea in safety, he conquered himself, / entering into it with spirit and zeal. The plan he proposed was crafty, his own part in it the principal. He spoke of disguising the prince as a female attendant on Monina; of his and O'Water's accompanying them along the river banks as soon as daylight.

"And wherefore not now? Or rather, wherefore even now do we not hasten to the Thames, and seize a boat?"

"Because," said Clifford, interrupting Monina, "his Highness's flight is already known; a line of boats intersects the Thames below London Bridge; and lower still every craft is on the alert."

Each one exchanged looks; the Knight continued: "You all distrust me, and I wonder not. I am in your power now; here are my unarmed hands; even a woman may bind them. Go forth yourselves; seek the path to the sea: before an hour elapses the Duke will be again a prisoner. You may in this wild spot plant your daggers in my heart to avenge, but that will not save him; for I have no power here. But set me free, confide to my care, and, by the / God that made me, he walks the deck of the Adalid ere the setting sun. I could tell you how this can be, and ye would not the more trust me, if I spoke of such alliance with, such power over, the rogues and vagabonds of this saintly city, as enables me to move strange engines to execute my will; even if you credited me, you would disdain that your hero should owe his life to such base means. Be it as you will: believe me; and I pledge my life that his Grace will ride the dancing waves beyond King Henry's reach to-morrow night."

"I accept the pledge," replied York, who had eyed him earnestly as he spoke. "I commit myself to your care; act speedily, without fear of balk or suspicion on my part."

Clifford's lips curled into a triumphant smile; because again he was trusted, or because again he would betray, it was hard to divine. "I must beseech your patience in the first place," said Sir Robert: "I cannot get the fitting disguises during the night."

"Night is no more," replied Richard, throwing open the casement; and the dusky room was / illuminated by the day. In the east there was a very fountain of light, which, welling up, flooded the flecked and broken clouds with rosy hues: the stars were gone; a soft azure peeped between the breaking vapours; the morning air was deliciously fresh; the birds chirped; a distant watch-dog barked. Otherwise all was silent; and security seemed to walk the earth.

"I will go seek the needful dresses," said Clifford. "Your Grace will await my return, even though my stay, lengthened beyond my expectation, give some reason for the distrust I read in every eye."

"It is but too natural," said the Prince, "that my kind friends should suspect you; for myself, I have said the word; I place myself in your hands: half measures were of no avail. If indeed you are a traitor, bring Tudor's hirelings here to seize their prey. I cannot fear; I will not doubt; and, if in my soul any suspicion lurk, my actions shall not be guided by it. Go; let your return be speedy or otherwise, I await you here."

Scarcely had the door closed, when Monina, / whose eyes had been fixed on Clifford's countenance during the whole scene, exclaimed: – "This moment is our own! Fly, my Prince; trust me – I know that bad man; if he find you here when he returns, you are lost."

"Hist!" Jane spoke the word, and a dead silence fell upon the anxious band. The steps of a horse were heard: Monina flew to the casement. "It is our faithful[30] Irish friend, my Lord; it is O'Water." The door was opened; and each one crowded round the visitant. He uttered a "By the mischief!" which sounded like a benediction, when he saw the Duke of York, adding, "all is well, all in readiness; I left the Adalid, after the storm yester evening, in safe anchorage."

"Oh yes, safety," cried the enthusiastic Spaniard; "safety or death! Trust not false Clifford – seize the fleeting, precious opportunity – O'Water's horse – "

"Is blown," said Richard, "he cannot carry me."

"And the ways strangely beset," said the Mayor. "Just now I saw a young gentleman / seized, much to his annoyance, by some patrol. He bribed dearly, but they would not listen – the whole country is alarmed."

"I will wait for Clifford," continued York; "and trust in providence. Some kind friend only bestow a dagger on me: I would not be taken like an unarmed girl."

"A tramp of steeds – they are coming, Clifford guides them hither; we are lost!" cried Lady Brampton.

"Oh, fly – fly – my liege," said O'Water, "expose not these women to the assault. Poor Rose Blanche can yet bear you fast and far."

The sound as of a troop of horse neared. The Prince saw O'Water blocking up the casement, and then draw his sword. Monina, wild with agony, fell at his feet: – "Fly, my Lord, fly for the Lady Katherine's sake: fly for mine own: must I see you die? I, who have lived – alas! how vainly. Lady Brampton – beseech – command – he must fly. O, they will be here – to seize, to murder him!"

"Here is my dagger, my lord," said O'Water coolly; – "Defend yourself – meanwhile – now / at our last hour – for surely it is come, Our Lady recommend us to God's holy grace."

The gallop of a troop grew yet more distinct; Richard looked round: Jane was kneeling, her face buried in her hands: Lady Brampton pale, but resolved, was ready to sacrifice the life she had spent for him. O'Water had resigned himself to the final act of a life of peril, sealed in his blood. The lovely Spaniard alone lost all her self-possession; tears streaming from her uplifted eyes; her arms twined round his knees: to fly – fly! was the only thought she could express. "I yield," said York; "throw open the door." O'Water's horse had been led within the hut; he vaulted on his back; he placed the dagger in his belt. "That way," Lady Brampton cried, "it leads to the river's side below."

A scream from Monina followed his swift departure. "He perishes – he betrays us!" cried O'Water. Richard galloped on; not across the fields away from town, but right into danger; there, whence the troop was certainly approaching. He was lost to view on the instant, / in a straggling lane which stretched out half across the field. A moment after, coming from the other side, unobserved till in the hut, Clifford entered alone. He bore a large bundle; his steps were cautious and swift; his look told that he was intent only on the object of his errand. "I have succeeded beyond my hope. My life on it all is safe. Where have ye hid the Prince? Oh, prithee, fear not, nor trifle: each second is precious."

The confused, wondering looks of all present replied to him. Clifford laughed, a short, sarcastic, bitter laugh: and then, with a fiendlike expression of face, he said, "The Prince has done well; and ye have all done well: and his Grace will thank you anon. Ye grudge me, maybe, the Duchess Margaret's bounty. She promised largely; 'twere pity to share the boon among so many. Now mark the event!"

These words displayed the baseness of his motive, yet vouched for his sincerity. He threw a menacing glance around, and then quitted the hut; and with hurried pace hastened across the field towards the town. /

CHAPTER XVI.

———

Full many a glorious morning have I seen,
Flatter the mountain tops with sovereign eye,
Kissing with golden face the meadows green;
Gilding pale streams with heavenly alchemy;
Anon, permit the basest clouds to ride
With ugly rack on his celestial face.

SHAKSPEARE.[a]

———

The Duke of York, urged so earnestly to fly, felt that to do so was to save himself at the expense of his friends, on whom Henry's vengeance would severely fall, when he found himself balked of his victim. He consented to leave Jane Shore's abode, with the resolve not of effecting his escape, but of securing, by surrendering himself, the safety of his defenceless adherents united under her lowly roof. He / directed his course as he believed into the very centre of danger, entering the narrow straggling street whence the sound of the advance of the troop of horse had been heard. He entered the lane; it was empty. The ominous sounds were still sharp and near; it seemed as if they were in some street parallel to the one which he threaded. He turned at right angles into another, to reach the spot; again he turned, led by the baffling noise, in another direction. It was just four in the morning; there were but few abroad so early: he saw a monk gliding stealthily from under a dark archway, and a poor fellow, who looked as if he had slept beneath heaven's roof, and had not wherewithal to break his fast. True to the kindly instincts of his nature, Richard felt at his girdle for his purse; it was long since he had possessed the smallest coin of his

---

[a] Sonnet XXXIII, ll. 1–6.

357

adversary's realm. "I, a Prince!" his feeling had been more bitter, but that his fingers came in contact with his dagger's hilt, and the conviction of freedom burst with fresh delight upon him. Free, even in spite of his intents; for the / tramp which had gradually grown fainter, was dying absolutely away.

They had probably reached the hut: thither he must return. It was no easy thing to find his way to it, he had so entangled himself in the narrow lanes, and wretched assemblages of dwellings huddled together on the outskirts of London. At length they opened before him; there was the dingy field, there the hut, standing in quiet beneath the rays of the morning sun, of the opening, summer, soft, sweet day. He was quickly at its threshold; he entered. Jane was within, alone, seated in her wooden chair; her hands clasped; her pale face sunk on her bosom: big tears were gathering in her eyes, and rolling down her faded cheeks unheeded. Jane's aspect was usually so marble (a miraculous chiseling of resigned hopelessness,) her mien so unbending, that these signs of emotion struck the Prince with wonder and compassion.

He knelt at her feet and pressed her thin, but little hand to his lips, saying, "Mother, where are my friends? Mother, bless me before I go." /

She dried the drops raining from her eyes, saying in a voice that expressed how occupied she was by her own emotion, "I am a sinful woman; well do these tones remind me of the same: those days are quite, quite gone, even from the memory of all; but once they were as the present hour, when so he spoke, and I was lost, and still am lost; for, through hunger, and cold and shame, I love, and cannot quite repent. Will the hour ever come when I can regret that once I was happy."

Many, many sad years had passed since words like these had dropped from poor Jane's lips; her feelings fed on her, possessed her, but she had been mute; overflowing now, her accent was calm; she spoke as if she was unaware that her thoughts framed speech, and that she had an auditor.

"You have paid a dear penalty, and are surely forgiven," said York, striving in his compassion to find the words that might be balm to her.

"Prince," she continued, "some time ago, – I have lost all date; now the chasm seems / nought, now a long eternity; it was when my poor heart knew nothing of love save its strong necessity and its delight; methought I would see your father's fair offspring, for I loved them for his sake. At the festival of Easter I placed myself near the gate of the royal chapel: I thought to be unseen. The happy Queen held her sons each by the hand; you were then, as now, his image, a little sportive blue-eyed cherub. The Prince of Wales had his mother's look; her large, dark eye, her soft, rosy mouth, her queenlike brow; her beauty which had won Edward, her chaste sweetness, which had made her his wife; my presence, I thought to conceal it better, was revealed. The Queen turned her face away; there was anguish surely written there, for the Prince darted on me a look of such withering scorn – yes, even he – his stainless, fair brow was knit, his bright angel's face clouded: the look sunk in my heart. Edward's beautiful, pure child reproved me, hated me: for three days I felt that I would never see the deluder more: you do not share his abhorrence; / you do not hate the pale ghost of Shore's wife?"

Such clinging to the past, such living memory of what was so absolutely dead to all except herself, awe-struck the Prince, "We are all sinners in the eye of God," he said, "but thy faults are surely forgiven thee, gentle one; thy tears have washed every trace away, and my brother, my poor murdered Edward, now blesses thee. Alas! would that I could soften this last stage of your suffering earthly life."

"'Tis better as it is," she answered hastily, "once I felt disgrace and privation keenly; perhaps that may atone. Now, would it were more bitter, that so I might wean myself from him whose very memory will lose my soul. You are good, and Our Lady will requite you. Now, listen, the damsel Monina and Master O'Water have gone towards Southend:[a] your remaining friends watch for you here. I shall see them again to-night: meanwhile it is to be feared that Clifford plots vengeance, and you must fly; you must at every hazard go towards Southend. Beyond the town, on the lone sands, there is a / wooden cross, telling where one escaped dreadful peril through the might of Him who died on it for us; the smallest sign, the waving of your cap, will be watched for by the Adalid, they will send a boat to take you on board. Now swiftly depart: your life hangs on the hour; this purse will furnish you with means: Lady Brampton left it for you."

"Bless me, mother, ere I go."

"Can a sinner's blessing avail? fear rather that God punish me through you, where my heart is garnered. Oh, may he indeed bless and save you; and I shall die in peace."

He kissed her withered hand and was gone; she dragged her failing limbs to the casement; he was already lost among the straggling tenements that bounded her field.

Again York was flying from his foe; again studying to elude pursuit, with how different feelings. Before, his flight was peremptory, for the preservation of others, while he blindly longed to deliver himself to slavery. Now liberty, for its own dear sake, was worth the world to him. He had tasted to its dregs the misery of captivity, and loathed the very name; whatever might betide, / he would never submit willingly again to one hour's thraldom. He felt his dagger's hilt; he drew it from the sheath, and eyed its polished blade with gladness; for eight months he had been living unarmed, under the perpetual keeping of armed jailors; what wonder that he looked on this sharp steel as the key to set him free from every ill.

He got clear of the town: the open sky, the expanse of summer – adorned

---

[a] Southend (or South End, p. 361), on the coast directly east of London.

earth was before him. It was the "leafy month of June;"[a] the far spread corn-fields were getting yellow; and on their weltering surface played the shadows of a few clouds, relics of the last night's storm: the sun was bright, the breeze balmy, already the very foot-paths were dry, and scarcely from its inmost leaves did any tree shake moisture: yet there was a freshness in the scene, a lightness in the air, the gift of tempest. The dazzling sun rose higher, and each island-vapour sunk on the horizon; the garish light clothed all things; the lazy shadows crept up around the objects which occasioned them, while both object and its shade seemed to bask in the sunshine. / Now over head the meeting boughs of trees scarce sufficed to shield him from the penetrating glare; now in the open path he was wholly exposed to it, as his diminished shadow clung almost to the horse's hoofs. The birds twittered above; the lazy mare was stretched basking, while her colt gamboled around; each slight thing spoke of the voluptuous indolence of summer, and the wafted scent of hay, or gummy exhalation of evergreens, distilled by the warm noon, fed with languid sweets every delighted sense. If paradise be ever of this world it now embowered Richard. All was yet insecure; his White Rose was far; but nature showered such extasy on him that his whole being was given up to her influence. Latterly the form of man had been ever before his aching sight under the aspect of an enemy; the absence of every fellow-creature he hailed with gladness – free and alone, alone and free! With the pertinacious dwelling on one idea, which is characteristic of over-powering feeling, this combination of words and ideas haunted his thoughts, fell from his lips, and made a part of the soul-subduing rapture now his portion. /

May it be added – we must address the unhappy and imaginative, who *know* that the future is so linked with the present as to have an influence over that present, when we add – that the intensity of the liberated Prince's feelings was wrought even to pain, by its being the last time that unalloyed delight would ever be his – the last when he might feel himself the nursling of nature, allied by the bond of enjoyment to all her offspring. He knew not this himself. Immersed in the sense of all that he now possessed, he did not pause to reflect whether this were the last time, that he, the victim of chance and change, might ever see the waving corn or shadowy trees, or hear the caroling birds, or the murmurs of the fresh free brooks gurgling round some pendant bough or jutting stone; but that so it was to be, gave poignancy to his pleasure, a dreamy halo to the whole scene.

It would appear, in spite of the precautions taken by his enemy, that the north bank of the Thames had been neglected. Richard met with no impediment in his progress. Whenever he caught a sight of the river, he perceived unusual / signs of activity. Little wherries shot hither and thither on its surface,

---

[a] Coleridge, 'The Rime of the Ancient Mariner,' l. 370, first published in *Lyrical Ballads* (1798).

revealing to him that keen and vigilant search was being made. Meanwhile he rode on, the broad stream for his guide, avoiding towns and villages. He ventured to purchase bread at a lone farm-house – he alighted in a little grove beside a rivulet, to rest his tired horse, and to refresh himself. The summer heat recalled Andalusia to his mind; and scenes and objects quite forgotten, wandered from their oblivious recesses back into his recollection. "My happy boyhood! My beloved Spain! Why did I leave the land of beauty, where with Monina – ?" The idea of her whose fate was so inextricably linked with his, of his bride, who had quitted her palace home to share his adversity, reproached him. But his imagination could not fix itself on bleak Scotland, its wild haunts, its capricious king: it could only build another bower among the folds of the mountains of Andalusia, and place his White Rose therein.

Again he pursued his way. The slant beams of the descending sun were yet more sultry, but it sank swiftly down; now casting gigantic / shadows, bathing the tree tops in golden dew, and flooding the clouds with splendour; now it was gone, and the landscape faded into a brown mellow tint. The birds' last chirp was given, the beetle winged her noisy flight, the congregated rooks had flown to the belfry of the church, or to their nests in the church-yard trees; silence and twilight crept up from the sedgy banks of the river, leaving the pale water alone to reflect the struggling farewell of day. In a little time the banks shelved away, giving place to broad yellow sand. Richard ventured to bend his course along the beach. There was a bark upon the dim tide, whose progress he had watched since noon, whose flapping or full sails were the signs by which he foretold the prosperity of his destined voyage. Now with swelling canvas it walked swiftly over the water.

He passed South End. He perceived the tall rough-hewn cross. Two figures were seated at its foot. He hesitated, but quickly perceiving that one was a woman, he proceeded onwards. The stars were out; the very west was dim; in the offing there was a vessel, whose build and / tall slender masts he thought he recognized. The broad expanse of calm ocean was there, whose waves broke in tiny ripplets on the beach. He reached the cross. O'Water and Monina saw his approach. The Irishman welcomed him boisterously, in his own language. Monina uttered a benediction in Spanish. The scene was solitary and secure. Every danger was past. There floated the caravel which ensured escape, and the stars alone witnessed their flight. Monina gave her white veil to O'Water, who contrived to elevate it on the cross. In a few moments the splash of oars was heard, and a dark speck floated towards them on the waves, from the direction of the Adalid. "They come; you are safe," murmured his lovely friend; "this hour repays for all." The boat was already on the beach: a seaman leaped on shore. "The White English Rose," he said: such was the word agreed upon; and, hailing it, Monina hurried to embark with her companions. The little boat was pushed from shore. O'Water gave vent to his delight in a shout, that resembled a / yell. Monina crept close to the Duke of York: that he was safe was a truth so dear, so new, that she forgot every thing, save her wish to assure herself again and again that so it was. At that moment of triumph, something like sadness invaded Richard: he had quitted the land for which his friends had bled, and he had suffered, – for ever: he had left his Katherine there, where all was arrayed against him for his destruction. This was safety; but it was the overthrow of every childish dream, every youthful vision; it put the seal of ineffectual nothingness on his every manhood's act.

While each, occupied by their peculiar reveries, were aware only that they were being borne onwards on the waves, a smaller boat shot athwart their bows, and a voice exclaimed in Spanish, "Desdichados, estais allá?"[a]

"My father – we are betrayed," Monina cried: and she threw her arms round Richard, as if by such frail guard to shelter him – another stronger grasp was upon his arm as he endeavoured to rise – a voice, husky from passion, yet still / Clifford's voice, muttered, "The day is mine – you – she – all are mine!"

"Thou fell traitor! What ho! De Faro to the rescue!" already the mariner had thrown a grappling iron – already the Adalid was in motion towards them. Clifford strove to draw his sword. York was upon him in mortal struggle; his keen dagger, unsheathed, uplifted; the boat lurched – his arm descended, but half the force of the intended blow was lost, while both fell overboard. The crew rushed to the boat's side to loosen the grappling iron, which concluded its upset. De Faro, who stood high on the bows of his own boat, had seized Monina. Now another larger skiff was seen approaching, "To your oars!" cried the Moor: they shot swiftly towards the Adalid, and while the sea became alive with craft, they reached the little caravel, who turning her canvass to the wind, dropped down the tide. /

---

[a] 'Wretches, are you there?'

CHAPTER XVII.

———

"Your love and pity doth th' impression fill,
Which vulgar scandal stamped upon my brow;
For what care I who calls me well or ill,
So you o'erskreen my bad – my good allow?
                                        SHAKSPEARE.[a]

———

On the fourth day of her restraint, imprisonment it could hardly be called,
Lady Katherine was brought up to Westminster; she was carried in a close
litter, and no familiar face or accustomed attendant came near. Her anxiety, her
anguish weighed intolerably upon her – sleep had not visited her eyes; she lived
in perpetual terror that each sound was freighted with fatal tidings. It was in
vain that even reason bade her nourish hope – a stronger power than reason /
dwelt in her heart, turning all its yearnings to despair.

As she approached the city she thought each step must reveal the truth of
what she was to suffer. Lo! the palace was entered – her habitual chamber –
silence and solitude alone manifested that some change was even now in its
effect; she had no tears to spend upon her grief; her changing colour, her
quickened respiration shewed that every faculty was possessed by terror. Two
hours, each minute stretched to a long long century, two hours passed, when a
little scroll was delivered to her; it came from the Queen, and contained these
words, "My White Rose! the tempest has past – leaving, alas, devastation: we
yet remain to each other – come –"

These expressions spoke the worst to her fear-stricken mind – no subsequent
agony might ever compare to the pang, that made her very life-blood pause in
her failing heart at that moment. Had the present and the future become void
for him, to whom she was wedded heart and soul? – wedded in youth, when
our hopes stretch / themselves not merely to to-day and to-morrow, but even to
eternity. In this state of human woe, we do not describe the disheartening and
carking sorrows of those who lag on life's high way – but the swift, poignant,

———

[a] Sonnet CXII, ll. 1–4 (loosely quoted).

363

intolerable agonies of the young, to whom the aspiration for happiness is a condition of being. The Queen had been accustomed to witness and admire Katherine's self-command and quiet fortitude; she was awe-struck on beholding the devastation of the last four days, and the expression of wild horror on her soft features. With feminine instinct she read her heart, her first words were, "Sweet love, he lives – and he will live – his life is spared, and we may still hope."

Tears at last flowed from the mourner's eyes, as she asked, "What then will be his fate? – Shall I ever see him more?"

"How can we guess the hidden purposes of the King? By your enforced solitude you have escaped his scowling brow, his violence, his sarcasms; again he smiles. My gentle Kate, my sweet courageous sufferer, hitherto we have played with the lion's fangs – they are unsheathed / in anger now – let us prepare: he will be here anon."

The Princess desired not to exhibit too humiliating a spectacle of misery to her cruel foe – she checked her weeping – she endeavoured to forget the burning agony that tortured her beating heart. "Let him but live; let me but once more see him;" and the unbidden tears flowed again. The King soon broke in upon them; his look was haughty even to insolence: an expression of vulgar triumph was in his eyes, that baffled the eager scanning gaze of the hapless Princess. He said, scoffingly, (and was it in man's nature, or only in Henry's, to look on the sad, but lovely countenance of his victim, and to mock her woe?) "We congratulate you, Lady, on the return of the gentle Perkin to our good city of Westminster – do not weep – he is in safe keeping now, very safe – it is no feathered shoe our Mercury[a] wears this day."

"Holy Virgin!" cried Katherine, "your Grace does not surely mean –"

"Fear not – he lives," continued Henry, his scorn growing more bitter as he spoke; "he / lives, and shall live, till the White Rose acknowledge on what base stock she is grafted, or he twist the rope by some new sleight. Is Perkin's honoured dame satisfied?"

"Oh no, no, no; some covert meaning you have; in pity for a woman speak." The agony her countenance expressed, was the mute echo of the frightful idea that convulsed her frame. "Oh, let me see him! you have tormented me too cruelly; even if my worst fears prove true, he suffers not more than I; and can it be that the young limbs of my own loved Richard are put to torture!"

Elizabeth grew ashy white; the King listened with a sarcastic smile, saying, "I had not thought of that; you are a silly girl to mention such things."

"I do not believe you," exclaimed the Princess, "your looks bely your words; let me but see him afar off, let me catch a glimpse of my princely love – is he in the Tower?"

---

[a] The fleet-footed messenger of the gods in Roman mythology.

"Neither the Tower, nor any royal palace detains your lord; he is taking the air, pleasantly I hope, in the high places of our town. To / finish this war of words, and your incredulity, will you visit your prince of plotters, and behold him on whom the King of Scotland bestowed your virgin hand?"

"See him! Oh, even in death to clasp his decaying limbs were better than this absence!"

An indefinable expression passed over Henry's countenance as he replied, "Be it as you wish; you must hasten, for in an hour the occasion will be past; it is but a few steps; you shall be attended."

At last she was to see him; this assurance filled and satisfied her; there was no place in her heart for any other thought, sinister as were her torturer's looks. Her eyes grew bright, her cheek resumed its vermeil tint, never had she looked more lovely; it was a dazzling beauty; one of those ineffable expressions, which, unless language could express music, or painting image fire, it is in vain to attempt to describe: an irradiation of love passed over her countenance; her form; something like it dwells in Raphael's Madonna's and Guido's Angel of Annunciation,[a] – Henry was awestruck, yet did / not falter in his purpose; he let the bright angel go forth on her mission of good and love, to meet on her way a sight fiends might rejoice over. Human life and human nature are, alas! a dread, inexplicable web of suffering and of infliction.

In Westminster, in sight of the Abbey where his ancestors had been crowned kings, the spectacle intended to be so opprobrious, was set forth. Henry, in his angry fear on his escape, in his exultation at his re-capture, forgot the soft tyranny of Katherine's looks; or rather he despised himself for the obedience he had yielded to them; and, in the true spirit of baseness, was glad to revenge on her the ill effects that had resulted to him through his involuntary enslavement. It was a triumph to him to disgrace the object of her care, for he was ill read, his understanding affording him no key to the unknown language, in that illuminated page of the history of feminine excellence, which tells the delight she feels in exhausting her treasures of devoted love on the fallen, because they need it most: he believed, that to present her husband / to her, under the very infliction of ignominy, would turn her affection to cold disdain – he permitted her to go. Attended by some of the body guard and a gentleman usher, she hastened through the courts of the palace into the open square: there was assembled a crowd of common people, hushed to universal silence: at a distance from the centre some were talking aloud, and the name of "Perkin" was the burthen of their speech; but pity stilled those nearest to the spot, towards which, to the surprise and horror of all, she hastened. The crowd instinctively closed to bar her advance; and, when forced to make way, in spite

---

[a] For Raffaello, famous for his madonnas, see p. 10n. Mary Shelley praised Guido Reni (1575–1642) to Leigh Hunt in 1819 (*MWSL*, I, p. 90), when she probably saw the Annunciation (1610) in the Cappella dell'Annunziata of the Quirinal Palace, Rome.

of the despotism of the times, the word "Shame" burst from the lips of many, especially the women. She was agitated by the obstacles, by the numerous uncourtly eyes turned on her; still she went on, and soon saw –

She understood not what – a kind of wooden machine in which the lord of her heart sat.[a] There had been a time when pride and royal majesty of soul had shed such grandeur over York, that, when exposed as a show, he had / excited reverence, not scoffing. Now he was evidently labouring under great physical suffering; his brow was streaked with mortal paleness, his cheeks were colourless; his fair hair fell in disordered ringlets round his youthful but wan countenance; he leaned his head against the side of the machine; his eyes were half shut; it was not shame, but suffering, that weighed upon their lids, and diffused an air of languor and pain over his whole person. Katherine hastened towards him, she knelt on the unworthy earth at his side, she kissed his chained hands. "You are ill, my love; my ever dear Richard, what has happened? for you are very ill."

Rouzed by such music from the lethargy that oppressed him, yet still overcome, he replied, "Yes; and I do believe that all will soon end, and that I am stricken to the death."

She grew pale; she called him cruel; asking him how he could dream of leaving her, who was a part of him, alone in the desolate world. "Because," he answered with a faint smile, "the world is kind to all, save me. No taint, / dear love, attaches itself to your name; no ill will mark your fate, when you are no longer linked to such a thing as I. God has spoken, and told me that this earth is no dwelling for one, who, from his cradle to this last shame, has been fortune's step-child, and her despised toy. How often have I been dragged to the utmost verge of life: I have felt indignation, anger, despair: now I am resigned; I feel the hand of the Mighty One on me, and I bow to it. In very truth, I am subdued; I sleep away the weary hours, and death will end them all."

With every expression of tenderness, Katherine endeavoured to recall him to life and to herself. She spoke of another escape, which it would be her care to achieve, of the solitude, of the paradise of love they would enjoy together. "My poor girl," he replied, "teach your young heart to seek these blessings apart from me: I were the very wretch Tudor stigmatizes me, could I live under a memory like this. Forget me, my White Rose; paint with gaudier colours the sickly emblem of my fortunes; forget, that, duped by some strange / forgery, you were wedded to – Perkin Warbeck."

In spite of himself large drops gathered in his eyes, swelling the downcast lids, and then stealing down. Katherine kissed them from his cheek: a thousand times more noble, royal, godlike, she called him; had not the best and worthiest

---

[a] The spectacle of Warbeck in stocks, first at Westminster, and then at Cheapside, was described in the chronicles.

suffered ignominious punishment; even our blessed Lord himself? His own acknowledgment alone could disgrace him; he must recal the false words wrung from his agony; this last vile act of his enemy must awaken each sovereign on his throne to indignation; each would see in him a mirror of what might befal themselves, if fallen. James, her royal Cousin, roused by her, should resent the stigma affixed to his kinsman."

"For your own sake, sweet, do so; my soul dying within me is alive again with indignation, to think that your plighted wedded love is he, who is exposed to contumely; but for that, methinks, I would call myself by that wretched name I dared pronounce, so that the annals of the House of York escaped this stain: yet even / thus I seem more closely allied to them; for violent death, treachery, and ill have waited on each descendant of Mortimer;[a] my grandfather bore a paper crown in shame upon his kingly brow."[b]

He was interrupted by the officer, who unclosed the instrument of disgrace. Richard, weak and failing, was assisted to rise; Katherine supported him as a young mother her feeble offspring; she twined her arms round him as his prop, and, in spite of misery, was enraptured once again to see, to hear, to touch him from whom she had been absent so long. "This is not well; it must not be; his Majesty will be much displeased," said the chief of the guard, witnessing the compassion her tender care inspired, "You must return to the palace, Lady."

"One little step," pleaded Katherine; "if I should never see him more, how should I curse your cruelty! I will not speak, as I half thought I would to these good people, to tell them that they may well honour him a Princess loves: drag me not away yet – one more good bye! – / farewell, noble York, Kate's only love; – we meet again; this parting is but mockery."

She wept on his bosom; the sound of wailing arose in the crowd; the Prince's eyes alone were dry; he whispered comfort to her; he promised to live, to baffle his foe again for her sake; the words revived her, and she saw him depart with hope, with new joy kindled in her bosom.

There had been another, the public gaze, till Katherine came to draw all eyes to a newer wonder. An emaciated, pale woman, in a garb of penury, who knelt, telling her beads beside York's prison; her face was hid; but her hands were thin and white to ghastliness; during the last scene she had sobbed to agony, and now as the place cleared, went her way silently, with slow, feeble steps. Many marked her with surprize and curiosity; few knew that she was the Jane Shore, whose broken heart whispered misery, as she thought that she beheld King Edward's guilt, in which she had shared, visited on his son. This cruel lesson of religion was a canker in her heart, and most true it was, as far as

---

[a] For Mortimer, see p. 116n.

[b] Richard Plantagenet, 3rd Duke of York (see p. 15n), mockingly crowned before he was stabbed to death; Shakespeare makes Queen Margaret, wife of Henry VI, an active participant in the murder (3 *Henry VI*, I. iv).

regarded her royal lover, that his light / loves, and careless playing with sacred ties, had caused the blot of base birth to be affixed to his legitimate offspring, and so strewed the sad way that led them to untimely death.

Henry, cruel as he was, had not the courage to encounter his insulted prisoner on her return. Katherine's feelings were wrought too high for any display of passion; her anxiety was spent on how she could sooth York's wounded feelings, and restore his health; it were vain to ask, she feared; yet, if the King would permit her to attend on him, under whatever restrictions, they should be obeyed; and this while poor Elizabeth besought her pardon with tears, for being the wife of her insolent adversary. She, a proud Plantagenet, was more sorely stung than the White Rose, by the indignity offered to her house; and she intreated her not to love her brother less because of this foul disgrace. "So doing," said the quick-sighted Queen, "you fulfil his dearest wish. While you are Richard's loving wife, he, even he, the fallen and humiliated, is an object of envy to his Majesty, who / sought, by making you witness his ignominy, to detach you from him."

"How strange a mistake," replied Katherine, "for one so sage as the King: the lower my sweet Richard falls, the more need he surely has of me. But that love, such as ours, knits us too indivisibly to admit a reciprocity of benefit, I should say that it is to make me rich indeed, to enable me to bestow, to lavish good on my Lord; but we are one, and I but give to myself, and myself receive, if my weakness is of any strength to him. Dear sister mine, your liege, wise as he may be, is a tyro in our woman's lore – in the mysteries of devoted love; he never felt one inspiration of the mighty sprite."

This was not quite true. For some few days Henry had been so inspired; but love, an exotic in his heart, degenerated from being a fair, fragrant flower, into a wild, poisonous weed. Love, whose essence is the excess of sympathy, and consequently of self-abandonment and generosity, when it alights on an unworthy soil, appears there at first in all its native bloom, a very wonder even to the heart in which it has / taken root. The cold, selfish, narrow-hearted Richmond was lulled to some slight forgetfulness of self, when first he was fascinated by Katherine, and he decked himself with ill-assorted virtues to merit her approbation. This lasted but a brief interval; the uncongenial clime in which the new plant grew, impregnated it with its own poison. Envy, arrogance, base desire to crush the fallen, were his natural propensities; and, when love refused to minister to these, it changed to something like hate in his bosom; it excited his desire to have power over her, if not for her good, then for her bane.

The Duke of York was imprisoned in the Tower.[a] No further measures were apparently in action against him. Katherine no longer hoped any thing from her

---

[a] 'June 15' (marginal note in *Abinger/Palacio*), the date of Warbeck's imprisonment.

foe; and day and night there lay beneath her eye-lids the image of Richard, wasting and dying in captivity. Something must be done, some aid afforded him; she was anxious also to learn the details of his flight, and how again he fell into the hands of his foe. Monina, who in a thousand disguises had been used to penetrate every where, / was seen no more. Still public report informed her of many things.

It was known, that Sir Robert Clifford, the old spy and traitor of the White Rose, had become aware of the measures taken by York's adherents to insure his escape from England. He had followed him down the river, and by a knowledge of the signs and countersigns of the party, decoyed him into a boat that was to convey his victim back to his prison-house. The deceit was discovered, and a mortal struggle ensued on board the tiny bark; it sunk, and many perished, Clifford among the rest. On the morrow his body was found upon the beach, stiff and stark; a gaping wound in his neck showed that the waters alone had not been his foe; in his clenched hand he grasped a mass of golden hairs, severed by some sharp implement from the head to which they grew: as if nought else could liberate his enemy from his hold. There he lay, bold Robin Clifford, the dauntless, wily boy, hunted through life by his own fell passions, envy, cupidity, and libertinism; they had tracked him to his death; his falsehoods / were now mute, his deceptions passed away; he could never more win by his smiles, or stab by his lying words; death alone had a share in him, death and the cold sands beneath which he was interred, leaving a name, the mark of scorn, the symbol of treachery.[a]

They had struggled beneath the strangling waves, Richard and his adversary. The Prince was wounded in the scuffle, and became enfeebled almost to insensibility before he could sever from his enemy's grasp the fair locks he clutched – he swam away, as well as he might, and, with the instinct of self-preservation, made for the shore – he forgot, that England was a wide prison – he only strove to master the fate which beat him to the ground. He reached the sands – he sought the covert of some near underwood, and threw himself upon the earth in blind thankfulness; exhausted, almost inanimate, he lay there, given up only to the sense of repose, and safety from death, which visited his failing heart with a strange sense of pleasure.

The following morning was far advanced, before / he could rouse himself from this lethargy. He looked upon the waters; but the Adalid was no more to be seen – he was quite alone; he needed succour; and none was afforded him. Well he knew that every field, lane, dingle and copse swarmed with enemies, and he shuddered at the likelihood that unarmed, and weak as he was, he should fall into their hands. He desired to reach London again as his sole refuge; and he journeyed, as he hoped, towards it, all unknowing of the route.

---

[a] The chronicles say nothing of Clifford's fate.

No way-worn traveller in savage lands, pursued by barbarous enemies, ever suffered more than the offspring of Edward the Fourth amidst the alienated fields of his paternal kingdom. Cold and rain succeeded to the pleasant summer weather: – during night he lay exposed to the tempests – during day he toiled on, his limbs benumbed, his heart wasted by hunger and fatigue; yet never, at the head of the Scottish chivalry, never in Burgundy or in England, did he feel more resolute not to submit, but, baffling fortune and his enemy's power, to save himself in spite of fate. He had wandered far inland, and knew not where he / was – he had indeed passed beyond London and got up as high as Barnes.[a] It was the fourth day from that of his escape – he had tasted little food, and no strength remained in him, except that which gave energy to his purpose. He found himself on a wide, heathy common, studded with trees, or desolately open – the rainy day closed, and a bleak east wind swept over the plain, and curled the leaden coloured waters of the river – his love of life, his determination not to yield, quailed before the physical miseries of his lot; for some few moments, he thought that he would lie down and die.

At this time another human figure appeared upon the scene. A Benedictine lay-brother, who in the freedom of solitude, in defiance of wind and rain, trolled a ditty, fitter for a ruffling swaggerer's bonnet, than a monk's cowl. He started not a little, on perceiving our wanderer leaning against the scathed trunk of a solitary tree; nor less did he wonder when he recognised the fallen Prince. It was Heron himself, the magnanimous mercer, who having / effected his escape with a well-hoarded purse, contrived to introduce himself into the house of Bethlem, at Shene, which was called the Priory. He was a little frightened to perceive his ancient leader; but pity succeeded to fear; and with many fair words and persuasions he induced him to permit himself to be conducted to the Priory. There, since he believed himself to be dying, he might receive the last sacraments – there perhaps, for some few minutes, he might again behold his Katherine.

Thus was the fugitive again led within the pale of his enemy's power. The Prior, a man esteemed for holiness, did not delay to make his sovereign acquainted with the capture of his rival. His awe of Katherine having vanished, Henry was left at liberty to follow the ungenerous dictates of his groveling spirit. Many a courtier, true man or false, counselled the death of the aspiring youth; and they praised their master's magnanimity, when he rejected this advice, and in lieu exposed him, whom he knew to be the descendant of a line of kings, to beggarly / disgrace. Thus worn and weak, the ill-fated son of York was made a public spectacle of infamy. But Henry went a step too far; and, when he thrust the Scottish Princess forward on the scene, he turned defeat to triumph.

---

[a] South of the Thames and west of the city's limits in the fifteenth century.

He was not to die – but rather to pine out a miserable existence – or had the sage monarch any other scheme? The high-spirited Prince was to be cooped up within the Tower – there, where the Earl of Warwick wasted his wretched life. Did he imagine that the resolved and ardent soul of Richard would, on its revival, communicate a part of its energy to the son of Clarence, and that ere long they would be enveloped in one ruin? Some words had transpired that appeared to reveal such an intention; and his order to the Lieutenant of the Tower, that, without permitting, he should connive at any covert intercourse between the two – his recommendation of a noted spy and hireling to a high trust, and the order this fellow had to bring each day intelligence to the palace from the prison – spoke loudly of some design; for Henry never / did aught in vain. It was in circulation also among the lower officers in the fortress, that an attempt to escape was expected on the part of the prisoners, and that rich reward would attend its discovery.[a] /

CHAPTER XVIII.

———

And bare, at once, Captivity displayed,
Stands scoffing through the never-opened gate;
Which nothing through its bars admits, save day
And tasteless food.

                              BYRON.[b]

———

The Lady Katherine, no longer trusting the good intentions of the insolent tyrant, was eager to communicate with her royal cousin of Scotland, to urge him to save from death or disgrace, if not to effect the liberation, of him to whom he had given her hand. The difficulty of finding a messenger was great. The Queen, all amiable and sorrowing as she was, shrunk from any act, which, if discovered, would enrage the King. Where did Monina tarry while her / friend was in this strait? Of all his sometime associates was there not one who

---

[a] Tudor chroniclers and later historians acknowledge that many believed Henry VII himself set the trap, although they acquit him of the charge.
[b] *The Lament of Tasso*, ll. 11–14.

would risk all to retard the last steps of fate. Since York's escape she had been so vigilantly guarded, that a thousand schemes she had formed for her own evasion proved abortive at their very outset.

Help was at length afforded her unexpectedly, when most despairing. Edmund Plantagenet stood before her: changed indeed from what he had been; she had not seen him since the siege of Exeter, where he was wounded; but slight was his bodily hurt in comparison to the death-blow his mind received.

Plantagenet was one of those concentrated characters, whose very outward show of softness and gentleness serves the more to force the texture of their souls to receive one indelible impression. He had passed a boyhood of visions, given up to mighty aspirations and engrossing reverie. His thoughts were stirring as the acts of others; his forest-school had so tutored him, that he could live in bodily repose, while his mind ruminated: he could be quickened to hope and fear, to lofty ambition, to generosity, and devoted / courage, feeling in his heart the keenest impulses – while around him were the mute trees of the wild wood and pathless glades. He could be satisfied with such dreamy illusions; so that action with him was never the result of physical restlessness, nor of youthful emulation, nor of that stirring spirit of life which forces us to abhor repose. It flowed from an imperious sense of duty; it welled up from the very sources of his soul. Other men perform the various parts allotted to them, and yet are something else the while; as is the actor, even while he struts in the garb of royalty: but Edmund yielded himself wholly up, and was the mere creature of the thought within.

To be great and good – great from the good he should effect, was his boyhood's aspiration. It is probable that, if he had not been subjected to extraneous influence, he would have devoted himself to religion, and become a saint or martyr; for his all, his understanding, heart, and person, would have been given up to the holy cause he espoused. His being led to[31] King Richard's tent, the night before the / battle of Bosworth Field, gave a new and inextinguishable law to his life. Unknown duties were imposed. The first and dearest was, to redeem his father's soul from the guilt of murderous ambition, by elevating his injured nephew to his original greatness. He devoted himself to his cousin. Soon he learned to love Richard as the work of his own hands. He had reared his tender infancy; he had been his tutor in martial exercises, teaching him to curb the fiery steed, to wield the lance, and, more than all, to meet danger in the field fearlessly; to be honourable, brave and kind. He had led him to war, and shielded him with his own body from the cruel Moor. If ever they were divided, his thoughts dwelt only the more carefully with him. Last, he had brought him from glorious combats in Spain, to conquer his ancestral kingdom, and set him up the rival of a powerful king – the mark of his vengeance.

It was all over. Edmund possessed no innate strength to rise from the blow;

he was a mariner on the wide ocean, without compass or rudder. The universe had one central point for / him; that was destroyed, and a total blank remained. York's first surrender visited him as a death stroke; he struggled against it. Enfeebled by his wound, more by despair, he passed over to Ireland; there he expected to find friends of the White Rose; he found only enemies of Duke Perkin: men eager to exculpate themselves, from the charges of ill faith or ingratitude, gladly adopted a phraseology, or a belief, that reduced to dust the golden glories of poor Edmund's idol. Perkin Warbeck! Oh thou flower of York! thou nursling of love, though child of calamity, is even thy bright name so to be tainted? Not by those immediately arrayed by self-interest against thee; but by the vulgar crew, ever eager to crush the fallen. There was no hope in Ireland. Keating, the Prior of Kilmainham, was dead. The Earl of Desmond was reconciled to the English Government. Lord Barry had fled to Spain. The Citizens of Cork were busy redeeming, by eager servility, their Mayor's disloyalty.

Overcome by these sad changes, a malignant fever seized on Edmund: in addition to every / other disappointment, he had the consciousness that his aid was necessary to his cousin; that his absence was probably misinterpreted by his friends as cowardly dereliction. York was calling on him in vain. Monina perhaps suspected his truth. Next to the sun of his life, the noble Richard, Monina lay nearest his heart. It was a mixture of many feelings; and even love, subdued by hopelessness, quickened them to greater intensity. As soon as he could rise from his couch, he directed his course to England. He arrived in London on the day of the Duke of York's worst disgrace. It was reported to him as the gossip of the town: at the fatal word a mortal change seized upon his frame: his limbs were as if struck by palsy; his cheeks fell in; his hair grew white. On his arrival he had taken up his abode in a monastery in the habit of a poor pilgrim: the sage monks who beheld his state, possessed no leech-craft to administer his cure: he lay with beating pulses and open eyes, while the work of the grave appeared already in operation against him: he wasted into a fleshless skeleton. And then / another secret change came over him; he conquered death, and crawled forth, the ghost of what he had been,[32] into the hopeless world.

He contrived to gain admission to the Princess. She did not recognize him, such was the pale disguise disease had put upon him. His voice, hollow as from a tomb, was altered; his dark, melancholy eyes, occupying too large a portion of his face, gleamed from under his streaked and wan brow. Yet his was a visit of comfort, for he could do her mission to Scotland, and invite the forgetful James to succour his friend and kinsman. Edmund listened eagerly to this proposal: a draught of soothing balm descended into his frame, with the thought that yet all was not lost. His physical energy almost returned: he hurried to depart – "How will you traverse this wide kingdom?" asked the lady. "Cannot the Adalid come as before, to aid and speed you on your way?"

"The Adalid is sailing on the far ocean sea," replied Plantagenet; "we are all as dead, in the eyes of De Faro and our Monina."

"Faithless girl!" /

With a trace of his ancient warmth and sweetness, Edmund entered upon the gentle maiden's exculpation. He related that a poor fellow lay on the bed next his in the convent hospital, whom he recognised to be an Irishman, who had escaped from Waterford, and sailed with them in the Adalid to Cornwall. From him he heard the tale of what had befallen De Faro and his child. He heard how the mariner had long haunted the English coast waiting for an opportunity to carry off the Prince; of the fatal night, when snatching his daughter from the watery peril, he saw Richard, as he believed, perish in the waves. What more had the Moorish mariner and his daughter to do with this miserable, guilty island? He called his men together; he told them his resolve finally to quit the eastern world for the golden islands of the west, inviting those who were averse to the voyage to go on shore at once, before the fair wind that was rising, should hurry them into the open sea. The poor Irishman alone desired to land: before he went he saw the Spanish damsel; he described her as calm and mild, though there / was something unearthly in her gleaming eyes and in the solemn tone of her voice. "If," she said, "you meet any of our friends, any who ask for De Faro and his daughter, if you see Lady Brampton, Lord Barry, or Sir Edmund Plantagenet, tell them that Monina lives, that she tarries with her father, and tasks herself to be his comfort and support. We seek the Western Indies; well may it betide us that we never reach the unknown strand; or we may be cast away in an uninhabited solitude, where my care and companionship may stead my dear father much; or I may teach the sacred truths of our religion to the wild Indians, and speak the dear name of Christ to the unbaptized of those wilds; or soften, as best I may, the cruel Spaniard, and save the devoted people from their barbarity. Tell them, whichever way I look, I perceive a thousand duties to which our great Taskmaster calls me, and these I live to fulfil, if so my feeble body will permit; tell them that my only hope is death; that, and that by my obedience to the Almighty will, I may / partly merit to join in Paradise the earthly angel who now survives there."

Tears choked further speech; she imprinted her words by a gift of gold. The boat which had been hailed, came alongside. The man on board, the sails of the Adalid swelled proudly in the gale; the little caravel ran lightly along on the top of the roughening waters. In less than two hours she was out of sight, speeding swiftly over the sea towards the wild western ocean.

Plantagenet departed; and the Princess was yet more cheered when she found that no further injury was meditated against her lord. Imprisonment in the Tower was his sole punishment. Her pure, gentle mind could not divine the full extent of King Henry's villainy, nor guess how he undermined the edifice he claimed praise for not levelling with the ground.

Nor could her resigned, patient, feminine spirit conceive the cruel, biting impatience of his lot that York endured. He had yielded at first to the over-whelming sense of disgrace, and felt that last, worst emotion of the injured, / which answers the internal question, "What have I done so to be visited?" in the poet's words, –

> ———— "I cannot charge
> My memory with much save sorrow – but
> I have been so beyond the common lot
> Chastened and visited, I needs must think
> That I was wicked."[a]

But soon his eager, eagle spirit spurned the tame debasing thought: he resolved again to struggle, and at last to conquer; the fire burned brighter for its short smouldering; almost with a light heart he laughed, as he resolved again to endeavour.

His prison life was more than irksome; it was unendurable. No change, which is the soul of enjoyment, varied it. No sympathy, the parent of content, came anear. In his young days he had trod on the verge of life's wave, watching it recede, and fancying that it would discover glittering treasures as it retreated into the ocean of eternity: now the tide ebbed sullenly; the barren sands grew dark; and the expanse before afforded no hope – what was to be done? /

He was in the Tower, whence he had twice escaped; where the Earl of Warwick was immured, pining in fruitless vegetation, rather than living. Should he do as he had done, and become a cypher, a forgotten prisoner, a mere thing to wake and sleep, and be as nothing? The very dog that guards a cottage-door from nightly harm, had more dignity and purpose in his life, than this victim of ambition. The bird that alighted on the sill of his iron-barred casement, and carried off a crumb for her nestlings, was an emblem of utility and freedom in comparison, which Warwick, cut off from all, must weep to mark. How different was Richard's fate; he had dear friends ready to risk all for him, whose life's sacrifice he could repay only by being true to himself: he had a wife, wedded to him in youth's early flower, whose happiness was unalterably linked to his. He had courage, fortitude, energy; he would not cast these gifts away, a thankless boon; he valued them at their price: if death crowned his efforts, it were well: he was a mere toy in the hands of God, and he submitted; but, as a man, he was ready to cope / with men, and though defeated never to be vanquished.

Not a month after his removal to the Tower he had observed his facilities, marked his instruments, and resolved to enter on his schemes: they were quickened by other circumstances.

Warwick heard of his cousin's arrival; and he believed this to be the signal of

---

[a] *The Two Foscari* (1821), IV. i. 164–70.

his own deliverance. His first chief desire was to have communication with him. Among his attendants there was one to whom he could apply; he was a lank, tall fellow, with little understanding and but one idea – gratitude to the Duke of Clarence. This man, called Roger, and nicknamed Long Roger,[a] his length being his chief distinction, had been very poor, and burthened besides with several infant children: accidents and a bad season brought them to the verge of starvation, when a chance threw him in the way of the Duke of Clarence, who got him made servitor in the Tower. When this unfortunate Prince was imprisoned within its fatal walls, Long Roger underwent a thousand perils to wait on him by stealth, and to do what service he might. / Long Roger had a prodigious appetite, and his chief delight was to smuggle dainties, cooked by his Madge, into the prison chamber of the Duke. The manner of Clarence's death, which Roger affirmed to accord with the popular tradition, alone consoled the faithful sympathizing fellow. Now he had turned the key for thirteen years on the Duke's hapless son: in spite of his watchful care and proffered cates,[b] he had seen the poor youth dwindle to a skeleton, when suddenly the progress of decay[33] was checked by Our Lady: it was a miracle to see Lord Edward grow fat and comely to look upon, changing his woe-begone looks into gracious smiles: by the Mass, there was witchcraft in it! Warwick often thanked Long Roger, and told him what he would do when restored to freedom and rank; which will never be, Roger said, except among the saints in Paradise; unless it pleased God to remove his Majesty, when my Lady the Queen should fully know how fervently her cousin prayed for her; and, forsooth, with sweet Prince Arthur, his royal mother would be all powerful. Long Roger's visions went not beyond. / He never imagined the possibility of effecting the Earl's escape; his limited understanding suggested no relief, save a bottle of Canary, or bunches of White Roses in June, which in fact was Dame Madge's feminine idea; and often had the simple flowers soothed Warwick's care. To this man the poor prisoner applied, to enable him to see and converse with the newly arrived Richard: two are better than one to a feast; and, the next time Roger meditated a dainty supper for his lord, he resolved to endeavour that York should partake it with him as a guest.

In his own guileless way, the simple-hearted man began to practise on and bribe one of his fellows, without whom it had been difficult to accomplish his desire. Abel Blewit had lately been appointed to his service: he was nearly a dwarf, with bushy eyebrows and red hair; there was something of ill omen in his physiognomy, but as the tall yeoman looked over the head of his comrade, his courage rose: "The whipper-snapper could not rebuff me," he thought, as he drew himself up to his full height, and began to / propound the mighty deed

---

[a] Long Roger formed with Abel Blewet, Astwood, and Strangeways (see p. 382), a quartet of Tower workers whose names occur in the chronicles.

[b] cates, 'choice viands; dainties, delicacies' (*OED*).

of conducting Perkin by mistake to the Lord Edward's chamber, on his return from vespers. Roger paused suddenly; for, in spite of his stature, he was appalled by the glance Blewet shot up from under his penthouses of brows: still he gave a willing assent, and even took upon himself the chief risk of the undertaking.

The following evening, while Richard was yet pondering how to commence his machinations, undecided, though resolved; and while he made up his mind not to betray his thoughts to the sinister-looking being before him, he was surprised to find that he was led through an unaccustomed gallery; and still more, on entering the chamber into which he was introduced, to recognise it as that where he had unexpectedly found refuge during his last visit to the Tower, and to perceive that Warwick himself was there expecting him.

Was this the thin, wasted being he had seen three years before? Had Warwick been then set free to hunt upon the hills, he had not regained more flesh and bloom than now that / hope had been his only medicine. His cousin York had inspired him with marvellous confidence; his last entrance into the formidable Tower, and his speedy exit, had appeared a miracle to the poor Earl, to whom these high walls and sad chambers formed a world, from which, as from the larger one, death only promised egress. He had pined and wasted in his appetite to be free, to be without those gates, beyond that fosse[a] and giant battlements that girded him in: these portentous, insuperable obstacles were mere cobweb chains to Richard. He had come in, he had departed, and all as easily, so Warwick thought, as the unregarded fly, that had perhaps flown from Westminster, from Elizabeth's chamber, to light upon his cheek. In all the subsequent tales of York's checks and overthrow, he smiled at the idea that one born to victory could be thus overcome. He laughed at the chains Henry had thrown over him; and his transfer to the Tower elated him with a firm belief that liberty was at hand. Dwelling on these thoughts Warwick ceased to be the dead alive; he was cheerful, erect, elastic in his gait, / his complexion glowed with health, while sickness still lingered on the cheek of the younger Plantagenet, and a more subdued spirit dwelt in his heart.

Long Roger beheld the cousins embrace: he heard the Earl call him, named Perkin, his liege, and most dear kinsman: from that moment the opprobrious name was banished from Roger's lips: he was convinced of York's truth, and the Lord Edward's friend became an object of reverence and of love. /

---

[a] ditch or moat.

CHAPTER XIX.

——

> Gentle Cousin,
> If you be seen, you perish instantly,
> For breaking prison.
>
> No, no, Cousin,
> I will no more be hidden, nor put off
> This great adventure to a second trial.
> TWO NOBLE KINSMEN.[a]

——

Quick on the first greeting followed Warwick's question. "And, noble Cousin, what have you projected? when shall we escape?"

Richard's being in durance with him, seemed sufficient pledge, that without delay they should both be free. While York, wearied by opposition to his mighty foe, just foiled in his endeavours to preserve his freedom, even when he had attained it, saw giant obstacles in his path; and, / although resolved to endeavour all, was fully conscious of the fatal end that must wait upon his too probable failure. His reply was dictated by these feelings; he was averse to drag one so inexperienced, and so unhappy, into the pit he believed that he was digging for himself. He besought the Earl well to weigh the value he set upon life; to place the fatal scaffold in prospect; to teach himself to know what death was, and to be ready to meet it, before he planned escape from the wily Tudor. Warwick listened with impatient wonder; but when Richard concluded with affirming, that he himself, in sober sadness, preferred hazarding all to the remaining in prison, and that he would be free, the Earl's countenance again grew light and gladsome. "But when, Coz, when?" was still his eager question.

Thus they had changed characters. Warwick, so many years secluded from the world, was in total ignorance of its ways. Had the Tower-gates been opened to him, he had trembled to walk forth alone; but restraint had made him feminine; and with his cousin he would have rushed upon an army of spears, in

---

[a] Shakespeare and Fletcher, III. vi. 112–17.

sure / belief that some unseen ægis would protect him. His position rendered him timid, indolent, and dependent; but he relied on Richard, as a woman on her lover. York beheld all things in their clear, true light; he was aware of every difficulty; of the means he possessed for overcoming them, and of the hazards he ran in using these means. A sentiment, born of the highest generosity, made him hesitate before he concerted any plan with Warwick. It was not alone that he was averse to risking another life; but he felt that his cause would receive advantage from this link with an undoubted Plantagenet; nay, that, in the prison itself, the attachment and respect felt towards the son of Clarence, by some of the very men he meant to use, would serve him. That he should reap benefit from exposing the ill-fated Prince to untried dangers, revolted his high and independent nature. Warwick had recourse to many an entreaty and persuasion, ere he brought Richard to consent that their fortunes should be joined, and that, last of the White Rose, they would rise or fall together. Still York was obliged to check his / cousin's impatience, and to show that they must slowly work out the end they had in view.

To gratify the Earl's greedy curiosity, York related his adventures; they afforded him an inexhaustible fund of surprise and delight. He sighed over his tale of wedded happiness; and half wondered that angelic woman, seated high on the throne of loveliness and love, should deign to devote herself for man. A pang, not of envy, but of regret, on comparing their fates, shot across him; soon the usual current of feeling returned; and, when he heard that his idolized, lost Elizabeth was the friend and companion of the devoted wife of York, his affection for Richard was increased. Night was far advanced before they separated, and then only in certain expectation of meeting again.

York's hopes grew brighter, and he indulged in visions of the future, which lately had been so blank. He verily believed that he might escape, though still he doubted whether he should. He remembered the fondness of the Duchess of Burgundy for her brother Clarence, and how she had deplored the hard destiny of / his offspring; he would present that son, liberated by him, to her. His junction with the Prince must revive the old Yorkists in his favour; this worst blast of fortune might be the gale to speed him to the harbour of his hopes. The royal cousins met again and again; nor was it long before their own desires, and Henry's craft, began to weave that fatal web which entangled them even in the very mode the hard-hearted king devised.

Summer was gone: quicker than he was wont, the sun withdrew his embattled array of light and heat; and cold and tempest, erewhile driven to mountain fastnesses, or to their own frozen kingdoms in the north, took courage and force, and broke with wild fury upon the defenceless world: the bleak winds were their coursers; savagely they yelled and howled over the land they desolated. First, the growth of flowers was their prey; the fruits, and then the verdure of the earth, while the sun, each day retreating, afforded further scope to their inroads. York resolved not to pass another winter in prison. He had quickly perceived that his purpose could / only be effected by corrupting their guards, and then all would depend upon the fidelity of these men. His first attempts were followed by an almost too easy success: good-hearted, dull-headed, Long Roger heard with unreplying credulity the assertions of Warwick, that Richard must succeed in all he undertook, and readily promised his aid. Abel Blewet, in spite of his dogged, sinister aspect, yielded at once to the seduction of a promised bribe. Two others, by his advice, were associated as necessary to their success. Strangeways, a ruffling, drunken fellow, who had been thrice dismissed, but whose pretty wife each time procured his re-appointment; and Astwood, a saving miser, who lent money to his fellow-servitors on usury. With these instruments the Cousins went to work: Warwick in full belief of success: York, perceiving treason and discovery close to them, but ready to defy these bloodhounds to their worst.

"And now, Coz," said Warwick, "in very truth there needs no further delay. Methinks were the drawbridge down, you would mistrust some gin,[a] and wait to throw an arch of your / own across the moat. Sooth, my Lord, I am aweary of your sloth."

There was a caressing sweetness in Warwick's voice and manner; an ignorant, indolent, confiding enthusiasm, so unlike quick-witted Clifford, or any of Duke Richard's former friends, that he felt a new emotion towards him – hitherto he had been the protected, served, and waited on, of his associates, now he played the protector and the guardian.

"My gentle Cousin," he replied, "even as you trust, so you shall find me – wait but a little, and all will be past. Yet I grieve to say, where you see escape, I perceive an ambushment of death; and, though ready to face the grim skeleton, we must arm ourselves against him. I wish I could show you even as I see, the dangers that environ us – perhaps you would shrink; and it is yet time. What do you do? Not only plan escape, but ally yourself, and give the sanction of your untarnished name, to one whom Tudor brands as an impostor, and abhors as a rival. His vengeance will fall heavily for this deed, if he reach you. While a few years, like the many / already gone by, may lead him to his grave, and you to liberty. I have too often met danger to be frightened by him: and I endure worse than death, each day I pass of youth, apart my sweet White Rose. You have no lady-love to beckon you across the path of peril. Bethink you well, my ever dear Lord, will you not regret this prison, when the cruel axe glitters before your eyes?"

"Do you refuse then to take me with you?" said Warwick, mournfully.

"Be the choice yours; to go with me is fraught with danger – to stay – "

"Hush, Cousin! cried the Earl, eagerly, "speak not the ill-omened word. Stay, – to endure days and nights of guarded doors; to eat viands served up

---

[a] gin, snare or trap.

KING ALFRED'S COLLEGE
LIBRARY

poisoned by the jailor's touch; to see the sky but through those iron bars; alas! in my dreams, when heaven and its stars are before me, they are crossed and paled by those accursed lines. Give me but an hour to tread earth a free man – or, mark, Cousin; sometimes I win good Roger to lead me to the roof of the White Tower; it is high, and overhangs the deep, dangerous river – The day you / quit my side, I seek that tower, I leap from its height, and the cold waters shall drink up my being, rather than I endure another hour my prison-life."

"My dear, dear Cousin," said York, "it is written by the Fates, and I yield – our fortunes shall be one. A few days now brings the hour; it will move along the dial; it will become a portion of past time – what it will leave us, is in the hands of God."

That hour came – full soon it came – the evening hour which preceded their escape. Long Roger served supper to the kinsmen, the last they were to partake within the fated walls. The poor fellow heaved a bitter sigh, as he waited by his lord's chair. "Thou art downcast, good Roger," said the Earl, "pledge me, my man, in this ruby wine of Burgundy – think of to-morrow, not of to-night – to-morrow the deed will be done."

Roger quaffed the proffered bowl – he set it down with another sigh, almost a groan, adding, "Better drown reason than life in the vat!" Then recollecting to what he alluded, and before / whom, he blushed scarlet to his very ears, and like a bashful man he made it worse by going on blunderingly, "I was never handy at these sort of things; it is for all the world like turning out of a warm bed on a cold snowy morning, only to think of them – and when they are about, – by the Cross, I thought no hole far enough or dark enough, when my Lord your father –"

"Roger!" exclaimed Warwick.

The wine had not decreased the man's terror, but it had opened his mouth, and taken away his discretion; he continued: "It was an awful night. We all knew what was going to be done. I am sure, as Thomas Paulet[a] said, we heard our very hearts beat. Then there was grim-faced Hobler,[b] who at the Judgment might be taken for the born twin of Master Abel, only he was taller by a span – even he looked uglier, nor spoke above his breath – 'Is he at his prayers?' asked he, and Sir Brakenbury was as white as the earth itself – it was the beginning of Lent; and the snow lay three feet deep on it." /

By no uncommon law of our nature, the dread design of the present night awoke keen recollection in the usually drowsy mind of this man. At first, with thrilling horror, Warwick interrupted him, but now the very terrors of the theme he chose, assumed an awful charm – he was fascinated to listen, while his knees knocked together – Richard felt also the magic of such perilous excitement.

---

[a] Unidentified.
[b] Unidentified.

"Oh, Lord Edward," continued Roger, "these walls have seen fiendly sights – the blood of many a Plantagenet, York or Lancaster, is on its pavement. Was it not in this room that the pious King, Saint Henry, as Father Piers calls him – you will not sleep another night in it, so there is no harm now, telling you that his poor ghost has been seen on the battlements coming from this very chamber, where he was murthered."

The night wind rushed round the massy walls, the autumnal wind, fierce and howling – York started up, "No more of this unreason, while we need all our strength, and God's grace to boot, to nerve us to our task. Oh, ghost of / Lancaster! if indeed thou hauntest this spot, where those akin to me did the foul deed, be thy pious soul propitiated now; many a mass shall be told for thy repose!"

Roger crossed himself, and said an ave; then in his usual voice he rejoined, "Would the thing did not require blood. Master Abel vows by the saints – 'twere better when men make bad oaths to swear by the fiends – that Sir John must die; old wrinkled Astwood squeaks out, 'By'r Lady, it were not worth while, with only promises for reward, if we have not the rifling of the Lieutenant's private chamber. They are bloody-minded men, my Lord; Mat Strangeways, when he is sober, and I, fasting or feasting, hold out that we might bind him, and get the keys.' 'Blockhead,' says Master Blewet, saving your presence, 'thou goest the way to hang us all.'"

Another goblet had set Roger talking. Warwick had quitted the table. He threw open the casement: it was very dark, and the wind howled fearfully – "Oh, iron bars of my prison house," cried the ill-fated Prince, "can only midnight-murder / wrench ye asunder? It is a dread act to disobey God's word, and lay the soul under mortal sin – must it be done?"

"My dear Cousin," said York, "do not mistake – a month ago the choice was yours; now there is no going back. We have no right to draw these poor men into peril, and then to quarrel at the precaution they take for their safeties. We said, aye, when the matter was proposed. Again I repeat the word; they must look to it, who so savagely have driven us to the fatal pass. When Digby[a] undertook the ungentle task of jailor, he knew that he must hold it at the hazard of his life."

"Sir John has ever been kind to me," said Warwick, "forgive the word, my Lord, I am firm now – away with mercy! To win an easy egress from these murderous walls, I could myself plant the dagger."

"We are not executioners," interrupted the Duke, who felt none of Warwick's vacillations, now sinking beneath the required tone, now wound up far above it, and was perfectly calm, though his heart, he scarce knew why, entertained / no hope of success. Warwick believed that he should win, and

---

[a] Lieutenant of the Tower during Warbeck's imprisonment.

mourned the losers in the frightful game. Richard knew that he might fail, and assuredly would, did he not meet each necessity and hazard with a dauntless spirit.

The sound of a bell from a neighbouring convent was brought fitfully by the wind – "They are ringing matins – there is our signal," cried Roger.

"And Digby's knell." The door of the chamber opened as Warwick said these words, and Blewet, with his usual catlike pace, slid in; he walked straight up to Roger, and casting on him a glance from under his brows, said only "Come."

"Are all at rest?" asked the Earl.

"Two hours agone," said Master Abel, "I have kept myself awake sharpening my steel;" he touched the handle of a huge butcher's knife stuck in his girdle, whose glittering blade did credit to his care. Warwick turned pale and sick. "It will be dulled anon," continued Blewet.

"Where are thy comrades?" Richard asked.

"They wait at the end of the corridor – / Master Astwood is counting his gains. Come, Long Roger."

Poor Roger followed him to the door, then turning to the Princes; "My royal masters," said he, "if this deed goes ill, and I never see ye more, by Christ and his Cross, I pray a blessing on ye; if I may pray, but by the mass I fear I shall never pray, nor sup more."

They were gone – Warwick strove to look, to be firm, but he grew ashy white – a door, clapped to at a distance, made him almost faint. Richard was pale also; but his hand shook not in the least, as he presented a cup of wine to his cousin. "Give me water rather," said the Earl, shuddering, "that cup is red – hark – it is his groans!"

"It is the wind around the turret, where my liege and brother died," said York, endeavouring to give other thoughts to the poor Prince, who cried,

"It is the hell-born laugh of fiends viewing the deed." With the breeze indeed came a sound of laughter. "Are we betrayed!" cried York: but the sound passed away in wailing. / Warwick was on his knees – "I cannot pray," he cried, "a sea of blood is before me."

"Hush!"

Steps now approached along the corridor, and Blewet, his stained, half-wiped knife in his hand, appeared – Again the monosyllable "Come," was pronounced – fraught with how different a meaning. A life had been torn from an innocent breast since then by that fell instrument. The Princes, awestruck, one trembling with dread, the other striving to quell his horror for a murderer, followed him, as he led through the gallery – at the end stood Astwood with a bunch of keys – there were no stains on his hands; he looked anxious, but brightened up when he saw the prisoners.

They trod stealthily along. Warwick's faltering steps scarce kept pace with their conductor's. After passing through many narrow high passages, they reached a low postern door. Astwood put the key in the lock – the sound was magical to the fearful Earl. "Farewell, old frightful walls," he cried, "farewell, dark murderous / prison house, the Foul Fiend possess thee! such is my benison."

Blewet looked at him – York marked the sarcasm, the scorn of his glance – the gate meanwhile was opened: at that moment a clash of arms was heard. "The sentinels at the Eastern gate," remarked Abel.

"God grant it!" cried Warwick, "God grant – yet can it be! and am I free?"

He rushed through the open door, intent to seize upon liberty, as Tantalus[a] on his forbidden feast – his first step beyond the threshold of his prison was followed by a shriek – almost a woman's shriek, it was so shrill and piercing. What he quailed before, gave presence of mind to York – experienced in ills. Whatever the new evil might be, he went out to meet it calmly. A party of archers and yeomen were drawn up in the court yard. "This truly is a mime," he said, "in which one at least wins. Our good Lieutenant is safe; we are lost."

Grim Sir John had much disliked even this masque of murder. He saw their seizure with a grin of delight. He abhorred Richard, as the / prime mover of the meditated assassination; but he hated Warwick more, who thus could lay in ambush for the life of one, who he believed had been a most courteous and soft-hearted jailor to him – he commanded his myrmidons to lead the royal kinsmen to the strongest ward-rooms of the Tower, with dogged, savage joy.

In dark and separate cells, in solitude and night, these ill-fated victims of craft and ambition were consigned to biting reflection and sinister anticipation. Warwick, worn out by the unusual excitement of the last weeks, by his eager hopes, and overwhelming despair, had no one thought, but ten thousand thoughts, making a chaos and hell of his poor heart. Richard felt more for his cousin than for himself. "But for me," he repeated internally, "he had still been a patient prisoner. Yet to break prison is not crime capital – he may yet be saved. Elizabeth will intercede; Tudor, for very shame, cannot do further wrong to one so near akin, so powerless and unfortunate. For myself; – I am / dead already: the Duke of York died, when first I became a slave. So that my memory survive in my own White Rose's heart – let the victor dispose at his pleasure of this mere shell of Richard." /

---

[a] Doomed for his offense against the gods (alternatively, feeding them his son, Pelops, or stealing their secrets or food) to stand in water beneath fruit-laden boughs that receded when he reached to eat or drink.

CHAPTER XX.

———

Tempestuous Fortune hath spent all her spite,
   And thrilling Sorrow thrown his utmost dart:
Thy sad tongue cannot tell more heavy plight
   Than that I feel and harbour in my heart.
                   SPENSER.[a]

———

The morning of the first of November dawned; a cheery day. Men went to their usual works: the earth, despoiled of her summer garniture, yet bore the change with sober content; for the sun shone, and soft airs, despite the coming winter, lightly shook the scant and altered foliage of the woods:

All rose to do the task He set to each,
Who shaped us to his ends, and not our own.
          And many rose
Whose woe was such, that fear became desire.[b] /

Among such fate-hunted victims was the Duke of York. Hope had died in his heart; and his few remaining days were only to be spent in celebrating her dark funeral. Morning opened its eyes on Prince Richard's dungeon, showing him vanquished by grievous overthrow and change. To look back through his tumultuous life, to dwell upon its chances, to think of the many who had suffered for him, were sad but fitting thoughts, to which he betook himself, till death became lovely in his eyes. But intermingled with such retrospection were other memories: his own sweet love was before him, in her tears or smiles; he looked into her dear eyes, he closed his own, and thrilling kisses pressed his burning lips, and soft, white arms were round him; at thought of such he grew impatient of his chains, and the fearful cutting off from all that awaited him. He began to calculate on the probability that his life would be spared, and grew cowardly the while; to feed upon those roseate lips, to drink life from those

———

[a] *Faerie Queene*, I. vii. 25.
[b] P. B. Shelley, 'The Boat on the Serchio', ll. 30–31, 34–35.

385

eyes, to clasp his beautiful, fond wife, feeling that beyond the circle of her arms[34] / nought existed worthy his desires, became a fierce, impatient hunger, to gratify which he would call himself impostor, give up fame and reputation, and become Perkin Warbeck in all men's eyes.

There was but one refuge from this battle of youth and life with the grim skeleton. With a strong effort he endeavoured to turn his attention from earth, its victor woes, and still more tyrant joys, to the heaven where alone his future lay. The struggle was difficult, but he effected it: prayer brought resignation, calm; so when his soul, still linked to his mortal frame, and slave to its instincts, again returned to earth, it was with milder wishes and subdued regrets. Monina's lovely form wandered into his mind; she was an angel now, a blessed spirit, he believed; for, what deceived her, deceived him; and he fancied that he alone had escaped from the watery perils of that night; she had arrived there, where he soon should be, in the serene immutability of eternal life; he began, in the revulsion of his thoughts, to pity those destined still to exist. Earth was a skaithed planet, a roofless, shelterless / home; a wild where the human soul wandered a little interval, tortured by sharp, cruel storms; lost in thorny, entangled brakes; weary, repining, till the hour came when it could soar to its native birthplace, and find refuge from its ills in promised Paradise.

His cell was indeed the haven of peace, compared to the turbid, frightful atmosphere in which his Katherine lived. Edmund had not returned; every attempt she made to communicate with Scotland or Burgundy, failed. She had past a summer of wretchedness, nor could the tender attention of Elizabeth sooth her. In spite of all, the poor Queen was almost happier than she had ever been; for many years she had been "the cannibal of her own heart,"[a] devouring her griefs in voiceless, friendless, solitude; her very joys, and they were those of maternity, were locked up in her own bosom. It was the birth of happiness to share her griefs with another; that other being so gentle, so wise, and yet so sensitive, as the fair White Rose, who concealed her own worst pains, to sooth those of one possessing less fortitude / and fewer internal resources than herself. Yet, while thus she forgot herself, she never quitted in thought her Richard's side; since the day she had seen him delivered over to ignominious punishment, pale and ill, he was as it were stamped on every outward object, an image placed between her and her thoughts; for, while those were employed apparently on many things, he, in truth, was their first, last, all-possessing idea, more engrossing than her own identity. At one time she spent every effort to obtain an interview with him in prison; and then she learned, through covert means, of the plots carrying on in the Tower for his escape, while the name of Warwick, mingling in the tale, roused the latent feelings of Elizabeth. When

---

[a] Adapted from Francis Bacon's 'Of Frendship', in *The Essayes or Counsels, Civill and Morall* (1597–1625). Versions of this quotation appear in *CC Journals*, p. 150; E. J. Trelawny, *Adventures of a Younger Son*, III, p. 304; as well as in *Lodore* and *Falkner*.

the last, worst hour came, it was less replete with pain than these miserable, unquiet days, and sleepless, tearful nights; the never-ending, still beginning round of hours, spent in fear, doubt, and agonizing prayer.

After a restless night, the Princess opened her eyes upon the day, and felt even the usual / weight at her heavy foreboding heart increased. The tale was soon told of Richard's attempted escape and failure: "What can be done?" "Nothing; God has delivered the innocent into the hands of the cruel; the cruel, to whom mercy is as unknown, as, methinks, it is even to the awful Power who rules our miserable lives." Such words, with a passionate burst of tears, burst from the timid Elizabeth, whose crushed and burning heart even arraigned the Deity for the agony she endured.

Katherine looked on her with sweet compassion, "Gentle one," she said, "what new spirit puts such strange speech into your mouth, whose murmurings heretofore were those of piety?"

"It is a bad world," continued the Queen; "and, if I become bad in it, perchance I shall prosper, and have power to save: I have been too mild, too self-communing and self-condemning; and the frightful result is, that the sole being that ever loved me, perishes on the scaffold. Both will perish, my White Rose, doubt it not. Your own York, and my devoted only / loved Edward. In his prison I have been his dream; he breaks it, not to find liberty again, but Elizabeth. Wretched boy! knows he not that he shall never again find her, who roamed with a free spirit the woodland glades, talking to him of the future, as of a scene painted to my will; faded, outworn, a degraded slave – I am not Elizabeth."

"Did you know the dearest truth of religion," replied Katherine, "you would feel that she, who has been tried, and come out pure, is a far nobler being than –"

"I am not pure, not innocent; much you mistake me," said the Queen: "wicked, impious thoughts harbour in my heart, and pollute my soul, even beyond the hope of mediation. Sometimes I hate my beautiful children because they are his; sometimes in the dark hour of night, I renounce my nuptial vow, and lend ready, willing ear to fiendish whisperings which borrow Edward's voice. I court sleep, because he wanders into my dreams; and – What do I say, what am I revealing? Lady, judge me not: you married him you loved, / fulfilling thus the best destiny that can be given in this hard world to woman, whose life is merely love. Though he perish in his youth, and you weep for him for ever, hug yourself in the blessed knowledge that your fate is bright as angels; for we reap celestial joys, when love and duty, twined in sisterly embrace, take up their abode together within us: and I – but, Katherine, did you hear me? – They perish even as I speak: his cruel heart knows no touch of mercy, and they perish."

"They shall not, dearest," said York's White Rose; "it cannot be, that so foul a blot darken our whole lives. No; there are words and looks and tones that

387

may persuade. Alas! were we more holy, surely a miracle might be vouchsafed, nor this Pharoah harden his heart for ever."

All her love-laden soul beaming in her eyes, with a voice that even thrilled him, though it moved him not, the White Rose addressed Henry. She had yet to learn that a tyrant's smile is more fatal than his frown: he was all courtesy, for he was resolved, implacable; and / she gathered hope from what proved to be the parent of despair. She spoke with so much energy, yet simplicity, in the cause of goodness, and urged so sweetly her debt of gratitude; telling him, how from the altar of their hearts, prayers would rise to the Eternal, fraught with blessings to him, that he encouraged her to go on, that still he might gaze on lineaments, which nobility of soul, the softest tenderness, and exalted belief in good, painted with angelic hues. At length he replied that his Council were examining witnesses, that her cause depended on facts, on its own justice; that he hoped report had blackened the crimes of these rash men; for her sake he sincerely hoped their guilt, as it was detailed to him, had been exaggerated.

For a moment the Princess was unaware what all this jargon might mean; his next words were more perspicuous. "Indeed, fair dame, you must forget this coil: if I consent, for the welfare of my kingdom, to sacrifice the Queen's nearest relative, you also must resign yourself to a necessity from which there is no / appeal. Hereafter you will perceive that you gain, instead of losing, by an act of justice which you passionately call cruelty: it is mercy, heaven's mercy doubtless, that breaks the link between a royal princess and a baseborn impostor."

A sudden fear thrilled Katherine: "You cannot mean that he should die," she cried; "for your own sake, for your children's sake, on whom your sins will be visited, you cannot intend such murder: you dare not; for the whole world would rise against the unchristian king who sheds his kinsman's blood. All Europe, the secret hearts of those nearest to you, your own knowledge, all proclaim your victim, your rival – to be your brother, and will brand you a fratricide. You are Lancaster, your ancestors were kings, you conquered this realm in their name, and may reign over it in peace of conscience; but not so may you destroy the Duke of York. His mother avouched him, the Duchess of Burgundy acknowledges him, I was given to him by my royal cousin, as to one of equal rank, and he upholds him – More than all, his princely / self declares the truth; nor can evil counsellors, nor false chroniclers, stand between you, and heaven and the avenging world. You vainly seek to heap accusation on him you term Crook-back's head: time will affix the worst indelible stain upon you. You cannot, will not slay him."

What were words to the fixed mind of Henry? A summer breeze, whispering round a tempest-withstanding watch-tower – he might grow chill at this echo of the fears his own heart spoke; but still he smiled, and his purpose was unshaken.

It became known that the Princes were to be arraigned for treason: first the unhappy, mis-named Perkin was tried, by the common courts, in Westminster Hall. When a despot gives up the execution of his revenge to the course of law, it is only because he wishes to get rid of passing the sentence of death upon his single authority, and to make the dread voice of mis-named justice, and its executors, the abettors of his crime.

When Tragedy arrays itself in the formal / robes of law, it becomes more heart-rending, more odious, than in any other guise. When sickness threatens to deprive us of one, round whom our heart-strings have twined – we think inextricably – the skill of man is our friend; if merciless tempest be the murderer, we feel that it obeys One whose ways are inscrutable, while we strive to believe that they are good. Groping in darkness, we teach our hearts the bitter lesson of resignation. Nor do we hate nor blame the wild winds and murderous waves, though they have drank up a life more precious and more beloved than words have power to speak. But that man's authority should destroy the life of his fellow man; that he who is powerful, should, for his own security and benefit, drive into the darksome void of the tomb, one united to our sun-visited earth by ties of tenderness and love – one whose mind was the abode of honour and virtue; to know that the word of man could still bind to its earthly tabernacle the being, voice, looks, thoughts, affections of our all; and yet, that the man of power unlocks the secret chamber, rifles it of all its / treasures, and gives us, for the living mansion of the soul, a low, voiceless grave: – against such tyranny, the softest heart must rebel; nor scarcely could religion in its most powerful guise, the Catholic religion, which almost tore aside for its votaries the veil between time and eternity, teach submission to the victims.

Days flowed on. However replete with event, the past is but a point to us; however empty, the present pervades all things. And when that present is freighted with our whole futurity, it is as an adamantine chain binding us to the hour; there is no escape from its omnipotence and omnipresence; it is as the all-covering sky. We shut our eyes; the monster's hollow breath is on our cheek; we look on all sides; from each his horrid eyes glare on us; we would sleep; he whispers dreams. Are we intelligible? Will those possessed by present tell us whether any bondage, any Bastille, can suggest ideas of more frightful tyranny, misery, than the cruel present, which clings to us, and cannot be removed.

"It is so; he attempted to escape, and was discovered; he is low in his dungeon; his dear eyes are faint from disappointed hope. He / will be tried. Tyranny will go forth in a masque, and with hideous antics fancy that she mantles with a decorous garb her bloodthirsty acts. He will be condemned; but he will not die! not die! Oh no, my Richard is immortal – he cannot DIE!"

"My royal Cousin, when you gave me to my sweet love, and pledged your word that in weal or woe I should be his; and I promised myself still dearer things, to be the guardian angel and tutelar genius of his life; and took pleasure, fond, foolish girl that I was, in the anticipation of misfortunes that I should rob of all power to hurt; no thought, among the many that strayed into futurity, told me of this desertion, this impotence of effecting good. Alas! how deaf and cruel man is: I could more easily tear asunder his prison-walls with my hands, and break with my weak fingers his iron chains, than move one, as liable to suffer and to die as even his victim, to pity!"

Elizabeth listened pale and silent to these complaints – bitter as they were, they were hushed to more heart-rending silence, when the hour of / trial came – she should only pray to die, before the word that spoke his condemnation met her ear. Accustomed as a Princess – a high-born and respected daughter of one most powerful, to be obeyed and served; to find herself destitute of all influence, seemed to place her in another planet – it was not men – not her fellow-creatures that were around her; but fiends who wore the mask of humanity. An uninhabited desert had not been more solitary than this populous land, whose language she possessed not; for what is language, if it reach not the heart and move it?

Richard, the wonder of the time, gathered courage as ill-fortune pressed more hardly upon him; in the hour of trial he did not quail, but stood in bold, fearless innocence before the men, whose thoughts were armed against his life. He was not guilty, he said, for he could not be guilty of treason. When the indictment was read which treated him as a foreigner and an alien, the spirit of the Plantagenet flashed from his eyes, and the very stony-hearted clerk, who read, casting his regards on him faltered and / stammered, overawed by a blaze of dignity, which, did we foster antique creeds, we might believe was shed over him by some such spirit as imparted divine majesty to the person of the King of Ithaca.[a] Proudly and silently Richard listened to the evidence on his trial. It touched only on such points as would afterwards be most material for inculpation of poor Warwick. In the end he was asked what he had to plead, wherefore judgment should not pass upon him – but he was bid to be brief, and to beware not to use any language derogatory to the high and mighty Prince, Henry, king of these realms. A smile curled his lips at this admonition, and with even a playful air he said, "My very good Lord, I ask for nothing, save that a little mercy be extended to the memory of my gracious uncle, my Lord of Gloucester, who was no child-murderer."

At the word he was interrupted, and sentence pronounced. As the ignominious words were said, Richard, who from the beginning had abstracted himself in prayer, so that his ears might be as little wounded as possible by an / unconquerable impulse put his hand where his sword might have been. Its absence and the clanking of his chains recalled him to the truth, and he muttered the words, "Oh, basely murdered York!" in recollection of his unhappy grandfather, to whose miserable fate he often recurred, as an example of suffering and patience.

---

[a] Odysseus (or Ulysses), Homer's hero.

Thus ended the bitter scene; one he had long expected, for which he had nerved himself. During nearly the whole, his look was as if he were absent from it. But who could read the secrets of his heart, while his impassive eyes and lips were no index to the agonies that tortured it? /

CHAPTER XXI.

———

So young to go
Under the obscure, cold, rotting, wormy ground!
To be nailed down into a narrow place;
To see no more sweet sunshine; hear no more
Blithe voice of living thing; muse not again
Upon familiar thoughts, sad, yet thus lost –
How fearful!

SHELLEY.[a]

———

"Speak to me, Lady, sister, speak! your frozen glances frighten me; your fingers as I touch them, have no resistance or life. Dearest and best, do not desert me, speak but one word, my own White Rose."

Katherine raised her blue eyes heavenward: as if the effort were too great, they fell again on the ground, as she said, in a voice so low that / Elizabeth could hardly catch the sound; "I must see him once again before he dies."

"And you shall, dearest, I promise you. Cheer up, my love, not to affright him by looks like these. Indeed you shall see him, and I will also; he shall know that he has a sister's prayers, a sister's love. Patience, sweet Kate, but a little patience."

"Would I could sleep till then!" replied the miserable wife: and she covered her face with her hands, as if to shut out the light of day, and sighed bitterly.

When our purposes are inflexible, how do insurmountable obstacles break before our strong will? so that often it seems that we are more inconstant than fortune, and that with perseverance we might attain the sum of our desires. The Queen, the weak, despised, powerless Queen, resolved to gratify this one last

———

[a] *The Cenci* (1819), V. iv. 49–55.

wish of her beloved friend. Many a motive urged her to it; compassion, love, and even self-interest. At first she almost despaired; while Richard continued in the Tower it was impossible; but on the twenty-third of November, / two days before the destined termination of his fatal tragedy, on the day of the trial of poor Warwick, he was removed to the prison of Ludgate.ª And here, at dead of night, Henry, being absent inspecting his new palace at Richmond, Elizabeth, timid, trembling, shrinking now at the last – and Katherine, far too absorbed in one thought to dream of fear, took boat at Westminster, and were rowed along the dark, cold tide to Blackfriars. They were silent; the Queen clasped her friend's hand, which was chill and deathlike. Elizabeth trembled, accustomed to hope for, to seek refuge in her stronger mind, she felt deserted, now that she, engrossed by passion, silent and still, the wife of the near prey of death, could remember only that yet for a little while he was alive. Their short voyage seemed endless; still the oars splashed, still the boat glided, and yet they arrived not. Could it last for ever – with one hope ever in view, never to know that he was *dead?* The thought passed into Katherine's mind with the sluggish but absorbing tenacity of intense grief, and at last possessed it so / wholly, that it was with a scream of fear that she found herself close to shore.

The necessity of motion restored Katherine to her presence of mind, while it deprived the Queen of the little courage she possessed. Something was to be said and done: Elizabeth forgot what; but Katherine spoke in a clear, though un-natural voice, and followed their conductors with a firm step, supporting the faltering Queen. Yet she addressed her not; her energies were wound up to achieve one thing; more than that it would have cost her her life to attempt. They reached the dark walls of the prison; a door was unbarred, and they were admit-ted. The Princess passed the threshold with a quick step, as if overjoyed thus to be nearer her wish. Elizabeth paused, trembled, and almost wished to turn back.

They crossed the high-walled court, and passed through several dark galler-ies: it seemed as if they would never arrive; and yet both started, when they stopped at the door of a cell.

"Does his Grace expect us?" asked Katherine. /

The turnkey looked as not understanding; but their guide, who was the chaplain of the jail, answered,

"He does not. Fearful that some impediment might intervene, unwilling to disturb by a disappointed hope a soul so near its heavenly home, I have told him nothing."

"Gently, then," said Katherine, "let our speech be low."

The door opened, and displayed the son of the proud, luxurious Edward, sleeping on a wretched mattress, chained to the pavement. The ladies entered

---

ª Warwick was arraigned on 21 November and beheaded on 28 November. The prison at Ludgate was on the main thoroughfare leading from Fleet Street to St Paul's. Warbeck was executed on 23 November 1499.

alone. Katherine glided noiselessly to his side; her first act was to bend down her cheek, till his breath disturbed the ringlet that rested on it; thus to assure herself that life was within his lips. Elizabeth fixed her earnest gaze on him, to discover if in aught he reminded her of the blue-eyed, flaxen-haired bridegroom of Anne Mowbray: he more resembled a picture of her father in his early manhood; and then again her aunt the Duchess of Burgundy, whom she had seen just before King Edward's death. He lay there in placid sleep; thought and feeling absent; yet in that / form resided the soul of Richard; a bright casket containing a priceless gem: no flaw – no token of weakness or decay. He lived – and at a word would come back from oblivion to her world of love. A few days and that form would still exist in all its fair proportion. But veil it quick; he is not there! unholy and false is the philosophy, that teaches us that that lurid mockery was the thing we loved.

And now he woke, almost to joy; yet sadness succeeded quickly to rapture. "My poor girl," he said, "weep not for me; weep for thyself rather; a rose grafted on a thorn. The degraded and disgraced claims no such sorrow."

Katherine replied by an embrace; by laying her beautiful head on his bosom, and listening with forgetful, delicious extacy to the throbbings of his beating heart.

"Be not unjust to thyself," said a soft, unknown voice, breaking the silence of the lovers; "be not false to thy house. We are a devoted race, my brother; but we are proud even to the last."

"This is a new miracle," cried the Prince. / "Who, except this sainted one, will claim kindred with Tudor's enemy?"

"Tudor's wife; your sister. Do you not remember Elizabeth?"

As these words were said, Katherine, who appeared to have accomplished her utmost wish, sat beside him, her arms around him, her sweet head reposing, her eyes closed. Kissing her soft hair and fair brow, York disentwined her clasped hands, and rose, addressing the trembling Queen:

"My sister," he said, "you do a deed which calls for blessings from heaven upon you and yours. Till now, such was my unmanly spirit, the stigma affixed to my name, the disgrace of my ignominious death, made me odious to myself. The weakness of that thought is past; the love of this sweetest sweet, and your kindness restore me. Indeed, my sister, I am York – I am Plantagenet."

"As such," replied the Queen, "I ask a boon, for which, selfish as I am, I chiefly came; my brother will not deny me?"

"Trifler, this is vanity. I can give nothing." /

"Oh, every thing," exclaimed the lady; "years of peace, almost of happiness, in exchange for a life of bitter loneliness and suffering. You, my dearest Lord, know the celestial goodness of that fair White Rose; in adversity and peril *you* have known it; – *I* amidst the cold deceits of a court. She has vowed never to return to her native land, to bear a questioned name among her peers; or perhaps to be forced by her father to change it for one abhorred. Though she must hate me as the wife of her injurer, yet where can she better be than with your sister? She would leave me, for I am Tudor's Queen; bid her stay with her Lord's nearest kinswoman; tell her that we will beguile the long years of our too young life with talk of you; tell her that no where will she find one so ready to bless your name as poor Elizabeth; implore her, ah! on my knees do I implore you to bid her not to leave me, a dead-alive, a miserable, bereft creature, such as I was ere I knew her love."

"What say'st thou, sweet?" asked Richard; "am I yet monarch of that soft heart? Will my single subject obey the crownless Richard?" /

Katherine stretched out her hand to the Queen, who was at York's feet, in token of compliance: she could not speak; it was a mighty effort to press the fingers of Elizabeth slightly; who said,

"Before heaven and your dear Lord, I claim your promise; you are mine for ever."

"A precious gift, my Bess; was it not thus my infant lips called you? I trust her to you; and so the sting of death is blunted. Yet let not too fond a lingering on one passed away, tarnish the bright hours that may yet be in store for her. Forget me, sweet ones; I am nought; a vapour which death and darkness inhales – best unremembered. Yet while I live I would ask one question – our victim-cousin, Edward of Warwick?"

Elizabeth could no longer restrain her tears as she related, that, however weak Warwick might heretofore have seemed, he appeared a Plantagenet on his trial. He disdained the insulting formalities of law, where the bitter Lancastrian, Lord Oxford, was the interpreter of justice; he at once declared himself guilty of / plotting to put the English crown on the head of his cousin, the Duke of York. He was quickly interrupted, and condemned to be beheaded.

"Generous, unhappy Warwick. Ah! is not life a misery, when all of good, except ye two angelic creatures, die."

The signal was now given that the interview must end. Elizabeth wept. Katherine, still voiceless, clung closer to her husband; while he nerved himself to support these gentle spirits with manly fortitude. One long, affectionate kiss he pressed on the mouth of Katherine; and as her roseate lips yet asked another, another and another followed; their lives mingled with their breath.

"We meet in Paradise, mine only one," whispered York; "through our Lord's mercy assuredly we meet there."

He unwound her arms; he placed her in those of Elizabeth. "Cherish, preserve her. Bless thee, my sister; thee, and thy children. They at least will, by my death, reign rightfully over this kingdom. Farewell!"

He kissed her hand, and then again the lifeless / hand of his wife, who stood a breathing statue. She had not spoken; no words could utter her despair. Another moment, and their fair forms were gone; the door of his cell was closed; and, but for the presence of the God he worshipped, Richard was left alone to solitude and night. /

CONCLUSION.

———

Love is too young to know what conscience is,
Yet who knows not, Conscience is born of Love?
Then, gentle cheater, urge not my amiss,
Lest guilty of my faults thy sweet self prove.
                                        SHAKSPEARE.[a]

———

*Time, we are told by all philosophers, is the sole medicine for grief. Yet there are immortal / regrets which must endure while we exist. Those who have met with one, with whose every feeling and thought their thoughts and feelings were entwined, who knew of no divided past, nor could imagine a solitary futurity, to them what balm can time bring? Time, the giver of hours, months, and years, each one how barren, contemptible, and heavy to bear to the bereft!

There was no consolation for Katherine, which could make her for a moment forget that her present existence was but the lees of life, the spiritless remnants of a nectareous draught. But Katherine was gentle, good, and resigned; she lived on, dispensing pleasure, adored by all who approached her, and gladly hailing any visitation of happiness, which might reach one whose affections were too fondly linked to the grave.

Years had passed, since the last act of the sad tragedy which destroyed her dearest hopes. She accompanied the Queen of England on a progress made by her, and they remained one night at Eastwell Place, the seat of Sir Thomas

---

* I do not know how far these concluding pages may be deemed superfluous: the character of the Lady Katherine Gordon is a favourite of mine, and yet many will be inclined to censure her abode in Henry the Seventh's court, and other acts of her after life. I desired therefore that she should speak for herself, and show how her conduct, subsequent to her husband's death, was in accordance with the devotion and fidelity with which she attended his fortunes during his life.[b]

---

[a] Sonnet CLI, ll. 1–4.

[b] Cf. Katherine's apologia and Mary Shelley's 'Journal of Sorrow' (*MWSJ*, II, 428 ff.), written during her early widowhood. The suppressed acts of Katherine's 'after life' (described in Mary Shelley's acknowledged sources) included acceptance of a pension from Henry VII and three successive marriages (to James Strangeways, Sir Matthew Cradock, and Christopher Ashton) contracted during the reign of Henry VIII.

Moyle.[a] There was a park, and / stately pleasure-grounds belonging to the house, undulating uplands, shady copses, and sweet running brooks to diversify the scene. A crowd of the noble and the gay were there, and the royal party was unusually mirthful; fireworks, masks, and dances were employed; and all joyously gave themselves up to the spirit of the hour. The chords of a harp, a well-known air, first awoke in the bosom of the White Rose that languid melancholy, so near allied to pleasure, so close a neighbour to pain. By degrees memory grew busy in her brain; she could no longer endure the laughter of her companions, their sallies, nay, nor their kindness; for Elizabeth perceived her dear friend's change of countenance, and was approaching, when Katherine, making her a sign not to remark her, stole away, and entering a straggling path, wandered on, struggling with the tears, which the beauty of the evening, and the very hilarity which just before she had shared, caused to gush, warm and fast from her eyes.

She reached a little streamlet, and was passing forward, when she became aware of the / presence of another in the scene. A labouring man, of middle age, (but his hair was grey, and flowed on his shoulders,) was seated on the rustic masonry of a rude fountain, reading; he rose when he saw the lady, and doffed his hat; she, with the cordial sweetness that accompanied her slightest acts, gave him an evening benison. Her voice, her look, her cordial manner moved to its depths a heart lately hardened against her. As she passed on, the man followed hastily. "Lady!" he cried.

It struck the Princess that this poor fellow had some request to prefer to his master, and that he wished to do it through her medium; she turned with a benevolent smile, "Can I do aught for you, good friend?"

His voice failed him; he stretched out his hand, which held his book, she took it: the tiny volume was no stranger to her eyes; as if a ghost had looked on her lonely watching, she trembled and grew pale, when she opened it, and saw written in fair characters, by a hand now dust, "La Rosa Blanca." The rustic knelt before her. /

"Lady Queen!" he cried, "Sole relic of the unforgotten! is it thus that we meet?"

"My cousin Edmund!"

"Hush! breathe not even to the silent woods the unknown word. Fancy not that I am Plantagenet; for all that was of worth in him you name, died when the White Rose scattered its leaves upon the unworthy earth."

"Ah! would that we had all died in that hour," cried Katherine: "why, when the ungrateful world lost him, did not all the good and true die also, so that they might no longer suffer!"

---

[a] Eastwell Court, Kent, seat of Sir Thomas Moyle (d. 1560), Speaker of the House of Commons in the 1540s and loyal servant of Henry VIII. Mary Shelley may have intended a reference to his father, John.

Plantagenet cast a reproachful glance on her, as he said, "Happy indeed are those who die. O God! when I think of the many and the beloved, who, a few years ago, were alive around me, and among whose low silent graves I now walk alone, methinks I am dead; it is but the ghost of him you knew that lingers upon earth."

"Yes, they are all gone," said the Princess; "all who linked me to the past, and were portions of my Richard's being. They are gone from before me. But are they truly no more, or do they live, like you, brooding over the lost, / disdaining to communicate with one who lives but to remember them? Of the death of several I have heard; but often I have longed with bitterness to hear of you, and of the Spanish maiden, Monina de Faro."

"Her gentle soul," replied Edmund, "has flown to join him for whom she lived and died. It is now two years since I was assured of this. A friar, whom I had formerly well known, visited Lisbon; and I entreated him to enquire for De Faro and his child. The commander of the Adalid was almost forgotten; at last, an old sailor was found, who remembered that, some years before, he had sailed for the Western Indies, and was never heard of more."

"His daughter accompanied him?"

"In the churchyard of a convent, placed high among the foldings of those lovely hills which overlook Lisbon, he was shown an humble tomb, half defaced; her dear sacred name is carved upon it, and half the date, the 14—, which showed that she died before the century began, in which we now live.* She could not have / survived our Prince many months; probably she died before him, nor ever knew the worst pang of all, the ignominy linked with his beloved memory."

"And you, my kinsman, how long have you wedded penury and labour in this obscure disguise?"

"Penury and labour," said Plantagenet, "are not confined to the humble occupation I have adopted. I was made poor by the death-blow of my hopes; and my chief labour is to tame my heart to resignation to the will of God. Obscure you may indeed call my destination. Would I could shroud it in tenfold night! Dearer to me is the silence and loneliness of this spot, where I can for ever commune undisturbed with the past, than a pomp which is stained by the blood of him, whom once I thought we all loved so well.

"When – Oh, let me not name the frightful thing! – when he was gone for ever, the whole world was to me but one miserable tomb. I groped in darkness, misery my mate, eternal lamentation my sole delight. The first thing that brought / peace to my soul, was the beauty of this visible universe. When God permitted, for some inscrutable purpose, moral evil to be showered so plenti-fully over us, he gave us a thousand resources out of ourselves in compensation. If I mingled with my fellow-creatures, how dearly should I miss him, who was

* Richard was put to death in 1499.

397

single among men for goodness, wisdom, and heaven-born nobility of soul. My heart sickens at the evil things that usurp the shape of humanity, and dare deem themselves of the same species: I turn from all, loathing. But here there is no change, no falling-off, no loss of beauty and of good: these glades, these copses, the seasons' change and elemental ministrations, are for ever the same – the type of their Maker in glory and in good. The loveliness of earth saves me from despair: the majesty of Heaven imparts aspiring hope. I bare my bosom to the breeze, and my wretched heart throbs less wildly. I drink in the balmy sweetness of the hour, and repose again on the goodness of my Creator.

"Yours is another existence, Lady; you need the adulation of the crowd – the luxury of / palaces; you purchase these, even by communing with the murderer of him who deserved a dearer recompense at your hands."

Katherine smiled sadly at these last words, which betrayed the thought that rankled in her kinsman's mind. "I thank you," she replied, "for your details. I will not blame you for the false judgment you pass on me. When years and quiet thought have brought you back from the tempest of emotion that shakes you, you will read my heart better, and know that it is still faithfully devoted to him I have lost."

"Ah! say those words again," cried Plantagenet, "and teach me to believe them. I would give my right hand to approve your conduct, to love and reverence you once again."

"Will you have patience with me then, while I strive to justify myself?"

"Oh, speak! My life, my soul's salvation, hang upon[35] your words."

Katherine raised her blue eyes to the now starry sky, as if to adjure that to be the witness of her innocent thoughts; and then she said, / "We are all, dear Cousin, impelled by our nature to make ourselves the central point of the universe. Even those, who as they fancy, sacrifice themselves for the love of God, do it more truly for love of themselves; and the followers of virtue too often see their duties through the obscure and deceptive medium, which their own single, individual feelings create. Yet we have one unerring guide; one given us at our birth, and which He who died on the cross for us, taught us to understand and to appreciate, commanding us to make it the master-law of our lives. Call it love, charity, or sympathy; it is the best, the angelic portion of us. It teaches us to feel pain at others' pain, joy in their joy. The more entirely we mingle our emotions with those of others, making our well or ill being depend on theirs, the more completely do we cast away selfishness, and approach the perfection of our nature.

"You are going to answer, perhaps to refute me – do not. Remember I am a woman, with a woman's tutelage in my early years, a woman's education in the world, which is that of the / heart – alas! for us – not of the head. I have no school-learning, no logic – but simply the voice of my own soul which speaks within me.

"I try to forget, you force me back upon myself. You attack; and you beseech me to defend myself. So to do, I must dwell upon the sentiments of a heart, which is human, and therefore faulty, but which has neither guile nor malice in it.

"In my father's house – and when I wandered with my beloved outcast, I had no difficulty in perceiving, nor – God was so gracious to me – in fulfilling my duties. For, in childhood I was cherished and favoured by all; and when I became a wife, it was no wonder that I should love and idolize the most single-hearted, generous, and kindly being that ever trod the earth. To give myself away to him – to be a part of him – to feel that we were an harmonious one in this discordant world, was a happiness that falls to the lot of few: – defeat, chains, imprisonment – all these were but shows; the reality was deep in our hearts, invulnerable by any tyrant less remorseless than death. If this / life were the sum and boundary of our being, I had possessed the consummation and fulfilment of happiness.

"But we are taught to believe that our existence here is but the stepping stone to another beyond, and that 'death is the beginning of life.'ᵃ When we reach the summit of our desires, then we fall, and death comes to destroy. He was lost to me, my glory, and my good! Little could I avail to him now. The caresses, love, and watchful care, the obedience and the heart's sacrifice, of a poor thing who groped darkling upon earth, could avail nought to a spirit in Paradise. I was forced to feel that I was alone: and, as to me, to love is to exist, so in that dark hour, in the gaspings of my agony, I felt that I must die, if for ever divided from him who possessed my affections.

"Years have passed since then. If grief kills us not, we kill it. Not that I cease to grieve; for each hour, revealing to me how excelling and matchless the being was, who once was mine, but renews the pang with which I deplore my / alien state upon earth. But such is God's will; I am doomed to a divided existence, and I submit. Meanwhile I am human; and human affections are the native, luxuriant growth of a heart, whose weakness it is, too eagerly, and too fondly, to seek objects on whom to expend its yearnings. My Richard's last act was to bestow me on his sister: it were impious to retract a gift made by the dying. We wept together – how long, and how bitterly – the loss of our loved one; and then together we turned to fulfil our duties. She had children; they became as dear to me as to her. Margaret I cherish as the betrothed bride of my ever dear cousin, the King of Scotland;ᵇ and, when I endeavour to foster the many virtues nature has implanted in the noble mind of Prince Arthur,ᶜ I am

---

ᵃ Probably alluding to 'Death the Gate of Life' (*Paradise Lost*, XII. 571).

ᵇ The great-grandson of this union, James VI of Scotland, became the first Stuart king of England, James I.

ᶜ 'Arthur died April 2, 1502' (marginal note at the bottom of III, p. 351 in *Abinger/Palacio*). Perhaps Mary Shelley would have incorporated Arthur's death into Katherine's epilogue in a second edition. The retrospective character and reflective tone of her 'favourite's' confession suggest that it was made many years after Warbeck's death in 1499. The references to Arthur, however, place the interview with Edmund before 1502.

fulfilling, methinks, a task grateful in the eyes of Richard, thus doing my part to bestow on the England he loved, a sovereign who will repair the usurper's crimes, and bestow happiness on the realm.

"Nor is this all – despise me if you will, but I confess that I regard others among those with / whom I associate, with a clinging affection that forbids me to separate myself from them. Did I not love the noble and good, even as he did, while Richard lived? Does he not now, in his heavenly abode, love them? And must my living heart be stone, because that dear form is dust, which was the medium of my communication with his spirit? Where I see suffering, there I must bring my mite for its relief. We are not deities to bestow in impassive benevolence. We give, because we love – and the meshes of that sweet web, which mutual good offices and sympathy weaves, entangle and enthral me, and force me to pain and pleasure, and to every variety of emotion which is the portion of those whom it holds within its folds.

"I quarrel not with – I admire – those who can be good and benevolent, and yet keep their hearts to themselves, the shrine of worship for God, an haven which no wind can enter. I am not one of these, and yet take no shame therefore: I feel my many weaknesses, and know that some of these form a part of my strength; the / reviled part of our nature being a portion of that which elevates us to the godlike. My reason, my sense of duty, my conscientious observance of its dictates, you will set up as the better part; but I venerate also the freer impulses of our souls. My passions, my susceptible imagination, my faltering dependence on others, my clinging to the sense of joy – this makes an integral part of Katherine, nor the worst part of her. When my soul quits this 'bower of flesh,'[a] these leaves and flowers, which are perhaps the growth of it, may decay and die. I know not; as it is, I am content to be an imperfect creature, so that I never lose the ennobling attribute of my species, the constant endeavour to be more perfect.

"I do not blame you, my Cousin, for seeking repose in solitude after much endurance. But unquiet should I feel in the unreplying loneliness, which forms your peace. I must love and be loved. I must feel that my dear and chosen friends are happier through me. When I have wandered out of myself in my endeavour / to shed pleasure around, I must again return laden with the gathered sweets on which I feed and live. Permit this to be, unblamed – permit a heart whose sufferings have been, and are, so many and so bitter, to reap what joy it can from the strong necessity it feels to be sympathized with – to love."

THE END. /

---

[a] *Romeo and Juliet*, III. ii. 81–2 (adapted).

ENDNOTES

The numbered notes refer to relevant passages in this edition which have been emended from the corrections and marginal notations made by Mary Shelley in a copy of *Perkin Warbeck* now owned by Lord Abinger. Because the Abinger copy could not be examined before this edition went to press, information has been taken from the census of changes made by Palacio (pp. 637–8). The text preceding the square bracket represents the reading taken from *Abinger/Palacio* and is followed by the reading from the first edition of 1830. Additional references to Shelley's corrections and marginalia recorded in *Abinger/Palacio* appear in footnotes on pp. 19, 32, 34, 39, 48, 50, 58, 64, 74, 89, 90, 100, 101, 103, 128, 130, 146, 148, 152, 159, 170, 181, 192, 205, 222, 238, 240, 242, 269, 271, 292, 346, 350, 368, 399.

[1] 1485] 1415
[2] cousin] nephew
[3] cousin's] nephew's
[4] go to the noble knight] go the noble knight
[5] slight figure] slight, stunted figure
[6] upon, partook of the enthusiasm] upon, the enthusiasm
[7] recommended to his chief] recommended his chief
[8] quitted] quited
[9] observed] oberved
[10] Noontide approached.] Noontide was approached.
[11] nurtured] nutured
[12] Warham] Wattam
[13] Warham] Wattam
[14] Warham] Wattam
[15] and it would not] which it would not
[16] delayed] layed
[17] take counsel] take council
[18] kinsman?'] kinsman?'"
[19] replied] replie
[20] particularly] partiticulary
[21] Stoke] Stowe
[22] enter?"] enter."
[23] colouring] louring

[24] Why] Why,
[25] men nor horses] men and horses
[26] Elizabeth.] Elizabeth."
[27] sprung, again] sprung again,
[28] yielding, again] yielding again,
[29] herself] himself
[30] faithful] faith
[31] His being led to] His being led him to
[32] what he had been] what he was
[33] decay] delay
[34] her arms] his arms
[35] hang upon] to hang upon

SILENT CORRECTIONS

The reading preceding the square bracket is the one given in this edition.

Page	line	
8	24	Fleur-de-Luce] Floeur-de-Luce
10	23	unexpected] un expected
14	23	having taken] having taking
19	4	posterity] posteriy
26	21	King.] King.,
26	27	bad] had
30	34	entertained] ntertained
33	18	besiege] beseige
33	19	neigbourhood] neighbonrhood
41	7	friend.] friend-
54	6	and] aad
58	19	gallant] ga ant
80	34	life."] life:"
88	25	magnanimous] magnaminous
89	19	though] through
90	29	tapered] taper
93	1	XII.] XI.
100	4	XIII.] XII.
105	19	XIV.] XIII.
106	3	employer's] employers
114	1	XV.] XIV.
120	6	XVI.] XV.
122	40	minutes'] minute's
123	34	O'Brien] O'Brien
123	35	O'Carroll] O'Carroll
124	23	O'Briens] O'Briens
124	23	O'Carrolls] O'Carrolls
127	13	XVII.] XVI.
129	15	days'] day's
133	1	XVIII.] XVII.
136	18	Chamberlain] Chambelain
137	30	impressions] im pressions

Page	line	
142	10	to him who] him to who
142	11	this] his
142	35	thread-broad bridge] thread-broad ridge
144	28	gallowglasses] galolwglasses
153	22	Poynings'] Poyning's
158	33	northward,] northward.
163	9	Henry,] Henry;
164	14	countryman] countrymen
199	13	be acted] he acted
201	35	Hythe. The] Hythe, The
203	20	ravine,] ravine;
206	5	O'Water] O'Water
209	20	magnanimity] magnaminity
222	6	friend's] friends'
227	25	hostile] ho tile
228	15	the errant] the the errant
243		page number. 277] 27
251	20	participating] participatin g
259	1	XVIII.] XIII.
269	22	from] rom
294	30	Hornbeck] Horneck
295	2	and] aud
298	23	army – a rout] army a rout
312	25	wove] wore
312	42	you] your
314	20	stubbornness] stubborness
316	15	steps.] steps
316	20	interrupted] interupted
319	10	will be here] will be he here
333	27	occurred] ccurred
334	19	woods] words
348	10	part of] part off
370	32	Katherine] Katharine
375	3	Question,] Question.
380	16	aweary] a weary
388	15	detailed to] detailedto
393	7	sleep] eep
398	34	others'] others

KING ALFRED'S COLLEGE
LIBRARY